The Chocolate Prophecy

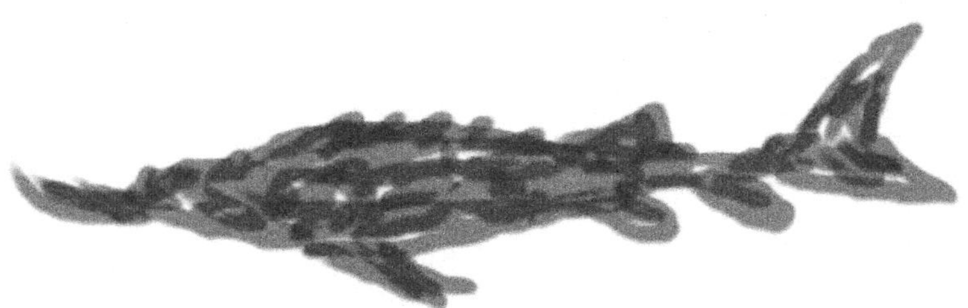

E. L. WARD

The Chocolate Prophecy is a work of fiction. Names, characters, places, and incidents either are the product of the author's imagination or are used fictitiously. Any resemblance to actual persons, living or dead, events, or locales is entirely coincidental.

ISBN: 978-0-578-75814-5

Cover Design by Daniel Schmelling

First Edition Cover Design: Rachael Van Baren

THE IDRIULTHORONTAN ARCHIPELAGO

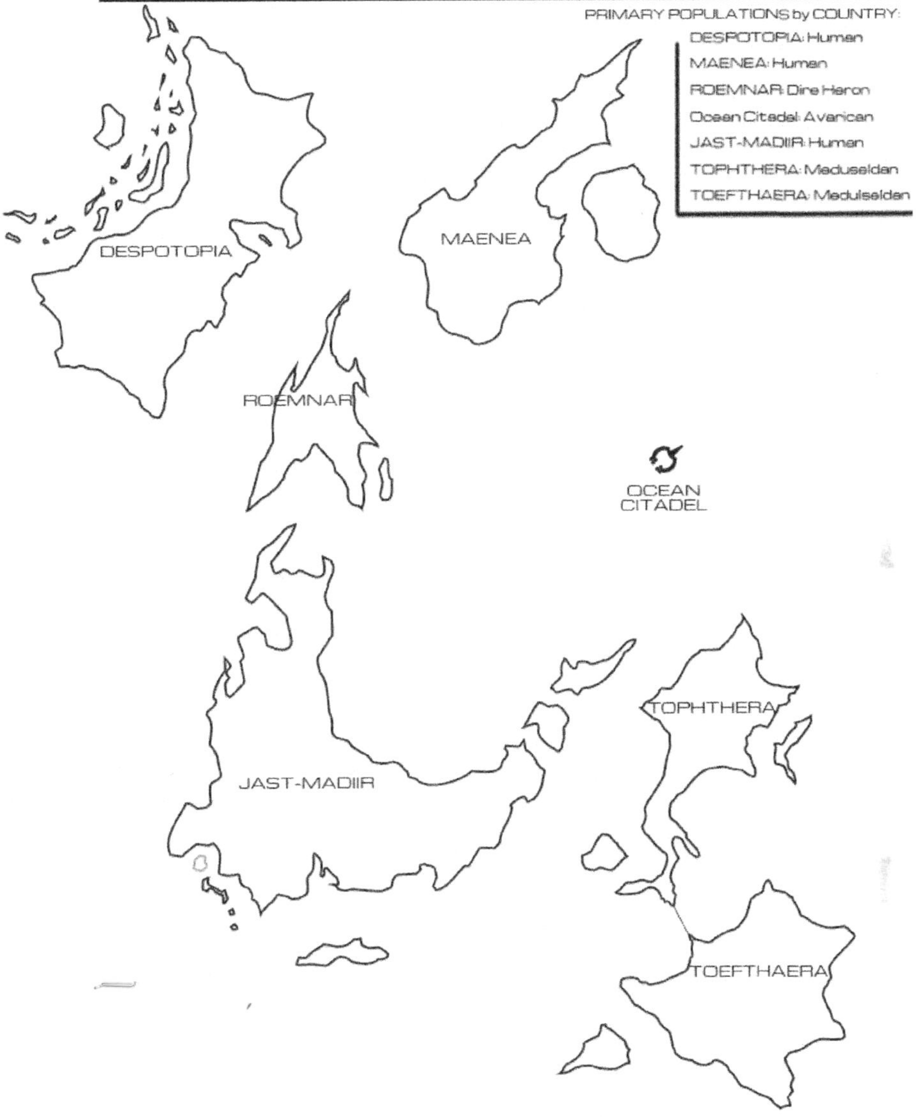

PRIMARY POPULATIONS by COUNTRY:

DESPOTOPIA: Human

MAENEA: Human

ROEMNAR: Dire Heron

Ocean Citadel: Avarican

JAST-MADIIR: Human

TOPHTHERA: Meduseldan

TOEFTHAERA: Medulseldan

DESPOTOPIA

MAENEA

ROEMNAR

OCEAN
CITADEL

JAST-MADIIR

TOPHTHERA

TOEFTHAERA

This book is dedicated to the people it is dedicated to.

Pronunciation Guide

Asiri (A-see-ree)
Avarica (Av-arr-ick-uh)
Baegulgog (Bagel-gog)
Berlberi (Burl-berry)
Berlie Beirel (Bur-lee Barrel)
Deacogal (Dee-koe-gal)
Despotopia (Dess-pot-oh-pee-uh)
Dyeus (Die-us)
Erukomë (Air-oo-coe-may)
Enscharaulgk (En-shar-awlk)
Ethon (Eeth-on)
Hienrechenshlagen (Hine-reck-en-shlog-en)
Idriulthoronta (Id-ree-ul-thor-on-tuh)
Irisa (Eye-riss-uh)
Jast-Madiir (Jast Mad-ear)
Jengadocea (Jenga-doe-see-ah)
Klinkofhenschmidt (Klinf-off-en-shmit)
Maenea (Mania)
Maricalgi (Mare-ick-al-gee)
Meduselda (Med-you-sell-duh)
Mesomelae (Mes-OH-mell-ay)
Mesomela (Mes-OH-mell-ah)
Murtaugh (Mer-taw)
Onyxadon (On-ix-a-don)
Pharonomagnus (Fair-on-oh-mag-nus)
Roemnar (Roe-em-nar)
Senahktenre (Sen-awk-ten-ray)
Schenburkreiga (Shen-burr-kree-guh)
Shontaulyin (Shawn-tall-yin)
Sowür Canpattel (Sour Can-pat-tell)
Tophtheaera, Tophthera, Toefthaera (Tofe-thay-ruh)
Valshaloli (Val-shall-oh-lee)
Variglew (Vaar-igloo)
Washoe (Wah-show)
Wuu Gappew (Woo Gap-you)

Table of Contents

Inspection Day

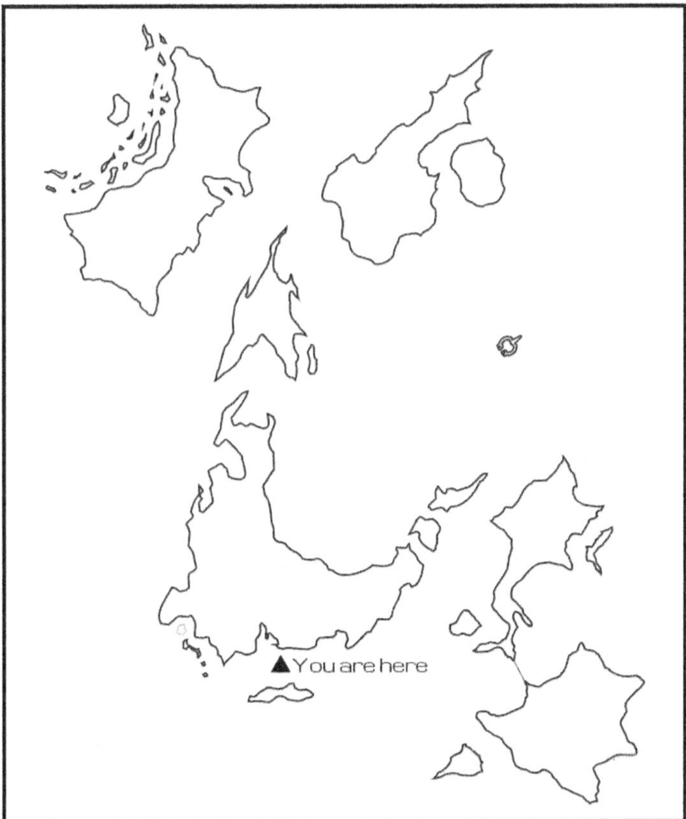

"If you are reading this, then you have Will, and you have Purpose.

"But what more do we know of these mysterious forces? We know this much: in Purpose consists all meaning and propriety, and in Will, all fallibility and failure. Purpose is silent and serene. Will is forever screaming its fickle nonsense. Purpose is irreproachable. Will is the great curse. Even the tiniest granule of Will can obscure a grand mountain of Purpose.

"It remains my sole hope and ambition that we may one day learn to divine the true Purpose within one another. Until that day comes, our only recourse is to conform to strict hierarchies. You would know them as states. The rulers must tell their peasants what to do, and the peasants must do it. Ideally the peasant should be given such a monumental task that he is not left with time to consider what he might otherwise like to be doing. Granted, the purposes rulers assign may be arbitrary. But even a contrived sense of Purpose is more to be heeded than Will..."

- Magormissahr, *Referendums on the World, Vol. 835*

AAAAAAAAAAAAAAAAAAA...

The subtle warning of the foghorn filled the modest estate house, volunteering its bluster to the prevailing sense of pandemonium. The floor quaked. Splinters flew. Furniture lay in shambles. The air bore a hint of some astringent odor. Watching all that was transpiring in the reception room with intense interest, Jek nervously patted his hair down and rubbed at the crust in his eyes again. A veritable eternity ago, he had been sleeping. But in real-time, he knew it couldn't have been five hours since he'd gone to bed in the first place...

KERSMASH!

Another dresser was no more. Jek had never stopped to consider just how many dressers there were around the house, until the Inquisitors had set about breaking them.

The next to go was a lampstand. It was a nervous business, but as Jek was forced to admit to himself, it was really rather impressive to see the cloaked creatures break his things with their bare hands. Three of them there were – two busily setting about searching for and destroying anything that seemed potentially excessive on the property, while the other looked on, arms crossed.

The pensive one had been instructing the others since their arrival. With some dread-curiousity, Jek found himself observing her, even as she herself observed the work of her subordinates. Occasionally she stopped them from destroying this or that, evidently guided by parameters too nebulous for Jek to reason out. Her speech was terse and infrequent, and though she proved attentive, he couldn't help feeling she seemed preoccupied. Though, she wasn't Human, and of this he was powerfully aware. That made it hard to even speculate about her true state of mind...

Presently her gaze wandered, and something by the far wall seemed to catch her eye. She strode heavily across the room on bare feet, nails as big as carving knives. Jek watched her pluck a particular clay knickknack up from a small display shelf. She turned back (in his direction!) even as she kept fixated on the trinket – small in her scaly grasp – tumbling it deftly in her hand to see all sides.

He wasn't at all sure how the chief Inquisitor could see what she was holding – or *anything*, for that matter. Her mask had no eyeholes. There was only a sharp slit about where he guessed the nostrils would be. And through it came pungent air, and blisteringly hot. The entire headdress was one shiny, elegant curvature that converged acutely to a sort of downward-facing chin, with an odd pair of panels gouging out of the flanks. The mask craned toward him...

As she approached, her footfalls menaced a series of creaks and moans out of the floorboards. She stood well over Jek, conservatively approaching seven feet. Standing there, letting her get closer and closer, had roughly the aspect of being voluntarily stalked by a dinosaur (and not the comfortably familiar egg-eating kind, either). She held forth the crude clay object in her hand...

"What is this?" she asked. Her voice was rich and metered.

How to answer? It was essentially a vase – or else a very misshapen bowl. It had been made by his father during a brief foray into the art of pottery. Jek was young when his father had made it, but he remembered that he had seemed rather proud of it, with just that noticeable hint of doubt that every creative person experiences when, deep down, they realize that their workmanship is actually terrible.

Jek started to construct his answer to the Inquisitor, but it was difficult to phrase. He felt obliged to answer with care. For there was a Human tradition, which held that one should always address one's superiors with special, high-falootin' grammar. But time was whiling away and he was only getting more nervous, so he had better start spitting it out...

"M'lady, thou hold'st'eth a work of pottery-craft which mine father did'st..."

Now she put forth her other hand... with one, long, knobbed, deadly-sharp finger extended accusingly. Her head stooped forward with a sudden, unnatural snaking action. On a conscious level, he was aware there was a long neck coiled back under the hood of her cloak. Veiled as it was, it created the deeply unsettling effect that her head was floating above her shoulders, and could spontaneously go wherever it chose.

"Do not speak to me in that fashion! I would not have you pay insult to my humility."

He blinked hard, banishing a bunch of apologies he instinctively fumbled for, deciding they too would probably make her upset.

"...It's a family heirloom," he answered simply.

She looked at the thing again – doubtfully – and then back at him. "Is it registered?"

"It – it is," he said. "Would you like to see the certificate?"

"That would be prudent, yes."

He felt silly that he'd even dared hope she wouldn't make him dig it up. "Alright, let me go get it; it's upstairs."

Suddenly he experienced a moment of relative relief, seeing this small errand would get him a moment away from the Inquisitors. He whirled around and started for the staircase, but he heard her footsteps behind him, over the sound of his own.

"I'll accompany you. We need to process your second floor as well." So much for relief.

As they started up the stairs, he felt a fresh wave of anxiety as the creaking behind him became so bad, he honestly wondered if she might fall through the simple cross-board steps. That would be horribly uncomfortable for all parties...

"We also need you to resolve a query about the layout of your first floor. What is the purpose of the room across from the master bedroom?" she asked. Jek's mind went blank. *The room across from the bedroom?* He never used it. But at last, he remembered what it was for...

"It's meant to be a nursery," he answered.

There was a pause.

"Your profile did not include a child. Will you be having offspring in the near future?"

His face turned ruddy, and he nearly laughed at the question. He couldn't imagine the day when he'd have time to raise a child...

"I suspect not," he said.

"In that case, we will be eliminating that room. You may rebuild it, if and when you should decide to procreate... provided you fill out the proper paperwork, of course."

"Thank you," he said – embarrassed – unsure what else to say...

For the remaining steps, Jek focused on his breathing, endeavoring to steal himself. He knew this kind of domestic demolition at the hands of the Inquisition was a naturalized part of life, even if it was still quite an uneasy ordeal. He remembered going through it once before when he was a boy. The Inquisitors of that distant memory had seemed hardly more huge, alien, and terrifying. As he was just a child at the time, one of them had been careful to delicately explain the process to him (even as the others began breaking things), taking a knee and resting an enormous claw on his back, as if to reassure him.

He could still recall the words of the Inquisitor as if each was a matter of life and death. Though, in reality, his short speech had to do with much larger concepts than that...

'Take heart, little Human,' he began. *'No doubt you are troubled and confused. But do not fret. All experience this, at their first purging. Still, you will have questions. Let me see if I can answer them, with a story...*

'Thousands of years ago, the Creators withdrew from our universe, moving on from infinity to infinity. They purposed to begin an entirely new *universe from scratch, ultimately finding in us a dissatisfying creation – fundamentally flawed. When this happened, seven of the world's most ancient dragons, who had borne witness to the works of the Creators longer than any other sentient beings, took it upon themselves to try to make what amends they could. It was their aim that if the Creators ever did return, they would find a more humble, penitent world than the one they left. These are the dragons now known as the Grand Inquisitors – they who founded the Inquisition, and continue to preside over it to this very day. To all citizens of every nation, we – their lesser Inquisitors – come at whiles, to curtail material excess – destroying your nonessential possessions with both care and comprehensiveness. But this is only one of many virtuous functions of our order. We have crushed countless uprisings, mediated as many international crises, uprooted heresies of all stripes, protected civilization from unrepentant dragons, and installed order over chaos time and again throughout the ages. But please, do not thank us. We only wish we could do more.'*

That was the story the enormous lizard-man had told him, anyway. But in Jek's part of the world, it was not entirely uncommon to run into someone who doubted the altruistic intentions of the Inquisition. Jek rejected the entire question. He just wanted to make it through the day.

Finally they reached the second floor. It was a drafty space that essentially consisted of one large room with many windows from which to see the grounds, and a door on the south side with an external staircase that led down to the road – and to the hill with the foghorn beyond. There was also an alcove in the opposite corner with a work desk. Apart from that, the floor was basically storage space.

As he rounded the desk that contained the heaps of paperwork, he saw something else that distressed him. The Inquisitor was looking in the other direction. She was looking at the *backup lens*!

And after all, how could she miss it? In the middle of the large upper room, there was a huge, deeply-ridged glass globe. It was used to amplify the simple torch that illumined the lighthouse...

Or rather, that *would* be its use, should their current lens ever fall into disrepair. Jek could feel the question coming...

"This is merely a reserve lens, in case the other one breaks, yes?" the Inquisitor plied. He really didn't want to answer...

"Yes," he answered, sifting through papers.

There was another short, perilous pause.

"Is it mandatory to maintain a reserve lens?" He definitely didn't want to admit that it wasn't.

"There was talk of making it mandatory. That's why we purchased this one, at great expense. But we haven't had an update to the inventory of equipment we're required to maintain on-site in months." All of this was true. Jek hesitated, bit his lip, but then came out with it anyway. "You're going to break it, aren't you?"

"Yes," she said.

But then in a concerted action, she very quickly produced a document, scrawling on it with impressive speed. After a few moments, she advanced on the desk and held the paper out to him.

"Here is a requisition order. If a reserve lens becomes mandatory, the Inquisition will foot the bill for the replacement of this one."

He was awed by two things. For one, the great sense of gratitude he felt to the frightening lizard-woman who was about to destroy his expensive backup lens. For the other, the clear sight of her hand holding the paper. Her long and deadly pointing finger had been impressive enough on its own before, but he hadn't realized just how inhuman her hand truly was until now. The scaly, elongated first and second digits weren't even the longest fingers... the knuckles of the third and fourth digits jutted out an inch or so beyond the others, and on the outside of the final knuckle was what seemed to be another thumb, oriented opposite the normal thumb. That thumb and the last two digits also shared webbing that reached all the way to the nails.

At length, feeling a bit boorish for staring so long at her hand, he accepted the paper. "Thank you," he said.

About the time he found the family heirloom certificate he was looking for, yet another thing began to go wrong. The blair of the foghorn was starting to weaken noticeably. He shot a glance out the window. *Still too hazy.* It would need more fuel again. He felt a bit of a relief once more. This time, he could surely excuse himself from the cacophony of shattering possessions and difficult questions for a while...

"Sounds like the foghorn needs more coal," he told the Inquisitor as he handed her the certificate.

"Of course, we do not wish to intrude on your duties," she said, evidently to excuse him, even as she scanned his certificate with great intent.

Jek tried not to look like he was rushing out the door. But before he could pass the threshold and start down the outside stairway, he found himself paralyzed with a word...

"Wait!" commanded the Inquisitor.

Jek reeled. What was wrong? What had he *done*!?

"Don't forget your firearm," she said.

Phew! She was just reminding him of the state of open warfare between the nation of Jast-Madiir (his nation), and the Dire Mantids that lived deep in its native jungles. Lighthouses were important fixtures, especially in an archipelago such as Idriulthoronta – they needed to be guarded in times of open war. This essentially meant that lighthouse stewards were required to carry a musket around anytime they went outdoors. The nearest jungle was perhaps fifty miles to the north... and to date, he'd never heard of an actual incident where Mantids had attacked a settlement. War with the Mantids cropped up every couple of years, and always went the same way. A troop was marched into the jungle against the savage insects, never to return. It was kind of a zero-sum arrangement, but deemed necessary by the Czarina of Jast-Madiir for the up-keep of proper relations with the Mantid tribes.

There was really no danger, but an ordinance was an ordinance, and so he hurriedly grabbed his musket, attached the bayonet, slung the weapon over his shoulder, and finally passed through the door.

*   *   *

As he hoofed up to the foghorn, Jek was surprised to see a stranger already there, shoveling the coal. He hesitated, but as he started forward again, he saw that he was only half-right. It was his wife.

She had her hair pulled back and she was wearing a green frock he hadn't seen before, so he could hardly have recognized her. Since they met (on the day of their wedding), they hadn't seen much of each other. As the sole stewards of Brighamok's Lighthouse, they each had to take a shift. Someone needed to be awake and alert at all times; constant vigilance was part of the job. You had to be sure the light didn't go out or stop spinning. You had to watch for fog, start the horn the moment there was any, and keep it fed. You also had to feed and care for the horse whose sole purpose was to pull the wagon that could carry one day's supply of coal back from town. You had to patrol the grounds – even when there was no war on – because naturally lighthouses were a known target of opportunity. And, of course, the cleaning, cleaning, *cleaning*. As the night-shifter, any time there was a foggy morning, Jek would end his vigil by starting up the horn and going straight to bed. Every morning was a foggy morning.

As she heaved another load of coal into the furnace that fueled the steam-powered foghorn, Jek glimpsed the face of his wife in profile. It was a nice face, he thought. Nothing to wax poetic about, necessarily... except that left cheek bone of hers. It was positively the most sublime cheek bone he had ever laid eyes on. The other one, though essentially identical, was nothing special.

Well, he'd told the Inquisitor that he was going to see about the foghorn, and regardless of his wife's getting there first, he figured he'd better follow through and shovel the rest of the coal...

"Hey!" he called out, waving awkwardly. She sort of half looked back at first, but evidently saw him and turned her full attention.

"What?!" she called back.

"Let me do that shoveling for you!" he shouted.

Uh-oh, he suddenly thought. *I bet she's the sort who'll be offended by my insisting on doing the shoveling just because she's a weak little woman, or something*. What rotten luck, his falling into an obvious faux-pas like that!

She squinted at him intensely. "WHAT!!!!?" she said.

Ah, good luck after all; she hadn't heard him over the horn. Maybe he could come up with a way to phrase the suggestion more delicately. He said it the best way he could think of...

"LET ME DO THAT SHOVELING FOR YOU!!!!"

Internally, he winced. Now he knew for sure he was an oaf.

"HEY, THANKS!" she said with a beaming smile. She abruptly handed him the shovel and walked away.

* * *

Wiping sweat from his brow, his grey skin blackened by coal powder, Jek was at last satisfied that the horn was adequately refueled. Shoveling was hard work now. With a twinge of yearning, he remembered his youth, spent working on a farm, when the greater physical demands of the job had kept him much stronger. He knew his former self could whip the tar out of his current self.

It was amusing to remember the end of that era – discovering that he would soon become a lighthouse steward – the excitement he had felt. Whenever he told people that he was finally moving up in the world, their shared enthusiasm had always seemed to fade noticeably, when they learned what exactly it was he would be doing for the rest of his life. Somehow, they must've all known better than him what he was getting into...

Jek was still propping himself up with the end of the shovel when he saw something else was afoot. Back down at the estate house, there were two soldiers standing at his doorway, looking out. Ahead of them was another man, demonstrating all of the conspicuous signs of impatience, looking straight back at him...

It was Rurik Howitzerov... the lighthouse inspector. Today was inspection day.

!!!

Jek ran full-clip back to the estate house. Wheezing and puffing, he watched inspector Howitzerov produce a clipboard and stare down his nose as he made some notes.

"Failed to welcome the inspector at the door at time of arrival," he stated. "A fifteen-point deduction."

It wasn't a good start. One hundred deducted points would mean execution!

Jek passed to the door and, inclining his head, wheezed out, "Thou art'est most welcomed unto this house."

Howitzerov grinned smuggly as he strode through. He certainly did not share the Inquisitor's qualms with being addressed as a superior.

Entering the house, the fact that it had been ransacked was immediately observed. What was not immediately observed, importantly, was the Inquisition. They had evidently moved on to a different part of the house. Jek swallowed. Out came the clipboard again.

"The furnishings are in substandard order," the inspector remarked, walking over to a smashed dresser.

"Thou should'st know'eth that the Inqui –"

"Ah-*ah*!" protested the inspector. "I did not invite an explanation," he said, scratching something else down, before kneeling in front of the dresser. He ran a finger along what would have been part of the top of the dresser. He looked at his finger, then rubbed it with his thumb, thoughtfully. "However distressed, this surface at least appears to have been properly dusted." He made another note. "You are therefore awarded only a total of 47 deducted points thus far." Jek sighed in relief. He had learned early that the dusting was a major deciding factor. Most lighthouse stewards were executed for lax dusting.

But wait! he thought. His mind suddenly returned to the small display shelf that his father's vase-bowl-thing rested on. He couldn't remember dusting it! It was a darned good thing that the Inquisitor had inquired about the pottery, because he probably would never have thought of that shelf otherwise...

He watched the inspector for a while to be sure he was preoccupied with some inspecty task... and then quietly, sneakily shot over to the shelf. He lifted the vase-bowl up in one hand as he wiggled a sleeve out past his fingers to swab the dust with the other...

But something was amiss. There was a clamor from the vase.

Brusquely he went ahead and whisked the shelf with a heavy brush of his arm before, more carefully, he brought the vase down in front of himself, peering in quizzically. He couldn't possibly have found anything inside which would have been more out of place...

Great Dianodes!

It was a zenithyst. An honest-to-goodness *zenithyst*. And a big one! He brought it gently out of the vase to be sure. The characteristic indigo color of the imposing gemstone could not be mistaken. His eyes were huge. This was a doozy. Jek had never been nearly so wealthy in his life as he was in this moment – the moment he spent holding what was, as far as he knew, the second-most valuable kind of stone in the world...

So many questions arose. *How? Why? Who? What? Where?* Admittedly, *what* and *where* were maybe not so much in question, but they arose just the same.

But there was no time for it! He pocketed the gem, turning back around to check on inspector Howitzerov. He remained providentially oblivious.

Before he could even count himself fortunate, the next calamity came with a piercing crash that made both Jek and the inspector jump into the air in unison. Howitzerov flailed wildly for a few seconds after he reached the ground. But Jek already knew what he had heard. It was the sound of the backup lens, shattering to a zillion pieces just above them!

Evidently his wife had been just outside the back door when the lens hit the floor. She threw the door open. "What in the *HECK* was –!"

She saw the inspector.

"What'eth in the Heck'eth was'est –"

"Never mind asking, dear," Jek cut her off. Her high-falootin' grammar just wasn't as polished as his was... and anyway, it was important that they get up the stairs in time to catch the Inquisitors in the act. They didn't have enough points left to take the blame for any more screw-ups. "Cometh along!" he said, waving both the other Humans after him to the stairway...

* * *

Jek had thought showing the Inquisitors to the inspector would make things better. Somehow now they felt worse. It had taken mere moments for the two parties to begin arguing, and the stress was mounting. Jek wondered where the inspector got the constitution to argue with an Avarican. But maybe that just came with being an important person...

"They *are* mandated to keep a backup lens!" Howitzerov insisted.

"No. I checked the inventory of mandated equipment myself. It is not as you say," the Inquisitor countered, producing the document.

"Let me see that!" Howitzerov said, snatching the paper. He zeroed in on a particular area, held a finger over it and turned the paper back around to the Inquisitor. "See that date? *Over five months old*! A Berlberi Clerk was supposed to hand-deliver an updated inventory no later than this morning!"

"Be that as it may, nothing was delivered. You should have sent it in the mail. Clerks are unreliable in these matters."

In their zeal, the lesser Inquisitors broke a window while the argument ensued. The sound of the foghorn was now sharply intruding into the already explosive environment.

"What are you doing!?" the Inquisitor demanded of her subordinates.

"It's almost midday! Turn that *blasted* thing off!" Howitzerov demanded of Jek's wife, indicating the foghorn. She shot off for the outside stairway. The door slammed behind her. Then it abruptly reopened as she reached back in for her musket, and it slammed again.

"Forgetting firearms during a time of open war!" Howitzerov called out. "Another deduction!"

"You could have reminded her *before* she rushed out the door... at your behest!" the Inquisitor insisted.

"And *you* could have stayed your minions before they smashed that window!" he snapped back.

Her head craned upward in her hood, and she took a few deliberately heavy steps – her bare feet crunching shattered glass – toward the inspector, who at last seemed to realize he was addressing a huge, powerful creature. "*You* do not need to place the blame on these people for my shortcomings... nor *your own*."

Though staring up into the mask of a several-hundred-pound killing machine, Howitzerov, lips quivering, somehow kept the verbal battle going...

"*You* need to replace this broken lens immediately!" he said, his voice cracking a bit.

"The requisition is already filled!" she insisted.

"That's not good enough!"

"What more could possibly be done!? Would you have us glue the entire lens back together?"

"I just might!"

And on and on the bickering went from there, with little obvious hope of resolution. It was a peculiar contest. She was an Inquisitor, with immunity to operate throughout the world. He was an agent of Jast-Madiir... just one of many states in the Archipelago... still he dared to stand on his essential, supreme authority over all things lighthouse in these parts. That their spheres of influence should overlap in this contentious way was certainly a unique misfortune. But at least the foghorn was starting to wind down. Jek tried to interject... to bring things back to a manageable intensity. He *tried* to make an opening in the argument, calling on his most advanced grammar...

"Thee... thine... thon... ye... yhine... yon...!" But it was no use.

Finally, outside stimulus once again imposed itself on the situation. There was a knock at the door. Jek was happy to answer it. Whoever it was – maybe a hostile Mantid, or even O'nyxon himself – could hardly make things worse...

Jek budged the door open. As it swung, it revealed a large jellyfish-like creature suspended about half a foot off the ground – self-illuminated with substantial cascading energies. It pulsated and thrummed with electric power as its seven tentacles – each gloved at the spade-shaped ends – wafted lazily in the air beneath itself. This primordial specimen was dressed in an extremely high-collared coat, as if to compensate for the fact that it had no head. To that end, it also wore a rather silly little hat, nestled in the midst of the collar, which was low-cut in the front, exposing the glow of part of the creature's central, bulbous body.

One tentacle wafted up... reached into a satchel... and snatched forth a piece of paper. This was the overdue Clerk. Jek hoped he was just here to drop off the inventory, and not to inquire about the upwards of two-dozen surveys he hadn't filled out yet...

"Good day to you, sir," the Clerk said, in a guttural but friendly voice, inclining himself in midair. "Permit me to introduce myself! I am Baegulgog, Clerk Second Class of the Clerical Dronehood of Berlberi. If you are a proprietor or resident of this fine establishment, then I have been tasked with delivering to you this updated inventory by the official Lighthouse Oversight Commission of Southern Jast-Madiir, LLC." Another tentacle from the same shoulder-type-area rose to the satchel and produced an entire wad of additional documents. "Please fill out these various waivers attesting to the fact that you are indeed a proprietor or resident and that you did in fact receive said inventory."

There was a tense silence. Jek received the inventory with one hand and the waivers with the other. "Thank you," he said.

Finally the floodgates opened and Howitzerov began shouting at the unsuspecting Clerk, followed nearly instantly by protestations from the Inquisitor.

Baegulgog floated slowly past Jek into the room, waving two of his tentacles in front of him. "Now, now, see here...!" he began, but soon what he was saying was completely subsumed in the din. Jek, standing in the doorway, decided he'd simply let them have it out, and stepped outside, pulling the door closed between them.

The sky had grown dark and blustery. Trouble was brewing outside as well as in. He had come out just in time to see his wife disappearing over the hilltop, toward the bay. Jek winced. She seemed to be in a big hurry.

More motion caught his eye, and he looked further up. In the sky over the coast, next to the light tower, there were dozens of encircling birds. It was an odd sight. They were *small* birds; much too small to be guls or vultures, though they flocked in true scavenger form. With the foghorn finally silenced, he could hear many chirping sounds – pleasing to the ear, yet agitated. It was a confused assortment of songbirds.

What in the wide, wide Undervoid is it now?

Gross expletives aside, he fumbled with his paperwork, stuffing it into deep pockets. The fitful wind caught one of the waivers and whisked it up into Jek's face, where it stuck for some seconds. Momentarily incensed, he finally snatched the document and crumpled it in with the rest. He *hated* when paper blew in his face! And it happened much too regularly. But brushing aside the moment of irritation, he grabbed hold of his musket strap and hurried down the stairs and up the hill.

Once again driven almost to the point of breathlessness, he gasped as the coastal winds burst on him. He had summited the hill, and he at last laid eyes on the source of all the new commotion. There – almost right at the foot of the light tower – was a beached fishing boat. The sails and mast were damaged significantly. And in the boat itself, an old man was flailing around desperately.

Jek's wife had nearly reached the boat, and he knew he'd better get there too, as fast as he could...

As Jek arrived at the scene, he joined his wife in trying to coach the old man out of the boat. It appeared well within his ability to simply climb out onto the shore, but the geezer had nonetheless planted himself in the stern of the boat, still flailing madly and shouting for help.

"Halp, *halp*!!!" he shouted for help.

At once, both Jek and his wife climbed into the boat, and continued trying to wave the man forward. They could hardly *carry* him out of the boat! But still he stayed planted and they were forced to come ever closer to him, hoping he'd soon regain his senses...

The old man finally fell silent, his jagged bottom teeth protruding through his scraggly beard as he huffed and puffed with wide eyes, which kept shifting between them and some elevated point behind them. Suddenly Jek heard shouting again over the wind and the crazed little songbirds, and he whirled around. The inspector, the Inquisitor, and the Clerk were on the hilltop now, evidently trying to get their attention.

Before he could make out what they were yelling, he felt a profound 'thud' on the back of his head. He had only enough time to be aware of falling into a heap before he was totally unconscious....

Twice Shanghaied

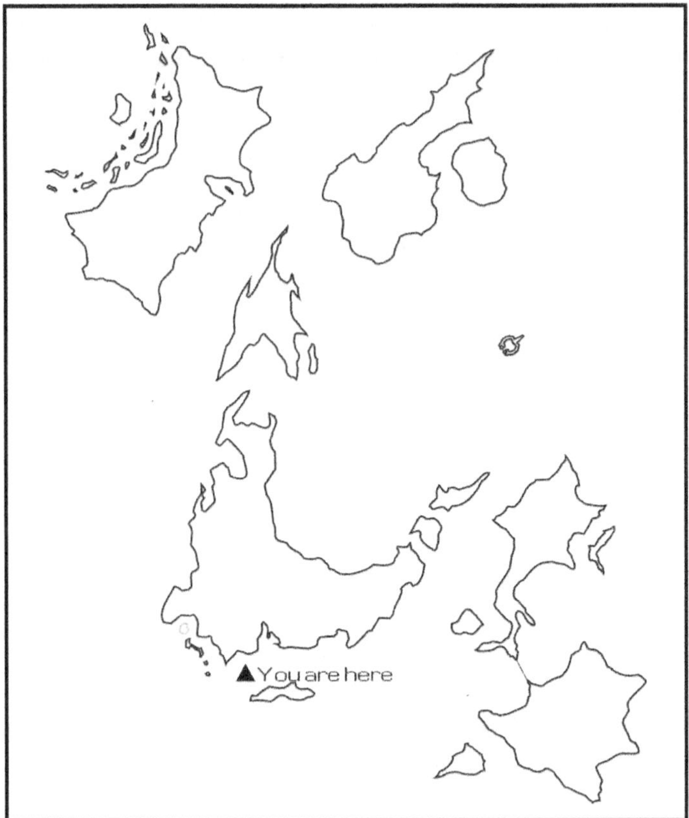

"The universe is both persistent and animated. We take it for granted, but these were not easy attributes to reconcile. The solution was to introduce two animating forces at a time – paired forces, diametrically opposed and balanced. We call them Dianodes. Their eternal clashing results in oscillations... what we observe most regularly as cycles and seasons. But really, the harmony of recurring themes in the universe can be observed at all levels for this reason, from the cosmic to the utterly trivial. If people find that their lives involve repetitive motifs, they needn't wonder about it."

- Practar Miflondi, *The Thirty-One 'O's: A Dissertation on the Origins of Music zzzzzzzzzzzzzzzzzzzzzzzzz...*

The old man's snoring was formidable. But each individual snore left a wide gulf of apnea before the next, which was filled with a chirping mania from some strange, disgruntled little birds nearby. It was kind of a sonic battle, between the birds and the old sailor. He was winning, but they never relented.

Audrey couldn't see it from here, but in the north-west, the sun was growing dim. As twilight ensued, she began to make out the oblong outline of the Other Worlds over the south sea, rimmed by light from an unseen source. Tonight, they appeared almost to be in line – like a guiding arrow, pointing the way to the next frontier. Or, so Audrey would have liked to believe. The past months of keeping watch over the southern coast of Jast-Madiir had been spent with the compelling knowledge that, anytime she looked out to the ocean, she was also casting a glance over the very edge of the map. If there was anything at all in the world further south than where she was right now, then no sailor she had ever met – however bold and enterprising – could say what it was. It inspired in her no small curiousity.

While she admired the great celestial disks, a pod of whales rolled gently by off the port bow. It was a beautiful evening, such as she had not enjoyed in a long time...

The fishing boat was drifting toward the coast again. Audrey lowered an oar off the port side to compensate. Adjusting the sail or rudder might have been more effective, but at least this way she could avoid the back of the boat, where her husband and their deafening elderly kidnapper were sound asleep.

They both had their reasons for exhaustion. Jek had been running on perhaps an hour's sleep. And he had borne the brunt of both the visit from the Inquisitors *and* the inspection, while she fed the horse and patrolled the grounds, warding off phantom Mantids. He had also borne the brunt of the smack from the oar that they both took to the back of the head, and it showed in the rather sizable bump he was now sleeping off...

Then there was that old man. Audrey didn't know much about him yet, except that he had pretenses of being a captain, that songbirds either loved or hated him (or his boat) well past any rationalization, and that he had a way of getting people to do what he wanted. As evidenced by her piloting his little boat while she let him snooze...

"Ye're a deserter now, *har ha-har*!" he had said, his nearly-interwoven bottom teeth put on nauseating display as he laughed at her expense. "Ye turn back, and they'll be chargin' ye with desecration o' duty... and *hersey*!"

It was a callously rendered point, but a good one. Being caught speeding off from your job on inspection day by a trio of witnesses consisting of the inspector himself, a Dronehood Clerk, and an Inquisitor sounded like the start of a bad joke. Being true, it was more of a recipe for certain execution. Sure, they had been knocked unconscious and taken against their will, but that was a matter of mere semantics. She knew the inspector and company wouldn't likely notice a trifling detail like that, nor consider it an excuse if they had. In their place, she probably wouldn't either.

So now they were fugitives. Sea-bound vagabonds without a country. It might have been stressful if it weren't pleasantly familiar...

'Pleasant,' however, was perhaps an understatement. This was more like a dream come true for her – a dream so unlikely that she had never even thought to dream it.

She loved the sea. She always had.

Audrey wasn't looking forward to finding out how her husband would take it though. He seemed like a worrier. They hadn't talked much over the course of their few months together, but she remembered their argument... the time she brought up the idea of making a minor addition to their family...

"We can't get a pet emu!" Jek had insisted. "It's all we can do to keep this lighthouse going!"

"But they are beautiful and majestic creatures!" she contended. He really hadn't said anything after that; undoubtedly he realized that she had a pretty good point. But she could tell he was still horribly unsettled about the idea. And in the end, they never did get that emu...

Land-folk were worriers anyway. Jek was an obvious land-folk.

Audrey didn't hold with worrying. It was her attitude that a minor mistake might be a matter of life and death... but then again it might not. And after all, what was there to worry about here? This was her *life* – a captive of the sea...

When Audrey was a child, her parents had sent her away on a ship – from where, or for what reason, she didn't know. All she remembered of that early episode was the horrible grief on their faces as they parted. If asked, she couldn't tell you the color of her mother's hair or whether her father had a beard, or how they dressed. The memory was a feeling only; like reading pure sorrow and later forgetting the words it had been written in. Not that she could read, or anything.

If their intention had been to speed her away from some grave danger, they were not altogether successful. The ship was soon enough beset by pirates. Not just any pirates, she later realized, but privateers – raiders on the payroll of Jast-Madiir. They weren't the adopting kind, so when they next met with their contact in the Jast-Madiiran navy, they were quick to pawn her off. The admiral had a well-rehearsed proposition for her. She could work on Jast-Madiiran ships and be paid with eventual citizenship. As a youngster, she didn't really know what the Heck he was talking about, but as with most who were being shanghaied – forced into working on a ship by the simple fact that she was *on* a ship and there weren't many other places to go – she ultimately ended up gainlessly employed for the next several years.

One might not know it, but a child could be of plenty of use on a ship. There were so many simple cleaning tasks, knots to check, and constant galley work. And before long you get old enough to tie some of those knots yourself, do shifts in the crow's nest, maybe help load or unload some cargo now and again – as long as the delivery was being made to or from another ship. She got to throw a line out to a guy that had fallen overboard one time. That had been pretty cool.

There were women as well as men serving aboard the *Cosigner* – the merchant ship she ultimately grew up on – and she enjoyed a host of mother and father figures. Though really, most of them were just doting elders; she didn't learn much from them – mostly some sailing stuff. As far as they were concerned, she was working, which demonstrated she had already learned life's most valuable lesson.

Finally, one day, she earned her recompense – she was allowed to leave the ship, making landfall on the southern side of Jast-Madiir, her new island homeland. Her first few weeks as a citizen were a flurry of paperwork. She progressed through the paperwork with remarkable speed – apparently much faster than new citizens who were literate. In this she took great pride.

Immediately following this brief transition period, she was married to Jek and began her new career as a lighthouse steward. It was the career that was supposed to have lasted her to the end of her life, barring any potential conscription to something else that might come up...

But now, just a few months of stewarding and several hundred wagon rides to town later, she was already back where she started. But instead of being a captive of pirates or an entire nation, now it was just a gnarly old geezer. And this was no proud merchant ship – just a fishing boat, and one that had surely seen better days. Not that she was complaining – merely observing. And there was plenty of damage to observe...

Up above, there was the mainsail. Audrey had helped the old man patch it earlier in the afternoon. It had been torn savagely – like it had been struck with a full-size cannonball!

Further down, the mast was missing a chunk. It told approximately the same story, appearing to have been clipped by speeding projectile. These were not your everyday maladies for a little fishing boat, and she couldn't help wondering how, faced with such an assault, a dinghy like this had ever managed to escape.

The most mysterious injury to the vessel was the one at the fore. The front-most and topmost section of the bow had been torn clear off. What made this particularly puzzling is that she could distinctly remember the bow being in fine shape when she had climbed right over it earlier that day. Whatever had rent the boat there had evidently done so in the brief time she was unconscious...

Watching the dusk gather, and satisfied that the boat would not likely run aground in the next few minutes, she decided to illuminate the small cabin at the center of the craft. Hanging by the rear entrance was a lamp, which she removed to the inside of the cabin. It didn't take much fumbling to locate the matches and the oil, and within moments the lamp was burning bright – the gloom of nightfall effectively banished.

In the new light, Audrey quickly saw that the cabin extended below deck. Curious, she secured the lamp and proceeded down the few steps. The small space was like a short hall with a door on either side. She pressed open the port door, finding it filled (to overflowing) with provisions and knickknacks. The starboard door had a handle, and featured a very nice painting of a duck. She found that behind that door was a toilet – a 'head' as her shipmates would have called it. *Glad to have one of those on-hand*, she thought.

Her attention returned to the short hall between the doors, where the steps emptied out. There were some curious little dark blobs on the floor that were hard to make out in the swaying light of the lamp up the stairs. Approaching with some caution, she felt a bit silly when she realized they were bed rolls. But this gave her pause... for she soon realized that there were *three* bed rolls. *Exactly* three. What was she to make of that? Foresight? Happenstance?

There was only one remaining feature in the hall. It was hanging on the far wall, furthest from the steps. A second painting. It banished all thought of the bed rolls.

She saw the features of the portrait plainly even in the low and shifting lamp-light as she arrived cautiously at the end of the hall. Examining it closely, a wave of the crisp night air brushed her from above, and she was chilled to the bone. Near the bottom of the painting was the silhouette of a seated man, appearing weary or downcast, hunched forward as he sat, almost limply. The vertical space of the portrait was dominated by his seat – a very great and imposing throne in bold relief with sharply carved inlays that extended beyond the uppermost bounds of the image. The man – or the shadow of a man – was shackled to it.

The painting was troubling in its apparent, confused proverbial pretenses. But that was as nothing compared to what really unsettled her. She knew this was not the first time she'd seen it. The subject and the context eluded her, but she *knew* the image. The image was a fragment, surely, of a time when she had been too young to boast a proper memory. It was an image, quite possibly, which held some great meaning in whatever forgotten nation had once been her birthplace. She dared believe nothing more fanciful than that.

Audrey reached a hand out toward the canvas, as if the tactile sensation of it would make her remember something more... but just as irrationally, she found she didn't have the nerve to touch it...

SMACK!

"Ye're desertin' yer duty for the secondliest time today!" shouted the old man.

She gasped and whirled around. The old man's hand rested open-palmed on the wall where he'd smacked it as he stood at the top of the steps, biting his lower lip, as if to hold back his dopey grin. "*Har-ha-har*!" he laughed at last. "I be joshin' ye."

She shot him an angry look, but she did it mostly out of courtesy to his simple sense of humor. It was a welcome diversion, after all. For the moment, she just wanted to put some distance between herself and that painting...

"How's Jek?" she asked, passing the old man as she ascended the steps and emerged from the cabin. "Did you check to see if the bump went down at all?"

"I be not much for nurse-maidin', I warrant," he answered. "Best check it yerself."

She did at that. The bump was still pretty easy to find with her probing hand. It felt like it had gone down a bit though. Probably. Maybe.

There was the sound of clumsy rummaging, and a very flagrant oath behind her. *"Heck,"* she heard. She stood and turned her attention. Back in the cabin, the old man was into the provisions, making such a clatter that she thought he might need help.

"Would ye care for some gallimimus jerky?" he called out, still hunched into the supply room, even as she started his way. Suddenly Audrey realized she was starving.

"Yes, thank you!" she said, walking up to the cabin.

As the old man emerged from the alcove, holding jerky in both hands, his eyes bugged, and he dropped the dried meat...

Audrey spun. Jek was on his feet! He had his musket... and they were in his sights!

"Aaliyah, step back!" he said fearfully.

"Audrey!" she corrected him.

"Sorry," he replied. He shifted unsurely as he continued to hold out the musket. Audrey didn't like all this mischief. They could hardly shoot the old man – especially without so much as finding out why he had kidnapped them in the first place. Nor did compelling him to take them back hold any promise. But she was suspicious of Jek's martial skill, so she stepped back just the same...

* * *

For several seconds, Jek just held the weapon, the old man staring back with his hands still up and out. His expression was not so startled now. It was mischievous, if anything.

"Ye made me to drop some mighty tasty foragin's," he said slyly.

"You monster!" Jek finally snapped. "Do you realize what you've done to us? We *can't* leave the lighthouse! We'll be hunted down! We'll be executed! We'll be branded heretics!"

The old man started slowly hunching down. "I better just be pickin' this jerky up here, a'fore the fifty-second rule pass us by..."

Jek rattled the musket, re-aiming. "Don't do it, old man! Don't reach for that jerky!"

"Got to, lad. I be one to cry over spilt meat, I warrant..."

"Leave it!"

"Just... about... got it..."

JOLT!

The boat was suddenly slammed skyward, as if buffeted by a rogue wave or a whale passing under. As the entire craft rocked violently, the gunwale caught Jek in the back of the legs. Tossing the musket into the sky in an ineffectual attempt to aright himself, Jek went tumbling off the boat and into the drink. Audrey ran to his aid. The old man snatched up the jerky, stuffed it in his pockets, and finally joined her by the side of the boat.

Jek had already righted himself in the water and Audrey grabbed one of his arms, the old man taking hold of the other. Audrey heaved hard, but Jek proved surprisingly effortless to extract. It was almost as if the sea were as cooperative now in giving Jek back as it had been conveniently inclined to capsize him moments earlier...

* * *

For a while they all just sat in the boat, though the old man quickly began to snack. He handed a stick to Audrey. Then he offered one to Jek. Still looking very bewildered and waterlogged, Jek ultimately accepted the jerky. "Thank you," he said.

Anticipant silence hung in the air for a while. There was explaining to do, and now that they were all finally awake, it seemed the unspoken consensus that the matters at hand be broached...

"Ye be havin' a lot o' questions, I warrant," the old man said, his face under-lit in a garish way by the lamp that was now in their midst. "Let me start by askin' one o' ye. Do ye recall Proconsul Zedulon's prophecy; the one he gave when last he visited yer island?"

Again the group fell silent. Audrey had certainly heard of Zedulon, the sovereign of the Dire Heron state of Roemnar, but his last trip to Jast-Madiir had probably predated her citizenship. She was sure she didn't know anything about his prophecy. But before she could admit as much, Jek remembered something...

"Oh, I remember it now. It was pretty tasty! Made for quite a lot of cleaning though. But I don't see..."

"Not *that* prophecy!" the old man said crossly. "It was t'other one before that! The one about the great evil coming back into the world!"

Jek frowned. "I guess I'd hoped the second prophecy excused the first one."

"Well, *it didn't,*" the old man said, bobbing his head. "That ain't how prophesizin' works! I seen the evidence me own self."

Jek stopped chewing and blanched. "You mean... you saw evil?"

"Aye, lad," the old man admitted gravely. "That I did." He got a very, very distant look in his eyes, and began his story. "There I was, at the helm of me proud ship and true, the *Sadie Hawkins*. We'd been driven along by the jet stream fer weeks. Rightly, I coulda steered the ship to safety even with me hands tied back, but I had more in me charge than me own fine ship. There was dozens in our convoy, and if I used me skills only to save me *Sadie*, the rest o' the ships would surely a-been dashed on the Mausoleum Peaks o' Meatgrinder Bay..."

"...You were north of Meatgrinder Bay?" Audrey interrupted. "You mean, you were coming from the continent... the mainland!?" It was a well-known fact that between the vast continent that made up most of the known world and the Idriulthorontan Archipelago (the sequestered island chain which Audrey and Jek knew as home) there was a jet stream that drove virtually all unwary (and many wary) boats bound for the islands to a grizzly fate on the Mausoleum Peaks. No one in the Archipelago would be sailing that way... with only the possible exception of crazed pirates. It was profoundly interesting that the old man had come from the continent. *No one* heard from the continent anymore...

"Aye, and I could tell ye tales of the goings-on up there that'd make yer grey hide stand on end!" Suddenly he looked unsure of himself, and scratched at the back of his neck. "That is... if I could but remember what them goings-on was..."

"Well never mind about that," Jek insisted, sounding a bit nervous. "I'm still more eager to get to the part that explains why you kidnapped us."

"Aye," the old man nodded. "As I begins to say, only by me braveliest o' efforts could the convoy possibly reach the haven o' Fool's Hope Isle. There weren't no other prayer for the poor lubbers. From the deck, I shouted out commands left, and I shouted 'em out right, and finally we was a-comin', one-and-all, to calmer waters. And yet, fer all me gallantry, it weren't Fool's Hope Isle we'd reached a'tall! Nay, we be still on the brink o' the Mausoleum Peaks. But to me wonderin' eyes, the seas was calm all the same! Seemed a plain miracle that we wasn't cut to ribbons on the jagged slopes! All the more when we saw the tangle o' masts and bows and bits o' ships stretchin' on between the Peaks, far as the eye could see all about. It was a dreadful sight – a parade o' death too somber for e'en a stalwart heart as mine."

At this juncture, the old man's arms flung out. "But our eyes was deceivin' us! Too late we realized the danger. Hidden ever-so-clever-like among the derelicts was *ships* – whole and sound – ships by the *hundreds*! New ships! Eldritch reekin' metal hulks – like Inquisition ships they was – all without sails, but they blacked out the sky with their smoke! They run down all the other vessels in the convoy. T'was the most I could do to save me precious *Sadie*, and t'was me only comfort that the others was captured, and so spared a watery grave, at least as I did watch."

The old man was noticeably sullen now, and had been spastically animated throughout the telling. It gave life to his story. Audrey was amazed. All thought of her own plight had flown for the moment, and Jek too appeared transfixed.

"How did you ever escape?" Jek asked.

Now the old man looked at him crossly. "Sailed south, then cut east 'round Roemnar. I figger'd any ships what was hidden that careful wouldn't dare make chase in Heron waters, where they'd be spotted sure. And right I was. But don't ye see? Ain't it plain, lad? There be a *Doom Fleet* out there! Hidden right where no one'd ever be thinkin' a lookin' for it – like a legion of assassins sprawled out in a valley o' the slain. I sawed a Doom Fleet in Meatgrinder Bay! That's what I been tellin' ye!"

"That's terrible," Audrey commiserated.

"But how could anyone build a huge fleet that close to Despotopia without them noticing?" Jek asked. Likely he was trying to reason away the old man's ill news, but he seemed to be avoiding the obvious conclusion...

"Are ye daft? Despotopia's the one's buildin' it, a-course!"

Audrey's heart soared at the mention of Despotopia. Of all the nations in the Archipelago, Despotopia was the one she had most hoped she was actually from. It was a remarkably productive and efficient island country that had extraordinary affection for their verbose Kaiser, who had done much to lead them to such great success in modern times. It was a nation of monocles and heavy industry. But it made her sad to hear that they were making a secret Doom Fleet...

Jek apparently was unconvinced. "I don't see how Despotopia could build an armada in secret, even in their own Bay. It would take an enormous labor force! Between the Inquisition and the Clerical Dronehood, there's no way they could stage that many of their people on the north-west coast without raising some suspicions."

The old man, going narrow in the eyes, waved a finger. "But they ain't buildin' the ships with their own people! They been seizin' on all the convoys comin' from the mainland, just the way they almost got me own self, I warrant. And there's all that business with Maenea to the east; that "Free-Dome" crisis be displacin' people by the thousands!"

That was a point that couldn't be dismissed. Some revolutionary movement known only as "Free-Dome" had evidently caught like wildfire in the nation of Maenea, and refugees were known to be fleeing the country in droves... sailing in overwhelming numbers primarily to Despotopia. Most others were turning up to the south on the shores of Roemnar, the next closest satellite. But this was a Heron nation, and not in a hurry to accommodate hundreds or thousands of new Human constituents. So these were ultimately being deported to Despotopia anyway. Allegedly the Proconsul had approved this arrangement with the Kaiser himself, who had expressed joy at the thought of welcoming the refugees to his own country. Suddenly it seemed there may have been a dark side to his hospitality. Even the Clerical Dronehood of Berlberi was having a hard time keeping track of all the displaced citizens, fastidious as they were in all things record-keeping. If Despotopia had access to phantom conscripts from Maenea, and apparently the mainland as well, then labor was no obstacle.

Audrey decided to voice her own reservations, for what they might be worth. "You have to understand, it's very hard to accept that a country like Despotopia would be up to anything sinister. Such a noble and hard-working people; so devoted to their Kaiser. They set a great example for all other Human countries. How could they be bad?"

"I felt the same way, a-course," the old man admitted with a sigh. "But Kaiser Heinrechenshlagen ain't no saint after all. He be the very evil what Zedulon was prophesizin' about... I'd stake me last plumb nickel on it!"

Jek huffed. "Now I know you're not making sense. Zedulon prophesied that a very great evil was coming *back* into the world. *Humans* don't just come *back* into the world! Even if they did, who would Heinrechenshlagen be? Or, well, *have been*... or whatever?"

The old man scratched his unkempt beard thoughtfully. "Mayhaps I didn't think that adequate through," he said.

"And anyway, what *is* the Kaiser planning to do with his Doom Fleet?" Jek asked. "Evil, sure... but what *kind* of evil? Who is he going to attack, do you think?"

Abruptly the old man jumped to his feet, stomping deliberately. "Heck if I knows, lad! And a'fore ye ask, Heck if I knows how they managed to calm all the seas what suffuse them Mausoleum Peaks! And Heck if I knows when the Creators is a-finishin' work on their second universe! *All I knows* is the Fleet be real – and dreadful so – and I has to stop it doin' whatever dastardly doin's it be made to do. But now me precious *Sadie* be sunk, and all hands lost but meself. That's what I needs you two for! I can't keep this dinghy goin' night and day! I's plug-worn'd-out!"

"But what can you do about it?" Audrey asked. "What can any of us do about an entire Fleet like that?"

The old man smiled at her. "But didn't ye reason it out yet, lass? We's on a Quest!" He looked into the distance again, eyes glinting in the lamp-light with inspiration. "Gonna save the world – and make a name fer ourselfs – all in the most classicalest way possibible. We're a-gonna find the Knights of the Indigo Lodge..."

Weight of the World

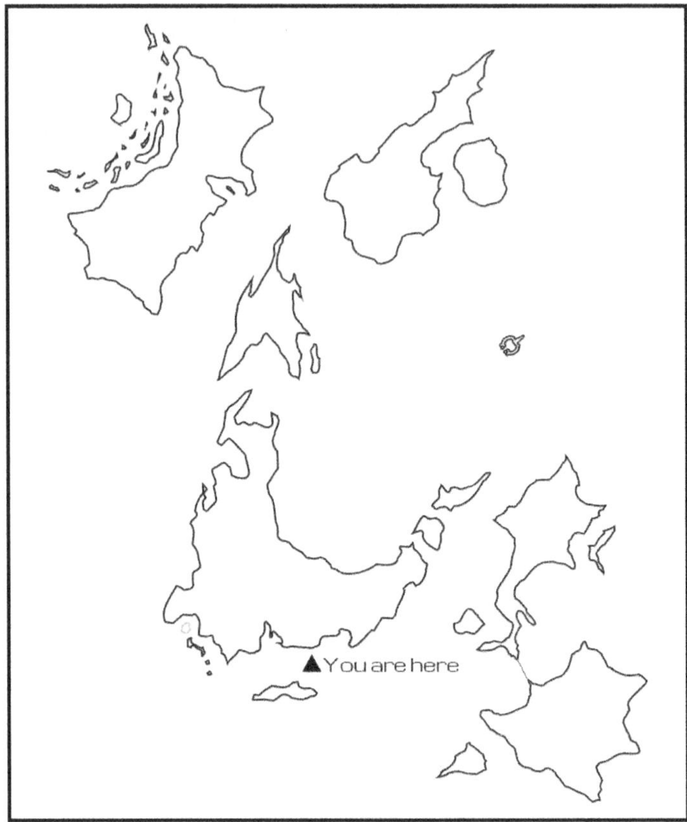

"First among sentient life were the Meduselda – colloquially (though not accurately) the 'jellyfish-folk'. Many are the drones of the Meduselda; their years are one-hundred and forty. Seven are the Queens; their years are seven-hundred and seventy. Kill a Meduseldan as many times as you wish, but they will never fail to return to the living, until their years are spent. Only at the end of their allotted time do they truly perish.

"Next among sentient life were the Avarica – colloquially (and accurately) the 'dragon-folk'. They are ageless, but can be slain. However, each Avarican is drawn to treasure… and if they possess any, and so long as they lay claim to it, they do not remain dead; they will reappear at the site of their treasure hoard, and will grow ever larger and fiercer with each regeneration.

"The final mode of sentient life is shared with that of beasts. One is born, and one dies. Why the Creators settled on this for the Humans, and all of the Enlightened races that followed, none can say…"

- Maribel Charnig, *Basics of Mortal Biology*

"Whoa-woah," said the cab driver to his horses, reining them in. But Parissah leapt from the bench before the wagon had a chance to stop. A half-day had been lost already.

"I left the fare in the seat," she called back over her shoulder, unknowingly turning her head back just a bit too far, causing the driver a shiver. He snatched up the paper note, redeemable for real money.

"Thanks," the driver replied weakly. Now Parissah shivered. She had received many thanks today, each as uncomfortable as the next. She held back a hand in final acknowledgement of the driver even as she quickened her pace toward the large, deadly warship that was moored just ahead on the twilight shore, anxiously awaiting her arrival...

Parissah had to negotiate her way through a crowd of gawkers gathered around the *Carroccio* – a Coup-de-Grâce-class heavy cruiser. Granted that modern Inquisition battlecruisers were an unusual sight on the southern coast of Jast-Madiir. It was essentially the edge of the world down there, and though the region had an unruly history, it had never seen any substantive naval combat. The ship could hardly have seemed more out of place if it had come from one of the Other Worlds. Even so, it struck her odd that so many people could find the time to stand and look at something.

Carroccio itself was a catamaran-style cruiser built around a huge central electromagnetic catapult. It was designed as a high-speed delivery system for implosive charges that could devastate single targets, or even crush entire small flotillas of closely-clustered ships or attack boats. The twin hulls also boasted powerful shorter-range defensive cannons. It was one of a hundred or so of its make, and there were many different makes and sizes of Inquisition warships – many smaller, but some even larger. The rig in front of her would have been extreme overkill for any potential seaward operations in southern Jast-Madiir all by itself. But it might prove indispensable in Parissah's next mission...

As she approached, she was met with Mariner Guards cradling full-size snail guns and escorted up the ramp of the ship. Once on the port catwalk, other crewmen promptly drew the ramp up behind her. Calls were given out, an alarm echoed down from the top deck, the mooring lines were cast off and the whole ship was thrumming away from the shore before Parissah had even entered the port hull. It was a reassurance. The crew met the highest standard of efficiency, and the ship could make up for much of the lost time, sailing at top speed.

She squeezed past busy crewmen in the spartan corridors, making her way to the lower decks. Skidding along some thick insulated piping, she came to a laddered hatchway that she took straight down the last few levels, her claws clinking in a flurry on the metal rungs.

The lowest deck was devoted to cargo and consumables. It was comparably spacious, and yet sequestered, with few having duties that brought them here. She came quickly to a refrigeration chamber. She opened the heavy door and found that the lanterns were already burning. This chamber had been hastily but effectively converted into an office for Parissah. It was unusual for a Primary Administrator to operate out of a specialized battlecruiser, so these kinds of accommodations had to be improvised.

She set her pack of forms and papers on the small desk and rounded it to sit down. Though the walk from the wagon to the ship was a short one, it was a definite relief (however unmerited) to be off her feet again. In the course of her duty that day, it had been necessary to lie, and she'd taken the prescribed penance – tightening her ankle-weights. It was not well-known among the other sentient species, but Avarica had weak ankles. Hers had already been hurting her from much earlier, when she found herself dashing full-speed down to the coast...

Parissah had started her day instructing two initiates in the proper disposal of superfluous belongings – a common task for Inquisitors of low rank. The subjects were an unremarkable pair of Human lighthouse stewards. This kind of training was well below her station by now, but she insisted on continuing it. She'd expected the mission to be quite routine, having instructed hundreds of initiates in her day. But there had been that unforeseen confrontation with the lighthouse inspector, whom she had found quite unpleasant. And then the arrival of the Berlberi Clerk... followed by the most incongruous flight of the stewards...

It hadn't taken long for them to notice that the stewards were gone. The inspector had been utterly wroth that they would leave him unattended during any part of the inspection. When he went to call for them, they caught sight of the male steward running down the far side of the hill toward the coast. Something seemed to be amiss and they all went to see what was going on. Reaching the hilltop, they oversaw the shore, where a fishing boat had beached itself at the base of the light tower. It had gained the rightful attention of the stewards, as well as the completely unmerited attention of dozens of tiny songbirds. The inspector, the Clerk and Parissah herself had called from the hill to see if any additional help would be needed. But they went unanswered... the stewards climbing into the boat...

It was at this point that Parissah took an active hand in the matter. She bolted for the boat. Even she did not know precisely why. Nonetheless, she intuited trouble. Maybe they would need her help. Or maybe, having already fared poorly on their inspection, they were attempting to *flee*. It was quite difficult to read the situation from afar, but in either case the matter seemed to call for her presence.

The flight down the hill was frenzied, and she couldn't be sure of everything that appeared to take place in the boat that lay far ahead of her. It looked quite as if the stewards had been assailed from behind by some old Human – a grubby little fellow that, by all signs, had been the very half-wit that ran the craft aground in the first place. By the time she neared the boat, he was the only one up and about, and it was clear that he was in a frenzy of his own, trying to get his dinghy back out to sea. He was having some success, which frankly astonished Parissah, for he looked quite small and weak. Regardless, he would have to be stopped! She couldn't very well let the stewards get away...

The old man beset her with an oar, which was effortlessly broken. She seized the bow of the boat, digging her claws in deep. In one great heave, she had negated all the old man's progress, pulling the craft back up the shore several feet. But, as she readied to heave again, she was quite suddenly struck by a massive tidal surge. She rooted her clawed feet into the beach for all that they were worth, and held fast to the bow, readying for the backlash of the rogue wave with every muscle. And rooted she remained. But the ocean would not be denied the boat, and the bow gave way in her grasp. She was left with two handfuls of splintered wood as the dinghy was whisked yards and yards out into the ocean. She went for her sidearm, but it was gone – decoupled from its holster by the force of the wave. The boat continued to retreat at surprising speed, trailing the little birds as it went. There was really nothing left for her to do… except to start calculating where the apprehension of these unlikely fugitives best fit into her schedule. By default, it was now her duty to see it done…

It seemed a terrible shame she would have to arrest and extradite the young lighthouse stewards at some point, to their sure execution – for they had come across as humble sorts, who probably weren't looking to get into any trouble, and had much more likely been taken against their will by the peculiar old man…

But, oh well.

There were more pressing matters at the moment. Though Parissah was sure the rogues had set out west, she was now sailing east…

* * *

Presently the heavy door swung open. It was her students – the initiates from the purging earlier that day. She had sent them back to the ship ahead of herself with word that she would be delayed; forced by the circumstances to go into town and send messages via carrier pigeon – and see to various other tasks related to the runaway lighthouse stewards.

"Reporting for debriefing, ma'am," they said.

She examined her students. They were pretty green; among the most undisciplined pupils she'd ever received. The Inquisition was in a stage of hasty recruitment of late, owed to a whole host of troubles that were cropping up all around the Idriulthorontan Archipelago. These two had made numerous glaring mistakes throughout the purging – breaking things they ought not to have broken, and missing other obvious targets. Worst of all, they had seemed to *enjoy* the job early on. There was nothing quite so unprofessional as Inquisitors that enjoyed breaking peoples' stuff…

Other aberrant behavior was already beginning to manifest, she could see. Young Deacogal was not even wearing his ankle weights. Parissah gave a hot sigh that sizzled the inside of her mask.

"Deacogal," she said, "why in all of creation are you reporting to me while *not* in full uniform?"

He stood there blankly for a spell. "Oh, you mean about the ankle weights? They were getting really uncomfortable," he told her matter-of-factly, "so I took them off."

"Of course they're *uncomfortable*," Parissah responded, metering her response as best she could. "That's the whole point."

"Oh," he said.

Parissah stood, producing the report on the day's purge from her pack, straightening the paper with a crisp snap. "The neglect of your ankle weights brings the total miscarriages of duty in today's mission to fourteen. We shall all have to be severely chastised when we return to the Ocean Citadel."

The initiates were silent, but apparently forlorn. Another rookie response. Parissah speedily reviewed the report for anything she had intended to expound on further...

"Maricalgi," Parissah began, "I especially meant to address your breaking of the upstairs window."

"Oh yes, I remember it well," she replied. "There wasn't all that much upstairs to destroy, so I just tried to improvise. I thought you might applaud my creativity."

Parissah folded the report. "No." She sat back down. "We're supposed to have our eye out for *superfluous* things... things without which the subjects' lives are not significantly disrupted. We're curtailing excess. Having glass in all the windows of your house does not constitute excess."

"Well, darn," Maricalgi said, hanging her head.

Parissah gave a cautioning point. "We do not tolerate such crass language within our ranks."

"Sorry," she said, much-dismayed. "I guess we're just hopeless screw-ups."

Parissah silently recognized the crucial tipping point in her training regimen. She got up from the desk, came around and set a hand on each of their shoulders, giving them an affirming look they couldn't see through her mask. It was clearly time to be nurturing now. "Don't despair. I was totally clueless like you people once. But after a hundred years or so of grueling discipline, I finally got around to being of some use. I have every confidence that, with a similar regimen, the two of you will also excel... eventually. If you survive our next assignment, that is."

She could see that their can-do spirits revived with her words. "What *is* our next assignment?" Deacogal asked eagerly. "Are we going to go blow something up with this ship?"

"The mission is a diplomatic one," Parissah explained. "But yes, the crew may have to blow something up. It will depend on the success of our negotiations."

From high on the wall opposite the door, Parissah pulled down a map that had been set in the room for review. The map featured the former Meduseldan nation of Tophthaera... a pair of large islands with a few small satellites apiece; one to the north and one to the south, each arcing toward the other in the west, but not quite meeting. In that area there was a line, which represented a very great bridge – it was named *Variglew* in the Elfish language. Parissah pointed to that very spot. "This is our destination – the Bridge of *Variglew*."

She moved her clawed finger to the westernmost side of the map, indicating a moderate-sized satellite island belonging to Jast-Madiir. "We will be coming to *Variglew* via the island of Fettonia, where we will make a brief stopover."

"What's in Fettonia?" Maricalgi asked.

"Reinforcements, with any good fortune," Parissah answered. "In any case, we plan to form an assault team to disrupt the Tophthaeran civil war at its epicenter... the great Bridge. The Twin Queens of the Berlie Beirels have been ignoring all of our stern warnings to suspend their conflict. So we are going to suspend it for them." She pointed to each of the main islands in turn. "Our ultimate objective is to stop the war for the time being. Based on analysis of prevailing Berlie Beirel psychology, we believe that if we engage the vanguard of both the north and south in the central battle-zone of the *Variglew* Bridge, they will listen to what we have to say – provided we can sufficiently frustrate their efforts to fight *each other*.

"If we survive long enough to prove our point to the local commanders, we must demand that they institute a ceasefire while we gain audience with the Twin Queens." She turned from the map. "In the event we are all killed in action, the ship *Carroccio* has been assigned to this mission as a contingency. It is ordered to shell *Variglew* into oblivion if we die."

"Cool," both Deacogal and Maricalgi said.

"...Except the part where we're dead," Deacogal stipulated.

Parissah shook her head. Such green initiates. They would learn, of course, not to think that things are cool... or at the very least, not to admit as much...

"Dying is not an option in this mission," Parissah explained. "Yet even for non-options, there must be contingencies. Because failure is even more not an option than dying."

The initiates looked at each other. "Can you explain that last part?"

"Just don't die," Parissah admonished serenely.

"Yes ma'am!" they agreed, and she dismissed them.

* * *

Seated again, Parissah thoughtfully considered her map. It was not the same map of Tophthaera, but a different one on the same roll. It offered a wider perspective, depicting the entire Idriulthorontan Archipelago.

In truth, the Archipelago was just a small, remote corner of the world. On paper it seemed orderly and manageable. But in practice, the area had become its own universe of unrelenting troubles...

There were the transitive difficulties, of course – the ones an Inquisitor could expect anyplace. Pirate attacks were ever ongoing. Watchfulness against the return of Onyxadon, and the threat of lesser dragons, had to be maintained. And there had been a recent, widespread heresy incident on and around Jast-Madiir's Fish Islands – a region that seemed to be always causing minor disturbances. The royalty of Jast-Madiir tended to neglect their southern coast, inaccessible as it was from the north – an inland band of mountains and dense jungles, populated by hostile Dire Mantid tribes, made it so. As such, the Czars and Czarinas mostly left it up to the Inquisition to deal with any serious situations which might arise in their own lower holdings.

Her thought wandered to those Mantid tribes – a trial all their own. Existing in indeterminate but considerable strength in mid-Jast-Madiir and in some areas of Maenea and Despotopia, these savage sentients refused to acknowledge civilized society, and were completely outside the Inquisition's supervision. That was a problem the Inquisition had long intended to remedy, just as it had many times in the past, whenever these kinds of rogue populations had been discovered. But in this instance, her order had suffered dearly for its outreach. They had recently lost a number of their best envoys in a desperate gambit to establish relations with the tribes.

And they had very bad need of skilled envoys right now. As she had just explained to her students, Parissah was entrusted with trying to negotiate a suspension of the Tophthaeran Civil War, until such time as Enscharaulgk himself could attend a summit with the warring Twin Queens. And, in but a few weeks' time, she would be meeting with the balance of their remaining emissaries to confront the armed revolt that was currently tearing the north-eastern Human nation of Maenea apart…

"Free-Dome," they called it… or, "Free-Dumb," to its detractors. At its heart was a proposal for a radical new type of civic order that allegedly intended to take terrifying abstractions, such as liberty and popular sovereignty, and *seriously* attempt to implement them as social virtues. The term "Free-Dome" was coined by Herz Bravado – a mysterious Maenean peasant, and the apparent mastermind of this troubling crusade. It was his battle-cry, and had already made the blood of thousands run suddenly cold…

Countess Jengadocea of Maenea had her hands full trying to stop the spread of Bravado's revolution. She was unable to prevent him from taking the secondary island of Magna Koepna in its entirety, and had very short-lived success at isolating the movement thereon. Being a sovereign who was already unusually lenient toward her subjects (having never even executed anybody), most external observation was quick to attribute the success of the radicals to Countess' own weak resolve.

However, anyone watching the situation very closely would note that something quite peculiar must be at work. The fact of the matter was, Jengadocea had sent entire regiments of highly skilled and zealous soldiers to eradicate Bravado and his band. But each successive wave had found members of the previous regiment swelling Bravado's own ranks! By now, he commanded a great company of turncoats. This was indeed baffling. Transcripts of Herz Bravado's various speeches about the concept of "Free-Dome" revealed a man of meager intellect and extremely substandard persuasive speaking ability. And yet, his personal army consisted more and more of some of the Countess' most loyal servants…

The crisis itself was two-fold. Not only was Maenea apparently falling to insurrection, but many of its inhabitants had already given up hope of being protected, and were fleeing en-masse to neighboring nations – in particular the reassuringly secure dictatorship of Despotopia. It was the Inquisition's only boon that Kaiser Hienrechenshlagen of Despotopia was doing all he could to alleviate the refugee situation. Without his proactive goodwill, the Inquisition would have been strapped well beyond their means. They almost were anyway.

In addition to all of these tangible troubles, there were also a few metaphysical concerns that her order was attempting to deal with. Most upsetting was the sudden emergence of *magic*…

Discovered on accident, magic was becoming commonplace much more quickly than was befitting of something that almost no one understood. Though briefed extensively on the matter, Parissah had to admit to herself that *she* was not even really sure how it worked. It had to do with alchemical manipulation of Purpose; she knew that much... and it was enough to leave her very unsettled about it...

Indeed, people running around with these new elemental powers gave the Inquisition great cause for alarm. One other time in history, sentient beings had gained sway over the governing forces of the universe, and that had led to perhaps the greatest cataclysm in the annals of the world. They called it the Great Regression, and it was the shimmering paragon of all that the Inquisition hoped to safeguard from ever happening again...

Magic was, admittedly, dissimilar from that dark historical episode by orders of magnitude. The forgotten Power of the time leading up to the Great Regression made magic seem quite a feeble little force by comparison (by all surviving accounts). And importantly, according to all experts, magic wasn't going to be getting any stronger. It simply wasn't possible.

Even so, it was still essentially a practice of mortals manipulating the elements. At the very least, it had to be regulated. But if they were honest, the Inquisition had no way of knowing *how* to properly regulate magic as yet. Enscharaulgk – their Grand Inquisitor – who had seen the Great Regression first-hand, and even escaped the era with his memory intact, would surely have all the answers... when again he lived. Until such time, Parissah and the rest of the Inquisitors could only do their best.

The other ethereal concern was Proconsul Zedulon's so-called "Chocolate Prophecy." He had delivered it nearly fifteen years ago in the Human nation of Jast-Madiir, and the Inquisition had spent all the intervening time on even higher alert than usual, knowing better than to take the prophetic words of a Heron Proconsul lightly – *especially* the words of Zedulon. Granted, a "Chocolate Prophecy" did not sound so ominous, and the eponymous effects of the premonition had already long-since resolved themselves. But on that day, the Proconsul's original, unprovoked foretelling had warned that, 'A very great evil will be coming back into the world'. Parissah was not alone in wondering if magic was perhaps that very evil. After all, he wasn't necessarily referring to a person. A practice or a skill could be an evil as well...

Of course, very little could be ruled out in the case of such a vague omen. The only elaboration Zedulon had given on his own prophecy was that he *hadn't* meant Onyxadon. It may be any of a million things, or more; *every* possibility had to be watched for, and it fell to Parissah and all of her compatriots to be the watchers...

But if anyone was up to the task of watching, she knew they were. The Inquisition had endured to see the rise and fall of many great empires. Almost without exception, each had ultimately come to dissolution out of simple complacency – taking for granted that their past achievements ensured future ones. There was nothing so dooming as the secure sensation of success. The Grand Inquisitors saw this, and had long ago resolved with great pains to elude the pratfall. Every tiny change in the status-quo had to be diligently scrutinized. Every victory had to be treated as failure. Absolutely everyone and everything had to be handled with healthy (if tempered) suspicion. That was the price to be paid for stability that would withstand.

Credos aside, the grave and unrelenting workload she was shouldering was Parissah's greatest comfort in a time of such uncertainty, when they were without the guidance of their Grand Inquisitor. They didn't have all the facts. In some cases they could at best buy time...

Enscharaulgk would know. She urgently hoped he would soon revive...

* * *

KNOCK

There came a knock on the insulated door of Parissah's office. She gave permission to enter, and at once, Taurnuren – the Captain of the *Carroccio* – appeared in her doorway.

For a moment, she just looked at him rather vacantly. His upper body was hunched under its own weight, mostly coming from his exaggeratedly long and sinuous arms. His head arced upward on the end of his neck several extra degrees, apparently over-compensating for the deep, downward turn of his wide shoulders. At the end of his arms one found gaunt fingers with bulbous joints that protruded at odd angles, not unlike a Human hand after many years of severe arthritis. Between the last two fingers and the auxiliary thumb, his elongated webbing had wavy ribbons of pale green and orange – the hues and patterning similar to lichen, and other creeping tree blights. In short – though it might not be her place to notice – he was a total hunk!

Yet the time might come when it *would* be her place to notice after all. For Enscharaulgk had suggested once that he might someday arrange for Parissah and the Captain to be married... each of them being touted as one of his finest officers in their respective fields. She was okay with that.

"Sir," she said, finally rising from her desk.

"Ma'am," he said, nodding.

What a voice!

For a few moments, they left it at that. Somehow the conversation had already come to an abrupt halt. It seemed neither knew what to say from here...

"...Is there something the matter?" Parissah finally asked. She hadn't expected to see him.

"Not at all," Taurnuren reassured her. "I was just concluding a guided tour of the *Carroccio*, with regards to your guest. I assume you have business with him, so I brought him at last to your office."

Another being floated into the room behind Taurnuren. It was Baegulgog – the unusually plump Meduseldan Clerk that had been late in delivering the updated inventory at the lighthouse earlier that day. She had sent him ahead to the ship along with her students. For he had been adamant to make up for his failure to perform his duties in a timely manner, and all the trouble it had caused. In payment of his goodwill, the unpleasant lighthouse inspector had tried to order the poor jellyfish-Clerk to glue the lens back together! But Parissah was quick in thinking of another, far greater service he could render. A not-unsubstantial amount of the work she had done in town was to secure leave for Baegulgog at his Clerical Dronehood office, so that he could be an acting liaison in her mission to Tophthaera... and perhaps later to Maenea...

The Clerk Baegulgog appeared to be in high spirits. His bright blue glow overwhelmed the lamps of her office as he glided along effortlessly through the air.

"Well-met again, madam!" Baegulgog said warmly, inclining himself. "I would, of course, remove my cap in your presence, were it not glued in place."

"Your manners are unimpeachable, Baegulgog, but there's no need to trouble yourself with such formalities." Parissah hated being on the receiving end of good manners, but even so she couldn't help being immediately fond of Baegulgog. She liked being around Meduselda in general. They were an older, simpler form of life with few vices. In other words, they were just better.

At this juncture, Taurnuren excused himself. "I leave you two to discuss your mission; I must return to the bridge." He half-closed the door, but then as an apparent afterthought, leaned back into the room and said, "Bye."

"Bye." Parissah said, followed by a delayed wave that she didn't think he'd seen...

She turned her full attention to the Berlberi Clerk. "As to our mission, Mr. Baegulgog..."

"I am most eager to learn what you have in mind!" he practically cut her off in his exultant manner. "Shall I be helping you to break peoples' belongings? I'm untried in that field, but more than willing to have a go of it!" He executed a lethargic karate-chop in the empty air as he spoke for a show of his readiness.

"Nothing so mundane," Parissah explained. "We're on a mission to the Bridge of *Variglew*. I want you to act as a diplomatic attaché. It may be prudent to have a Meduseldan representative. I trust this does not create a conflict of interest for you?"

"No indeed, madam," he laughed a bit nervously. "I am most certainly not a Berlie Beirel, if that's what you mean. I am a Sowür Canpattel!" Baegulgog spoke of his heritage. Since the beginning of time, there had been Seven Dominions of the Meduselda, each belonging to a different line of Queens. They were the Wuu Gappews, the Berlie Beirels, the Zye Karumbas, the Sowür Canpattels, the Prosketosa Daffadars, the Angus Dei, and the Taltaxikhomer Margaritamoarmonums. Berlie Beirels were the resident Dominion of the Tophthaeran isles, which belonged to their Twin Queens: Irisa and Asiri. Sowür Canpattels and all other Dominions were from the mainland, and each was somewhat distinct in its culture.

"I guessed as much, when you mentioned the glue on your hat."

Baegulgog absently patted his hat with a tentacle. "It is far preferable to having to constantly adjust the thing, and worry about it sliding off. I have a rather rotund frame; not the most stable surface to rest a little hat on."

"I had noted you seemed somewhat overweight. Do you have a medical condition we should be aware of?"

"Oh, no. I assure you I am at peak health," he said, his side-most tentacles lazily curling up in a sort of mock-bicep-flexing action. "But if it will be further relief to you, I once went to see a specialist in Roemnar about my excess weight. It was his determination that I simply eat too much."

Parissah was dumbstruck. She twisted her head in befuddlement. "But... Meduselda don't eat *anything*."

"Well, you see, *there's* my problem!"

Parissah could see she would enjoy working with Baegulgog very much indeed. But it interested her that he was not a native of the region. No one had heard tidings from the continent in some years. This too was a salient concern of the Inquisition. Their chapter in the Archipelago was quite self-sufficient, but no less than five of the original seven Grand Inquisitors lived on the mainland. Their insights would prove most useful in Enscharaulgk's stead, if only they could be reached...

"Tell me Baegulgog... when was it you last had word from the mainland?"

"Oh, full-many years, I'm afraid. I've worked here in Jast-Madiir ever since I finished my studies in Berlberi... perhaps a half-century ago now. That was only after I did a stint in the cavalry, I should like you to know. Like all Sowür Canpattels, my skills in the equine disciplines are unmatched! Unfortunately, my martial abilities left much to be desired. I didn't last long in that vocation. And not making rank as a mounted soldier, I'm afraid I soon discovered I was even more deficient in the musical arts." He flashed brightly. "You know, of course, that it was a Sowür Canpattel who first invented music!?"

"I know the tale," Parissah nodded. She was sure everyone knew of *The Refrain of Chordonoto*.

"Ah, good-good! I will not trouble you with the details then. At any rate, I was poised to become a pacer for a short interlude, but the need was not great enough. So finally, I was turned over to the Clerical Dronehood of Berlberi, to see if they might be able to whip me into some shape. Here I finally fit in, as I quickly learned I had a fondness for numbers... and they had a fondness for me. Surveys and statistics and calculating and crunching! It is all most invigorating to the spirit. And *counting,* madam! Counting is best by far – only *re*-counting is better. I have this favorite tree near my office in Yuffletown, and many days, when there is not enough paperwork, I will go out and count its leaves... and every time one falls... I get to begin the count all over!"

He laughed merrily.

"...But, well, just *listen* to me... going on and on about myself! Yet do not worry – I am as good a listener as I am a talker. Tell me, my good dragon-lady... what is your story? What brought you to the Inquisition?"

There was silence. Silence she couldn't prevent. *Such an inquiry...*

Baegulgog could not have guessed how much he had just caught Parissah at unawares. For although the Inquisition was the primary vocation of Avarica throughout the world, each individual one of them had to first volunteer their services. Such were the rigors of the job that the Grand Inquisitors had been loath to suffuse their ranks with half-hearted conscripts.

Even so, most Inquisitors came from a long line of Inquisitors. And rarely did they discuss their past life among themselves, since it was taken for granted that their stories were all essentially the same...

Parissah's was not.

"...Have I upset you? I beg your pardon!" Baegulgog said.

Drat! Parissah thought. She had klutzed around too long for a response...

"I should say you surprised me, anyway. Think nothing of it," she said, waving dismissively. She didn't want to, but in order to assuage Baegulgog, and because it was painful, she broached the topic... "To be quite truthful," she finally began, "I attribute my career in the Inquisition mostly to my father."

"Your *father*?" Baegulgog asked, seeming unsure of the term. Meduselda had no parents per se – only a Queen, in whose general vicinity they one day 'poofed' into existence.

"Yes... my immediate male ancestor."

"Ah, I see," he said, still sounding a bit unsure. "Was he an Inquisitor?"

A simple 'no' would have been enough. "I entertain the notion that he might have been a very great Inquisitor. But that was not his election. He found his work as a nacre whale tickler."

"Upon my word... a *nacre whale tickler*! What harrowing tales that must have made for! Diving into the deep – challenging the great molluskiform whales – surviving the struggle – tickling them sufficiently to spit forth their titanic pearl – capturing the stone and propelling its profound weight to the surface!" Baegulgog dramatically pantomimed the whole procedure.

"Yes, he enthralled us with many such tales early on. He was a great storyteller, and he was brave and generous. He kept only ten percent of the price for the first pearl he wrangled for himself, giving the rest away. There were many good years."

"Jolly good!" Baegulgog's amusement suddenly deflated. "But whence comes the Inquisition into this tale?"

"The bad years," she explained. "My father had a few brushes with death, you might say. He'd turn up at home; he grew larger and stronger... but ever more preoccupied."

"I'm not sure I follow," Baegulgog said. He was evidently somewhat ignorant of her people, the Avarica – the dragon-folk.

"All Avarica are natural-born treasure hunters, you see," she explained. "It is a curious aspect of our biology. We yearn for gold and gems, because they are a constituent element of our life cycle – somewhat like food for Humans and the Enlightened Races and lesser animals." Parissah determined she might better explain the whole thing. "You yourself will live to be exactly 140 years old, yes?"

"Indeed, madam – 140 years precisely, as your folk would count them!" The Clerk agreed. "That is the way with Meduselda. We drones cannot be denied our 140 years, nor the Queens their 770, no matter how many times we be vanquished!" It was true. If a Meduseldan perished, they would enter a ghostly form, and then, after a week's time, they would harden back into a solid state. They could not truly die until their years were spent.

"Our way is a bit like yours, but also a bit like Humans. It is also distinct. If an Avarican can claim ownership of gold and gems, he has an anchor-point in the material world. If he is vanquished, after a time, he will regenerate from the spot of his treasure hoard, provided the treasure is not taken from him." She waved a claw in the air, dismissing a sudden thought. "There's no sordid ritual or anything that goes along with it as some suggest! This is merely our life-cycle as it was designed; the ownership is enough.

"But each regeneration has rewards, as well as consequences. Every time we return to the world, we grow larger, stronger, until we reach a mature dragon form. But even then, we keep growing. The reward is in the body; the consequence is in the mind; for as we grow more beastlike in form, so also in thought. Our treasure is ever more our preoccupation – how we may add to it, how we may *secure* it – for if we should ever fall and our treasure be claimed, we can never again regenerate.

"I watched this happen to my father. The ten percent he used to keep for himself grew steadily to nearly one-hundred percent, and he began to argue with mother about what he really needed to send us for subsistence – only a little at first, but the arguments escalated by and by. The stories of his adventures grew truncated and obligatory. His time at home was ever more brief, and even when he was there, his mind was elsewhere. Finally the day came when he simply took his treasure and left. We had letters from him infrequently, but even those eventually ran their course. By that time, I had already joined the Inquisition."

Baegulgog just lofted in place, downcast. There was the tension of sympathy, but he couldn't find a way to express it. All of these things were quite alien to him.

"Maybe it's best explained this way: what I saw my father choose, I needed to choose the opposite. He might have lived forever... but he changed so much that, long before he ultimately perished, I lost him anyway... and nothing and no one in all the world could replace him.

"But *here*, with the Inquisition, I knew I would be taught to meet every day the same way – with the same tenacity, the same object, the same outlook. And *here*, I knew that, when my service was done, I could be replaced, just as I myself took the place of hundreds and thousands who came before me. *Here*, there should be no danger of living long enough to become... well, something else. I'm not sure that actually makes sense to anyone but me... but so it is."

"Oh, I understand, madam," Baegulgog assured her. "At least snatches of it here and there. I am sorry that such trauma has compelled you. But I suspect you made the honorable choice. You have my sympathy as well as my admiration," he said, inclining himself in the air. *Ever the gentledrone...*

"Thank you, Baegulgog," she replied, though his words stung. "But I should say it is high-time to return to work." She sat herself behind the desk. "You may have a seat if you wish."

"No, thank you," he said. "I prefer to float."

"Very good," she replied, unslinging her pack. "Before we do anything else, it has occurred to me that there will most certainly be an *In Absentia* trial for those runaway lighthouse stewards. My duties will make it quite impossible for me to attend, though I'm a primary witness. You wouldn't happen to have a waiver I could fill out to excuse my absence? For that matter, I'd better excuse yours as well."

As a member of the Clerical Dronehood of Berlberi, Baegulgog was both a peddler and an enthusiast in all things paperwork, just as he had earlier described. He reached into his satchel with a gloved tentacle and held forth a multi-page form post-haste.

"I keep one handy near the front of my stack... for just such occasions," he said. "Gladly, I would fill one out for myself, but since you have already volunteered to make my excuse, I will not deprive you of the pleasure."

As Parissah seized her pen and began filling out the form, she resolved to leave her ankle-weights tightened an extra rung for double the prescribed time. She hadn't lied to Baegulgog, but she fell well short of telling him everything. She probably should have. It may have been some relief. But then, relief was not the name of the game. But suffice it to say, her family history boasted a multitude of other dark secrets. There was surely no time to get into all that...

Noble Quest

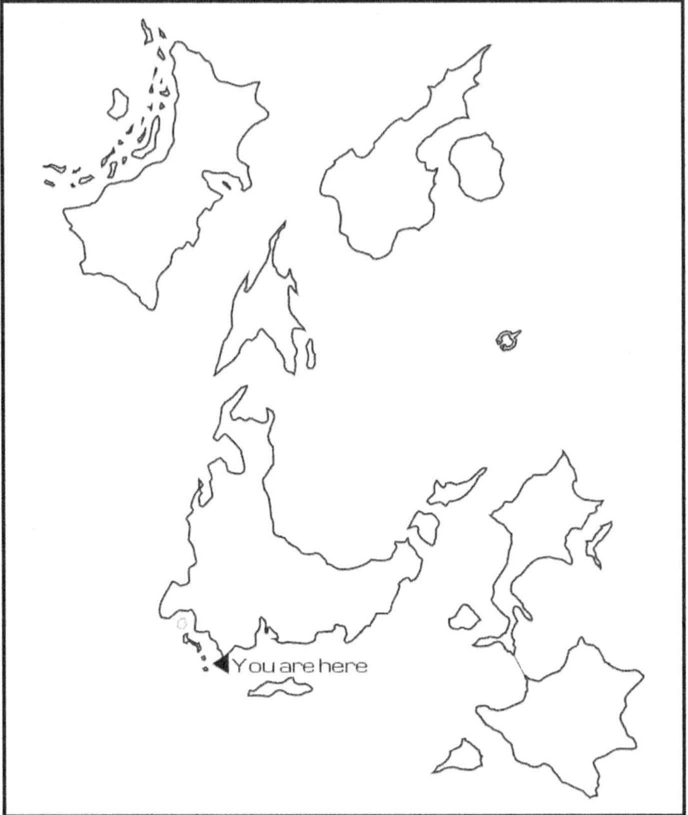

"If, upon the Great Looking-Back of all things, we are found to have done good, then let us have doneth the most greatest good that we could do. If we are found to have done bad, then let us have doneth the least worstest bad that we could do. If we pursued the good, may it have been so to attaineth it. If we pursued the bad, may it have been so to destroyeth it."

- The Pledge of the Knights of the Indigo Lodge

Jek's eyes were heavy, but they soon shot open. He was awakened by the furious chirping of the tiny birds that still hovered overhead. He looked one way and the other in the dazzling light, hoping he hadn't been caught dozing. It was early morning and he was the one who was supposed to be awake... and keeping the boat headed the right way. He twisted and peered over the edge of the boat. There was a sigh of great relief as he noticed that the shore was still off to their right a good ways.

Jek had never driven a boat before, but he remembered well the old man's navigational instructions. "Just ye keep the land off to yer starboard." Once Jek had verified that starboard meant the right side, he felt fairly confident of his ability to sail to the old man's satisfaction.

The night had been peaceful, if somewhat forlorn. It was beautiful being under the stars and the Other Worlds, and actually having time to appreciate them. But every so often, they passed by a lighthouse on the coast, and it reminded Jek grimly of what he wasn't doing. Brighamok's Lighthouse would be unlit that night, and it was his fault. He had spent much of the night struggling to push from his mind the image of dozens of ships piled up in a heap of splinters at the foot of his light tower. Few boats and almost no ships ever sailed by their lighthouse, but it would just about figure if a whole bunch of them had been passing through at just such an inopportune time...

...Especially if they were chasing the old man...

Jek had his suspicions, after all. It was clear that his fishing boat had seen action, but beyond that he couldn't be sure of the old man's story. It had been brilliantly rendered last night, and he couldn't deny that there was a frightening logic behind the plot to use refugees to build a secret Doom Fleet. But even if it was true, whoever sank his *"Sadie Hawkins"* might still be after him. In any case, the old man *was* their kidnapper, and thus, he probably ought to remain suspect.

And there were other reasons. For starters, Jek didn't know the old man from his elbow. And there were moments where he seemed only semi-coherent... though it might just be that he was eccentric. Most of all, it was something the old man had said, which strongly suggested that there were mysterious qualities about him which he hadn't told them yet...

"There be mysterious qualities about me what I ain't told ye yet," the old man had said grimly.

In spite of these many misgivings and reservations, Jek was certainly excited at the proposition of finding the Knights of the Indigo Lodge, distant as that possibility seemed. If their object *could* be realized, it would be wish fulfillment of the highest order! Every young boy grew up playing make-believe they were Indigo Knights. Jek fondly reflected on his own childhood games with his pal Teglo. They would spend approximately thirty seconds arguing about which of them got to be Carlos Washoe and which would have to be another Indigo Knight, before their folks all took notice and promptly compelled them to get back to work. *Darned* good times!

On top of that, the culmination of the Quest held with it a faint glimmer of hope. The Knights of the Indigo Lodge had got their start in a way not altogether different from Jek and

Audrey's own situation. One day they simply threw off all bounds and borders, purposing to do justice wherever it most needed done. They were hunted heretics at first, having forsaken their country. But such was the nobility of their quest that the Grand Inquisitors ultimately pardoned them, giving their budding order of Knighthood the full blessing of the Inquisition, and complete immunity to operate throughout the world.

That was thousands of years ago. Other such organizations had come and gone over the centuries, disbanding or falling into ill repute, but the Lodge remained stalwartly committed to good things. Not only could the Knights surely call the Despotopian Doom Fleet to the attention of the other powers in the Archipelago – most especially the Inquisition itself, which had unrivaled naval strength – but they could do so with the kind of legitimacy and clout that two runaway lighthouse stewards and a geriatric sailor could never wield. But more even than this, they could certainly secure the pardon that Jek and Audrey's lives depended on.

If – that is – the old man was telling the truth. If not, there was probably no hope for them at all.

* * *

Jek came to his feet. Standing up somehow aggravated the sore spot on the back of his head. He checked the bump. Even *he* had to admit that the swelling had gone down considerably. The cool, clear morning air eased the pain a bit. He was surprised just how little fog there was. He could see it up high in the hills on the shore, but nothing along the coast. A far cry from the mornings he knew. It must have just been his luck to run a lighthouse in an abnormally foggy spot.

He looked to the back of the boat. Audrey was there, sleeping soundly. He remembered the old man had offered her the cabin, but she had been adamant to be the one to sleep outside, for whatever reason.

Jek reflected on their time together the night before, after the old man had finished his account. She had still been concerned about his head injury.

"Do you want me to rub something on the abscess?" she had asked.

Jek's eyebrows furrowed. He didn't know medicine of any kind, and somehow immediately suspected she didn't either. "Like what?"

"I don't know; herbs or something." She called back at the old man. "Have you got any herbs?"

After a spell of rummaging, he called back. "I got some coriander... and paprika!"

"That sounds medicinal," she said. "Bring them both!"

Moments later, she was seasoning the back of Jek's head. It hurt, but it was the thought that counted, so he endured it gladly.

"Would you really have shot the old man?" she had asked him.

"I never loaded the gun," he admitted.

Seeing her sleep now, Jek regretted he hadn't apologized more thoroughly for calling her Aaliyah again. She just looked exactly like an 'Aaliyah' to him, and he was seldom wrong about these sorts of things. In the end, it probably wasn't that big of a deal. After all, he was fairly sure he had heard her call him "Jeff" once or twice. If they lived long enough, he was confident they'd get to where they knew each other's names.

Jek went to go get some dried fruit out of the pantry. That is, he hoped there was dried fruit. He didn't want to get scurvy just because he happened to be sailing around at present.

Suddenly, there was a loud, hollow thud, and the boat lurched. *Heck!* Could they have veered into the shore in so short a time? He'd seen it a hundred or so yards away only a minute ago!

There came shouting and swearing. Some of it was the old man's, as he shot awake and started struggling to escape his bed roll only feet away from Jek. But he also thought he heard more distant shouting and swearing. He didn't want to be in the old man's way as he was boiling over anyway, so he promptly exited the cabin and checked round to see where the other angry yammering might be coming from. Off – that is, *barely* off – the left bow there was a row-boat. A different old man – rotund and wearing spectacles, and not quite so elderly and unkempt as their own – was in the row-boat, along with a couple of youngsters – a little boy and a slightly older little girl. They all clutched fishing poles, which they waved vigorously in protest, and they were all wearing dorky matching cone hats.

"Why don't you watch where you're going, ya lubbers?!" the cone-hatted man demanded.

By this time, the old man was mostly out of his bed roll and had come to within arguing distance.

"Why don't ye watch yer language 'round yer grand-kinder, ye friggin' dolt!" he answered. That pretty much ended the argument. The cone-hatted man and his cone-hatted grandkids watched them pass by with looks of shock and aversion, but soon went back to their fishing.

Jek now saw that there were numerous other row-boats in the area, with quite a crowd a long ways off in front of them. All the ones which were close enough to see clearly had occupants with fishing poles... and a number of them were also wearing those dumb hats.

Jek guessed from all the fishing that they were nearing the Fish Islands. There were three Islands – two were pretty tiny little flecks off the south coast of Jast-Madiir, only just big enough to support a half-town on each, but the third was of moderate size. Most everyone who lived on the Fish Islands was a fisher. It's not that the fishing around the Fish Islands was especially great; really, it was kind of meager. But the name of the place suggested otherwise, and the Czarina thusly mandated a large fishing duty from the area.

Presently, Jek became aware that the old man was staring him down. He met his glance.

"Ye did a dumb thing then, lad," the old man said through his icky teeth. "Best do what he say and watch where ye're goin' next time."

Audrey was up now too, probing for crust in her eyes. "Why were those people we ran into wearing those silly hats?" she asked. Jek felt immediately validated knowing that she, too, thought they were silly.

"It be a bad omen, I'm a-feared," the old man began, rubbing his head, as if to smooth down some hair, though there was none. "There been an outbreak o' indigo *hersey* in these parts by all portents."

"What's indigo hersey?" she asked. "Is it contagious?"

"Indigo *heresy*," Jek corrected.

"Y'ain't never heard o' indigo hersey, lass?" The old man was flabbergasted.

"*Heresy*," Jek corrected.

"That's what we all been sayin'! Quit playin' canary and let me answer the lady's wonderin's!" He went quiet for a bit, stroking his beard, apparently trying to decide where to start. Finally he turned to Audrey. "Ye noticed, perhaps, that indigo be a color o' great distinction in the world? The Knights of the *Indigo* Lodge? The zenithyst... pertiest and most valuable o' gems... an *indigo* stone?"

Jek reflexively checked his pocket. He'd completely forgotten that he had come into possession of a *huge* zenithyst the day before! He was relieved to find it was still on his person. Although he was also *not* relieved, because that meant he had really found it yesterday... and he still had no idea what to make of it...

"Yeah, I suppose indigo gets its share of attention," Audrey said, a little unsure.

"There be reason for it!" the old man went on. "To rightly know why, ye have to journey back, deep in the folds o' time," he said theatrically, waving his hand and fingers through the air. "Back, back, back... to the late Meduseldan Era. Ye see, time was when there weren't no colors... there was only Light and Dark. Then the Creators gets this idea. Split the Light into the Seven Colors they did! E'en Red, Orange, Yellow, Green, Blue, Indigo, and Violet!"

"Alright, so it's one of the Seven Colors..." Audrey said.

"Nay, but it be *more* even than that! For one among the Creators did speak unto the Meduselda, sayin' that verily Indigo was greatest o' the Seven, and that only the most unwisest would neglect to take heed o' Indigo. Yea, for if one were to disregard Indigo, and fail to list it among the Seven, or to confuse Indigo with Blue and/or Violet, then just such a one would be called 'Dumbest o' Stupid Dunces'.

"So pleased was the Creators with their Seven Colors, that they went ahead and split the Dark into Seven varieties too! Only they was harder to differentiate... and anyway, that be gettin' off subject." He pointed fervently upward. "The main part be that it was a Creator theyself what said that Indigo was chiefest o' Colors!

"Needless to say, the Inquisition weren't one to take that lightly, for it be the only verbal ordinance what the Creators e'er gave! So, they police it most strict like throughout the world, and when they finds people what don't believe in indigo, or elsewise can't tell it apart from blue or violet, they gives them the dunce-cap! For five years, the hertic must wear the dunce-cap, and be kept under probation for another five. That be the terrible penalty what need be paid!"

Audrey seemed amazed by it all. "Wow! To think that they actually find people... well, that is... why would *anyone* reject indigo if they knew they'd get in that much trouble about it?"

The old man started to look downcast. "Most is driven by sheer ignorance or profane madness. There been times when peoples has not only forsaken, even *forbidden* indigo... but becomed so attached to their misguided ways that they tooked-up arms against the Inquisition, so's to erase all memory o' the great Color! Some mighty sad chapters in history, they was."

Jek looked around, feeling suddenly anxious. "You don't think... *these* people... might try to start that kind of trouble?"

The old man laughed. "Nay. Folks on yer side o' Jast-Madiir is often superstitious, and gets some funny ideas about a lotta things, but they's just under-supervised, and they ain't never done no harm, far's I know. Best not to mention our Quest though, should we has occasion to jibber-jabber with the locals again. Most 'round here got no love for the Indigo Knights; think they secretly controls the world! That they thrown in their lot with Wxldlr and them 'Non-Entities', and such."

"Who's-it and what's-it?" Audrey asked.

"Lands sake, lass!" The old man threw up his hands. "I ain't got time to 'splain all 'bout Wxldlr and the Non-Entities on top-a e'erything else! I *told* ye that all these folk bein' indigo hertics be a bad omen. Means the Inquisition be afoot nearby! They's sure to have heard about ye runnin' off, and they'll be lookin' for us! We gots to try to navigate 'round the Fish Islands fast-like, but also discreet. We gots to blend in with these here fishers!"

He rummaged through his pantry. Somehow his every trip to the pantry caused a great cacophony of rummaging. Finally, he emerged with a few fishing poles and a cornucopia. He handed each of them a pole, and then put the cornucopia on Jek's head.

"There," he said, admiring Jek's new headdress. "That be sportin'!"

"It doesn't look a thing like the dunce-caps!" Jek whined.

"Does if ye squint hard enough," the old man claimed. "Hopefully be effective from a distance."

* * *

The sun was bright on the east horizon. It was midday. So far, they had been successful at blending in. They had been considerably *less* successful at fishing... but that probably only boosted their anonymity. Occasionally they were met with some funny looks from the myriad other fishing boats they were navigating through. But so long as they weren't arrested, they endured it well enough.

"Hey, mister!" called out a kid in a nearby boat. "Why you wearing that cornucopia on your head?"

"Don't ask," Jek replied sullenly.

Jek was standing on the cabin, leaning on the mast. He slyly pretended to bait his hook. But really, he was the chief lookout, being up there where he could see all around, over the other boats.

The plan was to sail between the two smaller islands and out toward the deep sea, giving the larger island a wide berth, since most of the Inquisitors would likely be there. At present they were right in between the small islands. This was the gauntlet. Once they made it through this point, in theory, they should be putting more and more distance between themselves and the Inquisitors.

Suddenly Jek noticed movement off the north island, headed east. It was a boat – the size of a little row-boat – but it was moving *fast*! He climbed down off the cabin, walking up to the old man in the back of their boat. Audrey noticed and came to the back as well.

"Fast boat," Jek said simply, pointing it out to the old man. "*Real* fast."

"Get yer muskets," the old man said. "At that speed it be an Inquisitor patrol boat, er me name ain't..."

"Muskets!" Jek protested in a shouting whisper. "I'm not going to shoot an Inquisitor! We're supposed to be on a Noble Quest! Shooting an Inquisitor is one thing I'm *really* not going to do!"

"If worse come to worse, ye can shoot a hole in their boat, at least... give 'em somethin' else to worry about 'sides catchin' us. But by tunder, get them dang muskets loaded! They's cuttin' around towards us e'en now!"

* * *

The unearthly hum of the drive system on the Inquisition patrol boat throttled down to silence as the cloaked and masked Avarica neared the old man's fishing boat.

Jek whispered to the old man as they drifted closer. "I'm not sure I can do this. Resisting authorities goes against my very nature."

"Too bad," the old man assuaged him.

The patrol boat was getting pretty dang close... when suddenly it came to an abrupt stop. The Inquisitors seemed surprised and puzzled, since they'd clearly had enough coasting speed to come up right alongside the old man's boat. Yet now they were stopped a few yards behind it, for no apparent reason. Nevertheless, they carried on about their business, rising from their seated positions and calling out to their quarry.

"I beg your pardon," started the scary, powerful Inquisitor. "We are conducting a search for three fugitives. We ask if you have seen any Human people resembling what you see here." The Inquisitor produced a wanted poster, holding it out as far as he could, since they were still a ways apart. Jek, examining the image, saw three stick people in a boat – one with short hair, one with long hair, and one with just a beard. This was the general look of wanted posters in Jast-Madiir. It had long since been discovered by the Czars and Czarinas that, the more generic the rendering of a wanted poster, the more tips and leads that local law enforcement received. It might have been a help, because the cornucopia he was currently wearing concealed Jek's short hair, and so befuddled their stick-ish likenesses. Unfortunately, the boat they were in had been expertly drawn, showing all of the battle-damage. The sketch even had some small birds flying over them! These Inquisitors were likely just giving them a chance to admit their guilt and come peacefully.

"I can't read, so no," Audrey answered. Jek felt momentary relief. They were probably still going to die now, but at least her answer prevented him from having to lie to Inquisitors.

The Inquisitor hesitated, but finally took the poster in both hands and rolled it up. "I'm afraid you leave me with no choice but to be more forthcoming. We suspect that the three of you *are* the fugitives. We shall have to retrieve you for interrogation. You are under arrest."

"Open fire!" the old man shouted. Audrey grabbed up her musket from behind the gunwale without hesitation. Jek forced himself to follow suit. Audrey fired first, missing the patrol boat entirely, the shot splashing wide right. Jek saw the fault in her trajectory and made the mental arithmetic necessary to compensate. His shot splashed off to the left of the patrol boat.

The old man started a flurry of oaths. "Dianodes! Darn it all to *HECK*! Reload, ye lubbers, *RELOAD*!"

At this point the Inquisitors had long since produced their own side-arms – small pistol-versions of the snail gun...

Snail guns were an extremely advanced weapon that only the Inquisition possessed. Long ago, shortly after the first carpets and metal door handles came into the market, it was discovered that wearing socks and dragging one's feet could sometimes result in a static shock when one reached for the door handle. Naturally, considerable research went immediately into weaponizing this emergent phenomenon. The early snail gun, then, consisted of a large metal drum lined on the inside with carpet. In the center were four spokes that had socks on the ends, which met the carpeted surface. One need only crank the spokes for several seconds to generate substantial static charge. The trigger of the weapon would discharge the static energy along two forked electromagnets. The discharge in turn catapulted a magnetized projectile at speeds *far* exceeding anything that could be achieved with mere gunpowder. Between the large round drum and the forked barrel at its base, the weapon bore strong resemblance to a snail. Thus, the snail gun...

So, even as Jek and Audrey fumbled to reload their muskets, the Inquisitors stood cranking their snail pistols. There was a great confusion of tones as the two Avarica cranked. One of the modern innovations of snail pistols was that the cranking produced a tune, so that the user would know when their weapon was fully charged. They were progressing quickly through the jingles as they cranked with military intensity. Jek and Audrey were fumbling with their muskets as if they didn't know which end was the front.

The old man's gaze darted back and forth, forth and back from Jek and Audrey to the Inquisitors. He looked for any faint glimmer of hope that they could beat their opponents to the draw. There was none.

At last the old man snapped his fingers. "Looks like time to be takin' the cat out o' the fryin' pan!" he announced...

* * *

Mid-load, Jek heard a massive liquidy sound, like you might hear if you swished your arm just below the surface of the water with all your strength... only greatly amplified. He saw motion and dropped his musket as his eyes snapped up to see what was going on. Right out of the perfectly calm surf came a wave crashing down on the Inquisitors' patrol boat! It hit them broadside and capsized the craft. The Inquisitors emerged quickly, but they were in a confusion. They had lost their side-arms and were trying to ascertain where the wave had come from and whether to expect another one.

Jek was thrown toward the very back of the fishing boat as it suddenly leapt to speeds that might have shamed even the powered patrol boat. He lost his cornucopia disguise!

The Inquisitors tried to give chase, and were swimming with sufficient speed that they might well have overtook the fishing boat under any normal sailing conditions. But something extremely abnormal was at work...

Jek looked at Audrey. They were both on their hands and knees where they had been thrown by the speed burst. She looked back at him quizzically, and almost at once they both shot a glance to the sail. It was open in the wrong direction, scooping air as it rushed past the boat, actually causing drag. Even as Jek considered the implications of this, Audrey leapt up and deftly untied the sail at the base, letting it wave loose, rather than slow them up. Jek didn't think she knew what was going on any more than he did. But he was impressed; she had been quick-thinking enough to give them every assurance of maximum swiftness as they careened away from the Fish Islands.

The only one who didn't seem at all perplexed by their miraculous flight was the old man. He just stood there un-phased... appearing cross, if anything.

He had done this, Jek realized. Somehow, the old man had done it! He hurdled for possible explanations. It didn't take long to arrive at one... and only one...

"Magic!" Jek said. "You know magic!"

"Aye, Water magic," the old man grumbled. "How do ye think I out-sped them Despotopian ships o' Doom? T'was Water magic alone what made it possible."

Audrey heard it all. Her expression was awed. "Can you teach *us* magic?"

"Ye be not knowin' what ye're sayin' rightly," the old man said. "It ain't a matter o' teachin'!"

Jek was also alight with curiosity. "Well at least tell us how you did it... er, how you do it. How does magic work? What does it take? Until today I didn't even think it was real! Don't leave us wondering!"

"Ye want me to 'splain magic, eh?"

They both made fervent agreement that they did.

The old man's eyes rolled up in the air, his brows furrowing as he shrouded his beard with a thoughtful stroke of his hand. There were also vaguely discernable grunty noises. He was thinking *hard*.

Jek and Audrey's anticipation quickly waned as the contemplative repose drew on far too long. The old man looked at them blankly. He saw that he was about to lose his captive audience.

"It be a matter where's one takes some... well, there be the Purpose of the Dianodes and... th-they're the elemental forces ye see... but ye has somethin' else, so that has to turns into the other thing, and..."

He came to an unceremonious hault and silence fell again. The old man fumed.

"Well blast it! I be not *reticulate* enough to 'splain magic proper-like!"

"You mean, 'articulate'?" Jek asked.

"Aye... probably. And besides what, I still gots to keep part o' me brain set to work at movin' the boat!"

Jek looked back. They had already gone an incredible distance... well past the outermost fishing boats around the Fish Islands. "Seems like you could ease-off a bit now. We'll have some lead time if any other patrol boats come after us."

Suddenly the beleaguered fishing boat dropped and rocked, the squall of roiling water receding beneath it. The old man had stilled his magic.

"A mighty good suggestion. But then, even a blind pig be right twice a day." Jek frowned. The old man turned to Audrey. "Audrey lass, good bit o' thinkin' there, loosin' the sail! Could ye be a dear and tie it back up now?"

Jek began to protest. "But surely she..."

Eagerly, Audrey returned to the loose end and had it expertly retied in a flash. Jek was dumbfounded. He knew some things about knots. Knots had many schools, and all took time and practice. A sailor wouldn't be satisfied by just any knot; any more than a farmer would be indiscriminant about how his farm hands tied their lassos. Jek was learning something about his wife here. She had a background in sailing. It was a lesson that only made for more questions in the end...

"Thank ye, lass," the old man said. He made his way to the aft of the vessel and turned the rudder hard left. They were soon headed south-east. Up until this point, they had been sailing west.

"Where are we going now?" Jek asked, quite befuddled. As far as he knew, nothing in the world lay ahead of them on this new course...

"We're a-gonna cut eastward a while afore takin' a mighty lazy loop back 'round toward the Wading Isle. I gots a contact there what can maybe tell us where the Indigo Knights be. He oughta be a far sight better able to 'splain magic to ye than I could at any rate... and ye may well need to know! But if we's bein' watched, I'd rather it appear that we're a-headin' southeast for the moment."

A trip to the Wading Isle would certainly be interesting, Jek thought. He knew it was a stark contrast from the rest of southern Jast-Madiir – an idyllic retreat of singular interest to the royal family. The three of them would still have to be sneaky, he supposed, but an extensive Inquisition presence there was very unlikely... and that seemed a comfort.

"...Meanwhile..." the old man chimed, as an apparent afterthought, "... I see I needs to start to regiment ye in some real extensive martial disciplines. Ye shootin' at the Inquisitor boat was among the more pitiful sights me old eyes done ever seed."

He snatched Jek's musket, looking it up and down. "This be a *mighty* fine weapon... fittin' for hand-ta-hand combat much as for shootin'!" After a few more moments of examination, the old man abruptly leapt into a wide stance. He swung the weapon around awkwardly, making silly fighting noises. This continued for several seconds with little sign of ending.

"Are you winning?" Jek asked sarcastically.

The old man stopped and looked at him crossly. "Boy, how ye 'spect I can teach ye to use yer weapon proper-like 'till I done mastered it me own self? Let me get a feel for the balance and such! Ye'll have plenty o' chance ta make a 'jack-butt' out o' *yer* self when I's through with it." And with that he jumped immediately back into his fantasy battle.

* * *

Time ebbed along uncomfortably for Jek. They were in deeper, rougher waters now. It was hard to get accustomed to the heavier surf. It was especially hard for his stomach.

The waves didn't seem to bother Audrey or the old man at all. It seemed another sign that Audrey must have had a sailing background. Jek was curious, but afraid to ask. For all he knew about her, she could have been a *pirate*! It was exceptionally unlikely, but it would also be *terrible* news, which made it seem inevitable...

Jek took stock of what he knew about pirates, hoping he could rule Audrey out of being one. He was aware of the basics, at least – that their entire vocation was known to have originated by ancient dragons – dragons who had thrived and pillaged to their heart's content in the chaotic days before the Inquisition. But with the rise of that new order, these same dragons, who had enjoyed centuries of unchallenged domination, suddenly found themselves hunted to the far corners of creation...

Many chose to hide – to simply slumber through all the remaining ages with only the comfort of whatever portion of their treasure they were able to escape with. Many others were more feral than they were drowsy, and went on pillaging as they had before, compelled beyond any realistic appreciation of danger, often only to meet their doom. But the *smart* ones... *these* were the ones that founded piracy. Rather than loot treasures themselves, they kidnapped unwary seafarers by the boatload and absconded to their lairs, far beyond charted waters. They then set about turning their captives into private armies of buccaneers, who could raid in their stead. For the dragons, it was a perfect arrangement – the Humans, Herons, Jackals, or whomever they pressganged (sometimes even Meduselda and lesser Avarica) did all the work and accepted all the risk, while the dragons went on profiting.

Female pirates were a known phenomenon, and in fact were perhaps no more rare than male pirates. The dragons were indiscriminant in such matters, not caring who they endangered, as long as they had another pair of hands to carry back booty.

So Audrey *could* be a pirate. Why she would go through the trouble to attain Jast-Madiiran citizenship and pose as a lighthouse steward presented no small puzzle... but it might explain one thing. It might explain that zenithyst Jek had found in his father's vase...

If she had been hiding it from the Inquisitors, and set it in the vase after she was satisfied they were finished processing the first floor...

She *had* been just outside the back door when the backup lens came crashing down...

"Hey," Audrey said, causing Jek to jump back in surprise. Ambushed by the very person he was just having frightful misgivings about! "You look pasty. How about I see if I can make some stew?"

Jek regained enough composure to give her a brief blank look. "You think that'll help?" He'd never heard of stew settling the stomach... but then, he'd never heard of it *not* settling the stomach...

Audrey's eyes darted around a bit. "Um, sure, yeah," she reassured him. Then she called out. "Old man! Have you got something I can cook some stew with?"

The old man was still fighting his way through vast fictitious armies, but presently he fumbled, dropping the musket and taking one hand in the other. "Curses! Yer shoutin' done caused me to lose me sure handlin', and now I gots meself a cut to the fingar!"

"I feel like that would have happened anyway," Jek consoled him.

"Consarned weapon ain't proper balanced anywho," the old man continued to excuse himself. "What was it ye done wanted?"

"I wondered if you had anything I could cook some stew with."

The old man suddenly seemed not so concerned about his 'fingar', and he smiled broadly. "Sure do, lass. Ye couldn't tell t'is a whole galley I gots below deck?" Promptly he shot ahead of her to the cabin and started rifling for his stove, causing great racket. His excitement may have been ill-founded. The old man didn't yet know what Audrey's cooking habits were...

* * *

From the back of the boat, Jek overheard the old man and Audrey drum-up a conversation about knots. They were sharing favorite knots and discussing their merits and limitations. Soon they debated all sorts of knots in similar fashion. Jek caught only snatches – mostly silly names. "Finkley's four-fingered slipknot." "Choking pelican loophole." "Tri-line belaying octahedral spaghetti snarl." It was pure shoptalk, but they had evidently happened onto quite a shared field of interest.

Jek let his attention wander. He looked ahead of the boat. Off to the left slightly, the clouds were darkening; apparently readying to unleash some inclement weather. Probably they had plenty of room to begin their loop back toward the Wading Isle before they need sail through any rain. He looked back the way they had come. They were far enough from the Fish Islands that they didn't visibly stick out from the main isle of Jast-Madiir at all anymore; each was getting small and almost transparent in the haze.

But suddenly he became aware of something glistening. Actually two somethings. Jek leaned over the stern of the boat, the distant sparkles now having his full attention. It was hard to be completely sure, but it certainly appeared that they were moving. And not only moving, but *approaching*. Quickly...

"Old man!" Jek called. There was the sound of something heavy falling to the ground in the cabin.

"Gad-blame-it, lad! Why's ever'one tryin' to test me nerves all sudden-like!?"

"You better get out here!" Jek told him. "I think they're after us again!"

Very quick running ensued. The old man grabbed hold of the transom right next to Jek, leaning out to espy what he might. Jek watched his eyes widen.

"Sure 'nough! Good on ya, lad, for noticin'! T'is two more Inquisition patrol boats; they's in a mad flurry to catch us!"

"What's going on?!" Audrey called from the 'galley'.

"Brace yerself, lass!" the old man answered, "we's about to start off at flyin' speed!"

Jek himself hardly braced in time. The old man's Water magic buffeted the boat to sudden great velocity, just as before. It seemed likely they could outpace the patrol boats... but the sky ahead appeared ominous. Jek squeezed the gunwale as the old man began to guide them into the darkest quadrant of the horizon. It quickly became clear that he meant to lose the Inquisition in the mounting sea storm. Jek could hardly offer argument. Once more, he was at the mercy of much greater forces than himself. There was naught for him to do at the moment besides keep looking back at their deadly pursuers, and ahead at the thundering tempest...

Purely Mercenary

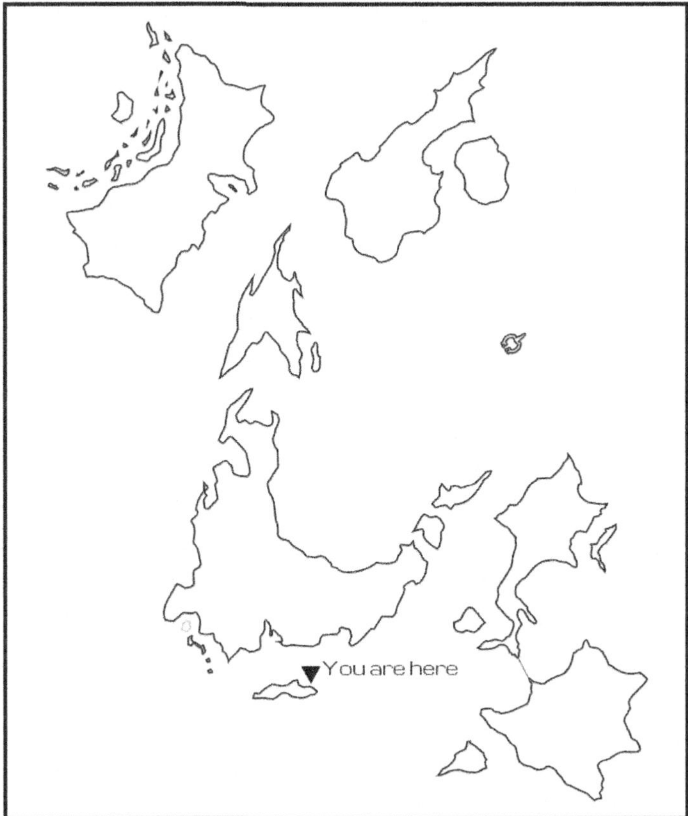

"It's hard work, you know... keeping the world working within its proper bounds. It's not comfortable and it's not celebrated. You're met constantly with resistance at every level. But you can be sure of this: either someone must, with all diligence, impose order on the world... or else, eventually, it always imposes order on itself. And while the former can be painful, the latter never fails to be cataclysmic."

- Unknown Inquisitor, *Minds Behind the Masks: Frank Interviews with the Inquisition*

Parissah flung the doors in. She eyed the room sternly under her mask, but privately her mind was still on the doors, which perplexed her. They were rather silly little things – far too short to fill the doorway or repel the elements – that swung back to the 'closed' position on their own. Once through, she could only hold one side open for Baegulgog as he floated in behind her. Sniffling, he let the other door run into him with a dull squish as he won his own way past.

The tavern had a strong odor. There was the sweet smell of spilled bubbly, of course. But mostly what Parissah noticed was the scent of a room filled with Humans – Humans unacquainted with soap, to be sure. She must have been more tired than she realized, because the smell made her hungry…

In ancient times, when Humans were first coming into the world, her own ancestors had been slow in realizing that they were a new sentient species. They seemed mere upright, grey-skinned mammals that didn't grow enough fur, and so were always taking it from other mammals – many of which were also just starting to appear in the world around this time. It was a pardonable mistake on the part of her dragonesque forebears. Humans were an aberration in the ranks of sentient beings – the first to be fragile and short-lived. They didn't possess the power to recover their life if they lost it prematurely… nor did they have obvious champions or overlords in their ranks. These had been presumed requisite characteristics of sentient life up until that point. The Meduselda in particular had a hard time with this, and they appointed queens over the Humans, so as to make them a more presentable intelligent race. This was a highly successful venture, for Humans continued to thrive under monarchical rule in one form or another to the present day. But the Meduselda also tried to teach the Humans how to not stay dead, and this proved far less successful…

In the millennia since then, Humans had, in their turn, taught the elder races a thing or two. Their fragility forced them to rely on cleverness and craft, and they were the world's first real technological pioneers. In merely trying to find ways to survive, they inadvertently revolutionized warfare, not only introducing weapons and armor and other impediments, but also the very idea of using skill to triumph in a battle, whereas strength and chance alone had sufficed in the past. To the very present, Humans could boast the balance of the world's most skilled warriors; they were rivalled in technical mastery of the martial arts by few other than the elite centurions of the Dire Heron states. Thus, Parissah's interest in bolstering her assault team with Human ranks…

Parissah continued her survey of the room. She was looking for mercenaries…

The mercs of Jast-Madiir made for a bit of a grey-area in terms of what constituted a punishable rapscallion. They weren't exactly state soldiers, and they weren't quite pirates. The profession took ground somewhere irritatingly in the middle. There were many registered mercenaries, who had to give the crown a cut of their wages – a worthwhile price to keep the Inquisition from giving them trouble. Jast-Madiir had been funneling tons of mercenaries into the Tophthaeran Civil War via the eastern board of Fettonia, to considerable profit. This came after the Czarina had already sold dozens of her own warships to the warring Queens, and had later sold them the lion's share of the building materials to construct *Variglew* after the naval frontier proved too costly to sustain indefinitely. Jast-Madiir was consummate at making money in all climates – but being neighbor to a seventy-year-long civil war was bringing in almost unprecedented cash. So it was a foregone conclusion that Parissah would find what she was looking for. The real trick was going to be to get them to cooperate...

Indeed, there were plenty of disreputable looking people in the tavern, and any or all of them could be mercenaries. Parissah zeroed-in on a table where the customers looked particularly tough. They were loud and rambunctious... and, importantly, decked out head-to-foot in weapons. She watched as one of them laid hold of a passing waiter's shirt collar.

"You expect us to drink *this*!?" the ruffian asked, swirling his glass mug in the waiter's face. He poured it out on the floor. "It's spoilt!" He flung the waiter in the general direction of the kitchen. "More grape juice! And this time make darn sure it's *fresh*!"

They were real hardliners alright. Only pirates were more roughshod; they'd actually drink the spoiled stuff...

The room grew hush as Parissah crossed it. The patrons had started to take notice that an Inquisitor was among them. Her quarry evidently hadn't yet caught sight of her; they were still rowdy – about the only rowdy ones left in the whole establishment. She made for a vacant chair in their midst. As she sat, they all shot out of their seats with much clatter of sliding wood and shifting iron, stricken silent...

Parissah folded her hands on the table. "You may sit," she told them. Cautiously, they all began to. She slid her chair a ways to one side to make room for Baegulgog as he coasted up to the table in his turn, before she settled back into her former posture. With everyone gathered in, she let a tense silence build.

"You are mercenaries, yes?" she asked at length.

"We're registered!" one of them squeaked.

"Shut up, Ned!" another one snapped.

She shifted in the chair, which was clearly not made for people with tails – even short tails. But no complaints – this operation was going text-book. "Very well, let's see your papers," she said, gesturing.

They all rifled around for their documentation. After a few moments, a big guy with a beard became particularly frantic. He blanched. "I think I left mine in my other armor..."

Parissah hesitated. She shook her head sullenly. "I'm sorry to do this then, but..." she said, reaching for her snail pistol...

"Wait!" he cried, urgently producing a wad of papers at the last moment. "Here they are!"

As she hoped. This was typical in her dealings with Humans. Tighten the screws too much, and they choked. Tighten them a little more, and they could seemingly pull off the impossible. Sometimes.

They all passed their papers to Parissah. She in turn handed them over her shoulder to Baegulgog. He shuffled through them with professional swiftness. "The paperwork is in good order," he said, sniffling.

As the papers made their way back to their proper owners, Parissah studied the mercenaries, searching for any sign of infirmity or other weakness. She was, after all, a predatory creature, and so had an instinct for such things. She noticed straight off that one guy had a missing arm, but it had at least been replaced by a sharp and deadly prosthesis, so she didn't think much of it. Besides that lone trifle, they all certainly seemed to be what passed in Human circles for healthy, able-bodied men.

She wasn't surprised that there were no women in the mercenary group. As she understood it, Human women were generally even weaker than the men, and so were usually relegated to occupations that didn't entail extreme toil and/or the high probability of a grizzly death. It was just considered good manners. Although, she also knew that Jast-Madiir had expended an enormous amount of mercenaries over the course of the Tophthaeran civil conflict, and there was talk that a general conscription might go out for both men *and* women, to replace the depleted ranks in the most cost-effective manner possible...

In her examination, Parissah was also able to determine the alpha of the group. He was seated to her right, sporting a wide, thick pair of steel shoulder pads with a prominent neck guard, as well as many nice scars. She would later learn from Baegulgog that his name was Grosdrev Trockelov, and that he was the leader of Guppy Troop, a very fine squadron of mercenaries indeed. He folded his papers and started to stand. "Been real nice checkin' in with you fine folk," he said. "I guess that'll be all then..." They all pushed away from their chairs.

"No," Parissah said.

They all sat back down.

Things were going very well indeed. By this time, they must have been about as exasperated as she could hope to get them. It was the ideal juncture for her proposition. "You needn't worry," she assured them, "I'm not here to disrupt your immediate plans... not very much, at any rate. You're still bound for *Variglew*. I only ask that you consider a change in employers. Instead of fighting for north or south, you could fight on behalf of the Inquisition."

They alternated giving her and each other looks of bewilderment. Still unsure they were going to dodge brutal punishment – deserved or not – it must've seemed some kind of cruel deception or fiendish trap to be told they could work *for* an Inquisitor. At last Trokelov spoke up.

"Tophthaera's been at war upwards of seventy years," he rasped. "What interest you folk have in it now, all of a sudden?"

"The Inquisition is always interested in everything that is happening everywhere," she qualified. "Admittedly we should have taken hand in this situation long ago. But as you can imagine, it hasn't been an easy job trying to decide what do about the Twin Queens dilemma..."

Trokelov leaned back, crossing his arms. "Personally, I don't see as it's much of your business. Meduselda have been fighting amongst themselves before the likes of your people or mine set foot in the world... from the very dawn of time. And mostly, you've been content to let them go on about it ever since. It's their nature, it is. This war's no different."

"You know well enough the difference," Parissah admonished. "Also since the dawn of time, there have been *Seven Queens* of the Meduselda. One for each Dominion. *Always*. Until now."

"She's right. One day, all of a sudden, there are *two* Queens of the Berlie Beirels..." the big bearded merc interjected, shaking his head in apparently earnest bewilderment. "How? How do you go about deciding which of them is the true heir?"

"That's exactly the impasse we've been in for the last seventy years," Parissah explained. "Each of the Twin Queens claims sole sovereignty of the Berlie Beirel Dominion. And by all historical precedent, there should *be* only one sovereign. But they both 'poofed' into existence at precisely the same time. They're both true Queens in every aspect of their nature. It's frankly impossible to decide which the heir is."

"Another fine reason to let the war go on, without interferin'," Trokelov said. "Let them work out the inheritance on their own, the old fashioned way."

"But the 'old fashioned way' isn't a permanent fix for the Meduselda. The Queens don't stay dead if they are killed, any more than their drones do. Finkley Twiggins and Ten Jeff Snorkel proved that ages ago on the very same islands which are now war-torn. And each of the two Queens might spawn a successor at the end of their 770 years. The conflict could go on for *all time*, if we don't find a way to resolve it."

"Don't seem any need to be in a hurry about it, then," Trokelov retorted, cradling the back of his head in his hands, slinking further into a relaxed posture.

"Supposing... they found a way," Ned put forth. "Supposing a way was discovered to *really* kill a Queen, *completely*..."

"Oh, perish the thought!" Baegulgog exclaimed.

Parissah nodded her agreement. Ned might have just asked a more urgent question than he knew. Not since the evil Queen Aedeloma herself had there been such impetus to devise a means to destroy the spirit of a Meduseldan. Above all else in this mission, Parissah and the rest of the Inquisition meant to discover whether the Twin Queens were pursuing such a line of research – and to stop them at all costs if they were. "Perish it indeed," she agreed. "And the Twin Queens may well be pursuing that very end. That, more than anything, cannot be allowed."

Trokelov laughed. "So, you admit you can't decide for yourself which of them is the heir, and you don't want them to fight it out until there's a clear winner, either. What does that leave? What's your play?"

"Armistice," Parissah said. "At least a temporary armistice. We plan to disrupt the ongoing warfare on *Variglew* long enough to win the cooperation of the field commanders.

We will demand audience with the Queens, and negotiate an agreement to suspend hostilities until there can be a summit with Enscharaulgk."

"Kick the can down the road, eh? Let the elder dragon figure it out for you."

She pushed aside his confrontational overtures and continued to speak as to the whole table. "The most critical decision would ideally be made by the wisest mind. The Queens might as well be made to wait and see what the Grand Inquisitor thinks ought to be done, at least. He's sure to revive soon."

"Aye," mocked Trokelov. "Enscharaulgkey's been asleep a long time, wouldn't you say? You better hope he's disposed to wake up in the immediate future, or that old *O'nyxon* is plotting the doom of the continent for his next trick," he laughed, "if there even *is* still a continent. If *he* wakes up first, and decides to hit the Archipelago again, you're going to be in a mighty pickle without your Grand Inquisitor."

Parissah grew tired of Trokelov's needling, and she shuddered ever so slightly at the mention of 'O'nyxon'...

"You're not wrong," she admitted. "But it is the responsibility of all good peoples to resist Onyxadon. The Inquisition should not find itself alone in that fight, as it seldom has before. But neither do *I* intend to find myself alone in the confrontation on *Variglew* Bridge. Which is why I'm prepared to pay for the services of mercenaries... and pay *well*. Either you can be the beneficiaries, or I'll go find another band. I'm sure it will not prove difficult to locate mercenaries here in Fettonia who are more receptive to the promise of a considerable bounty."

Grosdrev Trokelov sat up straight, blinking. "Bounty, eh? Well why didn't you say so!?" He even smiled. "I assumed you had a mind to make us party to your little mission whether we wanted it or not."

She nodded at the prospect. "I might have liked to at that. But the state esteems you to be legitimate businessmen, and so must I."

"Right you are, missy," the alpha agreed, shifting in his seat, the creases of his armor making considerable sound. "So... what's the fee?"

"The Inquisition is prepared to pay the Queen's price, plus fifty percent."

Trokelov's eyes were wide. "No foolin'? You're serious?"

This was a crucial juncture in the deal. Her honesty was being called into question! If she wanted to prove herself, she was going to have to speak their language...

Parissah seized the back of the Trokelov's head and slammed his face into the table. He cried out, and quickly obscured his nose with both hands. Looking up through watery eyes, his face was crinkled and flush.

"You broke my nose!" His voice was muffled but fierce behind his hands.

"Yes. It was my understanding that a display of toughness would be necessary to prove my resolve."

"Darn it all to Heck, woman! All you had to do was show us the money!"

"I'm sorry. I misread the situation." She looked thoughtfully at him. "Can I help you with that?"

With a wrenching motion, there was a gross popping noise, and away came Trokelov's hands from his nose. He reached for a spot on his sleeve to remove the blood. "Nah, I got it," he sighed.

Parissah turned to the Berlberi Clerk. "Baegulgog, could you draw up a check for these men?" She looked back at them. "I hope you're not fussy about wanting cash payment."

"Checks are fine; we know how to go to a bank," Ned answered.

"Let's see," Baegulgog said, "nine here, times one-point-seven..."

"I think you mean six, Baegulgog," she corrected his count.

"But there's *seven* in our troop," the alpha said from behind his sleeve. He looked around. "Here comes Nicolai now."

Parissah heard someone call out behind her. "Hey! Who took my chair?" It was evidently Nicolai.

"We got a lovely lady here in your seat, Nicolai," Trokelov grinned.

"A *lady*?! Well howdy ma'am! Nice... *YIKES*!" Parissah had instinctively turned her head about one-hundred-eighty degrees to see this Nicolai, to his immediate distress. "That's no lady! That – that's an Inquisitor!"

"A *lady* Inquisitor," Trokelov corrected. "She's also your new boss, Nic."

He just stood and gaped, drinks in his hand dripping on the ground. Undoubtedly it was a lot to take in at once. All of the mercenaries, as well as Baegulgog, shared a hardy laugh at Nicolai's expense. Parissah nodded her approval.

* * *

Arrangements were made for the troop of mercs to meet at the proper dock, and Parissah and Baegulgog left them to their final preparations. She had also tasked them with recruiting another pair of troops that they supposed were up to the job, for they had space and provisions enough on *Carroccio* to accommodate around twenty. Trockelov's troop – Guppy Troop, as they called themselves – had been quite amused at the prospect of trying to convince other mercenaries that the Inquisition was in the market for their services.

Parissah journeyed with Baegulgog down the street until they came across a cabby. The horse reared as Parissah approached, leery as it was of large predatory reptiles. Baegulgog waved with a pair of tentacles and gave a call, calming the horse. After a brief interlude where he expertly consoled the wary creature, they were ready to board the carriage, and the horse remained tranquil throughout the voyage back to the coast.

"They didn't seem very friendly with you at first," Baegulgog said as they clip-clopped along in the carriage. He sounded stuffy. "Downright inhospitable."

Parissah continued to look ahead impassively. "It's to be expected." She preferred to brush-off such subjects. She felt that, in a world where no one was entirely above reproach, it was only fitting that she be met with some reservation. Even being an Inquisitor was no guarantee of perfect altruism...

Baegulgog sneezed, but quickly recovered. "I admit those mercenaries set me thinking though. About Onyxadon, that is – when they brought that awful menace up. Mostly I got to wondering what sort of measures the Inquisition takes against his coming."

Parissah shuddered once more. There was that name again. That baleful name: *Onyxadon*! How she loathed it...

Excluding death itself, there was no more persistent threat to the inhabitants of the universe than Onyxadon. Interchangeably called "O'nyxon" in the Elfish tongue, meaning "Eternally Most Vile Dark Abomination of Impenetrable Enmity", Onyxadon was the menace of the ages, having arisen time and time again throughout history to conquer the world. Eldest of the elder dragons, he called no dragon 'father' or 'mother'... though there were some left in the world which he might call 'brother' or 'sister'. He reviled the Inquisition and was its sworn adversary, as indeed he was sworn adversary of all things which were not bound by his will. And his will was only this: to delight in the magnitude of his power, and in the using of that power to take over everything. And delight he did. There were perhaps no more conspicuously jolly entities in the world, and it was said that in this he held sway over some, compelling them to serve him by the sheer infectious potency of his sinister laughter.

But Onyxadon was not just another enormous and hyper-lethal dragon – not merely a creature of colossal sinew and flashing teeth and claws and incendiary breath. He took not the common forms of aerial reptile or aquatic serpent. But each Avarican adapts in form over the course of its regenerations to best suit the environment wherein it has stowed its treasure, such that very mature Avarica could range in bodily form from flighted creatures with many limbs to deep-sea titans with fins to immense wyrms far beneath the ground. Onyxadon had superior guile in this, for he hid his treasure where no other dragon had ever dared... in the cauldron of an active volcano. This served him well, for his gold, mingled irreversibly with the molten magma, could not be recovered by anyone – and as long as an Avarican's treasure remains unclaimed by another, they have their anchor in the material world, and so cannot truly, permanently perish. How he managed the willpower to surrender his treasure to such a sundering fate, where he could never again revel in its magnificence, none could say. But in so doing, he doomed the world to suffer him as an eternal fixture of chaos and mayhem.

So altered was his nature by this unthinkable place he chose as asylum that he had eons ago shed any semblance of a traditional body. Vaporous, he became – a living sulfuric aether – black and shapeless as the smoke that billows from a fire-mountain. Truly diabolical was his form; he could pass through the smallest of openings and yet reclaim at will enough substance to strike with full force! When assuming a recognizable shape, he was known to appear most unsettlingly as an ecliptic fire drake skeleton – dark and murky – brandishing a disarming grin.

Over the ages he had gathered many dark armies to his muster and had engaged in uncounted and widely-varied plots to dominate the earth. Somehow, he had never yet succeeded. Though the conditions of his defeat were as varied as his evil schemes, it had fallen to the Inquisition to overcome him many times. Enscharaulgk, The Grand Inquisitor of the Idriulthorontan Archipelago, could personally claim the balance of victories over O'nyxon, including the most recent one. Or rather, he *might*, if he had not been mutually annihilated in the process...

Concluding a short stint of contemptuous reflection on the villain, Parissah considered Baegulgog's initial question – what was traditionally done to guard against the coming of the Most Vile. She was glad few people ever thought to ask about it. "Ultimately there is very little we can do to predict where and when Onyxadon will strike next. He has become quite adept at shrouding his purposes until he is fully prepared to raise sheer havoc. He can go anywhere. He can pass right over head like a storm cloud and not arouse an ounce of suspicion. It is tragic to admit, but in all of our struggles against him, the Inquisition has almost never been able to take preventative action that amounted to much of anything." She looked at him. "But there is an omen we know how to interpret. There is one thing all Inquisitors do to maintain vigil."

"What is that?"

She gave him a resolute look through her mask. "We watch the sun."

Baegulgog fell silent, unsure what she meant. He might have inquired further, but presently, he sneezed hard, three times in rapid succession.

Parissah became concerned. She would have liked to offer him a handkerchief, but there was nothing to blow. "Are you sure you're not ill, Baegulgog?"

He sniffed. "Quite sure, madam. It's just that – *sniff* – today is a Tuesday."

At last she understood; it had been obvious all along. "Ah, yes. Tuesdays are the days that Sowür Canpattels shed their ectodermis."

"Indubitably," he confirmed. Once a week, a Meduseldan would molt an incredibly thin layer of ectodermis – a substance that was apparently half-way between ethereal and corporeal matter. It was a constituent ingredient in the biological process Meduselda used to harden back into corporeal form after every death – but they would shed it every week regardless. Each Dominion produced its sheddings on a different day of the week. Tuesdays happened to be the day of Baegulgog's folk.

He sneezed a few more times, and at last, with one final great 'achoo,' a cloud of tiny flakes puffed off of him, the balance of it ghosting directly through his coat. It wafted insubstantially into the sky – ever up and up – not to be seen again.

"Well, that's that!" Baegulgog said dismissively. He sounded quite his old self. Parissah was glad.

"It pleases me that you'll be on *Variglew* with us, Baegulgog."

"I'm excited at the prospect! All of this travelling around and engaging in rough-and-tumble intrigue may not be quite as stimulating as the mountains of paperwork I am leaving behind, but it is a welcome reprieve, nonetheless. And better still, those mountains will only grow ever taller as I am away!" He pantomimed the rising stacks with his tentacles. "I only hope that you are not counting on me to be much of a champion on the battlefield; such glory has never been my luck."

"What matters is that you live to report what you witness on *Variglew*, should the rest of us fall," Parissah explained.

"Won't you yourselves regenerate, and so survive to make such report?" he asked. She was dumbstruck by the question, having expected him to know the way of things. She hesitated, unprepared as she had been to address such a query...

"Inquisitors are *not* to have a treasure hoard of their own," she said categorically. "We don't regenerate."

The Clerk seemed rather taken back by this news. "Indeed? None has ever taken a treasure? Not in all the years of your order?"

She looked down rather solemnly, and spoke low. "I did not say that. There are those who have trespassed... and fallen away. But we do not speak of them."

Baegulgog thought, tapping the front of his body with a tentacle. "But Enscharaulgk – the *Grand* Inquisitor – you are counting on him regenerating, and doing so soon?"

"The Grand Inquisitors are different," Parissah explained. "They *must* have a treasure, whether they want it or not. Each maintains a modest hoard of their own. It is a terrible burden to them, but necessary to ensure that the Inquisition remains as it always has. And moreover, they are the only ones left in the world to keep the true memory of the Creators alive." She fact-checked herself, realizing with amusement that she wasn't entirely correct. "Then again, Onyxadon is old enough to remember the Creators first-hand as well. But since he is pure evil, he is hardly in the business of preserving their legacy."

"I see. So the seven Grand Inquisitors in the world are the same ones as began the whole show, and will *always* be the same?"

"Yes," she said. "There can be no others."

They were silent for a while again. It was a relief. If there was one thing she really didn't feel like talking about, it was treasures.

To guide matters back into better avenues, Parissah thought more about the ways she was hoping Baegulgog could be of help. "If our diplomatic mission to Tophthaera is successful, I hope you'll accompany me to Maenea to serve in the same capacity. We've lost many envoys on Maenea already. It may prove even more perilous than the Tophthaeran front. We really don't fully understand yet what is going on there. Whatever mysteries are at work, we must learn of them. Having a designated survivor is an indispensable contingency for that mission as well."

"I'll be only too happy to oblige, madam," Baegulgog said. "Survival comes ever so naturally to me. I have so far considered this venture as more of a vacation than a grave task."

Parissah suddenly remembered another thing she had best make the Clerk aware of. "On the voyage from Tophthaera to Maenea, we'll also have to make a stop in Roemnar. That is where I'll be apprehending the runaway lighthouse stewards."

Baegulgog turned toward her. His expression, if he had had one, would have been of great befuddlement; the cadence of his flashing glow revealed as much. "If that is so, it will be quite the trick."

"Not really. Such arrests have been made often enough in the past. You just have to know what the fugitive's objective is. From there, the rest can be easily calculated and controlled. It is only a matter of being in the right place at the right time. All fugitives... that is, all *Human* fugitives... eventually arrive at the same objective. So in truth it is all very simple."

Baegulgog's luminescence pulsated with reservation. "In any case I'll be interested to see what befalls in Roemnar..."

* * *

Some time later, the carriage arrived at the coast. There were boats and ships of many sizes on the docks and in the harbor – coming, arriving, waiting for a spot to make port. Improvised shop fronts lined the shore. There were all kinds of customers to be had in recent years – fresh mercenaries arriving at their staging ground, departing mercenaries on the way to war, haggard mercenaries who had narrowly survived to the end of their contract. So mostly there were mercenaries.

Not all of these faces were Human. Some of Parissah's own people were to be found, armed as for war, and the ones closest at hand were hunched under the bulk of their huge bodies, with winglet leathery digits folded back far behind the elbows, each probably on their second or third life. The sight of 'civilian' Avarica was not one Parissah greatly enjoyed. They invariably made her think of her father.

Clearly the prospective Avarican mercenaries did not escape Baegulgog's notice, either. "Would you look at that!" he said. "Dragon-folk have also come a-spoiling for war; bless my eyes... if I had any! I've reviewed the statistics since last we spoke, and so I know this is a rare sight indeed!"

"Yes," she answered simply.

He went on being bubbly. "It is rather an odd thing, when you think about it – almost a sight out of time. Not many of your folk dare to live in this way anymore. Here are some truly extraordinary stragglers! I admit I have wondered on occasion why your Order does not simply press-gang all Avarica into its ranks."

"That is a matter of policy which was not easily agreed upon by the Grand Inquisitors. Ultimately it was decided that, in order for commitment to an ascetic lifestyle to be sincere, it must be voluntary. That decision still has its detractors. I do not deny I question the wisdom of it daily."

Baegulgog continued to consider the Avarican mercenaries thoughtfully for some moments. "Whatever becomes of these enterprising sorts? I suppose eventually they all grow to proper dragons, if they're clever."

"They tend to. At which point they become the responsibility of the Inquisition anyway."

"And what is the responsible response to a dragon?"

"Sometimes we needn't do anything. Not all dragons grow ever more covetous. Some attain a measure of content, or else they become so afraid of losing what treasure they have that they can no longer bring themselves to bother about getting more. These are the best of cases. A content or a defensive dragon will withdraw to the most secret place they can discover, and there they will perhaps fritter and fret about finding ways to be yet more secret and secure... but the longer they sit upon their treasure hoard, the more tired their minds become. For once they are shored up as best they can be, there is nowhere for them to go, and nothing for them to do. They do not leave their treasure for any reason – even to hunt – so all of their vitality must then come from sleep. And sleep they do, ever more and more... weeks, months, years at a time. This is what is known as the 'golden slumber,' and it is as close to a final rest as some dragons ever get. For while they may yet on occasion wander into unpleasant dreams, they eventually reach a point where almost nothing can rouse them – even an attack."

"What of the rest?"

Parissah shook her head. "The rest become too greedy, and they make very awful nuisances of themselves. You understand the Inquisition is eminently concerned with combatting the sins of excess?"

"I do."

"There is no greater trespass of this sort than the wonton death a dragon can unleash in selfish pursuit. We have no greater enemy than the rogue elements of our own kind, and while O'nyxon is the very chiefest of our foes, we have special vehemence for all dragons who follow the old ways. We destroy them... and we track down their hoard and we make reparations of it before the offending dragon can return. We are all of us dragon hunters by trade. This is among the most earliest and important functions of the Inquisition."

"An Order of dragon-hunting dragon-folk," Baegulgog mused. "That is rather melancholy."

Parissah merely nodded. Perhaps it was better he never found out just how melancholy a business it could be...

* * *

Paying the driver and climbing down from the carriage, Parissah gave the horse a wide berth. Baegulgog, on the other hand, returned to the beast of burden, giving it a treat and a pat on the head, and it whinnied joyfully. He certainly did live up to the Sowür Canpattel legacy of horse whispering.

At the dock, they passed mast after mast, rigging after rigging, until they finally came to the ship with no masts – the ship made of metal – lighter in the water than any wooden vessel. They had returned to the *Carroccio*. The guards saw them up the ramp, and Parissah bid Baegulgog go to her office ahead of her, as she continued to the top deck...

There was a recessed area at about mid-ship on the starboard hull that berthed several small cages. She met the Chief Pigeon Keeper, who pointed out the animal that had been set aside for delivery of her outgoing mail. But she explained that her only interest at the moment was the incoming mail. He said she had received none. That was well. No further word of *Pharonomagnus* misbehaving. She had been adamant that she be informed if the thing acted up again...

Pharonomagnus was one of the world's great enigmas. It took up residence high in the principal tower of the Inquisition's Ocean Citadel, where it had been built, suspended curiously on countless balusters in a great intricate vault of glass. No one – not Tyxicalgra or Enscharaulgk, or even the builders themselves – could account for why it had been constructed in the first place, or who commissioned the daunting project, or even who had designed it. No blueprints or construction logs or plans of any sort were ever found for the titanic instrument, in spite of months of rigorous searching by the Clerical Dronehood of Berlberi. There was no paper trail whatsoever. But *there it was* nonetheless – the world's largest pipe organ by many orders of magnitude, fixed in the Ocean Citadel even more prominently than the Grand Inquisitor himself. And not a soul could say why...

No one ever played it. No one dared. But that didn't stop the colossus from voicing its own terrifying notes, when it deemed. Mostly, it could be relied upon to play a tune in harmony with the Avarican chorus that daily sung forth a new digit of Pi in the Elfish language.

But recently, at the conclusion of the Pi Chorus' recital, *Pharonomagnus* had done something unexpected...

It went like this. One day, the ascendant notes behind the Pi Chorus suddenly collapsed into a grave countermelody, the organ weaving a frightful cascade of furious keystrokes that branded all present hearts with foreboding. This continued each day for seven days, then ceased. And for a week after, things went as they ought – as they always had. But on the eighth day, the grim theme returned, and was voiced each day for two weeks running. After a second week-long hiatus, *Pharonomagnus* went back to its aberrant behavior for still another three weeks in a row. But after this apparently final string, the organ had acted nominally ever since – over a month had now transpired since its last episode.

There were two ways Parissah could think of to interpret the sign. Either you looked at the weeks, which formed one pattern:

1...2...3.

Or, you counted the days:

7...14...21.

This seemed more likely. It was the year 9021 of the Static Era, and the month of Novtober – the seventh and final month – was fast approaching. In lieu of this, she wasn't greatly looking forward to the fourteenth day of the month...

It might be nothing, and it remained entirely possible that she and her fellow Inquisitors had not yet unraveled the mystery of *Pharonomagnus'* delinquency. And it was just as possible the great pipe organ's ways might ultimately be completely unsearchable to them.

But in any case, the world seemed to be teeming with dire omens. Parissah was not above being a bit unnerved by it all.

Still, perhaps it was better than having nothing much to do...

Hours later, she oversaw the loading of the mercenaries, twenty-one in all. From her overlook on the top deck, they certainly appeared enthusiastic – no doubt excited by the prospect of making that extra fifty-percent. Little did they know – for she had only just resolved – that they stood to make a bit more money in the end...

The Wading Isle

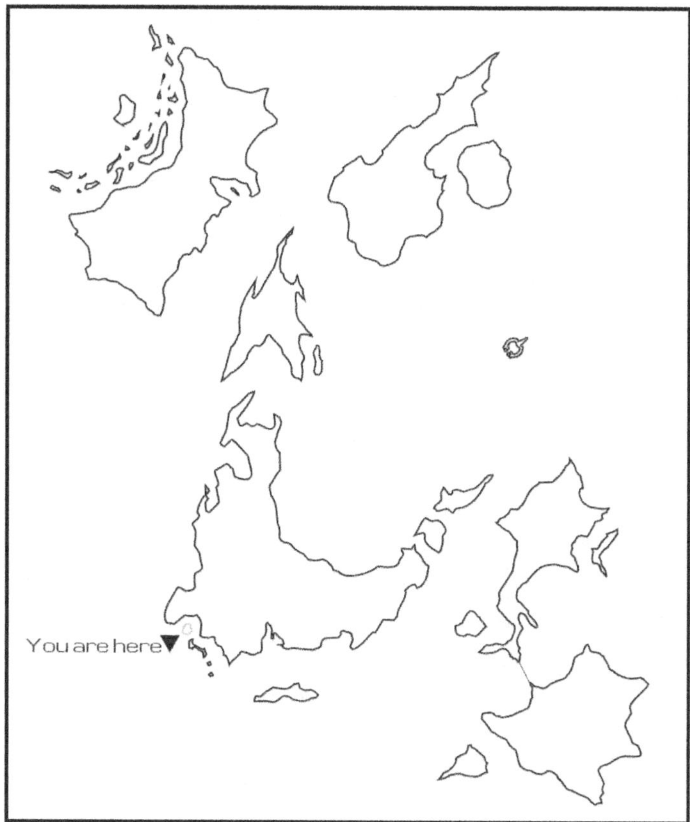

"The Heck I can't."

- Carlos Washoe

Jek fumbled trying to get hold of the hand bar protruding from the mast, already slicked by spitting rain. The old man wanted him aloft as a lookout. It hardly seemed called for; they could see their pursuers. Maybe it was just to give him something to do. Caught between a storm and a pair of technologically advanced military-grade patrol boats filled with dragon people, left to wonder which would be the danger that ended him, Jek didn't so much mind having something to do...

Thunder rolled distantly. He felt some relief that the sound was still far off. Perhaps they were farther from the really bad weather than it appeared. Immediately there came a fresh crash that may as well have originated in his own head, it was *so* loud! Jek had evidently misunderstood sea storms. They were big enough to be really far away *and* right on top of him at the same time.

Mutteringly and with caution, he advanced another few rungs up the mast, toward a half-bucket-thingy still several feet above him. He tried to spur himself to greater speed. There were more bars up there that he could cling to with greater security, and he figured he'd better get climbing now before the conditions for it got any worse. That is, before the rain picked up...

The rain picked up. But Jek reached the bucket thingy. There was iron barring over a foot out from the rim all the way around it. He frantically wrapped his arms around the bar and shut his eyes, collecting himself for a few seconds. The sheets of rain were cold and heavy. His breathing became momentarily panicked, his body reacting as if he had just been totally immersed. And there was the nausea of the dramatic swaying in all directions...

Jek tried to think outside himself to soothe his nerves. He could hear the commotion down below. The old man was shouting into the cabin.

"How is things in there, lass?!"

"Stew's not ready yet!" she replied.

There was a pause.

"Never ye mind the stew! Secure the galley!!"

There was a clamor of one or more metal somethings crashing in the cabin. "Ow!" Audrey said.

"See!" the old man chided her.

Jek saw the old man look up at him. "What can ye see up there, lad?!" Jek scanned around, still having no idea what he should even be looking for. He saw waves crashing into each other in wild trajectories all around. He saw lighter clouds beyond the darker clouds that swirled by at ghastly speed above. Every now and again came a blinding flashbulb effect. Not a whole lot he wouldn't have expected to see given the circumstances, and nothing at all worth reporting.

Still distant, he made out the patrol boats. They seemed steadfast to capture them, in spite of the storm. But at least they didn't seem to be gaining on them...

"They're still after us!" Jek announced over the din of the gale. He slipped a little bit but redoubled his hold on the barring in time. Numerous muscles protested. He'd been tensing them more than he realized. Suddenly he thought about the old man; in particular his mysterious powers they'd just learned about...

"Hey! What about your water magic!? Can't you do anything about... *all this*!?" he asked.

"Are ye jokin'?!" the old man protested. "I ain't the Water Dianode, such as could tame the mighty tempest! Me powers be a sight more humble than all that!"

"Fair enough!" Jek replied. "I don't mean *stop* the storm... but... couldn't you... I don't know... make it any better?!"

"I be makin' it as much *'better'* as I knows how!"

That, too, was fair enough.

"What else do ye see?!" the old man asked.

Jek hesitated. He didn't know what more the old man wanted from him. There was the storm and there were the patrol boats. "There's nothing else!"

"I was afraid o' that!" the old man said.

Jek was still watching the patrol boats, when at once, he caught sight of something odd. There seemed to be slivery flecks of something moving back and forth in traverse in the midst of the boats. The swaying and the confusion of his own situation made it hard to make out, but Jek even supposed he saw disruptions on the water as the flecks whizzed around. "Wait!" he announced to the old man. "I think there *is* something else!"

"I was afraid o' that too!" the old man said.

Jek was surprised as he quite suddenly heard a loud *'ka-floof'*! A hole tore in the sail near him, blindingly fast! *Heck*! What in the Undervoid had just happened?

The hole smoked at the edges, and he saw for the faintest moment a ghostly trail from the sail that stretched all the way back to the patrol boats. The Inquisitors had fired on them with a snail pistol!

A crunching sound emanated from the deck, and he saw that there was debris careening from the stern and the front of the boat simultaneously. A second shot had gone right through both... but it was wide on the right side, and so missed both the old man and the cabin entirely.

"Dianodes!" the old man cursed.

Jek tensed for more shots. He closed his eyes, but quickly reopened one. He felt it equitable that one eye would know what was going on while the other could remain blissfully ignorant. But presently he opened them both back up. The patrol boats were spinning around! In but a moment they were headed back toward the Fish Islands! Perhaps they decided that further pursuit was too reckless, and so had taken some parting shots before retiring. But the dancing flecks continued...

"Is they overtakin' us, boy?!" the old man demanded, hunched as he was in fear.

"No! They're leaving!" Jek was pleased to report.

Presently Audrey emerged from the cabin. "I've got the stuff in the galley tied down good!" she said, lightning erupting. The boat tossed sickeningly.

"Fine work, lass, and swift!" the old man doted. "How e'er did ye tie it all down? Did ye use the old 'octopus gauntlet multi-fastener'?"

"No. I tried it first, but the rope was six inches too short."

"Ain't that always the way of it?" the old man said, shaking his head.

"I know, right?" Audrey agreed.

"What did ye use?" He sounded eager.

"I went with a 'quadruple threadbare noose-loop' with a self-tightening 'Mobius pretzel knot' at the end."

"Jumpin' jackalopes!" the old man said, slapping his knee. "If that don't beat all! I ain't ne'er conceived o' such a knot!"

Jek's arms ached, and he was convulsing in the cold. "Can we get out of the storm now!?" he whined.

"Fastest way out is through, I warrant!" the old man called back.

"Oh great!"

"What about our pursuers?!" the old man asked.

Jek's face ruffled. "I told you they've turned back!"

The old man shook his head. "I don't mean the Inquisitors, lad! Didn't ye start to say ye saw somethin' else!?"

Jek blanched. He *had* said that...

Shifting his arms over the bar, he looked back in the direction of the patrol boats. He couldn't make them out anymore, and the flecks seemed to have gone too. But lower in his vision, he caught sight of the same pattern of side-to-side movement. This was considerably closer, and now he could make it out. The 'flecks' he had seen before were *fish*! Some sort of airborne fish with what appeared to be wide, wingish heads, leaping in and out of the water! It was a very large school, the concentrations of fish cropping up in wildly distributed spots. Jek would have found the sight of it all pretty neat... except he could somehow tell this was yet another sign that they were all dead meat...

"There are fi-!" Jek called to the old man and Audrey, but he was cut off by a deafening thunderclap. It seemed to take forever to dissipate.

"What was that?!" the old man asked.

"There are fish jumping around all over the place!"

The old man shook his head with crazed eyes. "T'isn't *fish* lad! T'is *hurdle sharks*!!!"

On cue, a great big shark swooshed over the rear of the boat. Audrey and the old man hit the deck. The head of the shark was *incredibly* wide; probably as wide as the whole creature was long! If the two of them had failed to throw themselves down in time, the shark would have tackled them both out of the dinghy. For that was the way of hurdle sharks; they were all but tailor-made to knock unsuspecting lubbers from their boats and into the water with their airfoil-like head, where they would be quite at the mercy of the swarm...

Jek blinked as he saw dozens of the things leaping all around the boat. The surf was much too rough to catch sight of them before they surfaced. It was all disastrously random!

Another hurdle shark shot out of the sea, but it didn't leap so true as the first. It landed right in the boat! Before there was opportunity to react, another, equally clumsy shark landed right on top of its compatriot from the opposite side. The old man and Audrey scrambled around the edges of the boat, desperate to avoid the thrashing of the big, frustrated animals. Audrey won into the cabin. The old man grabbed an oar. He yelled emphatically and started prodding and slapping one of the sharks with wild abandon. Audrey was more daring; she came back out with a frying pan and started beating the other shark at close range. From Jek's detached point of observation, the sight was almost comical in its futility. The sharks *wanted* out of the boat, but smacking them around wasn't going to get them there...

"That isn't doing any good!" he called to them.

Growling, the old man gave his shark a few final blows, then retracted his oar, leaning on it. "Ye're right! There's naught to do but tip them out of the boat! Grab the starboard gunwale, lass! We's about to pitch!"

Audrey's steps kicked up large splashes; a lot of water was coming into the rear of the boat through the hole left by the snail bolt. Just as she reached and seized the gunwale, she threw her feet out from under her and flopped into the deck, throwing water aloft. Jek started to warn her but it happened too quickly; another hurdle shark careened right through the space where her upright body had been the moment before. She must've seen it before he did. Jek heaved a sigh of relief when he saw she was still there after the shark passed over.

"Get ye ready!" the old man shouted. "I's about to throw the boat!"

Audrey tensed at the gunwale. Jek entangled his arms around the iron bar. They waited expectantly...

"Get ye ready!" the old man recited.

"We *are* ready!!" Jek called. "Just do it!"

Nothing happened.

"I hope ye'll forgive me hesitance! I'd do it straight away... only this is just how I lost me last two shipmates!"

Jek rolled his eyes. *That figured*. "Better do it anyway!" he called.

There came no further warning from the old man. He thumped the bottom of the boat with a wave of his own making, and it tossed the whole craft in a dramatic leftward reel. Jek's legs slipped out from under him! But his arms held tight. Tight enough, anyway. The pitch of the boat slowed, but now Jek's feet were almost within reach of the waves, the mast stretched out nearly flat over the ocean. Just in front of him, he saw a silver lump emerging from the depths. He curled his body up out of the way just in time to avoid the gaping jaws and the great ax-head of a hurdle shark that burst out of the roiling sea at him. The dorsal fin caught his back, and it stung like the dickens! But as far as Jek could tell, he was still alive, and that was some consolation.

The boat started to pitch back at last.

...But something about it was curious; disorienting...

Processing the sensation proved difficult for Jek at the moment, owed perhaps to the brush with death he'd just had. Slowly it dawned on him that his feet had caught handlebars *above* the bucket on the mast, in his desperate maneuver to avoid the shark. Now, as the mast drew up straight again, he was being inverted. It was kind of funny, really. But *no*... no it wasn't. It was terrible!

There was a cracking-creaking sound as the boat righted itself. Jek could feel it as well as hear it. Looking down – which happened to be the natural way to look in this peculiar orientation – he saw the missing chunk of the mast; battle-damage that had befallen the boat before he and Audrey had come aboard. He knew instinctively that it was buckling; the mast was failing under its own weight, and his. He hoped it would hold. As he continued to tumble skyward upside-down, he also hoped *he* would hold...

Jek looked over at the rear deck. The beached sharks had tumbled from the boat! It was good to know something had gone right. He saw that Audrey and the old man were looking back up at him. They seemed concerned.

"Dear, what are you doing?!" Audrey asked.

"Nothing I meant to!" Jek said.

The boat tilted past the full-upright position and started to pitch to the right. Jek seized on the opportunity half on accident; his feet losing their grip on the handlebars, his lower body tumbled into the bucket. He pushed off from the iron handle with his arms and soon found he was seated in the bucket, nearly being tipped out the other side! He grabbed hold of the mast, clinging to it absently...

When he next opened his eyes, he felt that the mast was mostly upright; though he wasn't sure how long he'd lapsed. But the storm wore on, and he could see that the hurdle sharks were still in a flurry. One plopped out of the air onto the bow, but managed to tumble off the gunwale back into the sea. Moments later, another shark flew over the midsection, clipping the mast with its enormous battering-ram of a head. The shark spun laterally and splooshed back in the drink, but the collision caused a serious 'crunch'. The mast was almost certainly critically compromised! He could be sure of it, because the old man had also taken notice...

"We gots to belay the mast!" he shouted. "T'is about ready to split in twain! If we loses the mast, I'll have to propel the boat meself night n' day!"

"...And I'll be *dead*!" Jek reminded him.

"Aye, that too! Hurry, laddy... toss us down yer rope!"

"What rope?!" Jek asked, but even as he inquired, he looked under his feet in the bucket, and saw a neatly coiled rope.

"There be a rope in the crow's nest with ye! T'is for tyin' yerself securely to the mast so's ye don't fall out in a storm!"

"Well that would have been nice to know about!" Jek said.

"We're going to need a good knot to belay the mast!" Audrey interjected, even as Jek started coiling one end of the rope around the iron handlebars above him. "What do you suggest?"

The old man scratched his beard. "Mayhaps an 'eternalock curlie-que'."

Audrey shook her head. "Those aren't reliable in all conditions."

"Aye, ye're right. We needs somethin' self-tightenin', robust and dependable."

"Maybe a 'Finkley's four-finger'?"

"I'd say t'is overkill for a mast o' this diameter..."

And on and on it went. Another great knot debate! Jek was already pretty sure he had this end secure. He was also sure the mast was moments from splitting and sending him down to the sharks. Looking down, he spied a belaying hook on the hull, opposite the missing chunk. His hands threaded the rope reflexively as he calculated for the extra weight, the wind, the distance...

I'll show them a knot...

Spinning the rope overhead in final preparation, Jek sent the loop flying for the small belaying hook on the ship's edge. At the last moment he caught the rope tight in his hands, tugging back. The rope held fast, secure! He had perfectly lassoed the hook! He cinched up the slack around the handlebars, waiting until the boat swung to the right, so the mast wouldn't slouch too bad. Now the rope was taught between the mast and the ship's base.

Just as he finished, he noticed Audrey and the old man weren't debating anymore. They were just sort of frozen, astonished. Jek realized that he, too, was surprised. Pleasantly surprised. He'd got to really contribute something! He gave his shipmates a thumbs-up.

But the exultant moment had to pass, and quick. The sharks were still afoot, and the boat was getting heavy in the water. It had been rained on considerably, partially capsized, buffeted by tall waves, and compromised in two places by snail gun fire...

"Back to business! We gots too much water in the boat!" the old man said, waving his hands emphatically.

Audrey still had her frying pan at hand. She bailed out what little water she could with it. The old man made a kind of throwing motion in the air, and pretty much the rest of the water flew up out of the boat and back into the ocean. Audrey blinked.

"What are we going to do about the sharks!?" Jek called down.

"Just keep not getting 'et!" the old man replied. "Ain't nothin' more can be done! This kind o' situation resolves itself after a spell..."

Before anyone could ask what he meant, the jumping intensified, but suddenly it was no longer chaotic. The hurdle sharks were all leaping in the same direction in some urgent flight! Just as one nearly cleared the boat, it was seized mid-jump by a lightning-quick tentacle with the girth of a cedar, and hurled back hundreds of feet. Jek followed the shark with his eyes, suddenly seeing dozens of tentacles curled up menacingly into the sky off in the distance. On a rough estimate he supposed they belonged to at least a pair of krakens. The hurdle sharks were running away from them for all they were worth! But Jek's heart sank. Because now, they were likely at the mercy of two or more hungry krakens!

"Okay... what do we do about *that*?!"

"These situations resolves themselves too!" the old man encouraged him.

Sure enough, within moments, Jek heard an eerie sound – a high-frequency moan like a thousand-foot trumpet being blown beneath the covering of the sea. There were several such calls, and they overlapped. He watched the terrible limbs of the krakens suddenly flail and pitch madly as they were beset by a pod of sword whales. Sword whales, of course, are not unlike their cousins, the narwhals... except that they are much, much larger, and utterly ravenous for the flesh of giant squid...

The battle of the titans was deafening in the distance. Great swells of tossed ocean and blinding flashes of lightning obscured much of the action, and soon all parties withdrew to the fathomless depths, not to be glimpsed again by mortal eyes for perhaps a century or more...

"Well! That be the food chain hard at work!" was the old man's final affirmation, as he brushed his hands together.

* * *

When the storm had died down, Jek climbed back to the deck, and laid down flat. He was in considerable discomfort, having performed a long series of acrobatics that his muscles were heretofore unacquainted with. Lying down stung. He'd all but forgot that scrape the hurdle shark had given him. It must've torn the skin. He hoped he wasn't bleeding out. He didn't feel like he was. He didn't *think* he felt like he was...

Jek wiped his face. It was still sprinkling. Blinking rapidly, he saw that the old man and Audrey were standing over him now, looking at him.

"Mighty, mighty good work tyin' the mast down, lad!" the old man told him. "I ain't never seen ropin' like that!"

Jek was a bit ambivalent. He was glad the old man was impressed. He was glad *Audrey* was impressed. But privately he knew it wasn't the extraordinary feat they supposed.

"I grew up on a farm, wrangling gallimimus all the time. Needed to be pretty handy with a lasso. Their heads are small and they bob around constantly; not the easiest targets."

The old man laughed giddily, pantomiming Jek's deft maneuver. "*Lassooin'*! Funny what one trade could learn from a'tother! If we gets occasion, I'd shore like to have ye teach me to lassoo!"

"Maybe later," he said, rasping.

"And we was both wonderin': What was the knot ye used!? T'is a fine knot!"

"It's just the ordinary lasso knot we were all taught. I don't even know what it's called. But I figured, if it was good enough to reign-in an angry six-foot-tall dinosaur, it might just work for the mast, if anything would." He smirked. "I guess you could call it the, 'gallimimus special'."

"I will at that," the old man said.

Jek sat up gingerly. He was still in pain, but it was contented pain.

Audrey must have seen his back. "Jek, you're injured!"

"I'll go get the coriander!" the old man leapt into action.

"I'd say we might even want to use some bandages this time," Audrey said. "Do you think you have any?"

"Like-as-not," the old man said. "I'll rummage around and sees what I find..." and he disappeared into the cabin. There was a sound of splashing. The water hadn't been properly exorcized from the cabin yet. Presently a tidal wave burst from below deck. The old man had bailed the water out with his magic again. Soon there were rummaging noises, as ever. "Yow!" they heard. After a brief hiatus, the rummaging started again.

Finally, the old man came onto the deck with a roll of bandaging and some seasonings. He looked befuddled at Audrey.

"Ye left the stove on? Durin' the sea storm?"

"Yeah," she said impassively. "I couldn't very well leave the stew half-cooked."

"We was bucklin' and pitchin' all o'er the place!" the old man retorted. "How's you to know ye wouldn't catch the cabin ablaze?!"

She shrugged. "I figured all the rain could put the fire out if it spread much. Besides, I remember what the old cookie on board the *Cosigner* used to say, 'If you're not burning something, you're not cooking.'"

The old man frowned. "That sounds wise enough, I warrant, but..."

"...I'm glad you reminded me of it anyway," Audrey said. "I'll get back to it as soon as I wrap Jek up."

It was another occasion where Jek couldn't help noticing what seemed like glaring deficiencies on the part of Audrey's medicinal acumen. She bandaged him up, that could not be denied. But she apparently hadn't felt it necessary to remove his frock coat or shirt to do it. Jek had thought it was traditional for the bandaging to not be the top layer. But he didn't much feel like trying to get out of the coat at the moment, so he let it be. At least he had talked her out of rubbing ground pepper into the wound...

As she got up to return to the galley, the old man stopped her. "Ye suppose the stew be done yet?"

"Not yet," she said. "It needs more gelatin... and sprinkles."

The old man blanched as she disappeared below deck. Jek smiled. It was one thing he had already known about Audrey. She had odd cooking habits.

*   *   *

Audrey took another bite of her stew. She kind of frowned. It was a real shame they hadn't had blueberries aboard. The way the other two were prodding their bowls, she could tell they too were lamenting the absence of the key ingredient.

"Mighty... *interestin'*... stew, ye got here, lass," the old man said.

Jek shrugged dismissively, and started shoveling food. The old man looked over at him with furrowed brow.

"Thanks," Audrey said, taking another bland, blueberryless bite.

"Ain't ne'er had a stew what was its own dessert."

Audrey smiled. "The old cookie always said, 'It's not hard to fit three courses in one pot. So why dirty three pots?'"

The old man nodded weakly. "I'd sore like to have a meetin' o' the minds with this here cookie o' yers," he said. He took one more tentative bite, and then set the bowl down. "Welp," he said, clapping his hands together, "Ain't got no more time for eatin'; gots to patch them holes in the boat back up."

Jek watched him grimly. "I certainly hope you don't blame *her* for all of this bad luck, old man."

The old man stopped, shooting Jek a look. "Blame who? *Audrey*?! Why in tarnation would I be a-blamin' her?!"

Jek smiled, relieved. "I'm glad you feel that way. It was my understanding that most sailors were really superstitious; that they maintained it was 'horrible bad luck' to have a woman aboard."

The old man reared back. "*Har ha-har*! It be just the opposite, lad! Me best mate, ol' Granite McFarlonger, always said t'was frightful *good* luck to have a woman along on a sea voyage. T'is why, when he done retired, and bought his own boat, he planned to take his wife with him on a grand tour o' the seas..." and he shook his head, frowning, "...rest their souls."

"What happened to them?" Audrey asked.

The old man looked very sullen. "Not an hour into their maiden voyage, they sprung nigh twenty leaks, ran aground on a sandbar, and then the whole boat went up in a huge fireball! Frightful sad, it was."

They all shared a moment of silence for ol' Granite McFarlonger and his wife.

The silence was broken by a familiar racket. Audrey could hear it coming closer. She stood and looked out past the stern of the boat.

"I'll be gosh-darned," she said absently.

"What is it?" Jek asked, slowly getting up. The old man also took interest.

"It's those little birds! Those stupid little birds are coming back! I thought sure we'd lost them in the storm..."

They all began to hear the chirping, tweeting, and cooing.

"Ain't been a storm yet what would keep them devils away," the old man said gravely.

Audrey and Jek looked to him searchingly. "What *is* the deal with the songbirds?" Jek pressed him.

The old man ran a hand along his bald head, shaking it. "They's Despotopian spys, they is. I know it sounds ridicalous, but t'is so. As I was roundin' Despotopia's southern coast, startin' to really put some distance 'twixt meself and the ships-o-Doom what was after me, along come these little tweeters, and they's been on me trail ever since."

Audrey actually began to feel apprehensive. Jek looked terrified. Up until this point, the old man's misadventure off Despotopia had seemed a distant narrative, hardly more dire than any of his anecdotes or 'splainations,' even if it was the apparent, direct cause of their Quest. Now it was revealed that the threat of Despotopia had literally been looming over them all along. Their reach had grown long indeed, and their devices clever and subtle. No one would ever have suspected little songbirds of such agency. How the Despotopians could communicate effectively with these little creatures was anyone's guess... but it didn't ultimately matter *how*. The resolution of the birds was obvious and unyielding, and Despotopia likely remained apprised of the old man's every move...

"We've got to lose them somehow," Jek said, expressing the consensus.

"I gots a way," the old man said, sounding forlorn. "After we done made our stop at the Wading Isle."

"How will we do it?" Audrey asked.

"Ye'll see."

* * *

The world began to turn red, draped in the early evening hours. Audrey grabbed both ends of her musket and heaved up with all her might. She deflected the sword from its mark in the torso... right into her own face...

"Ow," she said. She might've said more than 'ow', but she didn't want to alarm the old man. He was teaching her how to fight.

The old man retracted his sword into a defensive stance. He had the sheath buckled over the blade, as a much-needed safety feature. Likewise, they had improvised a way of wrapping her bayonet, and were very careful to empty all the gunpowder. So far, it seemed as if the old man could have done alright for himself without such precautions. His old head bobbed out a long ways on his old neck, which was strained with concentration. He might not have looked all that much like he knew what he was doing... but he did.

As Audrey recovered, he offered her some edifying, sage advice. "Try harder."

This time she swung first, committing totally to the attack. She felt she might've missed outright, the way he stepped to the side, but he caught her musket in a parry anyway, and still had plenty of time left to 'lop-off' her leg and club her in the back.

"Ow," she said.

The old man snapped back into his stance. "Again. Try harder."

Jek stood up. "Is this really the best way?" he asked. "Shouldn't you let her win once in a while... you know... to build her confidence?"

The old man looked crossly at Jek. "A fair heart never lets the faint maiden win," was his slogan. "Ye want her to have confidence? What good be confidence in a fight?! Ye think Despotopian soldiers is gonna be worried about woundin' yer confidence when ye both be battlin' them for yer lives?" He shook his head. "Nay. This be the hard way o' learnin', mayhaps... but the hard way be the only way when it come to the fightin' disciplines." He got back in his stance. "Again."

She tried, and failed. She tried again, and failed again. *Try harder. Try harder.* It was horribly awkward business, this fighting... and tiring. She hadn't made more than a dozen moves since they began, and already she was exhausted, taking her air in big gasps. Audrey swung for him one last time, and got only a wallop for it. She was struck from her feet, and she stayed sitting there.

"I'm not sure it's any use," she said. "I'd have to be a *lot* stronger to be any good in a fight."

The old man hunched by her, suddenly appearing sympathetic. "Ye'll need to build endurance, I warrant. But ye can't think of a fight as bein' about strength. Ye think I's winnin' because I's strong? Look at me. I'm old! And how about our ancestors? Ye think they survived wars with the Avarica and Meduselda a'cause they was able to match them strength-for-strength? Not hardly! Ye can be strong in a fight, and it can be o' some good. But *speed*... speed be a hunnert times better! Don't matter how strong yer opponent be if ye lands the first strike, and lands it good. And a heavy blow needs only be deflected a little ways to miss its mark. So, here be the lesson for the day..." he said, standing with upraised finger.

"...Try harder," Jek interjected.

The old man gave him a look. "Aye, that too," he said. "But the *real* lesson is... 'be faster'."

The old man helped Audrey to her feet. She was surprised by how encouraged she felt after getting clobbered. The old man turned to Jek, readying himself again.

"It be time for your whoopin' now, I warrant," he said.

The battle went similarly. Jek enjoyed no success and was showing obvious signs of fatigue from early on. But he was trying to be fast, and so demonstrated that he had got the general idea of the lesson.

"Well, I'm being fast," Jek huffed and puffed, resting a hand on his knee, leaning on his musket with the other. "So what's the problem?"

"Didn't say 'be fast'! Gotta be fast-*er*," the old man said. "Gots to have skill too."

"'Have skill'... that's the next lesson, I take it?"

"Aye, thereabouts. Not a bad phrasin' at that."

"Alright... you want to see skill?" Jek said, rising. "Put down the sword; let's settle it with our hands."

The old man grinned a snaggle-tooth grin, and threw down his weapon. "Alright laddy, if that be yer wish," he said, putting up his dukes.

They both bopped around like boxers. The old man took a swing, but Jek surprised him and grabbed him, wrestling him to the ground in a painful-looking tangle. The old man made considerable sounds of struggle as he tried to work loose, to no avail.

"Alright, *alright*!" the old man said, and Jek let him loose. "Ye had yer fun now. Wrasslin' ain't gonna do you no good on the battlefront though, I warrant. Why's ye so good at that anyhow?"

"Just another part of the job, growing up. Had to be able to get gallimimus off their feet by hand sometimes. There's a refined technique for it. I wasn't sure it would work on you, but, well... close enough apparently." He chuckled lightly.

"Aye," begrudged the old man, nursing a shoulder.

Audrey looked past them to the bow of the boat, and beyond. It was a clear dusk, with Mount Corsicarthal unshrouded, many leagues in front of them. But there was something else ahead that looked strange; something considerably closer. There were overlapping rectangular contours at the foot of the mountain... only they were clearly not attached to the land at all. The structure was fixed; it was not a boat. And as she observed it more closely, she was sure that it was far too large to be either a boat or a ship. It looked kind of like a village, if a village could be built right onto the water's surface.

"What the Heck is that?" she asked.

"What's what?" Jek asked, sounding worried.

The old man took his time getting to the front of the boat. "What ye be inquirin' about? The Wading Isle?"

Audrey shrugged. "If that's what *that* is, then yeah," she pointed.

The old man nodded affirmatively. "Aye, that be what that be."

Jek squinted. "*What the Heck is that*?" he asked in enchanted tone.

"Get the blubber out yer ears!" the old man said. "I already said that that be what that be, meanin' that be the *Wading Isle*!"

"I got that," Jek said, still transfixed by the oddity before them. "It just looks very odd. For instance... where's the *land*?"

"'Bout four inches under the water," the old man said. "Whole island's flat and submerged! What ye think they done called it 'the Wading Isle' for?"

Jek pursed his lips. "I never thought about it."

They all looked out at the mysterious Isle for a long time as it drew nearer. The structures that protruded from below the waterline were elegantly cloaked in a forest of hewn marble pillars and arches, which shimmered in the evening light as if freshly glazed. People, brilliantly attired, were plodding about to-and-fro between the buildings, and out in the open as well, trailing gentle ripples. The men's feet were obscured, but the women's dresses came all the way to the water's surface, and they seemed to coast along. Many were the fancy fountains, with arcing walls coming to hand's height between them. And the whole island appeared to be suffused with a resident population of peacocks and peahens, who perched all along the short walls and the fountains' edges, when not trailing their beautiful tail feathers back and forth through the tranquil sea. Audrey found it all so idyllic and beautiful that it was almost nauseating.

Off the port bow, there were a number of small boats that must have been moored to a low dock, judging by their neatly aligned proximity. Audrey looked around and found the old man had gone. He wasn't at the stern steering the craft, so she took control of the rudder herself, making for the docks. After several seconds, Jek too noted his absence.

"Where'd the old man go?" he asked.

There was a clatter from within the cabin. "I be down here!" he said.

Jek called back. "Going for seconds on that stew?! I'm afraid I already finished it!"

More clattering. "Nay. Gots to change me duds."

Jek looked quizzically at Audrey. She shrugged, returning the look.

As they approached the other boats, the docking came into view, and in no time Audrey had the boat tied off in a vacant spot. Presently an attendant came and harassed them.

"Hey, no vagrants!" he said.

Jek was immediately apologetic. "Sir, thou has'est mine sincereth-est apologies! We dids't not see-eth the sign!"

"Coulds't not have readeth it if I had," Audrey backed him up.

The attendant was still very cross. "There's no sign! Now get lost!"

"Nay! How's about *ye* get lost?" the old man said, treading heavily onto the deck. Audrey and Jek looked back to see a whole new old man! He was dressed in a very fetching blue captain's outfit, complete with awesome big hat.

"Wow!" Jek said. "That's a great costume!"

"T'aint a costume, lad!" the old man fumed. "T'is a *un-ee-form*!"

The attendant was evidently impressed too. "I doth sayeth sorry unto thee, sir," he said, nodding to the old man. "By-eth the look of thine minions, andst the shape of thine boat, I thought thee tramps."

"An understandable mistake," the old man said graciously, flipping a gold coin from his thumb up to the attendant. "Here's for the parkin'."

Jek shook his head in amazement. "You have money too?!"

"Shut yer yap, minion!" the old man scolded him. With a snap, Jek effortlessly assumed the role.

The old man climbed up onto the dock, with Audrey and Jek queuing behind him. The attendant was clearly agitated. "They can'st goeth into town so crude-eth-ly attired, good sir," he squeaked.

"Nay, I know it well enough. That's why I's gonna takes these poor blighters straight off to the duds shop. Come along now, ye dullards!"

They continued to file-in behind the old man. The attendant watched them for a long while, before either being satisfied that they were headed for the 'duds shop,' or else deciding there was nothing more for him to do about it in any case...

Audrey watched Jek take a hesitant first step off the docks and into the tranquil water that suffused the island. She shrugged. Having waded through the smelly bilge of the *Cosigner* on repeat occasions, this cool, clear stuff was no problem for her, and the ground below was smooth and level. Her feet still squished in her boots from all the excitement earlier in the day, so there was little new discomfort in any case.

As they came under the long shadows of the beautiful archways, they caught some rather skeptical looks, but weren't bothered anymore by anyone. Audrey looked all around, still taking in the spectacle. At her sloshing feet, peacocks and peahens were brushing by her ankles as she passed, and cooing pleasantly, like affectionate cats. Down the alleyways she caught sight of more than just Humans. There were occasional Avarica – fortunately not Inquisitors – rather they were obviously successful business folk. On her right, she also saw a small open amphitheater where Meduseldan minstrels were performing. As they had allegedly invented music, Meduselda were sought-after musicians. The audience even contained a small entourage of Dire Heron statesmen – possibly one or more Senators of Roemnar. Everywhere there were signs of merriment and peace of mind...

But on the left, she saw something altogether different...

Far down the alley, there was a big man in a sharp dress uniform. He wore a gas-mask with thick tubing coiled back toward the nape, and in his eye rested a monocle, reflecting a blinding red off the water. From the coils there suddenly rolled black plumes of smoke. This was unmistakably a Despotopian officer. He was looking right at them.

As if all of this did not bode ill enough, Audrey watched as the Despotopian unfolded his hands from the small of his back, holding out a rigid, gloved finger to his right. At once, a songbird alighted on his finger. It was highly agitated. From what Audrey could make out of bird psychology, it was as if the thing was desperately horrified to be in the company of the big Despotopian officer – much less perched on his finger – but was compelled to be there by a force far greater in magnitude than its own will. With the other hand, the officer produced a strange box with knobs and a coily rod sticking out of the top. As he held it out, the bird tweeted at it with furious intensity. The officer looked back at Audrey once more just as she passed behind a pillar, and she caught sight of him no more. She turned to gauge the reaction of her companions, but the old man hadn't seemed to notice. Jek definitely hadn't.

* * *

A little bell rang as they splashed into a lobby. This was evidently the 'duds shop', or else the old man had lied outright to the attendant at the dock. It seemed an odd place to buy clothes, because there weren't any shelves or mannequins or other such displays. There was just a big empty room with a high desk at the far wall, with a man and a woman standing behind it.

"Howdy-doo!" the old man called out to the storekeepers. They frowned.

"Howdy-doo," the woman at the desk answered, sounding rather unsure.

"Well, no time for chit-chat," the old man said, waving a hand around. "Gots to have some fancy duds for me little bilge rats here." He gestured at Audrey and Jek.

The man and the woman pushed the spectacles up their noses in unison and rounded opposite sides of the service desk. They held out tape measures at odd angles in front of Audrey and Jek, primarily along diagonals. The man approached the old man. "We art ready to proceed," he said, and then audibly sniffed. "Would-eth you also like a bath drawn for thineself, sir?"

The old man lifted his arm and took a sniff for himself. "Aye," he begrudged.

The storekeepers went back to their original place behind the desk, as they made up the old man's bill. He looked it over with bugged eyes before quickly trying to talk the man down. The man at the desk looked quite aghast; he probably wasn't used to haggling in his line of work. He was being as polite as he could, but wouldn't let the old man negotiate a smaller fee. Jek eventually grew impatient.

"I don't think it's any use," he told the old man. "You might as well pay him what he wants."

"A penny saved is worth a thousand words," the old man retorted.

"But it's not worth a thousand hours, which we don't have," Jek said.

The old man sighed. "Figgers ye'd take his side in this; ain't your penny what's not bein' saved," he said, turning to the man at the desk. "Here be the whole fee."

The man led Jek and the old man through one side-passage as the woman led Audrey through another. She showed Audrey a washroom and gave her time to clean up, and by the time she was done, the woman was waiting outside with her arms full of shiny dark-green fabric.

"Your frock coat was abhorrent of course, but I felt the color suited you, so I chose this for you to wear," she explained, indicating the fabric. "Try it on and see if you like it."

Audrey took it and changed into it. It was a beautiful gown with a high neck and a shimmering drape that hung nearly to her elbows. There had been no shoes laid aside, which, after a great deal of thought, seemed to indicate Audrey was intended to go barefoot... a welcome change from the boots, she soon discovered. The way the water of the island clung to the bottom of her dress was a bit awkward and uncomfortable, but for her feet, the immersion was actually quite refreshing. She came back out, and the woman tugged at the drape over one shoulder, nodding. "What do you think?"

What did she think? She loved it! She'd never had occasion to be dressed so lady-like!

"It's very nice," she said.

"Good," the woman said. "Now, onto the hair."

In another room, there was another woman waiting, apparently a hairstylist. She sat Audrey and started drawing her hair in various places – firmly, quickly, but expertly enough that she wasn't pulling so it hurt. She was tying her hair up some fancy way. Audrey asked her what knots she was using, but the stylist only paused briefly, and then set back to work, apparently dismissing the question. It was all done quite expediently, and with a gesture, Audrey was shown to another door. She picked up the stuff she came in with and proceeded to the exit.

More time had passed than she thought, for as she crossed the portal, she came back outside to a small courtyard and saw that it was now dark out, with only scant, moody lamps to illuminate the scene. She only just caught sight of someone passing through the shadows opposite her, when suddenly Jek emerged into the light. They both froze in their tracks at the sight of each other. He was decked-out resplendently in dark violet dress pants and a matching vest, with a white shirt underneath that featured ruffs and some big, snazzy cufflinks.

She had only the most fleeting moment to note how sharp he looked before she became irrecoverably fixated on his face. It was drawn back so comically in a look of pure astonishment that, clashing mightily as it did with his most dapper attire, she spontaneously burst out laughing at him. In moments between heaves of laughter, through teary eyes, she saw that he blushed severely. She had likely already wounded his confidence beyond repair, but before she could collect herself adequately to start apologizing, she heard him start to laugh as well – a rough snickering that steadily grew – resting his ruddy-grey forehead in a palm. Their shared laughter was self-reinforcing and soon became utterly raucous.

"What in the Undervoid be a-goin' on over here?!" they heard the old man call out. He ran up to them waving his hands aloft. "Just me luck that me new crew would turn out a pair o' slap-happy chuckle-heads!"

Audrey wiped away a tear of mirth. "Sorry, but... you should have seen his *face*!" And she wheezed with another round of laughter. Jek laughed again too.

"Now ye cut that out!" the old man demanded. "Ye gots to focus-up and start exudin' dignity, like I be a-doin'." He looked at them both. "Ye got yer other duds?" They both did. "Good. We gots to hurry along and throw 'em back in the boat. After all, if we needs to make a quick exit, ye can't be makin' the rest o' the voyage dressed like fancy folk!" With that he started off, and they followed. Audrey trailed behind, and looked at Jek again with a grin, stifling another laugh.

* * *

Soon they had their stuff unloaded, and they were journeying back into town.

"This seems like a lot of trouble to go through just to meet your old pal," Jek said.

"Aye, but t'is necessery. Ye heard the man at the docks; can't go around town lookin' all homeless like."

"If you think about it, we *are* homeless now," Jek replied.

The old man shushed him. "Don't be overheard admitting as much in these here parts! Not after the pretty price I paid to get it so's ye could go trapesin' around the island!"

"Who is your friend we're here to see?" Audrey asked. In all the commotion, she'd all but forgotten that they were on their way to learning about magic. She was keenly looking forward to it. "Is he another sailor?"

"Nay, not for full-many years. Did but a short stint on the seas, he did, afore he done got conscripted to be a thinker."

A thinker! Wow! To think that the old man was friends with a thinker! Among the many vocations one could grow up to have, Audrey had esteemed 'thinker' in her top five, even if it was among the most fashionable professions. And it wasn't easy, either, from what she understood. To be a thinker, one must master the continuous wearing of black turtlenecks as well as a variety of pensive expressions, and be able to sustainably stare into the middle distance. Also helpful was the use of bubble-pipes, and the coordination necessary to rest the ends of one's fingers against each other. And probably, they had to learn to read, too. But above most else, thinkers must think. You wouldn't want to be a thinker and be caught not thinking, because you would likely be executed for dereliction of duty.

She was aware that many a thinker had met with great career success using one or more of the following tactics:

1. Pointing out the possibility that an accepted universal truth may be wrong.
2. Singling out a respected figure of wisdom and implying they may be wrong.

3. Taking statements and rephrasing them as questions.
4. Stating a well-known cause-effect relationship in reverse order.
5. Employing tautological rhetoric.
6. Using between 5 and 70 big words in a single sentence.

Audrey nodded to herself, reflecting on all of this privately with a whole new anticipation for the meeting. Judging by Jek's reaction, she wasn't the only one...

"No kidding?" Jek said. "A real-life thinker! What's his name?"

The conversation skipped a beat. "...I don't reckon ye done never heard o' Zeph Bronzegloom afore?" the old man asked theatrically.

"*Zeph Bronzegloom*!?" Jek shouted. "Sure as shoot I've heard of him! He's very well-published; I've read his books! '*What if Magormissahr was Wrong*', '*What if Galahadron Mucolyptus was Wrong*', and the ever-controversial, '*What if* I *was Wrong*?'"

Even Audrey had heard of Bronzegloom. Though obviously, she hadn't read his works...

The old man chuckled softly. "That's right! I knows a famous person – even from afore he was famous! No doubt I played a definin' role in inspirin' much o' his profundliest insights what he's so well-knowed for now."

As they rounded a corner, the old man came to a sloshing halt. Audrey and Jek came up behind him and saw that they were at the threshold of some kind of large social function – a dance party of unknown significance. Music had wafted through the air from all quadrants since their arrival, and at the thought of thinkers and magic, Audrey hadn't even noticed that they were getting closer and closer to some especially full-bodied music, being performed by a larger orchestration. They looked out into the enormous courtyard. Mostly the dancers were Humans in elegant attire or in dress uniforms of Jast-Madiir, but also there were some who wore the colors of Maenea. Standing head-and-shoulders over the rest of the crowd, she could see some Avarica – and even some Jackal People, who were reputed true masters of advanced dance.

The Meduseldan orchestra was arranged at the rear of an elevated stage, and in front of them were seven professional pacers – other Meduselda, undoubtedly of the Angus Dei Dominion, whose exceptionally refined pacing technique was world-renowned, and a sought-after spectacle. Audrey was awed at the sight of their lazy floating – first one way, then the other.

An indefinite span of time later, her gaze wandered again, and she saw that the court was illuminated entirely by arrangements of scorch-dandelions – a perpetually-burning flowering weed – attained at significant peril from the deep jungles of Jast-Madiir. All-told, the entire party was another dazzling wonder.

Jek broke their collective trance. "We'd better go around," he almost whispered.

The old man looked back at him. "*I'll* go 'round," he said, and he grinned mischievously at them, "but the two o' ye is nicely outfitted to go straight through, I'd say. Go on then!" he commanded with hardly any delay, rushing behind them and giving them a heave into the courtyard. "Take some time and enjoy yerselves; embrace the romanticalness! Then meet me yonderways under that there arch," he pointed. And before Jek could protest, the old man vanished into the shadows of a side-alley.

Audrey and Jek looked at each other nervously. It was the first moment of 'romanticalness' they'd shared. That is, unless she counted that one time... when they were in their respective queues at the marriage office, waiting in line, counting back from the front to see who they were going to be paired up with. They had counted back to each other simultaneously. Jek had given her a timid, awkward wave. She had returned it.

Back in the moment, they set about trying to do as the old man had said. In unison, they each held out their right hands. Jek threw his down and picked up the left, and they joined hands, coming into a very loose embrace, attempting to dance. It was awkward business for many reasons, not the least of which that Audrey didn't know how to dance, and Jek clearly didn't either. And there was the four inches of water they were kicking through. But they seemed to be cohering at least enough that they weren't stepping on each other's feet, and Audrey soon began to relax a bit. Jek continued to seem very nervous. She decided to engage him with conversation, hoping it would calm him down.

"I don't like the way this dress trails in the water," she said. "It's rather irritating."

"It feels strange in pants, too," he said. And they said nothing more.

Well, that was a dead end...

She reached around in her brain for another subject. She needed something more open-ended. "Tell me about yourself, Jek," she said. He seemed to frown.

"Well, you already know I worked with gallimimus on a farm," he said. "Nothing much else comes to mind." There was a pause, but he arrived at an afterthought. "I did do some of the planting and weeding, and harvesting too, of course."

Again, they fell silent, plodding in a lazy circle. She accidentally stepped on the tail-feathers of a nearby peacock, and it shot away squawking. Audrey and Jek both tried to pretend as if they hadn't noticed, in order to save face. She was going to have to think of something else to talk about, and quick...

"Tell me something about the Knights of the Indigo Lodge," she said. He grinned a little. Audrey was glad; she must've found a good subject.

"Well, I know their pledge by heart," he told her. "I had it memorized by age six or seven, I think. But surely you've heard it."

"I don't think I have," she admitted. His smile broadened.

"Well, I could recite it for you, I guess. It goes like this..." He cleared his throat, and then began in a strange voice, where he seemed to make some effort to sound heroic, and yet didn't dare be too loud about it. "'If, upon the Great Looking-Back of all things, we are found to have done good, then let us have doneth the most greatest good that we could do. If we are found to have done bad, then let us have doneth the least worstest bad that we could do. If we pursued the good, may it have been so to attaineth it. If we pursued the bad, may it have been so to destroyeth It'."

She could hardly help baring her teeth a little. "Are you sure you memorized it? That sounds a little silly."

"It's not *silly*," he frowned. "I think it's very noble. It's all about doing good and not doing bad and stuff."

"I suppose you're right," she said. "What else can you tell me about the Knights themselves?"

He snickered nervously. "To tell the truth, I guess I don't know all that much about the Knights, when it comes right down to it – the deeds they've done, and the times they saved the world, and all. Most of the stories I know are just about Carlos Washoe."

The name registered, but Audrey couldn't really attach much to it, except a handful of juvenile jokes she'd heard, where Carlos would do some impossibly tough feat that somehow passed for a punchline. "Well, tell me about him. He was one of the Indigo Knights, I take it?"

Jek nodded emphatically. "Yeah; he was *the* Indigo Knight. Orphaned at the age of five... *minutes*. Raised by sharks. I'm surprised you don't know about him; there are so many great books on his adventures..."

She gave him a look.

"Right, sorry."

He lifted her hand aloft, evidently to let her do a spin move. Their fingers got kind of twisted, but it didn't hurt that much.

"I'll tell you a story my dad told me about one of the times Carlos saved the world," Jek continued. "It was a time when Onyxadon had once again ascended to the very point of world-domination, and... er, you know about Onyxadon, right?"

"You mean O'nyxon? Yeah, I'm sure everyone knows about him."

"Okay, good. So anyway, it was a very, very bad time... among the worst the world had known. Onyxadon's dark armies blanketed the lands. All hope faded, and absolutely everyone gave up. Except for Carlos. He single-handedly gave battle to O'nyxon's legions and bested the elder dragon himself in mortal combat, preserving the world and its inhabitants."

Silence.

"That's it?" Audrey asked.

Jek looked dumbfounded. "W – yeah... I mean... he saved the world from Onyxadon and like a hundred evil armies single-handedly. What more should there be?"

"I don't know. I just thought there would be more detail."

"I'm just telling you like I heard it from my dad. There wasn't much time on the farm for lengthy anecdotes."

"Ah, I see," she nodded.

"I'll tell you another Carlos story," Jek said. His enthusiasm was on the rebound. "There was this other time, when he found himself on a dark desert highway. As his sight grew dim, he came unwittingly to the purgatory-like sub-plane known as The Baja Inn: an otherworldly outpost believed to have been inadvertently formed by the damage caused to the fabric of time and space preceding the Great Regression."

"The Great Regression?" Audrey interjected. "That's another one of those things; I'm sure I've heard of it, but I don't know anything about it."

"I wouldn't be the one to explain it," Jek admitted. "I know it was *the* most apocalyptic event in the history of the world, but little more." He shuddered, evidently eager to push away all thought of the cataclysm. "Carlos wasn't around for all that. But anyway... there he was in the Baja Inn, right?"

"Right."

"Well, after spending one night, and enduring harrowing experiences like strange voices in the halls, perspiratory dancing, and a very, *very* abnormal supper, he was headed for the exit. Suddenly, he was confronted by all the weird and creepy people that resided there. They told him he could *never* leave! But he simply turned around, looked at them, and said, 'The Heck I can't...' and then he walked right out the door!!!"

Again, silence.

"What is it this time?" Jek asked. "Not enough detail again?"

"I just don't get it, I guess. So, he walked out the door. So what? That doesn't seem like a big deal to me."

"Oh, it is, *it is*! You see, he *couldn't* leave... but he did anyway!"

She was skeptical. "Well, but, how do you *know* he couldn't leave?"

"Because they told him he couldn't!"

"But who's to say they didn't make that up? I mean, are we just supposed to take their word for it?"

"Well, why would anyone make something like that up? I mean, how would you even *think* to make something like that up?"

Audrey shrugged, pursing her lips. "I don't know." She felt bad that these apparently grand epics Jek was trying to expound were not coming across to her very grandly. "I'm sorry, I don't mean to belittle your story."

"...Und a fine little story it is, too," intruded a tinny, masculine voice. It was deep, robust, but with an oddly exultant higher-pitched quality at the same time. "Can you imagine, mine fru... zee fugitives are telling stories of zee Knights of zee Indigo Lodge! Vhat an unusual subject to be on zee minds of such rogues, vouldn't you say?"

Audrey gasped. Dancing right next to them was the Despotopian officer she had seen earlier, and a lady Despotopian with him!

Suddenly, and not a moment too late, she could smell the burning coal from the small boilers at their backs. After so many generations of wide-spread coal mining in Despotopia, followed by the industrial age they had entered, where they burnt the stuff everywhere all the time to power their great machines, most Despotopians now needed to breath coal fumes constantly just to feel their best.

"Perhaps not so very unusual, mine Oberführer," the lady answered. Her dress was all angular, shiny black leather, and her hair was slicked back so tightly that it appeared the slightest tug would pull it all out. She too wore a gas mask.

It was probably no time to notice, but Audrey noted that they were a well-matched pair in their contrast. The onyx dress and the white uniform. The lady was small, slight, and sharp, and the man was big and bulging with muscle. The Oberführer's eyes were narrowed with oppressive skepticism, giving his face a death-grip on his monocle, clenched securely as it was between many deep folds of skin. The lady, on the other hand, had wide eyes, unrelentingly searching behind small round glasses with even smaller round loupes.

Audrey stole a look at Jek. He looked utterly astonished again, but it didn't strike her as funny at all this time. She might well look the same right now...

"Ah, but forgive me mine manners!" the Despotopian exclaimed. "Ve know all of zhis about you, but vhat do you know of us? Let me be having vith zee introductions. I am Oberführer Klinkofhenschmidt, und zhis is fru Schenburkreiga, mine vife."

"Glutentöffen," said lady Schenburkreiga. It was a way of saying hello. Despotopians spoke a cooler dialect of Claptrapanese – the common language.

"Your boat has led our agents on quite zee merry chase. My superiors vill be most happy to learn zhat zheir pursuit has now ended."

"You're going to kill us now," Jek said, too weakly to determine whether he'd meant it as a question or a statement of obvious fact.

"Ah ha-ha ha-ha," they both laughed in haughty unison. "Oh, no," the Oberführer said, spinning his wife. The Despotopians danced with disparaging proficiency. "It vould be most discourteous to do such a ting, und not altogezher expedient. By all means, dance zee night avay! Ve'll be sure to run into you again... vhen you have your old man vith you."

"*Then* you'll kill us," Jek whimpered again.

"Yes, yes," the Oberführer admitted. "Ve don't vish to let our manners mislead you. Ve *vill* kill you. Only not right here, vhere it would be socially ham-handed, und leave zee old man on zee loose." Suddenly they stopped dancing, and the Oberführer turned from his wife, standing over Audrey and Jek, who found themselves all but frozen in place. "Alzhough, to be quite fwank, Heck only knows vhy Her Ladyship is so insistent on zee messy vork. In my opinion, it vould be far more amusing to let you complete your Qvest. Let you find your Indigo Knights... only to learn zee more tragically in zee end zhat zhey cannot help you. No von can."

After an interminable period of being spellbound by the Oberführer's threat, they saw that his wife reached for his shoulder. "Come, mine Oberführer," she said. "Let zhem have zheir evening."

"Yaevogel, mine fru-fru," he said in the affirmative. With one hand tucked at his back, he bowed to them, gesturing widely with the other. "Until ve meet again!" And they parted Audrey and Jek's company, boogying resplendently back into sheer anonymity.

Audrey and Jek stared at each other. She could see that Jek was quite lost to his terror. She gave him a bit of a shove to get them dancing again, and almost mechanically it seemed to work.

"All things considered, that could have been worse," Audrey coached him.

Jek blinked rapidly, and his eyes darted around for a moment before settling back on her, focused. "I suppose you're right. They didn't kill us just now."

They danced just a few more feet around the outer edge of the courtyard, before they were yanked bodily out into an alleyway. Audrey was disoriented in the dark, unable to see their assailant, but she heard Jek say, "Oh, *thank the Creators* it's just you!!!"

"Aye, and who else should I be?" the old man said, sounding impatient. "Where has you two been?! Took ye long enough to get in snatchin' distance!"

Audrey, catching sight of him, furrowed her brow. "You told us to take our time and enjoy ourselves. We've been dancing maybe five minutes, tops."

The old man shook his head. "Can't ye hear yerself! Who's got five whole minutes to burn? Anyway, there's Despotopians afoot!"

Audrey nodded. "We noticed." Jek heaved a breath through his teeth and shook his head in apparent agreement.

"We needs to be off. I'd had a mind to get ol' Bronzee to put us up for the night, so's we could mooch off o' him for a meal or three. But in lieu o' these Despotopians, we might better pick his brain and vamoose!"

* * *

He led them ever deeper into the city, hesitating now and then at a few crossroads. The streets suddenly felt barren and desolate, and the music distant and ghostly. Once in a while they heard a flutter and a chirp echo down from the rooftops.

After what felt like an interminable labyrinth in the dark, they came to one row of houses that the old man really pondered over. He evidently couldn't remember which one belonged to Zeph Bronzegloom. Jek started to say something, but the old man shushed him. Audrey went up closer to the houses, searching for clues. At the second house, she saw something that seemed promising. She returned to the group.

"The front door of that house has some writing on it, but I don't know what it says," she whispered.

"What sort o' writin', lass?" All parties were whispering harshly.

She threw up her hands. "I don't know! It could be letters; it could be numbers; it could be pictograms or hieroglyphics or anything! But it's writing – I know *that*."

They crept up to the door to investigate. Jek read the type. "'*Not Zeph Bronzegloom's House*.'"

"See, this is it!" Audrey exclaimed.

"Nay, this be *not* it!" the old man argued. "Didn't ye hear the lad say, '*Not* Zeph Bronzegloom's House'?"

"But don't you see?!" Audrey insisted. "If you were a world-famous thinker, wouldn't you want to use precisely that kind of ingenious misdirection to keep people from constantly bothering you?"

The old man was scratching his beard thoughtfully. Jek, for one, reinforced her. “I think she’s onto something.”

Finally the old man nodded, pursing his lips with an intense gaze of resolution. “Aye, we’ll try it.” Slowly, hesitantly, he reached for the door. Then, he knocked...

The Battle on Variglew

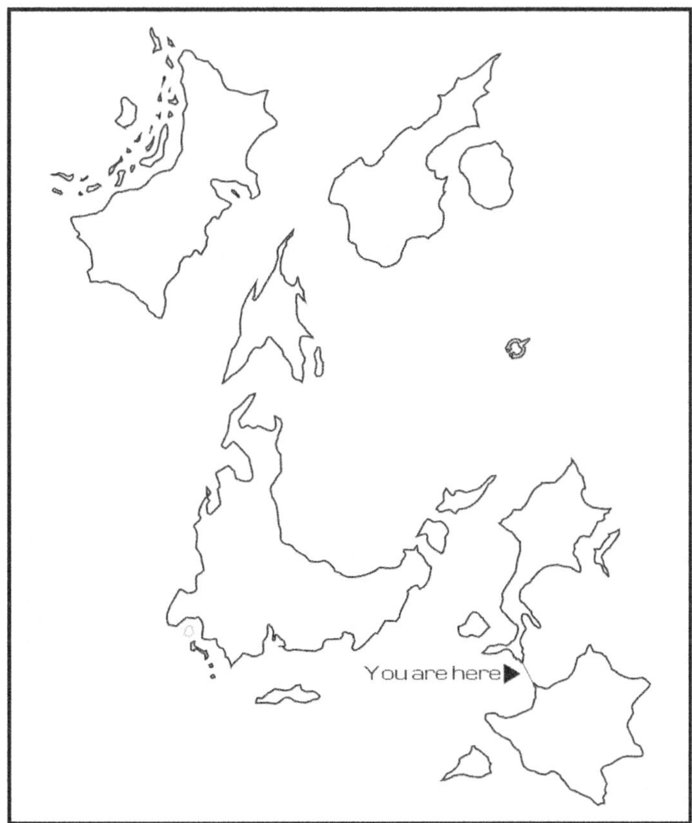

"Those of you with any knowledge of history will of course remember learning of Queen Aedeloma of the Berlie Beirels, and her ilk – the architect of the 770-Years War. And for all those ancient years of trial, widespread distrust of her Dominion endures to this very day. It is often wondered whether this is merited – whether after six generations of living at peace with the Berlie Beirels, we have any reason left to still be specially wary of mischief on their part. So I tell you now – we have certainly not yet seen the last of Aedeloma's brand of evil machinations. Her abominations and her vile ambitions will rise again from the Tophthaeran Isles... and her heirs who achieve this will know no shame in it whatever."

- Proconsul Zedulon, transcript of the Aedeloma Prophecy, as delivered in the nation of Maenea, circa S.E. 8930

The wind was chill as she stood on unsure feet at the epicenter of the Tophthaeran Civil War. It bit unpleasantly at her, but that was nothing compared to the fierce attack it wrought against the very great Bridge of *Variglew*. The frosty, hazy morning and the incredible elevation and breadth of the Bridge shrouded all the world. The ramshackle central disk they stood upon felt very much like its own private, ethereal plane – hastily constructed to allow the legions of the Twin Queens to join battle from across their divergent landmasses.

It was a struggle now seventy-five years in the making. Upon the death of the previous Queen of the Berlie Beirels, the new Queens, Irisa and Asiri, were born. From the very moment they were mutually aware of each other, there was no small disagreement as to which of them was to take up the mantle of the Berlie Beirel Dominion. Their personal duel leveled the original Tophthaeran capitol, and each fled in a more or less cardinal direction, with Asiri retreating to the southern Isle, and Irisa taking root much farther in the north. It was thus that the old nation of Tophthaera was split into Tophthera and Toefthaera – the northern and southern states, respectively.

For several years, the warring Isles depended on their navies, and they toiled fruitlessly to make gains in the gulf. In no time at all, their warships were decimated, only to be replaced as hastily as possible with ever-less-sea-worthy successors. Many of these ships crumbled and sunk while still in their berths. The Tophthaeran region had always been horribly poor in ship-building materials – for that matter, it was poor in useful resources of any kind – and it was not long before the only recourse was to buy ships from nearby Jast-Madiir. For a glorious while (though an incredibly short one) Tophthera and Toefthaera enjoyed elegant, ornate, and effective warships to supplement its few remaining homemade pieces of junk. But these were also quickly lost, and both Queens knew at once that the war on the ocean had come, unceremoniously, to its end.

So began the great undertaking. The warring Queens pooled fortunes to buy as much timber and sheet-metal as they could get their hands on from Jast-Madiir. Naval warfare was never a good fit for Meduselda anyway, whose background in conventional infantry battles stretched into the earliest annals of time. The rest of the war between the islands would be terrestrial, even if they would have to build miles of bridging to realize this vision. And that is precisely what they did…

Now Parissah found herself at the zenith of the titanic Bridge of *Variglew*, which had got its namesake from the Elfish language. In that tongue, it meant "Bridge Where We're Going to Settle This Whole Thing Once and For All and See Which of Us is the True Queen of the Berlie Beirels," appropriately enough…

The Primary Administrator, her three troops of mercenaries, six senior Inquisitor reinforcements and her initiate understudies, as well as trusty Dronehood Clerk Baegulgog (31 souls in all), were alone upon the centerpiece, which widened out into a respectable circular battleground. The whole thing was incredibly crude; even more so than was typical of Meduseldan engineering. Meduselda gave no thought to safety in their construction; there was really no reason for them to bother about it. Since they could build with such abandon, and do so around the clock without food and without rest, *Variglew* in all of its vastness (indeed it was one of the greatest structures on the earth) had gone up in a mere five years, and seen battle nearly every day since.

As Parissah steadied herself, she noted that it was a questionable sort of a miracle that the Bridge had endured to the present day. It quaked and rocked with lazy but dramatic ripples in the winds that were blowing clouds past her feet on all sides. Creaks and cracks filled the sonic environment. Retrospectively, she might just as soon have left the *Carroccio* at the Citadel. Probably *any* armed vessel could have proven adequate to bring *Variglew* down in a pinch; though it was reassuring to know that the keen and steady command of Captain Taurnuren was backing her up. There was no battle as yet, nor even a discernable sign of the opposing armies. But she could *feel* it; a primeval static charge hung over the Bridge. Just as a great lightning bolt strikes between the adjoined forces of Positive and Negative, so it was clear that the two Meduseldan armies would soon collide – with Parissah and her band of 31 in the very eye of the storm, compelled by duty to fight their way out...

"Well looky there," said Grosdrev Trockelov, the increasingly familiar alpha of Guppy Troop. She spun to look where he was looking. His eyes must have been keener than hers (though he did have the advantage of not wearing a helmet with a tinted visor). But soon enough, she saw what he saw. Through the mists came a soft blue glow – indeterminate at first, until it resolved into the weightless forms of dozens upon dozens of Berlie Beirel Meduselda, decked in ragged, ruined uniforms. These ranks floated to the bridge's peak from the south side, and wore violet accented by silver.

"They're all here," Maricalgi announced, unable to completely conceal her fear. Parissah looked back the other way. Sure enough, from the north, an equally phantasmal legion was emerging from behind the shroud – this group dressed in dark blue and bronze.

Virtually every Meduseldan soldier looked as if they had been mauled by a pack of raptors, at least in the way they were attired. But that only made sense. Uniforms were retrieved and recycled after every battle. It was well known that the war had had a profound effect on the Berlie Beirel culture. The current mode of their society held in greatest respect and status those drones who had the most impressive death count in the ongoing Civil War. Many had died hundreds of times in the conflict. Thus the ruined uniforms were more than frugal – they were essentially a badge of honor – displayed for all to infer just how many bad ends a soldier had come to.

But really, the Berlie Beirels had been thought a particularly warlike Dominion ever since their ancient Queen Aedeloma had declared herself the enemy of the entire civilized world generations ago. *Seven* generations ago, no less – and this was a matter not lightly considered. Indeed part of Parissah's purpose here was to see just how many of Aedeloma's diabolical tricks the current Queens Irisa and Asiri might be up to. It may well prove the culmination of another of Proconsul Zedulon's prophecies, which the Inquisition had already worried about for several years...

She shivered. The wind was yet cold and the silence of the great footless marching was eerie.

Presently something happened, which had not likely happened even once since the day *Variglew* went into commission. At the front of the Tophtheran and Toefthaeran armies, a lone drone on each side with a well-kept uniform held up a single tentacle, stopping all their subordinates in midair. These were the officers – the Field Marshals of north and south, and their vests were heavy with medals. Their glows pulsated such that Parissah could tell that they were considering her band. They had no reason to expect her to be there waiting for them. The Inquisitors and mercenaries had cabled up to the bridge from the deck of *Carroccio* (a harrowing episode all its own), and thus had not come to the center by way of north or south.

The thoughtful silence ensued, until the inevitable question was finally broached by one of the Field Marshals. "Say, there! What are you people doing here?!"

Parissah was obliged to answer. "We come as emissaries of the Inquisition, to seek audience with Queen Irisa and Queen Asiri!"

Contemptuous murmering began among the soldiers.

"Ain't no such no-one as any 'Queen Asiri!'" called a random northern soldier.

"Never has been and never will be no 'Queen Irisa,' you mean!" taunted a southern soldier.

"Quiet!" commanded the Marshals. And all were. The northern Marshal continued. "Explain your purpose, and you may find audience with Her Majesty in Tophthera. I can't speak for our counterparts in Toefthaera, of course."

"Toefthaera will certainly recognize any delegations Tophthera is not too dense to refuse," said the southern Marshal. "But pray tell what you want to discuss with Her Majesty?"

"We demand that all hostilities be suspended until the Queens can attend a summit with Grand Inquisitor Enscharaulgk," Parissah said.

Now, raucous laughter echoed across the Bridge.

"With all respect to the emissaries... why in *Heck* would Her Majesty the Queen agree to that?" asked the northern Marshal.

"Indeed," agreed the southern Marshal. "Our Queen is much better and more real than their Queen... but you can appreciate her ordeal. There is simply no reason to so demean herself as to enter into negotiations with the imposter in the accursed north. I'm afraid we simply must deny your request outright."

"That would be unwise," Parissah cautioned. "You don't yet appreciate how committed we are to this course. We will kill anyone who steps foot on this battleground."

There came more subdued laughter and snickering. "That hardly holds any menace to us," the northern Marshal said, and all agreed.

"I'm well aware," Parissah said. "Nevertheless, we will keep the forces of north and south from joining battle, until the last of us should fall. And if *that* should happen, this Bridge will be smote to ruins. Not an *inch* will be left standing! You'll have years of rebuilding ahead of you before the war can go on. Best to entertain our demands now, and save yourselves a most unpleasant report to your respective Queens."

They weren't laughing anymore. Yet they still appeared eager for a fight.

"Let's have that again..." a soldier plied, "...you're willing to fight us... to keep us from fighting each other?!"

"Yes," Parissah answered.

Many excited mumblings ensued. "That's the best news we've had in ages! Fighting with these simpletons has got mighty dull, and that's the truth of it!" exclaimed one soldier. "Aye! Some fresh opponents sounds just what the Heron ordered!" agreed another from across the way. "I want a go at that Dronehood Clerk meself," said another. "A right traitor I names him! Pushin' pencils when he ought to be servin' his Queen!"

"I say!" Baegulgog protested. "Neither of your Queens is any Queen of mine! I am a Sowür Canpattel, and certainly not one of you barbaric Berlie Beirels."

They jeered. "Oh, a Sowür Canpattel, is it?! Let your horse do all the fighting for ya, eh?!"

"That's not how cavalry works!" Baegulgog insisted.

"Take whatever action you wish, only understand the consequences," Parissah admonished the warring legions. "We are unafraid," she said, even as she looked back at her quaky initiates, and the mercenaries, who also appeared somewhat anxious. "...Or at least, we are undeterred."

Hesitation brought the Bridge to a humming tension, its magnetic components rattling under the electric energies of the soldiers upon it. Finally, each of the Field Marshals held a tentacle aloft again, and as one, pointed toward the center of *Variglew*. A hundred or a thousand shouts rang out. The armies floated slowly and gently toward the battlefield...

* * *

Parissah drew her snail pistol, and her initiates drew theirs. Behind them, five other Inquisitors assigned to the assault team also had their weapons drawn, even as they faced the opposite limb of the Bridge. As she drew, she began an aggressive march toward the northern army in step with another seasoned Inquisitor beside her, her students some paces behind. She was going to need to be closer to the edge of the central disk if she was going to get the most out of her shot, because of the rounding slope of the Bridge. She cranked up the pistol, hearing the internal perforated cylinder catch the familiar series of notes. Faintly behind her was the sound of other jingles – five of them in time, the other two breaking harmony.

Her own notes expired. She removed her other hand, holding the pistol out. She shifted a bit as she aimed down the sights, found she had an agreeable line of fire, and stopped. At last her students caught up on either side of her.

"Be sure to make the shot count," she told them. They shifted to the left or right, getting in line with a column of oncoming Berlie Beirels. She heard the crisp resonance of five shots going off to her back, and with it, the sound of her shot and those of her escorts...

With no discernable delay, four long columns of Meduselda erupted in front of her into a fine white mist wreathed in furious blue lightning bolts, vaporized as it were by the force of the electromagnetically accelerated projectiles. From the midst of the blasts, their uniforms flopped empty to the ground, and the ghosty forms of each soldier wafted above their compatriots. The ethereal jellyfish-folk all turned calmly away back to the north, floating over or through the rest of the warriors (who took no notice), as they had undoubtedly done dozens or hundreds of times in the course of the Civil War. In a week they would all be solid again, and ready to continue the zero-sum game.

The outer columns converged inward, hemmed to a chokepoint between the mercenaries, who had surged into position on either side of both points of egress from the central battleground. As the soldiers burst on the perimeter, Guppy Troop and their comrades cut them down, row by row. The Berlie Beirels offered only token resistance, hoping to extend the struggle with these new and interesting opponents. They had few if any forged weapons; the majority of their impediments were large, improvised wooden clubs or jagged strips of sheet metal – probably leftover pieces of *Variglew* itself, or else borrowed fragments. Many had no weapons at all.

Suddenly, a stream of Berlie Beirels won their way into the battlefield, trickling through a space left between the mercenaries. The first was unarmed, and Parissah leapt up to meet him with a snarl, pounding and clawing for all she was worth. Hand-to-hand combat with Meduselda was not easy, even for a dragon-lady. Sluggish as Meduselda were in their various movements, they had frightening strength in their seven tentacles, which could easily catch the unwary in a coil of bone-smashing constriction. They also had very high voltage coursing through their bodies. If the Inquisitors and mercenaries had not been very careful to equip insulated underwear prior to the battle, they would all be at risk of fatal electrocution…

Even after pinning him down, Parissah's opponent took bludgeoning after bludgeoning with elastic imperviousness. Finally her claws prevailed past the creature's surface tension, and he evaporated into a harmless apparition.

Victorious in her first exchange, she whirled in horror to see that Maricalgi was being lifted and contorted by another Berlie Beirel soldier, which seemed unsure which way to twist her in order to cause breakage. Parissah rushed to Maricalgi's aid and tore off a few limbs, saving the young initiate, and the two of them finished off the Meduseldan opponent. Deacogal, her other student, was having better luck, skirting the edge of the battlefield at speeds too great for the Meduselda to match while he re-wound his snail pistol. She couldn't be sure why, but it seemed to her that as he dashed around, she heard him mutter something like, 'Better part of valor, better part of valor…' over and over again to himself. Parissah gestured to Maricalgi and then to Deacogal so as to suggest she follow his example. Understanding, she took off in a musical flash, winding away.

Parissah drew her own pistol and started readying another shot. She only got a few cranks in before she was seized from behind. Southern soldiers had broken through in greater numbers, and her other squad of Inquisitors had been forced to break ranks. She tore away one tentacle, but another grabbed her arm. She tensed, trying desperately to overcome the grip, but she was not even sure she could prevent the creature taking *her* arm off, just as she had taken his.

Detachedly (not unlike how her arm might soon be detached), she noted to herself that the characteristics that made Baegulgog and other Meduselda so cheery and personable in lighter social situations were the very same that made them terrifying combatants – they had no understanding whatever of pain or consequence, and only a very remote and alien concept of death. She was about to get all she could bargain for of two or three of those things...

At that very moment, a hurricane-strength bluster buffeted *Variglew*. A loose slab of sheet metal was torn free of the battlefield, and Parissah heaved back with her legs, sending her assailant into its path. The sharp whipping sheet bisected the bulk of the Meduseldan, and his ghost flew away dejectedly, sending Parissah tumbling to the ground. The Bridge was pitching dramatically, its countless seams howling in the wind, and she only kept rolling, her free hand wildly searching for something to cling to. It should have been easy to find, with *Variglew* being such a carelessly cobbled-together mess – but often what she seized for gave way. It didn't help that the other hand had a death-grip on her pistol; she couldn't afford to lose it. Further and further toward the verge she careened, until she had only one last-ditch maneuver left in her battery. At the last she held fast to the Bridge, digging her foot-claws into a wooden beam. But she had reached the very edge, and was hanging over!

Suspended above the ocean and trying to gather her bearings, she blinked hard at the sight on either side of her. Up the slope, her fellows had mostly or all managed to secure themselves on the Bridge as it tilted to a roughly 30-degree incline. But the Berlie Beirels... they were being dumped by the hundreds off of the north and south ways!

It was an unspeakable relief to see so many would-be opponents thrown out into empty space. Parissah sighed heavily, bringing her mask to an orange-hot glow. The heavy breathing of her physical struggle had already gone a long ways to preheating it.

But even as she began to relax, and the great Bridge started to swing back the other way, all of her assurance unraveled before her eyes. It seemed that the Berlie Beirels weren't about to let themselves be idly cast into the sea after all. Aerially buoyant creatures that they were, they started to float skyward again, rounding up and alighting back onto *Variglew* like a two great rivers of loosed balloons! She shook her head at the sight. Her team would have to fight them all yet!

Parissah did a sit-up to aright herself and win back onto the surface of the central disk. It was a very great strain on her ankles, but the rest of her body was well able. In the end, the teetering and tottering of the Bridge had caused her team much greater difficulty than the opposing armies. The mercenary bands were now surrounded, hardly able to repel their opponents on three sides, let alone properly constrain the inward flow of oncoming soldiers. Parissah prioritized relieving Trockelov in his distress. With the leader of the pack free, he would probably be best able to help her reestablish the chokepoints.

As she darted, she heard numerous snail shots behind her, and that was well. She leapt onto an unsuspecting Berlie Beirel near Trokelov, and with an electrical pop, she tore the drone apart. The 'juices' of survival mode were really flowing at this point. She wondered if she was angry enough, and decided that she was. Parissah sucked in a huge breath – the biggest she could – and expelled a jet of flame from the nose-hole of her mask, incinerating three or four Meduselda. Trockelov, now free, was quick to express his 'thanks'...

"The fire-breath, that's a nice trick! And I'd give my whole wage for one of them snail pistols! But why in thunder are you going around whaling on them with your bare mitts? I'd expect you Inquisitors to come better prepared! Where's your iron? Where's your blades?"

"That's what you're here for," Parissah huffed, recovering from scorch-throat. "I don't have any training with those kinds of weapons."

Trockelov shook his head, reaching for various spots on his heavy armor. "Here, take one anyway; take a half-dozen! Pass 'em along to your pals. Just remember, cut the other guy, not yourself. There, you're trained!"

He unloaded a handful of long knives and an axe or two, and then charged off toward one of his squads. Parissah fastened the weapons under her belt, leaving one long knife in her hand. She found the thing an incredible help; she was able to 'cut-and-run', dispatching sluggish Meduselda as she darted about, relieving besieged mercenaries and arming her own Inquisitors. Soon they had the oncoming traffic well in-hand again – indeed, they were faring far better now.

All the while the Field Marshals looked on, flashing with interest, presiding over the battle with cold malevolence. They were within striking distance, and indeed would have been easy pickings in the opening volley of snail-fire, but as far as the mission parameters were concerned, they were firmly off the list of targets. Someone important would have to bring the Inquisitor envoys to the Queens, if that object could be realized. It had occurred to Parissah that the Marshals could still order the cease-fire and lead the way to the Queens just as well as ghost-Meduselda. Still it wouldn't be fitting to harm them. There was just something diplomatically callous about the idea of killing a commander and then expecting all that help of him...

Every so often, the wind picked up again, and they were hard-pressed, having to put forth a great deal more effort not to be blown from the Bridge, while the Berlie Beirels could move about rather freely. But for a while, the battle was sustainable, and became rather monotonous. Still the Marshals looked on without sign of relenting. Perhaps they had some knowledge of the fact that, if they kept the pressure on long enough, her group would eventually tire out. Meduselda were not usually aware of such foreign conceptions, but it was possible.

After one gust, Parissah stumbled to her feet, when suddenly one of her legs went straight through a hole in the Bridge! It hurt her ankle sharply, and was humiliating. Humiliation, of course, had its merits, but this was hardly the time for it. She thrashed around for a few seconds, trying to extract her leg from the pit, but succeeding in little more than pivoting in a semi-circle. Finally she stopped herself, and went about it more calmly, at last reclaiming her submerged foot.

In that short time, a gaggle of enemy troops were loosed on the battlezone. Her mercenaries were beset again, and she was going to have to make her way to them. Though soon she saw that a few of the mercs appeared to have slipped into the ranks of the Berlie Beirels, and were advancing on the center... as if they had suddenly switched allegiances. But as she looked closer, she realized they were not *her* mercenaries at all. These were recruits of Queen Asiri in the south! Parissah chastised herself. She should have expected to see enemy mercs!

She hurled herself into the situation. If possible, she wanted to dispel the Humans without killing them. It was perhaps impractical for her to notice or care, but it seemed to her that they had significantly more to lose if they died on *Variglew* than the Berlie Beirels did. Leaping in front of them with her claws extended wide, she craned her head high and snorted a jet of fire at their feet. This was a bold move for her, because all of these mercenaries looked healthy and fit, and almost certainly had greater skill in battle than she did. But *they* didn't know that... and anyway, she had observed that Humans were often easily intimidated by large lizards, such as herself. Sure enough, two of them peeled away from the group at the mere sight of her fire-breath, running for their lives.

One particularly brave mercenary with a nifty mustache jumped out in front of the rest of the group. There was fire in his hand – *magic* fire – and he brought it to an inferno. With an underhand whipping toss, he sent a fireball slamming into her torso. Parissah found it quite uncomfortable, but it ultimately did her no harm whatsoever. She was of the dragon-folk, after all – built to withstand fire within, and without.

The wind picked up. This was the opportunity she needed. Even as the fire in her middle receded and the mustache merc's eyes widened with the realization that he hadn't hurt her, she reached out and grabbed him up by the chest, throwing him bodily and sidelong into the rest of his troop. The bowled-over mercenaries rolled down the slope and off the Bridge, falling hundreds and hundreds of feet to the waiting ocean. Parissah nodded to herself, glad that she had been able to spare them death. It was well-known that you couldn't possibly die from falling into the water, no matter the distance. Just before she returned to the fighting, she did blanch at one thought... she hoped they could swim...

* * *

The fighting wore on, and time proved very hard to gauge on top of the world. The sun was still shrouded in the clouds, and if it hadn't been for the disparately colored uniforms flowing to the center from the north and south, Parissah might've lost all track of her cardinal directions. It was a timeless struggle up there, at the pinnacle of *Variglew*... or so it seemed to her.

She fought to relieve a group of her encircled mercenaries. One of the Berlie Beirels turned on her, wielding a very nasty looking shard of metal. She deflected a lazy attack or two with Trockelov's long knife, but she was unsure of herself in this mode of combat. One parry slipped, and her arm was gashed. The pain was sharp and hot, but the cut was rather superficial, and her fiery protestation flummoxed her floating assailant. She leapt on him with the knife, disintegrating him – feeling an odd tingling as the ghost of the drone sailed through her.

The mercs were safe for the moment, but one of them approached her. His breath was dramatic – his whole body seemed to be engaged in the action of getting air. It was a sign of exhaustion, she knew... though she hadn't expected to see such a thing yet...

"We're getting tired," he admitted in a truncated way, resting his hands on his knees. The little man was from Sickle Troop. Parissah was disappointed beyond the point of concealment.

"Already?" she demanded. It seemed incongruous. They were all seasoned fighters, and their armor was light, or so she reckoned. But *they* were Humans, after all.

"I've killed dozens so far," he seemed to argue, weakly, "*hundreds* between the five of us. They don't shy from the sight of their fallen brethren. They don't ease up... they don't retreat. They just keep coming! I've never seen anything like it."

Well, she had to take pity on the man, however much she'd hoped to get more out of her mercenaries. It was time for a fallback strategy.

"Retreat to the center," she told him, "you and everyone with you. I'll send the rest to you. A circle will be more defensible, and with the Berlie Beirels gaining free range of the field, they will begin to fight each other as well as us... much as I had meant to avoid it." She really had hoped to keep the fighting from breaking out between north and south today. But that was only an ideal, and had to be sacrificed now...

* * *

A light spitting rain blew over the Bridge from the west, and everything and everyone was rimmed in a sheen under the dull sky. Parissah had rounded up her mercenaries and fellow Inquisitors to regroup in a tight formation at the center of the disk. The fighting was much more intense now, but it burst around them rather than upon them, and so they were, for the moment, relieved. The din of battle had escalated enormously as the northern and southern Berlie Beirels came streaming unrestrained onto the battleground, and as she had anticipated, the balance of their strength was being expended each on the other. The Humans and Avaricans made for only a small island in the midst of a chaotic sea of warring Meduselda. It was bewildering to the eye and eerie in the ear. There was little sound of passion in the furious onslaught. To be sure, Tophthera hated Toefthaera with reckless intensity, and vice-versa... that much was so. But there were no cries of pain, no protests for mercy, no shouts of great effort expended in mad rage. There weren't so much as any jeers or sneers or insults or boisterous pronouncements of contempt... all such dialogue had long since become tedious after the long years of daily battle. They just killed each other. And the same time next week, they would do it again...

Often enough, the Meduseldan soldiers did break on her phalanx of mercenaries. The curiosity and novelty of the party's intrusion into their private war was easily enough to overcome the Berlie Beirels' belligerent nationalism. In a way, it seemed some of them were fighting each other just to get to the mercs and Inquisitors. But the formation made the confrontation considerably more manageable. A few mercenaries at a time could retreat into the circle and recover some strength, and a few Inquisitors would join them at whiles, crank their snail guns, and fire into the crowd of jellies, destroying all in the path of the shot.

But Parissah worried. She hardly caught sight of the Field Marshals anymore, being encircled by such a tumultuous throng. Her group wasn't controlling the battle any longer. The Marshals were all but free to forget her threats. Without benefit of sending them a clear message, the fighting would only go on... in which case their only hope of making an impression would be to outlast the entire pair of armies. Taurnuren might have to act on the assumption that they had all died and begin shelling *Variglew* into ruin long before that. She needed a gambit to alter the course of the conflict again... and *soon*, lest they all go down with the Bridge. But she couldn't think of anything...

Parissah withdrew into the circle and crossed over to Grosdrev Trockelov. In her estimation he was the premier military personality with her. Maybe he had some ideas...

"We're not accomplishing anything here," she told him.

"We're staying alive," Trokelov said, slicing into a Berlie Beirel, shielding himself from the electromagnetic eruption. "I don't know if that means much to you, but it's worth noting as far as I'm concerned."

"It's not enough. We have to settle this somehow before Captain Taurnuren initiates the failsafe plan."

"Which is?"

"He will use his ship to completely destroy *Variglew*."

"Oh great!" Trokelov said, shaking his head. "I thought that was just a lot of hot air, when you told the Marshals about destroying the Bridge. But I might've known you really had something like that in mind, bringing one of your fancy battlecruisers along." For a while he said nothing more. He watched Berlie Beirels struggling tither and yon. Finally he looked back over his shoulder at her, conscious of her gaze. "Well, don't look at me! I knew enough to give you folks some knives, maybe, but I certainly don't know how to change our fortunes against so many. Better hope your Captain is a patient man."

"Patient yes, but prudent too."

"Augh!" he groaned. "We're getting nowhere trying to stop one battle with another! I don't suppose you ever tried asking the Queens nicely to give up the war?"

"We did. Far *too* nicely... and far too long ago. We ought to have followed up with force earlier. Now we are doubtless working harder than we might have." Finally she thought of something. "If we can't make a power play, we should certainly try to send someone back to the ship; to let him know we're in for a very long fight."

He didn't reply.

"What is it?" she asked. "Did you think of something better?"

"*Blimey*," he said. He seemed transfixed. Finally he pointed south. "What in the Undervoid is that?!"

Her gaze followed his gesture. There was a light in the haze above the southern passage, arcing back and forth in a figure-eight pattern as it grew in size and intensity. There was little she could make out, except that it was *big.* She almost didn't notice as another mercenary behind her began calling out, "Look, look!" She twisted her head on her neck. She didn't know why, for it seemed plain the merc had caught sight of the same anomaly. But it was well that she checked, for she saw that he was facing north instead of south. And there, in the distance, was another dancing light of the same sort...

She had a theory about all of this. A terrible theory. But it fit the rumors coming out of the Isles. She would know soon enough...

Finally, through the mirk, the lights took up solid form before their eyes, emerging from the haze. She watched as the light to the south manifested a multi-bulbous body with an intricate series of intersecting muscular baffles in a pattern that was unsettlingly reminiscent of a rib cage, and a trailing plethora of enormous barbed tentacles. It stopped short of the disk, and began circling it in the air beyond the outer perimeter, coasting in aggressive arcs up and down, behaving half like a jumping fish and half like a probing bird of prey. The creature from the north did the same. These things were unmistakably Meduseldan. But they were far larger than drones. They were far *faster* than drones. Parissah knew exactly what they were. They were immense incarnations of sheer willful malice; manifestations of the rage and scorn of their Queens, each for the other.

They were abominations.

Only one other Queen had ever before learned the black art of generating larger and fiercer drones with which to subjugate her enemies – Aedeloma of the Berlie Beirels, may her name never fail to be strongly disliked! This confirmed some of the Inquisition's worst fears about the Tophthaeran Civil War. The Twin Queens truly had no shame in their mutual hate – or they would surely never have resorted to the devices of their most wicked ancestor...

The field was silent for some moments. The Berlie Beirels of north and south had also taken notice of the arrival of the abominations, and though they may have had no more cause to fear than they ever did, still for a time it gave them pause. Then the fighting resumed, markedly intensified. Perhaps they hoped to destroy as many of each other as they could before the abominations took hand in the chaos. Whatever the real reason, they were frenzied – as frenzied as such slow-floating creatures could be.

"What are we going to do about *those* beasties?" Trokelov asked.

Parissah might just as soon have asked him. But she felt she had a good idea how to proceed. "I'd say we do nothing. Not at first. This could be a boon for us. Remember, they're here primarily to fight each other."

"You all better have your pistols cranked! They might be just as keen about the new toys on the field as the first waves of drones – and then we'll be in a pickle!"

"We'll prepare a volley," she agreed. "Cover us." She withdrew into the circle.

"Naturally," he seemed to mutter to himself.

Even as she held her pistol skyward, turning the handle, hearing the tinny notes, she saw that the abominations, still circling, converged sharply into the disk. Now their huge shadows were cast over clusters of their comparably tiny brethren. Still they kept flying just above it all. Parissah stayed at the center where she could watch. The mercenaries didn't have the luxury of following them intently; they still had to be on guard against attacks coming from the infantry. She hoped to warn them all at the moment the titans committed to the battle...

They bobbed up, they glided down, trailing tangled death behind them, with valence energies coursing over their spiked tentacles. Their bodily glows pulsated like beacons, growing faster. They were becoming more and more agitated. Wherever their shadow passed, the drones came almost to a halt, and were drawn upward somewhat, like a rolling wave. They were being magnetically disrupted by their big cousins.

They circled and circled, sowing a little destruction here and there, whenever a rogue lightning bolt from their limbs happened to incidentally strike a Berlie Beirel soldier, vaporizing it. Their pulsations carried a powerful thrumming sound now that seemed to pluck the eardrums like a taught guitar string. It was dizzying and it hurt.

"I'm going to be sick!" called one of the mercenaries over the clamor. Parissah herself began to worry she might throw up in her mask. That would be very unpleasant.

The thrumming intensified. They all were struck faint, concussed by it. Some fell to a knee. Holding her hands ineffectually over the sides of her mask, Parissah hoped the accursed creatures would begin their onslaught soon...

Her hope was met. As her eyes followed, she watched one abomination pitch dramatically skyward, and she knew it was at last committing to a dive-bomb attack. "Brace yourselves!" she warned the group. And the great creature threw itself down onto the plain, crushing dozens of drones indiscriminately against the hodge-podge surface of *Variglew*, like a brick smashing grapes through a cheese grater. The enormous Bridge buckled and they were all tossed some inches into the air. The creature reared up again and repeated the attack, and whipped its tentacles around furiously behind itself, barbing Berlie Beirels all around and throwing lethal voltage out in chaotic arcs. The destruction was remarkable.

"Shoot them! Shoot them!" one of the mercenaries insisted.

"No!" Parissah called. "We have to ride it out! They can clear the field for us! The mission must prevail!" Her Inquisitor brethren held fast, though some had been ready to fire at the mere insistence of the mercenary. She had half felt like heeding him herself...

Time and again they watched the abominations erase clusters of drones. The central disk was emptying quickly of belligerents around the perimeter, and the great killing engines were yet converging. Some of the party wanted to bolt this way or that, but Parissah and Trokelov agreed they should stay at the center. By the time the abominations reached them, they would be quite close to each other, and would thus have bigger fish to fry...

But the havoc was getting very close. The feral tentacle attacks of the abominations were nearly reaching them! The collective flight reflex of the strike team was nearly insatiable. But they were all resolute enough to hold the middle amidst the striking and flailing and the terrible racket immediately before them on all sides.

"Duck!" someone called out, and they all threw themselves to the ground. A huge tentacle whooshed overhead, ridged barbs oscillating in search of stuff to kill. Lightning followed, striking in their midst. The electric force of it sent many metal elements of the surrounding area exploding off the Bridge's surface. Again, Parissah admonished herself for her misjudgment. They would all be swept away now, just as the northern and southern infantry had been wantonly brushed into oblivion...

But at that moment the chaos rescinded. Parissah saw that the abominations had resumed their lazy bobbing. They were conscious now of each other, circling higher as they had before, building steadily toward the inevitable clash.

To her surprise, some of her party leapt to their feet. A few Berlie Beirels that had survived the thrashing were converging on their phalanx. There were some dozens left on the field. But she ignored them; the others had the situation well in hand. She watched the abominations, readying herself to commit to one course or another. The things were clearly going to fight each other. She supposed it was smarter to let that play out; then they might have just one to bring down with a hail of snail fire.

The titans circled immediately overhead now. The thrumming resumed.

"Retreat!" she called out. Her group fled in all directions. Even as they made for the outer edges at full speed, furious crackling sounds erupted. In her mad dash Parissah suddenly threw a dancing shadow, as if a blue sun were jumping and flickering behind her back. Slashing a southern soldier, she reached a spot near the threshold and pivoted to see what was going on.

Energy poured from the opposed abominations in a thick blinding arc, with smaller bolts reaching wildly. It was a cackling surge of power, against which Parissah could tell that no amount of insulated undergarments could possibly have protected them. But the electric cascade wavered and eventually wore down and out, the creatures expending the balance of their charge on each other. Any pretense of drapery denoting faction had been utterly vaporized. The colossal entities were identical. Only they knew their own allegiances, for what it may have mattered to them.

Next came the fisticuffs, if it could be so called on that scale. The abominations pelted each other with tentacles, their barbs sticking and raking, and jumbles of lightning bolts sputtered from the tears in their hides like blood from a wound. They were oblivious to all such damage, just like their smaller counterparts, and so the flurried lashings extracted no protest. The only sound from the battle was the overlapping *thunks* of the tentacle strikes, each of which resonated like distant cannon fire. But the airborne struggle was tenuous; they tumbled upward one moment, spiraled downward the next. A disastrous collision with *Variglew* seemed inevitable. Having stood upon the Bridge for some hours now, Parissah had nothing but questions concerning its soundness. If the abominations hit the disk hard enough, she felt they would all be bodily ejected from their mission, and there might not be much left for Taurnuren and his *Carroccio* to finish off...

The thunderous contest wore ever on, and even seemed to escalate, as the Tyrannosaur-sized Meduseldan mutants gained unprecedented altitude. They flashed brighter and brighter again, and gave a faint blue cast to some of the lowest-hanging rainclouds in their midst. Their internal charges were building to exponentially lethal magnitudes again, and the lightning bolts that arced from their wounds grew apace.

Finally, something Parissah couldn't detect apparently triggered a simultaneous change in tactics. The two abominations flung as many tentacles as they could at each other, every barbed end holding fast in the other's hide like a fleet of anchors, and they hurled themselves earthward. Neither fought to break away; they surrendered to the freefall, building to terminal velocity...

"Get hold of something!!!!" Trokelov called out to all. Parissah went hardily along with the suggestion. She had been momentarily so transfixed by the spectacle that she honestly hadn't thought of doing anything so practical. Now she flopped onto the floor with all speed, digging claws in, hand and foot. And with her long, flexing neck, she snaked over her own shoulders to see what ruin would be wrought...

The abominations hit the Bridge and smashed straight through the epicenter like a cannonball through a trampoline, sending a shockwave through the disk that ejected hundreds of splinters and bolts, as if beating the dust off a drawn rug. Parissah held fast, but the reverberation through the field was concussive, and it knocked the wind clean out of her with a hot puff. She'd never had the wind knocked out of her before...

Once she got over the reflexive panic of wondering why she wasn't breathing, things began to normalize, and she rolled over and sat up, assessing the damage. The Bridge's poor integrity had been its salvation – the abominations simply tore a hole in the middle where they had fallen.

As she looked at the fresh pit, with shrapnel still tumbling loose around the edges, the beams of a great series of flashes emanated from below it – shocking and disorienting in intensity – and with it a warble of electric resonance that echoed off the ocean for miles.

She guessed she knew what happened. She heard the shriek of twisting metal and the crisp cracking of broken wood as a lone abomination won its way back through the puncture in *Variglew*. It hung calmly in the air for a spell as the other abomination came up silently after, absent at present from its mortal form. The ghost hesitated, and then withdrew to the north. Parissah's theory was confirmed. Now was the time to take hand in the battle once again...

"Open fire!" she commanded. And with practiced, swift action, drew and fired her snail pistol.

Her shot made a huge hole in the remaining abomination. Lightning coursed around the edges, as if to create some semblance of a seal over the wound. But several other shots quickly rang out, and it was more than the colossus could endure. It finally failed, erupting with the severity of the other abomination, now unchecked by the barrier of the Bridge.

All about were staggered for a good long while by the epilepsy-inducing explosion (even the few Berlie Beirels still on the field), so that Parissah only briefly glimpsed the second ghost as it disappeared down the southern path. But she sprang up, winding for another shot. This was their chance to reclaim mastery over the field...

*　*　*

...Or so she thought. Fresh northern and southern soldiers were floating in. It wasn't at all the onslaught it had been before; the ranks were thin and came in small groupings. But Parissah's assault team was depleted as well. A few mercenaries had been bucked clear of *Variglew* by the impact of the abominations. She could see that others of them had suffered injury. And they were having trouble regrouping; they could no longer hold the middle, and they might not be up to reestablishing the bottlenecks they had held earlier in the day, either.

Before she could decide what to do, Parissah noticed another, far subtler paradigm shift in the battle. A cluster of general infantry Toefthaeran Berlie Beirels were meandering across the field, half-concealing in their midst a soldier with an unblemished violet uniform; indeed it appeared completely spotless from what she could make out. And in each of his seven tentacles, the soldier held a forged weapon; the first she'd seen on any enemies beside the southern mercenaries. Seven swords, expertly crafted – honed and deadly.

Repelling a non-committal attack from a passing northern soldier, she surveyed the field, and sure enough found what she was looking for. An elite Tophtheran in immaculate blue attire was also prowling across the disk, and he too held seven swords, fanned out below him like the tail-feathers of a falcon swooping in for the kill. In light of the paired abominations, she was not surprised to see this. The Field Marshals had reenacted the Battle of *Variglew* so many, many times that by now, their actions were perfectly mirrored, with each committing his most terrifying assets to the fray at the same time and in the same fashion.

Parissah turned her attention back to the southern swordsdrone, watching him cut down a whole troop of northern infantry with shocking speed and finesse as his escort peeled away. She marveled at the sight of it, wondering where the drone had acquired such training. Perhaps in Roemnar; only tales of their most elite spearmen seemed to compare with the spectacle before her. This was not the wild carnage of the abomination attack. The swordsdrone was as finely sharpened an instrument of killing as was each of his shimmering blades – a paragon of precision and skill – an assassin's dagger that followed the demigod's hammer-stroke. Even Aedeloma herself had never enjoyed this kind of martial asset. No one would have been foolish enough to instruct her minions, neither would she have been capable of recognizing the value in such teachings, if they came from any source but her.

On top of all this, Parissah became aware of a frightful peril. The southern swordsdrone was cutting a swath which led directly to her students. She could tell they were quite unaware that a truly expert fighter was stalking them. They would never realize the danger in time! Parissah went for her pistol, but even as she did, she caught sight again of the northern swordsdrone. He had doubled back on her, having floated nonchalantly to the edge of her peripheral vision and changed course. She watched long enough to be sure... she was his target!

She had one shot, and two divergent courses. She could save Maricalgi and Deacogal, or save herself. Her students were not mission-critical assets. They had no diplomatic training. They showed little initial promise, and certainly could not be trusted to represent the interests of the Inquisition at their present level of instruction. Parissah herself, as a Primary Administrator, was an indispensable diplomatic resource, with full knowledge as to their designs for both this Tophthaeran Civil War and also the Maenean insurrection. She couldn't unduly jeopardize herself. All duty, and pragmatism, and a whole logical checklist some hundreds of items long said so... self-preservation imperative notwithstanding. There was only one correct choice to make here...

She aimed, and fired...

The southern swordsdrone atomized instantly. His ghost hovered over his empty, tumbling uniform, now tarnished by a big square hole. The apparition turned toward Parissah, flashing with befuddlement. He was not so quick to accept his defeat as his novice brethren. But at last, his disembodied form retreated elegantly to the south. Parissah looked at her students. They skirmished with other drones... still in *some* danger, but no longer doomed.

She put down her pistol and took back up Trokelov's knife, turning to her northern adversary, watching the wind tug at his popped collar and long coattails. His posture of challenge was obvious and unflinching. It was abundantly clear – she didn't have a prayer...

Parissah had not made the correct choice. Perhaps she was getting sentimental. Or, maybe it was just that she knew too well what it felt like to live with the correct choice...

Silently the swordsdrone dismissed his posse. There was no cause for further subterfuge; he knew that she knew. Parissah held out the long knife, creating what distance she could. She felt silly. She was sure her opponent could already measure her skill; she half expected him to laugh at her. But he just floated there impassively in the spitting rain. Finally, she realized that he was inviting *her* to make the first move. What a cold invitation! But she steeled herself. She had a puncher's chance, for what it might be worth...

Just as she was about to pounce, Trokelov and one of his Guppy Troopers leapt into the gulf, wildly but expertly striking at the swordsdrone. Parissah jumped into the fray as well; it would be most inconsiderate to merely receive their intervention, and quite possibly it would be for naught without her help.

The swordsdrone was altogether undaunted. He didn't give an inch. For after all, even against three opponents, he still had two-and-one-third swords to every adversary, and he used each with independent mastery. Being quite without a head, or eyes, or organs of any sort for that matter, he did not see as they saw, and could not be flanked, nor limited to tracking the movements of any one or two opponents at a time.

Still they tried fanning out, hoping to find a weak spot in the swordsdrone's defense. Parissah was almost directly across from the Guppy Trooper when she watched his axe get caught in the scissors of two of the swordsdrone's blades. He sliced outward with beastly strength, throwing the Trooper off of *Variglew*. But there was a quick, dull thud, and Parissah was distressed to see that the Trooper's arm had remained behind with them!

Trokelov jumped back, his face all in a horrific sneer. He reached into his high armored collar, and expertly tossed yet another of his seemingly countless knives at the swordsdrone. The drone literally caught the ballistic knife in swords, tipping it in the air from blade to blade, and finally deflected it right back into Trokelov's shoulder, all while fending blows from Parissah.

Trokelov buckled, staggered. But the knife was not in deep, and he quickly drew it out, and swung with it in one hand, his sword in the other. He was fierce in his rage but not at all sloppy or overcommitted. He wrenched a sword free of one of the drone's tentacles. It was a major victory for morale! But it passed in a flash, for even as the sword struck the ground, the drone's free tentacle hurled a fireball at Trokelov, striking him in the middle and sending him limp. The swordsdrone possessed magical Fire power, as if his great skill were not enough!

Trokelov's fate was uncertain, though it seemed rather hopeless, unless Humans were more flame-retardant than Parissah guessed. She continued her awkward attacks against the most horrible drone, unable to do anything for her fallen mercenary... even offer a fair chance of avenging him. The Berlie Beirel parried blow after blow, but made no reprisals, effortless as they would have been. The creature must have been hoping she would offer him some greater challenge if given enough chance.

Finally, he decided he had given her chances enough. He unleashed a furious assault, each sword now illumined by coursing lightning from the drone, and it was all Parissah could do to retreat from reach. But she stumbled on the cobbled surface of *Variglew*, and fell to the ground.

She was quite deep in the desensitization of survival mode, and did not at once understand what had happened, but when she went to get up, she found she could not – one leg was not cooperating. She looked at it, and was amazed to see that the swordsdrone had put a blade through the shin. That was really something. Of course, she was still free to sit up and fight, and a leg wound like that could heal well enough...

She readied for a lunge, but another sword caught her arm, and pinned it too. This limited her options. Total failure was closer than she knew. Indeed, she only guessed the swordsdrone's next move in just enough time to coil her neck out of the way of twinned stabs, the swords holding fast into the metal framework of the bridge, each no more than an inch from her throat.

Parissah had one attack left in her arsenal, which she remembered at last. It was a good one. She sucked in a great breath and ignited it, sending an immolating stream of fire at the drone. But this too he countered, meeting her jet of flames with a mirrored one from his tentacle, fighting fire with fire. And this attack he held against her for some seconds after her own flame had burned out, soaking her mask in sizzling heat. It would have been enough to sting terribly. But she was ever so dully aware of it, just as she could barely detect the blades in her limbs...

She felt far away... too comfortably far away...

She made no further move for a time, and the drone might have supposed her dead, not necessarily knowing that fire would not prevail against her. But she finally flopped thoughtlessly, and the drone now knew that she yet lived. She realized too late her mistake. The swordsdrone readied for a final stroke...

There was at last a transcendent twinge of doom. Doom for her mission. Doom for her career. A horrible, unfeeling doom...

A silent, blinding flash filled all her awareness. Parissah supposed she was dead, and this some metaphysical phenomenon of the hereafter. But to her surprise, the flash resolved, and there was everything – the sky, the swords lodged in the turf, and in her arm and leg... and an utterly glorious implosion above her, which jostled the world with its delayed, boisterous *POP*. The only thing she couldn't find anywhere was the swordsdrone...

It was incredible to believe, but as she realized it must have happened, she had been lying just beyond the implosion's outermost circumference. The swordsdrone, on the other hand, had been caught by the edge of the great destructive singularity, and eschewed into its epicenter at hypersonic velocities! Her foe was quite defeated... and not a moment too soon.

Another flash and *POP* came, and soon another – each erupting quite close to the Bridge, sublime in strength. Parissah craned her head up and stole a glimpse over the edge of *Variglew*. What she saw rekindled all her senses and her hopes...

Bless that magnificent man! she thought, watching as *Carroccio* unleashed incredible destructive power from its towering spinal cannon far below. Captain Taurnuren, in his aforementioned prudence (not to mention his substantial reserves of cunning), had evidently arrived at a revolutionary thought – showcase the magnitude of his ship's capability with a barrage of warning shots in clear view of the Field Marshals, rather than actually committing to the obliteration of miles of *Variglew*. The Marshals could scant afford to ignore Parissah's threat now. It was plain as day that the *Carroccio*'s ordnance could make mincemeat of the great Bridge's foundations, as effortlessly as putting a sledgehammer through a house of cards.

Parissah rested for a bit, heaving a heavy sigh of great relief. The cool rain felt wonderful. It was the rain of victory. Also it was the rain of not being dead. She only wished she had thought of Taurnuren's gambit before beginning the whole operation. She was quite proud of *him* for thinking of it. In her current abundance of emotion, she felt she might be very much in love with the Captain – but only in the most perfectly professional sense, of course...

*   *   *

She didn't know how long she rested there, and may indeed have lapsed into sleep. But however unconscious she may have been, she was snapped out of it instantly with a terrific sharp pain...

"*ROAR*!" she roared.

There were no attackers. Rather, someone had just pulled the sword from her leg. It was one of her mercenaries – but not *just* one of her mercenaries. It was none other than Grosdrev Trokelov! He had evidently lived, and she could tell immediately that he was still in good health.

"Sorry," he said, blinking, "Or, well, kind of, anyway. I half thought you were dead."

"Me?!" Parissah wondered aloud. "What about you? I saw you take a fireball to your thorax! I supposed Humans to be quite flammable..."

He laughed. "Fire's bad news for us, aye. But there's the advantage of working for a fire-breathing dragon lady I didn't quite trust." He looked at her. "You gave us a layer of electrically insulated underwear..."

"Yes," she agreed blankly.

"Well, I got a layer of fireproof underwear on over that."

Parissah finally decided that she appreciated Trokelov. He didn't trust her any more than she did him – and so was a man of discernment. She was only too glad that his suspicious nature had saved his life.

He pulled the sword from her arm. This time she held her protest down to a crocodilian growl, with just a bit of smoke. She stood up. "Thank you," she told him.

"Easy on that leg!" Trokelov cautioned.

"Don't coddle me overmuch," she said, looking at her damaged arm. "These wounds should be small enough concern, as long as they don't become infected."

He just shook his head at her. It occurred to Parissah that perhaps being impaled was a more grievous injury to Humans, tiny fragile things that they were. He looked at the swords he now held, pursing his lips. He seemed to like them very much.

"These are some real beauties," he said. "Which one you fancy? The one from your leg or the one from your arm?"

She thought for a moment. Looting swords hadn't so much been on her mind, she still being at best a novice with such things. But she didn't want to refuse his offer. The whole experience suggested she ought to learn the proper use of melee weapons, when next she got the chance... however many months or years hence that might be...

"The arm, I suppose," she said. He held the weapon out to her. She held out his knife in similar fashion.

"You can keep that too," he said. He seemed to anticipate she would insist otherwise, but he wouldn't have it. "I don't even like that knife very much, or I wouldn't have given it to you."

She nodded, and took the sword. "Thank you." As she tried to figure out where best to keep the weapons in her belt without great risk of jabbing herself in the legs, she turned to more pressing matters. "What casualties did we take?"

Trokelov's eyes were wide, and he nodded. "Not bad ones, all things considered. Bumps, bruises, breaks. Some of Firebrand Troop and almost all of Sickle Troop went in the drink, and a few of your Inquisitors too, but I figure they all made it back to the ship alright."

"What about your Trooper who lost the arm?" she asked.

He laughed again. "What, Ivan?" He went over to the arm, picked it up, and flopped it around. It made clinking and clanking noises. "It was just his fake arm. You'd be amazed how many times he loses the thing!" She saw now that it was the sharp and deadly prosthesis. In the thick of battle she'd managed not to notice. Trokelov tossed the artifice back onto the ground, rubbing the back of his neck. "I almost forgot though. We did have one fatality."

Parissah was solemn, but unsurprised; in such a battle they could hardly have hoped to fare any better. "Who have we lost?"

"...Not to fret, madam!" came a voice from beside her. "It was just little old me."

"Baegulgog!" Parissah said, turning and seeing the Clerk in his ghosty form. "I had all but forgotten you were here with us!"

"Oh I quite understand!" he said cheerily. "My contributions to the scrap were rather few and brief. I perished almost immediately." He pantomimed some punches. "But I got in my blows, so to speak... or at least I nearly did!"

Privately Parissah was most glad that if anyone in her team had to die, it was Baegulgog... but only because for him it was so trivial. She would have liked to say so, but there just wasn't any polite way of going about it.

Presently the rest of the occupants of the battleground began to converge on her location. Most of Guppy Troop, a few Firebrands, her students, four of the senior Inquisitors. And, of primary import, the Tophtheran and Toefthaeran Field Marshals were coming forth, amidst the escort of her own retinue...

"We have agreed to suspend the war effort for the time being," said the northern Marshal.

"But of course, your vessel left us little choice," the southern Marshal qualified.

"Thank you for your cooperation, in any case," Parissah said, and she meant it. "Now you must each escort us to your Queen."

The Marshals turned to each other, as if to gauge whether their counterpart was willing to go along with the demand. "Agreed," they said, and they turned and floated away, each to their own path, beginning their long trek back to their sovereign without any further delay.

Parissah gestured to the other Inquisitors to follow the southern Marshal, and they did so. But her students ran up to her.

"Where are we supposed to go?" Maricalgi asked.

"Go with them," she said. "They have less experience in diplomacy; perhaps they will need your help."

"But we have *no* experience," Deacogal said.

"Well..." she countered, "...do your best."

"Yes ma'am!" they said. "Except there's just one other problem," Maricalgi pointed out. "Granadar fell off the Bridge; he had most of the provisions."

Parissah gave them her pack. "Take mine. I can forage. It will be no trouble."

"Gee, thanks," Deacogal said. She was glad he was so eager, rather than roping her into a protracted contest of selfless charity.

"Now go," she said. They saluted, and began along the road south.

Baegulgog approached her now. He bobbed in the air a bit sullenly. "I hate to impose anything on you, madam, but I hoped I could enlist your help in bringing along my satchel and uniform. I'm afraid I'm unable to bear them myself, in my present state."

"Of course, Baegulgog," she said.

"Thank you very much, madam," he replied.

As she picked out his stuff on the battleground, and when she was just about to go retrieve it, she was stopped midstep by Trokelov.

"What about us? Where do we fit in now?"

"Your work here is done," she told him. "Return to *Carraccio*. Captain Taurnuren will ferry you back to Fettonia. I'm most grateful for the work you've done here, Trokelov. You and your men have earned your pay, by my reckoning."

Trokelov smiled. "I'll be glad to work with you again. Any time the Inquisition needs a leg-up from a bunch of mercenaries, just let me know."

"I will."

He walked over to the edge of *Variglew*. "I hope you do put a stop to all this. I don't much like the idea of those big terrible beasties roaming around. And I certainly ain't pleased to know there are jellies out there who are better fighters than me! The whole thing is entirely out of hand."

"We'll stop it. Even if we do ultimately have to destroy *Variglew*. Even if we have to destroy it a hundred or a thousand times."

"That's a lady," Trokelov said, and with that, he quite simply hurled himself from the Bridge. No cabling back to *Carroccio* for him!

Parissah took up Baegulgog's belongings, and the two of them fell in behind the northern Marshal, gathering an entourage of Tophtheran troops as they went. So began a new journey. It was a long road to Queen Irisa in Brittegonnen, and not at all a pleasant one, from all she'd heard...

Everything in the Entire Universe

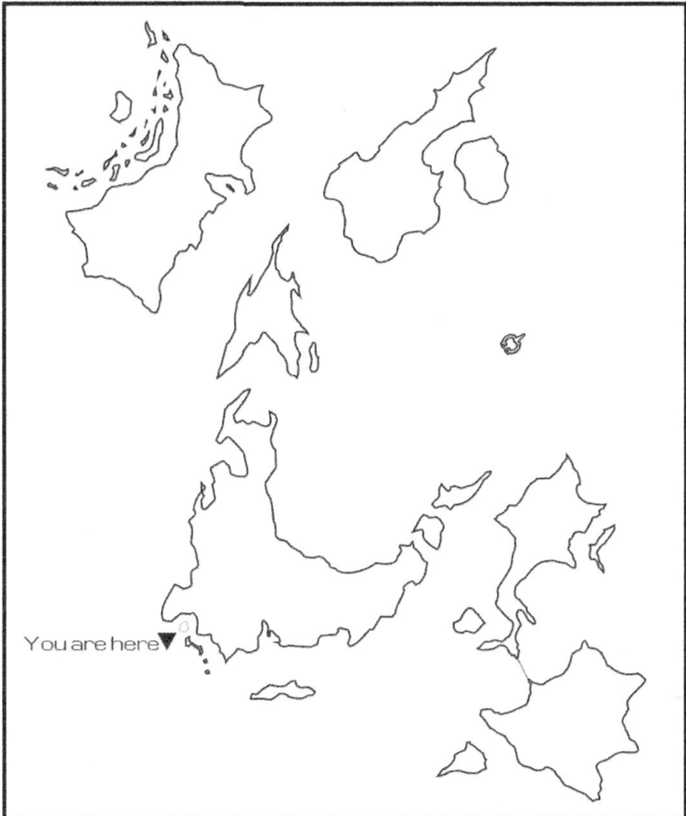

"Don't be too easily daunted by the thought of infinities, or multi-infinities. Infinities are as ordinary a part of our experience as anything can be (though admittedly some infinities are certainly greater and more daunting than others). But take a simple circle for example. Every circle is a derivative of Pi – a number with infinite *digits. (This is the very instance of infinity which the Inquisition daily celebrates as homage to the profundity of the Creators, and the long wait for their return). Thus every circle consists of this infinite number – Pi – multiplied by its diameter. A sphere takes the same infinity and multiplies it by even higher values ($4\pi r^2$, to be exact). This means that if you're like me, and you have two eyes, then brace yourself... there are two multi-infinities right in your own head!"*

- Zeph Bronzegloom, *What if Galahadron Mucolyptus was Wrong?*

Jek could hardly endure the suspense he felt on the stoop, waiting for the door to be opened... either by the estimable Mr. Zeph Bronzegloom, world-renowned thinker... or *not*. It was a rather crucial disparity, or so it seemed to him. As it was, his nerves were frayed quite to their capacity by innumerable other blistering attacks they had already endured that day. An afternoon spent dodging snail bolts and hurdle sharks. Trying desperately to beat the old man at swordplay, even while suffering a lash on his back. Learning of the malevolent purposes that drove the little songbirds to dog their every step. The confrontation with the dock attendant. Getting herded through the makeover place. Being dumbstruck seeing his own wife in all the splendor that might be due a Princess! The hastily improvised attempts at dancing with her. The awkward and stressful conversation during the dance, where she had asked about his past, and he had done what he could to avoid asking about hers (he was still very much afraid she was a pirate). And not least of all, the direct threats on their lives by Despotopians – who turned out to be many, many times more scary in person than even Jek himself had imagined.

Well, compared with all that, waiting for a door to open was perhaps a small thing. But he still didn't like it...

Above them, he heard the rustle of flittering little wings, and a tiny chirp. It was horrifying.

"Hurry up, old man," Jek whispered rather desperately.

The old man squinted at him in the dark. "Lad, I done knocked at the door. Can't rightly control how fast anybody comes to answer it. Iffen I could be asure that this be Bronzee's house, I wouldn'a hesitate to barge right on in and shout the lazy lubber out o' his bed! But I can't be asure." He shook his head in resignation. "I warrant I ain't hardly never dealt with such uncertainty as we is met with now..."

Jek gulped. The old man had a way of being the opposite of reassuring in times of doubt. He tried to steel himself against a few more seconds. And in the end, that was all he needed, for at last the door creaked open... ever so slightly, ever so slowly....

In the black crack of the doorway, a buggy eyeball seemed almost to leap out at them, darting all around in a flurry, which betrayed in an instant that the owner of the eyeball was just as unsure as they were.

The door inched open a tiny bit more, and a thin band of light reached the occupant, revealing a second buggy eye and other features of pure astonishment – though it was not quite enough to illuminate his whole face, and so give him a real clue as to the man's identity. Nevertheless, Jek scrutinized every detail he could make out of the man behind the door. His head looked to be floating; nothing below his chin could be made out. Looking up, Jek saw that the hairline was unnaturally straight across the man's forehead.... until he realized that it was no hairline at all, but a hat. And not *just* a hat... it was another indigo heretic dunce-cap, like the ones they'd seen off the Fish Islands! This *couldn't* be Zeph Bronzegloom....

"BRONZEE!" the old man announced, throwing his arms out, and the door in with them. The hunching little man was tossed back in alarm, shielding himself with his hands. But now there was more light in the doorway, and Jek saw that he wore a black turtleneck – the de facto uniform of thinkers!

Hoppin' hypsilophodonts! Jek thought. *This really* is *the real Zeph Bronzegloom!*

And it really was.

Still in a defensive recoil, Bronzegloom let his hands of widely curled long fingers come down an inch or two at a time as his eyebrows did crazy things above his eyes, now buggier than ever. He was still very astonished, but it had become the astonishment of familiarity.

"Oh it's *you*," Bronzegloom said, in an unnecessarily awed whisper, "Good golly, it's you." He scanned the strangers in his doorway with blinking eyes, then finally looked back at the old man. "What the Heck are you doing here?" If Bronzegloom was happy to see him, his tone did not make it very obvious...

"*Har, ha-har!*" the old man guffawed, coming over and slapping Bronzegloom on the back. "We's here to skin yer elbows and pickle yer kneecaps, *har-har*! What do ye ***think*** we's here for?" The old man's bad teeth caught his lower lip, holding back another impish laugh.

"Ah good, we're off to a leaping start with the thinker-puns," Bronzegloom commented stiffly.

Audrey, evidently satisfied that the two really knew each other, walked into the house. Jek shot in after, sighing in overdue relief as he closed the door behind him. The birds, of course, would still know their exact whereabouts, but he was only too happy to shut them out for a while.

"Well don't just stand there, Bronzee!" the old man commanded. "Ye's got customers, and what's more, *guests*! Get some light in this place! And mayhaps grab us some grub while yer at it."

Bronzegloom muttered some muttery noises. They were loud enough that Jek could tell he hadn't actually said anything. "*Meh-me-neh...*" he muttered, or something to that effect. He crossed the room, and taking up a matchbox, lit a lamp. "Understand this, old man," he said over his shoulder. "I'm too tired to throw you out right now, but don't expect any help, either. It's a matter of official policy – thinking hours are between sun-up and sun-down." He turned and crossed to another lamp, and laughed an annoying nasal laugh as he did so. "Only kidding." He lit the second lamp, and held it up by its handle. "Although, to be sure, I'm none too happy you were able to decrypt the cipher that is my door."

"T'was Audrey here what did the balance of the figurin'," the old man said, indicating her.

Bronzegloom approached her, holding forth his lamp, squinting into her face.

After some moments of scrutiny, he stepped back. "*Dianodes...*" he said, awed again. "To think that..." and his eyes wildly took stock of the room again. "Well, that is, we don't get many visitors of your importance these days, m'lady."

They all looked at Audrey. He *had* been talking about Audrey. Jek was baffled. It was a mighty incongruous statement, since everyone knew that the royals of Jast-Madiir spent a great deal of time on the Wading Isle. So did dignitaries from all around the island chain. It was the jewel of Idriulthoronta – a perfect coalition of natural wonder and artisanal hubris. Important people were there constantly!

Audrey was baffled too. Finally she just shook her head. "I don't know what in the world you're talking about..."

Bronzegloom looked at her again as if to be sure. "You don't know?" he said, suddenly grinning. He looked at Jek and the old man. "She doesn't know!" He considered their blank looks. "*None* of you know?!" They had no answer. Jek felt a pit in his stomach again. "Well, *I'm* not going to be the one to tell you," Bronzegloom at last proclaimed, heading for the adjoining room.

As they all joined him, he chucked a match into the fireplace, and the whole thing came at once ablaze. Jek was glad for a fire; the night had grown chilly. Idriulthoronta may have been quite tropical, but it was nearing the end of the year, and so was getting about as cold as it ever got.

The warm glow illumined plentiful pieces of comfortable furniture, and revealed arched walkways into a pair of rooms, one to the far left of the fireplace, and one to the far right. Palely, Jek could make out a stairway on the left, and a kitchen beyond. The room on the right was darker, but a bit of tangerine light from the kindled embers fell on columns of books, and it seemed entirely likely that this was a personal library. There were several other bookshelves arrayed around the den in which they now stood. Prominently featured was a very great and broad armoire of a bookshelf, containing dozens or perhaps even hundreds of volumes in Magormissahr's potentate series – *Referendums on the World.* The man had books. Jek supposed that made sense.

"And may I just say, madam," Bronzegloom continued, turning to Audrey as he went on lighting more lamps, "that you have positively the most radiant left cheek bone my eyes have ever gazed upon."

"Alright, ye old flirt," the old man interjected, shaking his head. "Show some modesty! She be a married woman, and here's her husband to prove it!"

"What, this guy?" Bronzegloom asked, pointing to Jek. He came up to scrutinize Jek as well. It was strange to Jek; he honestly couldn't tell if Bronzegloom was peering into his very soul, or staring blankly into empty space, or whether one eye was engaged in each of those activities at the same time. "Hmm, hmm..." he pondered. "Yeah, there doesn't seem to be anything remarkable about him at all."

Jek certainly felt he didn't know what to make of all these cryptic insights, but decided at once that Bronzegloom must be right – certainly as it pertained to him. "Is that not good?"

Bronzegloom turned away, stroking his chin in deep but professional consideration. "On the contrary, I suppose it is only too appropriate."

The old man became rather impatient. "Bronzee, we ain't known what ye's on about since I done started introducin' me tagalongs, such as they is. I figger that be a hallmark o' yer trade, but 'tis nonetheless irritatin', and all the more on an empty stomach. Now, if ye ain't gonna be bringin' us any grub in the immediate postmortem, I've a mind to go get it meself."

Bronzegloom pointed repeatedly at the old man in warning. "You stay out of my kitchen."

* * *

"Yes, I can certainly explain all about magic," Zeph Bronzegloom said, leaning over the folding table he had set up in the den. They had all eaten now (though the old man went on as if he'd skipped a meal [which, essentially, he had]), and had put to him the question of magic – what it was, and how it worked. Jek shifted uncomfortably in his chair. Somehow the back of it was agitating his shark wound, which had at least been properly redressed at the 'duds shop'. But he was most anxious to hear the ins and outs of magic directly from the mind of one of the world's premier thinkers; though Audrey may have been even more. It seemed to him she was very intrigued by magic indeed.

"It's a recent discovery," Bronzegloom continued, talking with his hands as much as with his mouth, "made completely by accident, and..." he took a moment of repose, "Er, well, maybe I'm getting ahead of myself. Do you know about how everything in the entire universe works?"

That seemed to Jek like a pretty expansive question... one deserving of an equally all-encompassing answer...

"No," Jek admitted.

"Well, that settles that! There's no sense at all in telling you about magic until I've first explained everything in the entire universe."

Before anyone could object, Bronzegloom threw himself up from the table, crossed into his library, and came out with a piece of paper and a paintbrush, as well as a well of black ink. He quickly and crudely scrawled a very basic silhouette, and then held it out to each of them. "Look at this and tell me what you see."

"I can't read," Audrey huffed. She had been forced to admit it rather a lot of late, and it was probably beginning to wear on her.

"Oh! Well that is most regrettable," Bronzegloom said. "We shall certainly have to do something about that later. Remind me about it. Though actually, don't bother, I'll be sure to remember."

"I can read!" Jek volunteered enthusiastically. One could hardly pass up a chance at impressing a famous thinker with one's intellectual achievements, after all.

Bronzegloom squinted at Jek. "Okay then, smart guy." He held the drawing out to him. "What do you see?"

Jek plainly saw the black figure of a fish, haphazardly drawn, and equally poorly colored-in. This was probably a trick-question, but he went ahead with the obvious answer all the same. "It's a picture of a sturgeon," he conceded.

"It's actually a trout," Bronzegloom explained, leaning in even further. "What *else* do you see?"

There you go, a trick question! He searched the painting over and over from top to bottom. The 'trout' was all Bronzegloom had drawn, and there were no two ways about it. It might be foolish to admit, but what else was there to say? "Nothing," he answered.

"Exactly!" Bronzegloom said, leaping in his chair with excitement. "I'm glad you're getting this!"

Jek shared a dubious look with Audrey. "I'm not sure we are," she said.

Bronzegloom changed aspects in an instant, readying for a more intense explanation. He stood now, hunched over the table, and sprawled out the silly fish painting, as if it were some kind of complicated blueprint, and he was about to point out its various components. "It works like this… you have the inky part," (he pointed to the fish), "which is the *something*… in this case, the form of a trout." Now he moved his finger in orbit of the fish. "All around that, you have the blank paper, which is the *nothing*… in this case, the form of the *absence* of a trout. The nothingness defines the somethingness, but the somethingness also defines the nothingness. So you see, neither has any definition apart from its opposite. Each exists only as a counterpoint to the other."

Jek thought that was rather profound, but Audrey was shaking her head. "But if you cut that sturgeon out of the paper, it would still be a picture of a sturgeon, wouldn't it?" she asked.

"It's a trout!" Bronzegloom rebutted with some minor annoyance, finger to the sky. "But that's not entirely the point. In any case, even if you cut the trout out, it would still be recognizable as a trout, as long as there was surrounding, distinct space." This time he traced the fish carefully. "Now say the bounds of the entire universe were the edges of the trout. You'd never be able to discern the shape of a trout, because there would be no external nothingness to define it." Now he took the painting and rolled it up. "Fortunately things in the universe aren't like that. There is an equal counterpoint for each force at work in the cosmos – a non-trout for every trout, so to speak. That's how everything in the entire universe works."

Jek finally felt he knew what Bronzegloom was trying to demonstrate. "The Dianodes!" he ventured. "You're talking about the Dianodes."

"Yes, the paired elemental forces," Bronzegloom agreed, further qualifying. "I'm not sure how much you know about Dianodes already, so let me give you the basics. They *are* the elements – the forces that act on matter in the universe. And they are *also* a kind of entity – not sentient life, exactly, but they do possess *some* of the characteristics of sentience.

"There are a number of known Dianodes… Fire, Water, Life, Death, Up, Down, Positive, Negative, Light, Darkness, Space, Time, Knowledge, and Ethon. There are also inferred and false Dianodes, but that's for a different lecture.

"Each of these forces is a self-aware being, and exists only to resist its counterpoint, and in this way animate the universe. This mutual resistance is *crucial*. Before the beginning, the Creators had tried to introduce only one force into the universe… spinning. But everything promptly spun apart and they had to start over! They hadn't introduced anything to moderate the spinning! After that they learned their lesson, and instituted paired, mutually-opposed forces from then on." He gestured widely. "So now here we are, essentially at the focal point of about eight or so eternal games of cosmic tug-of-war."

Jek, characteristic of himself, responded to this revelation with a considerable sense of sudden vulnerability. "That sounds like kind of a fragile system."

Bronzegloom shook his pointy-hatted head. "It's actually very robust. People have tried – *very hard,* in fact – to disrupt the balance of Dianodes and so destroy the universe. They certainly appeared to be succeeding for some time, but they ultimately failed, and things pretty much went back to normal. That was during the Great Regression crisis; we don't really have time to get into all that, either. Suffice it to say that when any one Dianode grows too powerful, its opposite grows proportionately, becomes aware of the overreach of its counterpart, and acts accordingly, eventually reducing both elements in strength to a sustainable level. This is the Balance system.

"As an example... if, say, Fire were to burn all the lands to a crisp, Water would become aware of the magnitude of the problem, and rains or tidal waves would surely come along to put things out. Conversely, if Water swallowed up all the lands, Fire would know of it, and would belch molten rock from the submerged volcanos until land once again rose from beneath the covering of the seas."

Jek's mind went ever bleaker at the thought of all of these cataclysms. "It's more than a little unsettling to know we're at the mercy of elemental beings that want to burn the lands to a crisp or swallow us up in the ocean."

Bronzegloom waved a dismissing hand. "No-no, it's not like that; the Dianodes don't *want* anything! They're incapable of want." Then he snapped and pointed. "But you bring me to my next subject – Purpose and Will – the two forces in the universe that transcend the Dianodes and are not mutually opposed."

"*Not* mutually opposed?" Audrey asked. "But you were insistent that 'everything in the entire universe works that way'." Jek was rather surprised at her challenge. She seemed at times to be rather unimpressed with Zeph Bronzegloom. But then, she had never read his books. And not everyone had a healthy appreciation for famousness, anyway...

"Yes..., Bronzegloom agreed, "I said 'everything in the entire universe works that way'. And so it *does*. But now I'm telling you about the two things that don't...

"Purpose and Will. Put simply, Purpose is what you're *supposed* to do, and Will is what you *want* to do. Sometimes these forces are in harmony, sometimes they're at odds. So they're not Dianodes. They simply are... whatever they are. I'd diagram it for you, but I have yet to come up with any fish pictures that do justice at trying to explain the concept of Purpose and Will."

"Maybe try a flounder," Audrey suggested. Jek couldn't tell if she was being sarcastic.

"I'll take that under advisement. Anyway, Will isn't important to understanding magic. You can use magic according to your own will once you have it, but they're otherwise unrelated...

"*Purpose*... Purpose is key."

Jek had token familiarity with the semi-dichotomy of Purpose and Will. He was given to understand that it was a matter of considerable philosophical import to the Inquisition. Ironically most of his exposure to the subject came from reading *What if Magormissahr was*

Wrong? But about all he had really gleaned from the book was that the whole thing was impossibly confusing. If magic involved being transcendentally aware of what his own purpose was, Jek feared he had no chance of ever mastering it...

"Well, that might be a problem," Jek admitted. "I'm not sure I know what my purpose is... that is... what I'm *really* supposed to do. I thought I was supposed to look after a lighthouse, but..."

"...You don't know your purpose, and I don't know mine," Bronzegloom interjected. "Most beings never do. Things obscure it; Will especially makes it hard to discern. And every being has a purpose that is at least somewhat distinct from every other, so there's really not much room for pattern recognition either. And talk about a wide gamut! You might have a purpose like Carlos Washoe – to save the world 201 times or so. Or you may *never* – as long as you live – have anything more important to do than pass the saltshaker. It's all very mysterious!

"What we *do* know about Purpose is, it has substance. In order to fulfill your Purpose, whatever it may be, you have to have the right *stuff* in you." Bronzegloom pointed to an area in his upper abdomen roughly between the appendix and the black bile reservoir. "The *stuff* one has varies in magnitude and composition from one being to the next, just as the Purpose itself does. You need different *stuff* to save the world 201 times than you do to pass a saltshaker, and a Heck of a lot more of it, too. But!" Bronzegloom exclaimed, making everyone jump, heightening the anticipation of his next point...

"...What if... you could change some of your *stuff*?"

At this, the old man laughed a hardy laugh. "*Har ha-har*! Ye's a world-class thinker indeed! Here ye is, 'splainin' magic... and ye resorts to a word like '*stuff*'." And he went on chuckling.

"I don't make the jargon, I only use it," Bronzegloom explained with all seriousness. "Purpose is so poorly understood that when biologists finally discovered that there was a pouch in the abdomen that contains a related substance, they didn't know what else to call it, and so eventually the term "*stuff*" just stuck."

"But what do you mean, 'change some of your *stuff*?'" Jek asked. "Change it to what?"

Bronzegloom sat back down at the table, holding his hands out as if cradling an unseen crystal ball. "Well, you see, it all comes back to the Dianodes. Magic, as you've probably noticed, is the practice of using elemental powers... that is, *Dianode* powers. Dianodes, as I said, don't have the capacity to *want* anything. That is because they were created without Will. They don't have any Will, and they can't. What they *do* have, in essentially infinite quantity, is Purpose. Their Purpose is to shape the universe in whatever way is native to them, and to resist and be resisted by their equal opposite. We know the Purpose of individual Dianodes, because it can be clearly observed and can't be disguised by their personal whims, since they have none. And *now*, their corresponding *stuff* is also becoming known, and so can be manufactured! What made magic possible, then, was the discovery that a sentient being can change some of their own *stuff* to match the *stuff* of a Dianode, through a simple alchemical process... namely, by just drinking an elixir. With a little bit of the *stuff* of Fire, I could hurl a fireball at you people. A bit more, and I could make the room spontaneously combust!"

Jek reeled. It was all very metaphysical and nebulous to him, and not very comfortable to think about.

But Audrey was still keenly interested, and set forth a new question. "So then, the idea is probably to turn all of your *stuff* into Fire *stuff*, and then you can be a really powerful fire sorcerer, right?"

Bronzegloom's eyes grew very wide again as he shook his head. "No! Not actually. Changing all of your *stuff* is an extremely terrible idea!" He laughed nervously.

He got up again, and withdrew to his library, quickly finding and retrieving a prefabricated chart. There were four pictures on the chart, showing a progression. The first picture was of a Human silhouette holding out his hand. There was a question mark in his hand, and a matching one in a chamber by his stomach area that was greyed out. The next picture showed essentially the same figure, but now he had some red in his stomach chamber, and also a small flame in his outstretched hand. The third picture showed the same figure holding a pretty dang big fire in his hand and smirking, and his chamber was now mostly full of red, but with a tiny bit of grey left. The final picture, however, just had an enormous fire where the Human had been, with the lone addition of a tiny dialogue cloud protruding from the flame. It read, 'Whoops.'

"You see," Bronzegloom began to elaborate, "If you have no *stuff* other than that which allows you to wield fire, then you simply aren't able to do *anything* else. Anyone who has ever changed all of their *stuff* to Fire *stuff*, whether intentionally or by accident, instantaneously disintegrated into a 'fire-sprite' – a little self-propelled spirit of fire." He shook his head sullenly. "It really is a pitiful fate, because you retain all of your old Will, but no ability outside of the properties of Fire with which to pursue it. So becoming a sorcerer is a very dangerous business! Because you never know just how much *stuff* you have. You can't add to it or take away from it. You can only make a gamble that however much *stuff* you're changing isn't all you have. Because if it is, you'll be going through the eons as a sad little spook!"

There was a moment of silence in the room. Zeph seemed to sense that the point had been difficult to digest.

"The self-disintegration part baffles some people, so here's another way of looking at it." He reached onto the table and snatched up a saltshaker he had put in front of them while they were eating. "I've already mentioned a saltshaker. If a saltshaker contains only salt, you can't very well use it to pepper anything. That's why you *mustn't ever* change all of your *stuff*!"

This was all far and above what Jek could handle. He hadn't known that magic involved so much gambling and uncertainty, and the distinct possibility of a very horrible doom. "Well, I'm glad you explained magic," he said, "because now I can say for certain that I never want to have it!"

Audrey paid Jek no mind for the moment. She was still curious. "And, all this... you said it was discovered on accident?" she plied.

"Most extremely profound and complicated things are," Bronzegloom admitted.

"Supposing we did have occasion to become sorcerers, just how would we go about it?" she asked. Jek stared at her. He couldn't believe she would wonder such a thing, knowing what they now knew! Further, he couldn't believe that she would phrase the question with '*we*'. How presumptuous!

"Recipes for *stuff* conversion have become pretty common among alchemists in the last couple of years," Bronzegloom explained. "You can go into most any old alchemy shop and pick up an elixir. Most know recipes for Fire *stuff*, Life *stuff* and Death *stuff*. Fire and Death have the most straightforward uses on the battlefield, so those recipes are in high demand among foot soldiers. Life magic is naturally pretty helpful for medics."

Well, that was even *more* than too much! "***Life*** and ***Death*** magic!?" Jek protested. "Those sound pretty extreme!"

"Not as much as you might think. Life and Death magic are basically only good for restoring or draining vitality; I haven't heard of anyone who got strong enough in those types of magic to actually straight-up kill or reanimate anybody. But that brings up something else I should mention. Obviously the strength of a given elixir is a consideration. Half-ounce solutions are pretty safe. Almost no one has disintegrated themselves on a half-ounce solution." And at this, Bronzegloom looked at Jek. "I wouldn't recommend any higher dosage than that for you, smart guy."

Jek just kind of disgustedly shook his head. No one seemed to be listening to him anymore. He'd already quite decided not to chance anything beyond a *zero*-ounce solution.

"What kind of magic do you suggest we get?" Audrey asked. *'We' again*!

Bronzegloom gave her a blank look. "I mean... I dunno. You have to take into consideration: I still have no idea who you guys are or what you're doing, or why you're having me explain all this junk. I haven't even seen this old man in ages! Seems like a lot of trouble to go through – to find me, just to have all this explained."

"Didn't go to no trouble!" the old man insisted. "We was headed this way, and I figgered on makin' a stop here anywho, on accounta I gots another question what I thought ye might shed some light on..." He stood heroically. "A much more importanter question! The *second* question!"

For all his own antics, Bronzegloom didn't seem to appreciate why the old man was suddenly being so dramatic. "Okay, what?"

The old man was undeterred. He leaned in, looking around as if to make sure what he was about to ask wouldn't be overheard by the bookshelves... then he started, low and discrete: "Where do ye – with all yer inside-information and like-what – suppose the Knights of the Indigo Lodge is to be found?"

Bronzegloom blinked madly.

"Oh, no-no-no-no," he said with a waving finger and a nervous snicker. "You're not implicating *me* as an accessory to some madcap Noble Quest! I'm in plenty enough trouble with the Inquisitors as it is!" He pointed insistently at his cone hat. "Truth be told, I think they've been gunning for me ever since I published *What If Magormissahr was Wrong?* I've got almost five years before I can publish again!"

"You should have thought of that before you committed Indigo Hersey," Audrey reproved him.

"*Heresy,*" Jek and Bronzegloom corrected her. After they got over the momentary flummox of having jinxed each other, Bronzegloom went on to excuse himself. "Look, it was an honest mistake. They held up a color swatch, and I could have *sworn* it was blue!"

The old man snickered, crossing his arms. "That's what they all says."

"I guess at any rate I should have known better than to go the Fish Islands right in the middle of that big sting operation they were putting on over there," Bronzegloom admitted. Suddenly his eyes bulged again, and he snapped his fingers, pointing at all of them. "Hey wait. Wait-wait-wait! Ho, no! If you're on a Noble Quest... *you're* the ones from the wanted poster!" He ran into his library and returned with one of the same stick drawings as was presented to them by the Inquisitor off the Fish Islands. "There you are, in living color!" (The poster really had been made with a vibrant assortment of colored pencils). "Go ahead and deny it!"

"Nay, yer right, 'tis us," the old man sighed. "But don't ye go turnin' yer nose up at our Noble Quest just yet, for *'tis* noble, I assure ye!"

"Okay, try me," Bronzegloom challenged.

The old man grinned smugly; he was absolutely certain of the import of his mission, and that he had the persuasive flair to get his acquaintance from of yore to feel the same. "Well first off... do ye recall the latest prophecy of Proconsul Zedulon?" Jek rolled his eyes.

Bronzegloom patted his stomach. "I certainly do."

The old man was immediately furious. "Don't be a dullard! I ain't talkin' about *that* part o' the prophecy! I is talkin' about the evil comin' back into the world!"

"*Evil*?!" Bronzegloom took on a breathless fright. "You think you found an evil?"

"*The* evil, Bronzee," the old man corrected.

"Oh, not good. Not good!" His posture was becoming very defensive, as if he expected the evil to suddenly pounce on his back at its mere mention. "Wh-what did you find?"

"T'was a Doom Fleet I done found... off the north-west coast o' Despotopia."

"*Despotopia*! Oh, not good at *all*!" He grabbed his head, almost as if to cover his ears. "If *Despotopia* is building a Doom Fleet, I'd say it couldn't be much worse! They don't like us Jast-Madiirans one little bit you know! We've won too many wars against them, imposed too many reparations, won too many wars *over* the reparations, and so forth! I wouldn't be a bit surprised if we were their first target!"

Jek hadn't previously considered the matter from quite that perspective. "It does sound pretty bad when you put it that way," he agreed wholeheartedly.

"That isn't even the worst of it," Bronzegloom lamented. "I've heard that they burn books now in Despotopia. It would be very, *very* grim indeed to be taken over by a regime that burns books!"

"Because it directly threatens conventional wisdom and reverence for the past?" Audrey asked.

"Well, that too, I guess," Bronzegloom said. "Mostly I was thinking of how hard it would be to get published ever again."

"Now maybe ye sees why ye ought to help us," the old man said. "Our Noble Quest is the only hope ye has!"

"Oh great!" Bronzegloom said. He threw himself into a slumped recline, resting his face flat on the table. They waited for some response. The old man tried to say something more, but Bronzegloom immediately shushed him. He made pitiful whimpering sounds as he postulated the potential trajectories of his future, few and glum as they now seemed. Finally, he calmly sat up. "Alright. I've already sheltered you and fed you, so I'm in this one way or the other. It won't hurt to help you a little more. The irony is, I wouldn't ordinarily have any idea where the Indigo Knights are."

"Why not?" Audrey asked. "I mean, haven't you ever *thought* about it?"

"Oh yes," Bronzegloom said, "to no small degree. But I could *think* about it night and day, and still not *know* where they are." He laughed nervously, rubbing the back of his neck. "It's actually kind of a trade secret, but there can be a world of difference between thinking about something and knowing about something." Audrey nodded as if she'd just learned a profound truth, even as Bronzegloom waved dismissively. "Anyway, there was an irony I was driving at." And here he paused, to make sure he had their full attention, proceeding with a low voice, much as the old man had. "It just so happens, that in the last few days, I've heard talk that the Knights have been spotted... working out of Cape Gulph, just south of Port Sanoi..."

Jek was awed. They had a destination! The Knights could be found after all! It filled his heart with the light of a joyous hope he'd never known before. It was the hope of a foolish dream suddenly made attainable – tangible even, if still a ways out of reach. And, if only for a glorious moment, all thought of murderous Despotopians and wicked little birds and peril on the high seas was banished...

But the moment did pass quickly, for he saw that the old man was unsettled by the news...

"But that be in Roemnar!"

It was a point of some anxiety. Roemnar was about the closest neighboring state, but it was a *Heron* state, and not predisposed toward welcoming Human visitors. The three of them would be quite conspicuous there. Supposing they weren't immediately identified as fugitives, they could easily be mistaken for Maenean refugees, and shipped post-haste to Despotopia, where the birds would give them away sure. *The birds!* Those tweeting menaces had already attracted more trouble than they could handle. The Oberführer and his creepy wife were still out there waiting to kill them!

"Hey," Bronzegloom objected. "They *could* have been infinite other places! They could've been in uncharted waters, or on the continent, or the Down side of the earth, or one of the Other Worlds, or on the far side of Galahadron's Gate, or even right in the fastness of

Despotopia itself, for all I would usually know about it! Just you thank your lucky stars I happened to overhear where they really are, and that it turned out to be *not* any of those other places."

"But what are we going to do about the Oberführer?" Jek insisted. His mind had quite fixated itself on that danger once again.

"The who?" the old man asked.

"Oberführer Klinkofhenschmidt," Audrey explained. "He's a Despotopian who told us he was going to kill us."

The old man was momentarily stunned. "Ye *met* the Despotopians whats been casin' the island?"

"Yeah," Audrey nodded. "They seemed to know all about us. At least, they knew we were here with you." Her eyes rolled up to the ceiling as she endeavored to remember the substance of the conversation. "They said they were going to wait and kill us all together, so they could be sure no one slipped away."

"Well how informative!" the old man scoffed. "And all awhile I thought we might yet slip by them unnoticed. Next time ye runs into the enemy, I hope ye tells me straight off, so's we have more time for figgerin' out how to stay livin'!"

All along in the back of his mind, Jek had been carefully formulating a clever gambit to that effect. Now seemed the appropriate time to reveal his master-plan. "Why don't we run like Heck for the boat and just sail away as fast as we can?"

The old man scratched his beard. "Could work, except for a lot o' things. First-wise, the boat is ezactly where they's gonna be waitin' in ambush for us. And number two, them birds is givin' away our every move, so's we can't even sneak up on 'em!"

"Dang, you're right," Jek said, deflated. "I guess strategy is a lot harder than I hoped it would be."

"It was a decent first try, kid," Bronzegloom said, patting Jek on the head, "but as long as you're here, why not leave the thinking to the professionals?"

Jek smiled broadly. "You mean you're going to help us?"

"As I said, I'm already implicated in this thing. I don't think you guys can possibly succeed, but I might as well see if I can think your way through the immediate danger. I only ask that, in the off-chance you do find the Knights of the Indigo Lodge, and they vouch for the Inquisition to pardon your Quest, just remember to mention I helped you. Who knows but that they might also pardon my heresy, and I could get my new book published!"

"You have a new book?" Audrey asked, if only politely curious.

"Yes, yes I do," Bronzegloom said with furrowed brow. "You'll be leaving here with an advance copy, if you live, I can assure you of that." Jek was befuddled. Bronzegloom was speaking directly to Audrey – the known illiterate.

"What's the book?" Jek plied. He was curious too, and certainly didn't want to come across as less curious than his wife. Of the two of them, he *was* the one who had familiarity with Bronzegloom's other works, after all...

"You'll see," Bronzegloom said enigmatically. "But for now, we need to get down to brass tactics." He once again indicated their wanted poster. "Let's see if you were paying attention earlier. Here's a perfect diagram of what the Despotopians are focused on – the three of you, and the boat. But what *isn't* in this picture???"

"Nothing," Audrey guessed.

"Incorrect," Bronzegloom shook his head. "There is plenty of nothing in this picture, but you can't read, so I'll excuse the answer. What isn't in the picture, then, is *everything else* in the entire universe... with the exception of these little birds up here."

"I might better tell ye about them birds afore we solidify any plans," the old man said. "But what do ye have in mind?"

"We know what they're expecting," Bronzegloom said, gesturing to the poster once more. "As I said, it's all right here. All we need to do to catch them off guard, then, is confront them with the one thing they *aren't* expecting."

"We're going to confront them with everything in the entire universe?" Audrey asked sardonically.

"That would take some doing," Bronzegloom answered with perfect seriousness. "You don't have quite all that on-hand. What you *do* have... is me."

* * *

Curfew befell the Wading Isle, and all through the village, lights dimmed, music retreated, and an anxious restfulness prevailed. A brisk evening had matured into a cold night, but the Oberführer took no stock of it. Another obsidian puff from his breathing apparatus, and he was deeply and contentedly warm from the inside out, keeping unblinking vigil over the immoderate island. He had spent a decent interval wondering how Jast-Madiir had ever managed to construct a monument to whimsical artistic panache and splendorous beauty such as the Wading Isle in plain sight of the whole world, without the Inquisition coming along and tearing half the place to shreds. Finally, he concluded that the Isle must've been twice its current self at its inception. The Oberführer had some familiarity with Jast-Madiiran cunning; it was not outside the norm for them to sacrifice a dime not to be begrudged a penny, so to speak... for they had full many dimes and pennies. And no shortage of those coins had come from years of extorting, usurping, and bullying none other than his homeland – Despotopia itself.

Klinkofhenschmidt hailed from a country of humble foundations. There were only two resources of notable abundance in Despotopia: kidney beans, and coal. Kidney beans, of course, were an extremely hardy plant that grew most everywhere, and so had no market value. Despotopia's entire gross domestic product, then, hinged on coal sales.

Coal had basically one widely recognized use – to be burned for heat. The tropical nature of the Archipelago therefore made local trade a merciless buyer's market, and indeed, most of the stuff was only bought for resale to the distant mainland. Despotopia had the misfortune of being almost entirely unable to trade directly with the continental powers;

their island had to be given a very wide berth by traveling convoys, lest they be dashed against the Mausoleum Peaks of Meatgrinder Bay by the relentless jet streams that plagued the area. This had forced the Despotopians to sell their coal to the trade hub of Jast-Madiir's Great Harbor for eventual resale... and Jast Madiir made considerably more off the coal than did Despotopia itself under this arrangement. The Kaisers of the past had bravely vowed to make the Czars atone for their underhanded dealings, but this had only manifested in costly wars that ended in reparations paid *to* Jast-Madiir, rather than by it. The peoples' only comfort in these times had been their extreme fondness for their dictator, and a number of years of fair kidney bean harvests...

But all that was a world ago now. The paradigm had shifted much in the last fifty years, and indeed far more so than anyone in Jast-Madiir yet guessed. Misfortunes had become opportunities; curses had become blessings. Despotopia's every weakness had been turned to great, potent strength. Worthless coal begat towering industry. The rich continental states no longer fed off indirectly undersold Despotopian exports... now, indeed, it was Despotopia's privilege to prey off the mysterious miseries of the world to the far north. And Jast-Madiir – pathetic, insignificant place that it was – could be so handily crushed beneath their boot now that it didn't even seem worth the effort. The aspirations of the nation had grown in step with their power, so that even centuries of prior grievances no longer entered into the scope of their ambition. There were bigger fish to fry than Jast-Madiir. Much, much bigger fish...

But of course, in order to fry the big fish, you sometimes had to screen the little tadpoles. That was more or less what the Oberführer was engaged in. All during the execution of their bold scheme to manufacture a Doom Fleet, they had been utterly fastidious and totally successful at keeping a tight lid on the secret of Meatgrinder Bay. That was, until a single vessel – one of inexplicable speed and evasion – finally slipped the nets.

The Oberführer now stood immediately between the two remaining threads of this loose end: the little dinghy behind him, and the old man and his accomplices somewhere ahead in the rising mists. They were keeping him waiting, but wait he could, and indeed he knew as well as anyone that patience was among the chiefest killing virtues.

Anyway, he saw that he did not have to wait long now. Darting among the rooftops, he could make out the weaving pattern of the little birds that were Her Ladyship's spies, as they were helplessly compelled to demark the whereabouts of the fugitives.

They were darting ever closer to him.

After minutes of watching the birds in their fluster, he kept his eyes fixed directly into the alleyway ahead, and lo and behold, a lone man shrouded under a great wide captain's hat came trudging into view, and the splashing sound of his footfalls mingled with the tweets of the spies. It was the very same hat the old man had been wearing into the city. The regrettable elder sailor hadn't been present when Klinkofhenschmidt confronted the pair of young fugitives earlier that evening, and may well be returning to his boat entirely unaware that certain death was waiting for him. But of course, he would have to keep an eye out for the other two. There was no sense whatever in underestimating the resourcefulness of a cornered animal. *Any* animal. So Klinkofhenschmidt merely stood and watched with his weapon nigh at hand, ready. Ready for the old man – ready for his companions, if they showed themselves. Ready for anything...

...Except what he found, as the man strode up to him, right into arm's reach...

He sensed much later than he should that something was seriously afoul, and snatched the dark hat from the head of the walking man. Under that hat was *not* the old man – it wasn't even the young lighthouse steward! It was some other unidentified man with big buggy eyes and a dark turtleneck, who looked up at him as with sudden surprise. The Oberführer may well have looked equally surprised. A bird swooped in and trilled angrily, as if it too was only just recognizing its error...

"Vhat are you doing here?" The Oberführer scowled, squeezing his monocle in his facial muscles.

"That's a good question, son," the little man said weakly. He walked a few paces away as if in a trance. "It-it was some strange old man... he was acting so odd... he just came up to me demanding to know if I had a boat... said he'd trade me his." He looked back hauntedly at Klinkofhenschmidt, pointing waveringly. "He... he even threw in that nifty hat you're holding."

The Oberführer cast the hat down to the dock. "But *vhat* are you doing here?" he insisted.

"I..." he began. "I came to find my new boat... to take it around to the other side of the island, where I usually park." He turned and looked directly at the old man's boat. "Ah-h! There it is..." And so he trudged over and climbed into the boat. The Oberführer didn't stop him. But he watched furiously. He couldn't tell the verity of the man's story. He didn't know if the fugitives might have already given them the slip, sailing on in some other boat. But he would soon find out...

The little man nervously set about decoupling the vessel from the dock. He really meant to paddle it away. "I... I'm leaving now," he said.

"Niet, ve are staying right here," came a voice from behind the little man, backed up the sudden appearance of a dagger before his throat. The Oberführer nodded warmly. His wife had taken the man by surprise; she was waiting in the cabin of the boat all along. "Go, mine Oberführer," she said. "I should have no trouble extracting zee truth from zhis man vhile you check zee ozher docks."

"Vünderschnogg," the Oberführer acknowledged. "I vill return wizhin zee hour."

He never got around to leaving. Klinkofhenschmidt turned with only enough time to watch helplessly as the loophole of a sturdy rope snatched him by the throat...

* * *

Bullseye! Jek thought to himself. The lasso had caught the enormous frightening Oberführer in just the same way he'd seen it fly from his hands and lay hold of ornery gallimimus countless times before. Jek had this one talent available in his arsenal, and they had planned to use it shamelessly – and Bronzegloom's befuddling ruse had given them only just opportunity enough.

Jek reigned in the Oberführer. It was at once electrifying to have the enemy at his mercy, but through the whelming adrenaline he also felt shame. He didn't like to see the man choke. But Jek was immeasurably grateful that *he* hadn't choked! So much of their survival had, in that moment, hinged on his roping mastery. It was a lot of pressure in the tensest situation he could have ever imagined... and yet somehow, he had come through when it counted most. Perhaps this was a life lesson. Jek would have to remember to be less anxious about things in the future. He would certainly have to *try* to remember...

The Oberführer's plight was of obvious and immediate concern to his creepy wife. Bronzegloom had shot an arm up between her dagger-hand and his throat, which was a life-saving boon; had she been unresisted, he maintained she might well have eviscerated him even as she took her first bounds to the aid of her husband.

She was *fast* – faster than they had counted on. A wave leapt up at her (the *real* old man was somewhere nearby in the shadows), but was ineffectual and largely missed; the shallow water made it hard for him to gather up enough to strike with force, and anyway the dock was dry in many places. The creepy lady seemed determined to be an uncontrolled variable in spite of all their careful pre-planning. Bronzegloom had, in fact, tried to do a *lot* of thinking about her before they would commit to any plan. He was aware – or had at least heard tell – of Despotopia employing women in espionage, training them rigorously in the disciplines of assassination. And at any rate it was quite common for soldiers to pass their martial instruction onto their wives. No version of this surprise attack could be drafted that would take her for granted.

The old man, who had swapped hats with Bronzegloom as an integral part of the gambit, pounced from a set of shadows opposite Jek, brandishing a sword – not his own, which was in the boat, but one of 'Bronzee's'. But he didn't pounce soon enough to keep her throwing their plan into disarray. She slashed the taught rope and Jek gaped as he watched it go slack in his hands. He no longer had any restraint on the Oberführer! The hulking man kneeled, coughing and sputtering coal smoke, but Jek knew he would not be staggered for long, and was already starting to pull the coil around his neck loose...

Bronzegloom had apparently assessed all of this as well. He stumbled from the boat, taking an oar to the Oberführer. But he was quite helpless with it, and Klinkofhenschmidt was not about to be caught at unawares again so soon. He flew to his feet and snatched the oar in midswing, wrenching it upside Bronzegloom's head and launching him from the dock into the deeper water with no discernable effort.

Jek had no idea how to react to all of this... which is perhaps the biggest reason he found it quite baffling to discover he was already running full speed into the fray. He was two paces behind the Oberführer when the idea struck him: there *was* a second talent in his arsenal!

In the next instant, the Oberführer was laid out on the ground, caught mercilessly in Jek's famed triple-Nelson wrestling maneuver. It was another trick he managed to pull off without a hitch in the moment of need! But Jek hadn't time to congratulate himself for being a man of action. The Oberführer was ***strong***, and Jek knew that no amount of superior leverage would avail him long. This was exacerbated by the fact that the Oberführer was wearing a boiler pack on his back... it stymied Jek's reach, and in places it was uncomfortably hot, as one might imagine.

Jek looked around desperately for some sign that help might soon come. He saw the old man and the scary lady dueling under a street lamp. It was more than a little impressive, though not at all hopeful or helpful, to see her fending off his sword slashes with just a dagger. He knew Audrey should be somewhere just outside the beams of the lamp; waiting darkly in ambush while the old man feigned (or didn't feign) retreat, putting the Oberführer's wife right where she could clock her on the noggin from behind with a frying pan. The old man had expressed extreme reservation at the thought of actually wounding a lady. Despite all of his earlier lecturing about the life-or-death struggle of combat, he maintained that he was far too chivalrous at heart to do something of that nature. If the fight was half as demanding as it appeared, chivalry might be the least of his concerns at present. Audrey obviously had no restriction in such matters, and as she had already proven a willingness for clobbering things with a pan in a pinch, her part in the whole skirmish was drafted easily enough...

Jek strained and watched as the swashbuckling regressed into the shadows beyond the lamp. He still heard the clatter of metal weapons crashing into each other. The blows seemed hours apart as he waited and *waited* for the sound of Audrey's pan striking true. His hold on the Oberführer was reaching critical compromise...

Finally the bulging man snapped it, and before Jek could even recollect his wits, he found his throat in the Oberführer's steely grip. He tried to scramble away, but his legs were soon treading air, as he was held aloft by one great knotted arm. He beat desperately on that arm, but he might as well have been punching a tree trunk. He tried to think of something else to do, but he was horribly distracted by all the little stars flying around in his eyes, which made it rather impossible to see anything...

The next thing Jek knew, he was on the ground, and the Oberführer was laid out senseless just in front of him. He gasped air as he was now able, and sprung on his arms to sit upright. His frantic eyes sought some explanation for the fact that he was still living, and he found Audrey, who had evidently changed the plan on a whim and snuck over to Jek's own aid. She stood over him and the Oberführer, still huffing with Bronzegloom's frying pan in a white-knuckle death-grip.

For a while they just looked at each other in some solemn way that only people who have shared a battle for their lives could understand. Jek never forgot that moment. It evolved their relationship in a way that might have otherwise taken years, or more. Never again were they two strangers who had been incidentally roped into a series of cooperative efforts – first marriage, then the care of a lighthouse, and then to serve the whim of an old coot. There was something more to them. Though Jek was not yet sure what to call it...

"Halp!" the 'old coot' cried. They at once returned to reality and remembered what exactly it was she had gambled to help Jek. It was well that he called out, because to remain oblivious of such imminent consequences would have been utterly inexcusable on their part. Indeed, if Audrey had risked anything beyond the safety of the old man, they did not know how they might have forgiven themselves...

They sprang to action. Jek went for the sundered rope. He felt rather exploitive, having to rely on the same trick twice, but sometimes you just do what you have to. He wound a lasso knot, and the two of them advanced on their remaining adversary, hoping they would not be noticed. Jek found the situation hopelessly hectic; even the thrashing of a feisty gallimimus compared favorably with the unpredictable darting moves of a knife-fighter.

Jek couldn't wait for a sure opportunity – he tossed his lasso, forced most unpleasantly to trust his gut. He caught the Despotopian woman almost as expertly as he had caught her husband! But it availed nothing; her dagger arm was still quite free, and she was out of the rope as quickly as she had got in...

Suddenly the whole rest of the battle played out in Jek's mind in an instant, as if he had become at once clairvoyant, or some sort of combat savant. Here's how he saw it would go. Audrey had already charged in to finish the woman off with a pan-stroke, and it was too late for her to hold back now that the rope gambit had failed. The Despotopian would see that she now had two opponents in her reach, sense the weaker of the two, and cut her way past Audrey. She would then overtake Jek, paralyzed as he was with his moment of shattering grief and horror, and then he also would be dead. Then she would have all the time in the world to wear down the old man and get him too. In one false step, they had negated their three-to-one advantage! And in their failure, they had condemned the world to – well, whatever it was that Kaiser Hienrechenschlagen had in mind for it. Most likely oppression... and not the good and healthy kind of oppression, either...

Things began to play out in real time just as Jek had seen. Audrey stopped short, seeing the rope fail. The Despotopian woman took stock of Audrey, even as the old man also hesitated – he too seemed to see what was about to happen, and he was struck dumb for a crucial hal- an-instant. But he was still in this thing, and not about to let it play out that way if he could help it! Jek charged in too, though he could not get there with enough time, except to put himself at a more convenient striking distance in the bitter end. And anyway, he had nothing to defend himself against her blade. The old man swung hard, as if to prevail by the sheer forcefulness of his rejection of all that was unfolding, but in this he overcommitted, and she broke his slash and he faltered. But in the moment she raised the dagger so to fall on Audrey with it, something unforeseen played into the fray. There was a '*hwooshhh*,' and the Despotopian woman was wrenched out of the way, the shaft of an arrow sticking in her shoulder.

Jek stumbled with a crash and a splash. The proximity of the arrow as it had whizzed by caused him to trip himself up. He came up coughing water and trying to shake it out of his eyes. Finally, through blinking beads of ocean water, he could see... just in time to witness

Audrey knock out the stunned and wounded Despotopian lady with a none-too-friendly swing of the pan.

It was *over.*

But how was it over? Jek turned around, and there was Bronzegloom – soaked, huffing, and clearly more surprised than anyone that he'd made the shot. He was cradling a repeating crossbow, which belonged to the Oberführer, though he had not had occasion to use it himself. It had been leaning on a post for the entire battle.

"What a shot, Bronzee!" the old man said, nursing his collar bone. He had a cut or two.

"Thanks," Bronzegloom said, still aghast. And, for a prolonged moment, there was only the sound of dripping.

"Where's me hat?" the old man finally asked.

"*Your* hat?! Forget your dumb hat! Give me mine back!" Bronzegloom insisted, waving him over. "I don't even want to think what will happen if I'm caught without it."

Jek was a little surprised with their behavior. "Hey! We all just about died, and you're talking about hats?"

"That's part o' life, lad... best try and get used to it," the old man instructed him.

"What's part of life?" Audrey asked, eager for clarification, "almost dying, or talking about hats?"

"Both," the old man said.

* * *

Soon the old man and Zeph Bronzegloom had their proper hats back, and Jek and Audrey took segments of the rope and bound the Despotopians hand and foot.

They all might have parted ways then and there, being so close to the boat. But Bronzegloom was adamant to provision them, and though they were pressing their luck to continue skulking about after curfew, ultimately they went along with it, following the thinker back to his house.

Once there, they loaded up what non-perishable foodstuff he was willing to part with. For being so insistent, now that they were in his house, he suddenly seemed considerably more tight-fisted about his edibles. It soon became apparent he had lured them back with a different gift more in mind...

"I haven't altogether forgot about the problem of your illiteracy, Ms. Aaliyah," Bronzegloom said.

"My name's Audrey!" she objected.

"Are you quite certain of that?" he asked.

She hesitated. "Well, I mean..."

But Jek had overheard, and interjected. "Wait, what did you call her?"

"Aaliyah, of course," Bronzegloom said.

"No kidding!? I always thought she looked just like an Aaliyah!"

At this, Bronzegloom searched his face most skeptically, lifting his eyelids one at a time. "What do you know that you're not letting on?" he plied Jek.

"I – I don't know anything," Jek said, very confused about being suddenly put on the spot again. "I just have a bit of a knack for knowing what peoples' names are by looking at their face. Usually, anyway... if I can see it well enough."

Bronzegloom's eyes were still very narrow. "Alright then, what's my middle name?"

Now Jek examined Bronzegloom. "Horatio."

Bronzegloom snapped. "Lucky guess."

"*Har ha-har*!" the old man laughed. "Don't let him fool ye Bronzee! Remember he's read yer books; probably knew it from one o' them..."

"Obviously *you* haven't read them," Bronzegloom retorted, not averting his searching glance. "I never made mention of my middle name in any of my books. Not even an initial!" But suddenly he realized that another test was presenting itself. "Now you tell me this one smart guy, what's *his* name?" And he pointed to the old man.

Jek's eyebrows shot up. He had not even thought to wonder or consider what the old man's name was up until this point. He checked his face. The old man looked back at him with a very sudden, strange intensity, as if he had great personal investment in what Jek might be about to determine. But to Jek's surprise, the search came up oddly blank. "I have no idea."

The old man seemed to deflate in that moment. Bronzegloom, on the other hand, looked at once rather amazed. "You're even better at this than I could have imagined," he said, and he sounded as if he meant it. Jek shook his head in bewilderment. He felt quite privileged to have met a famous thinker, learned things from him, and even had his life saved by him. Still, he could not avoid the conclusion that Bronzegloom was a bit of a looney after all...

Now Bronzegloom withdrew to his library once again, talking back at them. "Anyway,' *Audrey'*... I simply cannot let you leave here without this." He returned from the dark room full of books, and held out a fresh hardcover volume to her.

Audrey took the book hesitantly. "Well, thank you," she said sheepishly, trying to sound as grateful as she could, and not like a snake being given a pair of mittens. "But, you know I..."

"...can't read, yes," Bronzegloom interjected. "That's exactly my reason for giving you this. It's an advance copy of my next book. I call it *Literacy for Knuckleheads*. As an author, I have long been extremely disgusted by the thought of all the illiterate people out there who ought to be reading my books, but they can't. So I did the only logical thing and wrote a book to teach people how to read." He reached for the book and opened it in her hands. "See, here's page one."

She looked at it, and with little delay, she read it. "Aaay," she read.

He flipped another page for her. "Here's page two."

"Beee."

Jek protested. "That's impossible! How can somebody learn to read from a book?"

"The first several chapters are written in pure phonetics," Bronzegloom explained.

Jek marveled. He'd never thought of that obvious solution! He looked at the book to see for himself. "Ooooh," he said.

"No, that's not until page fifteen," Bronzegloom corrected. And then, he moved on to the old man.

"Now I'm also going to entrust you with this," he said, handing the old man a peculiar little metal box with a coil sticking out.

"What in tarnation be this here gadgetry?" the old man whined.

"It's a two-way radio," Bronzegloom said. "The Despotopians had them, and I took them after the fight! I figure this is the best gift I can possibly give you guys. You can use these to get a hold of me anytime and pick my brain about all the question's you'll no doubt be having!"

Jek felt sudden disappointment. "You mean, you're not going to come with us? You're not going to become part of the Questing party?"

"Not a chance in Heck," Bronzegloom qualified. "I got involved in one scuffle, and I think that will have to be enough. I'm not generally much use in a fight, and even less so in various other survival scenarios."

"The same could be said for us," Audrey reasoned, and Jek quite agreed.

"Oh well... you're young, you'll learn," Bronzegloom assured them. "At any rate you better put any thought of me going along out of your heads." He snickered. "It ain't gonna happen."

With that, the thinker sidestepped again down the line, as if to continue his gift-giving. "Are you going to give me anything?" Jek asked.

Bronzegloom struck a posture of repose. "I could give you this," he said at last, holding out the repeating crossbow he had also taken from the Despotopians.

Jek looked at it questioningly. "I mean, I already have a musket; I might better stick to that."

"Aye," the old man agreed. "We'll be hard-pressed enough to get ye proficient in one weapon."

"But it has this cool boiler-powered oscillating retractable double-saw-blade feature!" Bronzegloom contested, hitting a button that made the limbs of the crossbow snap back even as a tiny boiler sprang to life and shot out paired saws past the end of the weapon that reciprocated with great, ferocious speed. It was a rather overwhelming display of doodad-ery. Jek winced.

"No thanks," he said.

"Okay, cool, I'll keep it myself then," Bronzegloom said.

"But what about this here 'radio'!?" the old man insisted. "I don't much comprehend its workin's."

"It's very simple," Bronzegloom explained. "Let me show you..."

This of course began a requisite several-hour-long process where the two of them fiddled around with the radios to try to get them to transmit to each other. They argued about all kinds of things – the channel control, the volume control, the signal strength, the AM/FM/PM, how to turn the 'darg-blasted' thing on in the first place...

Jek quickly and unabashedly settled into a shallow sleep even as this situation escalated, and so did Audrey. All it took was merely sitting down. He had never learned so much in one day or been in mortal peril as many times. It was the hardest-earned rest of his life. Still he woke repeatedly, only to privately wish the old man and Bronzegloom would argue more quietly, and then fall right back off...

* * *

A beam of light struck Jek in the eye, and finally he was really awake again. It was morning! And he could still hear Bronzegloom talking! How had he and the old man let time get away from them this way? They probably were still trying to figure the radios out. Perhaps they would be there for weeks...

But he listened to see whether it was as he suspected. What he heard was curious. Bronzegloom was engaged in some kind of mock-use of the high-falootin' inflection of grammar...

"Can'st thou hearest me now, over?" Bronzegloom said.

After a moment there was a startling 'bleep'ish noise that was rather unlike anything Jek had heard before, with the possible exception of the tinny voices of the Despotopians in their masks. And then there was the voice of the old man – but this also had the peculiar quality, as if the sound of his speaking was somehow being mashed through metal, or something.

"-oger, I hearest ye, ov..." the old man said.

"You're still pressing the button too late and releasing too early, over," Bronzegloom answered. They evidently had got the radios working, and were just playing around with them now.

"-is any better? Ov..." the old man tried again.

"No. Over," Bronzegloom replied.

Jek was suddenly aware that Audrey was propped up on his shoulder. It was very nice. He didn't want to disrupt her, but it was clearly high-time to get going, so at length he nudged her gently. She woke with a start, and began tousling streaks of her hair that had come out of the fancy knots and into her face. Jek shambled to his feet, more sore than ever.

"Geezer one, the lamp is back on in the lighthouse, over," Bronzegloom said.

"-at are ye yammerin' about? Ov..."

"The stewards are awake, over."

At once the front door flew open, and the old man barged in. "'Bout time ye woked up; we's wastin' daylight, when we shouldn'ta even wasted night-light!"

"You could've woke us up any time," Jek said. "Why did you spend all night playing with those radios?"

"Not *'playin'*! We was testin' and figgerin' the radios, so's we could get proper use o' them! Don't try an' make this my fault when I already done made it yours! That's just plug argumentative."

"Well, okay. We're ready to go now; we better just go."

"Not afore we eat again," the old man declared, much to Bronzegloom's surprise.

"You already had a breakfast," Bronzegloom reminded him.

"It be most unbecomin' of a host to remind their guests how much they done already et."

* * *

No further attempts were made to talk him down; they all ate a hurried breakfast and sloshed out to the docks. As they went, they were dogged as ever by the tweety birds, but they also gathered an ever-greater muster of peacocks and peahens in their trail. And the great beautiful terrestrial birds trumpeted angrily up at the darting little flying ones, as if to drive them off. It was a curious and somewhat aggravating racket.

When they made it to the docks, they saw that a crowd of people had gathered, and to their particular amazement, the Despotopians were still bound where they had left them! The local law enforcement was there, ready to seize the tied-up foreigners for obvious breach of curfew, but they refused even to question the Despotopians, and were simply loitering. They had to wait for the town gawkers and criers to finish their job. It was the established protocol, after all. In order for town gawkers and criers to adequately perform their duties, the law could not be enforced too quickly.

A young man ran up to them. He was weeping. "Hey, look! Look at that!" he wept, pointing to the Despotopians. He was clearly a newly-hired town crier. Most criers who were new to the job made the mistake of believing that in order to properly discharge their responsibilities, they had to cry, in the sad sense of the word.

All the hubbub began to be too much for Jek, and he found himself for the first time very glad at the thought of being soon back in the boat, sailing away from the weirdness. This was multiplied considerably as he noticed the Oberführer had spotted him, with cold steely death in his eyes. But the old man wasn't budging from where he stood.

"What's the hold up? Let's get going, while all eyes are still on the Despotopians," Jek suggested.

"Nay, there be an opportunity here what we can't rightly pass up," the old man said gravely.

"What are you talking about?"

"We gots to let these people know that there be a Despotopian Doom Fleet what's out to murder everyone," the old man explained. He continued before Jek could form an objection. "There's many a danger left on the road betwixt us and the Knights in Roemnar. The secret o' the Despotopian's fowl scheme might'a perished with us last night! We can't take that sorta chance no more. We's gamblin' with the fate o' the world! Someone else has to know, even if it's these here morons."

"Bronzegloom knows," Jek argued.

"Aye, but he's a hertic right now, so's that don't count for nothin'. Now stand back! I's gonna tell all these here people and ain't nothin' ye can do to change me mind!"

He gave the old man the room he wanted, and his old hands shot up in the air as he endeavored to cry over the din of the other criers. "Hear ye, hear ye!" he shouted. And before too long, he had the ear of everyone standing around. The old man put on his very best air of public speaking, looking solemnly into the eyes of the crowd. Though his look was also rather blank, as if he didn't know how to begin, now that the time for his speech had come...

"Dearly beloved," he began, and Jek rolled his eyes, even as he saw Bronzegloom wince and dig his knuckles into his brow. "We is gathered here today to tell ye a story o' woe, which will surely shiver ye by yer very timbers," he continued. "But first... have ye occasion to recall the prophecy o' Proconsul Zedulon, which he done delivered to yer very fine nation o' Jast-Madiir nigh on fifteen years ago?"

There was a great happy murmur among the crowd. "We remember!" one person spoke up. "Who could forget such delicious flavor?"

The old man was hopping mad, literally. "Not *that* part o' the prophecy, ye pea-brained..."

But Audrey tugged on him, and caught him midsentence. "Look, you've tried that introduction over and over, and it never works. We need to get right to the point!"

And she stood on some crate, and immediately had everyone's full attention. The whole moment had an odd gravitas Jek couldn't explain. The peacocks froze attentively. The little birds fell silent. Even the Despotopians appeared spellbound. It was like the entire world stopped breathlessly, in anticipation of her stentorian potency...

"Listen up, everybody," she imparted to the masses. "There's a Despotopian Doom Fleet out there, and you're all gonna die."

Moments ebbed silently by. Every face remained awed. And then finally, the substance of the message penetrated the trance, and everyone began running away and screaming, as if the Doom Fleet had just fallen out of the sky on top of them. Jek himself began to bolt, until he remembered that he had already known about the Fleet, and was doing what he could to stop it perpetrating the Doom it was intended for...

As the terrified crowd emptied out into the unsuspecting streets of the Wading Isle, leaving their midst in a foamy, wavy fluster, Jek looked back at Audrey. She had a very confounded and disgusted look on her face.

Jek and the old man helped her down from the crate. "Ye mighta not put it quite as bad as all that, m'dear, and cause such a panic," the old man said.

"I don't get it," Audrey said. "I know I didn't exactly mince words, but... I didn't even think they'd listen to me. That was the *last* thing I expected them to do!"

Bronzegloom laughed nervously. "The *last* thing? Well good gracious, what on earth *did* you expect?"

"I don't know! I thought they'd laugh it off! I thought they'd ask for proof, or something!"

She was quite beside herself, and Jek could see that. So he came to her defense, as the old man and Bronzegloom still appeared deeply perplexed and troubled.

"She did what you wanted," he said. "There's a whole crowd of people out there to cast suspicion on Despotopia now. Let's just be glad of it, and get the Heck out of here while the coast is clear..."

Even as they turned to go, another voice stopped them in their splashy tracks.

"Bon voyage, mine little fugitives," the voice called to them. It was Oberführer Klinkofhenschmidt! "Ve vish you all zee best!"

The old man grimaced at them. "Aye, now that ye done failed yer mission, I don't doubt it! Yer only hope now is fer us to find the Knights and put a kibosh on yer country's fowl dealin's, afore ye gets extradited, and executed!"

They laughed. "Oh, no. Zhere is no hope vhatsoever of zhat. It is as I said before, I zhink it will be far better if you find zee Knights. Our victory vill only be zee more glorious, if zee world has occasion to spend all of its last, desperate hopes in vain."

Bronzegloom did something unexpected here. He got very close – dangerously close – to the Despotopians, looking into their faces searchingly, as was his apparent wont.

"There can be no lasting victory for a nation that hates knowledge enough to burn books," he said.

But the Despotopians were quite unmoved. "Niet, ve do not hate Knowledge," Klinkofhenschmidt argued.

"Ve prize it above all else," lady Schenburkreiga said, completing his thought.

Bronzegloom was quite stricken by this. "That is even far worse," he said fearfully.

The Oberführer looked dismissively past him. "Your Qvest is waiting for you. Do not let us furzher forestall it!"

* * *

They didn't. Bronzegloom threw the rather small bag of foodstuff into their boat, and they cast the mooring lines and started to shove off, while the peacocks and peahens lingered in great rows of silent witness. It was a moment of sorrowful farewell, as the party was sundered from their new friend, the thinker. Waving with great solemnity, Bronzegloom rendered a most eloquent word of parting.

"Bye now," he said.

"See ya later, Bronzee," the old man waved back, hardly much looking away from his saily chores.

Bronzegloom walked away muttering.

The Case of the Stolen Stewards

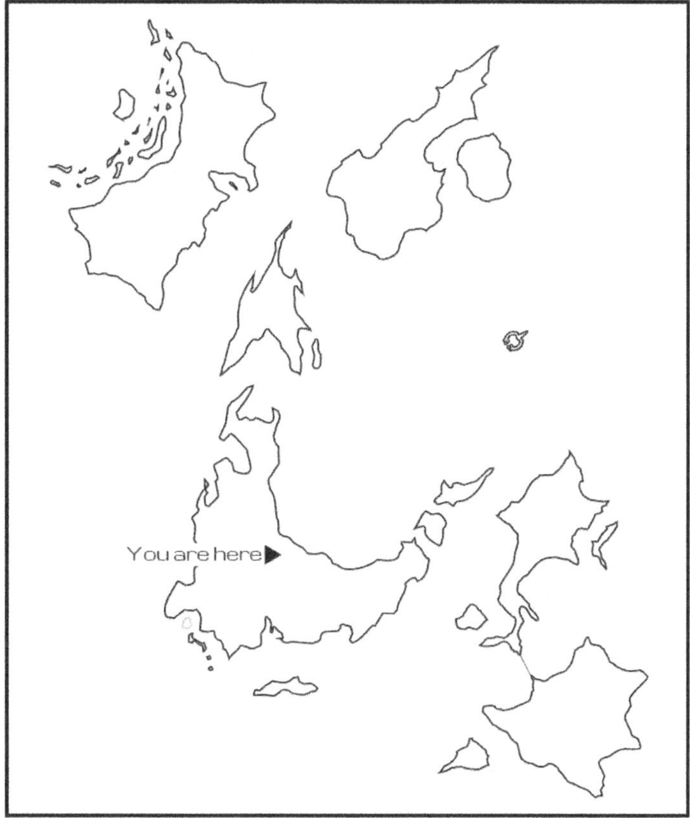

"If a law is to be unfair, then let it be unfair to all."

- Horus Templar, *Bar Thesis*

Horus Templar tugged again at the collar of his jacket, trying in vain to seal out the elements. Perhaps the chill did not approach the frigid desert nights of his youth, but the tropical air was so moist that even a mild nip seemed to cut to his very bones. He shivered as he watched his breath pour in plumes from his long snout, and in a moment of whimsy he felt somewhat like a dragon.

He was no huge lizard, nor one of their folk. Even so, he stood almost two feet over the Humans that were coming, and the Humans that were going. They were also breathing trails of mist as they passed him by urgently on all sides. The night was wearing on, but that scarcely slackened the bustle of these dazzling urbanites. They were the proletariat of a truly modern city...

St. Argonsburg. It was a metropolis of a very rare and exciting new breed – one of the very finest – and as a rule it never slept...

Still chilly, he buried his furry hands in his deep pockets, hoping his sharp, curled nails wouldn't get caught in the lining again, and he rocked back and forth on his feet, stretching his neck out as far as it would go above his massive, robust frame, trying to catch a glimpse of the train he was waiting on. He heard it first. The moan of the night whistle disrupted the flow of pedestrian traffic, with groups of people clustering under flickering street lights, preparing at once to board the cars as they pulled up.

Now the light of the command car emerged through the tunnel some few hundred yards down the track, and Horus' ears folded back reflexively as the bright beams caught his keen eyes unguarded.

Soon the command car pulled past, and the long, long line of drive cars – two-man pump trolleys powered by burly Humans heaving up and down on the sea-saw lever for all they were worth – came and went in its wake, followed by the passenger cars. Attentive conductors swung out with the doors and started punching tickets. But the conductor he approached didn't reach for any ticket from Horus. He just gave him a cautious nod.

"Evening, Mr. Templar," the conductor said.

"Good evening, Sergio," Horus answered as he passed him by.

He wiped his smallish shoes off on the matt as he stepped through the car's threshold into the bright cabin, eschewing street gunk, if there was any. It was more than just a courtesy to the train and its caretakers. He had a personal interest in the tidiness, for along the train – just a few links ahead of the caboose – was a car set aside for his use. It was, in fact, his office. The door even had his name on it, in very fine monograms:

Horus Templar – Public Defender.

But he wasn't headed to that car just yet. He snagged a bench about midway down the ordinary passenger car and sat down, scanning the people that passed by. Their somewhat unfriendly demeanors showed they had scanned him too. Many quickly buried their faces in the nightly newspapers. A lady in a very puffy and impressive fur coat paused at his bench, sticking her nose in the air and giving a very disdainful 'hmph,' before continuing on. He nodded at her pleasantly. He could tell at once that she was a professional busybody. The city employed hundreds of them to patrol the public sector, rendering their conspicuous disapproval wherever it seemed called for. Horus' line of work put him always in their crosshairs. Many were the *'hmph'*s and *'harrumph'*s and *'well I never'*s that he endured in the course of a week. But he did so with a healthy appreciation for the importance of their work, and it did not at all upset him...

The truth of the matter was, the duty of Public Defender was not a popular one – not by any means. It was universally understood that the law existed to protect the right, not of the *people*, but of the *state* – the right to be orderly and judicious, and to use every expedience at its disposal to put down unrest. This was of course the purview of the prosecutors, who were the obvious heroes of the legal system – the agents of the state itself, passing swift judgment on the unruly. The fact that anyone would be appointed to argue the opposite point – to take up the cause of the ordinary citizen, as if to appeal to the mercy and understanding of the court – seemed a horrible flaw in an otherwise efficient and admirable system. This was Horus' part to play. He was the fly in the ointment. He was the heel.

If it bothered Horus that he was doomed to such an inglorious job, it never showed. He understood the importance of his own work too, even if the public he defended did not so much. And anyway, he was very enamored with a thing. It was a rather pesky, fanciful thing called *justice*... a second-rate ideal, perhaps, but an ideal nonetheless. At any rate it had apparently meant quite a lot to Carlos Washoe, the great hero of the past. Horus felt that had to count for something...

So, on he sat among the commuters, ostensibly fishing for cases. This was just about his only means of exposure to clientele. There were many freight cars between his office and the passenger section of the train, and ordinary people were not allowed to traverse those freight cars, unless they had already scheduled an appointment with Mr. Templar. But the only way to set up an appointment was at his secretary's office, and her car was the one immediately ahead of his. If he had thought about it, Horus may have been forced to conclude that the powers of Jast-Madiir had knowingly obstructed the public's access to his legal counsel. So, he just didn't think about it.

Of course, sitting there didn't get him much work, either. People were loath enough to ask for his help, let alone in full view of everybody. Most folks preferred execution over being known to associate with a Public Defender... even when they were wrongly accused. Sometimes, Horus would try to press his luck, and would go around the cars asking people if they needed an attorney. But it was little use either way, and most nights he just sat.

Soon the train was loaded, the drivers were given their allotted five minutes' rest, and the wheels creaked back to life. Horus watched the world inch past him on the other side of the window, soon faster and faster. Before long, the train would come to another jutting root of Mt. Norvein – a rather wide and stunted thing, as mountains go, but certainly much more habitable for it than a rigid snow-capped peak. And then it would enter another tunnel that would weave up and double back on itself at a higher altitude.

But before all of that, he came to an otherwise featureless stretch of track that had been of considerable interest to him of late. He found himself pressed up against the cold window with anticipation. Even now, he was passing it on the rail again – those remains of some poor dumb animal that had got in the way of the train, and was now in a shape that made it quite impossible to identify. His stomach leapt within him even as he eyed the heap of roadkill. It began to look irresistibly tasty! But then, appearances can sometimes be deceiving. *I'll give it one more day*, he thought...

* * *

Scarcely had his mind begun to settle into a holding pattern, when he heard the door to the car behind him swing open. He was not so far away that he couldn't feel a blast of cold air whiz around the cabin. He didn't look back, but something unconscious told him this development had to do with him. Something was right...

"Fine evening, isn't it, Miss Boulevard?" Sergio the conductor asked most courteously.

"If you say so, Sergio; it's a bit cold for my liking," said the viscous voice of a very lovely lady. "But it is nice to see you, as always."

Sergio adjusted his hat a bit bashfully, being so complimented by such a prominent and respected lady. Everyone quite adored Deborah Boulevard. And how could they not? She was the most famous secretary in the whole world, having attained to measures of secretarial mastery previously unimagined. She was so admired, even the fact that she now worked for the questionable likes of a defense attorney did nothing to negatively affect her celebrity. If anything, people were *more* gracious to her, feeling unexpressed sympathy for her bad luck...

She delicately set a clawed hand on Horus' shoulder, as he continued to play at being oblivious to her arrival. He turned to look at her as if surprised. Her dainty snout rumpled in a warm grin. She was of the Mesomelae – the Jackal People – as he was.

"Another busy night?" she joshed him.

"Maybe twice as busy as last night," he said, standing and moving down to let her be seated. "I was just admiring my new favorite stretch of track."

"You noticed that too?" Deborah asked, burying her own hands in her pockets as she ruffled her jacket against the draught and sat down. "The dead deer, I take it?"

"Oh, I don't know. I rather thought it used to be a hypsilophodont," Horus said, also sitting back down.

"We shouldn't speak of such things now. I'm already famished." She looked questioningly up at him. "You read the paper?"

"Not as yet."

With a grunt – probably from the effort of getting a claw unstuck from the lining of her pocket – she reached into her coat and produced a rolled-up newspaper, which she handed off to him. Horus spread the paper out and snapped it upright. "The front page story ought to jump right out at you," she told him.

He whipped the paper again even as it attempted to fold itself at a corner. "Tophthaeran Civil War Suspended," he read. "Well, that is quite a development, isn't it?"

"*Yes*," she bobbed her head impatiently. "But that's *not* the story I meant."

Horus searched the page up and down again with a stern look. "Limes Ruled-Out as Cause of Lyme Disease," he read. "You know that's very old news. They probably just keep reprinting it because people are still dreadfully afraid of limes." He looked sternly back at the paper. "That's the kind of mistaken thinking that can take centuries to reverse, I fear. People still blame oranges for the Orange Plague."

She took the paper back from him and rolled it up quick as a flash, and hit him over the head with it. "Now would you *please* take a break from your sarcasm?"

Grinning, he gave the paper one more look. "Lighthouse Stewards to be Indicted for Dereliction of Duty." All of the headlines read matter-of-fact in this way. Newsmen were proscribed from ever using adjectives or adverbs in their parlance, under penalty of death. It was a lesson hard-learned and long ago that, if you gave a newsman an adjective – let alone an adverb – they would at once succumb to delusions of grandeur. By the end of the day, they would be fledging doomsday-poets. Within the span of a week or a month, there was no telling what they could esteem themselves to be, or which individuals or institutions they might deign to build up or destroy on the slightest whim. Needless to say, royalty didn't hold with that sort of radical element. Horus didn't go on to read the actual story below the headline, because there wasn't one. Stories were, as a rule, kept to a twenty-word limit. This was sort of a self-imposed guideline – newsmen knew that the longer the story was, the more likely they would succumb to the powerful temptation of using sensational language. One word, chosen from the wrong etymology, could cost them their lives, and it was too easy to make a mistake. Some *still* made it, on occasion, whether on accident or simply because they couldn't help themselves. Horus shook his head at the thought of past cases, in which he had represented wordy newsmen. He had fought quite valiantly and expertly in their defense, and in the end, they had all been executed. *The poor saps*, he thought...

"That's the one," Deborah said, confirming he had read the right story at last. "Could be an interesting case."

The newspaper across from them folded down, and to Horus' great surprise, the man behind it turned out to be none other than Artimus Mallard – his go-to private investigator, and another of their folk – the Mesomelae. "You got that right," he said, looking solemnly at Deborah, but his serious expression soon melted. "And by the way, hi there, sweet baby," he added, characteristically.

She nodded back at him. "Art."

Mallard looked now at Horus, and his face was urgent again. "Horus, you didn't hear it from me, but the D.A.'s office is gearing up to have a field day with these Lighthouse Stewards."

"Now where *have* I heard a line like that a hundred times before, if not from you?" Horus goaded him.

Mallard reached into his own coat – of course a marvelous coat of the trench variety – and got out his pipe. "Don't give me that," he said. "It's too darned cold a night." Horus still marveled at his detective's ability to hide in plain sight. No newspaper published for mere mortals could hope to conceal his great bulk... and yet, with the pages open, he could achieve perfect anonymity. Art Mallard really was the perfect private eye. He was tough, he was smart, he was stealthy... and most of all, like the city itself, he never slept.

Horus watched as Art poured soap into his pipe, got out the little wand, and started mashing it around in the bell end as if it were mortar and pestle. It was strangely aggressive.

"I tell ya, this new stuff they're forcing on us," Mallard muttered, bemoaning the soap in his pipe.

"It's supposed to be healthier," Horus qualified.

"Healthier my foot," Mallard said, still furiously stirring.

"Does beating it like that really help?" Deborah asked, eager to be party in giving Mallard a hard time.

"I don't know if it does anything for the quality, but the violence makes me feel better," Mallard answered. He was finally satisfied, and he took the pipe in his muzzle, where his shiny onyx coat had turned an early grey. His ears turned out with some conspicuous relief as a stream of bubbles wafted from the bell. "You know one of these days, they aren't even gonna let us puff these things indoors," he said through his teeth, whipping the excess soap from his wand.

"I've heard that one before, too," Horus said. "Now what of these lighthouse stewards? Apparently you know something."

"Yup," Mallard said, and he blew another long series of bubbles, sinking back into his seat. He finally began to appear a bit less agitated. "It's one of the more audacious incidents I've come across in a long time. Guess these two stewards up and took off right in the middle of their own inspection, in full view of the inspector, *and* a Berlberi Clerk, *and* an Inquisitor!"

"Scandalous indeed," Horus nodded.

"There's more. They escaped in a boat, you see, on the southern coast." He paused for his next point. "They haven't been caught yet."

Horus grimaced, revealing a hint of a few fangs. "And the prosecution is going to go right ahead with the case anyway..." he concluded.

"You got it."

He sighed. "An *In Absentia* trial." No wonder the two of them were going to such theatrics to get him on the scent of this case. They knew he abhorred *In Absentia* trials. It was a loathsome trial format that featured the full array of normal participants... with the notable exception of the defendant, who would be tried and convicted in their absence...

Horus may have been an unpopular man with an unpopular opinion, but to his mind, a conviction lacked for legitimacy when a suspect was not even given a chance to plead guilty. And he was absolutely steadfast that being present for the pronouncement of a sentence was every bit as important as being present for the carrying out of that sentence. Horus resolved that one day, he would prove it... and he had never yet shied from a chance...

"There's a whole stack of related papers already on your desk," Deborah told him.

"This begins to sound like a conspiracy," Horus grinned. They were both looking at him expectantly. "I guess tonight will be a busy night after all." And he stood, and with his associates in tow, began the long cold jaunt to his office...

* * *

Horus and company had to watch their step as they went single-file against the rest of the train. It was a regular trip, but they were careful never to take it for granted. Especially tonight, because they were making it earlier than usual, while the rails were still on a steep climb and arcing further up the mountain. As a matter of fact, they were currently arcing *through* it. The train was in another long tunnel, cut into a huge ridge that formed the westernmost bound of St. Argonsburg. By the time they emerged again, they would be far enough south to overlook the whole city...

It was quite impossible for the average passenger to tell if they were close to the end of the tunnel, because it wasn't demarked, except by bright orange torch lights at regular intervals, far too numerous to keep count of. But Horus knew on a gut level (from his hundreds of past rides on this route) that they were fast approaching the open air. He paused between cars, standing right on the coupling...

"What's the hold-up?" Deborah asked.

"This is my other favorite part of the trip," Horus said.

"We make this loop every night, you know," she reminded him.

"I know. But I've never yet tired of the view."

And the train burst from the tunnel, seemingly into space, for there was an immediate drop-off of some hundred feet where the great hole in the ridge emptied out, and they passed over a skeletal but sturdy bridge. Horus beheld the bright wide arms of St. Argonsburg, flung out to hug the contours of the coast far beyond, its thousands of points of light reflected in dazzling streaks that mingled with the stars off the Farjean Sea. Only the Palace was not in sight from here, unless you looked the other way, yet further up the slope.

The view – a truly glorious spectacle – was the precipitating purpose for building the capitol of Jast-Madiir in this location to start with. From this distance up the mountain, on a clear day, you could overlook hundreds of miles worth of the Great Harbor, though not all of it – there probably wasn't a high enough mountain in the world or a clear enough day to see the entire crescent of the Harbor. Both this great outlook and the terrain made the area incredibly defensible – amphibious landings would require enemy troops to climb for a mile to reach the city, and there be confronted with a high, sturdy northern wall that spanned the breadth of the settlement. It was much too far inland for the cannons of enemy ships to support their raiders – only the infamous static-powered guns of the Inquisition armada stood a chance of reaching the wall.

Of course, Jast-Madiir had never been at war with the Inquisition, nor had any legitimate state besides the fallen Berlie Beirel Dominion under Aedeloma thousands of years ago (the very scourge who of old destroyed the last of the Jackal People nations, may her name be forever strongly disliked!). But Jast-Madiir *had* endured many wars with Despotopia, and more than a few with Maenea. Even one or two with Tophthaera, for good measure. St. Argonsburg was, in fact, such a formidable bastion that Jast-Madiir had intentionally feigned retreat to it in several past wars, enticing the enemy with the hope of a headshot, only to route all comers and send the survivors back in disgrace.

All of these tactical elements only leant to the beauty. The city was admirable in its practicality as much as its aesthetics – rich in history as much as anything. And it was a *very* rich city, being the nerve center of the world's most vast trading hub.

"There it is," Horus said simply. There really weren't words for it.

"Don't go all to pieces on me, boss," Deborah said, teeth chattering.

He smiled, and he soaked in the sights for only a few more seconds. "Alright," he said, "let's get out of the cold."

"You said it," Mallard agreed. It might be that neither of his compatriots had a sentimental bone in their body. Horus wouldn't have it any other way.

* * *

Soon they were in Deborah's office car. As Horus opened the final door before his own, he looked back at his secretary. "Are you coming the rest of the way, or do you have your own business?"

"My schedule is your schedule," she said. "I won't have anything to work on until the next thing you give me."

"Come on then," Horus said. "Since I was the last one to find out about all this, you might as well help me go over the documents you dug up. Besides, as I recall, you were hungry."

Her ears perked. "Well if you have food, that settles it."

So they all continued to his car.

With some surprise, as Horus pushed open his door with the fine monographs, he found an uninvited guest – another face shrouded in the nightly news... sitting opposite them... behind Horus' own desk! But the jet-black fingers with deadly nails clutched around the paper revealed that his visitor was yet another Mesomela... and Horus immediately had a guess as to who had come calling. Suddenly recognizing the coat on the hanger next to him, there could be little doubt...

The next moment confirmed his theory as the paper was flung flat on his desk. Revealed was the chiseled face of Hamilton Blackforest, Horus' ultimate foil – the brilliant and unswerving district attorney of St. Argonsburg, his very self. He looked right at Horus with the signature gaze of a courtroom genius – beady eyes with a steely stare that could induce truth-telling at fifty paces. His intensity and his sharp features gave him the aspect of a Pharaoh from the days before their people's exile, and this was only exacerbated by the short, tight coil that Blackforest wore for a beard.

Now, of course, there were no Pharaohs. The most exalted Mesomelae in modern times were the Viziers, who presided over the national and international courts. Jackal People tended to fill out nearly the entire legal hierarchy of the various nations of the world (notwithstanding police, for though Mesomelae were imposing creatures, they preferred jobs that were almost entirely cerebral) and made up a fair percentage of adjoining trades (as evidenced by Horus' associates, the secretary and the investigator). Like most of the other species, Enlightened Jackals had a shared, inborn aptitude for a particular social function – a niche that almost any member of their race could fill and excel at and be glad. Phage were postmen. Herons were plague doctors. Mesomelae worked the law.

Blackforest stood now, adjusted the hem of his suit, and set his hands on the desk on either side of the paper, leaning over it with the air of both a suave sophisticate and a predator prepared to pounce. "Good evening, councilor... Miss Boulevard... Mr. Mallard." He nodded to each of them in turn.

"Good evening, Hamilton," Horus replied. "I'm glad to see you've made yourself at home," he said, with not more than playful sarcasm.

"Feel free to return the favor any time," Blackforest said, a smile curling up over his finely sharpened teeth. His voice had a very authoritative gravelly-growl quality, and it certainly bespoke his many years of blowing pipe soap. He stepped aside, and with a gesture welcomed Horus to his own chair.

"No I insist," Horus waved. "We can all sit out here." And so they took up chairs in front of the desk, arrayed a bit like the passenger benches, but facing the back of the car, for that of course was where the desk was. There were windows by each of the seats, slightly glazed with crystalline patterns by the cold air outside. Blackforest sat on the side of the car facing north, and Horus and Deborah sat opposite him, leaving Mallard to default to the north as well.

"So what brings you here, Hamilton?" Horus asked. He was more used to being ambushed by the D.A. in the process of calling witnesses than in his office car.

Blackforest's hand reached out and seized the newspaper up again. "I think you know by now," he said, and he put the rumpling sheets back on the desk. "Your secretary is certainly due all of her worldwide acclaim, but even *she* can't get copies of case filings from my office without my hearing about it."

"I wouldn't dream of trying," Deborah said.

"Of course not, my dear," Blackforest replied with a dubious grin. And he fished out his own pipe, preparing it absently. "Horus, I hope you won't misunderstand me, but I'm going to get right to the point. I don't want you involving yourself in this Stewards case."

"I'm more than idly curious what involvement *your* office is supposed to have in it," Horus deflected. "I know almost nothing as yet, except that the suspects fled the southern coast. A bit out of your district, wouldn't you say?"

"Well, you know the south side," Blackforest snarled, blowing his first series of urbane bubbles. "The district these stewards abandoned doesn't belong to *any* district attorney, because there isn't one assigned down there – never has been. I'm sure I don't have to tell you how thin the resources of the law are stretched, south of the jungles."

It was true. The south was unprofitable, and therefore undermanaged. Beside the military and a few crucial local enforcement bureaus (of which the Lighthouse Oversight Commission of Southern Jast-Madiir, LLC was one), organization was sparse, and the Czars and Czarinas had always leaned heavily on the Inquisition to moderate the southern populations for them – at least, to keep them getting crazy ideas of armed revolution, or other insurgency.

"Alright," Horus said, linking his fingers in front of him. "Now suppose you explain why you don't want me involved. Afraid of losing?"

"Darn it, Horus!" Blackforest cursed, striking the arm of his chair with his free fist. "I'm trying to help you... much as you make me wonder why. You know I respect the work you do, but outside of the people in this room, you don't have many friends. This case is going to be a big one. I don't want to see you on the wrong side of it."

If he had any remaining reservations about taking the case, Horus' professional pride had pretty well eradicated them by this point. He certainly didn't like being told ahead of time which side of a case was the right one.

But there were other avenues by which he could pursue justice for these suspects, and he was not about to let pride or his contempt for prejudicial overtures get in the way of exploring them first...

"If you insist on excluding me," Horus bargained, "then why not simply wait until the suspects are apprehended before pressing charges? That would all but eliminate any special interest on my part."

"That's not my decision to make, and you know it," Hamilton insisted. "The *state* is pressing the charges."

"Strange... I thought you *were* the state."

"Very funny. At any rate I can't do anything to delay the prosecution, much less expedite the arrest of those stewards. My hands are tied."

So much for that option. Horus knew now he would *have* to take the case. It was a matter of principle. But how to break it to Mr. Blackforest? "You know how I feel about these *In Absentia* trials..."

Blackforest scowled. "Yes, they're your 'pet-project'... I'm aware. Well, I'm not exactly wild about them myself. But you're not looking at the big picture here."

Horus' ears perked. "Aren't I?"

"No, you're not." Blackforest stood, ostensibly to begin a lecture. "The fact of the matter is, there've been too many of these kinds of cases lately. A rash of indolent behavior is plaguing the country. Folks south of the jungle are starting to act as if they can get away with anything... and that attitude seems to be working its way north. The royals want a high-profile conviction; they want it fast. They want to show the people that they're not going to put up with anyone who doesn't take their job seriously... not even in the southernmost reaches of Jast-Madiir. Leastwise not anymore."

At this Horus laughed. "Honestly, Hamilton, if I didn't know you better I'd say you were bucking for a promotion with that kind of rhetoric." Never mind that he was already district attorney of the greatest megalopolis in the Idriulthorontan Archipelago. "Don't you think you're being a bit stagy?"

"You don't have to see all the reports coming through my office every week," Blackforest pointed accusingly, and returned to his seat. "Why just yesterday I took a statement from an alchemist who had *fifteen* late orders the month before. *Fifteen*! You know what his excuse was? He said that the demand for magic elixirs had him so backlogged that he could barely find time to sleep anymore. It was all I could do not to laugh right in the man's face! *Sleep*. When you and I were working to pass the bar, you think we could have excused a late paper with a little thing like sleep deprivation?"

"No, we certainly could not have," Horus admitted.

"And that's just one lucid for-instance. I could give you a hundred more. Chain-mail forgers suing for a career change because they 'couldn't take the sight of another circle'. Mercenaries wanting to go on disability over a single lost limb. Dozens of fishers in the Fish Islands behind on their duties without much of any excuse at all!" He shook his head, casting a blank look out the frosty window. "It's enough to make me wonder sometimes if civilization is coming unbolted."

It was a troubling thought indeed. Few things seemed to bode the sudden collapse of society quite like an epidemic of idle hands. But Horus still had his principles. He didn't like people being made an example of by the courts, unless it could be confirmed beyond any reasonable doubt that they deserved to be made an example of. *In Absentia* was bad enough without show-trial overtures to go along; show-trials were notorious for putting the cart in front of the horse, so to speak. Whoever these stewards were, they'd have a fair trial, if Horus had anything to say about it. He owed his principles that much...

"Well, I'm afraid I can't back down now," Horus told Blackforest.

"And why is that?" Blackforest asked at length, more than a little dismayed that his gambit to keep Horus out of the proceedings had completely backfired.

Horus made his best stern face. "Because justice, Hamilton."

For a beat, there was nothing more said. Finally Blackforest smiled his sharp smile again, and grabbing his coat, made for the office door. "Alright, Horus. If you want to make a real case out of it, be my guest. I'd say it should be good for society at large, either way it goes. If I win, it'll send a stern warning to all of those shiftless characters out there who think the world's gone soft and they can get by without pulling their weight."

"Well, that does sound beneficial. And, if I win?"

Blackforest opened the door, stepping half out. "You know I hadn't seriously considered that possibility." He nodded and gave a subsumed wave, and with an arctic gust, he was gone.

* * *

They spent the next few hours sifting papers. First the incident report. Then the personal files associated with the suspects. The man – Jek – was thoroughly documented, but the woman – Audrey – couldn't be traced back more than a few months. Her file had all the earmarks of a shanghai scenario, though he couldn't prove it with what he had on-hand, should it become important to do so.

They had accounts from all three witnesses in brief, and were cross-referencing them extensively. The inspector's telling was not incredibly helpful – most of the descriptive language centered on his personal outrage rather than on the events themselves. The Clerk's account was also little help because he had arrived late and was immediately hurled into confusion. The Inquisitor's report, on the other hand, proved extremely comprehensive, and went a good ways to creating a complete picture of what had happened – as complete as could be arrived at without benefit of the defendants' own testimony, anyway.

All three witnesses spoke at least in passing of an unidentified old man. The Inquisitor suggested he might have been responsible for the whole debacle and taken the stewards captive in the discharge of their duties. Of course, arguing that they had been unexpectedly kidnapped would make a laughably lackluster defense, even if Horus could prove it was true. Still, every little bit helped.

The other major document that Deborah had mined from Blackforest's office was an early draft of the prosecution's list of witnesses. Horus felt a pang of foreboding when he noticed that the Inquisitor was not on that list. He knew there had to be a reason, and a good one. Hamilton Blackforest was not one to try to pad his case by intentionally leaving out witnesses he thought might strengthen the defense. Quite the contrary – he enjoyed and welcomed a strong defense; it gave him something to dissect. Horus could think of no witness more likely to lend some vitality to the defense than this Inquisitor... and she was, apparently, unavailable for in-court testimony. Only two out of the three primary witnesses were on the list. It was beginning to look like a whole new level of *In Absentia*...

"Art, I'm going to need you to be on the first train back into the city," Horus said. "I need to find out why this 'Parissah' won't be appearing in court. And while you're at it, you might as well dig up whatever you can about all three eyewitnesses. And see about the woman – Audrey – whether anything about her past can be reconstructed." He thought for a moment. "We're eventually going to have to see if we can identify this 'old man' they mention as well..."

Mallard huffed. "Same approach as always, I see. Find out everything about everything."

"Well, if there's time for it," Horus said.

"Speaking of time, when were we going to eat?" Deborah asked. "Don't forget you alluded to something about food a while ago..."

Horus was amazed he had forgot such a thing. "My goodness, yes. We'd better take care of that right away!"

He rounded his desk, and opened the bottom drawer on his right. Not surprisingly, the meat therein gave off a very strong pungency. His nose and his eyes and his stomach alike were very glad to see the moldering meat was still there. More than a few times in the past, just as the stuff was beginning to age very finely, he would find that his secret pantry had been emptied! For a while he suspected Deborah of eating it out from under him, but eventually he learned that it was all some sort of misunderstanding on the part of the people who cleaned the train cars...

He drew out some rancid dinosaur flesh and set it on plates with fine silver trim before producing knives and forks in neatly rolled napkins. Next they drew up chairs and ate about his desk, as soon as he set some very nice candles. They were all starving, but naturally time had to be made for civilized supping.

Later, as he finished enjoying a chewy grizzled mouthful, Mallard wiped his paling jowls with his napkin and cleared his throat. "You know I do believe the world *has* gone soft, like Blackforest said. Here we are eating with silver utensils and finery while our progenitors are out there somewhere chewing dry bones on the ground."

He was right about that. In truth, the Mesomelae were an offshoot of traditional jackals – granted intelligence, and remolded into an upright form that allowed them to make better use of that intelligence. This had been the mode of the Creators for the ages spanning between the creation of Humans and the eventual Supreme Exodus... the time known as the Enlightenment Era. Prevailing theology maintained that by this Era, the Creators had started to become quite discouraged – disenchanted even – with their own universe, fearing that it would never please them and that they might be better off starting over. However, for some centuries they evidently held out at least some hope of still improving on what they had. Even so, they couldn't bring themselves to invest the same level of effort in the project as they had before. The Enlightenment Races, then, represented their final attempt to further enrich the world. Their emergence had a sort of creative economy: the Creators didn't need to invent wholly knew species any more, but simply fashion intelligent variants of some of the life-forms they had already made over the eons, and make minor structural changes where necessary, often at least making the Enlightened creatures a bit bigger than their progenitors. Thus was the origin of the Mesomelae, the Dire Herons, the Dire Mantids, the Phage, and a number of others.

No one was sure exactly how many of the lesser order of creatures was ultimately modified in this way. Some Enlightened species produced prominent civilizations, while others never ventured from the deep wilderness they originated in, and were only ever encountered by chance. Every possibility remained that there were yet more Enlightened species, still to be discovered in the remote and secret places of the world...

Of course, a Mesomela or other Enlightened creature could, if not careful, succumb to a certain amount of existential angst, knowing what they knew about their humble origins. But rarely did they dwell on it or let it make them gloomy. Other than an occasional whimsical comment about what their 'dumb cousins' might be up to (not unlike Art Mallard's musing about chewing dry bones on the ground), the subject hardly, if ever, came up. But Horus had, from time to time, supposed that Mesomelae might yet have some character traits in common with the brainless species they had come from. Savoring another bite of rotting carapace, though, he couldn't begin to conceive what that common ground might be...

"I wouldn't worry about anything as abstract as the condition of world society, Art – not more than you can help – there's not much use in it," Horus said, once he finished chewing. "We all do our part, but in the end these systems have to work themselves out. If the world ever does go too soft, I daresay something will come along to toughen us all back up, eventually. In the meantime, who else wants some more meat?"

If You're Going Through Heck….

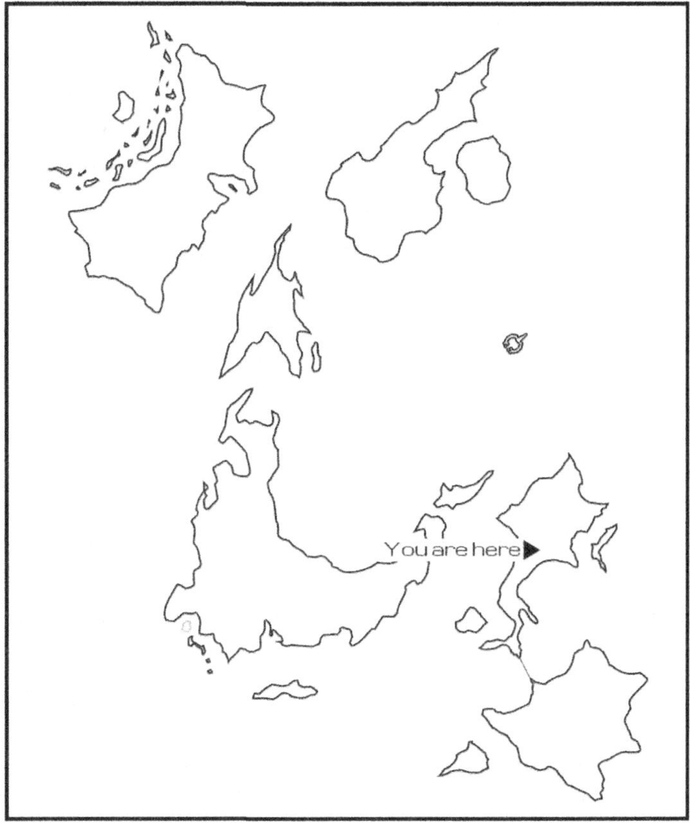

"Perhaps the best evidence of the immortal soul is this: There are too many debts to be paid in a single lifetime."

- Magormissahr, *Referendums on the World, Vol. 254*

Six days. Six full *days since* Variglew...

Parissah reminded herself, feeling in need of a reminder. *Full* days indeed! Though, she disdained the sort of melodramatic thinking that would make those six days out to be an eternity. A day was merely 21 hours. *Period*. If she felt like she could have fit a hundred years into every one of those hours, she knew it was merely a trick of the mind...

Even as she thought this, a rare ray of daylight lanced across the black wastes, as if to split them open and expose yet another river of lava. This confirmed that it was indeed *day* – a fact otherwise only hinted at by the lighter-grey band of gloom on the horizon. A blanket of volcanic smoke and ash from many towering spouts and vast open chasms was drawn over the sky like a very heavy eyelid, and all the dark land of Tophthera was in a kind of restless sleep, filled with nightmarish visions of desolation.

Parissah had known ahead of time that the journey to the capitol of Tophthera would take some days. She knew that there was no rushing an army of Meduselda. And this was no figure of speech – Meduseldan drones have a very low maximum float speed, hardly faster than a shamble – roughly a mile per hour. This fact, she had carefully calculated into her schedule. What she *failed* to anticipate was the cruel whim of the landscape. Having never visited inland Tophthera before, Parissah now understood that there were two sovereign governments on the island – the monarchy of the Queen, and the oligarchy of the volcanos... and the volcanos seemed Heck-bent to demonstrate at every turn that they were certainly not the lesser of the two regimes...

In this blistering environment, 'Heck-bent' was no idle phrasing. Tophthera was an infernal world straight out of allegory. Walking across it was like stepping into the darkest chapters of many great epics from of yore...

Parissah recalled the story of the two brothers – one good, and one turned to evil – who dueled across a molten river...

She thought of the tiny people, who bore a most wicked ornamental accessory back to the fires of its origin...

But mostly, she thought of Heck itself – a proposed ethereal plain of punishment where everyone was believed to go after their time in the mortal universe was no more. It was a concept introduced by a now-defunct sect of the early Inquisition, and had enjoyed great popularity for a time. It was held to have been of particular interest to Magormissahr, who homaged it in many of his writings. Ultimately, though, the idea of Heck could not be proved, since the Creators had never mentioned it before they left, and so it was steadily given less and less thought over the intervening centuries. In modern times, Heck was little more than a strong expletive. But to Parissah, in the heat of the moment, it did not seem so far-flung. Heck was eminently real, and she was walking right through it.

She faltered a bit as she gimped onto stiflingly hot ground that gave way under her foot like wet sand – though it was pure rock – and tried not to be unduly distracted by the smell and the steam and the aggressive sizzling noise. There were veins of freshly belched molten stone strewn everywhere, which, after cooling for only a few minutes, were just as black as the rest of the ground. No matter how close she watched her step, she couldn't discern cool, solid ground from spongy, immolating ground. Rather than even try, once she had realized from the first misstep that her body could withstand the heat (with hardly any damage beyond transitive agony), she simply let her feet be scalded over and over again.

Anyway, the sensation in her wounded leg, where she had been stabbed by the swordsdrone, was quite dull at this point… and so it was with her wounded arm. In the hot fetidity of Tophthera, the deep punctures had evidently enjoyed ample opportunity to fester. Indeed, with her finely honed predatory nostrils, she could vaguely smell the spoiling of some of her own flesh over the reek of sulfur. Eventually those wounds would have to be addressed. For the moment, she was rather glad to be desensitized in two of her limbs…

After days of urgent scanning, she was forced to conclude that her bacterial infections were the only growing things in the whole inland region. Parissah was, as she had told her students before giving them her provisions, a very expert forager. If there had been *anything* to forage – anything at all – she would have caught it and ate it by now. But there was nothing living here. Nothing could. There wasn't so much as a patch of ground for a hundred miles that wasn't being buried and reburied in endless coats of lava on a weekly or even daily basis. The Meduselda alone were able to endure such a place – they who felt no heat, knew no hunger or thirst, and had still in their essence the memory of the infancy of time, before night and day, when all was dark and featureless, and they were alone upon the earth. Tophthaera was a perfect home for Meduselda. Perfect for them, anyway, in the sense that it would never have done for anyone else.

But even the Berlie Beirels had not always called the northern and southern Tophthaeran Isles home. Their coming to the Archipelago was just another way that the mideeds of their diabolical Queen of seven generations past had changed the course of history forever…

Queen Aedeloma's life span was one of the truly great trials of world history. Her attacks were unrelenting for the entire 770 years of her existence. And she did not hold with the pattern of other Meduseldan Queens in waging wars of lazy but persistent pressure. Unlike her colleagues, she didn't do war just to pass the time, or give so much as a thought to fair play, or limit herself to opponents who were mutually interested in a fight. She fought to *win*. For reasons known only to her, she dedicated her life to world conquest. She made great strides in strategic thought and the use of unpredictable tactics. With time, she also learned to generate more and larger and fiercer drones (the *original* abominations, which Irisa and Asiri's own modern variants were no doubt patterned after). This was a frightening testament to the singularity of her will, for no other Queen before her had even dared to imagine she could tailor her drones to her whims. And with all her ilk, it did not take long for her to prove that there is almost nothing in the universe more fearful than the onslaught of a truly ambitious and intent Meduseldan Queen. A number of realms during this time were engulfed, never to arise again. The one saving grace was that Aedeloma insisted on attacking all realms within her reach continuously, expanding her influence outward in all directions at once. If she had focused on but a few at a time, it is possible that none but her kin would have endured the full 770 years of besiegement…

To make matters worse, there was also Onyxadon. He had the deepest and most sincere admiration for Aedeloma, seeing in her a kindred spirit. He beseeched her that they should join forces, and it was among the world's few good fortunes in that time that she refused with all possible fervor. This, of course, did not altogether discourage Onyxadon from continuing to engage in his own pervasive attempts at world domination. And so civilization at times faced these two great perils at once. But this tooeventually proved to be a boon, because in time the various realms became better at baiting the forces of O'nyxon and Aedeloma into close proximity, and then quietly stepping out of the way to let them fight each other. It was this strategy – combined with the heightened efforts of the other Meduseldan Queens to try to hold Aedeloma at bay – which allowed Humans, Avarica and the Enlightened races to endure to the end of her life. There was never hope of anything more than merely riding out the storm...

Upon her death, Aedeloma's immediate successor, De'Ankamori, fortunately was one more in keeping with the better tradition of the Queens. So moved she was to make amends for the crimes of her predecessor that she commissioned the Clerical Dronehood of Berlberi to make and distribute a form letter of apology to all citizens of all nations. It was really a nice gesture, and copies of this form letter later became the prize of many collectors of historic memorabilia. However, many peoples were not sufficiently encouraged by their mail, fearing that a strand of evil may have wound its way irrevocably into the bloodline of the Berlie Beirel Queens. And so, De'Ankamori did something even more concessionary than the form letters, if that were possible. She uprooted herself and many of her Berlie Beirel drones, founding a new and remote colony on the twin isles of Tophthaera.

This move was greatly celebrated among those on the continent... but to the relative chagrin of the newly-burgeoning population of Idriulthoronta. Ironically, many of its residents had recently immigrated to the far-away region in direct flight from Aedeloma. But the population of the mainland was still much greater... and after all, the needs of the many outweigh the needs of the not-so-many. Yet with time, all began to seem mended. The Clerical Dronehood of Berlberi continued to operate independently out of the old Berlie Beirel capital, now less tied than ever to a particular state. And De'Ankamori and her successors caused little enough grief in their new adopted home...

That was, until the present day. With the emergence of the Twin Queens, Aedeloma's old machinations appeared ready to pick up where they left off, over five thousand years ago...

* * *

Parissah started as a shaft of lava burst sidelong from the ground some hundred yards away. The incandescent liquid stone poured out in a viscous fury, gathering into a gully that snaked between two great mounds of dry rock and cascading on from there in a newborn river. The volcanos were asserting themselves again, as they had already done many times, for the river formed an obstacle directly in their path. Fortunately, this time it was only a minor one. But even small obstacles formed wide detours. The Field Marshal and his retinue, though they could not possibly experience pain, gave all free-flowing lava a wide berth. They could still be killed by it, after all, and that would be rather inconvenient. But this was the whole hitch in Parissah's plan. The straight road she had expected to take to Brittegonnen was but a convenient fantasy, she now knew. The real way – as the Meduseldan floated – turned out to be an impossibly organic series of twists and turns and double-backs.

She reproached herself for not foreseeing these problems and planning accordingly. She reproached herself for having not taken greater care in supplying the journeys; she should have had everyone pack their own consumables. She thought back to the battle itself, and the way that Taurnuren had resolved it… and how, if she had been as tactically savvy as she needed to be, his brilliant employment of strategic warning shots should have been the plan all along. Retrospectively, the whole fight on *Variglew* was a waste of time and energy, and an unnecessary gamble and expense. Her plans were growing more and more shoddy of late, though they were crucial plans on which much depended. She was making too many mistakes. She was getting horribly tired and she was making stupid mistakes. Worse than that, she realized, she was now making *excuses*…

But she *was* quite exhausted. The impossibly slow caravan of warrior-Berlie Beirels to which she was attached held her speed to a crawl. But, perhaps worse, the procession went entirely without interruption. Meduselda never tired nor slept. So she had to coax herself into the relentless shuffle day after day, night after night. Turning aside to rest would have been a waste of precious time, and a display of weakness she was sure she could not afford. She didn't suppose the Berlie Beirels would understand, nor feel inclined to wait up for her. She couldn't hope to impose her needs on an entire army (no more than she already had), nor would she have tried. And though she could, in theory, have charged ahead and got to her destination ages ahead of them, it would not have done to enter the fastness of Brittegonnen without the escort of the Field Marshal. She relied on his authority to give her passage through the city gates, and grant her audience with the Queen.

It would have helped so much if there was only something to eat. For Avarica, sleep and food were essentially interchangeable, in the way they restored the body. Totally famished, Parissah thought of eating even more than of sleeping. More than a few times, she considered asking a nearby Berlie Beirel soldier if she could eat some of his tentacles. In many ways it was not an unreasonable request. It would cause no pain and not be permanently damaging. And she knew that Meduselda, despite all of their unusual aspects, were good for eating. But no matter how much she thought about it, there just wasn't any way of asking diplomatically to eat somebody's limbs…

She wished there was more to divert her attention. She felt rumbles and churns in the earth below, and heard distant blasts, and ever there was the gentle pitter-patter of brimstone. But unless a geyser of lava went off right in her midst, it was all just an apocalyptic white noise after a few days' march.

There was only one thing she could see that really gave her something to process, and it was troubling. Many of the Meduselda in her midst (not the least Mr. Baegulgog) were still ghosts. It wasn't that she was specially unnerved by the thought that she was participating in a slow and somber parade of the dead in Heck on earth. What upset her was that she was meeting some of these ghosts *on the way* – that even as she was headed north, some passed her by on the way back *south*. She couldn't easily account for that. There was no war in Brittegonnen – all the fighting had been on the Bridge for the last several years. Why would a steady trickle of ghosts be coming *from* the capitol?

She had a theory, which only leant to her fear. Having already seen some of Aedeloma's playbook at the battle on *Variglew*, she worried that the Queens were up to even worse tricks than the abominations. It could be that they were capturing enemy soldiers and hauling them back to their cities for experimentation. If this was true, then her only comfort was the fact that the ghosts kept coming. All of this would have to be investigated, when finally she came to the end of her road…

That could yet take some days…

* * *

Finally, they were rounding the spout-end of the river of lava that had sprung to life in their way. They found that they had been more fiendishly made sport of by the landscape than they could have guessed from downstream. A low ridge had only just concealed from view that the spring was merely a puncture made by an elevated pool of lava that stretched on for miles, and was actively engaged in trying to flow freely to lower ground, even as it churned. At the sight, the Berlie Beirels autonomously doubled back to give the boiling lake more elbow room. They would have to take a wide eastward arc around it. Most of this arc, unfortunately, was sunken-in, and Parissah knew that more rivers could easily spring in their path along the way. Indeed, some of the gentle ridges along the eastern coast could be concealing streams of their own already. They could perhaps lose a half day or more just trying to get around this open pit!

She was sorely tempted to complain furiously, but it would have been fruitless to try. The delay meant nothing to anyone else. She plodded on.

For a while she let the Field Marshal take quite a long lead, so she could save herself snaking back if he suddenly found an obstacle and they were all forced to turn further aside. She had had no words with him since the Bridge, or he with her. The entire army had been silently and anxiously marching all the way. She could read uncertainty in their glowing pulsations. Doubtless they wondered what would become of them if the war was really over. But it was no use asking or planning or predicting amongst themselves. There was only one way to know what was going to happen. They would have to wait and see what their Queen decreed…

Baegulgog had also been uncharacteristically quiet. He kept close to her along the way, feeling not at all at home among Berlie Beirels. But he had said so little. His ghostly form just pulsed, and it was a pulse like that of the soldiers. He was distinctly anxious about something. Parissah could hardly imagine what. She knew he had an eating disorder.

Perhaps he was hungry. She didn't think ghosts could be hungry... but then, it made no sense for a Meduseldan in *any* form to be hungry. Finally, she decided to simply ask...

"Baegulgog, is something the matter?" she asked, and cleared her throat. The hot and dry fumes were cracking her gills, and her voice had faltered. "Your constant flickering would suggest anxiety."

"It is surely nothing, madam," he said, but his voice belied him. "Don't let me disrupt your peculiar walking. I will be quite fine."

"You'll forgive my curiosity, I hope. It is no small wonder to me what would give a ghost a fright."

"In that case, I shan't leave us both in suspense. I confess I have been ever watchful of that great peak in the far nor-east. We are headed nearly straight for it now."

Parissah looked up into the distance, and there was a very great volcano there; easily the most vast of all the ones that could be espied. It had a particularly wicked look about it, with a curled-back summit beyond the spout, and another further down and facing the other way, spilling lava into empty space, onto the very feet of the mountain. It was like a pouring vessel for a Moon-Moth about to make a meal of the island, soaked in a lava-gravy. The most and the richest vapors in sight emanated from its warped cone in roiling heads rimmed garish red from below. All the height of the mountain was behind a gradient of smog that bespoke the miles of its girth. The sight of it stole away mortal strength, and you could not endure to look at it long, unless your vitality was already long forgot.

"It is certainly not pleasant," Parissah admitted. "But it is only a volcano."

"The volcano itself is not what troubles me," Baegulgog explained, "but rather what might be living within. Is it not maintained that Onyxadon makes his dwelling in such doom? If I were as evil as he, I think I should want that volcano for my home before all others. I do not know if I could imagine a more terrible one."

Parissah found it rather remarkable that Baegulgog had such a fearful fixation on Onyxadon. The old dragon may have been the Most Vile of all things the world had known, but he held no special danger for Meduselda... except that he might corrupt their hearts, if he deigned, and if they were not strong enough to resist the gravity of his persona...

"I do not believe Onyxadon lives anywhere in these Tophthaeran Isles, Baegulgog," she explained. "You are not the first to wonder. These lands were under the continuous vigil of the Inquisition for centuries, for that very reason." She paused, wishing there was nothing more to qualify. "But I will not deceive you, and have you believe that we can be certain of anything when it comes to Onyxadon. He may yet live here. Though we feel confident that he does not."

Her words seemed to fall flat, even in her own ears. So much for comfort. Rather than encourage him, the doubt had only passed to her. And she imagined now that the rolling rumble she heard came not from the ground below, but from living smoke and ash that filled the sky, even as it looked down on her, laughing at her plight. At any rate, she hoped it was only her imagination...

* * *

Time went on far more slowly now. It was all an endless loop. Left foot, right foot... left foot, right foot... and her pulse rose and fell with each heavy step. It would beat in her ears and then regress, so that she felt faint. Feverish constriction plagued her body. Once she heaved, but her stomach had nothing to expel. It gave her an instant fright, which she almost as quickly forgot.

Eventually she heaved again, and was dimly reminded of the first time, as of a distant memory. The significance of it all finally registered. She was taking ill.

Baegulgog, though still somewhat adrift in his own worries, took notice. "Beg your pardon, madam, but you do not walk as you should, and you have made some odd noises. Are you afflicted in some way?"

"I'm afraid so, Baegulgog." And she hesitantly knelt by a small fissure with flowing rock inside. A horrible chill came over her as she stooped to the ground. "Something is going to have to be done about my wounds, or I will grow still sicker."

He floated over to her side even as she sat and examined her arm and her leg. The punctures were indeed swollen and turning interesting colors. She sniffed, and it was more than her sensitive olfactory center could handle. She dry-heaved again.

"I say, that is a bit unusual, isn't it?" Baegulgog remarked.

"Yes," she answered. "I've never had such simple punctures fester so badly. It's rather extraordinary."

"What is to be done about it?"

She found she had to think about it, though it was a simple matter. "I'm going to have to cauterize them."

Baegulgog chortled, and it nearly startled her. "Might I suggest the use of some lava, madam! It seems to me I just saw some nigh at hand, somewhere hereabouts..."

His sarcasm didn't inspire much levity. There was of course loads of lava everywhere. But lava was probably well in abundance of her need. She was intimately familiar with the sting of fire, but molten rock struck her as a bit extreme...

"I don't know if I'm up to all of that... sticking my limbs into boiling rock. I'm honestly not sure it won't do more harm than good."

"I see," he sighed. But soon he clapped, and upraised a tentacle, signaling inspiration had struck. "You could breathe your own fire onto the wounds! That ought to do nicely, I should think."

"Yes, that is what I mean to do. But I will need your help, Baegulgog."

He flashed with new uncertainty. "Hrm, well... I am not yet very corporeal, I fear. But I will certainly help, to the extent I am able. What must I do?"

"I can't just breathe fire at will, exactly," Parissah explained. "I need to be stressed in some way. I need to be upset... angry... whatever. But suffice it to say, unless you can trigger the fight reflex in me, I'm not going to be able to breathe fire."

He hesitated. "You... you want me to make you very angry?"

"That is what I *need* you to do, yes."

He hesitated yet more, pacing through the air. "You understand I am not very confrontational by nature..."

She tried to coach him, even as she fought a wave of nausea and dizziness. "I understand. I hate to even ask it of you, but the need is great. Now, I would be most grateful if you would begin angering me."

He paced a bit more, though now she was sure she had convinced him. He was just trying to devise a strategy. At once he spun and pointed at her. ""You're a terrible person!" Baegulgog reprimanded.

"That's true," Parisha nodded.

"I mean it! You are deeply objectionable!" Baegulgog insisted.

"I couldn't agree more."

There was quiet as Baegulgog flashed thoughtfully. "Well, come now! We shan't get anywhere if you keep going along with everything I say."

More dizziness. "Keep trying," she said. She had no other ideas. She felt nothing but exhaustion. Even the pain and the stench and the hunger were now dull by comparison as she sat there on the ground.

"Very well." Baegulgog agreed somberly. "You make me sick!" He continued to point a tentacle admonishingly.

"I'm sure you don't mean that, but you should," she said.

"As bad as you are, your mother was twice as bad!" Baegulgog continued.

At this, Parissah felt a small stir of heat in her gut. She didn't care so much for this line of insults. "She had her faults, no doubt, but..."

"...And your father was perfectly awful!"

She snorted an incendiary blast

Her wounds sizzled. The pain was impressive. But the flesh was clean...

* * *

It wasn't easy later, getting back up, continuing on. Just a few minutes off her feet had made her head swim with an aggressively oblivious feeling. She saw that it confused the Tophtheran soldiers to see her sitting there, beside the convoy, as they all continued on without her. But it didn't take long before she hardly noticed or cared, and it was the most she could do not to lapse into sleep. She let the last of the soldiers pass her by before she finally came to her feet, resolving to jog back to the front. She hoped a little bit of jogging might make her feel better. It most certainly did not. She felt aware, for the very first time, that her body had considerable weight of its own. The prospect of propelling it at any great speed began to seem like gambling at long odds against overexertion. She *could* faint, and if she did, there was no telling how long she might be delayed in waking...

It was just as well. She forgot that Baegulgog couldn't possibly keep pace with her. She didn't like the thought of leaving him behind in the wastes, so she quickly abandoned all thought of jogging.

Back to the shuffle.

Her ghosty friend the Clerk was soon by her side again. She could see he was pondering something else now. She hated to think what.

Maybe it was just the setting, or her ailing mind playing tricks on her, but her own thoughts were drifting on a steady current of paranoia, as if she was under a seeing glass. It felt like her every weakness was being individually put on display for merciless scrutiny. And everyone seemed to be looking in his turn. The soldiers were wondering about her. Baegulgog was wondering about her. And still she imagined Onyxadon overhead, melded with the vapor that smothered all the land, fiendishly delighting in her suffering...

These feelings were soon reinforced, as Baegulgog broke the tenuous silence between them. "I am sorry for upsetting you, madam."

More niceties. She felt more than ever she didn't want to bother about polite chatter. Especially since this confirmed that Baegulgog really was still pondering over her outburst. Still, polite he was, and polite she must be in return. "Do not be sorry. You did what I needed you to do... and I know I asked something very difficult. You have my deepest gratitude."

He stammered. "Perhaps... I could be of yet more help. You tried to make me feel better about Onyxadon before. I don't understand what it is that troubles you so deeply about your father. Indeed, perhaps I can never understand it. But if you wish, you may certainly speak to me about it, and I will console you if I can."

Suddenly – unaccountably – Parissah was conscious of her ankles. Not surprisingly, they hurt terribly. The weights had dug them savagely during the battle now six days past. But until this moment, she'd never given so much as a thought to relieving herself of them. There were just some weights you needed to carry in life. No such burdens could ever simply be cast off...

But, maybe, some could be *shared*...

...If only once...

"You are a kind soul, Baegulgog. I have already spoken to you about my father much more than I ever intended to speak of him again – as long as I lived – on the day I met you, no less. But you are right if you guess that there is much I withheld even then. There is more to the story. There is the matter of our final parting."

He paused for a moment, as if mustering emotional strength against whatever she was about to reveal. "Very well, then... let's have it."

She started easily enough. "It came at a time when my life was becoming quite stable. I had some years in the service of the Inquisition, and more than a few since he last wrote to my mother or me. Memory has a way of exaggerating irony, but I could almost swear I had only just begun to really put the sadness of our sundering behind me. Life as an Inquisitor granted me the comfort of structure. I had moved on. I was content.

"Then, one day, I was recalled from some mentorship duties, to help address an urgent matter that had suddenly arisen. A nearby village was besieged. It was being menaced and scoured by a raiding dragon.

"As I once told you, an Inquisitor is a naturalized dragon-hunter. These were the sorts of calls we dreaded, for there never failed to be great pain and death wherever a dragon came to usurp the wealth of the defenseless. But it was also by this time a familiar part of the job. I knew all of the logistics and the tactics and the execution by heart. I knew I could depend on everyone in my team, and they on me. I wasn't afraid or hesitant. The mission would go over like clockwork, as it had a dozen other times in a dozen other places..."

Finally, she reached a hitch. The story grew difficult in the telling all at once...

"Only this time it *was* different. Because when I finally caught sight of the monster, I knew at once that it was *him*. It was my father."

Parissah tried to swallow, but there was nothing in her throat except a dry vacuum. It was hard – far harder than she could have imagined – revisiting all of this. But she knew she had to go on now, rather than leave Baegulgog an opening, in which he might feel he needed to jump with some clumsy words of sympathy...

"Besides all that it did go quite like clockwork," she continued, and surprised herself with a bit of a quake in her voice. "I oversaw his demise and I was put in charge of hunting down and dispersing his treasure hoard." Suddenly it was all she could do not to completely break down. So she tried to make light of a humorless irony. "It was rather a windfall, really... having me there. Locating the dragon's hoard can be nearly impossible business for us in many cases. But I guess I knew him well enough, after all..."

"My dear," Baegulgog said somberly, shaking his body back and forth in sorrow. "What can I ever do to take back the horrible things I said?! If I had known, I should never have..."

"It is alright, Baegulgog. You described my father quite accurately enough – as he was in the end – when you called him perfectly awful. It pains me to remember. But I think what actually haunts me most is the memory of the generous man he was at the start." Her strength nearly failed her, and she took a moment. "Indeed, it is my doom to remember him by what he gave away, and not what he later tried to take for himself."

"Whatever is the end of such a matter?" Baegulgog asked, apparently exasperated. "Perhaps an Inquisitor would know. Is it really possible that the evil deeds, committed nearer the end of one's journey, fully undo the former good deeds? For that matter, can any good deeds, done later in life, truly erase the evil that came before?"

Parissah hardly knew how to answer; it was one of those questions too basic to the condition of life to ever be fully grasped. She could do naught but admit her own ignorance. "I do not know. It is far beyond me. But I can say that in my own reckoning, no ending could *yet* be made of it... for even the early deeds of my father have quite outlived him. The Knights of the Indigo Lodge maintain the concept of 'The Great Looking-Back of All Things.' Until such time, I don't suppose any matter is ever truly closed."

Baegulgog had more hard questions yet in store. "You... you feel very responsible for your father's death, I take it... though he himself provoked it?"

"I do. You will remember, it *was* my responsibility."

He considered her answer, and how he might yet try to salve her, though she would not be moved – leastwise where it involved her accountability. "It is a harder thing that you did... far harder than any I had ever known to be asked of anyone. But I hope it is of some solace that you fulfilled your duty faithfully." Suddenly he took on a feisty aspect. "Let one stand here and *try* to say that you did not do the right thing! I would at once slap him with all seven tentacles, upon my return to solidity!"

Parissah really did appreciate his bravado. She actually laughed a single laugh, but it stung in her parched throat.

"You might have to slap *me*, Baegulgog. I did not do the right thing that day. But I learned. I learned the most difficult lesson I have ever learned."

"What is that?"

"I learned that, while there are always many wrong things to do, sometimes there is no right thing to do."

Baegulgog muttered some sort of harrumph. He was clearly unprepared to be confronted with an idealess axiom like that, particularly coming from an Inquisitor. "I respectfully disagree. Though perhaps I would feel differently, if fate were ever so cruel as to compel me to raise a tentacle against my own Queen, albeit for the good of all... perish the thought! But that is quite the closest I could ever get to really knowing for myself what you went through."

"It is as you say... perish the thought. Don't allow your imagination to menace you with any shadow of the guilt I know, which I would wish on no one. It is enough, and indeed far *more* than enough, that you have helped me to bear it."

"If indeed I have helped at all, then I am most glad of it. But I suppose now we should not dwell on such dreary matters any longer. You are not well. And I suspect you feel – as I do – that this is not a very fine place."

"I feel that way, yes. And you are right; we should speak no more of it."

They continued on. After some moments of reticence, Baegulgog drifted into conversation again. "I do wish there was more I could do to lighten your mood. I would sing you a song, except I am horribly tone-deaf, which is a very sad state of affairs indeed for a Sowür Canpattel. Still... perhaps this is an occasion to clear my own conscience. You'll remember, I have the rather peculiar habit of snacking?"

Snacking, she thought, and dearly wished he hadn't brought up anything that would remind her of food. Still, it was easier being reminded of the pit in her stomach than the one in her heart. "I remember."

"I shall tell you the tale of how I became acquainted with food, if you will agree to hear it – only be warned that it is yet another unpleasant memory."

"I am not sure a pleasant memory could be recalled in a place like this. But go ahead with your story, Baegulgog."

He began with an *'ahem'*, and gestured widely and lazily. "Picture me in the full glory of my cavalry days, tearing about the countryside on a great charger. Indeed, I had the finest steed in the entire 17th Division! His name was Charles... and if ever there was a finer, friendlier, more loyal and courageous horse, then all the annals of history are shockingly moot about it. We won many races together."

Parissah thought she could detect where the unpleasantness was coming in. She decided to set him up for it. "What ever became of Charles?"

"That is the rub of it, madam. You see, I was hopeless as a fighter. It didn't matter how fast I could charge into the teeth of the enemy, if every charge only ended in my immediate skewering. When they finally lost all patience with me... and I was discharged... poor old Charles was put out to pasture, too." Here he paused, rallying for a harder truth. "I... I was later told.. that they used him to make *soap*!"

Parissah blinked in her mask.

"It was my understanding that horses were traditionally used to make *glue*."

Baegulgog sniffled. "Yes. It is a fact that only makes the whole story that much more tragic!" He floated now in a very dejected slouch. "Anyway, I was grief-stricken. I didn't really know what to do to assuage myself, until one day I simply turned to eating. That, after all, is what most other sentient life forms do when they are quite miserable."

"There again, I think that is not right," Parissah corrected. "Most turn to *drinking*, if I am not mistaken." She wished she was being more sympathetic. But after all, she couldn't let him build a habit on false pretenses.

"Even so," Baegulgog sulked. "I fully mean to give up snacking, I hope you know. Perhaps it would be made easier, if I could but think of something constructive to do, in order to honor the memory of Charles the Horse."

"If I think of anything to that effect, I shall let you know," Parissah assured him. "Right now I am not much for thinking. But if it is any help, your expertise in the equine disciplines has not escaped my notice. Doubtless you are most discerning in these matters. So, if you say that Charles was a horse of great distinction, then I am very sure it is so."

"You are too kind, madam," Baegulgog whimpered. "It gives me great solace to know that someone beside myself will now remember Charles. Thank you for helping me to relieve my great sorrow!"

"Thank *you*, Baegulgog. You first helped me with mine."

In spite of what she told him, Parissah couldn't decide if she really felt better now, having aired some of her deepest pains. Her feelings were doing impossible acrobatics, even as her various other bodily systems were still up in a tumult. It was typical of the whole experience. Chaos within and all about – but still she had to keep sojourning on, inch by inch, with no discernable end. Finally, she resolved that she *would* be glad she shared her troubles with Baegulgog – as glad as she was able to be.

...But still, she had held something more back...

* * *

Hours passed, eventually. Day turned to night, but it did so without the invigorating promise that dusk usually brought. Night in Tophthera was not true night. It was dominated by dull ruddy light, hardly unlike the day. Even when the sun at last became completely dark, she felt no change – not even the slightest stirring of life in her hunting instincts. Ultimately, it didn't matter. There was still no prey to pounce on...

Parissah had come to the point where she mostly watched her feet, to be sure that they were still doing the right thing. Her head continued throbbing and all her muscles wanted to quit. She had waited far too long to address her wounds, and the fever wasn't going to let up now without a fight.

That particularly oppressive volcano that had given Baegulgog such a fright was quite firmly on their right now, and so they had made some measureable northward progress. But every step was so exhausting, it felt like trying to summit that horrible mount in a single bound. Yet somehow, she was still managing step after step... if her eyes did not deceive her.

Gaze fixed down, she despaired to make herself believe that Brittegonnen was actually getting closer, when suddenly she had to stop herself. She caught sight of tentacles in front of her just in time to avoid walking straight into the Field Marshal! He recoiled himself, and fluffed the hems of his uniform.

"You ought to rejoin me at the front, if you wish to gain passage to the Queen, as you claim," he told her, and turned briefly to Baegulgog as well, as if to include him. And without further chatter he spun and led the way.

Parissah was caught nearly breathless. Perhaps the city was close! Her eyes fluttered but she saw nothing except the same endless desolation. Still she hurried ahead, and it seemed suddenly less hard. She could not further excuse herself lagging behind the Marshal. Not after an ultimatum like that.

They were climbing up a rocky ridge now, and she marveled as she realized that it was proper stone she was shambling over. She had not perceived it, but she looked back and saw that they had been working gently uphill for some time, and the higher ground was here emerging out of the igneous ocean. It was tumbling under-foot and it was trying to subvert her, but she would have crawled on her belly to get over that ridge and see if there was anything on the other side of it...

And at last, she saw there was.

Reaching the top, she now overlooked the capitol of Tophthera – a jagged and ramshackle series of spikes that resembled the *Variglew* Bridge its apparent architectural theme of pure speedy abandon. It was at the bottom of a deep valley with a high ridge encircling – indeed it appeared to be at the heart of a huge crater, either left behind by a long-defunct molten pit that could have passed for an inland sea, or some sort of cosmic collision. There weren't any lights in the foreboding city of Brittegonnen. Not light *fixtures*, anyway. The lights she saw were ghoulish and moved about, and it was clear to her after a few moments of bewilderment that these tiny lights were the citizens of the city, passing to and fro.

It was a very alien feeling that came over her as she looked down into the valley. The only feeling she could attach to her impression of Brittegonnen… was *cold*…

"This way," the Field Marshal said, though it was beyond obvious. But before she went on, Parissah stole a look back. She gazed across that vast wilderness of despair, and though it was now behind her, she felt the disquieting aspect of looking ahead.

A final assault of metaphysical overtures drudged up in her weary mind. Her eyes were mesmerized one more time by the ever-rolling funnels of smoke and the gently wafting ash, even as her mind flipped through the invincible pages of her past. She wasn't sure what she really deserved. But all this felt like a start.

Circumventing Corsicarthal

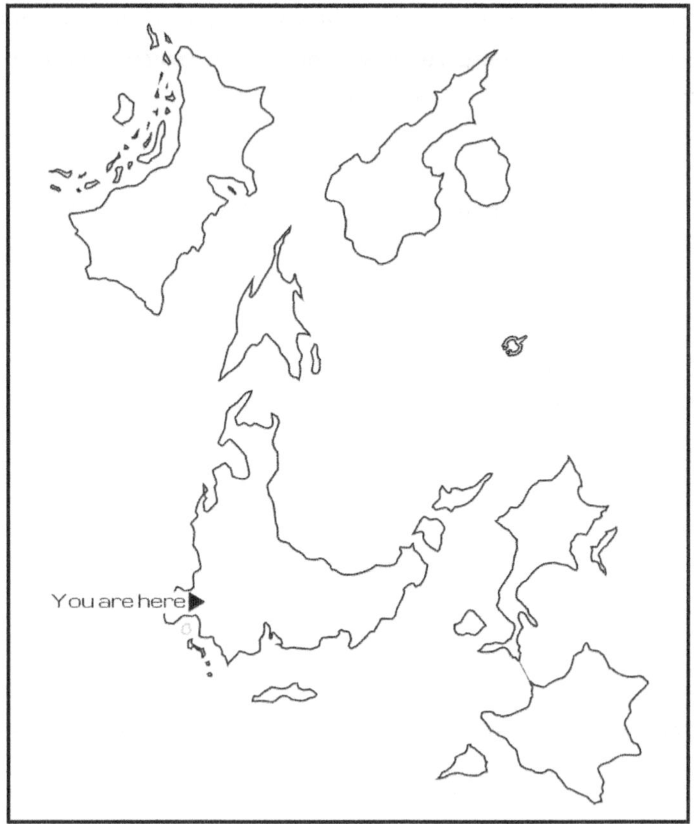

"Discovery is where you find it."

- Unattributed, *Compilation of Unhelpful Quotes and Witticisms*

They sailed all morning. It didn't take long to round The Wading Isle, and as they made west and gently north, the countenance of Mt. Corsicarthal loomed large from the main body of Jast-Madiir. The enormous notch in the mountain – the very one that nestled The Wading Isle, which had kept it safe from all hazardous weather since its founding – held off their starboard side almost unchanging for hours. The Isle may have been the culmination of refinement, but it was hardly more than a few stones' throw away from proper wilderness. There were sea-trees growing in the shadow of the mountain to the west, which had never been cleared. It was hard enough felling trees that grew in the ocean, but harder still when there were jagged rocks hidden all in their midst. Moreover, it was expensive. The Czars and Czarinas had never bothered to foot the bill, and simply sailed around the Snaggletooth Forest, as it was called. The old man, on the other hand, insisted on passing through it deliberately, and he set about trying to find the shallowest neck of the woods, to keep Corsicarthal in view, so they would not lose their bearings. It seemed to him a worthwhile route, just in case they were being followed.

Of course, they *were* being followed – by the unflappable birds, who seemed to greatly enjoy the change in scenery. With branches to dart between, and progress being so slow, they obviously found their pursuit of the fugitives more relaxing than ever, and they chirped down at them mockingly.

Audrey watched them, shaking her head. "You had some way of getting rid of those birds, didn't you?" she asked, turning to the old man.

"Aye," he said, and he sounded glum, not taking his eyes from Corsicarthal. "We'll be comin' to it when we comes around the mountain a bit more."

She wondered what he had in mind, but she wasn't going to prod him about it. Jek was of another mind; he wanted to know, and he got up gingerly from where he had been resting against the cabin. Audrey felt bad for him. He had put his body through the ringer the day before, and been remarkably courageous (compared to usual, anyway). But being on the water was still unfamiliar to him, and he seemed unable to get back to sleep, though they had encouraged him to, in the hopes of returning to a system of rotating watches. It probably didn't help that they were continuously bumping into stuff.

"What *is* your plan from here, old man?" Jek asked.

"Ye is nervous?" the old man goaded him. "Mayhaps a'cause sailin' for Roemnar means sailin' almost direct towards Despotopia from this here direction, eh?"

Roemnar, Audrey thought. Heron country. She had heard sailors talk about it a lot growing up. It was fairly and inconveniently in the middle of the Archipelago. Inconvenient, that is, in that Roemnar was pretty isolationist and didn't engage in a lot of commerce. This made it both a grave obstacle as well as an easily dramatized enigma for commercial sailors to gossip about, who had otherwise been most everywhere and seen most everything else in the island chain.

From what she knew about the place, and from a distance even seen for herself, there was no more thoroughly subverted land in Idriulthoronta. The Herons had come in ages past to the island, in the hopes of creating a wintering home for their race. The rest of the

Archipelago was by this time fairly well picked-over. Humans inhabited the tamer isles, and the Tophthaeran region was too barren and volcanically active to be of much interest. That left Roemnar – the most overgrown and perilous of all the islands in its day. The outskirts teemed with lethal dinosaurs. If you could win your way further into the island, you would find impenetrable jungle, and the unfriendly Dire Mantid tribes that lorded over it. But in those Imperial days, the might of the Herons was indomitable. They drove out all the Mantids and tamed even the biggest dinosaurs for house-pets. The tangled jungles were harder to subdue, but even those soon yielded to the will of the Herons, utterly leveled.

Audrey cast a longing glance south once again, as she tended to when she thought no one was watching. She still cherished a private wish to sail that way, beyond the reaches of every previous expedition, past all that was known, just to see what might be found. She couldn't make out the horizon for the body of oceanic forest in the way. All the more, she lamented that Roemnar was to be the final end of their Quest. For though it would be yet another new and exciting place she'd never been to, she couldn't help regretting that it was a land without wilderness...

She didn't yet know it, but she was about to get all the wilderness she could bargain for, as the old man was poised to reveal...

"You bet sailing toward Despotopia makes me nervous!" Jek said. "They came close enough to killing us once already, and we were nowhere near their country!"

"Well don't get yer crickets all in a jiminy," the old man told him. "Cause we ain't gonna sail toward Despotopia much longer. Ain't even gonna continue circumventing Corsicarthal a'fore long."

"*Circumnavigating*."

"*Potato, topato*! Point is, our sailin' is about through, I'm a'feared."

Now Audrey was perplexed. "How do you mean?"

The old man sighed. "Well, the way I figgers it, ain't no place we can go under an open sky where's we can be rid o' these birds. Only way to duck 'em is to go where they won't follow. And I knows a way through Corsicarthal – a *tunnel* – what tunnels right to the other side o' the mountain! I can't figger what power in all the world's drivin' the birds ta badger us so, but whate'er it be, can't very well be strong enough ta get 'em to follow us through an underground labyrinth. No little tweeter would dare, I warrant."

"I'm not sure I dare," Jek said.

"Oh, ye dares alright! Lest ye wants to sail me boat all the way round to the feet o' Mount Norvein on yer own!"

Jek fumed for a bit, apparently trying to find the best way to rationalize with the old man. "Look, avoiding the Despotopians and ditching the birds is one thing; hardly anything would make me gladder. But you're swapping one road that leads straight into the teeth of certain death for another!"

"How ye figger?"

He pointed to the mountain twice, as if to point straight through. "What's on the other side of Corsicarthal?"

The old man pondered, working his jaw. "Trees."

Jek laughed mirthlessly. "That's a very diplomatic way of putting it! 'Jungles' is more like it. You know what's in those jungles?!"

"I think I done already answered that: *TREES*!"

Jek was ticked. And no wonder; Audrey knew well enough that the old man was avoiding the mention of a pretty significant obstacle. But Jek held himself to a minor implosion, and spoke calmly again. "Trees... yes. But also, there's the matter of homicidal tribes of Dire Mantids. I'm sure you sailors get a lot of stories, so tell me: have you ever heard of anyone that went into the Mantid jungles and made it out alive?"

"Nope," the old man flatly admitted. "Don't need to. The way I knows through the mountain is safe! Don't go by no Mantids; empties out too far north."

"I suppose you've gone through it yourself?"

"Nay, but I done had the tunnel pointed out to me from the shoreline by another sailor who gone through it, and he made it out livin' enough!"

Jek mused for some seconds again. "Okay, so assuming we find the way, and we're able to take it without getting lost forever underground, and we don't get eaten alive by giant bugs... what then? We'll have to trek through some of the most thoroughly policed areas of Jast-Madiir to reach the coast, where I suppose we'll have to steal a boat, because *nobody* is going to be sailing for Roemnar. So even if we make it past all the cops, we're going to have to commit larceny just to get where we need to go!"

"Larseny?! Ain't gotta light nothin' on fire, lad!"

Jek facepalmed. "I'm just saying I don't want to steal a boat, and add another capital crime to my portfolio."

"Too bad," the old man explained. He went over to Jek and patted him on the shoulder. "Think outside yerself, boy. Ye think I likes to go around criminalizin' everywhere? I don't! But we gots to do what we gots to do to save the world. And we gots to accept a mighty high danger quotient too. Tis a Noble Quest we's on, and Noble Quests is required to be dangerous at every step. That's just how these things works. So man-up, and get ready to do some rock-climbin'!"

Jek said no more. He couldn't argue with the old man's logic, much less his illogic.

* * *

When they emerged from Snaggletooth Forest, it was a little after noon. Time progressed more quickly from there, as they did. The mountain still turned slowly, for it was very immense, but they were making strides that they could now easily discern. Audrey looked over the mountain repeatedly. She'd seen it in the past, from a great distance – it was tall enough to be visible from their lighthouse on a clear day, if you went up the light tower. And there were some ports they had sailed to on the north-west coast in her younger days where it could be espied. She found that the further they sailed around its western feet, the more unfriendly it got. Angry clouds had crashed up to its head on the north side and seemed to be working round and down to meet them. She fancied she heard distant thunder, but it was so subdued that even the gentle splooshing of the boat through the water made it hard to be sure she'd heard anything at all.

She was not the only one eyeing the mountain. The old man was watching and studying it unrelentingly, looking ever more nervous. He despaired to find the tunnel, she knew.

Jek also noticed the old man's disquiet. He looked like he was about to ask or say something, but Audrey shook her head at him, and he thought better of it. They had no trouble reaching an unspoken consensus that the old man should be left to his search, and not have any outside pressure put on him.

Finally, he stirred, and hesitantly pointed up a steep slope. "There it be," he said. They followed his point, and there was sort of, kind of an impression in the bare rock which might be an opening.

Jek's face drew back. "You're sure?"

"I'd rather not say."

* * *

Now they were out of the boat. It was somber business, unloading for what they knew was the last time. Even Jek was clearly moved, knowing he was looking his last on the little fishing vessel that had been his prison and his home. The old man was verging on a breakdown.

"Nay, no sense in tyin' it off, lad; why bother?!" His eyes were moist, and his lip was buckling. "We ain't gonna be comin' back this way. Leave her unbound, so's she can go sailin' on one last voyage into the horizon, if she feels like it."

Jek silently let the ropes slip from his hands.

A small eddy in the current lapped up and drew the boat gently out toward the sea. Audrey wondered if it was a natural phenomenon, or if the old man had used his magic to give his boat a nudge into its eternal journey. Overcome, he turned and plodded toward the mountain. "Best stop blubberin' and start climbin'," he said. Jek and Audrey exchanged a sorrowful look and followed him up.

They were trudging over mountain stone within feet of leaving the shore. It was a steep mountain, and very soon it engaged their arms as well as their legs. The sky gathered ever dimmer and greyer, and there was no longer any question about the thunder. But Audrey was still thinking about the dumb boat. They all were. She tried to force herself to be less sentimental.

She surprised herself when she soon succeeded. For at once she remembered something unsettling that she had been pushing away the whole time they were aboard. She remembered the *painting* – the one at the far end of the space under the cabin. The terrifyingly familiar, and yet unfamiliar, painting of the dark man resigned to his massive throne...

Audrey mined for resolution. She realized at once that she should ask the old man about the portrait she dreaded, while it was firmly on her mind. If it was a clue to her origins, she didn't want to forget it entirely. It had to be faced...

"Old man," she asked, "there's something I meant to ask you... about your boat. Who is the man in the painting? The man in that painting you had at the back of your cabin?"

The old man looked back at her, and his eyes were searching, and he at once took on a stern aspect as his beard wisped ghoulish in the wind. *"That be no man,"* he whispered. It was chilling, and it was cryptic, and he almost seemed to run his words together. Her resolution failed her, and she dared not ask any more...

She just looked over her shoulder, back at the boat, seeing that it had already coasted a good ways to the south. And it struck her, because it now pointed in the direction it was floating, and she even squinted as if to see if some phantasmal figure had manifested in the boat to steer it aright.

The old man apparently looked back at the same time. Because she heard him mutter something to himself from higher up the slope.

"Farewell to thee, me *Sadie*."

Audrey hurt for the old man. And watching it sail unrestrained for the southern sky, she envied the boat...

* * *

The rain poured and the wind howled as they clung to the mountainside. They had climbed for hours and were in the dregs of the evening, or so she guessed by the way things kept getting darker. It was cold and wet and slippery up there, suspended tenuously over hundreds and hundreds of feet of sheer jagged rock. This was not their most pleasant day. Audrey listened absently as Jek and the old man argued.

"Old man!" Jek called out over the weather. "Are we getting close to that blasted tunnel yet?"

"Heck if I knows, lad! Should be 'round here someplace!"

"Why is it every time I get above ground level, we get a rainstorm?!"

"Ye got me, sonny."

"I feel really light-headed for some reason! Does anyone else feel light-headed?!"

"A bit," Audrey admitted.

"Aye, me too," the old man grumbled.

"Well... why is that?!"

"I DON'T KNOW – BLAST IT, LAD! Ye think I done much mountain-climbing in me long sailin' career!?!"

Jek seemed to relent. But it was only a feint. "What do we do if we can't get to shelter before dark?!"

"Let go o' the mountain and lean backward, for all I cares!" the old man said, amidst thunderclaps.

It was bad like that for a good long time. But it eventually got worse. The little birds faired a bit better in the weather, being small and able to shelter themselves in crannies here and about. But they were getting agitated, and Audrey guessed that they had some idea what the three of them were up to, and were being driven to the point of desperation to keep them succeeding...

The birds were *very* agitated indeed, and emerged with a new stratagem. They started dive-bombing at Audrey and Jek and the old man!

First, they merely flew by their heads and tweeted infuriated tweets. But soon they grew more and more bold and determined, and resorted to pecking and clawing. A particularly pretty little blue bird just about took Jek's ear off.

Each of them faltered under the increasingly feral attacks from the songbirds, and was nearly plunged to a rocky death. They grunted and yelped and swatted and tried absolutely fruitlessly to repel the critters. Audrey was driven to an anger she'd never known before, and in the horrible surge of it she cried out:

"STOP IT, YOU BIRDS!"

It was not a particularly poetic culmination of fury.

...But... to her utter bewilderment... it worked!

The birds relented, and peeled away to the open air, darting about in a confusion. They tried to attack again, but couldn't seem to take more than a couple flaps in their direction, before banking off with indecision...

Jek and the old man looked dumbstruck at Audrey.

"Ye... ye got them to quit," the old man stammered. "How? How did ye do it?"

As if she would know. She *never* knew. "I don't know!"

"There be only one 'splanation I can think of..." the old man brooded. "Tis known that *Princesses* is natural-born-capable of cahootsin' with little tweety birds!"

Audrey looked at Jek. He had that same annoying terrified look on his face that he always did when anything about her past was inferred. She was reminded at once of Zeph Bronzegloom, and how she had really expected to find their visit interesting, but how he had virtually scuttled the whole experience from the start by making such a fuss about her. She didn't know why, but she hated to be fussed over, let alone made out to be important... which to her dismay was a more and more prevalent theme lately...

"I'm not a Princess!" she protested. "I'm not an important person! I don't want to be celebrated for solving any more door-riddles! I don't want to give any more impromptu speeches on random crates! I just want to be along for the ride! I just want to be a quiet tag-along and that's all! Don't make me into royalty! Don't make me a *leader*! Please just *don't*!"

She huffed in the rain, trying to steal back her breath in the damp cold. The other two were staggered for a bit, which only made her feel worse. But finally, the old man grinned, and regained himself.

"Not to worry, las. I's still the one in charge o' this Quest, as far as I's concerned. But if ye got some sort o' power o'er the tweeters, then for Dianodes' sake, use it! Stop 'em peckin' our eyes out! I'd be sore appreciative if ye'd do that much."

Now she did feel bad. "I mean, don't get me wrong," she said sheepishly. "Don't think I don't want to contribute. Just don't make a big deal out of it, okay?"

"Shore thing, lass," the old man laughed, and strained to go on climbing. But Jek just stared. It was a frightened, alienating stare... like he didn't know who she was all over again. And after they had shared that moment while they fought the Despotopians... that moment where she felt so sure they had understood each other on a deeper level. It made her ache to see him look at her as a stranger again...

* * *

Gloom and cold became increasingly dominant as they climbed higher and higher. Holding fast to the slope didn't exactly give them a very availing vantage point with which to spy out any caves or tunnels. Again and again the birds mustered and marshaled against them, and again and again she shouted them away. Rocks tumbled in their grasp, the clamor in the air made the whole mountain tremble, and the rain slicked everything. The situation appeared critical. She winced as a stream of water from outcroppings above caught her in the face, and she coughed reflexively, leaning her head on the stone, water still dripping from her nose.

But she heard the old man call out. "I sees somethin'! I sees somethin'!" She blinked to drive out the water and looked up, and saw him pointing to their left. There she saw muddied stone; almost a ruddy beard on the side of the slope, and at the top of the beard there was a mouth! It was a clear opening in the rock, and a big one! They were not a hundred yards away! Without further dialogue they made for it as quick as they dared.

The old man clamored into the cave, and helped Audrey up over the lip. Soon they both hauled in Jek, who had been lowest on the mountain. They collapsed and heaved air for a while, getting some well-deserved rest, while the birds shot around angrily outside the tunnel. It was as the old man had wagered – the birds appeared quite unwilling to pass the threshold! At last, they appeared to have given the horrible little spys the slip! The three of them might've enjoyed some taunting at the birds' expense, but they were too exhausted to bother about it. And it was *cold*, so they all huddled belaboredly against a wall. Audrey remained cold, but soon was only faintly aware of it. She heard the breathing of the other two relax, and before she knew it, she also passed into sleep...

* * *

She woke with a horrible shiver. Her whole body quaked. In the next moment she was startled again by a nearly deafening snore from the old man, who was hunched awkwardly against the stone, looking none-to-comfortable, but sound asleep. Jek was already on his feet again. He was looking deep into the tunnel, which fell off at a steep angle only a dozen feet or so from the opening. Audrey didn't want to move. But then again, she didn't want to take another ballistic snore in her ear, so she got up and walked over to Jek. She rested a hand on his shoulder, hoping he wasn't still feeling horribly unsure about her. He did give her a faint smile that reassured her a bit, but he was quickly back to brooding. Though it was clear it had nothing to do with her. It was about the *cave*.

It was an ominous sight. Not totally black as she'd expected. Rather, there was a wavering red light far down, down into the mountain – and the source of this light couldn't be seen from where they stood. Her instinctive guess was lava, which wasn't exactly hopeful. But there were other odd signs to interpret. A pair of metal rails spaced by wooden planks ran the length of the tunnel, all the way to the opening. She hadn't noticed it as they came in... but at that point she wouldn't have been likely to notice anything, short of a hungry rex staring them in the face.

"What are you thinking?" she asked Jek.

"I've seen rails like that before," he said. "It's like train tracks. Northern Jast-Madiir has rail trains it uses to freight people and goods around."

"I've heard of them. What do you suppose they're doing here?"

"It's a mining trick. The deeper you dig, the further you have to cart the dirt and rock out of your way. Whoever dug this hole must've had a mining cart... and a big one, if the rails are any hint."

They *were* big rails, and far apart...

"You think that's torch light down there?" she asked, in light of the new facts. "You think the miners might still be here?"

"I don't know. I kind of hope not."

"I thought it might be lava."

"That sounds bad too."

"It be called 'magma' when it's still under the ground," the old man said, coming astride them.

"Good to know," Jek said. "Your friend the sailor mention anything about magma or torch lights when he told you about his tunnel?"

"Nope, not neither one. But whichever it be, at least it gives off heat. I's cold down to me inmost bowels. Let's get down there and out o' this here draught!"

Audrey heartily agreed. The heat was worth the foreboding... and anyway, there was no turning back...

* * *

The downward march was surprisingly tiring. Audrey considered suggesting that they simply roll down the slope, but though she couldn't put her finger on an exact reason against it, still something told her it was probably a bad idea.

Yowling echoes bit at their backs. The wind was snapping now at the entrance, and they could hear it ever more hauntingly behind them. The air was increasingly warm, which was nice, and the exercise did much to bring them back up to a reasonable temperature. But their boots still squished and squalled with rainwater. Audrey couldn't much feel her feet. This made the trek harder.

Also they were far from stealthy. It was quite impossible to step quietly down into the hollow, which carried rumor of every small squirm for miles. Jek had swung his musket around from his back, marching with it from the start. Audrey did likewise, and the old man had his sword ready. They had no idea what they were getting into. Between them, no one knew of any mining operations on Mt. Corsicarthal. Not that they tended to know much of anything between them. Still it boded ill. And it was clear that anything waiting for them at the end of the path would have plenty of warning...

Eventually the air got downright stifling. Audrey began to suspect the lava again. There wasn't any sign of Human presence, present or past, no matter how far they went. Nothing besides the endless rails.

The only other thing they began to find were some very odd plants, snaking along the walls and the ceiling... first in patches, and then in ever-greater tangles, until the cave was simply covered in them. They were plants with a very unpleasant look. They were wilty and browned, and came to a kind of bisected flowering head with spiny bristles at the outer edges, roughly twenty inches across. It was eerily mouth-like.

Audrey wasn't the only one to notice.

"I don't like these plants one bit," Jek said.

"They's 'venetian flytraps,' I warrant," the old man explained. "I heard tell o' them. They catches flys in they's mouths... that's how they gets most o' their vitality."

"Why should a plant eat flies?"

"Heck if I knows, but they do. The Creators made some mighty zany things in their day, and these is one o' them."

Audrey decided to test the old man's information. She reached out to a plant, setting a finger right on the maroon-colored spongey pad of its 'mouth'. After a moment of pressure, sure enough, the hemispheres closed, slowly but firmly, and Audrey withdrew her finger with a start. *Zany, alright.*

* * *

The tunnel finally leveled out. By now they were hot, and mostly dry, and the echo was less concentrated. But there was still a lateral bend in the tunnel that prevented them seeing where the now-intense red light was coming from. They could faintly discern a kind of grinding sound in the distance. Audrey noted that they were all walking with slower and smaller steps the closer they got to the leftward turn. None of them was in a hurry to find out what lay ahead.

They found themselves bunched up close to the wall, though not against it; for the walls were still coated in flytraps. Audrey waited, expecting someone in the group to peak around the corner. Neither of the others did...

Finally, she took it upon herself. However much she despised to lead, she ultimately wasn't afraid to...

"Wait," Jek motioned, and she stopped even as she took her first step. "I'll check it out. I need to do more brave stuff."

"Aye," the old man nodded.

Jek shut his eyes hard, apparently marshalling bravery, and then leapt out awkwardly with his musket into the open, staring ever more wide-eyed around the bend.

"*Dianodes*," he muttered, the musket going slack in his grasp.

Seeing he didn't die instantaneously, the other two walked out for their own look. Immediately around the corner, the tunnel opened into a colossal antechamber, where the track split into several shoots, each with a mining cart the size of a stegosaurus docked against the walls. The antechamber naturally led into the main chamber, which looked large enough to hold a whole other mountain inside. Audrey couldn't even begin to take stock of all the features and pieces of equipment and torches and forking paths on level after level of the hollow. The sheer size of the room alone was too much to process...

As if they could have been more surprised, the walls in their midst immediately started flailing and snaking and winding. The 'venetian' flytraps sprang to life! They were not rooted to the walls as they had appeared to be, and were freely and speedily encroaching on Audrey, Jek and the old man from all sides in countless droves.

"Intruders!" the plants exclaimed, in overlapping voices, accusing them shrilly.

Jek shook his musket at them, and the old man flashed his sword, and Audrey aimed down her sight, though she hadn't a clue which one of them to shoot, or even where one plant ended and the next began...

"Stop!" Jek warned them all, and they did slow to a stop, but by then the three of them were quite encircled. "We do not wish to fight you!"

After a few moments' hesitation, one of the infinite plants spoke in answer. "I don't doubt it."

Though the three Humans were beset with the distinct fear of death, the mood immediately brightened in the silence of the stalemate that followed. These beastly plants were apparently willing – and *able* – to communicate. That meant there was at least a morsel of hope...

"Audrey, quick, talk to them!" Jek said, still holding his weapon out, turning back and forth, to be sure they weren't flanked.

"*Me*?! What am I supposed to say to a bunch of plants?"

"I don't know! Negotiate!"

"Better do what he say, lass," the old man chipped in. "This ain't no time to shy away from yer public speakin' acumen!"

"I'm not going to talk to plants! I don't have any experience!"

"Ye think *we* gots experience?!"

"Well, we wish somebody would start talking to us," a plant said.

Jek tried to get a feel for the situation. Slowly he set his musket on the ground. "We lay down our arms," he said, putting his hands in the air.

"We do?" the old man protested.

There was a narrow parting in the great legion of flytraps, and a lone flytrap crawled to the front of the encircling battalion. He looked eyelessly at a flytrap to his left, who returned the look. "They're onto us, sir," the second flytrap addressed the lone flytrap. "Should we kill them?"

"Are you joking?" asked 'Sir Flytrap'. "They have soldier weapons. What if other soldiers come looking for them? We can't kill them! That would tend to render transparent the sinister overtures of our secret plans."

The other flytrap stole a glance at their Human captives, and quickly turned back to his superior. "Should we even be discussing the existence of our secret plans, given the present company, sir?"

"Ah! No indeed! Good thinking."

"Beg yer pardon, me photo-syncretic little friends," the old man butted in, "but now we's the ones what feel left out o' the parley. What is it ye's on about?"

"My apologies, good sir," answered Sir Flytrap, in a surprisingly groveling fashion. "Do not let us further consternate you with the private mulling of secret plans, which need not be considered by you whatsoever, since we do not in truth have any such plans. Particularly not that would interest you in the least, let alone give your nations cause for alarm."

"Yes," agreed the second flytrap. "And may I just add that we *definitely* do not harbor an imperative desire for the complete eradication of the surface world."

"Very smooth, lieutenant," nodded Sir Flytrap chummily.

"Thank you, sir," said the second, apparently *Lieutenant*, Flytrap.

There was a beat of silence, where the words of the strange sentient subterranean succulents hung in the air. And they all seemed anxious, to see how their uninvited guests would react...

"Well, I be mighty glad to hear it!" the old man said, grinning with bared bad teeth. "What with all this muster, and the sheer scale o' yer hidden constructions, I hope ye can excuse us gettin' the wrong idea, and thinkin' ye was plannin' mischief."

Sir Flytrap exchanged a knowing look with Lieutenant Flytrap, and generated a cackling round of laughter that could have passed as megalomaniacal, in the right context. "Oh, certainly we can excuse it!" And he succumbed to mirth once more. "And yet, despite all appearances, if we had even the *slightest* of military intentions for meticulously constructing this unimaginably vast network of tunnels, leading to various strategic points all across the islands of the Archipelago – and about which the nations of the world are *hopelessly* unaware – then we would certainly have told you at once."

Notwithstanding his very friendly demeanor, Sir Flytrap quickly began to seem like a lot to keep up with at times. Jek appeared to think so as well. "Okay," he nodded with pursed lips.

Now the old man began laughing hardily. And the flytraps returned the laughter, if rather tentatively. "I don't know *what* we was thinkin'! Can ye imagine?! A secret army o' Enlightened Venetian Flytraps... seizin' control o' the world by strikin' from below! *Har ha-har*! What a redicalous idear!"

"And horribly unoriginal," Jek added, with a still-nervous giggle.

"Ha-ha ha-ha," Sir Flytrap laughed, more robotically than before. "Oh my, I don't know about all of that. In fact, I might contend, rather, that it is a *very* original plan, deeply rooted in reserves of subtle genius the likes of which mere mortals could not possibly conceive. Ha! But that is pure conjecture on my part, since we are talking about plans that obviously do not exist, because no one has ever so much as dreamt them, least of all our Dread Master... if indeed we *have* a Dread Master... not in the sense that you think I admitted as much, because I didn't... since we don't."

"*Har-Har*!" the old man continued, very joyful indeed –the unexpected pleasure of not being killed still whelming his brain. "I don't got a clue what ye little plant fellers is talkin' about, but ye didn't murder us straight off, so's I'd say ye are mighty fine folk! Mighty, mighty fine!" And he bent down and patted Sir Flytrap on the head.

"I thank you roundly for your patronizing compliments," Sir Flytrap responded.

"You are welcome, Sir Flytrap," Audrey said, trying to climb aboard the diplomatic party, now that it seemed to be sailing steadily.

"Oh! Forgive my bad manners. You needn't address me as 'Sir Flytrap'. My name is Aaouuaaiooaauuo. Feel at liberty to call me thus at any time."

"...Aye..." the old man said. "But maybe we oughts to stick to callin' ye 'Sir Flytrap'... fer short. And permit me to introduce ourselves... this here's Jek an' Audrey."

"It is a pleasure to meet you all," Sir Flytrap nodded to each of them. "You'd be surprised how few visitors we get here in our undiscovered labyrinth. But O! Pray tell, what brings you here? We are most anxious to learn that. I hope and trust it has nothing at all to do with counter-intelligence and government-sanctioned investigations into suspected subterranean paramilitary activity?"

"Nah," the old man waved dismissively. "We ain't got no part in that sort o' fancy business. We's just tryin' to get to the other side o' the mountain, is all."

"*Wonderful*," Sir Flytrap said, his mouthy face curled up in a way that almost appeared deviously pleased. "In that case... right this way..."

And where Sir Flytrap led, a path for them opened in the sea of other plants. Audrey was very taken back by the whole thing. She had known about and even encountered many Enlightened species... Dire Herons and Dire Mantids and Jackal People, and even the Phage. But she had never heard of Enlightened plants before! As far as she could tell, they were the first Humans to make contact with such creatures...

And the more she thought about it, the more she liked it. Maybe she'd never get to sail south... though she could still hope against hope for it. But she was delighted to be shown there were still many undiscovered wonders of the world, even within its old and well-traveled borders and bounds...

*   *   *

Sir Flytrap led them through the main chamber. It was a guided tour far beyond any Jek could have imagined. He led them past a dozen or so armories, stocked absolutely full of a vast array of exotic military equipment they had no plans of ever using. And everywhere about, flytraps by the hundreds drilled in rank and file, practicing for non-martial purposes, the exact nature of which Sir Flytrap had temporarily forgotten. Each of them crawled on approximately four appendages that branched from their lateral stem-body; these were spindly limbs like insect legs, but with dry and brownish leaves here and there. The flytraps were all skilled and orderly, marching up and down the floor and even across the vaulted thousand-story walls. It was quite grand.

Apparently knowing well where he was going, Sir Flytrap brought them to a tunnel quite like the one they had entered in, when they finally reached the far wall of the incredibly enormous chamber. He was only too eager, by all appearances, to help them reach the other side of the mountain. It was a turn of fate that was marvelous in its convenience.

Still, nagging reservation kept brushing around in the back of Jek's mind. He couldn't put his finger on it, but something about these Venetian Flytraps struck him as mildly suspicious – despite their repeated (and sometimes unsolicited) insistence that they were not acting suspicious at all. Jek tried his best to be satisfied with that. The adventure so far had shown him that he often fretted in vain – that he needed to be less defeatist, if he could...

It wasn't easy. True enough, he had begun to find tiny granules of daring within himself. Even so, he still had some considerable doubts... chiefly his capacity to become a true man of action. But what kept troubling him most – and more and more consistently – was not knowing who his *wife* really was. She made pretense of not knowing herself, but he worried whether he could really believe it. Things just couldn't seem to stop happening that made him bode ever stranger things about her...

For a while he was sure she was a pirate; a hypothesis he now felt very stupid about. Because more recently, the portents were suggesting she was *royalty* – even a Princess! Jek didn't find that improved his plight much. If she had been a pirate, he certainly would have been distressed to share his life with an unscrupulous character. But if she was a *Princess*... then how in Heck could he presume to have anything to do with her at all?

He thought about the giant zenethyst he was still smuggling around. In his mind it had gone from being illicit booty to a royal heirloom overnight. But it was all still merely conjecture. Nothing had been proved. He was desperate to know the truth about it, and about her. But equally desperately he feared what he might learn, and how it would affect their relationship...

Walking a few paces behind in the dim and dismal cavern, wrestling again with a foreboding that peril of some sort lay close ahead, Jek looked at Audrey with a sick feeling. Like any married man, he had always hoped he and his wife would come to know each other well... and even, in time... perhaps... to love each other. But the road to Roemnar was still long and deadly dangerous, and all other concerns aside, he worried they simply wouldn't live long enough to know such fondness and devotion...

Jek looked away, quite angry with himself. He hadn't shook his defeatism yet...

* * *

They reached a fork in the road, and to their surprise, Sir Flytrap and his lieutenant came to a halt. Jek felt a quick pang of doubt. Perhaps even the founders of this underground maze could get lost in it! But Sir Flytrap turned to address them.

"Before we continue," he began, "I wish to express with all explicit clarity how incredibly much I find it amicable to help you reach the north side of Mt. Corsicarthal. *However...*" he paused, and grinned, "I wonder if first you might help *me* with a very minor errand. You see, we are not altogether alone down here in the depths. We have... a *neighbor...* of sorts. She lies in this direction..." and he indicated the right fork in the path. "We came across her while attempting to tunnel that way. We have tried to reason with her, but she has been quite rudely adamant that we not conduct our work in her midst. This has led to some trifling disagreements that I fear we have yet to resolve. So, my proposition is this. If you could negotiate with our neighbor on our behalf, and get her to stop pestering us, I will lead you the rest of the way through the mountain. Does this arrangement agree with you?"

Jek's misgivings immediately prevailed upon him. He sensed some kind of misdirection here. He was sure the others felt it too...

"Sounds terrifical!" the old man announced jovially. "We be mighty glad to help ye out!"

"I am so pleased you feel that way," Sir Flytrap said. "You may continue on to your right at your own peril... by which, I of course mean, your own *discretion*."

"A'course," the old man agreed, and already he was leading the way down and to the right, even as Jek mounted the unnoticed protest of shaking his head.

"Won't you be coming with us, Sir Flytrap?" Audrey called back to him.

"Ha-ha! No way! But I will do this much for you: I promise to remain here with my lieutenant for a few hours, in case you are able to make it back."

"*Able*?" Jek repeated. "Why wouldn't we be able?"

"You'll see!" Sir Flytrap explained, and as they continued on without him, his voice already began to echo after them. "Best of luck to you!"

"I don't like this," Jek told his companions, low enough not to be heard by the flytraps.

"What's to like?" the old man asked. "What could be more simpler than resolvin' a teensy residential kerfuffle? Least we can do for the nice little fellers." Jek harrumphed. The old man took notice. "Ye can always stay behind, I s'pose; we can take care o' this without ye, I warrant."

Jek thought about it for a moment. "No, that wouldn't be good Questing form," he admitted. "I don't like walking blindly into things, but I'll do it."

And so he did.

* * *

Aaouuaaiooaauuo snickered maliciously to himself, listening to the Humans traipse loudly and stupidly to their doom.

"I thought you didn't want to kill them, sir," his lieutenant, Ooiiaiiaaooi, said.

"But don't you see, lieutenant, it's perfect! This way, they don't live to breathe a word about what they saw here, and even if other soldiers come after them to investigate their disappearance, we can blame *her*, and not even have to lie! Not that we aren't devilishly good liars – we learned that much today..."

"What if they actually succeed, sir?"

"In reasoning with *that* creature? I doubt it strongly! But even if they do, then all the better for us! We'll simply show them the way out, as I promised, and then we'll have their trust through-and-through! It can't fail!"

"But don't you think they'll trust you a little less, when they see who you sent them to negotiate with?"

At this, Aaouuaaiooaauuo became quite impatient with his lieutenant. "Go back to the principal fortification! I'm tired of looking at that face of yours!"

"My face looks exactly like yours, sir."

"Don't remind me."

* * *

The red light of the caves was actually growing brighter the further they wandered from the main chamber where most of the torches had been, and it was now *oppressively* hot. The track down this stretch of tunnel was torn to shrapnel and there were deep gashes in rows three across on the floors, the walls, and the ceiling. There were eddies of dried leaves swirling around in the hot air currents, too...

"Am I the only one seeing all this?" Jek asked.

"Seein' what?" the old man huffed.

"Total devastation, by the looks of it."

"Tis just what neighborly disputes usually comes out lookin' like," the old man explained.

Jek was unconvinced. He kept looking at the clefts in the stone. They were just about like claw-marks... if claws could be that big, and cut through solid granite. There were black marks on the bare rock as well in places, like it had been scorched.

But even as he was scanning the floor, he realized suddenly that his were the only footsteps he heard. He stopped too, and joined the other two in simply staring straight ahead. They had reached the end of the downward-sloping tunnel already, and it opened out to a vast, natural cave, wherein there flowed a river of magma! Other frightening features included those pointy rocks that hang from the ceiling and stick out of the ground, and a sulfuric odor that was disorienting in potency. It was an infernal place. Jek new instinctively that this was the den of the 'neighbor'...

"Best see if anyone's home," the old man said, and plodded right out of the tunnel into open space. Jek didn't know where he got his bravado... or whatever it was that made him oblivious to the terrors ahead. Audrey followed. Jek just blanched and followed suit.

Coming into the cave, it was some comfort at least that the bubbling and churning sound of the flowing molten rock was strong enough that they couldn't hear their own steps. Jek didn't feel distinctly that they were being watched. Yet he *did* feel there was something at hand which could watch them, if it had known to. Jek thought that that was an unusually specific feeling to have...

They walked as close as they dared, and the heat permitted them, to the river's edge. They were all squinting, trying to discern a far wall of the cave. Not one of them suspected they had already passed what they were really looking for.

Suddenly, there was a deep and prolonged rumbling sound. Jek's flight reflex was immediately kindled, but he couldn't reach a decision where to run and so flailed in place for a few seconds. The rumbling might have been from unseen volcanic activity. But it sounded terrifyingly like a *snore*. A snore, that is, as it might have sounded to an ant as it crawled around in the mouth of a slumbering grizzly bear...

They all turned around slowly toward the tunnel. And there – almost right next to where they had come in – was a vast living mound. It had appeared to them only as bare rock as they passed it, but now, as the enormous creature slowly exhaled thousands of cubic feet of air, they could make out the shape of a dragon!

Jek was more than a little inspired by the sight. He'd never even seen a tyrannosaurus before (for which he was immeasurably grateful), but he knew immediately that this was much larger than that. He wanted to get extremely far away, but he found he forgot how to move, or even what moving was. It hardly mattered, for in the next moment, the colossus stretched out in a fit of restlessness, and its tail conveniently sprawled across the entrance to the tunnel. They couldn't possibly get out without climbing right over!

"Upon me word," the old man said, in a voice that was not nearly hushed enough, though it was but a whisper.

"That's a dragon," Audrey said, even more carelessly than the old man.

"Aye, and more than just *a* dragon, I warrant! Could it be possible?"

"What is it?"

"I think this here dragon might be *Faucette*, her own self! By tunder! She ain't been spotted since the Idriulthorontan Archipelago done was founded. But that's her alright! Ye can tell, on account o' the distinguishin' marks what everyone knows about! This here dragon's got 'em all!"

"Are we really talking right now?" Jek interjected. "How could we be talking at a time like this?"

"Who is Faucette?" Audrey asked.

"Ah, another tale what ye don't know, eh?" the old man said, stroking his beard with a whimsical look in his eye. "Best to tell ye, I warrant, so's ye gets some idea o' the historical import o' this discovery we done made."

"We are going to die," Jek whispered gravely.

"It all started some time like a zillion years ago," the old man began, and he went on to tell the entire story of the founding of the Idriulthorontan Archipelago. It went more or less like this:

> There was once a nation on the coast of the continent, called Gilgamphonor. Following a significant island discovery west of her realm, Queen Sharaasi IV sent out a decree to commission commoners to sail themselves over to and settle the new territory. This she did with great haste, to secure the island from other powers in the region who might try to lay claim to it. She deemed it simple enough for great masses of inexperienced peasants to sail themselves in the right direction, hoping to avoid tying up significant naval resources in the settlement effort.
>
> One man gladly volunteered to helm a voyage of these self-guided amateur colonists, whose name was Argon Moteph. He did this because a past decree had already conscripted him to become a rutabaga farmer, which he had since tired of, because the climate made it quite impossible to grow rutabagas in the realm.
>
> With great excitement and enthusiasm, Moteph handled much of the preparation for the voyage himself, most importantly including the procurement of his navigational equipment. He went to the market one day in search of a compass, but he encountered first a small sundial, and mistook it for his quarry. He set this critical device in his cabin where he could read it by the light of the lamp…
>
> On the day the voyage began, Moteph's crew noted that all of the other boats of colonists were headed in a significantly different direction than they were. Moteph laughed at the fools, who clearly did not know how to read a compass. And so, as the other ships departed in the proper westerly direction, Moteph sailed south-east…
>
> After many days of holding this course (full many days longer than they expected), they came to the island now known as Maenea, luckily missing the jet streams that blow ships approaching from the north toward Despotopia's Meatgrinder Bay. After weeks of finding no evidence of prior colonization, and no one else showing up behind them, the crew finally realized that they had come to an entirely *new* island!
>
> Naturally, 'Captain' Argon was eager to be hailed as a great man of discovery, and so set sail to return to the mainland. This was unsuccessful, and Moteph's ship instead put in at Roemnar, *another* uncharted island! So he struck out in another direction and wound up on the south side of Despotopia – yet *another* uncharted island! It was really quite a boon, but Moteph began to grow very weary of making history… and anyway it

> would be rather in vain if he could never find a way back whence he came. Fortunately for Moteph, before he could sink too deeply into despair, his crew was attacked by *Faucette*, a flighted dragon! Faucette was mature and strong, but retained some higher thinking; she recognized quickly that the band of 'explorers' were mere impoverished peasants – with no real treasure to be had – and so relented her assault before too many grievous injuries were imparted. Moteph, having nothing really to lose, appealed to the dragon, offering her riches if she were able to guide them back to the mainland. This offer she accepted with great enthusiasm. With the help of Faucette, Argon and his crew returned at last to their home country...
>
> Dubbed a hero of the realm by the queen, Argon Moteph was allowed to name the Archipelago he had uncovered. He named it in honor of his trusty pet Emu, Idriulthorontus Maximillius.
>
> Moteph was also awarded vast wealth. He fancied somewhat the notion of keeping the money and being extremely rich, but he fancied even more the notion of not being dead, so he bequeathed his fortune to Faucette.

"...And when she got her loot, she done vamoosed, and weren't never seen or heard of again, even in all the years since Idriulthoronta been settled," the old man concluded. "We's maybe the first Humans what laid eyes on her in millenniums!" And he slapped his old knee. "If that don't beat all!"

Jek sat down, woozy. It was a story long in the telling, and the old man had told it ever more boisterously as he went along, and by now Jek was faint with suspense, having expected each new exclamation from the old man to wake the slumbering titan in their midst.

"Jek, you look pale!" Audrey said, coming to his aid.

"I'm just a little tired out, I guess," Jek said softly. "No one else in the group really seems to appreciate danger. It can be a lot, worrying for three."

The old man was immediately huffy. "Ye's frettin' for nothin'... as per usual! If Sir Flytrap sent us down here to settle some dispute he got with Faucette... why, that oughta be reason enough to be sure we can do it! Maybe we done just met that feller, but I feels I knows him, just as if I'd planted him meself in me own little garden. He wouldn't steer us wrong! Ain't no way!"

"Maybe you're right," Jek said, recovering some courage. "Either way, we're going to have to find out. There's no way out of here, except back the way we came... unless we could somehow cross that molten river... and who knows where we'd end up? But there's no way to go back through the tunnel, either... unless we wake the dragon. Her tail is blocking the exit!"

The old man looked, and when he saw they were cut off, he laughed. "How do ye like that?! Well, ain't no question about what's to be done, then. But I warn ye, this ain't gonna be easy."

"*Pshaw*," Jek agreed.

"I don't mean the negotiations, neither. Nay, the firstest hardest part is gettin' the dragon awake." He stood thoughtfully for a moment, and then cupped his hands, and shouted. "Hey Faucette, ye blunderin' oaf!!! Get ye over here and eat us!!!"

Jek waved his hands emphatically for the old man to can it, but he heedlessly shouted the whole taunt. And, to Jek's amazement, the great dragon went on slumbering...

"See? Done told ye there weren't cause to fret. T'woulda took me singin' her life story at the top o' me lungs, with a whole orchestration accompaniment, a'fore she'd given much thought to wakin'!"

"I didn't know dragons were such sound sleepers," Audrey said.

"Ain't all of 'em what sleeps like this. But this here dragon's been restin' by her treasure for ages! She's in the 'golden slumber,' as they says. Takes real stimuli for to get her awoked."

"Where *is* her treasure?" Jek asked, even as he marveled at their situation. He'd certainly never anticipated trying to figure out how he could wake up a dragon...

"She gots it stashed in an alcove in the wall, what she can sleep up against, so's to keep it hid and inaccessible, I wager. A shame too, a'cause takin' from her treasure would be the easiest way to get her woked up. Although, t'would be the most dangerous way too, I warrant."

"Do you have any other ideas?" Jek asked.

The old man thought again for a spell. Finally, he took up a big rock, and flung it into the dragon's face...

It was a good sound hit, and sure enough, Faucette was immediately roused from her deep sleep with a concussive snarl and the hiss of steam. As she shifted, her whole body emanated sounds like the felling of immense trees – her ancient bones and thick scales all in a protest to come unset. There came a smolder and smoke at her belly, which was gorged with fire, ready to be spat in an incendiary stream at whatever fowl nemesis had struck her. Faucette's bright and keen eyes burst open with their own radiance, and in one flick she had the three of them in her crosshairs.

Another jet of vapor shot from her nostrils into the air, and it rolled at the ceiling in a fury. She stared at them with disarming accusation for several seconds. Jek did all he could to mentally prepare himself to die...

Then... her eyes glossed... blinked... and sagged...

She tossed her head. Her maw opened wide and slack – like the disjointing of a snake's mouth as it engulfed prey bigger than its head! And there was a great and deafening beastly sound, and a stench to go with it – the stench, Jek intuited, of a hundred rotting flytrap carcasses...

But this was not a roar.

It was a *yawn*.

And the next moment, she fell flat on the ground, asleep again.

The old man wiped the terrified look from his face and scowled. He threw another rock that struck her right on the flank of her snout.

"I'm awake! I'm awake!" Faucette rumbled as she sprung up again. And she glowered at them, looking twice as cross as before. "In Heck's name!!! Pray tell what you mean by disturbing *me*?!" The cavern echoed and trembled with her anger.

"Beggin' yer pardon, madam," the old man began... and Jek was relieved that he was beginning to act a bit more courteously, now that the dragon was really and definitely awake. "We comes as emissaries of his High Flytrapness, sir Aaooeeoo."

"I think he said his name was Aiiuuooaeeoi," Audrey corrected.

"Aaouuaaiooaauuo!" Jek exclaimed. "His name is Aaouuaaiooaauuo!"

Faucette's wings brushed out in a wide and thunderous flash, and the whelming wind knocked them all down. "Shall I endure such nonsense!? Come to a point, or die instantly!"

"The flytraps, madam Faucette! The flytraps done sent us to parley with ye!"

The knuckles of Faucette's wings struck the ground and shook the earth, dislodging many stalactites, but she seemed to return merely to a simmer. "Oh, those little *pests*! How they have filled my days with restlessness! Ever they drill and drill and drill their silly holes, and they shake the mountain with their fowl contraptions, and break stalactites off the ceiling that strike me in my sleep! And *now*... now they come bothering me with witless envoys! Whatever is to be the end of it? Must I slay them all just to get a good night's rest?!"

"Nay, ye mustn't! Peace, madam! The answer be peace!"

Now she *did* roar, and fire illumined the cave, so that afterward they staggered in the dark. "*Peace* is what I had *before* they came to my sanctum! I would not endure them at all, except that I cannot *reach* them! Their burrows are too small." She snaked her head around, and tested the air with a tongue-flick. "I wonder why I endure the three of you, even now." Faucette growled, and it sounded a hungry growl. "You know and respect my name, and that is some redemption." She grinned in a universally devious way. "What more? What have the flytraps sent along with you, in token of their goodwill? With what would you ransom yourselves, let alone pay for the disturbances of your naughty little friends, both past and future?"

Jek knew at once the answer. He didn't want to part with it. He hadn't even wanted to let on he knew about it. But the sense of predestination he felt was too clear to question for even a second. He reached into the pocket of his dirty frock coat, and held out the dragon's ransom...

"We offer this," Jek said solemnly. And he watched as Faucette's eyes bulged. She was incredulous. Audrey and the old man were stunned, too. Their eyes looked almost as big as the dragon's...

"Whence comes a treasure like that?" Faucette asked in awe. "Queen Sharasi herself never offered such an exceptional prize!" She craned around, trying to catch all the different ways the facets of the enormous zenithyst shimmered in Jek's hand.

"Is it enough?" he asked.

Now Faucette produced a third deafening sound. This time, it was a laugh.

"I should say it is! So long as they do not go on digging *forever*, I would consider all their mischief well worth a bounty like this!"

"It's yours then," Jek said.

Shifting her colossal weight, she reached with a foreleg, and Jek forced himself to remain standing in place with his hand out. Two of her nails converged on the gem, each as long as his upper body, but honed to a point fine enough to write a letter with. She crashingly stood out of the way of her treasure, which as the old man had guessed, had been hidden in an alcove in the wall behind her bulk. It was a very great hoard; perhaps not legendary, but full many times in excess of the amount of money Jek had expected to see in a lifetime. She set the zenithyst gently on the pile of gold, where it could be easily looked at any time she wished, on the rare occasions she was awake to look at it. She admired it again for a little while, then plopped back down in the snug way she had been before.

"I hope you will excuse my behaving so rudely," Faucette told them. "You understand it is unpleasant to be awoken unexpectedly – particularly with a rock to the snout. And I didn't get the idea right off that you were such skilled negotiators."

"Aye," the old man agreed. "I didn't know it meself." And he furrowed his brow at Jek.

"You must tell me about yourselves," Faucette insisted, determined to be polite now. "I have not seen a Human since I returned from the continent."

The old man was very happy to oblige, and started their story from his own harrowing tale out of Meatgrinder Bay. He wove in as many grim details as he could to really capture the horrible doom that was sure to come over all the world lest the three of them complete their Quest. Through it all, Faucette blinked heavily, shifted to get more comfortable, and tried to hold back perhaps a dozen yawns. Finally, there was nothing more she could do, and she fell hard and fast asleep. The old man looked rather sad.

Audrey patted him on the shoulder. "Don't feel bad. I'm sure your story wasn't *that* boring."

"Nay," the old man remarked. "Tis only natural. A dragon what's been slumberin' by her treasure for thousands o' years is a powerful drowsy kind o' critter. If anything, 'tis a mark o' me storytellin' excellence that she didn't fall asleep no sooner than she did."

Jek began to feel very tired too. Stress had run higher in this latest misadventure than ever before, and with them so very far underground, he couldn't even begin to guess what hour it was, or how long they had been out of the sun. "Maybe she has the right idea," he said, stretching.

The old man looked cross. "Hold on there, 'mister moneybags'! Ain't no more sleepin' for you till we practice fightin'!"

"You want to do that *now*?"

"Got to. The Despotopians mighta had us, and we wouldn'ta faired well 'gainst Sir Flytrap's men, iffen they had fighted us! And ye shore ain't no dragon-slayers. We needs to practice today and every day, no matter how tired we gets!"

"We don't even know if it still *is* today," Jek argued. "It might be tomorrow or the next day by now."

"All the more reason," the old man said. Jek didn't offer further argument. The old man considered it a matter of duty, and duty always came before rest.

* * *

They fought each other until they couldn't fight anymore. Jek had felt flashes of what seemed like clarity and balance, and he saw that Audrey also made some improvement. It was reassuring, and only leant to his overall drowsiness. They might've all fell on the ground and slept right then and there, but something else came up first...

"Excuse me!" they heard from within the tunnel. Sir Flytrap emerged. "I was wondering how things were going down here. Since I heard no blood-curdling screams, I thought perhaps you had survived my little errand. I am pleased to see that it is so!"

"Well hi there, Sir Flytrap!" the old man said. "We done just as ye hoped! Weren't hardly no trouble after all." He waved him forward. "Come on in! She promised she ain't gonna bother ye no more... so long as ye don't dig forever, she said."

"Oh, we won't, I can assure you of that," Sir Flytrap said, coming into the cave with a troop of his comrades. His voice waxed authoritative and eloquent. "Our centuries of tarrying underground shall come to a definite end; I believe it will be soon. We shall carry out our mission, and live and thrive once again under the sun. And what a *great* and *glorious* new era it will be! Perhaps it shall come all the sooner... thanks to you. I cannot adequately convey my gratitude for your assistance in this matter. You have forever altered the fortunes of all the peoples of the world."

"Ye're welcome, little buddy!"

Sir Flytrap stopped in their midst, and he looked up at each of them with an eminent smile. He really did seem incredibly pleased. "Shall we continue on through the mountain now?"

"Nay," the old man said weakly, propping himself up on his sword. "Me old bones ain't goin' no further afore they gets a good night's rest."

And they really didn't. The old man immediately set about readying to sleep, and so did Jek and Audrey, awkward as the business was, there in the den of the dragon by the magma flow. It wasn't exactly comfortable lodgings. The stones were hard, as stones are wont to be, and they jutted out all over the place. Only the ground around Faucette was appreciably smoothed-out. She had quite possibly bedded down there for hundreds or thousands of years, after all. Ultimately, they all ended up resting themselves propped-up against her forearm.

* * *

Jek was exhausted, but found sleep impossibly elusive. Going right from having never seen a dragon in his life to using one as a pillow wasn't a very natural progression for him. The old man had gone out like a light, and that made sleeping even harder. His snoring was domineering, as usual, and there was the added stress of wondering if he might get loud enough to wake Faucette.

"Seee…" Audrey said in a low creepy voice, giving Jek a start, and he sprung up with his musket.

"What – see *what*?" he demanded, looking all around for some sort of new danger.

"Oh dear, nothing," Audrey said, and he looked back at her. "I was just reading page three of my book." She held it out for him to see.

Jek sighed in great relief, and returned to his reclining spot. "Having trouble sleeping too, huh?"

"Just a bit preoccupied I guess."

Jek laughed. "Yeah, it's hard not to be preoccupied when you're wedged between a dragon and a river of magma."

Audrey was quiet for a moment. "I hadn't really thought about it."

"Well, what were you thinking about?"

"Just one of those pesky existential questions that crop up every so often."

Jek hesitated. Existential questions weren't his flavor; he preferred to avoid them where possible. "Which one?"

"Well, flamingos are pink only because they eat salmon, right?"

He felt immediately unsure where the existentialism was coming in. "Umm… yeah, right."

"So then, what makes the salmon pink?"

She certainly had him there. "That's what's been bothering you?"

"Not bothering, exactly. It just kind of makes you think."

Jek marveled at her ability to remain detached in times of danger. He credited it to her as a character strength, feeling confidently hopeful that she wasn't actually a clueless flake. "I wish I had an ounce of your bravery," he admitted. "All these scary things keep happening and it shakes me to the core every time. Hardly anything ever seems to bother you."

She gave him a sympathetic look. "Don't worry, Jek. You're just still getting accustomed to a life of adventure. It's only easier for me to deal with all this because to me, it's normal."

"Negotiating with tens of thousands of Venetian Flytraps and a giant dragon miles underground is normal for you?"

She laughed. "Well, no… not precisely. I just mean what I said before – a general kind of adventurous life. I'm used to peril. You'll get used to it too, and then it won't bother you so much; I'm sure of it. There's nothing special about me."

Jek doubted it. And he wondered again about her past life; what had made it so adventurous. At once it reminded him of the zenethyst – *her* zenethyst – that he had presumptuously given away. He had better apologize. He had better just be ready to find out the truth, once and for all…

"I'm really sorry I gave your zenethyst to the dragon. I hope you agree I had no other choice."

She looked at him astonished. Just as astonished as when he had produced the thing in the first place. "*My* zenethyst?!" Her mouth curled up but remained wide with amazement as she searched the middle-distance. She was undeniably flabbergasted. "What in Heck makes you think it was mine?! Where did you even *get* that thing?!"

"I found it in the house! You mean it *doesn't* belong to you?!"

"Ha!! Are you kidding?! No!" she insisted. "For crying out loud! I've watched a lot of money change hands in my years, but I've never even *seen* a gem like that before! Where on earth do you think I would have come across it?"

Here it was – she was setting him up to admit his suspicions – and he'd better go along with it. "I... well, I thought for a while that you were... that you were a pirate."

"*What*?!" and she smiled awkwardly again. "Me, a pirate?! Boy, you sure get some ideas." She held out a curled finger, like a mock hook. "How many times have I ever said, 'Arr'? Where's my eye patch and peg-leg?"

"I'd say that's getting a bit stereotypical. At any rate, I just thought, maybe, since you were so good at sailing, and you had a great big gem stone – apparently, anyway – I figured you must be a pirate."

"That's crazy!" She thought for a minute. "Did you *hope* I was a pirate?"

"No! Not at all! That would be extremely controversial! It's the last thing I wanted. But I think that's what made it really easy to believe."

She gave him a smile, and patted him on the shoulder reassuringly. "Well then, cheer up, Jek. I'm not a pirate. And I'm not a Princess either, if you were wondering. I'm just a former merchant-marine. I'm just me. Get some sleep, alright? And try not to worry so much."

With that she turned back, and shut her eyes, resting her book open in her lap. And Jek settled in too. For the first time in a while, he found that sleeping was not so hard, after all...

* * *

'I'm just me.'

The words still echoed in her head, even as she wondered what that really meant anymore. Was she reassuring Jek, or herself, when she said that? She looked over at her husband, and saw that he was now fast asleep. She smiled weakly. It really wasn't any wonder who she had reassured, after all.

Princess.

Pirate.

It was eminently frustrating to be doing so little and yet be so idealized. And no idle musings about flamingos and pigeons and other beautiful avian specimens could long distract her from her bewilderment. It wasn't that she feared importance or notoriety. She just didn't like it. It wasn't her culture. Growing up on a ship gave one an appreciation for the simple things – the minutiae that could be easily overlooked without vigilance. She had done so many hundreds of seemingly trivial little tasks on the *Cosigner* in her day – polishing belaying hooks, washing dishes, checking the same knots dozens of times. But those knots never came undone in a pinch, the hooks were never compromised from rust, and nobody ever got botulism. It was those silent victories Audrey lived for. She thrived in the anonymity of a crew – as just another pair of hands on the deck. Her pride had always been in trying to spy out the mundane details everyone else missed and quietly make them right.

But in being conscious of all of this, she was reminded of one thing that gave her solace. Today, they *had* found some things that everyone else missed, on a scale that defied credulity. A fathomless army of sentient Flytraps underground! Not that they were really an *army*, mind you... as Sir Flytrap had expressly pointed out many, many times. Discovering this enormous hidden colony of alien creatures in all of its benevolence was, in a sense, the very thing she had dreamt of every time she set her eyes on the southern sea...

But it could not sate her wondering what was to be found there. If anything, now she was more curious than ever. If all of this could be hiding in plain sight, what strange new phenomena might yet be found in the undiscovered country?

Slowly, but steadily, her waking dreams about such wonders progressed into sleeping ones...

Ancient Cataclysms

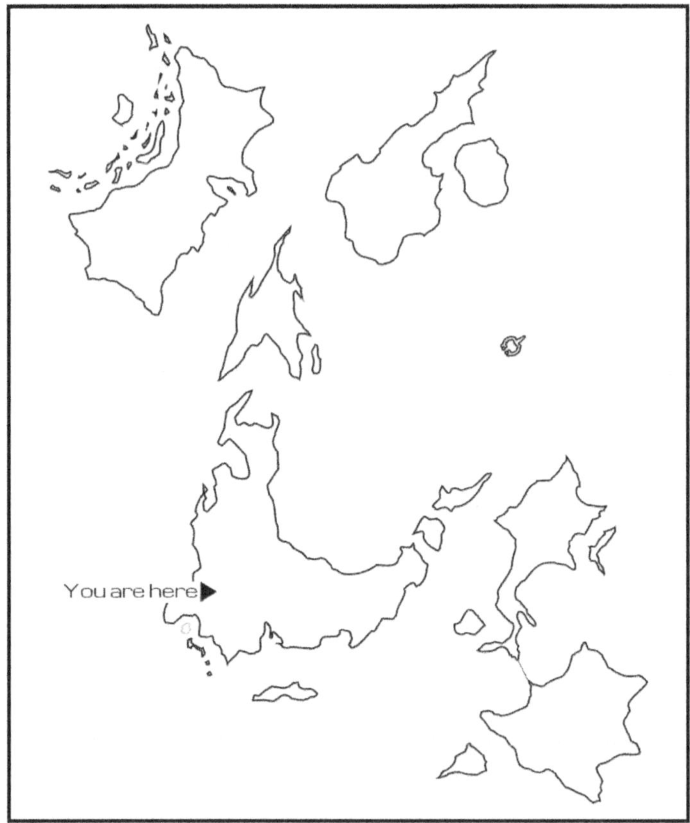

"Destroying something is base. Anyone can destroy something. And you're only gratified if you don't live long enough to see whatever you destroyed come back. Changing something is little better. It requires a bit more imagination and finesse, but it's no more permanent than destroying. Creation – pure and true creation – is the only exclusive power. But in order to create – really *create – you must first learn to* really *destroy. Then you must* really *change. That is the course of things. Anything else is regression, or what might be worse – stagnation."*

- Princess Bellanchora, *The Surviving Theology of Princess Bellanchora*, curated S.E. 6650

Jek started awake, as if he'd come hard and fast to the very end of all the sleeping there ever was to do. He was so thoroughly rested that he became immediately anxious. Never in his life had he had such a deep sleep, and he recognized at once that it had been a horrible mistake to rest against a dragon – that her mystical slumber must have extended to them – that he may have been out cold for days...weeks... or years!

Jek looked to his companions, who had apparently bolted upright as well. He just hoped they wouldn't look a decade or so older. He saw first the old man, which was inconclusive. But Audrey looked the same, and so he was relieved.

Faucette shifted restlessly. It caused Jek to remember that she had already twitched once, and *that* was what had waked him – and in fact *thrown* him to his feet. A dragon of her size twitching was no small event. It was fortunate that her first stirring had got them all up, because with her second she would have rolled over just enough to crush them to jelly. Some Venetian Flytraps that had been resting higher up on her belly scampered down in fright and narrowly avoided being snuffed out themselves. Faucette's cedar-like neck curled around and the power of her yawn filled the cavern. Her legs stretched and flexed and she helped herself upright onto them with her great wings and tail, almost disastrously heedless of the tiny fragile fellows in her midst. She made a guttural sound like clearing her throat as all the people and the Flytraps scampered out of her way. She turned out away from the wall so that she could look into the alcove that contained her treasure. As she considered the heap of wealth, she held rigid for some seconds – motionless as only lizards can be. And there was another sound, which made Jek think of purring.

"Ha!" Faucette exclaimed at last, shaking the cavern with an echo that was slow to die. She looked around, and saw that the others were still in the den with her. "I fancied I had a dream that some poor dullards gave me a huge zenethyst – and there it is! And here you all still are! Though I remember it now, I can scant believe it really happened." She yawned again, and her tongue flicked. "This is all quite a bit more excitement than I've had in ten thousand years! Imagine that I should wake twice to see the same few Humans! What with your busy and pitifully short little lives, I thought you should have long ago scampered off." Her tongue flicked a few more times. "But no. I see that I have slept no more than a few days. That is quite the cat-nap!"

And still a few more times her tongue probed the air. "There is something here that does not belong." Her eyes swiveled around independently, and she quickly caught sight of what offended her sense of smell. "Ah, the unwelcome houseguests!" It was the Flytraps she spoke to now.

"Forgive us, O great Faucette!" groveled Sir Flytrap, who seemed oddly accustomed to groveling to dragons just then. 'We meant thee no trespass. We only intended to remain among the Humans until they were ready to depart from the mountain, as was our pre-arranged agreement. As they have assured thee, it is our sincerest wish to have no further quarrel with you." Jek was incredulous about Sir Flytrap's high-falootin' grammar. It seemed very off-key, like he had almost no idea how to phrase it properly.

"And so you shan't," she growled. "But do not make fast friends of us. I will *tolerate* your infernal digging, digging, *digging*... but I hope it is not prolonged overmuch."

"That is our hope as well," Sir Flytrap agreed.

She huffed. "You were wise to send these creatures in your stead to do your bargaining. Still it is well that you have come here yourself afterward, to give me your own assurances that you do not plan on playing in the dirt for all eternity." Faucette looked over all present. "But before you leave – and I *do* expect you all to leave – perhaps I can enlist a bit of your help." As she spoke, she settled back onto the trodden ground. "If I am to meet the rigors of deep slumber, I shall need to get some proper rest first. That is the trouble of excitement, you see. This new zenethyst is a great blessing in the aggregate... but at present, it seems to have cursed me with restlessness. So, if one of you could bore me back to sleep, I would be much obliged."

"I'll pick up wheres I left off in recountin' our Quest!" the old man volunteered at once.

"Please don't," Jek said.

"Why ever not, lad?"

"The point is for *her* to sleep, not all of us. We already know that story. Couldn't you tell something that would have educational value?"

The old man pondered a bit. "How's about the tale o' the Four Voyages o' Flannigan Oswald?"

"A pirate story?" Jek asked pointedly. "Won't that involve treasure?"

He snapped. "Aye... wouldn't be none too restive to a dragon what just got a gargantian new gem."

"Deeeee," Audrey said.

"No readin' from yer book, neither!" the old man protested at her. "There's bored, and then there's *bored*. The dragon like-as-not already knows her letters!"

"That I do," Faucette agreed.

"Sorry," Audrey said, and closed her volume of *Literacy for Knuckleheads*.

Suddenly, Jek had an idea. "Hey, hey!" he said. "Bronzegloom! Zeph Bronzegloom gave her that book!"

"Aye," the old man said impatiently. "We's all there when he done it."

"Right! But that's not the *only* thing he gave us!"

The old man pointed at him knowingly. "The radio! We ain't made no use o' the radio yet!" He fumbled for it in his coat, twisted some knobs and started calling into the speaker. "Bronzee, Bronzee are ye there?! Over!"

"What is he doing?" Faucette demanded.

"It's an invention," Audrey tried to explain. "We can talk to somebody else far away who has another one of these things, and they can talk back to us."

Faucette's shimmering eyes narrowed. "That sounds like a horrible nuisance. But... if the man with the other box has a boring story to tell, then so be it."

"He does, I'm sure of it," Audrey assuaged her. "If I've met anybody who would have a bunch of boring stories, I daresay it would be him."

Jek frowned, not overly pleased with the thought of qualifying Zeph Bronzegloom's vast troves of thinking as 'boring'.

But Faucette nodded. "That is good to hear. Let us hope the boring man can be reached."

The old man continued trying to raise Bronzegloom for some time, becoming more and more obnoxious in his attempts. "Bronzee Bronzee Bronzee Bronzee *Bronzee*! Over!"

For a split second Jek swore he heard something come through, but the radio beeped and there was nothing again. "Pick up the durned radio, ye lubber! Over!" the old man shouted.

"Let me see that," Jek told him.

"Nay," the old man recoiled. "I don't need no youngins tryin' to show me how to use technogoly!"

Jek reached for it anyway, and they tussled for a few moments before they dropped the thing. As it came loose from the old man's grip, there could be heard the tinny garbled likeness of Zeph Bronzegloom's voice. He was shouting angrily.

"-o let go of the transmit button you old imbecile! OVER!" he said.

The old man gave Jek a look of defeat, and Jek took up the radio. "Hello, Mr. Bronzegloom – we got your message. Over."

"Oh thank Heck! I was just about to chuck this thing out the window." There was a beat of silence, where they thought they might have heard a low sigh of relief. "What is it you people wanted? It's getting late you know."

"Actually we *don't* know, over," Audrey said.

"I have to press the transmit button for him to hear that," Jek explained to her, even as he pressed it. "Over," he added as an afterthought.

"Yes, you do," Bronzegloom agreed impatiently. "And skip the 'overs.' Just tell me what's up."

"Well, it's hard to explain," Jek started.

"Try me."

"We have a dragon here that needs a bedtime story," he said, wincing at how ridiculous it sounded. There was no immediate response.

"...Okay..." Bronzegloom said. "Well, I can certainly talk about most anything you like. Even if I don't know about it, I can just as well tell you what I think. Any requests?"

"We don't have anything particular in mind."

"Alright. Let's start by picking a category. There's theology, mathematics, migration, wars, national histories, ancient cataclysms..."

Audrey reached for the radio. "Oo, ancient cataclysms ! Let's have ancient cataclysms."

"-at was that?" Bronzegloom said, as Jek let Audrey have the radio. "I didn't get the last thing."

"I want to hear about ancient cataclysms," Audrey said.

"Oh good! Ancient cataclysms are the spice of life, I always say. You've got to hand it to our ancestors... they were really good sports to endure all of those huge disasters so we could romanticize about them. Now there's two main categories of ancient cataclysms – Onyxadon cataclysms, and non-Onyxadon cataclysms. Which will it be?"

"Non-Onyxadon, I think," Audrey said.

"Good, because I don't have all night," Bronzegloom replied.

"Hold it!" Jek said.

"What's wrong?" Audrey asked.

"Aren't we supposed to be helping Faucette sleep? How are a bunch of scary stories about the world almost coming apart going to be any good for that?"

"Sounds alright to me," Faucette chimed in.

"There," Audrey said, "the dragon has spoken. Besides, you said yourself that you wanted an educational story. I want to learn about ancient cataclysms."

Jek could offer no further argument.

"What was all that over there?" Bronzegloom asked. It was pretty hopeless carrying on a very fluid conversation with him.

"Nothing," Audrey said. "Go ahead."

"Okay, let's see..." Bronzegloom began. "Well, I could tell you about the grand-daddy of all the cataclysms – the Supreme Exodus. But I suppose that's grade-school. Everyone knows about the Creators leaving the universe to go start a new one. It is a very unique cataclysm though, I've always felt – certainly one-of-a-kind. It didn't involve huge death tolls or the rearrangement of the cosmos or anything we would conventionally think of as disastrous. It was just that – one moment, the universe was ever-changing, ever-evolving, filling up more and more all the time with new creatures and new features and new forces and dangers and wonders. One moment, you marveled not only at all there *was*, but at the apparently endless promise of what *would be*. And the next... it was finished. Finished without warning or sense of completion. The pen was set down; the lathe was turned off; the project was shelved. Everyone felt it at once. They felt the *static*. We, of course, will never truly know what that felt like. But I think that's what makes it so darned interesting."

"You describe it well, distant speaker," Faucette said, and Jek was reminded at once of her incredible age. Her eyes took on a sad quality. "I do not have the words for it, myself. It was an unhappy time, you may be sure. Especially for us dragons, who had lived through many centuries of the Creators' work." She sighed an uneven sigh, filling their midst with even hotter air. "It is very hard to be reminded of such things, even now. Perhaps you could continue with a more uplifting cataclysm?"

"Erm, right," Bronzegloom said, and took some moments of consideration. "Well, I guess another good one to talk about is the Orange Plague. That one left the world with so many darned misconceptions! Anyone who doesn't know the truth about the Orange Plague is sure to benefit from hearing it..."

And Bronzegloom went on to describe the entire pandemic. It broke out not long after the Supreme Exodus itself. Such was the magnitude of its devastation that it was, at first, going to be called "The Black Plague". However, everyone agreed that naming a very awful tribulation 'Black' seemed rather cliché, and so it was renamed in honor of a more original color. This was a choice that had lingering consequences to the present day. Since mass contagions were otherwise unprecedented in the world, the term 'plague' was often misunderstood, and many illiterate folk continued to labor under the delusion that the Orange Plague was some peculiar historical episode where a great army of sentient oranges took up sword and spear and ravaged the countryside. After all, practically every other dark chapter in world history took this form... the part about Enlightened fruit notwithstanding.

Of course, the *actual* Orange Plague really was an insidious disease – one which spread through all races – and had nothing at all to do with oranges, sentient or otherwise. Even the Meduselda were not spared; some of them died many, many times of the infection.

It began with the rather dramatic appearance of large bacteriophages. They were among the last of the Creators' works, and had generated considerable interest among the civilized peoples, who thought that the 'Phage' were an entirely *new* sentient race (that is, without unintelligent progenitors) – the first in centuries. However, the Phage were quick to explain that they were descended from microscopic viruses. No one really knew what they were talking about, except that it eventually became clear they were rebuffing the idea that they were a new species, and so the excitement about them wore off after a century or two.

The Phage were, of course, quite naturally drawn to the postal professions, and so found a comfortable niche in international society. Unfortunately, the EXTREME size change the Phage underwent to become a macroscopic race had unforeseen consequences. In time, their large protein chambers made incredible incubators for a savage strain of bacteria that went widespread and undetected among their people for quite some time – certainly long enough for them to deliver a *lot* of mail. Many an unsuspecting possessor of a mail or P.O. Box became gravely ill before the Phage themselves were noticeably affected.

In this way, the contagion reached most of the world. The eventual salvation of civilization came from the Dire Herons – a particularly grave, meticulous, and intelligent species, gifted with peculiar powers of insight. Out of necessity they advanced medical technique and knowledge by very great strides in but a short time, becoming the de facto plague doctors of the earth. Operating out of their small, sequestered nation of Kanaedia, all of civilization quickly became heavily reliant on their expertise.

This led to towering medical bills. It was not a very happy arrangement for any of the parties involved, and came to some hard decisions on the part of the Dire Herons. Eventually, the debt grew so outstanding – so *titanic* – that the Dire Herons were left with no choice but to take over the world. It was really the only thing they could do to settle the accounts...

"...We're stemming from ancient cataclysms to general world history at this point," Bronzegloom said. "The Herons whipped the Plague alright, and the Kanaedionic Empire was born. They had supreme power throughout nearly the entire world for a very very long time. I'm sure we all know well enough about that."

"I must've slept through it," Faucette said, sounding slightly embarrassed.

Bronzegloom hesitated to respond. "You guys *really* have a dragon there with you? I guess I still feel unclear on that."

"Never mind, Bronzee!" the old man demanded. "Just ye keep regalin' her with yer fanciful stories."

"Okay," Bronzegloom agreed. "I've got one more cataclysm in store, and then I hope you'll let *me* go to bed. It's the *big* one."

"I thought you said the Supreme Exodus was the big one," Audrey insisted.

"No-no, that was the grand-daddy. *This*... this is the *big* one," Bronzegloom explained.

Jek gulped. "He means the Great Regression," he said.

"Right you are, smart guy," Bronzegloom confirmed. "You can be sure it was the big one, for many reasons. For one, the universe was falling apart. Or rather, it was being *torn* apart... deliberately. For another, it's the only time we know of when a Dianode intervened in world affairs, coming forth in his harbinger form."

"That does sound serious," Audrey admitted.

"To give you an idea *how* serious, let us consider what your average day would have been like if you'd been around to see the Great Regression...

"First, you would wake up at twilight, because it was always twilight. The sun, the Other Worlds, and the Phantom Light were all frozen in place.

"You wouldn't have had to worry about the foghorn or the light tower, because there was no sea-going traffic. There was no *sea* – unless you count the billion-foot-tall pillars of raging water the oceans had been formed into. That would have made for an interesting sight as you walked out of your house to start the day.

"You might want to watch your step though, if you did bother to walk out of your house. There were portals and tears in space, leading anywhere you could think of, and nowhere at all. Portals could be seen, easily enough, but the tears were tricky. Whereas portals went someplace, even if that place was deep space or the bowels of one earth or another, the tears were rends in reality itself, beyond which you couldn't see light, or dark, or anything, because there was none. Some were very small, and some could have swallowed the world.

"And there were other strange phenomena abroad. Windows through time; spontaneous elemental transmutation; strange creatures walking around, neither alive nor dead. It was all rather unsettling."

Jek found that he was rather unsettled indeed. "How did all of this come about? I mean, what could have disrupted everything so bad?"

"*We* did," Bronzegloom explained. "What else?"

"How?"

"We *learned* how. And the importance of that *learning* cannot be overstated. It was the key to our disemboweling of the universe, and also to its eventual restoration. Our knowledge grew to the point that we had sway over the Dianodes themselves. Those that had the knowledge had the ability to manipulate the elements the utmost extent of their power." Bronzegloom snickered. "This is why I find it fairly comical that people nowadays conflate modern magic with the Power of the Great Regression. It's about like confusing a little butterfly with a Moon-Moth."

"Okay, so we learned the key to unlimited power," Audrey said. "Why were we being so dumb about it? What was everyone thinking, causing all that chaos?"

"Like-as-not they wasn't thinkin' a'tall," the old man suggested.

"Oh, they *were*, and you might be surprised how much," Bronzegloom insisted. "There was a lot of very interesting theology and philosophy that came out of the Great Regression years. It was a time when anything suddenly seemed possible, and much of it was. And when anything *can* be done, the question rightfully rises as to what *should* be done. But that was where the chaos really came into play... because everyone and his brother had their own ideas about what *ought* to be done, and what's more they had the Power to try and do it...

"Prominently, you had the champion philosopher Galahadron Mucolyptus, and the schism he created in the Inquisition. He felt that the emergence of the Power was crucially tied to mortal destiny, as did many others. But his belief was that it should be used to find a way to traverse The Undervoid – that is, his term for the beyond-infinite nothingness between our universe and the second universe.

"His vision and sacred charge was to cross over to the second universe, which he would then make war on and destroy, winning back the attention of the Creators, in most dramatic fashion. He had been raised an Inquisitor, you see, though he was Human. But he decided that patience and penitence were not enough – that if we had the means to reach the Creators and demonstrate our jealous zeal for them, then we would be in the wrong not to.

"Mucolyptus' theology was promptly labelled heresy, and he as its champion was excommunicated from the Inquisition as quickly as could be. The vast majority of the Inquisitors found it easy to dismiss his notions as being radical and defiant, whereas the aim of the Inquisition had always been to respond to the disinterest of the Creators with humility. Plus, it all seemed rather wacko. But Galahadron dealt their order a heavier blow than they might have imagined. His proactive approach had broad appeal both outside of the Inquisition, and ultimately, within it as well. As Mucolyptus went on to his own independent prominence, he was often defended in open summits of the Grand Inquisitors by Opepci, one of their own number. The rift grew until eventually Opepci sundered herself from the Inquisition, and a number of like-minded Inquisitors left with her.

"Subsequently Opepci and Galahadron formed the Dark Inquisition, and formally declared open war on the Second Universe... though of course they still possessed no means of making their war, or even conveying their declaration of hostilities. They couldn't reach the Second Universe at this point. Even so, many flocked to their cause, and a very great host readied to invade the new reality... as soon as it became possible, that is.

"Galahadron and Opepci experimented with warping space until they were confident of their ability to reach through both the void and The Undervoid. To this day, a great rift in the universe, known as Galahadron's Gate, remains open in a deserted area of the continent. Eerie accounts of this abandoned wasteland are a mainstay. None know whether the Dark Inquisition and its frightful army of zealots ever reached the other universe, or whether it was possible to reach it in the first place… or even if, upon reaching it, they could exist there at all, much less make war on whatever they found. It is just one of those sorts of great mysteries in life, and most shudder at the thought of it…

"…But not all. Though the Power that facilitated Galahadron's quest is now forgotten, much of his teaching survived the Great Regression, and a steady trickle of new followers across the ages have sought out the Gate, never to return."

"That's really darned scary," Jek said.

"I thought you might think so," Bronzegloom said. "Anyway, I digress. Mucolyptan cosmology was hardly the only set of ideals set forth during these days that caused utter havoc. Whereas Galahadron was intent on destroying the Second Universe, there were others that believed the end of our own universe was in order."

Jek found himself incredulous. "You kept alluding to that. You kept making it sound like there were people *trying* to rip our universe apart. Why ever would they want to do that?!?"

"Believe you me, I wish I knew. Because if I did, I'd be *really* famous. People have been trying to piece that mystery together since the Regression itself. There were many Masters of Knowledge – our rather simple term for the people that lorded it over the elements, and seeded cosmic devastation. Among Humans, it's believed there were none greater than Princess Bellanchora. She was most clever and lethal and willful in her mastery of the Power, and she often exercised her ability on the grandest scale that she was able. Her deeds were equal parts whimsical and unabashedly destructive; she it was who formed the oceans into pillars, and she tore the most and the largest canyons in reality herself. Historical accounts insinuate that there was some sort of guiding philosophy behind these actions; that she was aware of some apparently dreadful secret of the cosmos, which inspired her to mock its form and seek to dash its very foundations. It's even popularly held that she possessed the Pamphlet of Unknowable Things, and learned all sorts of dreadful stuff – that she might have even discovered the Power from it in the first place. The trouble is, we just can't be sure of anything. Whatever dark truth, or *truths*, she unearthed from the Pamphlet is now forgotten along with the Power… driven forcibly from all minds by Ethon."

"Who is Ethon?" Audrey asked. "And what is all this forgetfulness about? How did we just happen to forget everything that this entire cataclysm hinges on?"

Bronzegloom chuckled over the radio. "Those questions answer each other. Ethon is Forgetfulness itself – the Scourge of Knowledge – Guardian of the Unknown, and the Unknowable. A legend, an eldritch terror, and a by-word, whose coming was hazily foreseen by numerous sovereigns of the Yellow Dynasty, when the Kanaedionic Empire was crumbling and many terrible things were predicted."

"I don't understand," Audrey admitted.

"Well, I could tell you forthright, but I can't help wanting to do some justice to the mystique that surrounds Ethon. To this day, some believe him to be an omnipotent punisher sent from the Second Universe to menace intelligent life for displeasing the Creators ages ago. Others think of him as a patron emancipator – a willing savior figure that benevolently delivered us from our darkest hour. He is neither. He's one of the Dianodes. You'll remember, I told you we *learned* how to influence the elements?"

"Yes."

"Well, you see, that's *Knowledge.* Our comprehension of Knowledge and our ability to wield it had grown to cosmic levels. But as I've also explained to you before, there is no force in the universe which is not balanced, and Knowledge is no exception. Knowledge is a Dianode too. It has an opposite, and that opposite is Ethon. As we cultivated the strength of Knowledge to dominate all powers, so too grew Ethon.

"The Masters of Knowledge had neither known him nor predicted his intervention – or if they did, it availed them not at all. For he *did* intervene, as was his Purpose. He came forth and bade them forget their accursed learning."

"What, and they just went along with it?" Audrey asked.

"No. Needless to say, there was a battle. But not until they first tried to subdue Ethon and make him a slave to their whims, as they had all the other Dianodes."

"What prevented them succeeding?"

"That's a tricky question, since we don't ultimately know what they did to enslave the others – as I said, that knowledge is lost. Retrospectively, though, it's understood that no craft of Knowledge could be brought to bear on he who is the Scourge of Knowledge.

"When they failed to sway him, they resolved to destroy him completely. But every attack failed, even as their strikes continually intensified. Worlds and time and space were rent but all of their contrivances could not bite their foe. They could no more succeed against him than they could have outmaneuvered their reflection in a mirror." Bronzegloom snickered. "It's why I tell you, the Balance system is robust – although a word like 'robust' falls short. In fact, if the Regression crisis proved anything, it's that the universe is all but indestructible. Because even when we brought it to the brink of collapse, it recovered just as dramatically."

"But then how did Ethon succeed?" Audrey asked. "How did he overcome them, if they couldn't overcome him?"

"Well he wasn't alone. The Inquisition backed him. Oh, I admit that didn't add any remarkable strength to their cause, since the Inquisitors flatly refused to learn the Power, much less practice it. But the Masters of Knowledge were so intent on destroying Ethon that they didn't even take notice of the Inquisitors until it was too late. Whatever elemental fury they may have been capable of, they were still flesh and blood, and their host was routed. They were too single-mindedly focused on Ethon and too confident in their strength, and they underestimated their lesser enemies – who as you know included some of the world's oldest and most powerful dragons. All of the Grand Inquisitors were present for the fight – except Opepci, who had already gone with Galahadron. It's maintained that Enscharaulgk and Bellanchora mutually annihilated each other... but he being a dragon with a treasure, and she just a Human, you can see who got the better end of that deal."

"Did they all die? All of these Masters of Knowledge?"

"No. Many of the greater ones survived; they chose surrender and obfuscation over death. It was then that Ethon's real job began. He went to each of them, and throughout the earth, and erased all memory of the Power... in print, in mind, and in every form... and shrouded the years leading up to the calamity in forgetfulness. Last of all, he went to his de facto allies, the Grand Inquisitors, to cause them to forget. But they resisted him."

"They did? They turned on him after all that? Why?"

"They didn't consider that they were betraying him. The Grand Inquisitors, as you may know, tasked themselves ages ago with keeping alive the direct memory of the Creators. They didn't allow Ethon to purge their minds, lest any trace of their memories of the Creators be incidentally damaged."

"How could they prevent him doing it anyway?"

"Well, by this time, Ethon was greatly diminished in strength, for as he caused the abundance of Knowledge to depart from the world, so too his own power declined. He may well have tried to drive out their memories by force. But their minds were adamant, and he failed."

"That must've made him pretty angry."

"Not at all. Remember, Dianodes have no Will, only Purpose. Without Will, I doubt very much he could react emotionally to his failure. At any rate, the Grand Inquisitors bade him trust their resolution to keep the world on the proper course, and to curtail any future efforts by mortals to exert their own will over the natural forces. Ethon had naught to do but take their word for it, and return to the obscurity whence he came. The rest of the Dianodes, freed from the influence of the Masters, resumed their proper shape soon enough. The universe has never quite been the same, it's true, but apart from some fairly minor rearrangements, it's back in functioning order, and has been for many generations."

The old man sniffed. "I loves a happy ending."

"That's really more of a status-quo ending, I'd say," Jek needled.

"They be one and the same, lad."

Jek huffed. "I guess I always thought of a happy ending as being where something new happened that made things better than they were before."

The old man shook a finger at him. "In fairy-stories, mayhaps. But ye know what they says about new things."

"What's that?"

"'Everything new is old.'"

Jek just shook his head.

"I think that pretty well wraps-up the telling," Bronzegloom announced in his tinny voice, even as he yawned. "It's always a struggle to get through the Great Regression crisis... it's pretty esoteric and hard to explain. If I wasn't tired before, I sure am now."

"Well, I don't know if you really made me understand it or not," Audrey admitted, "but either way, your story was a success."

"How's that?" Bronzegloom asked. Jek himself wondered for a moment, but he looked back and saw that Faucette was fast asleep.

"You bored the dragon," Audrey explained, "and that was the main thing."

"Oh, good," Bronzegloom said. "Then I can really go to bed. Tune in for next week's fireside chat. Over."

"Thanks again, over," Audrey signaled, and handed the radio back to the old man.

"Not to press the issue," Sir Flytrap interposed, "but would you perhaps be amicable to continuing on your way at this time? I admit that further delay would begin to impinge on my other duties."

"Shore thing, Sir Flytrap," the old man said, standing up and stretching. "We needs to keep to our own tight schedule, and get the world saved afore it's too late for savin'."

"In that case, the world would just save itself, if Bronzegloom knows half as much as he says," Audrey joshed.

"Aye, and it's a reassurance. But I finds its best not to count on it."

* * *

It proved a good thing that Sir Flytrap had been there to guide them out of the mountain. The forks in the road were shockingly numerous; it would have been quite hopeless for them to find the proper way on their own. And it was a *long* journey. They stopped to sleep again on the way, long before there was any rumor of the outside world...

But finally, the stagnant heat in the air steadily diminished, and Audrey found herself buttoning her frock coat, and walking with her hands in her pockets wherever the grade of the tunnel was not too steep. The atmosphere became fresher, cleaner, and scented. It was clear they were nearing the surface...

But the road got progressively darker, too. She decided it must be night out, or else the end of the tunnel was covered over. In either case the light of day was not waiting for them ahead, and the light behind them was getting ever farther away. They were hindered as they groped around in the dark, trying to be sure of their bearings. Sir Flytrap seemed unimpeded, and almost a bit annoyed at their difficulty. Perhaps not having eyes made for better night vision.

At last there was a stirring up ahead, and an urgent voice.

"Halt! Who goes there?!" said the voice.

"At ease, lance corporal," commanded Sir Flytrap. "It is I, Aaouuaaiooaauuo."

"Oh, it's you, sir!" Lance Corporal Flytrap said. "I haven't had word from your command in some time, and I was more than a little baffled to see these Humans coming up from our secret lair. But I suppose you must've remembered me after all, and brought me a snack. Many thanks!"

"They are not for eating, lance corporal. They are our guests, and trusted liaisons. And I'll not have you spouting mindless nothings about any 'secret lair'... a rather ugly term, that. I prefer to think of it as our 'benevolently obscure sanctum'."

"Whatever you say, sir."

"Now, if you wouldn't mind, kindly make way for our friends, to whom I was just showing the way back to the surface world."

"Yes, sir! Immediately, sir!" And Lance Corporal Flytrap quickly scurried and unlatched a covering too dim to make out, swinging it free and revealing the pale night sky.

"This is where we must part ways, my comrades," Sir Flytrap said to the Humans, the outline of his fearful mouth just dimly decipherable by the light of the stars. "Be very mindful in the lands beyond. There are creatures which rove this territory that I would be remiss not to warn you about. They look extremely tasty, but do not let that fool you! They are horribly, deadly dangerous, the lot of them."

"Thanks for the warnin', and for everthin', little buddy," the old man said, giving the small creature a very heartfelt thumbs-up. "Been a real pleasure, knowin' ye!"

"Likewise, I'm sure. Fair thee well! And good luck in your Quest to save the surface world! We would certainly much prefer to find it peaceful and unsuspecting when at last we return to it."

* * *

As Aaouuaaiooaauuo gave one final wave of his foreleg in dismissal to the Humans, Iiaaoaa resolved with some boldness to address his superior.

"What do we mean by letting Humans see our 'sanctum' and live to speak of it, if you don't mind my asking, sir?"

"I suppose you have some right to be curious, lance corporal, but you needn't worry. The Humans are oblivious to our designs, and have actually helped us a great deal. Besides, I have released them into the jungle. They are at the mercy of the Mantids now. I wouldn't worry about them living to speak of anything."

"We could just as well have eaten them ourselves."

"I am aware. However, you know it is not for us to begin working our hostilities on the surface-dwellers... not before word from *him*."

"Your devotion is truly remarkable, sir."

Aaouuaaiooaauuo smiled, gazing into the middle distance with his lack of eyes. "You would understand if you had ever seen him, young Iiaaoaa. I have lived to watch many generations of our folk labor without comfort of the sun on their foliage or the taste of flies on their pads. But I count it all well-worth every moment of suffering, if it will but please him, and help him in the realizing of his Vile purposes. That which he has banished us from, he shall soon return to us, and grant us much glory in battle besides. And you also will count yourself privileged to have been any part of this great undertaking, when at last he reappears, and you behold our Dread Master... Onyxadon."

* * *

Parting with Sir Flytrap was indeed sweet sorrow, and not just because of his endearingly earnest qualities. They were unprepared for the bitter cold of night. But they hurried on briskly, and soon their exertion kept them warm. Still, on the whole they advanced slowly in the thick woods where they had emerged. The trees were all but matted together and the underbrush was treacherous, soggy, and thick. Their rustling through the knee-deep leaves caused a proper racket – every step was like the rap of a whitecap against a rock wall.

"What are all these leaves about?" Audrey asked to no one in particular.

"I's glad ye asked," the old man said. "Ol' Bronzee's not the only one what can expunge on a yarn, I warrant."

"What does that mean?"

"Means I's about to tell ye a story. Ye see, there be all kinds o' trees in the world. Mostly there's three kinds: big, small and medium. But botany done gets even more intricater than that in some regards. Particalarly there be places in the world what gets mighty more cold than hereabouts. I'm sure ye heard o' winter."

"Yeah, and snow, and all of that," Audrey agreed.

"Well, winter ain't so kind to the trees, and every year the trees what gots to make it through the winter gets kinda dead, and their leaves get mighty pertyful, and then they falls off. That's about rough-like what's goin' on in these here woods."

Audrey pondered that. "Why would any trees in Jast-Madiir be shedding leaves for winter, when we never get a winter?"

"A'cause these trees is mighty confused. They heard about winter hunderds o' years ago, and they been preparin' for it e'er since. Only it never comes... so they just keeps spittin' out more and more leaves forever. It's a mite sad, when ye thinks about it."

"It is," she agreed.

"There's something a lot sadder about these woods," Jek volunteered, "something you've neglected to mention. They're actually *jungles* – the very jungles we were supposed to avoid. Mantids live here! The Flytraps didn't lead us far enough north! We're doomed."

"Oh, frogshair!" the old man said, waving Jek's remark away. "I always done said, Sir Flytrap never put us in no danger what we couldn't easy enough weasel out of. Iffen he dropped us off here, I got no doubt we'll fair just fine."

"He even warned us about the Mantids, if you were paying attention," Jek said. "And this time I'm fresh out of zenithysts."

"Well, it be night time. And with any luck, they's sleepin', and won't even hear us."

"With any luck, the *Despotopians* won't hear us. Darn these crazy leaves! I couldn't make more noise if I tried!"

"Don't ye go tryin' anywho. Ye got me a bit afeared o' them bugs now."

"I suppose we should keep an eye out for them," Audrey conceded. "But it would help if I knew what to look for."

"They looks proper invisibible, until they pounces on ye, from all I hear," the old man said. "They's powerful camouflaged... and it don't help matters none that it be the nightly hours."

"Maybe we should turn back and ask your pal Sir Flytrap if he has another tunnel that goes straight to Roemnar," Jek posited.

"I'm sure ye're bein' sarcastical, but it don't strike me as a bad idear a'tall!"

He stopped at once, and so did Audrey and Jek, but as they watched to see if he was really going to turn back, they heard a *snap*.

"Quiet," the old man whispered gravely. "I done heard a *snap*."

"*They're here*!" Jek despaired in his own whispery voice. "I just know they're here!"

They surveyed about themselves in silence for some seconds, each gripping their weapons.

"I don't see them no place."

"But you said they're invisible," Audrey said. "Not seeing them is probably the surest sign they're here."

The old man reacted to her logic with solemn confirmation. "On three we makes a run for it," he said.

"Back to the tunnel?" Jek asked.

"Aye. To the tunnel."

They waited tensely for the countdown to commence.

"THREE!" the old man called, and they bolted.

Audrey was very caught up in the adrenalin rush of running for her life, but a calculating and oddly serene quadrant of her brain knew for certain that the effort was futile. There would be no navigating the jungle back to an obscure hole in the ground in the middle of the night. Even if there were no Mantids at all, they would at best succeed in running until they exhausted themselves, and then have to double back north again twice as far. But she resolved not to consider it further. She was thinking too much like Jek.

The ordeal was over soon enough anyway, and quite beyond their control. Jagged limbs of trees were flying out at them from all directions. Except they weren't tree limbs at all – she knew they must be the probing claws of a great host of Mantids! She narrowly avoided one set of pincers, and rather than keep bolting, she surprised herself by stopping to fight. Audrey turned and faced the pincers, and finally made out the discernable form of a 6-foot insect. She struck it in the shoulder with the bayonet end of her musket, and the blade stuck in the creature, though it caused no detectable harm.

She heaved a breath in to redouble her strength, even as the protestations of Jek and the old man echoed behind her. As if to avenge them against the whole company, she focused all her strength into a twisting remise, and the bayonette audibly cracked through the insect's thick carapace, and it squealed in pain.

But before she could even begin to contemplate her next move, her legs were swept out from under her, and she fell face-first into the ground, and knew nothing more...

Secrets of Brittegonnen

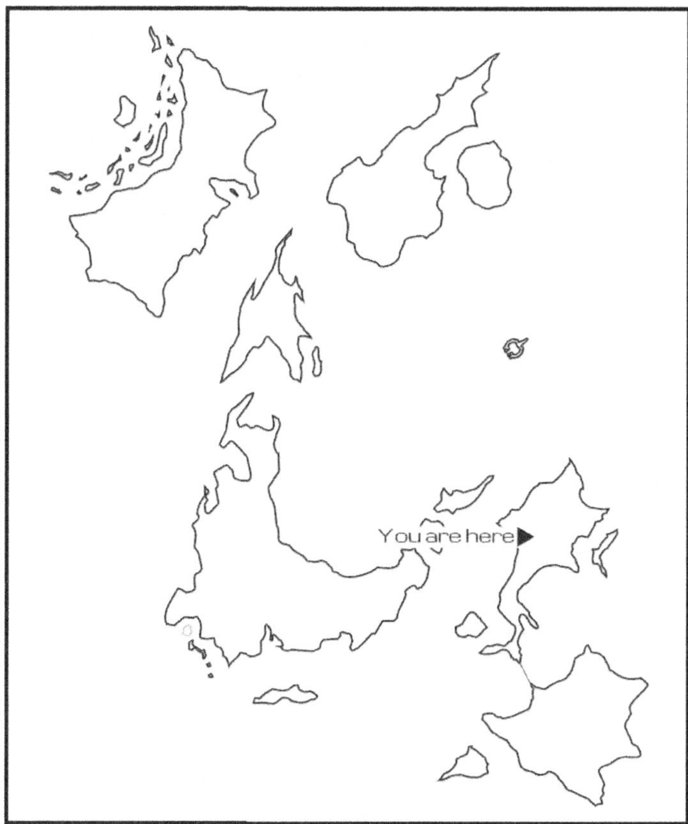

"Something tither, something yon
Somethings ever on and on
Count the one and all the others
Therein lies the Dronehood's druthers"

- attributed to Queen Jemimilia of the Berlie Beirels, *Dedication Plaque of the Archives of Berlberi*

♫♫♫♫, thought Baegulgog. It was a fine time to hum. Although, to his reckoning, there was never *not* a fine time to hum...

So long as he kept it to himself, anyway. The Clerk was well aware he couldn't carry a tune aloud – whether humming, singing, whistling, or fumbling on an instrument. He hated to bother people with his tonal impairment. Moreover, it was a great embarrassment to him. After all, music itself had been brought into the world by his most famous forerunner, Chordonoto – a fact he still enjoyed reminding himself of, as well as any he encountered, in spite of his own unfortunate break with that great legacy. Indeed, a Sowür Canpattel who had no musical acumen was about as envied as a Dire Heron missing half his tail feathers.

But this much gave him solace: while his faculties might be hopeless, in his mind there was forever a great and tireless orchestra, whose myriad melodies told the story of his life. They galloped the overture of his *Daily Float to the Office*! They syncopated the rhythmic theme of *Counting Stuff*! They burgeoned the heroic anthem of *Doing Paperwork*! His retinue of imaginary musicians had a tune for every occasion. And Baegulgog himself, humbly but happily, hummed ever along. He was a true Sowür Canpattel in that much, at least!

Of late, he had been introduced to a number of new and fascinating orchestrations. It was his distinct pleasure to be party to the sublimely sad and courageous *Requiem for Parissah*. *The Battle Theme on Variglew* was the most frantic, suspenseful, and energetic anthem he had yet known (apart from the aforementioned timeless classic *Doing Paperwork*, of course. Some of his old *Cavalry* tunes also ranked high). He had not, however, cared overmuch for the brooding undertow and discordance of *The Rumor of Onyxadon*, which had hung over him all the time they were passing through the burning wastes of Tophthera...

Now hovering through the courts and causeways of Brittegonnen, amidst gaunt and dim walls hastily constructed, that theme had finally given way to a homier intermezzo... even if he supposed he felt a vague current of bitterness within the city walls...

Though Baegulgog did not have fond thoughts for Berlie Beirels up to this point, he had to admit he found their architecture pleasant. It was distinctly Meduseldan, transcending the Dominions. Brittegonnen reminded him very much of Berlberi, the ancestral capital of all Berlie Beirels, which they had abandoned after the reign of Aedeloma, and where Baegulgog himself had studied many years ago, while apprenticing as a Clerk in the Clerical Dronehood.

He didn't like the thought that his beloved Dronehood owed its very existence to the Berlie Beirels of old who had founded it. They seemed quite a brutish lot to him, and hardly the Dominion best suited to have carried forth the bright and shining torch of statistics and paperwork to all of civilization. But the city of Brittegonnen was slowly disarming his prejudices. He couldn't help but see that between its precarious triangular buildings – patched together as they were by sparse and cheap building materials – there was a clever and subtle mathematic precision. There were nine different buildings meeting each at a corner in a sprawling tile fashion that spread across the city. Every time he reached such an intersection, he could see down each of the nine paths all the way to the encircling walls.

Nine, of course, was a tricky number, Baegulgog knew. It had two distinct meanings. There was the *original* math – Meduseldan math – wherein you counted in one progression: 1,2,3,7,8,9,10. Then you had *Human* math, which added several numbers in the middle, so that the count went like this: 1,2,3,**4,5,6**,7,8,9,10. For whatever reason, most of the world besides the Meduselda now counted in this second fashion. Occasionally, Baegulgog wondered whether this minor mathematical nuance ever occurred to the Humans and other creatures that made use of the Dronehood's statistics. A Human lord over a population that had been reported by Dronehood census to number at 20,000, for instance, might be a little surprised to learn that, according to his own number system, that same population would read a seemingly more modest 4,802. But that was a rather trifling sort of discrepancy, and Baegulgog didn't let it worry him. *Data are for collecting, not interpreting*. That was his slogan, anyway...

Nine really was a fascinating number to Baegulgog. He had long ago observed that if one were to add up the digits of any multiple of nine, the sum of those digits *would be* nine, or one of its multiples. As an example, 7 x 9 = 33, and 3 + 3 = 9. Even more interestingly, this phenomenon could be worked out in Human numbers as well. For Humans, 7 x 9 = 63, and 6 + 3 = 9. Deeply, he wondered how many different number systems could be devised where the multiples of the base number minus one would always have digits adding up to that same number or one of its lesser multiples. It was something he meant to investigate one day, and, of course, document thoroughly...

It would have to wait. The 'road trip' (which had not actually featured roads, until their arrival in the Capitol) was ending, and his adopted role as a diplomatic attaché was about to come into play. He and Parissah were being led by the Tophtheran Field Marshal down the central path to the principal structure at the far north side of the city. This was of course the Queen's residence, built into the face of a sheer cleft in the huge crater where Brittegonnen was seated. If you removed the city itself, the valley of Brittegonnen would be very much the shape of a pie pan, with one slice of pie left in it. It was the jagged end of that pie slice where the Capitol building stood, tall and concave, rather like an enormous hourglass.

The thought of pie made Baegulgog wish for a snack (still an odd habit as it was, for a Meduseldan to eat), and then he knew he was definitely his corporeal self again. And so much the better! Now he could appear as ambassador before Queen Irisa in the relative pomp of his Clerk uniform, rather than as a bare ghost.

"I do hope they will give us a moment before we are taken into Her Majesty's presence," Baegulgog admitted to Parissah, as if hoping she could do something to make it so. "I feel I am ready to don my vestments once more. And with any luck, I have not nearly come to the end of my supply of hat glue! Ever I seem to run out of it at the least opportune times."

"We will find time for you to dress, Baegulgog," Parissah said, and her voice along with her stride seemed somewhat improved to him, though he understood little of physical weariness. "The Field Marshal will go ahead of us to seek our audience with the Queen. But dress as quickly as you may; we will have need of that time! You saw the southbound ghosts as well as I did on the road?"

"Indeed I did," Baegulgog said.

"We must learn for ourselves where they were coming from. You must bear witness to it. Even if our diplomatic efforts should be entirely scuttled, we *must* get at the truth of those ghosts."

Baegulgog was once again blindsided by Parissah. She certainly had her own sense of priorities. "What do you suspect?"

"I think those ghosts were southern soldiers, captured for scientific experimentation."

That did sound ominous. "To what end, I wonder?"

"The worst end, I'm afraid. It is obvious that the Queens would gladly destroy each the other, if they were able. I expect they have picked up where their ancestor Aedeloma left off, trying to learn a way to totally destroy the life force of a Meduseldan."

The mere thought made Baegulgog fearful, even dizzy. It was difficult to conceive of a drone living fewer than 290 years (140, by Human reckoning), or a Queen living fewer than 2180 years (770). And moreover, it was an affront to the natural order of things – one that he understandably took rather personally. He made a noise like clearing his throat, though of course he did not have one. "You are thoroughly convinced they would try to contrive such evil?" He asked in a low voice.

"It has ever been my greatest fear with regard to this war. Waiting at the end of any indefinite arms-race is a weapon that changes the world. And there is no greater breach in the mission parameters of the Inquisition than to allow the world to change. The Queens must not find a way to really kill each other. All other concerns are secondary."

Baegulgog contemplated all this for a moment. "I concur! But what are we to do about it? There have been no more ghosts for some hours. We shan't very well be able to trace them back to any secret laboratories, if they have all passed us by. What other means do we have at our disposal to root out the conspiracy?"

"I wouldn't fret about it, Baegulgog. There is a Magormissahran proverb: 'The road you are not intended to walk will never fail to present itself.' To be sure, Queen Irisa does not mean for us to walk into her secret labs. Which is why we may be confident that we will have occasion to do so."

Baegulgog made no answer. Her 'plan' was apparently to trust in rhetoric. But then, rhetoric was generally pretty trusty... particularly the rhetoric of very ancient dragons...

* * *

Now beyond the comb of basic city structures, they passed a legion of stationary troops along the entry to the main gate of the capitol building, and came into a reception hall. A strong scent of cooked pineapple suffused the air. Baegulgog thought he had detected the smell of it as they passed throughout the city, but here it was absolutely unmistakable. He knew at once what that meant. The Berlie Beirels had been harvesting their ectodermis sheddings – in finance of their war, no doubt.

Ectodermis had considerable monetary value in some circles. This is because it was subject to the force of Up, rather than Down. As such, a great enough volume of ectodermis could lend aerial buoyancy to vehicles. Only old Kanaedia and its offshoots ever made substantial use of ectodermis in the production of airborne attack ships. But ironically, no one consumed more of the stuff than the Inquisition, who used it to keep their enormous fleet of naval vessels light in the water, so they might be unnaturally fast and agile.

Though it was endlessly renewable, ectodermis had a couple of good reasons to be expensive. For one, it would take many, many sheddings to be able to lift even a few pounds. For another, Meduselda rarely harvested it. They didn't tend to bother about it – after all, they didn't tend to need money. And anyway, the process was rather tricky, since ectodermis is halfway between existing and not existing. Very few substances could be used to collect it, because it passed directly through almost everything. The most common harvesting method was a tarp coated in pineapple oil (not, mind you, to be confused with pineapple juice, which didn't work at all).

There seemed to be no shortage of folk in Brittegonnen to collect sheddings from. Having already passed a great muster outside, now all about Baegulgog there were many more soldiers – enough to fill the hall with a wavering blue light. And Baegulgog noted that this rather vast garrison of royal guards was far better equipped than the front-line soldiers, with most or all actually carrying a weapon. It was unconventional to see so many resources committed to guarding the Queen's dwelling in wartime. Queens, after all, were not helpless.

Prominently in the midst of the troops, with a pair of those elite swordsdrones at his sides, was another drone attired similarly to the Field Marshal. This, evidently, was the Captain of the Guard. Baegulgog watched as he floated forward to confer with the Field Marshal. He couldn't quite make out their exchange, but snatches of it sounded rather heated. Baegulgog understood that the war had gone on very steadily for many years, and so the sudden and unplanned withdrawal of the forward Command and the ceasefire must've come as quite the unpleasant surprise to the Captain. Baegulgog shuddered to think how the Queen would soon react...

He turned to Parissah, to see how she gauged the response of the Captain of the Guard. But she paid no mind to the conference of the Captain and the Marshal. Her head was swiveling all about on its long neck. Baegulgog determined she must've been engaged in trying to deduce where they might be stowing some secret laboratories in the palace. After a few moments, something held her gaze.

"Look there, Baegulgog," she said, pointing.

"What is it, madam?" Baegulgog asked.

"There are Humans over there," she answered, "and Herons."

There were indeed – a small group of them down a corridor on the left side of the reception hall. They were in some sort of fluster, and fumbling with a good deal of luggage. The Herons were all in their plague doctor attire, and the Humans were dressed similarly.

"I spy a Mesomela as well," Baegulgog said, "and not a few armed Berlie Beirel guards herding them all about. What do you make of it?"

She raised her snout, as if testing the air. "Smells like science."

With this, she began to stride for the corridor. Baegulgog was at once shocked by her boldness. There were rows and rows of troops in her path, and they were leaving the retinue of the Field Marshal, even as he was trying to get them in to see Queen Irisa. "Do you really mean to investigate *now*?" he asked. "I'm at best unsure they will approve."

"You may be sure they won't. But this is the opportune moment. The Marshal is tied up in the debate with the Captain of the Guard, and will yet have to go before the Queen herself ahead of us. We must seize the opportunity afforded us by the bureaucracy."

He felt rather unconvinced. "Might you better use the time to rest? I understood your people do that sort of thing."

"We do. But I would appreciate it if you didn't remind me."

Baegulgog followed her lead. He might well have stayed behind, so that at least one of the folk who had come calling on the Queen would be there for the benefit of the Marshal to point out. He might very well indeed... except that she still had his hat and coat...

"Halt!" commanded a Berlie Beirel soldier as Parissah drew near. He raised a sword, and Baegulgog saw that there was lightning in his tentacles.

"Stand aside, soldier," Parissah replied. "I am a Primary Administrator of the Inquisition, and my associate here is a Berlberi Clerk. Your palace is being audited."

The soldier hesitated. "I... I can't allow you to pass. There're secretive things this way."

"Those are the things which we are here to audit," Parissah explained.

"...Oh..." the soldier said, his glow pulsating with contemplation. "In that case, go right ahead."

"Thank you," Parissah said, and she and Baegulgog pushed past the many rows of the Guard.

Reaching the corridor, Baegulgog began to hear snippets of the conversations between the gathering Humans and Herons. They seemed distraught.

"...humiliating enough that I never passed the bar, and had to resort to a career in the sciences," said the Mesomela he had spotted earlier. "Now this! I can't take any more disgrace!"

"'Least ya have a home to go back to, m'lad," said a little Human woman. "Me own kinfolk up and fled for Despotopia months ago, and I dunno if I'll e'er be able to find 'em again! I'm just a simple xenobiologist maself; I canna very well go home and face them awful 'Free-Dome fighters' all alone!"

"Technically I *don't* have a home to go back to, since my species was displaced thousands of years ago," the Mesomela replied.

"Well then, *technically* I feel sorry for ya," the Human woman, apparently from Maenea, remarked. "Now be a lad and let me get back to feelin' sorry for *maself*!"

"I don't see what the fuss is about," said a Heron woman. "Things have worked out the very best way they could, in the end. Did you want to labor to your dying day in that lab, chasing ever more oblique hunches and getting nowhere? It was a fool's errand from the beginning."

"Ye're always such a ray o' sunshine, Tersairah," the Maenean said.

"What is the meaning of this?" Parissah demanded, reaching this small grouping of scientists. The three of them, though masked, seemed more than a little surprised at her sudden appearance.

"By golly, an Inquisitor!" the Mesomela said at last.

Parissah pointed at him. "You watch your language." She pivoted her head aggressively. "And you – small Human – explain yourself! What are you people doing here?!"

Baegulgog noted to himself that he was rather impressed with Parissah's questioning. She was so direct that even *he* almost forgot she really had no business asking anything.

"We – we're just sciencing, ma'am," the Maenean answered meekly. "We're just doin' our job we were hired to do. Or at least... we were. I'm afraid we just got the axe."

"The axe?" Parissah repeated.

"We got canned, ma'am."

"Canned?"

"She means we've just been fired," explained the Heron, Tersairah.

"Hmm," Parissah considered. "That is hopeful. But it reveals very little. I should like to know what you were 'sciencing' when you were fired. In fact I demand to know."

No one volunteered a word.

"Well?" Parissah coaxed them impatiently. "Will no one so much as admit that you were attempting to devise a Meduseldan-killing weapon of some sort?"

"We'd like to, ma'am," said the Mesomela. "We certainly don't want any trouble with the Inquisition. But we would be in violation of our contract to tell you anything."

"Under penalty of death, I suppose?" Parissah asked.

"Naturally."

"I see. Still, I can't help noticing you did nothing to deny that you *were* working on a weapon, such as I described."

"*Darn*," the Mesomela huffed, realizing too late how she had tricked him.

Parissah appeared ready to scold the Jackal for his casual use of obscenities again, when suddenly a Berlie Beirel guard who had been among the displaced scientists arrived to investigate the disturbance. "What is the meaning of this?" he asked, and like the guard who had earlier barred their way to the corridor, this one looked ready for a fight.

"I have already put that question to them," Parissah told the guard, "and I suppose they have answered it as well as could be hoped."

Her response flummoxed the guard, but he soon regained himself. "I mean to say, what are *you* doing here? And what makes you think you can question these scientists?"

"That is none of your concern!" she answered. "This is Inquisition business!"

"It's little use trying to conceal our work from the Inquisitor," Tersairah further reasoned with the guard. "She seems to have already had some inkling what we were up to. At any rate, we failed. There hardly seems any secret worth keeping in failure."

"Queen Irisa alone may decide which secrets are worth keeping and which are not," the guard retorted. "You should know better than to reveal anything about your research. Don't you remember the eighty non-disclosure agreements we had each of you sign?"

"I was sure there were only thirty-five," the Maenean mused.

"Never mind how many there were!" the guard exclaimed. "You are in breach of all of them. I'm afraid you shall all have to be executed."

"Dang it," the Jackal sighed.

Parissah walked by him on the way to the guard. "With a mouth like that, you ought to have been a sailor," she told the Jackal, before turning her attention back on the guard. "And *you* – you may do as you see fit! You can kill me; you can kill my associate the Clerk here; you can kill all of these people, if you wish!" Baegulgog noticed that the scientists were apt to silently protest the part about killing them. "It matters little now. Baegulgog the Clerk is under my express orders to return to the Ocean Citadel and report that your nation has been researching illegal weaponry – as a ghost, if need be."

"I am?" Baegulgog asked.

"You most certainly are," Parissah told him, and homed in on the guard again. "And when the Inquisition comes here to raze Brittegonnen to the ground and rid the earth of your illicit science, it will fall to you to explain all of this to your Queen!"

The guard hesitated. He lowered the point of his sword. "Well, that does sound like a lot of unwanted trouble," he admitted. "But what would you have me do? I am duty-bound to enforce the non-disclosure agreements."

Baegulgog at once had a thought, and floated forth triumphantly. "Perhaps I might be of some service in resolving this matter. I am a Clerk, as you've heard – well-versed in non-disclosure agreements, and all other forms of paperwork." He examined each of the scientists in passing. "I am sure one of you at least has their copy of the agreements on their person?"

"Of course!" the Mesomela exclaimed, ears perking. "I'd never go anywhere without them!" And he quickly produced a healthy stack of papers from a pocket within his heavy lab coat.

Baegulgog took the agreements and flipped through them with great speed. "I see that all of these forms are part of a larger contract. May I have that as well?"

"Certainly," the Mesomela said, and handed him an even larger stack of papers. Baegulgog merrily but deftly examined the contract from beginning to end, a very condensed 921 pages in all.

"It is just as I suspected," he announced at last.

"What is?" the guard asked.

"This contract does not include the EReg73013-J form."

The guard flickered with deep thought. "I – I'm not sure I'm familiar with that form."

"Suffice it to say, without the EReg73013-J form, the signees are no longer considered bound by their non-disclosure agreements after their contracts have been annulled upon the termination of their employment."

Again, the guard went alight with consideration. "What does that mean?"

"It means, now that we're fired, we can't be executed if we accidently blab about the research," the Mesomela interjected proudly. "I may not have passed the bar, but I learned that much about legal mumbo-jumbo, at least."

"Beside that rather glaring oversight, I would say this is a superb contract – wonderfully written and a distinct pleasure to read," Baegulgog said, reluctantly surrendering the document back to its owner.

"So... I can't execute any of you?" the guard asked.

"No," Parissah instructed. "And furthermore, you won't prevent these people showing me to their secret laboratory.

"I won't?"

"No. You won't."

The guard seemed unsure. "Is that also in the contract?"

"Not exactly," Baegulgog admitted. "I'm afraid there was little language pertaining to showing visitors around the secret laboratory. But how about being a good sport and giving us the benefit of the doubt, would you?"

"Well, alright," the guard agreed at length.

"Very good," Parissah said, sounding at once much more agreeable. "I thank you for your cooperation." She turned to the scientists. "Please lead the way."

* * *

Passing through a variety of secret doors revealing secret windows that led to secret walls, they descended a secret stair to the secret floor where the secret laboratory was built. It was a sprawling facility, surprising in its vastness and its alien construction. The architecture was different here – unaccountably precise – the way Humans and Avarica and such tended to build things. The walls and ceiling were immaculate. The floor was less so; things had been dropped on it, and guards were currently overseeing scientists cleaning it up (there were several guards and scientists still in the lab). The space was a flurry of urgent activity. It was clear from the general manner of everything that the plug had been pulled on the Queen's pet project hastily and without prior warning. Those left in the lab looked quite bewildered as they tried to improvise a means of disposing of their own work. Beakers and flagons and scientific glass tubes of every stripe were being poured down drains. Small stoves and turntables and other unidentified little bits of paraphernalia were being hurled into bags. Baegulgog watched in horror as great stacks of papers were tossed in the trash! It was a sight nearly unbearable for a Clerk, and it was all he could do to keep from crying out...

The guards in the lab itself naturally didn't take to interlopers much more than the others had before them. But the guard from the hall – Hubblefro was his name – and the three scientists they had got to lead them – Tersairah, Shailey (the Maenean) and Naucratis (the Jackal) – did most of the negotiating this time. Parissah didn't wait around to see how that played out, and Baegulgog did what he could to keep pace with her, as she wove past a long series of enormous glass vats, examining them. Baegulgog was sure that these had been holding tanks for the southern soldiers that were being experimented on – a most unpleasant thought. He was glad that each of them had merely been killed by the experiments, as opposed to *really* killed...

"Here is the lab – the very proof of the Queen's wicked deeds and intentions," Baegulgog said. "What more? Should we perhaps now go back, and be ready to face Her Majesty?" He was, after all, still rather anxious about snooping around the palace. He didn't like the idea of displeasing a Queen one bit, whether it was his own Queen or not.

"We can't return yet, Baegulgog," Parissah said. "One mystery has run into another. I have to know *why* they shut down the project. Surely Queen Irisa is not yet satisfied that her goal is impossible. To this day we don't well understand Meduseldan Queen psychology, I admit. But impatience has not historically been one of their quirks."

Baegulgog was mildly miffed by that language. He wouldn't readily think of Queens as 'quirky'. But Parissah was right, of course. It would not be wise at all to merely accept that the research was over. There had to be a reason...

Past the vats, they came to a series of offices running darkly in a long row on both sides. Baegulgog had far underestimated the breadth of the intersection. After a very brief survey, Parissah quickly doubled back toward the primary lab. Baegulgog couldn't match her speed, but managed not to get too far behind by the time she returned to the triumvirate of scientists that had brought them there.

"Why did you get the can?" Parissah demanded of them.

"Nay, ma'am," Shailey corrected. "We *got the axe*. Alternatively, we got *canned*."

"Well never mind about that," Parissah said. "Why were you all fired? Why has the research been abandoned?"

They were all silent for a time.

"We – we don't rightly know, ma'am," Shailey admitted. "Wish we did. Truly I do."

"All we know is that we did not succeed, and that we were in no danger of succeeding," Tersairah added. "But you should speak with our Project Director. He is still here, you may be sure."

"That is what I meant to do," Parissah agreed, "only I don't know who he is or where he is. Perhaps you could find him for me?"

"Anything for the people that got us out of being executed," Naucratis said. "I find I am a bit grateful for that."

"Never mind that they also nearly got us *into* being executed," Tersairah said. "Still, we would be glad to help."

"You have my thanks," Parissah told them.

* * *

The unemployed scientists led Baegulgog and Parissah back to the offices, down the left way and around two corners. Apparently the Project Director's office was quite removed from the main lab, but seeing as he was preeminent over a very secret facility, this seemed not entirely inappropriate. Finally, the scientists slowed, and came to a stop.

"His is the one two doors down from here," Tersairah said, rather quietly.

"I suppose you don't wish to see him," Parissah mused.

"Not especially. This is a shameful occasion for all of us... but after all, it was *his* project. He must bear the brunt of the failure. It is not what I would consider a good time to come calling."

"Darn straight," Naucratis agreed.

Parissah cast him a look over her shoulder. "I wish I had a bar of soap..." then she started as if she'd caught herself in her own words, and turned to Baegulgog, "...if you'll forgive the expression, Baegulgog."

"Quite alright, madam," Baegulgog replied, "I've made my peace with soap, I believe."

"What does that mean?" Shailey asked.

"There's no time to explain," Parissah said. "In any case, you are all free to go. I thank you again, and wish you well. And do be careful crossing the molten wilderness out there."

"Oy, I'd all but forgotten about that until ya said something," Shailey lamented, as they all turned and began back. "This day just keeps gettin' better."

* * *

Baegulgog and Parissah approached the Project Director's office. Before the door was an enormous window, and Baegulgog was not sure whether he was relieved or dismayed to see that the Director was indeed still perched behind his desk. He was a Dire Heron, which was little surprise. Heron personalities tended to be the most meticulous and brilliant in the world. They also tended to be the dreariest. Small wonder his subordinates didn't want to disturb him.

Baegulgog considered the large bird. Unlike all the lab hands, he didn't wear a plague mask, though he did sport a heavy medical cloak. He was intently considering a phial in his talon, such that he didn't appear to notice as they came up to the door and pushed their way in. Even Parissah now seemed reticent to barge right in and get her answers. The door creaked slowly in her claw.

"Excuse me, Director," she said, and Baegulgog became rather unnerved. He couldn't be sure if she was actually anxious about confronting him, or if she just wanted to show a bit of tenderness in the man's unhappy hour. Either way, it seemed a peculiar approach for her.

"Do you know what this is?" the Director asked in a low voice, indicating his phial. It was filled with orangish goo.

"I'm sure I don't," Parissah responded.

"Neither do I," the Director admitted. "When I was quite new to my studies, I mixed some chemicals in this phial. But I neglected to make record of the materials I used. And by the next day, I had entirely forgot." He reached out and set the phial on his desk with great care. "Every time I meet with failure, I retrieve this phial, and I attempt to recall what chemicals I mixed that day. Even though, in my heart... I know that I can *never* remember."

Baegulgog felt a pang of sympathy for the Heron Director. He had heard that some Herons were so naturally gifted at melancholy that even the merriest mind could hardly resist being pulled down a ways with them. He now knew that this was true.

"Director, I know this is a bad time..." Parissah began, but trailed off.

"– Not at all. You remind me that there is much I must yet see to. As the captain goes down with his ship, so I should be supervising the dereliction of my research." He fluttered to his feet, and walked right past them out the door.

They followed him a few paces behind, sheepishly, until Baegulgog saw Parissah give herself a shake – apparently mustering some of her old manner – and come up alongside the Director. "Director Issrius," she addressed him (having read his name tag), "I take no pleasure in pestering you now, however relieved I may be that your project has turned out a complete botch. But you must know better than to try to ignore an Inquisitor, when we come inquisiting."

He stopped, holding motionless as few other than birds are able. Baegulgog worried how ugly the confrontation might get. He knew that Herons historically felt they had an axe to grind with the Inquisition – that the relationship there had been under some strain from as far back as Kanaedia...

But finally, the Director turned to them, and Baegulgog saw that he was too downcast to long hold his gaze to either of them. "Yes, you are right. You must forgive my petulance. It is hard enough answering to myself at the moment, let alone anyone else. But there is no use making excuses. Come with me, and I will answer all of your questions, if I can."

He hurried along again. By now they were nearly back to the glass vats.

"I have only one line of questions," Parissah said. "I must know why your research was cancelled."

Director Issrius rested a talon on one of the vats as he came alongside it, his claws tinking on the glass as he considered the question. "Why indeed. That is rather difficult to qualify." Suddenly his talon shrieked as he whisked it down the vat. "I never saw it coming! We weren't fast enough, I suppose. Not nearly fast enough..."

Parissah began to reach out, as if to grab him by the shoulders, although he really didn't have any. And she couldn't very well grab his neck, so in the end she just knelt by him to be at eye-level. "Get a hold of yourself, Director! You're speaking in riddles. What did you not see coming?"

"The technology," he gasped. "It's out there. Someone else has already got to it ahead of me! And it's been promised to Queen Irisa. Don't you see! She does not need me because she is already getting what she wants."

O horror of horrors! Baegulgog thought. A Meduseldan-killing weapon! That he should live to learn of something so abominable!

"Who?" Parissah asked at length. "Who has promised this weapon to the Queen?"

The Director's feathers puffed, and his beak shook. "I... I don't know. They never told me. You'll have to ask the Queen herself. I don't know..." His vacant look of utter disbelief was terrible to behold.

* * *

After they had gathered themselves and Baegulgog had once again donned his Dronehood uniform, they left the lab, escorted back through the secret ways by the guard Hubblefro. It was a sullen march. Baegulgog felt nearly as beside himself as Director Issrius. Parissah was right – the arms-race had changed the world. Even if the Weapon was only ever used to return the count of Queens back to ten – indeed, even if it was *never* used – its mere existence altered the balance of power, and in ways too subtle and cosmic to guess. He couldn't get over the audacity of it all. The *hubris*! And he, too, was determined to know who this unpleasant fellow was – the scoundrel who had created the Weapon, and meant to put it in the hands of the belligerent Queen of the north...

"I do hope you found whatever you were after," Hubblefro began, unbidden. "You may have got me into a lot of trouble after all, now that I'm an accessory to your investigations."

Baegulgog was indignant as he floated through yet another secret door. "Indeed, quite a lot more trouble than you guess, perhaps. The Queen may soon have you executed if she wishes... and *permanently*."

Hubblefro hesitated. "Then the scientists succeeded after all? That is well. The war can now end as it ought... with the destruction of that southern imposter!"

At once Baegulgog became more indignant than ever. "Is that all you can see!? An end to your own little squabble? What will the world be like afterward!? Suppose other folk get ideas about how to use the new Weapon. Suppose the number of Queens goes from ten to nine, from nine to eight, from eight to seven, from seven to three! And so on! Shall we then hear 'that is well' from the guard Hubblefro? I can scant believe the state of you modern Berlie Beirels! What has become of your older and better legacy? Where are the mathematicians? The counters and the registrars? Where are the ones like those who of old built up the great Archives of Berlberi, with its many shimmering paths of filing cabinets stretching on miles long and stories high? I am a Sowür Canpattel, yet I daresay Berlberi is more my home than yours!"

"You shame me, sir Clerk," Hubblefro confessed, dejectedly. "I admit I have never even seen Berlberi, our homeland from of yore."

"That is obvious," Baegulgog laughed mirthlessly. "If you had, you would not have such brutish thoughts. Your soul would be too full of the joy of numbers and paperwork. Instead you harbor only the ire of Aedeloma." He shook his body back and forth in woe. "If it were up to me, I would send the lot of you – *north* and *south* alike – back to Berlberi straight away! I think it would do you a world of good. But alack, I am only a Clerk. And anyway, I suppose it is too late. The damage is done."

Parissah stopped dead in her tracks. She turned to Baegulgog and grabbed hold of him by the shoulders. "Baegulgog! You're a genius!" she exclaimed. It befuddled him greatly.

"Dear me!" he replied. "Surely not! I cannot even conceive what I said to make you think so."

"You will see!" Parissah promised, still unsettlingly jubilant. "When the time comes to meet with Queen Irisa, you will see!"

Just about as Parissah let go of him, Baegulgog felt a fresh wave of anger. It was not his own anger he felt – that much he knew. It belonged to someone else...

"You shall have to meet with her very soon, I think," Hubblefro said, resting a tentacle on the top of his body, as if he were woozy. Baegulgog knew at once that he had felt the foreign anger as well. "She has just learned of the ceasefire you imposed on her, if I don't miss my guess."

The next moment, the whole palace shook with a crash.

"...Yes, I believe you are right," Parissah said, hunched defensively. And they continued on their way back to the reception hall... though much more sheepishly now...

* * *

Baegulgog and Parissah stood in awe in the deep red light of Queen Irisa. It had taken some time to reach her. There was a substantial, nearly-vertical climb that separated the reception hall from the Address Level of the royal chamber. Beneath the rough grate below them that formed the circular Level, they could espy hundreds of feet of her coiled tentacles. And above, stretching unsearchable heights into the upper recesses of the palace, continued the vast upper body of Irisa. Little could be made out, but it appeared that she had a sharply ridged shape, very wide but flat – quite distinct from the bulbous body of drones. Baegulgog hadn't expected that. Indeed, he hadn't even expected the bold red hue of her luminescence. He reeled that in all his time he had never so much as heard that Queens were red...

He did not intend to advertise it, but this was actually the first time Baegulgog had ever seen a Queen of his own race. Drones generated by a Queen could poof into existence anywhere within a roughly hundred-foot radius, and so it was not unheard of for a drone to materialize on the other side of a wall, or even several rooms away. That is precisely how Baegulgog had come into the world. So this was for him a solemn moment.

Rapturous occasion though it was, his mental orchestra couldn't seem to so much as impose a note of its own music on the situation. For while Baegulgog was quite amazed, he was also much-diverted. A powerful current of annoyance had a hold of him, and he was hopeless to break with it. As with the anger he had felt in the secret places beneath the halls of Brittegonnen's palace, he recognized at once that the feeling was foreign. Now in the Queen's presence, he knew it was *her* annoyance that was finding real estate in his mind. This was an ability of Meduseldan Queens. They did not control the minds of their drones (let alone drones belonging to other Dominions), but they gave off such a powerful and intricate electrical signature that any drones in their midst (who of course also had strong internal currents) could not help picking up an empathetic resonance. He felt what she felt... and so did every other Meduseldan in the area...

Baegulgog took stock of the scene. There were several guards and a number of swordsdrones... and even abominations. So Baegulgog hoped Parissah would not make Queen Irisa overly wroth... lest all of these forces converge on them in a fit of sympathetic rage!

"It is remarkable, Baegulgog," Parissah whispered, almost choking the words out. Baegulgog understood that she was out of breath from the climb, and also possibly robbed of it by Queen Irisa's imposing presence. There were evidently many ways that breathing creatures could be short breath. "If I had not seen Enscharaulgk for myself many times in the past, it would have been difficult to believe that something so enormous could be living."

"Truly momentous," Baegulgog quietly agreed. He too was still quite taken aback by how many bazillions of times larger the Queen was than he. Taken aback enough that, even being a Clerk and so a consummate math whiz, he resorted to the figure of 'bazillions'...

"I hear you speak," burgeoned the voice of Irisa. Parissah and Baegulgog recoiled, though the voice seemed to come from everywhere, leaving few places to recoil to. "I have never considered that I was enormous... only that all of you are so very small."

"Forgive me, Queen Irisa of Brittegonnen," Parissah kowtowed. "It was most ill-mannered and unprofessional of me to speak of you behind your back just now."

"Never mind," Irisa said. "You are not behind my back... but rather, you are in front of my front. If indeed this is my front, as I strongly believe it to be. But you should not call me 'Queen of Brittegonnen'. I am Queen of the Berlie Beirel Dominion!"

Baegulgog felt absolute resolution that this was true. But he knew that it was her resolution and not his own.

"Your Highness," Parissah began, "Far be it from me to deny you any of the honor you are due. But you know as well as any that the title of 'Queen of the Berlie Beirels' is in dispute, and it is not my place to make judgment between you and Asiri of the South."

Now there was a very great and fierce anger! Baegulgog watched as the Berlie Beirels in the room went into a fluster. He then realized that he too was flustering mildly, and at once he stilled himself...

"That usurper!" Irisa growled, and the metal in the palace creaked and warped with the electromagnetic intensity of her sudden fit. "Such a name should never be spoken here! I would see that it is never spoken *again*! Indeed, I should say that I was well on my way to making her answerable to her treachery, before *you* came and interrupted my war! Why have you done this? If not to name me rightful and undisputed Queen, as I so obviously am, then *why*?!"

"Because there must be negotiations," Parissah answered. "Certain hard truths must be accepted, and considered rationally, if at all possible. Like it or not, you and Asiri are both Queens. You both possess all of the qualities of a Queen, from greatest to least. You both are able to generate full compliments of drones. None of these objective facts are in dispute."

"Perhaps not," Irisa said in an even tone, though Baegulgog knew the great contempt that she was withholding. "Though I am not sure all of your objective facts and mine are in agreement." Pulsing red filled the entire wide disk about Irisa as she waxed thoughtful. "Even so, the war has not yet yielded the results I have sought, and I grow weary. If you have an expedient solution in mind, I will gladly hear it."

Parissah hesitated. "I'm afraid I don't have anything *expedient* to offer. My mission was to convince you and Asiri to attend a summit with Enscharaulgk. He alone may possess the wisdom to decide whether one or both of you is the rightful Queen of the Berlie Beirel Dominion, or whether the advent of twin Queens spells the end of all Berlie Beireldom for ever, and each of you must begin her own, new Dominion."

"Unconscionable!" Irisa exclaimed. "You dragon folk do not understand these matters. There can be no *new* Dominions! And the Berlie Beirel Dominion must certainly not come to an *end*!" She seethed with an ever-growing outrage. "And most assuredly of all, we cannot *both* continue the legacy of the Berlie Beirels!"

"But perhaps you could," Parissah suggested. Baegulgog could hardly believe the limb she was climbing on. There was no more objectionable thought to Irisa – he was sure of it.

"How *dare* you," Irisa said, beside herself with the arrogance of her guest. "How can such a legacy be yoked between two heirs?"

"Because, as my associate the Clerk has just reminded me, the legacy of the Berlie Beirels is already at a crossroads," Parissah answered. "Long ago, your ancestor De'Ankamori settled these Isles of Tophthaera. The Berlie Beirels are a firmly established cornerstone in the canon of this, the Idriulthorontan Archipelago. But in yet older days, your home was Berlberi, and that great domain endures. It is still yours – or Asiri's – to reclaim, if you wish. And Berlberi may well be the better for it. Imagine the Archives once again under the administration and protection of a Queen!"

Baegulgog's thoughts were swirling. And he could see that Irisa too was awash in deep consideration. Her tide of epiphany spilled into his mind, and all the Meduselda present flashed rapidly and brilliantly in uniform mental processing.

"This is actually a good idea," Irisa admitted at length. "Certainly worth consideration. Another Queen of the Berlie Beirels would not so greatly offend me, if she were very far away." She gave a single laugh of exultant thought. "Continental Berlie Beirels and Island Berlie Beirels! It has a rather pleasant sound about it..."

Baegulgog was overjoyed that the negotiations were going so well. Parissah seemed to have a knack for getting people to be compliant by first exasperating them. But even as he was about to sigh his final relief of the whole ordeal, he felt Irisa's emotions plunge back into bitterness...

"Still..." Irisa started softly (softly as any being that fills a tower may start), "...still, suppose that I wish to return to the continent, and Asiri does as well? Or suppose I decide to remain here in Tophthaera, but the vile charlatan resolves the same? No. No... this may not hold the promise I hoped..."

"My original advice remains the same," Parissah said urgently. "You should treat with Enscharaulgk. At least now there is a possibility for peace worth exploring."

"Yet now perhaps there is a better possibility to explore," Irisa said, and Baegulgog objected to her feelings of venomous delight. "I might just as well go ahead and destroy Asiri, as I had planned from the first... then claim Berlberi once again, and rule over both the domains of the Berlie Beirels, old and new alike!"

"That *would* be a respectably direct approach," Parissah conceded. "But this... this talk of destroying Queens... it is ill-founded. Does one breach in historical precedent call for another – indeed, a worse one – to set it right? I know you are pursuing a secret Weapon. And where you should not be! I cannot duly discourage it. It simply must *not* be done."

"But it *is* done," Irisa retorted. "The Weapon is made. I have but to receive it."

Parissah seemed in that moment to decompress. Baegulgog felt very sad for her. She had come so close to getting the Queen to see reason, but at the last it had all fallen apart. And he worried afresh about the course of the future, reminded potently about the inevitability of the Weapon by the remorseless feelings of Irisa.

But Parissah looked up again. "Whence comes your Weapon, pray tell?"

In the moment that followed, Baegulgog was surprised how the Queen reacted to the question. She felt no compulsion to conceal anything. "It was promised to me by the Glowy Lady."

Parissah was dumbstruck. She stood and convulsed with a quick birdlike twitch. "Who in the H..." she began, but caught herself. Her mask seemed to glow dully orange with sudden heat. "That is – I mean... whoever is *'the Glowy Lady'*?"

Queen Irisa mulled it over for some moments. "Oddly enough, it didn't occur to me to get her name. Perhaps I ought to have. But I'm surprised you do not know of the Glowy Lady. She seems very much the sort of person your Inquisition would make it their business to know about."

"She does at that," Parissah agreed. "Indeed, I should like to hear all there is to know about her, if you would be so kind as to enlighten me."

Irisa endeavored to remember what she could. "She appeared Human, I think... but taller and more conical at the top. And she glowed green."

Parissah stood silent for several seconds, apparently inviting more information. "Is that *all*?" she said, and she dared to sound somewhat impatient.

"Yes, I'm afraid so. I don't know where she came from, or any of her other business. She simply showed up one day and asked if I wished to destroy the southern imposter. I told her I wished that very much... and she promised to return with the means."

"I don't suppose she said anything about when?"

"She did not. Perhaps any day. I really don't know. But I meant to continue the war in the meantime, of course." She paused for a moment of thought. "I think I will continue it. Unless you remain intent to stop me, that is. But you should know it is futile. Once I have the Weapon, you can be sure I'll find a way to use it... whether *Variglew* stands or not."

"There is nothing I can do to restrict you. I have neither the time nor the means to destroy your Bridge any more at my disposal," Parissah admitted.

"Then the war shall go on," Irisa imparted, and at once some drones went out to inform the Field Marshal. "But fear not – I will see it comes to a good end, and as soon as can be managed."

"Then I take my leave of you," Parissah said. "But I hope you will yet pay mind to your alternatives. I hope you will recognize the colossal mistake you're making, and help us to eliminate all of this wicked technology before it is used carelessly, in ways you have not yet imagined."

"Don't hold out any great hope of that," Irisa replied, and Baegulgog felt emotionally crushed by how calmly resolute the Queen was. She could not be moved. She would have her victory over Asiri, no matter the cost. "Farewell."

* * *

"Do you have even the first notion who 'the Glowy Lady' might be?" Baegulgog asked Parissah, the two of them removing themselves from the palace and the encircling city. None of the Berlie Beirels paid them any mind now. Word had evidently preempted them that the Inquisitor had come up short in her defiance of the Queen, and was leaving in disgrace. Or, such was the smug way they seemed to be ignoring them, in Baegulgog's estimation. He left there wishing very much to wash his tentacles at Berlie Beirels, once and for all...

"I don't," Parissah sighed. "And there is so little time to look into it as I ought. It will have to be handled by others. Once we reach the coast, I can get word back to the Ocean Citadel. They must learn of this – as indeed I must also let them know my negotiations with Irisa have failed. My plan is that they should blockade Tophthera in the hopes of keeping the Glowy Lady from returning. It does not guarantee anything, of course... and in the end, we must certainly find her and destroy her research. Still, at least it allows us to put our swollen navy into play – it is the one resource the Inquisition has over and in abundance at present. But after that, I have to continue on to Maenea at once; that situation is also very dire. Countess Jengadocea will soon be utterly besieged by the forces of Herz Bravado, if she is not already!" She shook her head. "There is just so very little time to waste. We will have to make for the coast with all speed. Lest I forget entirely, I still need to work in a stop-over at Roemnar on the way to Maenea. Those runaway lighthouse stewards must be arrested."

Baegulgog was surprised. "Do you still consider that of any import? It seems a very little thing, next to all the international intrigue we are already mixed up in."

Parissah slumped, and shook her head. "If I thought that way, many little things would never get done."

Considering the road ahead, Baegulgog suddenly felt like dead weight. He had been some help to her in investigating the secrets of Brittegonnen, and that was well. But now she had need of speed, and he could only float so fast. "I fear we will reach the coast no faster than we reached Brittegonnen," he admitted. "I am going just as speedily as I can. Perhaps you should rest before you do anything more. I can at least float ahead of you, and you can pass me on the road. If you feel the need, leave me behind – I will understand. I have been of little enough utility thus far, and probably have scant to offer in Roemnar or Maenea."

"I mustn't rest, Baegulgog," Parissah said, and he could tell she meant it through and through. "And anyway I am not so tired as I was. This whole business with the Queen and the mysterious 'Glowy Lady' has me quite incensed. It fans *the fire within*, and I have revived... somewhat. You of course remain free to go, if you feel that all these errands might be in vain, as indeed they may be. But if you still wish to help, I would consider it of great value."

"My soul would speed me forward to your aid! But alas, as I said, the body will not propel me any faster."

"That's no obstacle at all," Parissah said, resolutely... all the while taking out and putting on an electrically insulated glove. "You cannot quicken yourself, but I can! Take my hand, Baegulgog!"

With a hold of one of his tentacles, she took off across the barren, molten wastelands of Tophthera at great speed, bound for the northwest coast, Baegulgog in tow behind her...

In Absentia

"Justice is yet another product of mortal vanity. We invent what we think is fair, so that we can feel entitled to it."

- Magormissahr, *Referendums on the World, Vol. 304*

"The court will come to order," bellowed Vice-Vizier Senahktenre amidst his gavel strikes. Up until that very moment, Horus Templar had held out some hope that the defendants – the Humans Jek and Audrey – had been arrested... and that the authorities might actually parade them out into their own trial. His heart sank as court convened, the seats next to him still empty. *No such luck*.

And yet, he knew he would be all the more vested in the case for it. He still had his axe to grind. He would defend the Humans by prosecuting *In Absentia* itself. For him there was no conflict of interest. Indeed, with what little he had found, it might be the *only* avenue of defense available to him...

Expediently, the him-haw and the pitter-patter of all the witnesses, jurors and spectators fell silent, and everyone took their seats, lastly the judge – the Vice-Vizier himself...

Horus considered Senahktenre. He was looking much older and more grizzled than the last time he saw him, and his droopy jowels worked with suppressed panting from the exertion of convening court. Though he was certainly becoming rather feeble, Horus was not at all surprised that Senahktenre was the judge of choice for this high-profile case. He had a lifelong perfect record of the death sentence. He made every charge stick in the end, even when the jury dared disagree with him. He embodied what was popularly understood as the way the system was supposed to work. Horus had to admit to being a bit intimidated, if not impressed.

"Does the prosecution have an opening statement?" judge Senahktenre asked.

"We do, your Honor," Hamilton Blackforest said, rising, adjusting his excellent suit. "The state intends to prove beyond any reasonable doubt that the defendants, Jek and Audrey, are guilty of one or more capital crimes, including dereliction of duty. The state will present definite testimony from multiple witnesses who saw first-hand as these criminals fled their post – Brighamok's Lighthouse – on the southern border. As deemed prudent, the state will also introduce into evidence any or all other facts damaging to the overall character of the defendants at its disposal. The state *will* – unequivocally – demonstrate the pressing need to sentence these villains to a swift and sure execution." Blackforest was an excellent speaker. The words themselves were but garnish over the icy stare he gave the jurors. Having quite got his point across, he sat back down.

"Very good, Mr. Blackforest," nodded the judge, and he cleared his throat with a hoarse cough. "Is there also an opening statement from the defense?" he asked.

"There is, your Honor," Horus said, coming to his feet. He didn't bother to look at the jurors – only grave-faced at the judge himself. "I hereby object to this whole proceeding as a farce and a miscarriage of justice, and move that it be held over until such time as the defendants can be brought forward."

The room was uncomfortably silent.

Finally, Senahktenre's long jowels flapped again in kind of a weak cackle. "The court is well aware of the public defender's distaste for *In Absentia* proceedings. It cautions the jurors to not be influenced by Mr. Templar's misguided attempts to distract them with questions of ethics, which are not on trial here. Objection overruled."

The gavel struck.

Horus sat down. He saw Blackforest shake his head at him, disappointed.

"Let the prosecution call its first witness," the judge declared, and Blackforest stood again.

"I call inspector Howitzerov to the stand," he said.

Horus urgently shifted in his chair to look back at the assembly. It was his convention (which he observed quite strictly) to always catch sight of witnesses in the first few seconds of being called forward. It was, after all, a disarming moment – and you never knew what you might be able to glean about someone, seeing how they reacted in such a moment...

Horus saw the inspector rise. He had an eager look about him, as if he had been waiting a long time for this. Horus guessed that he was probably prejudicial against the defendants, but otherwise honest. At any rate he looked too confident to be planning to conceal anything.

Horus heard the court recorder catch up on his typing just prior to the court officer intercepting the inspector to swear him in.

"State your name," the officer instructed.

"Rurik Howitzerov," the inspector recited.

"Do you swear to tell the truth, the whole truth, or whatever portion of the truth best expedites the final ruling of this court, so help ye Creators?"

"I do."

"Be seated."

As the inspector sat, Blackforest circled in, resting a deadly claw on the oak railing between him and his witness. "Before the state begins its line of questioning," Blackforest said, still announcing, "it is my intention to invoke the Witness' Rant Clause."

Horus blinked and ran a long nail across his whiskers. *The Witness' Rant Clause*. It was rarely invoked, being rather a stuffy formality and not actually admissible as evidence. In practice, the Witness' Rant Clause gave a witness the chance to preface their testimony with a series of negative observations about the defendants. There were no restrictions about how many of these observations a witness could string together, nor was it even required (or expected) that they confine themselves to insults pertinent to the case. A reticent witness might only have a few mean things to say and then be done. But every so often, a witness specially possessed of oration could improvise a character-assassination-filibuster that went on for hours or even days...

The defense council had only one ground for interrupting the Clause: if the witness used any indefinite articles, the corresponding insult would be ruled as speculative, and impeached... and the prosecution would have to immediately proceed to its questioning.

This was a rather odd move for Hamilton. Horus could only deduce that he was invoking the Clause merely for the sake of adding to the overall sense of scandal about the case, so to better please the Czarina and her administration.

"Hum, yes, alright... let me think..." said inspector Howitzerov, suddenly seeming unsure of himself. Horus became hopeful. "Where to begin? The defendants were certainly not punctual or attentive. They incurred numerous deductions in their inspection. Their house was filled with rubbish. The woman did not take homeland defense as seriously as she ought. They were both getting behind on their hygene; they seemed... a bit smelly, I guess..."

"Objection!" Horus leapt in. "The witness' use of the indefinite article, 'I guess,' results in improper testimony."

"Objection sustained," Senahktenre carried. "The comment about the smelliness of the defendants will be stricken. Proceed with your questioning, Mr. Blackforest."

"Yes, your Honor," Blackforest said through his fangs. He was noticeably disappointed that his witness had got no further in his Rant. But he mustered his full composure in a flash and began his questioning. "I understand, sir, that you are an agent of the Lighthouse Oversight Commission of Southern Jast-Madiir, LLC."

"Twenty-one years in, yes, that is correct," inspector Howitzerov agreed. "It is the reason I was present on the day of the crime. I was there to inspect the defendants' lighthouse."

"Indeed. You mentioned they had a number of deductions," Blackforest mused. "Did they ultimately pass inspection?"

"They would have, yes... if they hadn't carelessly wandered off," Howitzerov grudged to admit. "But not by much. It was a low score, I daresay."

"I'll object to that as well," Horus challenged. "Is the prosecution trying to pad his Witness' Rant? The relative score of the inspection has no bearing on the charge of dereliction of duty. It is irrelevant, and immaterial."

"I'm afraid he's right, Mr. Blackforest," judge Senahktenre cautioned his prosecutor. "Unless you can prove relevance."

"I believe I can do just that, your Honor," Blackforest said. "The State is attempting to demonstrate motive for the defendants' criminal act of abandoning their post. It is entirely possible they fled in expectation of failing their inspection, hoping at all costs to avoid the punishment of execution."

"Objection," Horus chimed once again. "Pure speculation on the part of the prosecution."

Senahktenre wheezed another chortle. "The defense is certainly spirited. I have not yet passed judgement on your *other* outstanding objection."

"Never mind, your Honor," Blackforest conceded. "Proving motive, or even the possibility of motive, is of marginal importance to the State's case, in the end."

"Very well, then," Senahktenre said. "*Both* objections sustained. The last question from the prosecutor and its answer will be stricken."

The court recorder blinked hard under the strain of so many strikings.

"Let us proceed directly to the point, then," Blackforest said, leaning heavily in the direction of inspector Howitzerov. "Is it true that you saw the defendants board a fishing boat, which then sped away from the scene?"

"It is true," inspector Howitzerov nodded enthusiastically.

"And is it also true that this happened in spite of your own expressed insistence that the defendants return to you?"

"I did shout after them that they should return immediately, yes... even before the boat departed. They had gone down to the coast, ostensibly to help the poor oaf that had beached his little vessel. It was all rather improper from the start – lighthouse stewards ought to know better than to concern themselves with trifling boat crashes when they are supposed to be cooperating with their inspector."

"Of course. Furthermore, is it not also a fact that an Inquisitor was present – that she even attempted to retrieve the boat as it was putting off?!"

The inspector cleared his throat, seeming suddenly a bit agitated. "Yes. There certainly was an Inquisitor there that day. It was apparent she tried to stop them."

"Objection," Horus called. "The presence or absence of an Inquisitor is irrelevant. It does not affect the severity of the alleged crime against the state. If Mr. Blackforest wishes to introduce the Inquisitor, he should have her give her own testimony by producing her as a witness."

"I don't believe it's so irrelevant, your Honor," Blackforest argued. "The State is merely interested in demonstrating that the defendants were given more than ample warning that they were acting in the wrong. Indeed, they persisted in their crime even after forceful attempts were made to stop them."

Senahktenre nodded. "The prosecution's point is well taken. In any event the Inquisitor could not be present to give testimony. The defense council knows this. Objection overruled."

The gavel struck.

"Now, Mr. Howitzerov," Blackforest said, more gently but still clearly. "To put a very fine point on it, I ask that you explain to the court one final thing. Under what circumstances is it considered legally excusable for lighthouse stewards to abandon their charge during an inspection?"

Howitzerov grinned, and shook his head. "There are no such circumstances."

Blackforest's nails rapped on the rail, and he gave his witness a nod. "No further questions." He about-faced confidently to his table, calling out, to nowhere in particular, Horus' priviledge. "Cross-examine."

Horus stood, a bit slowly and deliberately. He needed every moment he could buy himself to concoct a defense. His numerous sustained objections from only a minute earlier now rung in his memory as dull moral victories. Blackforest was already triumphant in establishing that the defendants had left the lighthouse, and that in doing so they had committed a crime... with no room left for ifs, ands, or buts. Anything beyond this point would be argumentative and immaterial. It was a complete and utterly darning testimony. Horus *could* try for witness impeachment. But he didn't have anything to go on there. Perhaps the best he could really hope to do was grasp at straws and try to bide enough time to force the judge to reconvene at a later date. And then hope to Heck that the stewards would be arrested in the meantime, so they could face their trial as they ought. But how to buy such time?

Better embrace the argumentative and immaterial, Horus, he told himself...

He reached the railing of the witness stand. He stared very seriously at the inspector, as if to search the depths of his psyche. But really, he was still just stalling. Psyches, after all, are often quite voluminous, and he didn't know what to look for anyway. Finally, a line of questioning came to him – one that might at least cast some doubt on the situation, or win a modicum of sympathy for his clients in the eyes of the jury, for what that might be worth...

"Mr. Howitzerov," Horus began. "While we're in the business of introducing key players in the alleged crime whom the court is unable to produce, I point out that your testimony hardly made any mention of the occupant of the fishing boat. Is it not true that there was an old man in the boat – apparently distressed – and that it was *he* who put the boat back out to sea?" He quickly doubled-back to his desk, and produced a manuscript – the inspector's own report of the incident. "Furthermore, in your own account of the events," he said, holding forth the manuscript, "did you not admit that it appeared the old man assaulted the stewards prior to fleeing?"

"One moment," judge Senahktenre interjected. "Do I hear an objection from the prosecution? Perhaps on the grounds of irrelevant and immaterial questioning?"

"No objection, your Honor," Blackforest answered. "If Mr. Templar wishes to present the court with a more complete picture of the incident, so be it. In fact, the state is willing to stipulate the existence of the old man, and his apparent attack on the defendants. That is, if defense council will also stipulate that the defendants, even if taken forcibly against their will, still have no legal grounds to excuse themselves."

"The defense will *not* stipulate," Horus resolved. "And if there is no objection, then I insist on an answer from the witness."

"Very well," Senahktenre conceded, after waiting some more moments for Blackforest to object. "The witness will answer."

"There was an old man piloting the craft... and yes, it appeared that he struck the stewards with an oar. But of course, I was rather a good distance from the action. I may not have seen things as clearly as I suppose."

"That works both ways, inspector," Horus reasoned. "If you admit to some doubt about what you saw, how then can we sure of *any* of your eyewitness testimony, whether for or against the defendants?"

The inspector looked unmoved. "Whatever I saw or didn't see, the fact remains they are gone. That is measurable. I spent the better part of the day filing reports."

"Even so," Horus argued. "Without being able to swear to exactly what you saw, the actual sequence of events cannot be firmly established by your testimony alone."

Horus heard Blackforest rise. "I still offer no objection, your Honor... though I'll admit the defense council is dabbling in the argumentative. At any rate, the State has another witness to call who can corroborate the testimony of this witness... and will do so, if it will please Mr. Templar."

"I'll thank you to do that, Mr. Blackforest," Horus said. "After I've finished my cross-examination."

Blackforest revealed a wide, sharp smile. "Defense may proceed." He gestured and sat back down.

Horus gave the inspector another stern look. "Tell me, Mr. Howitzerov," he began, "are you familiar with the term *corpus delicti*?"

"It is legal jargon for 'body of the crime,' I believe," the inspector answered, a tad on the smug side, evidently pleased with himself for knowing something technical outside of his own professional sphere. "Defense attorneys are known to bring it up when they think they can sow some doubt about whether a crime has really been committed or not. But as I just told you, I have spent considerable time dealing with the consequences of these stewards abandoning their lighthouse."

"But where *is* the 'body of the crime'? How can we rule that a duty has been derelicted if we cannot produce the derelictors?"

The inspector looked at once very displeased. He was not the only one.

"Objection!" Blackforest called out. "The defense council is blatently trying to appropriate his own interpretation of *corpus delicti*. This is clearly just another jab at trying to cause a legal stink over the *In Absentia* trial system!"

Senahktenre huffed angrily, but addressed Horus. "So there can be no room for misinterpretation: is it truly the intention of the defense to suggest that the court must produce the defendants in order to prove that they are missing?"

"It's absurd!" interjected the inspector. "There's an empty lighthouse in southern Jast-Madiir right now to attest to their absence!"

"Then produce the lighthouse!" Horus demanded.

The whole courtroom became aflutter in shocked mutterings.

"Order!!!" Senahktenre commanded, absolutely outraged. "Provided the prosecution can, as he claims, produce a second eyewitness to corroborate the testimony of this witness, the court *will* have sufficient ground to accept that a crime has indeed occurred. We need not move any buildings around or sit on our hands while the defendants are brought to account! The prosecution's objection is sustained!" Senahktenre pointed his gavel accusingly at Horus. "And the court cautions the defense council – if he persists in trying to challenge the legality of *In Absentia*, it is well within my priviledge to rule council in contempt of court, and have him executed along with his clients, when at last they *are* arrested."

"Understood, your Honor," Horus said, and his voice had no fear.

"Good," Senahktenre huffed. "Now is council quite finished with this witness?"

"Not yet, your Honor. I have one final line of questioning."

"Please get on with it," Senahktenre barked. Horus obliged.

"You've proven some knowledge of legal terms," he said to the inspector. "Tell me, are you also familiar with the Knights of the Indigo Lodge?"

"Of course," inspector Howitzerov nodded. "They are the great heroes of my race."

"They are," Horus agreed. "History holds that, interestingly, these great heroes got their start in a way oddly similar to the defendants, wouldn't you say?"

The inspector cleared his throat again. "I suppose that's true. They did leave their nations – in pursuit of a higher ideal, hoping to bring security to the world at large."

"And until they obtained to that ideal, they were considered fugitives and criminals, were they not?"

"...They were."

"It was only in receiving pardon from the Grand Inquisitors that their organization was considered legitimate, and their crimes of forsaking their homelands forgiven, is that not so?"

"Yes."

"Why, then, should we judge the acts of these stewards, until we can learn definitely why they did what they did? Is it not at all possible that we are wasting our time here? That whatever judgement we pass on the defendants now might simply be overruled at a later time by Enscharaulgk?"

"Objection, your Honor," Blackforest challenged. "That's not only pure speculation on the part of the defense, it's amateur fortune-telling! It is certainly not for the court to suspend its ruling merely to allow for the *possibility* of being overruled by the Grand Inquisitor. If Enscharaulgk does see fit to pardon the defendants one day, that's his prerogative. But there are no facts yet in evidence to suggest the defendants might be pursuing a Noble Quest! And even if there turns out to be such evidence, it is irrelevant for the sake of our intents and purposes here."

"I'd go further than that, Mr. Blackforest," Senahktenre said. "The defense may well be implying that the case lacks critical evidence, because we are not able to learn the true motivations of the defendants in their absence. I fear that he is once again trying to subvert this entire trial by discreetly turning it into a referendum on the system itself, despite my stern warning. Will you object to the defense on grounds of challenging *In Abentia*, so that I may rule him in contempt of court?"

Blackforest stood dumbstruck – his eyes wide and his ears pinned back. He looked at Horus. Horus looked back impassively, offering his leave to Blackforest to do as he felt best...

"No, your Honor," Blackforest said at last. "The State objects only on grounds of speculation and irrelevant questioning by the defense."

Senahktenre was noticeably disgusted. But he was powerless to rule more severely than Blackforest was willing to object. "Objection sustained," he said. The gavel struck.

"No more questions," Horus said, returning to his table.

"The prosecution will call his next witness," the judge said.

Blackforest stood. "I call Clerk Second Class Baegulgog to the stand."

* * *

Horus mused, studying the Clerk Baegulgog as he was first called to the stand. Something about those first moments struck him odd, though he couldn't put his finger on what. Horus had limited experience with Meduselda, though he had studied the cultural differences between their Dominions, in order to better understand the nuances of each of their nations' distinct laws. And he had only the most basic on-paper knowledge of Baegulgog himself – that he was a Sowür Canpattel who had scrubbed out of the 17th Cavalry and the Royal Orchestra. That didn't give him much to go on. If Meduselda had a 'tell' – some tick or other sign that they were nervous and might be planning deception – then Horus had to admit he didn't know what it was. As he watched, this Baegulgog had simply floated some inches higher as if to rise when called, flashed a bit, adjusted his hat, and glided from the back row up to the stand, where he was now being sworn in. It was all utterly mundane... yet Horus could not shake the sense that something in these few simple acts was horribly amiss...

He'd have to think more on it later. Blackforest was about to circle in...

"Well sir," Baegulgog began unbidden as he took the stand, in a rather plain midtone voice, "I'll attest to the fact that the defendants were indeed rather smelly. And also dirty and..."

"...Well never mind all of that, Mr. Baegulgog," Blackforest interrupted. "I'd rather proceed directly to the questioning, if that is alright with you."

"Very well," Baegulgog agreed, almost sheepishly. Perhaps he felt quashed, not being allowed to spiel petty insults as the inspector had...

"You were also an eye-witness at the scene of the crime, were you not?"

"I was. I had been sent to deliver an updated inventory checklist to the stewards, I believe."

"What can you tell us about what you saw?"

Baegulgog hesitated. "I can tell you that everything happened just the way the inspector told it. You may be sure of that."

"Then you do knowingly – under oath – swear to the series of events that inspector Howitzerov described, just as he described them?"

More hesitation. "Yes. That is exactly what I mean to do."

"Very good, Mr. Baegulgog," Blackforest nodded. "I would say then that Mr. Howitzerov's testimony has been duly established. No further questions." He shot back for his table. "Cross-examine."

Horus had an idea just then. It was another juvenile trick, but at this point he might as well try anything...

"Your Honor, the defense has no questions for this witness at the present time, but asks that it may reserve its right to recall him later. The defense also wishes to roundly object to the prosecution's qualification of this witness as an *eye*-witness, since it is a well-known fact that Meduselda do not have eyes."

"Another purely semantic argument from the defense, your Honor," Blackforest contended. "It is also a well-known fact that Meduselda have the ability to perceive visual phenomena, regardless of whether they have eyes or not. Surely defense council can't presume to impeach this witness' sense of sight!"

"Can't I?" Horus challenged.

"No," Blackforest said, flatly. "You can't."

"Very well. In that case, the defense *does* have one question for this witness, if it may yet reserve the right to continue its cross-examination at a later time."

"I have no objection," Blackforest said.

Horus turned to the Meduseldan Clerk. "Alright then, Mr. Baegulgog. Let's put that sight to the test..." He raised his hand with all his fingers extended. "How many fingers am I holding up?"

"Eight!" the Clerk answered with all confidence. There was a murmur in the crowd again. Senahktenre looked utterly aghast.

"Eight indeed," Horus said. "Let the record show that the defense was holding up only *five* fingers. No more questions," He whirled triumphantly to his table.

But as he did so, Horus saw that his success would be quite short-lived. He saw Blackforest's face. His fangs were all in a grin.

"One question from the prosecution on redirect, your Honor," Blackforest said. "Will the witness please count aloud to the number eight?"

"Well, okay," Baegulgog said, sounding rather perplexed. "One, two, three, seven, eight."

The crowd whispered its amazement once more.

"One, two, three, seven, eight," Blackforest repeated smugly, almost to himself. "It seems to me there is nothing at all wrong with the witness' sight. It's his numerals that are a bit on the peculiar side."

Dianodes, Horus cursed to himself. It figured that Blackforest would also know the rather obscure fact about the Meduselda going by a different number system. *This really isn't my day*, he further noted. He was being outmaneuvered at every turn...

"The witness will float down," Senahktenre instructed. "And the prosecution will call its next witness."

What other witnesses could he possibly need? Horus wondered.

"I call Postal Squire Raphael de Lafayette to the stand."

* * *

A postman, Horus thought...

This was the spot he liked least to be in... the spot where he had absolutely no idea what Hamilton Blackforest was planning to unveil next. There had been no postal carrier at the scene of the crime. All first-hand witnesses other than the unreachable Inquisitor had already given their testimony. This was going to be something altogether different, for which he could not prepare himself...

Horus watched as a bailiff installed a booster platform under the witness' stand seat in order to help the little Phage postman see over the railing. Then when that was done, Raphael clambered up the wooden rungs on his multiple insect-like legs. Like the Clerk, he wore a hat – this one was a feathered cap, to denote his squire-hood. Horus wondered how the hat stayed on as the postman vertically scaled the witness chair...

Hats, Horus pondered. *Something about hats...*

It would come to him later. He would make sure of it...

Unfortunately, this was another 'fresh-faced' witness, the countenance of which Horus couldn't read at all. Because once again, the witness had no face to speak of. His 'head' was a very simple polyhedral of tiled triangles. Such were the Phage: the race of enlarged viruses. Horus mused sarcastically to himself that Blackforest could take his witnesses and form a very nice poker team. It was far from a helpful thought, but at least it diffused some of the suspence of agonizing over what evidence Blackforest might be about to introduce...

"Mr. de Lafayette," Blackforest started. "I understand that you deliver mail regularly to Brighamok's Lighthouse – the property of the defendants, is that correct?"

"It's on my route, yes sir, Mr. Attorney," the young Phage agreed.

"Thank you, young man," Blackforest said, momentarily amused by the youth's enthusiasm, and being referred to as 'Mr. Attorney'. "You did make a stop at Brighamok's Lighthouse later in the afternoon of Juvember 20th – the very day of the crime – did you not?"

"It would have been around four hours past noon," Raphael explained. "That's when I usually get there, sir. But I didn't see any crimes..."

"That's alright, son," Blackforest assured him, as he went for a pocket on the inside of his suit-jacket and retrieved an unopened letter. "I show you now this letter. Do you recognize it?"

"Yes, sir, I do sir. It's the letter I delivered to the Lighthouse on that day. Government envelope. Very official-looking. They got that along with seventeen Clerical Dronehood surveys."

"You seem to have an excellent memory, Squire."

"You could say I've got more in my head than just complex protein molecules, sir."

"I suppose you could at that. Now, as to the letter. The state has awareness of the contents of this letter, and its subpoena to have those contents entered into evidence against the defendants has been approved at the highest level. I ask you now to open this letter and summarize its contents to the court." He held the envelope out to the witness.

"Oh, no sir!" Squire de Lafayette recoiled in sudden terror. "I couldn't possibly open someone else's letter, sir – with or without any fancy legal permission! It would be a violation of a very sacred trust. As a postman and an adherent of our paragon Klaiven, I simply must decline."

Blackforest nodded, taking back the envelope. "Very well. Then with the court's permission, the state asks that it be allowed to enter this letter into evidence itself."

"Permission is granted," Senahktenre pronounced. "You may open the letter."

Blackforest's deadly sharp nail effortlessly sliced the envelope. He unfolded the letter, perused it for some moments – apparently to make very sure it was the letter he reckoned it to be – and then addressed the court. "Let the record show that this letter is an official notice from the Czarina's office – an emergency conscription notice – reassigning both of the defendants to mercenary duty forthwith."

Horus blanched. He had heard that such notices had begun to circulate – that the Czarina's administration was in the process of cataloguing the nation's civilians with jobs considered to be of little importance, and conscripting them as mercenaries. This was due to the high demand of mercenary work in the Tophthaeran Civil War, and the rapidly declining supply of registered mercenaries. As the tenants of an obscure lighthouse on the disused southern coastline, Jek and Audrey were obvious candidates. But Horus did not know they had been conscripted, as Blackforest had obviously learned. He hadn't even thought to look into it!

"I ask that this letter be entered into evidence as prosecution exhibit-A," Blackforest said, handing the letter to a court clerk with a stamper.

"For the sake of clarity," Senahktenre interjected, "the prosecutor ought to explain to the court his precise intentions for entering this letter into evidence."

"Double-indemnity, your Honor," Blackforest announced. "By failing to report as state mercenaries, the defendants are liable to not one, but *two* counts of dereliction of duty."

"Objection, your Honor!" Horus challenged. "Surely the defendants weren't expected to be mercenaries *and* lighthouse stewards simultaneously. That is not how conscription usually works, anyway. It is the opinion of the defense that this letter invalidates all of the prosecution's past evidence and testimony. As this letter decrees, the defendants were no longer lighthouse stewards, and so cannot be held accountable to *that* charge of dereliction of duty. Further, I feel that this case should be dismissed as a mistrial, so that the state may pursue the *valid* charge of dereliction of duty... without being mired in a second charge that the state itself has just proven no longer applies."

Senahktenre scowled. "Does the defense dare to try his luck again? 'Mistrial,' he says! Yet another scheme of yours to forestall sentencing until your clients can stand trial, I warrant."

"On the contrary, your Honor," Horus argued. "It is my duty to so move under these circumstances. The defense cannot help that the prosecution has founded its case on a false pretense."

"There's no false pretense here, your Honor!" Blackforest insisted. "This notice of conscription goes into effect upon delivery. I have already established that the notice was *not* delivered until after the first crime was committed! Therefore, the defendants first derelicted their duty to the lighthouse, and then, mere hours later, derelicted their duty as mercenaries. No other interpretation of events can be put forth."

"Your Honor, the prosecution is now involving *himself* in semantic arguments," Horus further argued. "The notice is in effect 'upon delivery,' you say? Tell me Hamilton: are letters to be delivered to properties, or people? The defendants have not received this notice! It is therefore not in effect, and irrelevant. But in light of this, I admit I am forced to retract my movement for a mistrial."

"'Properties or people,' eh?" Blackforest recited. "Well since you asked, let me give you my interpretation, if it please the court: it is the duty of the mail carriers to put the letter in the box, and the duty of the recipients to get the letter out of the box. Who then, if not the defendants, is to be blamed that the letter has not reached its intended recipients? I tell you, *they* are at fault! First for abandoning their lighthouse... and second for failing to return to check their mail."

"The point of the prosecution is well-taken," Senahktenre announced. "Objection overruled. The defendants now face two capital charges of dereliction of duty."

The gavel struck. Twice.

Horus swallowed hard. This was a new low for him. He'd had many clients who were ultimately executed in the past. But he'd never before faced the distinct possibility that a client of his would be *double*-executed. Now, barring a miracle, it looked like this case would end in *two* double-executions...

Blackforest sighed. His perpetual victories seemed to be tiring him out. "I have no further questions of this witness." He returned to his table and sat heavily.

Horus was beside himself. This witness was the most unimpeachable yet. The squire simply had a letter, and he delivered it. Horus couldn't think of any avenue of attack. He couldn't think of any way of maintaining reasonable doubt, or even unreasonable doubt. And he had little cause to think that Blackforest had many, if *any* other witnesses to call. After this cross-examination, the state might well rest its case, and then it would be on Horus to present his defense. Then would come the sentencing. And on top of it all, Horus *had* no defense to present...

He needed time. Time to think – time to strategize – time to try to turn the whole thing on its head, if there was any possibility of that left at all. Yes, the only thing that could possibly avail him now was more time. But *how* to get it?

He had one final trick in mind.

At last he stood. "Your Honor, I anticipate a lengthy cross-examination of this witness," he said. "I move for recess, so that the cross-examination may be had in its entirety on the next court date." It was perhaps his most desperate gambit of the day.

Senahktenre hesitated. "Court has only been convened for twenty minutes," he said, suspiciously. "Are you sure you need *that* much time to cross-examine this Postal Squire?"

"As sure as if my life depended on it, your Honor," Horus answered. "Or if not my life, then somebody's."

Senahktenre huffed, but ultimately relented. "Oh, very well. Court is adjourned! It will reconvene on Monday, the next."

The gavel struck.

Everyone slowly started getting up and shuffling out of the courtroom.

* * *

Horus sat, even more heavily than Blackforest had done. His eyes darted back and forth across the table as he searched inwardly for inspiration. He had held off sentencing until after the weekend, at least. There was *some* possibility now that his clients would be arrested in time. But it was not anything he could rely on...

He felt angry with himself – even righteously indignant – as he remembered that his whole reason for taking the case was to have another swing at *In Absentia*... to see if he could finally start to dismantle it. Without even realizing it, he'd already abandoned that high notion, and was now thinking pragmatically – hoping just to see justice prevail *this* time, with no thought of the next. He abhorred the idea of letting himself be bullied by the Vice-Vizier. Still, Horus recognized that he was at a distinct disadvantage here. His agenda against *In Absentia* was too well known, and there wasn't much he could do if Senahktenre was very determined to shut him down. Anyway, he probably had no chance whatever of changing the system if he couldn't even win the case...

While he was still mulling all of this over solemnly, Deborah sat down next to him. She smiled at him – just like it had been any ordinary, pleasantly mundane day on the rail tracks. It made him feel instantly better.

He quite adored Ms. Boulevard. *Why don't you just marry her?* he asked himself. Of course, he knew why. Even though he had the liberty to propose marriage to her (a liberty unique to the Mesomelae), he didn't dare exercise it. She was just too well-liked. It was far bad enough that she'd had the misfortune of becoming a public defender's secretary. *That* was a necessary evil – it was, after all, the job assigned to her, and so there was nothing at all to be done about it. But if she agreed to *marry* him... that would be something altogether different. That would mean she actually *approved* of the work Horus was in. He didn't want that kind of black mark for her. He saw that everyone treated her very well wherever she went... and to him nothing could be more fitting, because she deserved it. He just didn't have the heart to dream of people thinking badly of her on his account...

She reached into a briefcase. "I brought you a steak," she said, showing him a very nice cut of raw meat, although a bit on the fresh side...

"I'm grateful," he said, "but certainly not hungry at the moment."

"Oh it's not to eat," she said, closing the steak back into the case. "It's for the black eyes Hamilton's been giving you all morning."

He grinned. "It was that bad, huh?"

His heart skipped a beat as she suddenly changed aspects. Deborah pinned her ears back. She was upset – badly upset. He'd never seen her upset. "Horus, I'm worried. I think we should've taken Hamilton's warning more seriously. Senahktenre's really gunning for these stewards, and I think nothing would please him more than to get you caught in the crosshairs along with them."

He gave her his best confident look. "I've worked around Senahktenres all my life, Deborah."

She put her hand on his shoulder. "There will always be other cases, you know. Other chances for you to fix things. Maybe some other time; with a different judge – a trial where the stakes aren't so high. You're playing too dangerously. If it had been anyone other than Blackforest on the other side, they'd have had your skin..." She looked away and shook her head. "Anyway, I think you should just throw the whole thing. There's no question now they can get the charges to stick. But you shouldn't have to go down with the ship. It won't solve anything."

"Deborah," he appealed, speaking gently. "Believe me, I appreciate your concern. It means the world. But this isn't about who lives and who dies. It's a matter of principle."

She hesitated, but eventually she rallied to fix a weak smile on her quivering jowels. "You are a man of principle, Horus. But the living and dying part matters to some of us. Try not to let them kill you, if you can help it."

"I certainly will," he said.

Eager to change pace, Deborah rifled into a different compartment of her briefcase. "I have some gifts from Art. He mined the waiver that the Inquisitor used to excuse herself from making a court appearance. He also got me a revised list of material witnesses for the prosecution."

Horus blinked hard. "Blackforest has *more* witnesses to call?"

"Well, do remember, it *is* a show-trial. The Czarina's people don't just want a high-profile execution – it needs some pizzazz. At any rate I'm sure they think a few more days of headlines and gossip will go a lot farther than a knee-jerk conviction. That's probably why Senahktenre let you get away with your early adjournment." She gave him a mocking smile. "Or did you really plan upwards of eight hours worth of questions for that poor little Squire? I can't help wondering what you might have asked him..."

"Nor can I," Horus agreed. "But at the moment, I'm much more curious where Blackforest is getting his supplemental witnesses from."

She handed him the documents Artimus Mallard had unearthed. "The Wading Isle, mostly," she said. "Have a look for yourself; there's a name on that list you're sure to notice."

Horus' eyes widened. He saw the name, alright. "You're not kidding."

"Art's going to try to get in touch with him, but he's being held by the state... and Blackforest's office isn't *all* revolving doors. He hopes he can get some lead as to the identity of the strange old man, or possibly the lady lighthouse steward."

"Nothing on those fronts at all yet?" Horus asked.

"I'm afraid not. I guess the old man is a total phantom. His fishing dhingy had no markings... nothing to identify it by but battle-damage. And Audrey, well... Art got a hold of her certifications of citizenship, but of course they were the 'shanghai special'."

Horus knew exactly what she meant. Jast-Madiir had specially commissioned the Clerical Dronehood of Berlberi to make a custom line of citizenship certifications for immigrants – certifications so spartan that they didn't even have fields for prior identity or nationality. This made it so that the Jast-Madiiran navy and merchant fleet could press-gang more indiscriminantly, since they had no need to keep track of where they were getting their forced labor from. Since all of those forms were handled by the Dronehood, and therefore universally accessible, it only made sense not to include that sort of information, just in case other countries decided to audit Jast-Madiir's citizenry and didn't like what they found...

"Well, there's some hope for the stewards yet, then," Horus said. "Or at least, for the woman."

Deborah looked skeptical. "There's hope because Art found out nothing?"

"Precisely. If he had learned anything at all, I would have been very displeased."

"Well I wouldn't go telling that to Art, if I were you," Deborah said.

Just then, a formidable presence rested its deadly digits on Horus' table. Hamilton Blackforest was standing over them. He appeared very angry. Horus rose to meet his gaze.

"Come to gloat, Hamilton?" Horus asked, grinning. "I'll concede you won the day. But don't assume things will be so easy when Monday morning rolls around."

"I've already seen what you think of my warnings," Blackforest said, ignoring Horus' playful egotism and remaining grave. "But here's another one anyway, just in case you're listening this time: don't count on me to pull you out of the fire anymore! If you keep goading Senahktenre like that, he'll find a way to get your head on a platter – with my help or without it. Do I make myself perfectly clear?"

Horus mused for a second, scratching under his chin. "There is something you said earlier, Hamilton, that I wish you would clarify. Something to the effect, I believe, that there were no facts *yet* in evidence to suggest the defendants were pursuing a Noble Quest. Should I expect any such facts to come up in future testimony?"

Blackforest looked ready to blow a gasket. But, after a moment of glowering, he retrieved his composure, and actually looked around sneakily, as if to be sure they weren't overheard. Then he leaned in to say something discretely. He had Horus' complete attention.

"Well, if you can believe it... there've been some startling allegations related to this case, coming out of The Wading Isle."

"What sort of allegations?"

Blackforest checked around again. He went on in hushed tones. "According to a prominent witness, the defendants claim to be trying to thwart some kind of Despotopian conspiracy... a 'Doom Fleet,' he called it..."

Horus was incredulous. Up until this point, he had privately romanticized the notion that his clients might be unlikely heroes. But *this* sounded pretty sketchy... even kind of dumb. "This allegation... you believe it's credible?"

"The witness certainly does. In fact we have the statements of dozens of other, very frightened witnesses from The Wading Isle who will attest that the defendants spoke publicly and very convincingly of the threat, even invoking Zedulon's Chocolate Prophecy. On top of that, we have a Despotopian statesman and his wife in custody that can't be made to breathe a word... even to deny the plot."

"That is all very odd indeed," Horus nodded absently. "But all it amounts to is hearsay and suspicion."

"Very *serious* hearsay and suspicion," Blackforest insisted. "Certainly worthy of further investigation. You know this country's history with Despotopia; if they have anything sinister in mind, you can be sure St. Argonsburg is their target."

"I don't feel I can be sure of anything, Hamilton," Horus said. "This is all news to me."

"Horus, this is very important. If anything can be brought to light about this alleged plot in the course of our inquest, we need to pursue it with all of our resources."

Horus almost laughed. "Are you proposing some sort of truce?"

"Whatever you want to call it, yes," Blackforest said, becoming impatient again. "My office isn't for international capers. It's not really the purview of the regular police force either. But if there is even the most oblique threat to the state, then we – as responsible and highly-motivated residents – need to learn all we can about this."

On one level, Horus agreed with him. But on another, he resented the double-standards in play here. "I'm happy to be any help I can," he began. "But if you want to get in the business of using the case to delve into side-issues, you might help me with mine while you're at it."

Blackforest set his jaw. Then he began to chuckle. It was a scary kind of chuckle. "Still have *In Absentia* on the brain?" Suddenly he looked far less amused. "After my warnings; Senahktenre's threats?! Are you really going to refuse to help me preserve national security unless I agree to stick my neck out along with you?"

"You apparently had some sort of deal in mind when you came over here," Horus said. "So let's make a deal. I help you get to the bottom of your supposed Despotopian conspiracy, and you help me bring the injustices of *In Absentia* to light."

"Nothing doing, Horus," Blackforest shook his head. "And don't pretend like you're in any position to name terms here. We both know this could have ended today. If I really wanted my conviction, I could've had it before lunch. But if there's *any* chance your clients are onto something about Despotopia, then it's worth extending the case. What's the matter with you, anyway? Don't you appreciate the importance of what I'm trying to do?"

"I'm sure I do," Horus agreed. "You're trying to do the right thing. But so am I."

"Oh you're impossible!" Blackforest said, tossing his hands and storming away.

"Hamiton," Horus called after him. "Thank you." And he made it clear he meant it.

Blackforest stopped, not quite looking over his shoulder all the way. He seemed for a moment prepared to say something, but then stormed on.

Deborah set a hand on Horus' arm to get his attention. "Are you really not going to help Blackforest with this espionage business of his?"

Horus smiled. "I never said that."

Deborah smiled too. "That's what I thought."

* * *

Horus was left with a lot to think about. He didn't easily accept the idea that Despotopia could be planning anything that threatened the nation of Jast-Madiir. But he knew better than to dismiss it.

And for all his inflated rhetoric, he did realize that further uninspired challenges of the *In Absentia* system would only result in his unceremonious martyrdom. Anything he tried on that front from here on out was going to have to be clever, as well as convincing...

There were new witnesses to investigate... but he would also have to reconsider the witnesses already called...

So very much to think about.

His eyes went to his table, and in a moment of clarity he decided to start with what was directly in front of him. He picked up the files Deborah had handed him a minute earlier and flipped through them. Mostly it consisted of the Inquisitor's waiver. He was glad to have it; he noticed immediately that she had been as meticulous in filling out the waiver as she was thorough in her incident report. She had veritable essays in many fields that would have been left empty by almost anyone else... excluding Clerks...

Clerks, Horus thought. *There was something about that Dronehood Clerk...*

This thought happened to coincide with him seeing the word 'Clerk' in one of the fields of her waiver – a field for additional allowances, wherein the applicant could beg the court's excusal for more than just their own absence. It was almost unheard-of to see this field filled...

Horus read the field. He read it again. He read it a third time to be sure and then there was no doubt – he had happened on to something that would change the entire course of the case!

"*Hats*," Horus said aloud.

"Beg your pardon?" Deborah said, still by his side.

"You heard me," Horus said. "I said, 'hats'."

"Okay, 'hats'..." Deborah imitated. "What on earth about them?"

"It's what the whole case comes down to, Deborah," he answered. "A tip of the hat."

Zedulon

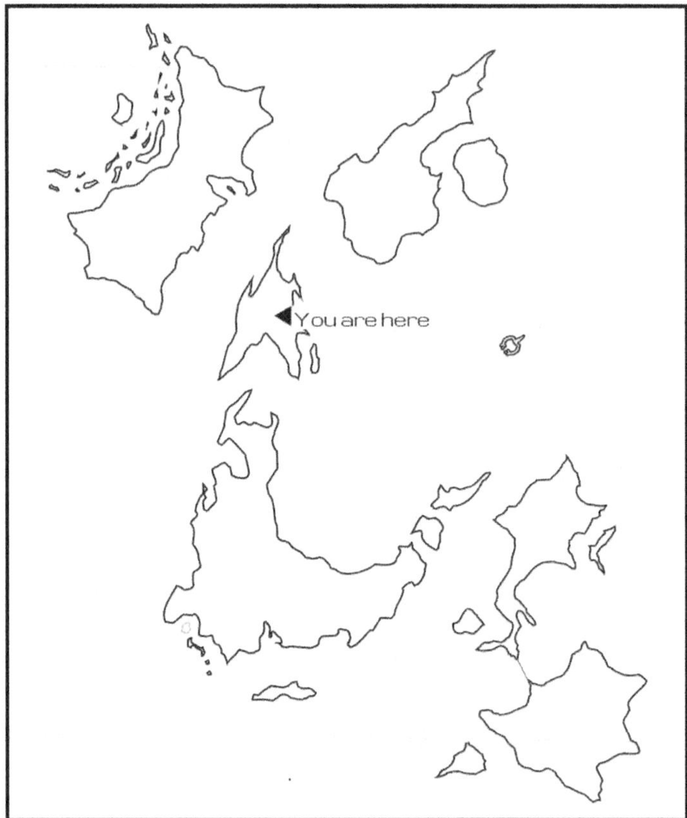

"By now, word has reached the far-flung corners of the earth that the Empire is finished. Let me begin by confirming what you've heard. It is clear to me you do not wish my rule. For my part, I never wished to rule you! I do not believe any of my predecessors ever did. Therefore, I am doing the expedient thing and ending all of this as quickly as I may. Yet you came here expecting a Prophecy, and for me to portend the fall of Kanaedia would hardly suffice. Those wheels have already been turning for weeks. Rather, I would have you know this: What I unmake now, another shall remake, one day. The tyrant you imagined – the one you have made me out to be – he will live and walk the earth, and he will make it his own. How many generations lie before now and then, I cannot say. So may your children's children, and their children, live to fear the day of his appearing. But go now, and rule yourselves while you may, if that pleases you."

- Emperor Omengan, transcript of the Resurgent Prophecy, as delivered in the nation of Kanaedia, circa S.E. 1309

The pale blue shafts of night fell upon strewn petals of violet blooms long-dead as they rustled in a ghostly dance, carried on the distant howl of a chill breeze. Light and air alike intruded from the three small open portholes high above on the ceiling of the great, dark hall. A deep rest had claimed the sentinels of this imperious place, whose great strong lungs helped to stir the wilted petals as they slowly heaved their slumbering breaths. Keeping eternal vigil in their stead were paired rows of tall, arced pillars, all wrought of thick proud steel that had been bent – bowed inward – frozen in a kneeling shape on either side of the path down the length of the hall that led to the *tree*...

Like the pillars themselves, the tree was pale, and smooth, and polished. It, too, was bowed... presenting its trunk and its boughs toward the outer court, not unlike an arm held out with upturned hand. It, too, was cold as death... less alive than even the old blooms fallen at its feet. It was the only tree in all of Roemnar that stood above the ground. And it was made of stone.

The flowers, of course, had not come from the tree itself. Even in all its prominence and distinction, the tree was merely a stand – a platform for a work of craft far greater and older. For nestled atop its boughs in a thick but sprawling weave was Alphozar's Wreath – a very ancient vine, descended from a progenitor plant of the same name. The original Wreath had been the very seat of power whence the dynasties of the Dire Herons had overseen the old Kanaedionic Empire, in all of its past glory. Grown of *Wisteria Draconis* – a deadly-strong constricting plant, and nearly indestructible – the flowering vine had once been as beautiful as it was secretly perilous. Only a worthy ruler might perch upon the tangled vine, and not expect to be crushed by it most unpleasantly. Whatever science or mysticism or other virtue had been set on the Wreath to render it so discerning and shrewd was, at best, a closely guarded secret – or perhaps more likely, one lost to the ages. But this imposing plant had both decided and delineated the sovereignty of all the Dire Heron Emperors and Empresses... and later the Proconsuls. It had flowered in crimson for generations, followed by bright orange, and yellow. These were the three dynasties of the Kanaedionic Empire. After the great nation of Kanaedia came to dissolution, shoots from the original Wreath were taken to grow thrones for the Proconsuls of each of the smaller Dire Heron states that resulted. The second generation of Alphozar's Wreath had flowered in four cooler dynasties – green, blue, indigo... and finally, violet. Through all of these ages, the seat of each ruling Heron had been most lovely to behold – a spectacle sought by many far and wide...

But now, few visitors came before the Wreath. It was not well-known – nor did the elite of Roemnar wish it known – that the Wreath had withered for many years, casting off its once-vibrant blooms. By now, the bare, knotted vining was nearly as pale as the lifeless stone that supported it. No one seemed to possess the skill to interpret this omen, beyond the obvious fact that it was really, *really* not good...

Though sickly, the Wreath still stalwartly and sturdily held its shape, at least. It was woven in the form of a canopied nest, such that, from the entrance of the hall, it resembled the vacant lids of an eye...

Perched within Alphozar's Wreath was Zedulon.

His thoughts were deep and drear in the shadow of his sinewy shelter. Hour upon hour he hunted from his place of prominence, trackless as the air howled and the petals swished and the immense breath of his slumbering pair of pet tyrannosaurs whiled endlessly on around him. His quarry was a single point – a moment in the ebbs of time he bent all his thought to identify. A moment not yet past...

Like all the Proconsuls, and the Emperors and Empresses before them, the future tended to reveal itself to Zedulon. It was not so much a skill for him to cultivate. Indeed, Zedulon reckoned it more like an affliction. He gathered that, to other beings, time had continuity and clarity. He envied this greatly. His powers of foresight were far more chronic than they had been in his predecessors, and if that gave him any edge, it was not without its cost. There was no special place in his mind for the future to insert itself, so it was often intruding where memories belong, masquerading as the past. So he had to be ever-vigilant about time's great sequence, and this was for him a constant struggle – one that had caused him some embarrassment in his long years. For instance, there was that time, perhaps not so long ago, at a garden party put on by Lady Mathelda – one of the Senators of Roemnar. He had approached her with his condolences...

"I was sorry to learn of your husband's untimely demise," he had said.

The feathers of her neck ruffled in alarm. "My husband isn't dead..." she replied.

Well, what does one say in the midst of such a gaffe?

"Hmm..." Zedulon had said.

Many were the incidents like this he had endured. His entire relationship with the future was a nuisance and a logical snarl. At times he could remember something yet to happen to the last detail, just as clearly and effortlessly as if he were recalling what he had eaten for breakfast the previous morning (and he was not one to lightly forget what he had for breakfast). Even more than this, at times he felt so in tune, it was as if he were penning the future himself...

Other times were nebulous. Other times lacked context. Some premonitions were at best half-remembered. And though it might be aggravating, in the past he had managed well enough to weather the insights however they came...

But not this time.

Zedulon had had a vision unlike any before – grave and alarming beyond all attribution. So great an impression it left on him that he had been utterly engrossed in it for much of the last two decades, like some sort of clairvoyant detective that refused to let go of a cold case. He had seen much, and yet not nearly enough. And in his dogged old heart he resolved he would not move again until he learned all he wished. On this hung a very great doom. If it were at all possible to wrest what he needed from the clutches of Time, then he knew he must not fail...

It had all begun with the glimpse of *her*.

Zedulon had no idea who *she* was, or even what. The vision was not clear. He saw the shape of high-helmed armor, like a Human might wear. But this was luminous – green and ghoulish – gashed deeply (even lethally) in the torso. And within all the armor was nothing discernable – no face, no head... no sign of a corporeal form at all. He felt and heard the very air about her, thick as it was with an ageless melody. What the notes were, he couldn't say. And yet, he had heard it before. He had heard it a hundred times. A thousand times. Surely millions upon *millions* of times...

If there was anything behind or about her besides empty space, Zedulon did not recall, such was his focus on *her* alone. But he knew this vision was no transcendental portrait of an entity – Zedulon perceived the future, and nothing more abstract. This was him seeing *her* through his own eye in some moment yet to come. And for all the mystery, he remembered at least what manner of moment he was seeing. It was not a moment of profound revelation – but rather, the moment just *after*: the moment the mind beats itself into a new shape as it is forced to reckon with a previously unimaginable truth. But for all of Zedulon's strength, he could not make himself remember what that truth would be. He *despaired* to know. But he could not...

Equally oppressive, the question remained who *she* was. Though he fought it, he could not quite shake the awe of her. It was an experience. It was beholding one who knew everything and so feared nothing – one so in tune with the deeper music that suffused her presense, she may as well have written every note...

But even if she was, in some exceedingly profound way, at one with the universe – or what might be larger still – then it did not make her peaceful or passive. He knew she had some cosmic agenda, if only by the way he felt his own centuries of scheming shrink to utter inconsequence in her shadow. And he felt with certainty she had the audacity to realize her designs, though they were much too grand... and to demand absolute satisfaction, though nothing in the universe could grant it...

Ultimately, the feelings were what he remembered most about the vision. And behind all of these very particular and esoteric sorts of feelings, he knew in his soul it was *fear* he was left with. Fear in its most essential form. Fear of the End. Fear of the *Truth*...

The premonition had come to him at a curious time. Zedulon had been travelling south to the nation of Jast-Madiir, there to give a customary prediction of the future. In ages past, it was the convention for the sovereign Heron of the Kanaedionic Empire to deliver some kernel of prophecy to his or her Human subjects, once every twenty years. This tradition had outlived the Empire itself, and Zedulon was tasked with rendering such predictions to the neighboring Human nations of the Idriulthorontan Archipelago. From his brief glimpse of this mysterious woman, he saw that he had something most urgent to reveal to the Humans. But since the meaningful details eluded even him, as he stood before the awed throng of people that stretched far as the eye could see, he could only forebode that, "A very great evil will be coming back into the world..."

All the Humans took this to mean that Onyxadon would return, and they began to get very panicky. Zedulon had rolled his eye. "Yes, Onyxadon will return," he had said, "...and it *will* be horrible. But that is all very obvious, and so not worth prophesying about. I speak of *another* great evil..."

Well, at this, everyone was very exasperated, and started complaining that prophecies never fail to be downers. "You would like an agreeable Prophecy, would you?" Zedulon had asked, and all agreed they would. "Very well... in two weeks' time, it will rain chocolate." And so it did.

For quite some time after that relatively futile episode, Zedulon had fixated himself much as he was doing now. The identity of this troubling apparition had to be learned, and he could think of little else. For years, he would frequently remove himself to the Wreath so to struggle for some morsel of further insight, forbidding interruption... lest the wrath of his tyrannosaurs be loosed.

All the while the Wreath still withered, and he saw that his Senators and Prefects were growing more and more suspicious of him. It needn't be wondered about, since the first fallen bloom of the Wreath had coincided with Zedulon's rise to power. But as far as he concerned himself with the matter, they could think whatever they liked. They still owed him their utmost allegiance, for the fact remained that he had perched upon the Wreath, and it had not crushed him...

But the inward search was consistently unrevealing. Zedulon dearly wished he could contrive some way to use the impressive resources of his nation to bring the quest for the phantom from his vision into the material world. Only there was nothing to go on – no clues and no starting point from which to launch a manhunt that could span the earth, or even the cosmos. Crossly, he eventually suspended the entire effort, coming not into his throne room... except to feed his pets, or on the occasions that matters of state made it necessary. And this was to be his way for two or three years. And the elite of Roemnar wondered what his deal was all the more...

Only then came the *second* vision. It burst on his mind with more detail than he had hoped to process. Rain and smoke and waves and thunder and confusion and doubt... and behind that, the ecstasy of sated vengeance. It was a very great battle on the ocean. More – it would be *THE* battle on the ocean, eclipsing even the notorious Battle of Aqualoo, famed of so many paintings.

The second vision proved informative in all the ways the first had been moot. Though this premonition was at high sea, the exact location of the conflict was immediately plain. For he saw, as it were, the titanic Citadel of the Inquisition – hanging on the horizon, towering dark and eerie in the storm...

It was burning.

At this, Zedulon had laughed. Unfortunately, this all had the serendipity of coinciding with his attendance of Lady Mathelda's husband's funeral, which made it a rather poor time to laugh, and he quickly excused himself. His flight back to his neglected Wreath was a dizzy one. He would not have previously imagined the arrogance necessary to strike at the heart of the Inquisition. It was the very summit of conceit! But he needn't have imagined it. Because he knew instantly that he had felt it once before...

Now Zedulon once again perched upon his Wreath – doubling, tripling, quadrupling, and *quintupling* his efforts to learn something more. He had learned the *where*... who and why no longer seemed to matter. He needed to know *when*. *WHEN*! Only with that knowledge could he play the part he had determined to play in this calamity that would define an era. Only with that knowledge could he set his own audacious new scheme in motion...

He needed to know. So he tried harder, and harder, and *harder*...

...And, at the last, he knew...

"Novtober 14th, S.E. 9021," he muttered to himself in astonishment.

So soon!

Suddenly there came a pitter-patter. It was not the petals. It had the sonorous quality of rapid footfalls. Zedulon looked out to the mouth of his court, clutching in one talon his royal spear. A young Dire Heron was running headlong towards his throne. He was clad with the garb of a plague doctor, mask and all. It was one of Zedulon's own attendants. All of his attendants were fully trained plague doctor's. It was appropriate enough: Medical training was widespread among the Herons, and as he now approached the years allotted to a Meduseldan monarch, Zedulon was certainly old enough for his physical health to be a potential consideration...

The Proconsul was immediately annoyed with the impetuous appearance of his attendant. He was sure it was in answer to his muttering to himself. He was being watched – and listened to – much too closely. This confirmed that his Senators had already begun spying on him...

The attendant had apparently done more than just annoy Zedulon's pets with his abrupt intrusion. Roused from sleep, Cutholan heaved upright and filled the hall with a roar of unanswerable challenge. Zimetra quickly followed suit. This was enough to make Zedulon himself boil over. His false eye flashed bright orange as he sprung to his feet.

"Sa'kholo!" he bellowed, issuing a firm command to his tyrannosaurs in the Elfish tongue. Roughly translated, it essentially meant, "Do not kill, ye great and deadly beasts, lest I be displeased with you, and things go badly for you, and a curse be set upon your spleen – yea, a curse of many years, plus a month or so."

He heard the deep echo of his command, and nothing more.

Then the pitter-patter began again – slower now, more cautious. The attendant hesitated, looking furtively at the rexes on either side of the Wreath, and then finally addressed the Proconsul.

"My lord Zedulon, I beg you would pardon your servant, for he did believe he heard you call for assistance," the attendant groveled.

Zedulon's displeasure had not yet subsided, and there was a smoldering in his voice. "My servant's ears are too keen for his own good. You have listened in on your lord more closely than you ought... at the behest of the Senate, no doubt. Do not deny it, and make yourself a liar as well as a spy!"

The attendant bowed most low. "The Senate only worries about my lord the Proconsul. He has been most withdrawn and preoccupied."

Zedulon's neck fluttered at the admission, thinking of his upstart Senators. *Such irreverence*! "Is the Proconsul's behavior now a matter for the Senate to debate? Is it for them to decide when I have been *too* withdrawn and *too* preoccupied?"

"Surely not, my lord. The Senate would never be so bold as to..."

"...As to what? As to quietly disapprove of my manner? *Bold* indeed! I only wish they would be bolder! Instead of putting you up to mere eavesdropping, perhaps they could better reassure themselves by setting you on the throne in my stead. Let one who is so young and driven and intelligent and capable fill my station, and then let us see how his success compares with mine!"

The attendant bowed again. "May it never be, my lord Zedulon. I am most unworthy, and would immediately be crushed by the Wreath. May my lord the Proconsul live forever."

At this, Zedulon huffed... and at length, even laughed a horrible little laugh. He stayed his spear and sat back down, his feathers smoothing as his rage subsided. "Your own boldness disarms me; that you would wish something so mean-spirited on an old man." This sudden change in aspect was not inauthentic. The anger he felt truly was for the Senate, and not this unfortunate errand-runner. "In fairness to you, my lad, though I had not summoned you hence, I admit I was about to. I must have you relay my commands to the Fleet Admirals. They are to draw up battle plans for the 14th of the following month. Let them coordinate a full-scale aerial attack. I want the plans brought before me for final approval within a day's time."

The attendant rose. But he hesitated, and responded unevenly. "It will be done, my lord. But, let not his Excellency send forth his servant to the Fleet Admirals with only a time of attack. They will demand of your servant a target as well."

Zedulon would have smiled a roguish smile at this moment, if it were possible with a beak.

"Our target area," Zedulon imparted, "is the Ocean Citadel of the Inquisition."

Praying for Daylight

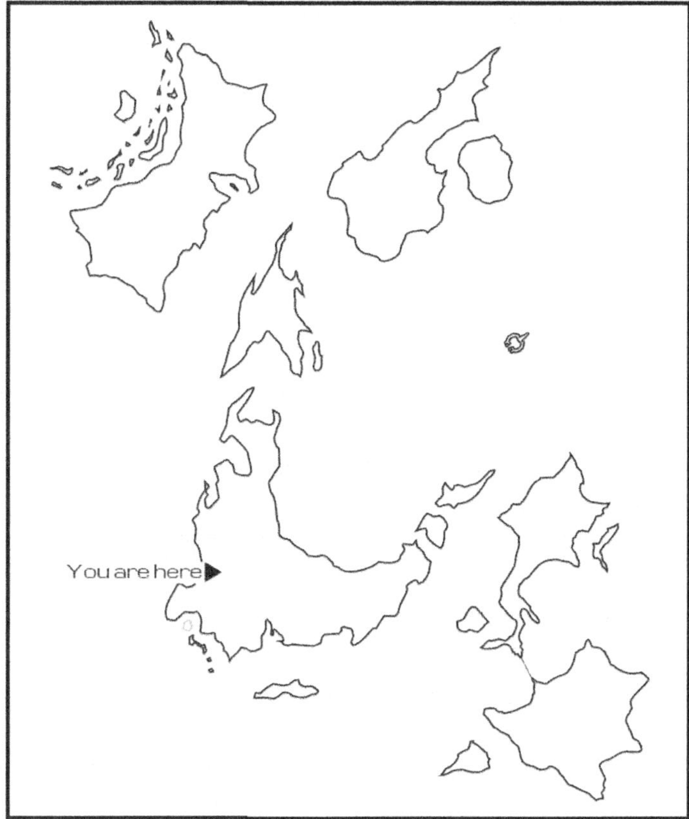

"The only kind of change that isn't horrible is the kind you notice in time to change it back."

- Eurydice Inhapi, *Too Many Referendums: Philosophy Abridged*

Jek was scared. It may have had something to do with being dragged through the woods in the dark by huge insects – known enemies of the state, and of Humanity, and civilization itself – and from whose captivity no one ever returned...

He yelled and yelled until he winded himself. From there, he started trailing off into some intermittent yowls, a few isolated yelps, and finally inaudible whimpering, before at last holding silent.

It wasn't just that he wore himself out. He started to notice between his cries that the Mantids were making a clicky-chittery sound every time he acted up. It was an alien sort of sound, but Jek found it unsettlingly as if they were *chuckling*. Eventually he decided it was enough that he was facing his certain demise. He didn't appreciate being laughed at to boot...

A multitude of other astute observations slowly began to dawn on Jek over the course of what felt like (and may well have been) hours of his mobile captivity. Firstly, he realized he was in some sort of net. Secondly, that it hurt much less to be dragged on his back than on any other hemispheres of his body. Third, that he still had his musket! He tried to draw it through the tangled mesh and get at his bayonet, but it was hopelessly snagged somewhere, and even with all his strength, he couldn't maneuver it the right way...

There was little more he could make out. The leaves were still probably two feet deep, and so he was basically immersed in them as he was drawn ever along. He caught fleeting glimpses of outside motion, and once in a great while, he got an obstructed (but frightening and unmistakable) view of nearby Mantids in the bluish gloom of the night. He didn't know about the relative land speed of Dire Mantids, but it seemed like they were in a hurry. And after all, why not? They had a Human to kill now – no doubt in the most painful fashion imaginable – and the night was wearing on. They would naturally want to begin the whole fun process as soon as possible, so they could enjoy their cruel deeds to the fullest while still under cover of darkness. That was how Jek imagined wicked, savage creatures would think, anyway...

Fresh horror set in as he realized that Audrey and the old man might have fallen to the power of the tribal Mantids as well. They could be doomed to share his fate, or have already met their own. He hoped they had somehow managed to get away, and that he alone had failed to evade the big bugs. But he soon found that hope far too unrealistic, and settled morosely for hoping that they had been dispatched quickly and with minimal pain.

What a terrible end! What a cruel trick! They had already come through so many harrowing experiences where they obviously should have died. They had already travelled far through sea and over and under land. They had *learned*. They had *grown*. They had braved wind and rain, darkness and dragons, and endured every kind of nonsense. They had done everything people were supposed to do in Noble Quests, and as close to the exact way they were supposed to do it as they could manage. For their efforts, they had even been rewarded with the knowledge they needed to complete their mission: the whereabouts of the Indigo Knights! Everything for them was coming together. But O, how quickly it had all come apart instead!

Suddenly, Jek heard a cough. Or rather, he *registered* a cough. He realized at once that he had been hearing it for some time, but that it had seemed farther off, and he had not deduced what the sound was. After all, he was under rather a lot of stress, and the sound of his own body bulldozing through an endless ocean of leaves obfuscated some of these things...

The coughing quickly grew in cough-likeness and severity. It was spirited and full-bodied enough coughing that Jek recognized a familiar surly rasp about it. It was the old man!

"Old man!" Jek cried out, too caught up in the glee of recognition to realize at once how terrible it was that they were both hopeless captives. "Old man, is that you!?"

"*Cough, cough*," the old man coughed. "Aye, tis me."

It was! Jek wished he had a million questions for the old man, but couldn't come up with any. He wanted to ask what had happened... but of course, he already knew that much. They had been ambushed and kidnapped by stealthy Mantids in the deep jungle – the very heart of Mantid territory. He wanted to ask what they should do now, but that seemed moot, and he expected the old man would have some rather stinging codgerly insults for him if he put forth such a question. There was only one other thing he was desperate to know – so desperate, in fact, that he didn't dare ask about it. Until, at last, he did anyway...

"Where's Audrey?"

"I'm here too," said Audrey's voice from close by.

He couldn't help being glad to hear her. Jek would have preferred that she live on, of course... but selfishly he found comfort in the thought of dying in good company.

"You are? I didn't hear either one of you!" Jek said. "I hoped you had got away!" He wondered at their quietness. "Why didn't you call out?"

"Well, for my part, I thought you were doing well enough on your own," Audrey said.

"And fer me, I thought I done start ta felt a tickle in me throat, what I didn't feel like agitatin'," the old man said. "*Cough, cough*!"

"Oh old man, you're coughing!" Audrey declared, distraught. "Are you alright?"

There was a moment of silence.

"It's nothing," came the old man's voice, brusquely.

"Don't you give me that!" Audrey said, suddenly indignant. "I've worked around plenty of old people! I know that when they start to cough, it's never nothing!"

"I say there ain't aught to be worryin' about!"

"There's plenty to be worrying about!" Jek said, even as his musket caught a snag and the stock end was nudged unpleasantly into his face. "No offense to your cough, old man, but I'm more concerned about being dragged to a grisly death! That's what's happening right now."

"Aye. We's in a mighty pickle!"

"What are we going to do?" Jek asked.

"*Cough*! Now don't ye start haranguing me about it! Why don't ye come up with a stratagem o' yer own fer once, ye pea-brain!" So came the codgerly insult.

"Don't stake this on me!" Jek insisted. "I don't know how to survive things! But you do! Or you wouldn't be so old!"

"Well, I gots none too few idears at present," the old man said, a bit less surly. "T'ain't ezactly the ideal time for thinkin', while ye's gettin' keel-hauled like this! *Cough, cough*. Might best wait till they's got us where they's takin' us to start formelatin' a plan."

"*Pleuu, pleue, plfew*!" Audrey said.

What could that have been about? Jek and the old man listened tensely for something more from her. "What was that, Audrey? Didn't quite make it out..." the old man inquired at last.

"I got leaves in my mouth," Audrey said.

* * *

After many eternities, the tides of dead, soggy, discolored leaves receded, and Jek was hauled into a clearing. A cool breeze caught him unawares, overpowered his squalid coat and chilled his wet body to the bone. With this, he realized that he had been cold for a long time. Checking around through the blank spaces in his matted net, he glimpsed the light of fires far ahead and reasoned that he would soon be warm again... and probably far in abundance of what he might wish for. Provided, of course, that Mantids did not eat their prey raw...

Freed of the constant rustling, he heard distinctly for the first time the footfalls of the Mantid that had borne him these many miles without relief, and he watched the narrow limbs treading on either side of him. It sounded and looked just like sticks hitting the ground. Each leg was gnarled and knotted, matching exactly the shape and texture of wood, and the joints creaked as would a tree in the wind.

Of the rest of his captor, he had a rather poor view. But he looked to his right and saw another Mantid plainly – the one he supposed was dragging the old man along. It was a more ghastly creature than he had ever imagined. The entire body of it appeared to have been patched together from the raw stuff of the jungle itself. Its main bulk was woody like the legs, but flaked with moss, and fraught with ragged loose edges that mimicked dead leaves. Even its huge purplish eyes were like prickly pears, nestled in a bed of greener foliage. They were pointed at the tops in sharp folds and set at steep diagonals, totally exasperating the maniacal look of the creature.

Jek blinked hard as he began to lose his focus on the Mantid. His eyes frantically tried to correct themselves. It was like the bug was getting blurry... although it truth, it wasn't. More like it was getting... *line-y*? The hard but dim light of night was catching the creature differently now, if Jek's sight did not deceive him. Even as he watched, it looked like the body of the Mantid radically changed texture, appearing now smoother and shimmery, streaked with millions of slowly undulating threads. Jek was astonished. The thing had completely resurfaced itself to match the grassy clearing! Small wonder that no soldiers had ever returned from the jungles. Mantid camophlage, as he now saw, was a true marvel of the natural world!

* * *

After a spirited exchange of chirts and chortles between the troop of Mantids and another group nearer the fires, Jek, Audrey, and the old man were finally dropped off by some vessels and baskets in the midst of what was clearly a very large encampment, their own captors continuing off without them in some tangeant. There were several large fires, and simply hundreds of small ones.

Jek discovered that many of these small fires closer to the ground were merely native scorch dandelions. That did not, however, account for the ones that were a good ways *off* the ground. But as Mantids came and went, he saw that those fires that were higher in the air were actually the eyeballs of the encamped Mantids themselves! Their eyes had dynamically camophlaged to mimic small bouquets of scorch dandelions!

At this, Jek shook his head. If it hadn't been terrifying enough at the mercy of giant homicidal bugs whose chittery language could not be understood, now their eyes were on fire...

"*Cough, cough*!" Jek heard the old man say, each of them still bundled up on the ground. "Upon me word! Them varmints got eyes like demons!"

"That's really nifty," Audrey agreed.

"We've got to get out of here!" Jek said.

"Can't, lad. *Cough, cough*. Ye might as well accept that we's gonners; ain't no gettin' away from this many bugs, what with us right smack in the middle o' the clearin'! Ain't no cover for a hunderd yards 'r more!"

"Well, we can get out of the sacks, at least," Audrey said, effortlessly opening the gunny end of her net. It was another rather surprising development.

"Jumpin' G. Wilkers!" the old man exclaimed. "We isn't even tied off!" He popped out of his net with unexpected spryness. He and Audrey brushed off some of the leafy residue. They watched for Jek to come out of his net, with quickly waxing impatience.

"Well come on, lad!" the old man said in a shouting whisper. "We's waitin' on you!"

"Are we sure we want to do this?" Jek said motionlessly from within his net. "I don't think we're liable to achieve anything except to make them angry."

"Suits me, *cough, cough*," the old man said, wrestling his sword out of the net. "I'd rather go down fightin'!"

"Oh, alright," Jek resigned with a sigh, and he too got out of his net.

Though they hadn't been watched closely, their sudden, armed emergence naturally attracted some attention. There were Mantids everywhere. From the improved vantage point of actually being on his feet again, Jek quickly decided that they must be in the midst of an entire tribe! Opposite the vessels they were huddled against, he saw many motionless, firey eyes fixed on them a few dozen yards away. Mantids had stopped between seemingly every row of tents to watch them...

"Load yer guns," the old man prompted, quiet as a mouse.

Jek obediently fumbled with his musket, forgetting it was already loaded. But disaster! He saw that the flash pan was stuffed with wet mud. All those miles dragged on the ground had taken a toll. He tried to clear it with his finger but it was useless – the touch hole was also stopped up, and he would need *minutes* to properly clean the thing before it could possibly be used...

"It's no use," he announced.

"I know ye's a lousy shot, lad, but with so many, the two o' ye is bound to hit somethin'!"

"No! I mean the gun is stopped up! It won't fire!"

"*Cough... cough-cough*," the old man lamented. "Mercy me, but this is a pickle we's in!"

A disorienting buzzing sound filled the air. A troop of Mantids struck the ground all around them, their wings kicking up dirt and ash. The confusion of this surprise attack and the blinding particulates left Jek swinging his musket senselessly, hoping the bayonette would strike something. As he blinked the dust out of his eyes, the barrel did catch, but it was in the iron grip of enemy pincers, and he was wrenched to the ground. It knocked the wind out of him, and his weapon was levered from his grasp.

He lay motionless, trying to breathe, practically paralyzed as one of the creatures leaned over him, all flaming eyes and pincers full of barbs long as nails. This close to the fire, it had a sandy complexion, and the ends of its limbs were black and blanched like burnt timber. Its mandibles worked and chittered, and there was thick green saliva between them, probably poison.

In a surprisingly effortless fashion, Jek resigned himself to the fate of being a big evil bug's late dinner. His one remaining hope was that he wouldn't be eviscerated first. It was his cherished notion that guts – particularly Human guts – belonged on the inside. But whatever was about to happen, he willed his eyes open... at least part of the time, part of the way. It was, after all, his last chance to show a pinch of bravery...

The creature continued for countless ages to not eat him. Jek's eyes were twitching maniacly with effort and his breath came and went in chokes, but no matter how he tried to will it over and done with, still he went uneaten. Finally, the bug leaned back upright. Jek shut his eyes and gasped air. The thing was *not* going to eat him. At least, not at present. Jek really hated not knowing where he stood with these Mantids...

From a slightly more comfortable distance, his assailant kept watching him intently, perhaps even inquisitively. Jek felt almost as if it was waiting for *him* to do something. But he really had no idea *what* to do, or what it might want him to do. Finally, the Mantid turned and looked in the direction of some distant chattering, and before Jek could begin to muse about it, it turned back on him, springing forward and brushing him with a snarl and a screech. Jek was whisked to his feet. The bugs standing over Audrey and the old man did the same, and they were quickly corralled. They maneuvered such to herd the Humans in a particular direction. Jek found himself almost thrilled to cooperate. This felt like communicating. There was still much uncertainty, of course. Were they simply being taken *somewhere else* to be eaten? Possibly. Probably *quite* possibly. But Jek surprised himself with this thought: Maybe... just *maybe*... they weren't...

* * *

Soon they were led past great crowds. All eyes were fixed on them. There were eyes above the six-foot level and eyes around the four-foot level. Jek was surprised to suddenly see all these shorter Mantids.

"Who are all the little guys?" Audrey asked, as if reading his mind.

"They *is* the guys, lass, or so's I wager," the old man answered. "Male bugs is often smaller. And that's the least o' they's problems. Tis told that the ladyfolk eat their mates!"

"*Bleah*!" Audrey remarked.

Jek was also appalled at the savagery, but didn't voice it. If cannibalism ran in the Mantids, then it seemed all the more hopeless that he and his fellow Humans should endure much longer uneaten. Still, he found himself trying to piece it together over and over again. Something here was wrong. The camp wasn't in any mode of observing ritual sacrifice. Their mood was neither celebratory nor solemn. They were just watching the Humans walk through their camp. Silently, unflinchingly watching. Almost as if they, too, agonized over the question of what was going to happen next...

Jek returned his gaze to the fore. He saw that ahead of them, Mantids were working at assembling or erecting something. He had a clear view of it – clear enough that he could see there were clever little feelers that worked at the end of the Mantids' pincers, giving them at least passable dexterity. But he couldn't figure out what in Heck the object was. When after a few moments they finished their work, it came out looking like some sort of peculiar, ornate hammock on short stilts...

At this moment, the parted crowds of Mantids turned to face front and hunkered down. Jek intuited that the hammock thingy must be some semblance of a throne – that a prominent Mantid – a ruler of whatever sort the Mantids observed – was arriving. Jek plummeted back into despair. Probably they were just being offered as a meal to the queen...

Sure enough, emerging from the shadows into the firelight came a shiny troop of armored protectors on either side of a taller Mantid with great, spectacular antennae, an impressive chitin at its back that swept out beyond the shoulders like a set of false wings, and a necklace fashioned of mummified pincers. This singular Mantid opened its wing covers, spread huge moth-like wings and leapt with a buzz over its hammock, where it then sat. The armored protectors filed in ahead of the ruler and fanned out to the sides. The nearby fires caught in the eyes of the royal party.

Jek, Audrey and the old man were herded to about ten feet in front of the monarch, at which point, all activity ceased. For many moments, absolutely nothing else happened.

"Could it be that we're supposed to say something?" Audrey asked in a grave whisper, as if there was any chance they might not hear her.

"Well, go ahead, lass! Ye're the gifted speaker!" The old man answered.

"Augh! I knew you were going to say that."

Inspiration struck. "You should stand on something," Jek suggested.

"What? Why!?"

"I think it amplifies the effect of your speeches."

"Well, whatever. But there's *nothing* to stand on!" Audrey rebutted.

"Stand on Jek," the old man suggested.

"What!?" both Audrey and Jek asked in unison.

"Aye, ye heard me. Stand on Jek. He can get on the ground and ye can stand on him. We gots to give ourselfs every advantage! Tis our very lives at stake, and the future o' the world too!"

Jek looked at Audrey. She looked back at him gravely, apparently convinced that the old man was right. Jek groaned but he got on the ground. The old man came over to help Audrey steady herself as she stepped up on Jek...

"I don't have any idea what to say," Audrey admitted.

"Best say it anyway," the old man advised.

Jek waited many uncomfortable seconds as Audrey came to some decision about what to say. He looked around, as he was able. He could see that she had their attention, much as she had taken captive her audience back on the Wading Isle. That much was a good sign. Now if she could just arrive at some eloquence...

"Okay, bugs," she began. Jek winced, and not just from being stood on. "I don't have much to say, except to express our fondest wish that you would not eat us. It is actually really important that you don't! You will probably think I'm just making up junk to fool you, but the three of us are on a Noble Quest – one that might affect the future of our civilization, and yours."

"*We* – are ***not*** – civilized," came a voice – clicky and gurgly and with an odd timbre, but a *voice* nonetheless. It was a bit like the voice of an old woman, slow and easily enough understood, but still obviously alien. The monarch of the Mantids rose, and Audrey rather sheepishly stepped down off of Jek. "But," the voice of the monarch continued, "If you have come to help us in this late hour, then I hope you have brought many more of your soldiers with you."

Soldiers? thought Jek, as he got up off the ground and dusted himself.

"What are you talking about?" Audrey asked plainly.

"There is no time for feigning ignorance, important Human!" the monarch barked. "But perhaps you would have proof that we are ourselves and not our adversaries, before you would speak openly of these things." The monarch turned to the guards on her left, and clickety-clacked an urgent command.

With flighted leaps, the guards dashed away, and soon returned, dropping piles of great, stout bones at the feet of the Humans. Jek was horrified and bewildered. He couldn't interpret the savage show being put on before him...

"These are the bones of the dragon-people your Czarina sent forth some years ago, in vain attempt to civilize us," the monarch explained. "What would the foreign usurpers know of this? I am Chief Katydid of the Dyeus Tribe. Is that identification enough for you?"

For some time, they could provide no answer. "I don't understand," Audrey admitted at last.

The crowd muttered in their clickety language. They were deeply troubled by something. Chief Katydid herself slumped and sighed. "You are not sent of the Czarina, in answer to our plea for help, then?"

"No," Audrey answered. "I'm afraid not."

"Blast it, lass!" the old man called out. "Why'd ye answer that way?"

"Because it's true. We're not from the Czarina."

"Aye, but better they *thought* we was! Now they've no cause not to eat us!"

"Fret not, old Human," Chief Katydid said, with much sadness still in her voice. "We are very uncivilized, but we have no plans to eat you."

"Oh, what a relief!" Jek said, almost reflexively.

"Is this why you make trouble in the camp?" The Chief asked. "Is this why you have pathetic looks of great fear? You have thought all along that we will eat you?"

"Well... yes... of course," Jek said. "It's well known throughout Jast-Madiir that no one ever returns from your jungles. There are many terrible stories about the barbarism of your people."

To Jek's amazement, the Chief seemed at once to cheer up. "There are?! 'Terrible stories', you say? Are they quite gruesome?"

"Yes, they're horrifying," Jek admitted.

Chief Katydid nodded, and there were similar nods and murmurs throughout the tribe. "This, at least, is something good to hear! It is true that we have eaten very many of your soldiers. We are very, very uncivilized, you see. But perhaps we are not as scary as you think. In truth, we do not much like the taste of Human. It's a texture thing mostly, I think. We eat only the ones we have to."

Jek found this very hard to accept. 100% mortality rates seemed to contradict any sense of restraint on the part of the Mantids. "Then how is it no one ever returns? Not one... ever."

"It is a complicated thing," the Chief explained. "We have kept up our end of the war throughout the ages, as a courtesy to your Czarinas. They have always maintained at least an occasional interest in the war... and we, for our part, do what we can to oblige them. Though we hate more than anything to leave our jungles, and so *this,* we have not done. But we are fastidious in ambushing all the Human soldiers who come to us. Many fight, but often others surrender. We are most uncivilized, but we honor their surrender, nonetheless. But this is where we have other problems..."

"What kind of problems?" Audrey asked.

"The Humans that we take prisoner… we always try to send them back. But they do not go. Once they have seen our simpler way of life, closer to nature, they become enchanted by it. They quickly forsake their own culture and insist on joining us." At this, the Chief sighed. "It is a very pitiful thing, to see a Human try to live like a Mantid. In the end, we are forced to eat them."

Jek felt another nervous spell take hold of him. He looked around. There wasn't much going on at the moment, but they *did* seem to have an alluringly simple way of life, from what little he could make out. He worried that he, too, might succumb to it, and force the Mantids to eat him, as they had all the others…

"So, you let Humans surrender, and you only eat them when you have no other choice?" Audrey plied. Jek wondered where she was going with this, but was glad for the distraction from the magnetism of their lifestyle.

"Yes," the Chief answered.

"And you're organized into a tribal structure and you have tools and things."

"Yes, yes," Chief Katydid answered, becoming rather impatient. "What of it?"

"Well, are you *sure* you're not civilized?"

Chief Katydid's pincers clicked nervously. "Oh, yes. *Very* sure. For instance, we are often getting into many wars with other Tribes."

"Human countries go to war with each other all the time," Audrey countered.

The Chief's mandibles chattered with frustration as she tried to think of something else. "But you! You people cook your food! We eat our meat raw!"

"So do Jackal People," Audrey reasoned. "And they are *extremely* civilized."

The Chief sat quietly for some moments, agonizing. She fumed and clicked in frustration, but could think of nothing more. "Well, suppose you tell us something you have heard we do that is uncivilized, and we will have that much, at least."

Jek snapped his fingers with sudden epiphany. "We heard that your women eat their mates!" he said.

Chief Katydid looked around as the tribe chattered. It seemed like news to them. "I do not know where you heard this," the Chief replied. "We are very, *very* uncivilized… but we do not eat our mates. Although… we could certainly start… if you think it would help."

The males began to behave rather sheepishly.

"Nah, that's alright," Audrey said, diffusing the tension. "I'm sure you're plenty uncivilized somehow."

"We are indeed," the Chief agreed, but seemed forlorn again. "But there is no time left to prove it. When word spread that you were in the camp, the Tribe was hopeful that you were here to save us in our time of great need. I was certain that any help now would be too little and too late, and in any case I was correct. But for the sake of the Tribe, I have granted you audience. Now we must dissolve this parley and be swiftly on our way."

"Where are you going?" Audrey asked.

The Chief shook her head. "I forget that since you do not come from the Czarina, you would not know of our troubles. We are fleeing from the invaders – the rival tribes who have come from the island you know as Despotopia."

Jek blanched. "There are Mantids from Despotopia on Jast-Madiir?"

"Yes. They are *all* here."

It was an astonishing revelation. Whole secret populations of Dire Mantids had swelled the ranks in the jungles of his own country, apparently without anyone being the wiser. "But why?"

"The new Industry of Despotopia has allowed the Humans to flatten all the jungles. This is the same calamity that brought many Roemnari tribes to our lands hundreds of 'long-primitive-time-increments' ago. Some of the tribes that have come here are now twice-displaced. They are all competing with us for land, and we do not have the strength we need to resist them. Now we too must leave our home. We must leave, and hope to find some other place to go."

Jek just shook his head. He had only just begun to learn about his scary neighbors. And now they were *leaving* – driven out by probably even scarier neighbors. As he considered it, a pit formed in Jek's stomach. His childish plans for saving the world had been revealed for what they were. Even if they ultimately found the Knights in time to prevent the conquest of the Doom Fleet, Despotopia had already wrought damage that could not be undone. For these Mantids and for many others, the Noble Quest had failed before it even began...

"Oh, that's horrible!" Audrey lamented. "That's the very thing you said you would hate more than anything to do."

"Yes," Chief Katydid answered. "We hate it more than anything. But to go on hating it, we must live... and to live, we must leave."

"Where will you go?" Jek asked.

"We will go in boats," the Chief answered with resolve. "From there, I cannot say. Roemnar has no jungles. Despotopia has no jungles. Maenea, we have heard, is in a state of madness. The Mantids from Despotopia would not go there. Perhaps it is not long before the Crazy Humans destroy those jungles too. We do not know where to go."

"Did ye consider Tophthaera?" the old man asked, still holding back his coughing jags as best he could.

"The islands of molten rock?" the Chief asked. "Only the Jelly People may thrive there."

"I think you *should* go to Maenea," Jek suggested. "It's a terrifying place, but it sounds like your only option. Where else *can* you go?"

"You could sail south!" Audrey exclaimed. Jek was surprised. The idea didn't strike him, but she seemed strangely resolute about it...

"South?" Chief Katydid asked. "What is south?"

"I don't know!" Audrey said. "But that's the point. There's nothing charted below the southernmost reaches of Jast-Madiir. Nothing at all! So whatever you might find down there, you can be sure it won't be civilization. Who knows but that there might be a wide open jungle somewhere in the south just waiting for you?"

"Hmm..." the Chief said. She sat thoughtfully for some time, chewing debris from her wrist while contemplating in what was otherwise total stillness. "I thank you for your counsel. It is perhaps not good counsel, but anything helps. I remain undevoted to any one course. There will be time yet for that decision."

"Wait!" Jek said, and surprised himself. He too had just had a thought that might be helpful. "There's somebody else who might be able to offer you some advice. Someone who's more experienced at thinking than any of us."

"Who might that be?" the Chief asked, looking around, curious about how these three hapless Humans might have kept someone else in reserve. Audrey and the old man wondered too, by the look on their faces.

Jek pulled the radio out of his duffel. "We can use this thing to speak with Zeph Bronzegloom – a very famous mind among our people!"

"Aye!" the old man snapped, exuberant in his sudden understanding. "This here's a magical mystical box we gots, what can let us flab our gums with folks halfway 'cross the world!" He was dramatic in his rendering, evidently expecting to awe the bugs with the wonders of technology.

"Don't put us on!" the Chief warned. "We are extremely uncivilized, but not superstitious. And anyway we are not entirely ignorant in matters of magic, which have cost us dearly."

"But it's true," Audrey insisted. "At least, kind of true. You'll see."

The Chief said no more, evidently giving her blessing that they should demonstrate. Jek primed the instrument. Finally, he hailed Bronzegloom. "This is Jek calling Zeph Bronzegloom... are you there? Over."

There was no immediate answer.

"Mr. Bronzegloom, can you hear me? Over."

"'Over' what?" the Chief inquired.

"I don't know, but I guess you're always supposed to say that," Audrey said.

Jek grew nervously impatient very quickly. If Bronzegloom didn't reply, it would be pretty humiliating. Moreover, he still felt the diplomatic overtures of this unexpected audience with the Chief were tenuous. She had, after all, admitted to eating people many times in the past for behaving in a piteous way...

"*Please respond*. Over."

Just as he was really starting to lose his nerve, static came through from the other side. It was intermittent at first and then persisted for a few seconds. "What do you want, kid?" came Bronzegloom's voice, in a harsh whisper. "Make it fast! This is the very definition of a bad time!"

Jek wondered and worried what was up, but was at least relieved that he had not entirely made a fool of himself in front of the bugs. "Okay, long story short, we have a tribe of Mantids that need a new home... somewhere off the island. Where do you think they should go?"

There was more intermittent static, and what sounded like other voices far off. "Mantids now?! You guys sure keep strange company! Look, I can mull it over, but right now I have to *go*!" His voice was strained with urgency.

Jek hated to press the matter, but this also seemed important. "I don't know what you have going on, but there's no time to wait. Is there any advice you can give just off the top of your head?"

The intermittence of the incoming signal escalated sharply. "Darn it, kid... or... ick head! I can give you one or two... ers, but th... First, they... opal... zuly... malp... orthward. Secondly... tude... lemon... zonk... for another thirty miles. Now I've got to *GO*!"

"Hey, you!" Jek also heard distinctly through the radio.

After that, there was nothing. It was another great moment in demoralization. Jek cradled the useless piece of scrap in his hands. They were cut off now from their only source of wisdom. Perhaps forever...

"Well," Chief Katydid said at length, "that was interesting, if not at all helpful. Still I am thankful that you would try to use your silly contrivances for our benefit." She rose to her tiny pointy feet. "Now we must go without further delay," she announced to her tribe, extending her pincers over the crowd. They obediently broke rank and set about the business of mass exodus...

* * *

Jek watched the bugs go every which-way as he and his companions stood in place, feeling very lost. He didn't know what to do, and there seemed to be no way he could help. He just tried to stay out of their way.

"Whatever will become of them?" Audrey lamented.

"Can't rightly say," the old man answered, and unleashed a very hoarse cough. "But don't go frettin' overmuch about it. They's big bugs, what can take care o' themselves. But we still gots our Quest that needs finishin'. Won't do these folks no good to let Despotopia take o'er the whole world, and maybe leave them no jungles no place. Best we slip quietly away now and make our way north, I warrant."

"You'll do no such thing!" commanded the voice of Chief Katydid, as she emerged from the scattering throng into their midst. "I'll not allow it."

As one would expect, the Chief was a very imposing specimen up close, even among the army of other 6-foot-tall invisible killing machines over which she was master. Every contour of her exoskeletal structure was razor-edged, and she had prickers in her pincers as long as rail ties. Jek was mortally terrified at her sudden aspect of hostility.

"B-but... but we..." the old man stammered.

"...You will travel with us," the Chief explained. "It would be death to you if you were to do otherwise. We have made many traps along our pathway. You would fall into them without our guidance. Or worse... you would be caught in the pincers of our enemies. They are not far away. You will want to be with us when they attack."

"Attack?!" Jek asked. "We're going to be attacked?"

"Oh yes, definitely," Chief Katydid nodded. "We are at war with them, you know, and attack is integral to war."

"But where are we going with you?" Audrey asked.

"We have our boats moored at the northwest edge of our jungle. If we reach the docks, you will not have far to flee to be beyond the trees. Our enemies hate to leave the jungle as much as we do. Outside you will be safe. But in the meanwhile, you will travel with me, for I am the only one who can render your speech. When the battle comes, my Champions will defend your lives as well as mine, if they are not too busy."

Jek was truly inspired by the hospitable heart of the Chief. So much so that, in a sudden spell of grit, he snatched up his musket and set at scooping the mud out of the touch hole and flash pan. "And we will defend *your* life, and the lives of your people, with our last ounce of strength if need be," he said, resolute.

To his surprise, the Chief laid a pincer on his musket, stopping him. "That is appreciated," she said. "But don't get carried away now. It is a long road, and at the end you must be steadfast to go your own way. Don't become too zealous for us, and force me to eat you."

Jek blinked. He didn't know what had come over him! "Right... of course..." he said, at once frightened and embarrassed. He continued cleaning his musket, but he made a point of doing it with less selfless devotion to the tribe in mind...

Before long, they were all marching out into the black, leaving the campfires behind, still burning. Jek found his spirits shrink as the warm light diminished, even venturing forth in firm alliance with full arrayed strength of the very bugs he had feared most to find. The irony may have escaped him later that he should pine for the comfort of fire, when next he came across it...

The Radiant

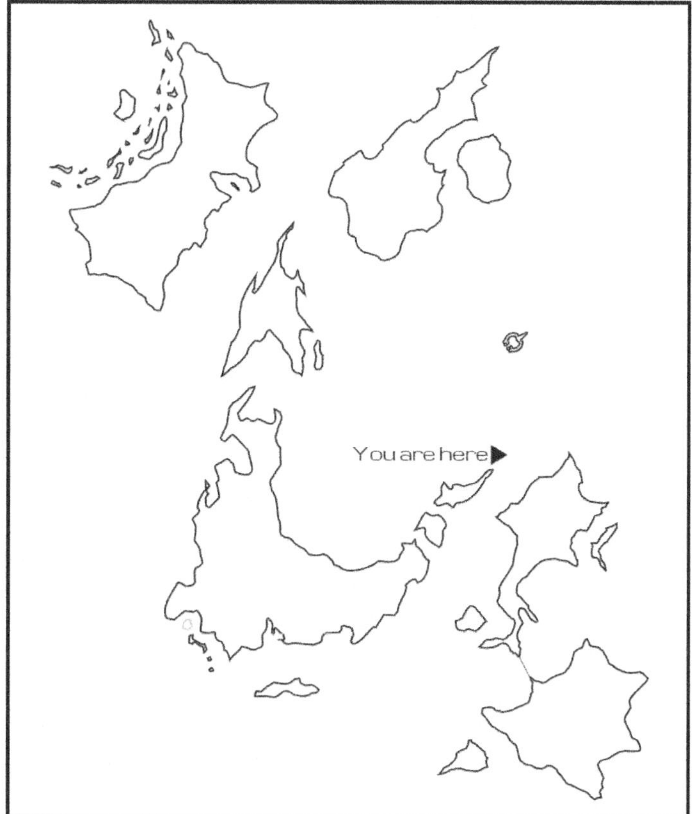

"There are others in my place who have tried to suggest that plundering is a legitimate part of commerce. But I would never so degrade myself as to agree. We were plundering long before anyone bothered to dream up commerce."

- Sultan Parcarox of the Porcelain Lily Band

She ran with new urgency as she finally abandoned all doubt that she could smell the coast. The sea was on her tongue! It was, surely, just over the next charcoal ridge. Other senses confirmed it. She saw patches of lichen and small sprouts here – new growth that must have spread over the hill from the shore. At last, Parissah's breath ran cold. There was no need to dig any deeper for the rage that had driven her this far. The exhilaration of being mere steps away from the end of that otherwise endless molten wilderness was enough...

Summiting the last band of igneous, she indeed found herself overlooking the ocean, glittering deep colors under a dusky sky. But there was still a wide and overgrown cape between her and the sea. Here on the coast, farthest from the inland volcanos, plant life was abundant and thriving.

Scanning the land beyond, Parissah caught sight of ramshackle buildings and stumps beyond a thin veil of palm trees. This is what she had hoped to find – a settlement. There were Humans living in some of these coastal oases of Tophthaera – descendants of an old pirate plot gone awry, wherein the famed Pirate Lords, Ten Jeff Snorkel and Finkley Twiggins, had combined their forces in the hopes of driving the Meduselda from the isles. It was a dumb plot, foundered in much liquor, as even Snorkel and Twiggins would later admit. But it had the distinction of being the only time in recorded history that anyone had ever killed a Meduseldan Queen, and it proved beyond any shadow of a doubt, once for all, that Queens would regenerate when killed, just as surely as their drones do. So the adventure was not without its historical import, at least...

"Upon my word, the coast!" Baegulgog exclaimed. The sound of his voice surprised Parissah. Though she had hauled him all this way by one of his tentacles, she had all but forgotten he was with her, silent and pensive as he had been since Brittegonnen...

"Yes," she confirmed, amidst heaving air. "Now if we can only find a ship."

"I should prefer that we did," Baegulgog said. "It would be a most unpleasant float from here to your Ocean Citadel. I gather your folk do not mind a swim, but my people are rather averse to big water..."

Parissah blinked. "That is some news to me, Baegulgog. Given your resemblance to jellyfish, and some of the famed expeditions of the Taltaxikhomer Margaritamoarmonums..." (she needed another breath after that mouthful... "I would have thought Meduselda had an affinity for the ocean."

"Not at all, madam – it is quite the opposite. Floating over the water is uncomfortable business for us. We find it dreadfully slippery."

Still struggling for enough air, Parissah simply huffed and shook her head. At times, the peculiarities of Meduselda were as bewildering as they were endearing.

"I say, is that the boat you were hoping to find?" Baegulgog asked, and his question caught her unawares. She scanned the horizon again. Only just in time, she got a glimpse of the stern of a ship, as it silently passed by a narrow but high and overgrown cleft, east of the settlement. Instantaneous recognition told her she had seen the rear of one of her Inquisition's own Destroyers – light and fast capital ships. It was precisely the sort of ship she had expected to be dispatched to await her arrival...

Within moments, the Destroyer emerged from behind the elevated ridge. It was not the most reassuring sight. The ship was sailing fast! Immediately she realized it was probably moving on, to search further up the coast for her. She was behind schedule, after all... and anyway it was hard to coordinate an exact rendezvous point ahead of time, since the Human settlements of Tophthaera were nameless and known to meander, as lava might necessitate. There might be other settlements to check...

Parissah tried to dredge up some more anger to power her limbs for a fresh dash, even as she began a charge down the hill, without so much as a word of warning to poor Baegulgog. She was going to have to cross through the village and try to overtake the speeding Destroyer, or else be forced to watch it slip unwittingly beyond her reach! There was no telling how much delay that might entail. She couldn't let it come to pass...

To her horror, she found spurring herself any further to be nearly impossible. She had allowed herself to become far too relaxed in the brief time she spent standing on the summit overlooking the ocean! The frustration of the past week and the stress of the moment didn't seem enough to sustain her much longer. She was getting colder and colder. Total exhaustion was imminent. But she kept running. She *had* to keep running...

Still in a mad scramble, Parissah entered the village with Baegulgog in tow. It was a desolate scene up close. The buildings were stripped and gutted, and there wasn't a soul in sight. Grisly as it seemed, the mystery was a welcome diversion from continually taking stock of her own depleted reserves of strength. But it didn't take long to arrive at a likely explanation for what had happened here...

"Good gracious," Baegulgog said, as if on cue. "I don't like the look of this. Whatever has become of the townsfolk?"

"Pray they might still be here, Baegulgog," Parissah wheezed. "This is a Human village, after all – and yet, these Humans would be under the sovereignty of Irisa. She will have conscripted them to the war. But perhaps some have endured here, in hiding. I do not doubt they would want to conceal themselves from us, even now."

"What of their buildings? Humans customarily build things to look sounder, I should say..."

"Another part of the war effort, I suspect. The Queen will have cannibalized these structures as fodder for *Variglew*..."

"Ah, yes," Baegulgog agreed, free tentacles flapping in the wind. "It all begins to add up now."

Parissah wished she might've saved her breath for the running. But she couldn't very well have left Baegulgog unassured. As she bolted down what must have been mainstreet and rounded a disused fountain, she fought back an urge to check around for another glimpse of the Destroyer's progress. She could ill-afford a misstep. She had to keep her eyes to the front...

Finally, a side street emptied out to the very shore itself. She ignored the boundary and splashed and splooshed right into the ocean, up to her knees. Only then did Parissah stop and take stock of the situation. She realized almost too late that it would be foolish to venture much further out. If she was too submerged, the Destroyer would have almost no chance of seeing her. And anyway, the chilly water was sapping her little remaining body heat...

But they had come out ahead of the ship, thank the Creators! She waved emphatically and called out, and Baegulgog did likewise, in his somewhat lazier fashion.

But the sound of her calls beat hard in her own ears. She winced with chest convulsions as her heart began skipping rhythm. All over, she began to feel tingly. And, perhaps worst of all, by now she was very cold...

The last thing Parissah remembered was taking a moment to look at her hands, which were swollen and puffy. And then, the splash...

*   *   *

ZAP!

An impressive electrical impulse jolted her awake.

In a frenzied fit of reflexes, she lashed out! Something tore away in her grasp, and she was startled by the sound of snarling... until she realized it was her own.

Finally, her senses began to rally. Her first moments of true consciousness revealed that she was in a typical Inquisition infirmary. She looked down at what she had in her claw, and saw that it was a Meduseldan tentacle...

"Aha! She lives! Good morning, madam!" said the former owner of the tentacle.

"Baegulgog!" Parissah exclaimed. She found him beside her cot, and a few Inquisitors with him. There were many questions to be had... but mostly she was instantly horrified that she had tore one of Baegulgog's tentacles off! She almost tried to hand it back, for what it would have been worth. "I'm so sorry about your limb! If I had only been more..."

"Oh, not to worry!" the Clerk replied, quite unphased, and indeed very merry. He waved a new ghostly appendage at her, to remind her just how superficial was the damage. "It shan't be missed long, I suspect... and in any case it was worth losing to see you well again! You weren't very much yourself after you flopped into the water."

"I..." she faltered, struggling to remember what he was talking about. "Yes... yes I must've fainted. My strength gave out on me after all. But the ship! Did we make it to the ship, Baegulgog? Is that where we are now?"

"Yes," answered one of the Inquisitors – the captain himself, it appeared, as she examined his uniform. "Your friend here was quite intrepid. He carried you to us himself, and indeed he intercepted us only just in time."

Parissah was amazed... perhaps unduly. "You carried me, Baegulgog?"

"Oh come-come, it is not such a great feat I performed! It seemed the very least I could do, really, after *you* had borne *me* nearly all the way."

"But you braved the slippery waters! You completed an integral phase of the mission when I was too weak to complete it myself!" She nodded to him, and it was a rather emotional nod. "I am greatly indebted to you... my friend."

Baegulgog muttered, as if embarrassed. "Pish-posh! I'll entertain no notion of any debts. It is an honor to have finally leant hand to your endeavors... in the most literal sense."

"*My endeavors...*" Parissah essentially whispered to herself, working at remembering her list of priorities in the proper order. "The blockade!" she recalled, and turned to the captain. "Captain, we must send word to the Citadel – Tophthera must be blockaded... and Toefthaera too, while we're at it! No one is to get in or out!"

"The word has been sent," the captain assured her. "The Clerk was quite urgent on that point as well. You seem to have made quite the effective synergist of him."

Again, Parissah was pleased with Baegulgog beyond her ability to express. He had indeed proven abundantly trusty. "I can't take any credit for the help he has been, Captain. He is a stout fellow by his own merits."

Baegulgog succumbed to more embarrassed guttural noises. "You must all stop fawning over me at once, or I may be compelled to become an Inquisitor myself."

"If you did that, we would certainly have to stop praising you," Parissah said. Satisfied as she was that the immediate business was well in-hand, she sprawled back flat on the cot. Her muscles were achy and unsteady. She deduced she had had a few hours' rest, but it was far from what she really needed to recover from the total exhaustion she had driven herself to...

"You are still not well, I fear, madam," Baegulgog said, concerned.

"That is true," she agreed. "But it is nothing that some more rest, or perhaps a fine meal, will not remedy."

"The food is being retrieved," the captain explained. "I had the Clerk resuscitate you so that you could feast, and so recover expediently. But in the meantime, I should like to know more about this 'Glowy Lady' that Mr. Baegulgog mentioned. After all, we shall be commiting extensive naval resources to barring from the Tophthaeran Isles."

"I should like to know more as well," Parissah replied. "We know that she has promised a Meduseldan-killing Weapon to Irisa. We can infer that she would be just as amicable to making such a deal with Asiri, if we leave the south unguarded. At any rate, we certainly cannot afford to dismiss that possibility. As for the Lady herself, we are told she appears somewhat Human... but glows green."

"The Queen also said she had an elongated conical top, if I recall," Baegulgog imparted.

"Yes, thank you, Baegulgog," Parissah nodded. "But that is all we know as yet."

"Hmm," the captain mused. "We will certainly have to learn more than that, if we can."

"I will do everything in my power to that end," Parissah assured him. "We are making for Roemnar with all speed, I hope? Perhaps there we can glean something."

"We should be there by the tenth hour on the morrow," the captain said. "But do you have any reason to suspect the Roemnari would know anything of this?"

"Not any concrete reason, I fear. But you know Herons. They have more than their share of esoteric insights. It will be worth asking around, if we find the time."

"Agreed," the captain agreed.

Presently, a great smorgasbord wheeled into the infirmary. The smell of it was very sensational... as one might expect when one has not eaten in over a week.

"I leave you to your food," the captain excused himself. "Join me on the bridge when you have revived."

"I shall," Parissah said, even as the captain walked out, and the rest of the Inquisitors with him. She turned to Baegulgog. "Perhaps you should take your leave as well, Baegulgog. I shall have to scarf down immense quantities of food in short order. It will not be an exceptionally polite spectacle."

"As you wish, madam," Baegulgog said, "though I am not sure I would appreciate the difference between one manner of eating and another."

* * *

After gobbling the sizable feast with peak efficiency, Parissah at last came to the bridge of the Destroyer, enjoying reserves of strength again, the likes of which she hardly remembered having had in the first place. She struggled not to let the shortcomings of her mission to Tophthera suddenly seem too small and distant. Feeling so revitalized, it was hard not to be optimistic. She had a particularly fast ship to take her to Roemnar, where she would finally put the side business of the lighthouse stewards behind her. And she had learned that numerous veteran envoys were already with her on the ship, having been recalled with great pains from various missions to meet the increasingly critical challenge posed by the insurrection in Maenea. Zalkothal and Grenthegaen, to name a few. Most remarkably, they also had Primary Administrator Hihvnor aboard! He had been presumed dead for weeks – among the latest casualties in a long series of failed outreach missions to the Mantids of the Jast-Madiiran jungles. Evidently, he had narrowly survived, only to be cut off and nearly immobilized in the wilderness for many days. With such help now at her disposal, Parissah felt great confidence that the Inquisition would quickly arrive at an expedient solution to the Maenean problem. And with the fleet deploying to ward off the Glowy Lady, she was assured that the Twin Queens did not yet possess the means to do any lasting harm. When Enscharaulgk returned to life, they would both still be around for him to set straight... with any good fortune at all. Things were really looking up...

Parissah took stock of the bridge of the Destroyer – *Radiant*, as the ship was named. It seemed an oversize command deck for a vessel of such limited scope. There were causeways to various stations that passed over a huge recessed disk. The whole round base of the deck was set with three-foot-tall teeth, like a giant inverted gear... and indeed, there were enormous ratchets set along the circumference. With the primary gunnery stations set into wings on either side, four barrels across, the bridge doubled as an enormous turret. Stout engineers stood by the ratchets, ready to rotate the deck, each dutifully eyeing an elevated central dais, with a dial that the range-finding officer could set in any direction. Their job was to keep the bridge in line with that dial at all times. In spite of their access to electrically-powered motors, there were many systems throughout Inquisition ships that demanded this kind of manually-intensive operation. Indeed, even the drive motors on ships were usually supplemented by manual power, in the form of jogging turbines. But Avarica were creatures of impressive strength, and it only seemed natural to channel that strength into their work wherever possible…

Presently, Captain Veshinkir saw Parissah and waved her forward. She went to meet him at the front of the bridge, by the wide viewport. The night had fallen very thick – to the point where, if she had not known better, she might have thought the viewport to be merely a big black wall. Reaching the cold glass, there were some points of light on the deck below, but the view was otherwise just as dark and featureless as it had been from across the bridge.

"However do you navigate in this blackness?" she asked.

"We have the compass," he assured her. "And if there was anything out there to run into, there should be a lighthouse to go with it."

"Fair enough," she conceded. "What news from the Citadel? Has Enscharaulgk revived?"

He hesitated to answer. That, of course, meant no. "Not yet," he framed it.

"And *Pharonomagnus*?" she plied.

"It continues to function nominally," he answered. She was glad. Though of course, the 14th of Novtober was still some weeks off. She couldn't very well abandon all reservation about the great pipe organ until 7-15-21…

"You seem to be in nominal condition yourself, now," the captain continued. "What more can you tell me about the Tophthaeran mission?"

"I can tell you it was enough to confirm nearly everything we feared," Parissah admitted. "The scorn of the Queens has given rise to huge, abominable drones, the likes of which we have not seen since the 770 Years War. And they were researching worse things, as you know. At least, Irisa was… but there is hardly any room for doubt that Asiri has been similarly occupied. From what we observed, they seem to mirror each other perfectly…"

"'Twin Queens,' indeed," Veshinkir mused. "That brings us at once back to the mystery of the Glowy Lady. Do you remember nothing more, now that you are quite recovered?"

Parissah hung her head. "There is nothing more. Queen Irisa was nothing if not indiscriminate about whom she hoped to receive illicit technology from. I pressed her for more details. But when she made her deal, she evidently had not bothered to learn anything – not a single fact beyond what you have already heard."

Veshinkir shook his head. "In any case, we seem to have a new enemy."

"Or an old one," Parissah speculated. "She could merely be a front for some new scheme of Onyxadon. I hesitate to consider what else she might be…"

The captain studied her. "For instance?"

"We still have Zedulon's Chocolate Prophecy. Some great evil is supposed to be coming back into the world, whether sooner or later. I know it is a hopelessly vague omen. Still I cannot help my suspicions…"

"In a way I hope you are right, so that we may have an end to that Prophecy, at last. I see now why you planned to seek more insight in Roemnar. We will have to see if we can contact the Proconsul himself, while we are there. Perhaps the description will register with him. Then again, perhaps it won't."

"Indeed. But I don't know which outcome to dread more."

As if her brooding could have taken tangible effect, the *Radiant* lurched suddenly, violently! A horrible clatter resonated throughout the metal hollows of the vessel, as the whole ship quaked in aftershocks. Parissah and the captain steadied themselves on the railing, so not to go crashing through the viewport...

"Goodness!" Parissah exclaimed. "Have we run aground?!"

"We certainly seem to have struck *something*," the captain answered. "A rather bitter irony, I daresay." He turned to his officers. "What of it, ensign?! Raise engineering at once."

The ensign took up a small bell-shaped phone-end attached to a cable that evidently ran all the way to the engineering section and beat on it with a stick three times. Then she held it in front of her. "Engineering, this is the bridge. Make report." After that, she held the phone up to her ear. Waiting on some answer was no small feat of patience for Parissah and the captain. But finally the ensign returned the phone to the front of her face and said, "Understood." She looked at the captain. "An explosion, captain. Engineering believes that the propeller struck a mine. The drive shaft is still turning but we have no propulsion. The hull is compromised, but not beyond repair."

Another phone cord made a dull clatter. The ensign interacted with it. "Understood," she said, and made another report: "The deck officer confirms the explosion, captain."

For her part, Parissah was incredulous. Working in the Archipelago for over a hundred years, she'd never chanced on a mine before!

"Signal combat alert," captain Veshinkir instructed. The ensign produced a hand crank and set it in a beam running through the top of the deck. As she cranked, a howling echoed down over the ship. The alarm was raised.

As she searched inwardly for some logical answers to all of this, Parissah was surprised to have the captain turn to her. "The fleet will be passing by us in mere hours," he recounted. "We need to send warning to them about this minefield we seem to have found. Can you get to the Chief Pigeon Keeper?" Even as he said this, he scrawled something. "Give him this; it details our whereabouts. He must instruct the fleet to give us a berth not less than a mile in radius."

"But our drive system is scuttled," she said. She hated to question the captain, but she had her own missions to consider. "Won't we need extraction?"

"It will have to wait until we can deploy minesweepers. I think we can affect repairs, but it is no use trying to get anywhere until we can be sure our path is clear of mines. I am sorry for the delay; the urgency of your mission is not lost on me. But it can't be helped. And we may be fortunate if delay is all we experience. There is likely much danger ahead."

Parissah was apprehensive. She thought she knew what he was getting at. "You suspect pirates?"

"I do," he answered. "Though I can't imagine what would possess them to operate this close to the Citadel."

She thought she had an answer at once. "The Berlie Beirels have been harvesting their ectodermis to fund their war."

"...And we're sailing along a trade route," the captain mused. "That would seem to put any question of pirates to rest. Hurry with the message! You may be sure the mine is not the end of our tribulations here."

Parissah took off without so much as another word, even as he told her to hurry...

* * *

In the corridors of the *Radiant*, it was an upstream battle. Parissah had need of haste, but the ways were densely packed with crewmen in the flurried activity of combat alert. Soon, she took to holding the note from the captain up in front of her and yelling, "Orders for the Pigeon Keeper! Orders for the Pigeon Keeper!" in hopes that the crew would get out of her way. She met with some success.

Running down one corridor, she chanced to meet Baegulgog.

"Prithee, madam!" he called out to her. "Whatever is all this commotion?"

She ran right by him. "No time to talk, Baegulgog. I'll catch you on the way back."

"Well... okay..." his voice echoed after her.

Finally, she reached the hatch she was looking for and climbed out onto the deck of the Destroyer. Here the howling of the alarm was quite potent, and the crewmen on deck were shouting back and forth to win over the tumult. It was so chaotic that it was easy to forget they weren't actually fighting anything. Yet...

She reached the Chief Pigeon Keeper.

"I bring word from the captain," she said. "You must warn the fleet to give us a berth not less than a mile in radius. We've struck a mine, as you must know by now." She handed him the note from the captain. "This details our latitudinal and longitudinal coordinates."

Even as she finished speaking over the alarm, it faded away. For a chilling moment, the whole deck fell silent.

"The alarm has stopped," she said at length, regretting to point out the obvious. "Does that signal that we are in the clear?"

"I'm afraid not, Administrator," the Pigeon Keeper answered gravely.

She took her leave of him and started back for the bridge. About the time she reached the hatch, a series of eruptions filled the night air! Parissah looked back to behold the dazzling white flashes of cannon fire bursting in the sheer blackness some hundreds of yards away, shallowly on the starboard side. Calls from the crew overlapped each other.

Resolving not to let the startling event leave her dumbstruck, Parissah climbed back down into the ship. She would hurry back to the bridge. Though, she feared she would be no help there, either...

She passed Baegulgog going back. He started to say or ask something else, but she cut him off. "Meet me on the bridge, Baegulgog!" she told him, whooshing by. Rounding another corridor, she had a thought: she hoped he knew where the bridge was...

Coming to the wide-open space below the bridge's fitting, she checked for its orientation, so she would know which hatch to use. Curiously, she found that the bridge was still fixed directly forward. Hurriedly, she climbed into the bridge. In times of combat, to make that climb was to take your life in your own hands. If the bridge's engineers started ratcheting, you might have the misfortune of being pinched in half...

She made it to the command deck in one piece. What she saw then baffled her. The bridge was sedentary... not a soul was doing anything. Shots had been fired by the enemy, but there was no response!

Parissah quickly crossed the gulf between her and the captain, he still at the front of the bridge, now scanning the darkness with a rangefinder. It was as if he and everyone on the command crew were oblivious. A confused multitude of emotions sprang up... some very cross. But she meant to give them the benefit of the doubt...

"The Chief Pigeon Keeper has received his orders," she reported. "And the enemy attack has begun."

In any case she would have expected such a postscript to inspire some urgency. But the captain merely replied, "So we have observed," and kept spying through the viewport.

Before Parissah could formulate some sort of objection, the barrage started all over again! Another intense round of cannon-fire, still vaguely audible from within the bridge – and quite certainly *visible* – was unleashed by their otherwise invisible adversary. She watched in horror as the crew silently ignored it.

"Captain, surely you mean to return fire!" she moderated herself. "How can you let the villains go unanswered this way?"

"I take it you are not familiar with old pirate tricks," the captain replied, still keeping his vigil. "This is a decoy attack they enjoy pulling in the dead of night. They sail a rowboat out with a load of specialized firecrackers to feign an attack. We waste our response on the decoy. Meanwhile, their actual ship circles round to hit us in the flank. And by then they can confirm our location by watching our muzzle flashes, ensuring maximum damage."

Parissah felt suddenly very shamed at having assumed the captain and crew were impossibly dense. It was very much the opposite. Even as she cursed the cleverness of pirates and her own fallibility (finally noticing that the *Radiant* had not sustained any hits), she was thankful to be in the hands of experts.

Captain Veshinkir at last retired his rangefinder. "They are listing eastward. Set the turret bearing to 270 degrees."

The range-finding officer set the dial on the dais, and the engineers finally began ratcheting the bridge toward the west.

"Slow and steady now," the captain instructed them. Amidst the surprisingly gentle lurches and the deep, low clatter of the huge ratchets, Veshinkir shuffled to the port side of the viewport for another intense gander. His range-finding officer joined him, as did Parissah. She did not know if the keenness of her eyes would compare with theirs, but another set of them searching for the *real* enemy would not hurt...

Tension built and built as the bridge slowly swiveled. Parissah deeply understood the value of waiting for the right shot, but this was on a scale she was unaccustomed to. She wondered what the pirates would do now that *Radiant* had gone so long ignoring the bait of the decoy attack. Hopefully they would presume that they had mined an unarmed trade ship. An assumption like that could lead to some careless decisions on their part. She couldn't help wanting them to make some decisions like that.

Of course, an Inquisition Destroyer – even one with a derelict engine – should be able to take a pirate ship in a fight. A *fair* fight, anyway. Still, she hated being in any way at the mercy of devious enemies, especially in a theater of combat she was unfamiliar with...

The engineers had nearly pivoted the bridge the full 90 degrees counterclockwise. There was still nothing out the window but unyielding black. Parissah deflated at the thought of an endless standoff – both ships daring the other to fire first. Captain Veshinkir whirled around. He was not about to have that, either...

"I want Starboard Cannon Four to fire on my mark."

"Ready sir," said a gunner from within the starboard wing.

Veshinkir returned to the window. His range-finding officer returned to the dial, keeping trained on the viewport as well. "All stations monitor," the captain instructed.

"Aye sir," somebody said.

"Fire."

The right-most cannon of the ship erupted with strength enough to pitch the ship a few degrees off level. Parissah took a step to steady herself, even as she saw, for the briefest instant, the enemy ship – dangerously close – revealed in the muzzle flash!

The range officer adjusted the dial. The engineers ratcheted, not slow this time, pivoting a jarring narrow arc. All of the cannons swiveled in their sleeves, with seven guns still at the ready.

The pirate ship shot first. It was a wide salvo, but not more than two decks tall. Immediately, the difference between a decoy attack and a real one assaulted Parissah's senses. This was a close volley, and the hull buckled and reverberated with the striking and bursting of the cannon balls. But some of the shots were wide and erratic – they had flummoxed the pirates somewhat after all! At this range, Parissah supposed they *had* indeed mistaken them for a trade ship, and might have been making preparations to board and loot, rather than exchange fire.

In a moment, it didn't matter much what they thought...

"All batteries fire!" the captain ordered.

The remaining cannons tore down into the pirate ship with devastating accuracy. As the blinding flashes cleared, an eruption under the enemy deck replaced their brilliance, and huge charred splinters were thrown back at *Radiant*. Their prolonged, sonic hailstorm showered the ship's metal frame as proud masts with burning sails tumbled before her eyes.

It was quite a spectacle. Parissah had never actually seen a ship go up like that before. The destruction was total.

Veshinkir turned to his range officer. "Get topside," he ordered. Parissah intuited this latest development. The captain meant to check for more enemies. As much as she would have dearly liked for that lone engagement to be the end of their troubles, there was really no telling how many pirate ships could be skulking around out there, ready to prey on the victims of their mines. Now was the ideal time to find out. The ruined hulk of the pirate vessel continued to burn on the water, illumining the whole area like a great big campfire. At last, they had a light to see by. Unfortunately, that worked both ways...

The range officer's claws clanked on the rungs of a ladder that ran up to a dorsal hatch. He swung it open and crossed the threshold with his upper body, his toes still cluthing the last rungs. For a while, they all just watched his legs, waiting with bated breath for his report...

Finally, he came back down, signaling from the ladder. "Two contacts. One at true 11 degrees, 5000 feet out, heading west. One at true 104 degrees, 1500 feet out, heading north."

The captain walked over and set the turret dial himself – toward the 104 degree mark. That ship was easily close enough to engage. The ratcheting began again, this time in the other direction, even as the cannons were reloaded. Parissah absently shook her head. She knew the situation was not ideal. They would have to turn their turret nearly the full 180 degrees to bear down on their next adversary.

"They could hardly have positioned themselves any better," she admitted to the captain.

"Indeed," he agreed. "And we're silhouetted against the burning derelict, and immobile. Their next attack will be most accurate."

"By Jove," came a voice from behind them. "Whatever does transpire? How did we find ourselves in the midst of this skirmish?" It was Baegulgog. He had caught up with Parissah at last.

"Pirates, Baegulgog," Parissah explained.

"'Pirates,' you say!?" he reeled. "That is a poor turn of luck. I hope you are giving the scallywags what-for!" His fisted tentacles engaged in boxing the air.

"We have done well enough so far..." the captain said, but at once enemy cannon fire rang out to spite him...

The attack was a deafening affair, not unlike standing with your head inside a bell as ten different pendulums struck. The pirate galleon seemed to have all guns trained on the bridge. It was a smart move for them, considering their disadvantage. Wrought of thick, rounded metal, the Inquisition Destroyer was largely impervious to their cannons, deflecting many shots, but not all. With the ringing of shot over shot squeezing her head, Parissah watched as some cannon balls punched dents into the wall of the command deck over a foot deep, and others exploded on contact, sheering the hull. Before she had time to be impressed, other enemy ballistics came directly through the viewport! They rebounded off the inside walls and smashed heavy scaffolding before errupting, sowing confusion and casualties.

But in all the chaos, the ratcheting of the engineers did not relent for a second. They were exceptionally disciplined and drilled, perfectly alternating between two teams of five, one team always moving the bridge while the other team recharged its ratchets. They would soon have the enemy in their crosshairs. The range officer adjusted the dial to account for the advance of the pirate galleon...

At that moment, a particularly unfortunate shot ricocheted into the starboard gunnery wing, smashing the housing for the innermost cannon and throwing back the gunners. When the enemy attack had ceased and the ringing died down, the captain demanded a damage report.

"Starboard Cannon One's fitting is irreparable. Starboard Gunners One and Two have sustained minor injuries."

Of course, more of the bridge had been damaged. The captain was taking his own scan of the situation as the gunners made report. He saw that the ensign's seat was empty. "Where is the ensign?" he asked.

"I'm okay," said a waving hand, protruding out from under some fallen scaffolding. She threw off the twisted metal and gingerly returned to her station.

The captain turned to Parissah and Baegulgog. "We need to keep all of our cannons in play, if we can. Could the two of you help the gunnery team steady Starboard Cannon One?"

"Indeed, good sir!" Baegulgog saluted. Parissah merely nodded and headed for the cannon.

They arrived even as Veshinkir was giving the order to prepare to fire. The ratcheting stopped as the turret aligned with the dial. They were still leading the galleon by some yards. It would give Parissah and Baegulgog a few moments to hoist the cannon...

Parissah took the far side. Once Baegulgog had a coily grip on the cannon, the injured gunner took charge of the situation. "Are you ready?" he asked.

"Ready," they said.

"Heave!" he instructed.

Parissah and Baegulgog lifted the cannon, levering it against the base of the sleeve through which it protruded. They had to struggle against and ultimately break loose shattered pieces of the fitting. Ten or twelve feet long, it was an *extremely* heavy piece of hardware, but Parissah found she was able to belay it steadily. Baegulgog had to brace himself against the ground with his lowest tentacles, but he too was up to the task. The gunner took hold of the cannon at the back, aiming it as they held it up for him. He stood a bit unsure, trying to decide where to put his legs. "Be ready for the recoil," he warned. Parissah adjusted her own stance, and Baegulgog wrapped one of his tentacles further down the barrel.

Parissah could see that the galleon had slipped into view of the cannon's sleeve. She held her breath, knowing the captain would give the firing order at any moment...

"All batteries fire!" he ordered, even as the enemy guns started up again...

The cannon in her arms went off savagely. The recoil was incredibly powerful! She and Baegulgog were thrown against the wall, but the gunner had smartly managed to throw himself clear of the cannon just before it set off.

Buffeting and rolling to the floor, Parissah could detect muscle strains and bruising, but nothing more serious. She turned to the gunner. Fortunately, he did not appear to be much more injured than he had been before the shot. Baegulgog got the worst of it, with another of his tentacles being torn asunder, smashed between the cannon and the wall. Now on merely five limbs, the Clerk was running low...

"That was rather exhilarating," Baegulgog said as he righted himself in the air. Parissah privately found she agreed.

Enemy fire kept trickling in for a few more seconds. The bridge crew sheltered themselves as best they could, with the viewport now pointed directly at the enemy. There were many holes in the window pane by now. But the hail of shots was thinner this time and truncated. Soon enough, it stopped.

Parissah returned to the cannon sleeve to see what had happened. It took some squinting, but in the light of the other ship still ablaze, she could see that most of the starboard side of the enemy galleon was in shambles. Even so, the damage was substantially less than what had befallen the first pirate ship. No providential shots had ignited anything combustible this time.

"Reload, double-time now!" captain Veshinkir ordered. Surprised by the urgency, Parissah, Baegulgog and the gunner wrangled their loose cannon on the ground and set to reloading it.

At first she thought they were just getting ready to engage the third pirate ship. But the angle of the dial was not being set that way. Indeed, the range officer turned them further *back*. In the midst of their struggle to ready the cannon once again, Parissah stole a glance out the sleeve. They were still tracking the second ship. But now, it was curling around to expose its port cannons. She shook her head in protest. Their first volley had *quite* fallen short of dealing the critical damage they needed! Now the galleon was doubling back, to try to draw their fire further into the rear quadrant, and spite them with the undamaged rows of cannons. The wily buccaneers probably did not have time to succeed in their maneuver, but the longer they could delay the *Radiant's* response to the third and final pirate ship, the greater was their peril...

Awkwardly finishing the reloading process, the three of them levered and steadied their cannon. The galleon had nearly fully exposed its port, and was already taking intermittent shots with small but accurate swivel guns on the bow. The bridge crew was sheltering as a result. But the captain saw that all gunners were ready, and gave the order once again...

"All batteries fire!"

This round resulted in pulverizing. That is, it pulverized the back of Parissah's head when she was thrown to the wall for the second time. She was disoriented and dizzy only for a few seconds, but on the whole, the experience was certainly much less fun than it had been the time before. Which was just as well, in her estimation...

As she belatedly came to her senses, she found that Baegulgog was holding her up, steadying her. He was trying to tell her something...

"Didn't you hear me, madam? The second ship! We've destroyed it!"

"Oh, that is good, Baegulgog," she said, shaking the cobwebs from her brain.

"Quickly now," she heard the captain caution. The engineers were ratcheting furiously to get the third ship in *Radiant's* sights.

"We'd better reload," Parissah told Baegulgog.

"It's no use," the gunner said. "That second strike against the wall damaged the firing pin. We won't be firing again."

Parissah tried not to be too relieved. With her duties here unceremoniously finished, she returned to Veshinkir...

"Starboard Cannon One is out of commission, Captain," she told him.

"That is unfortunate. Even so, your help was not vain. Without the extra set of hands and tentacles, we would not have got those last two rounds out of it."

She nodded. Veshinkir was gracious, but his mind and his eyes were really elsewhere. He stepped forward to the very edge of the dilapidated viewport, trying to catch an early look at the final enemy around the bend. Parissah found his behavior at once unsettling. He seemed to anticipate something dire. She wondered. The first two ships had been hectic enough, but the Destroyer had weathered them. Really, only the initial mine strike had caused truly catastrophic damage to *Radiant.* What nastiness did Veshinkir think the pirates might still have in reserve?

Even as she wondered, Veshinkir whirled. "All haste!" he commanded. The engineers went deep into their stores of strength and began ratcheting even faster, though now the pace was quaky, and at once Parissah feared the whole cadence was in danger of collapse. While she was still flummoxed, the captain physically shoved her. "Make for cover," he almost whispered. It was frighteningly affecting, but she obeyed...

The next moments were of the sort that gets permanently, finely etched into one's memory.

The viewport turned to reveal a very large ship, sailing at them, bow-to-bow. Nestled in its forward hull was some sort of horrible cannon! Though really, it was too huge – too garish – too caricatured to be *just* a cannon. Only the Inquisition's own Coup-de-Grâce battlecruisers had a larger gun. But this was no precision instrument like theirs. It didn't cap off with a forked pair of electromagnets. It came to an enormous, yawning bell-end. If anything, it was shaped just like a...

"Blunderbuss!" the captain shouted. "All hands, brace!"

That was all they got before the pelting.

A flash and a rolling explosion – almost a *roar* – filled their senses, even as thousands of assorted chunks of shrapnel embedded themselves into the *Radiant's* every surface. Whirring, darting, clinking and thunking bits showered their entire vessel for endless seconds. The improvised ballistics ranged from nail-size to barbed masses a yard or so across. The calamity of it all was heightened by the enormous amount of glass and other secondary debris the attack dislodged in the bridge. A frothy smoke rolled in, even as more shards arrived late to the party.

Finally, there was just stunned silence...

Firebrand

"Running away is a nuisance, but then, so is dying."

- Unattributed, *Compilation of Unhelpful Quotes and Witticisms*

It was a *long* night. Perhaps the longest that there had ever been. It had been the same night when they climbed out of the Venetian Flytrap tunnel a lifetime ago. They had walked through the woods, been dragged through the woods, endured two skirmishes and lengthy negotiations since then. And now, countless hours later, they were still marching under cover of dark through the dense trees and the even denser piles of leaves under each of them. The Mantids travelled almost silently on their slender legs. Jek felt like a triceratops in a china shop by comparison as he sloshed through knee-high leaves. It was hard going. They had to keep up with bugs that were only encumbered by the rather meager supplies they were carrying. All the while the battle the Chief had fortold was still hanging overhead, waiting to burst on them. Panting with every step, Jek almost hoped it would happen soon, lest his 'last ounce of strength' be about all he had left when the fighting started...

Despite the Chief's reassurance that it didn't make much difference, Jek felt pretty bad about all the noise they were making, between their heavy footfalls and the wheezing and hacking the old man was engaged in. He worried about the old man's sudden rapid decline, but every time he pressed him about it, the old man maintained, "It's nothin'."

By now, they had fallen some strides behind the Chief's entourage of 'Champions' – her armored protectors. Jek wondered about them too. Upon close inspection, they didn't seem to be wearing armor at all. More like their bodies *were* armor, as if they had camophlaged to a jungle of steel... and now they wore that 'camophlage' wherever they went. Only their eyes seemed to change to help them blend in. It had piqued Audrey's interest too. Jek had overheard her ask the Chief about it.

"I cannot reveal the secret of our Champions," the Chief had answered. "If I did, your people would soon use it to your own advantage." Jek highly doubted that, but he didn't press the matter...

There was one other mystery that was building in his mind as he watched the party march ahead of him. The Champions were not so much clustered around the Chief herself, who was kind enough to keep step with her Human companions. At present, they were guarding another group of indistinct Mantids, both males and females. Finally, he asked about this, too.

"Who are your Champions guarding right now? Is that your family or something?"

Katydid chittered some dreadful laughter. "My family?! No indeed! They are our enemies from of old," the Chief answered.

"Your enemies?" Jek repeated.

"Yes. They are the last of the Yeeyu Tribe. They came here from Roemnar many generations ago, when the Herons drove them out. They have been our sworn adversaries ever since."

"If you don't mind my asking," Jek said, blinking, "why are you guarding them?"

"Only for the most obvious reasons," the Chief answered. "We could not wish for finer and more devoted adversaries. I will not allow these Despotopian tribes to destroy them completely, if I can help it. The last of the Yeeyu will come with us wherever we go. In time, perhaps their Tribe will grow again, and we may have many more good wars. That is my cherished hope."

Jek was a bit incredulous.

"The 'Yeeyu' are from Roemnar, and your new enemies are from Despotopia," Audrey recounted. "What about your Tribe? Did you come from somewhere else too, or have you always lived on Jast-Madiir?"

"We have lived here always. Ever since the Creators gave us intellect and enormousness – from the very genesis of our people – this jungle has been home to our Tribe, and several others. We know every inch of our land, just as you would know... whatever it is that you know very well, if anything." She cast a glance back over her shoulder chitin, and sighed. "We will miss these trees horribly. They were dumb trees... but they were our trees." Jek could tell it was a very heart-felt epitaph.

Presently, a big falling leaf blew across Jek's face. He waited in vain for it to blow away, and eventually had to whisk it off by hand. Audrey evidently noticed, because he heard her snicker. But she noticed that he noticed that she had noticed, and turned more somber. "Sorry," she said.

"No problem," Jek replied. "I might laugh too, except I'm used to it. My face seems to catch blowing debris all the time."

"Yes, you have a good face for it," Chief Katydid reassured him. "I do not possess great powers of foresight, like Heron leaders are said to have, but I think it will serve you well to have such a face."

Jek grimaced. Again, the wisdom of the Chief eluded him...

Suddenly, there was a call, like that of a bird. Jek mechanically shielded himself with his arms over his head, his reflexes remembering the evil little songbirds that plagued them before the journey through Corsicarthal. All the Mantids reacted, too. They came to a dead stop, such that when Jek opened his eyes again (satisfied that no little birds were going to swoop in and try to peck them out), it appeared that he was alone in the woods with just Audrey, the old man, and the plated Champions. With some effort he began to see where the Chief and various other Mantids were. The old man hunkered down and signaled Audrey and him to do the same. Evidently the bird call was a signal.

"There is trouble ahead," Chief Katydid whispered. Jek had reasoned that much, but the confirmation was unsettling.

"Looks like an enemy camp," Audrey whispered back, and Jek was surprised. As he probed about though, he homed in on what she was talking about. Faint points of firelight were visible through the dense foliage.

"It is not a camp," the Chief said. "It is the vanguard of our enemies. The fires you see are their Revenants."

"Revenants?" the old man asked coarsely. "Ain't never heard of it."

"It is a vile contrivance of our enemies," Chief Katydid explained. "They loot the magical solutions your Human soldiers carry. Then they choose some of their folk to drink the solutions until they become fiery ghosts – invulnerable spirits of destruction!"

"They would do that to their own people?" Jek asked, incredulous.

"My gosh," Audrey gasped. "It's just like Bronzegloom was explaining about! It's the *stuff*!"

"It's absolutely barbaric," Jek lamented.

"Yes," the Chief agreed, "and in that at least, we admire them. But we have lost much to these Revenants. I fear this battle will go badly."

"Get me lots o' water," the old man said. "I can handle it for ye."

Jek and Audrey looked at him, amazed but very doubtful.

"You don't understand," the Chief said, also clearly skeptical. "They are *spirits*!"

"*Fire* spirits," he corrected, holding in a cough. "Don't overthink it, yer ladyship."

She did think about it a bit. "But why do *you* want the water?"

"I gots Water magic! Can't nobody douse these spooks more handily as I can!"

"Very well, we'll try it," the Chief resolved.

At that moment, the jungle filled with light as raking tides of fire swung blindly in wrath. Dozens of trees were charred. Jek choked in the wave of heat.

"Yes, we'll definitely try it!" the Chief said, leaping up and leading the way to the supplies. The Humans came chasing after.

"Too late for second thoughts then, I warrant?" the old man asked. But the question was rhetorical, and went ignored...

* * *

The chaos built more slowly than Jek would have ever thought, especially after such a dramatic opening attack. The Mantids were both experienced in stealth tactics and unflinchingly brave. They didn't move until a Revenant was nearly on them, relying on their camophlage for as much as they possibly could. The main thing was to not start the entire Tribe into flight. If they all started to scramble at once, the Revenants could stream incendiary fury right into the densest groupings, and they would certainly lose many. Still, every probing torrent of fire sent Mantids in flying leaps on all vectors. They were too close now to miss...

The dampness of the jungle was a salvation. Even the intense fire did not catch for long on the ground. If conditions had been dryer, Jek imagined that everything within a square mile or so would already be blazing. Instead, there was merely an overpowering reek of smouldering leaves. That much could be managed...

The Chief had to lead them in a wide arc to try to keep from being seen by the Revenants. Finally, she got them to a party of Mantids who were packing out vessels full of water. She had them follow her to the front. It was a painfully slow process. They couldn't advance quickly, but had to sneak. Jek hated to methodically stalk vengeful fire spirits.

"I hate this," he admitted to the old man. "We're tip-toeing into firey death."

"Afraid again, is we?" the old man retorted.

"As a rule, yes."

"Well, get a grip, lad. Just ye keep tellin' yerself, 'It could be worse'."

What dumb advice!

"It could be worse... it could be worse..." Jek chanted under his breath. He didn't believe it, but it was some small comfort to have something to keep repeating to himself. It bothered him to be a part of this surprise attack at all, since he had nothing to contribute. But he had to remain with the old man. They had to stay together, or they might never find each other again in the escalating disaster. And anyway, being close to the old man was probably the safest place to be, given that he was their best hope...

Apparently, the only method the Mantids had ever worked out to 'fight' Revenants in the past was to try to goad them into over-exerting themselves in their rage. Evidently there was a point at which they could expend too much of their own fire, which was their life-force, and finally they would fizzle out. Defeating them in this way didn't make for a very appealing fallback plan. Particularly given that there were perhaps a dozen Revenants on the battlefront...

With stinging smoke in his eyes, Jek struggled to make out exactly where their enemies might be. Once everything around them was ablaze, the Revenants had a nasty way of blending in – in effect they were just as stealthy now as they had been in life. It was surprisingly difficult to find them, even in the midst of their assault. A couple of times, the old man drew out and fired a vessel worth of water at what was merely a burning bush or a snapping twig that he mistook for an adversary. It was a bit demoralizing...

Ducking behind a tree, trying not to brush up against the embers, Jek took stock of his surroundings again. The swath of burning in the forest seemed to be fanning out. The Revenants probably had some plan of trying to work all the way around the Dyeus Tribe and hem them in. Not being a master strategist as yet, Jek couldn't tell if that meant certain doom or afforded them some hope for a brilliant countermove. But of course, he suspected the doom more.

"They's spreadin' out," Jek heard the old man confirm.

"This is the tipping point," the Chief answered. "Neutralize the Revenants in the middle, if indeed you can. I will try to lead my people through the gap. Then you must be quick to press your attack against their eastern wing! We will need to be able to swing to the east in our flight, or we will soon be bottlenecked between their ranks, and roasted on both sides."

"Are ye leavin' us?" the old man asked, noticeably fearful.

"Yes. I must return to my people and spur them on. But I will leave you with sound advice: Remember that this is only the vanguard of a traditional fighting force! Wait for our advance and follow us northward, if by chance we all endure these awful spirits. Otherwise, you will surely charge into their waiting pincers. And watch for traps!"

"Traps?!" Jek petitioned. "You keep mentioning these traps, but how do we watch for them? What do they look like?"

"They look like the ground," the Chief explained. "Now I must go, but do not fear. I'll not forsake you without first making some distraction..."

She leapt far into the air, her wings propelling her at a great speed (but she could not sustain flight... it was more of a fantastic jump). The dramatic move was easily enough spotted by Revenants. Tongues of fire raced after her. Jek held his breath, hoping the Chief could escape, but in the confusion he could not be sure of her fate...

He started as a fire jet came from behind him, shooting into the air. It was a wide shot, obviously intended for the Chief, but it came close enough to be painfully hot, and Jek rolled out of the way, wondering whether he might be on fire. Audrey was startled too, but tried to retaliate. Skidding down to one knee, she fired her musket into the blazing spirit. To Jek's amazement, the lead ball wafted a hole right through the blinding core of the Revenant!

"What a shot!" he said. It was a great improvement over her last display of marksmanship. Never mind that the thing was only about ten feet away.

The hole filled back in with fiery essence and the Revenant, reforming itself, swatted the tree that Audrey had been crouched by. She leapt for another tree and managed to get behind it in time.

"Now you shoot it!" she yelled to Jek.

With no thought of attack, he made for another tree for cover too. "It's no use! If your shot didn't hurt it, mine won't! Muskets don't work on spirits!"

"Well then what good are they!?!" she asked.

"Not much at the moment!"

The shouting was probably ill-advised. The Revenant rounded the tree Jek had put between them. Not knowing what to do or where to go, for a second he did little beyond get his first good look at the thing. Jek hadn't enjoyed much time to consider what a fire-mantis-ghost would look like prior to this moment, so he didn't know if he was surprised by the sight or not. It was definitely very much made of fire. But its form was strange and sporatic – it appeared as dozens of thin luminous bands constantly knitting themselves into a larger, undulating charicature that was little more than vaguely reminiscent of Mantid physiology. Jek intuited that the creature was deliberately directing its own firey energies in an effort to doodle its former mortal body, which it had been forced to forfeit by its Tribe. But it could no more capture a convincing likeness of its old self than a novice artist of meager talent could make an accurate self-portrait, without so much as benefit of a mirror. Its proportions were loose, and its movements unnatural, with its 'legs' simply trailing on the ground, or *most* of the way to the ground. More prominent, there was also a bluish, blinding singularity nestled in the upper thorax, where the sketchy flaming strands all seemed to emanate. This core, he thought, was the Revenant's true form. The rest was mere vanity...

Jek was about to turn in a futile retreat when the spirit vanished in a hissing steam cloud under a hood of water. A faint glimmer of the core tried to spark back into existence, but after a few false starts, it went up in a tiny streak of steam. *The old man!* Jek realized. He had destroyed one of them!

"Old man, you saved me!" Jek exclaimed.

"Aye, and not for the first time! Told ye the water would work!" He charged eastward in search of the next Revenant, with numerous laden Mantids appearing suddenly to follow. Jek was often amazed at the old man's spryness. He thought old age was supposed to make you slow. But even with his sudden downturn in health, the old man was hard to keep pace with when he got moving. Already many feet behind, he chased after him...

The farther they got into the scorched earth that the Revenants had passed through, the ash of the leaves was thick, and the ground treacherous. Jek tried as best he could to skirt the edges of smouldering piles, until he saw that the old man was simply charging over them. Having never run through embers before, Jek hadn't known how his boots would hold up. But if his feet were burning, he didn't notice. Mostly it was his lungs that felt like they were on fire. But he had to keep up!

As they passed through a clearing, he noticed Audrey running clumsily beside him. He checked and was astonished to see her attempting to reload her musket on the run.

"What are you doing that for?" he plied.

"I'm reloading at an opportune moment," she said, short of breath. "I thought that was good practice with muskets."

"But why bother if it doesn't help?" It was rather pitiful to see her try. Reloading standing still was something they hadn't mastered yet, let alone while sprinting through the woods. He chanced to glimpse her pouch full of gunpowder, and it was only then that he noticed how much she was really struggling. "Anyway your gunpowder is leaking," he pointed out.

"Ah, dang it!" she said.

A fireball whizzed past them from the right! There was a Revenant flanking them!

"Run for it!" Jek called, hanging a narrow left turn.

"We're already running for it!" Audrey said, but she turned the corner with him.

Just ahead, a burning tree fell into their path. Foolishly they looked back at the Revenant, hoping to see they would have time to flee another way. They could find no escape!

But as the spirit made for them, its essence caught Audrey's trail of mislaid gunpowder and was whisked speedily away, caught like a train on a rail! It became obviously furious, flashing bright colors and lashing out with flaming jets as if to grab hold of something and anchor itself. In a final surge of rage, the Revenant burst like a bomb, filling a twenty-foot radius with toppling, immolated trees. The shockwave of heat and shower of twiggy debris was most unpleasant, and Jek and Audrey were knocked from their feet...

Propping himself back up, Jek assessed the disaster. The flames on the blasted trees were all wafting inward toward a central point, where the Revenant had been. It looked as if they were trying to regroup! Faintly, in the epicenter, was the same sort of blue spark he had seen go out after the old man had defeated the first Revenant. This one held on longer, and the flames surged with every flicker. But finally, it gave out... and its hold on the surrounding flames relented. The spirit had spread itself too thin in its rage! It was no more.

"*Dianodes*," Jek muttered, as they drew near the blast radius. "You got one!"

"Wow," Audrey gasped. "I guess I did. Kind of."

Just then, they heard a chattering. Looking about, they caught sight of a Mantid on the ground within the blast of the Revenant – a Dyeus male that had been carrying water for the mission. It was clearly hurt. They rushed to it, without so much as considering that there was almost certainly nothing they could do for the poor creature...

And there wasn't. By the time they reached the Mantid, it was already quite lifeless. Another couple of laden Mantids buzzed into the scene, their wings rattling the yoke of their vessels – a startling sensory event that mere hours ago would have put Jek's heart in his mouth...

But now, it was there anyway – not out of fear, but out of remorse. Up until this point, death had only been hovering over their Quest, never quite bothering to actually reach in. Now, finally, Jek was confronted with it again...

Looking on as the other Mantids assessed their fallen brother, Jek knew some of the sympathy he felt was borrowed from past experience. The whole scene recalled Jek's dad's final hours. He remembered finding him in a heap on the ground, where he had been stomped in a gallimimus-wrangling accident. He had been conscious, calm, even reassuring... if too broken to move. By the time Jek and his mom got him back to the house, it had actually seemed hopeful that he would recover...

They lost him some time in the night. Jek didn't hope much after that. He found it hurt less not to hope, and maybe be surprised...

"This is all my fault," Audrey said weakly.

Jek looked at her. Her eyes appeared blank as she took in the scene. He needed to reassure her, though he knew it wouldn't help.

"He was just in the wrong place at the wrong time. It was nothing you did. Anyway if you hadn't destroyed the Revenant, it would have gone on to kill many more. Besides, this is really my fault."

Shook from her solemn stupor, she gave him a look, and not a very kind one. "How in the world is this *your* fault?" she asked.

He had to think about it. "I don't know," he admitted, vacantly. Still, somehow he couldn't help feeling that it was...

"Where are ye, ya lubbers!?!" the old man bellowed from afar. Jek and Audrey were recalled immediately to duty. If there was going to be a time for their sorrow, it would have to be later. They needed to press on.

For their part, the Mantids sprung into action even more quickly than the Humans. Jek had a thought that caused him some hesitance, but it wasn't the time for indecision, so he forced himself to reach out...

"What are you doing?" Audrey asked, as Jek crouched beside their fallen comrade.

He struggled to unsling the earthen vessels the poor dead Mantid had been toting water in. "I'm going to carry on the work this bug was doing. I think that's all we can do."

"I guess you're right," she admitted.

Jek loosed a pitcher, and handed it to Audrey. "Go ahead with this, I'll get the big one."

Audrey looked doubtfully past him. "Okay," she said, reluctantly, and charged after the old man, who was still shouting incomprehensibly in the distance.

Going for the 'big one' – a formidable bulbous jar about a foot and a half in diameter – Jek heaved, and his eyes bugged. It was even heavier than it looked. But he stumbled to his feet with it, and on comical legs he made his best eastward beeline...

It was not long before the echo of the old man was lost in Jek's own sloshing, rustling, and labored breathing. He couldn't even clearly see Audrey anymore, but dared not lose a step more trying to find her. Running was his only prerogative now. Running, and feeling like a doofus. But for all the impracticality of it, he couldn't bring himself to let go of the big dumb jar. It was now his sacred mission, and his only lifeline if he was ambushed by another Revenant – which in the smoldering wood seemed inevitable...

Moments or hours later, he *was* ambushed, after a fashion, by none other than a bunch of bushes, which had sneaked into his path as he was huffing and puffing for all he was worth. The irony was perhaps lost on him as he tried to deduce the fastest way past the burning snags. He ran a few feet one way, and then the other, with no clear convictions. He felt like the world's stupidest fireman.

Fortunately, in this dark moment, Audrey reappeared, coming back around the thicket from the north side. She was waving her hands (and the pitcher) in the air, apparently to get his attention. She had already got it, but seemed not to notice and kept waving anyway.

"Over here, Jek!" she called. "This way!"

Jek tried to respond but was too winded to call back. He willed himself back into forward motion. "Where's the old man?" he wheezed, when he got closer.

"I don't know," she admitted. "I couldn't catch him. I think he got into another fight, but when I reached the spot, there was no him and no Revenant."

"Hopefully that means he won and kept going," Jek huffed, setting the jar down for a moment's rest. He figured he might as well. If Audrey had lost track of the old man, they probably had no hope of catching up to him now anyway.

"I guess I shouldn't have come back this way," Audrey said, her shoulders sagging as she looked around. "There's burning further south now. I probably couldn't find him because he probably veered to the south..."

"Shh!" Jek said, hunkering down, suddenly aware of their exposure.

Audrey crounched and came in closer. "What is it?" she whispered.

"I think you're right," he whispered back. "We shouldn't be this far north! The Revenants were working their way around the Dyeus Tribe, to surround them. But Chief Katydid expected the rest of the enemy tribe to attack afterward! They are probably making their way south now too!"

"They are," Audrey confirmed. She was looking north.

Breathlessly, Jek tried to match her gaze, scanning the northern woods for signs of enemy Mantids. He scanned and scanned, until he finally caught something he feared could not be mistaken. There was a pair of small burning spots, very close together, weaving in synchronous toward them. They were *eyes* – eyes that captured the firelight of their surroundings, just as the eyes of the Dyeus Mantids had. The eyes kept dancing forward until Jek was sure he could make out a body behind them.

"Did you manage to get your musket ready?" Jek asked under his breath.

"I haven't got the little ball in yet," Audrey answered in kind, "and I think I'll need some of your powder."

"Take it," Jek said, handing her his pouch. Then he swung his own musket to the fore, taking it in both hands, steadying for a shot. "Mine's ready."

They were both very tense as Jek let his target encroach. He couldn't possibly afford to miss.

"Do you want to take this shot?" Audrey asked. "Maybe it doesn't know we're here."

"It knows," Jek said. "It's stalking us!"

And he was right. The Mantid was actually not very far away, and not in any great hurry to reach them. At first, Jek had thought the way the eyes danced meant the creature was running through the woods. But the more clearly he saw what was going on, it became evident that this was a slow stalk. The Mantid, with its powerful instincts of camouflage, was weaving its upper body as it advanced in order to make its luminous eyes mimic the lazy flight of ashes in the breeze.

At whatever speed, it was coming directly at them – far too directly to be by chance. It saw them, just as sure as they saw it...

Now just a handful of feet in front of them, the Mantid stopped, chittering something vile. Any remaining pretense of hiding by either party was forfeit. Jek and Audrey came cautiously to their feet.

The Despotopian Mantid, for its part, stood its ground, chittering menacingly at intervals, besieging their nerves. Its shape and the way it carried itself was surprisingly distinct from its Dyeus cousins. This Mantid had a hunched back and a very low posture, and so seemed even more easy to mistake for a base predator. Of course, it was in truth highly intelligent, if savage. Jek and Audrey did not guess their true peril...

"Is your shot ready?" Jek asked.

"It's ready," Audrey confirmed.

The Mantid, which did not know their speech, evidently was in no mood for them to be exchanging secret information. In a flash its wing covers flung open and it pounced for Jek.

Scantily a split second later, a shot rang out! Jek's heart leapt in surprise, though the shot was his own...

The Mantid landed heavily on Jek, and he collapsed on the ground. The beating of wings echoed off the trees, or so it seemed, until two more Mantids suddenly appeared! The Mantid they had seen had been distracting them from the approach of the others! Jek valiantly struggled to wrest free of the first Mantid, who in spite of its successful tackle hadn't killed him yet. He heard another shot, and a frightening howl, but couldn't see what was going on in the chaos of his own contest of strength.

Finally, he threw the Mantid off of him, and it rolled onto the ground with a *thunk*. It was only then that Jek realized his shot had actually killed the Mantid in the first place, and it had landed lifeless on him. Jek had never killed anything intelligent before, but he did not have time to be solemn about it – life and death still hung in the balance for him and Audrey!

He quickly learned that her shot had wounded one of the Mantids and she managed to flee past it. The first Mantid's pounce had actually been a salvation – when she recoiled from that attack, it had caused the other two to miss their mark in their coordinated landing. Now she had only the bayonette between her and the remaining healthy Mantid, but it stalked cautiously, not necessarily knowing that muskets could fire only once...

Jek seized the opportunity to catch the stalking Mantid off guard. But the wounded one cried out, evidently alerting its comrade. Jek pressed himself to get in one good jab before the thing could turn to face him. Cleverly, the Mantid threw open its wing covers, one of which actually caught the barrel end of Jek's musket under the bayonette and deflected his thrust. It fluttered as if to stun him, but the wing cover had already effectively staggered his assault. In fact, he had overcommitted, and fell headlong, landing astride the Mantid's abdomen.

With terrifying swiftness the Mantid swung around and made a clearing stroke with its extended pincer. But it too was momentarily dazed, since Jek had apparently disappeared...

By the time it figured out that Jek was on the ground beside it, it was too late to prevent Jek taking the next move. His musket was hopelessly awkward on the ground, being so long, so he could not slash upward at the Mantid. But he swung laterally and took one of the creature's tiny feet.

The Mantid protested and faltered, but was too ungainly on three legs to make an effective retreat. It would have to retaliate. Jek held his musket out across his body.

When the bug struck back at him, it raked with both pincers. He held his musket just where it needed to be to keep him from getting shredded, but the sheer force of the attack doubled back his fully extended arms and drove the wind out of him. It was a dizzying blow and he could not hope to repel another like it...

Fortunately, it did not come. Audrey stuck her musket into the back of the Mantid's thorax. It was a rather superficial wound, where the exoskeleton was thick. But it was enough – the bug threw itself in a panicked reel to the ground, tumbling chaotically away and slashing senselessly into open air.

The bayonette of Audrey's musket had hardly wanted to come dislodged, and now all three of them had been thrown down. But Audrey was quick to get back up, and Jek also surprised himself with a swift return to his feet, though he still felt dazed, and not at all sure what condition his arms were really in. They rallied, and as the bug got up, its fierce eyes could not hide its uncertainty.

"Let's get out of here," Jek told Audrey. There was no point in continuing the battle, and they were still behind enemy lines. Hundreds more Despotopian Mantids could be just out of sight. She didn't bother to say anything in agreement. They just ran.

But before long they stopped short. Sure enough, more Despotopian bugs were staging into their path! With the bushes still blocking a direct southerly retreat, now they couldn't double back to the west. They cut and made for the eastern route around the thicket, but of course that move was also anticipated, and more Mantids leapt in their way. They could still flee north, though it was obvious that would be just as suicidal as any other direction. They looked from east to west in their desperation, hoping to pick a route with fewer enemies, but there were already dozens on both sides, creeping in slowly, probably hoping to drive them north into the woods, where they could be snatched in the dark without a fight.

Jek sighed. Somehow he could not bring himself to believe that the Noble Quest was over, even though he knew certainly that he would not survive to see it through. Clenching his musket, he steeled himself for another fight. Perhaps by some crazy chance Audrey would make it out with her life, and she and the old man would complete the Quest. Yes, he honestly believed that would happen somehow! Whatever else might yet be unclear, he knew Audrey was important. This would not be her end, though it would be his. He intended to make it the best one he could...

Yet maybe it was not to be that way after all. Even as more Despotopian Mantids sprung to the front, suddenly there was buzzing coming up out of the *south*. Jek and Audrey were all but thrown back as a massive burst of sound and air washed over them. Chief Katydid herself alighted in their midst, with her Champions clinking heavily to the ground on both sides. She threw up her pincers and trilled some buggish warcry, and hundreds of the Dyeus tribe flooded into the north, leaping and bounding thirty feet or so at a time. They were at last running the gauntlet between the Revenants!

The Despotopian Mantids shrieked in fear and hate, but they refused to give ground. The Dyeus Tribe was still in a sort of retreat, after all, with most alighting only long enough to take another spectacular leap forward. But the Chief was not advancing with them. She meant to stay and cover the Humans. This presented an opportunity to the Despotopian Tribe – a battle of long odds, perhaps, but worth the gamble. It was a chance to kill an enemy Chief.

When Jek got over beaming with joy at Katydid's timely and dramatic intervention, he set to work loading his musket again, and Audrey did likewise. He was aware of an enraged charge forming in the enemy lines, but he tried his best to ignore it. There was buzzing and beating and chittering everywhere, and he tried to ignore that too. He realized now that battle was a lot of chaos, most of which had to be tuned-out. But he had to hope that his instincts were good enough to tune correctly.

He needn't have worried, for though the enemy advance was very swift indeed, they could do nothing to penetrate the wedge formation of the Chief and her Champions. They broke against her and her guard twice before Jek and Audrey were reloaded, but they were turned back by the impervious Champions in their glimmering metallic exoskeletons, and had no answer to Katydid's superior reach and her precision, honed over many years on the front in wars against the Yeeyu.

After the third charge, Katydid called back to Jek and Audrey. "Are you quite finished tinkering with your contraptions?!"

"Yes," Audrey answered on their behalf.

"Good. Then let us press on!"

With a chittery command her phalanx advanced to the north.

Jek scanned the battleground. Dyeus were still flocking through everywhere, with Despotopian Mantids near and far struggling to engage even one Dyeus before they could leap again, to their great consternation. When that proved too frustrating, they would either spring northward themselves or rally to the cause of trying to eliminate the Chief. They kept up a valiant fight along the front of the wedge formation, but Katydid's forces still managed a steady advance.

Perhaps only just in time, Jek realized the potential problem. What with their winged blitzes, there was nothing to keep the enemy from catching them in the rear. He decided that the Mantids had the front covered well enough, and so began to watch their flank. Audrey, always alert to such cues, also trained her musket to the south.

Almost as if prompted, some Despotopian Mantids leapt at their haunches from parts unknown. Jek resisted the reflexive urge to shoot on sight, and waited until he knew he had a bead on the enemy. He took his one shot, and it proved true. Audrey fired scarcely a moment later, but to no obvious effect – the shot probably went wide. It didn't make much difference in the end, because there were too many for two muskets alone to repel the attack. But the Champions were alerted now, and some moved back to handle it...

Audrey started another reload, still on the move. Jek was amazed at first that she would try it again, after the way she faired before. But she was admirably committed to getting it right, even if it had cost them one pouch of gunpowder. It took a long time, and there were some hairy moments where it looked like she might have to drop everything and the two of them spar for their lives, but the Champions remained stalwart, and when she completed the job, she gave the pouch back to Jek. He found it tricky too, trying to back up and go through the whole process at the same time. And he was extra careful about the pouch. If nothing else, he didn't want to make the same mistake...

There was a frightful ruckus off to his right that stopped him up. Chittering rang out like mad and whole trees sounded like they were going over. Jek felt the earth quiver, and then some other great bellowing noise demanded his full attention. He looked up and saw a fresh wall of fire coming at them, and ahead of it a charging brachiosaurus! The westward wing of the Revenants was closing in, and had evidently driven an enraged dinosaur from its sheltering in a nearby marsh.

Other Despotopian Mantids seized the moment and threw the Chief's party into a confusion. The formation was breaking! Jek could hardly abandon his reloading in time to see he was exposed... with enemy Mantids closing in! He thought he could hear Audrey shout something at him from behind, but it was drowned in the din of the brachiosaur. Jek leveled his musket and backed away for all he was worth, but another Despotopian Mantid pounced at him, and this time he had no shot to take...

The impact was savage. Jek couldn't tell if he had skewered the Mantid or not. He was only aware of the force of its body slamming into him at seemingly a hundred miles an hour. It was a very odd sensation – for a split second he could almost swear the ground had given way behind him, and he was in free fall. Then a sharp pain in his leg – so sharp that it overrode all his senses. Almost instantly he blacked out completely, and knew nothing more...

* * *

Pain, he thought...

He kept trying to remind himself that the boat needed righting, but he couldn't think past the *pain*. He didn't know why there should be so much of it...

Here he was, in the midst of many Indigo Knights. He tried to recall how he had found them, but it eluded him. And ultimately it didn't seem that important. They were found, and yet there was *so much* left to do. *Why was there more?* He looked at their weary faces. Each Knight, though heroic in stature, seemed leached of their strength by great doubt. What was wrong? Where was Audrey? Where was the old man? And *how* did the little birds find them again?

The birds!

Jek fixated on that thought until the anxiety brought him back to consciousness. He shot up with a gasp, and knew that he was awake, if still dazed. The night terrors receded, leaving only the vestige of bird-song, which still met his ears. His sight was filled with dazzling noise. His head swam and his leg throbbed molten agony. Yes, far and above everything else, he felt his right leg. He couldn't see it yet – and he despaired to think what he would find when his sight cleared, if indeed it would...

Frantic to learn something of it, no matter how bad, he groped around in the dark, where he felt something hard and sharp. He pulled back his hand and tried to focus on the spot. Dimly, he began to see the face of a Mantid!!! His pulse raced even higher, to the point where he might have blacked out again... but as he watched, nothing happened. He mustered resolution and reached out, touching the head again. It was lifeless.

Jek sighed among his strained breaths. The Mantid was dead. But he was still prone, in the dark, apparently alone and lost. He tried to assess anything he could about his surroundings...

Above, there were points of brilliant white light. They were hard to make out in his state, and focus came only with great effort. But eventually he made out rays and decided that light was peaking in from the sky – that he was under some sort of very dense, dark underbrush. Suddenly he remembered: *the traps*! Chief Katydid kept warning them that they had traps set in the woods. Naturally, he had fallen into one when he least expected. Really, he had been *tackled* into one by the charging Despotopian Mantid, he realized, as he continued to reconstruct the battle. Apparently the Mantid had got the worst of it. The more Jek looked, he began to see that there were spikey things in some spots on the ground. The Mantid had undoubtedly found some. But as his sight cleared yet more, Jek realized that he had found one too. The one that was sticking through his leg...

So now the truth was arrived at, but it brought no comfort. He had at least one extremely serious injury. He hurt everywhere, but nowhere more than the leg, so he guessed it was his only puncture. Anyway, he could move everything else... if only a little, and at the cost of getting very dizzy and sick to his stomach.

Quite immobilized and forsaken, he couldn't help contemplating the various miserable fates he had to choose from. He could maybe make it out of the pit and get eaten by Mantids, which sounded like a stretch in the shape he was in. Or he could bleed to death or starve. Yes, it would probably be one of those...

Before he even had time to turn to his other great worry, he heard her say, "Are you alright, Jek?"

Needless to say he was rather startled. He yelped, causing her a bit of a yelp.

"Audrey, what are you doing here?" he asked, finally dimly catching sight of her beside him in the dark, sitting in a ball with her musket propped up against her legs.

"I saw you fall," she said flatly. "I couldn't move you. So I just stayed with you."

Jek groaned. This was perhaps worse than he feared. He could remember earlier being prepared – truly prepared – to go out in a blaze of glory to help buy her escape, so she could complete the Quest. Now here he was instead – alive, but totally dead weight. How relieved he felt that she was here! How much it meant that she had kept vigil over him through what must have been hours of warfare raging on all around! But now, he would have to find some way to convince her to go. How was he going to do *that*? It was the very thing he least wanted her to do...

"Oh, Audrey," he started, struggling for something more to say. He surprised himself by laughing first. "This is all wrong," he continued. "It's not the way it's supposed to be at all."

"What do you mean?" she asked.

"Don't you see that this is all about you? You're an important person, Audrey. Zeph Bronzegloom knew it. Everything that's happened since only reinforces it. I don't doubt the old man found you for a reason. This whole Quest might only be a stepping stone toward your true purpose..."

"No, really – I..."

"...Listen. I appreciate your modesty, but you're going to have to own-up to this sooner or later. I've read some stuff about Purpose, and granted, I don't fully understand it, but..." he strained for some illustration, "...well, it's like Bronzegloom said: there are people destined for big things, and there are people who will never do anything more important than pass the saltshaker. *That's* what's wrong here! I'm the saltshaker guy! But *you're* protecting *me*!"

"What are you trying to say?" she asked urgently.

"I'm saying you need to leave! Leave me behind! I'll never make it, and even if I could, I'd just be a fugitive on a bad leg. You'll only forfeit your life if you stay with me. You need to find the Knights! And I believe you can do it. I don't have any doubt."

"But what about you? You're part of this thing!"

"Me?" Jek sighed. "You're right. I *have been* some part of a Noble Quest. It still amazes me every time I think about it. The truth is, I've already made it farther than I ever thought I could. It's been a greater adventure than I've dared to dream about since I was a little boy. But I knew all along that reality would catch up with me. I've been preparing myself for this from the start. So just leave me now. Finish what we started! I can't ask for more. I wouldn't."

Audrey just looked at him for a long time with piercing, glassy eyes, pale and keen. Jek realized, if he never had before, that her face hid so much more than it told...

"You think we're so different," she said, shaking her head. "I don't know. I don't feel like either one of us has been much of a Questing hero. We aren't great at fighting, or negotiating – we're not especially brave or talented... and we usually have no idea what we're doing. But somehow, between us, we've always had just what we needed to get by...

"Now granted, it could be just like you say. I hate to admit it, but... maybe I do have way more *stuff* than you do. I *could* be very, very important – and you might just be the saltshaker guy. But, even if that's true..." and here she paused, as one does when they reveal something enlightening, "...maybe you aren't finished passing the salt just yet."

Instantly, Jek was overcome with a bizarre serenity. She didn't know it, but Audrey had just fomented how he saw himself in a way that would last until the end. The *real* end – whenever that might be. At the same time, she had changed his thinking – in a nuanced way, but a powerful one. Perhaps it was not so much that he was *expendable*, but rather, that he was destined to be *expended* – instead of just a footnote, he might be the kind of person that gets to make the noble sacrifice in the critical moment! The thought of it filled him with warm resolve. He knew he could be making a horrible conceit... but it was one worth living for...

"Okay," Jek snickered, hiding his enormous discomfort at trying to prop himself up. "I guess we can give this 'saving-my-life' thing a try. Where do we start?"

"We start by taking that big spike out of your leg," Audrey declared, and she began to move for it...

"No-no-no!" Jek rifled, waving urgently. "Let's not start with that."

"Why not? It *has* to come out! Don't forget, I've done all the doctoring on this trip so far."

"Yes, you have," Jek agreed. "And so far I've managed to avoid telling you that you don't know the first thing about doctoring."

She huffed. "Okay then, enlighten me – what is the first thing?"

"The first thing is, you don't take things out that are impaling people. Because then they start to bleed until they run out of blood."

"...Oh..." she said. "Well, what about the second thing?"

"The second thing is, it's too bad we don't have a wet washcloth."

"What do we need that for?"

"Well, from what I can tell, dabbing a wet washcloth on somebody's forehead is kind of a home-remedy cure-all. I've seen it done before many times."

Without hesitation, Audrey ripped the cuff of her sleeve off and spit on it repeatedly. Jek winced, but he went along with it without further complaint. It was an off-color thing to do, but probably appropriate for wilderness survival.

She dabbed him on the forehead for a while. The spit hardly seemed enough to wet the cuff. But Jek still fancied he felt a little better.

"Now what do we do?" Audrey asked.

"Now we need to get me out of the pit, I guess..." he said.

"How are we going to do that?"

Before he could give it any thought, he heard an eerily familiar sound echo into the trap. Not the birds singing in the forest, but something else – like distant spirited cursing. Could it be the old man?! Was he really within earshot?

"Did you hear..?" Jek began to ask, but Audrey was already scaling out of the pit. She knocked some of the covering away, and Jek winced at the sudden surge of light and the twigs falling on his head.

"OLD MAAAAAAAN!!!" she cried out from above. The sound rang in Jek's ears. But all the discomfort seemed rather superficial now. Maybe with two people they could get him out and reach some village by the jungle. Anyway, the pain was dulled. Though he began to be aware of feeling rather cold...

"Audrey!" they heard distantly. "Where is ye, lass?!"

"OVER HERE!" she answered.

"Where in blazes is that?!" he called back.

* * *

Jek zoned out for much of the remaining confusion, until he heard Audrey shuffle back down into the trap. He looked up, and he saw the old man, who was looking right back down on him. He appeared very troubled, but it didn't stop Jek being glad to see him – much gladder about it than he ever expected to be.

"It's good to see you, old man," he admitted.

"Shut yer mouth, lad!" the old man replied. "Don't go exertin' yerself! Ye's grievous hurt and delirious, like-as-not." Jek blinked. The old man was as reassuring as he was sentimental.

"How can we get him out?" Audrey asked.

"I still gots a length o' rope," the old man indicated. "Ne'er leave the sea without it! And for gosh sakes, don't ne'er leave land without it!"

For some time, they set about weaving the rope into a harness for Jek's upper body. They disagreed somewhat on how to thread it around his arms, and naturally debated which knots to use, if only for the joy of the debate itself. Jek paid little attention. In fact, attention seemed to be in short supply...

"That oughta hold him," the old man said, standing and folding his arms. "Best get topside and commence at tuggin' the lubber outta here."

"Old man!" Audrey suddenly said in surprised tones. "I just noticed... your cough is gone!"

"Aye," the old man agreed haughtily. "Told ye it was nothin'."

* * *

Jek missed most of his own extraction. What he did experience of it was a lot of pain and a head full of sparkling stars. He was aware that they argued and rummaged some more, but eventually Jek found himself being dragged along on some kind of improvised sledge. The forest was still smoking, but the sky was not so bright and clear anymore, and a gentle drizzle glazed the land.

In his moments of clarity, Jek wondered about the Dyeus Tribe. He hoped they were safe. He hoped they were keeping warm. It had got so cold. So strangely cold...

* * *

Audrey looked over her shoulder again as she hauled the mist-slicked branch – her fork of the sledge they had frantically fashioned out of brush, rope, leaves, and their overcoats. She watched for any sign of movement from Jek. He had been right about what to do with his leg – just dislodging the spike from the ground had been enough to start him bleeding again, and taking it out would have surely done much worse. By the time they had started packing him out of the jungle, he was already in a noticeable delirium...

Seemingly for the first time, she really despaired to think what might happen. In spite of much past peril, she was not very familiar with disaster, beside the one she had been too young to remember properly. Perhaps her years aboard the Cosigner had been more sheltered than she guessed. Jek's words in the pit still dogged her. It wasn't just that he had actually asked her to leave him to die. Not only was he prepared to meet a tragic end, but apparently he had expected nothing else from the first. Audrey shuddered. It was all far too morbid for her. And it made her worry still more. Jek needed to hold on. But how hard would he cling to his life if he already considered it forfeit?

Presently, Audrey lost her footing and veered into the old man. "Whoops," she said, and set back on the right course.

"Eyes to the fore, m'dear," the old man said solemnly. "If ye keep lookin' back, t'will only slow us down."

"Do you think help will be very far off, once we're clear of the jungle, old man?" Audrey asked.

"Couldn't rightly say. Surely don't know this neck o' the woods." He laughed half-heartedly. "I guess there ain't many Human folks what do." He fell silent for a moment, nodding thoughtfully. "Would that we was already out sailin' again. I done well enough for meself on this here cross-country jaunt, but it sure ain't me element."

O, to sail again! Audrey found the thought a very welcome diversion. Without meaning to, she remembered the moment on Corsicarthal, where the old man had turned back to his boat, and bid adieu to 'his *Sadie*...'

This brought to mind some interesting questions. By his account, the old man had fled Meatgrinder Bay in a *ship* – not a mere fishing boat. Whatever had become of that ship – the *Sadie Hawkins*? She intended to find out...

"Old man," she began, "What happened to your ship?"

He hesitated. Then he huffed. "Ye got memory problems, lass? Ye was there when we done cast her off..."

"Not your *boat*..." she said, "...your *ship*."

"Oh... right... me *ship*," he started. "'Fraid she was sunk by pirates, lass. There just weren't nothin' for it. When ye's got a Doom Fleet somewhere behind ye, the last thing ye's expectin' is to run smack into pirates! They sprung on me ship some leagues north of Tophthaera. T'was only by the skin o' me teeth that I done escaped that second peril in the boat. Ye seen what rough shape she was in! Weren't the Despotopians what did that – t'was the pirates."

"What in the world were pirates doing north of Tophthaera?" Audrey asked, rightly perplexed. "Wouldn't that put them dangerously close to the Ocean Citadel? To Inquisition waters?"

"Aye," the old man lamented. "And it don't bode well that them buccaneers was gettin' away with their lootin' right under the nose o' the Inquisition. Don't bode well a'tall. They's missin' too many things, what with Enscharaulgk out to pasture..."

Audrey was sure he was right about that. If there was a consistant theme of the Quest so far, it seemed to be that there was an awful lot going on that no one knew about.

She didn't get to muse about it for very long, because it was at this point she heard some kind of groan from Jek. It unsettled her, but the old man was apparently unmoved. Maybe he didn't hear the groan. She felt she'd better call attention to it...

"Sounds like Jek groaned," she said simply. "That must be a bad sign."

"Ney, t'is a good sign," the old man answered. "Ye gots to be alive still to groan."

That was scarcely a comfort. But before she could ruminate too much on it, she glimpsed a large, unbroken patch of daylight peaking onto a wide green void between the trees. Perhaps they had reached the forest's edge!

"Old man, look! There's a clearing up ahead! I think we're almost out!"

"Aye, looks promisin'," he agreed. "Let's chance a bit more speed..."

The Unlikely Skipper

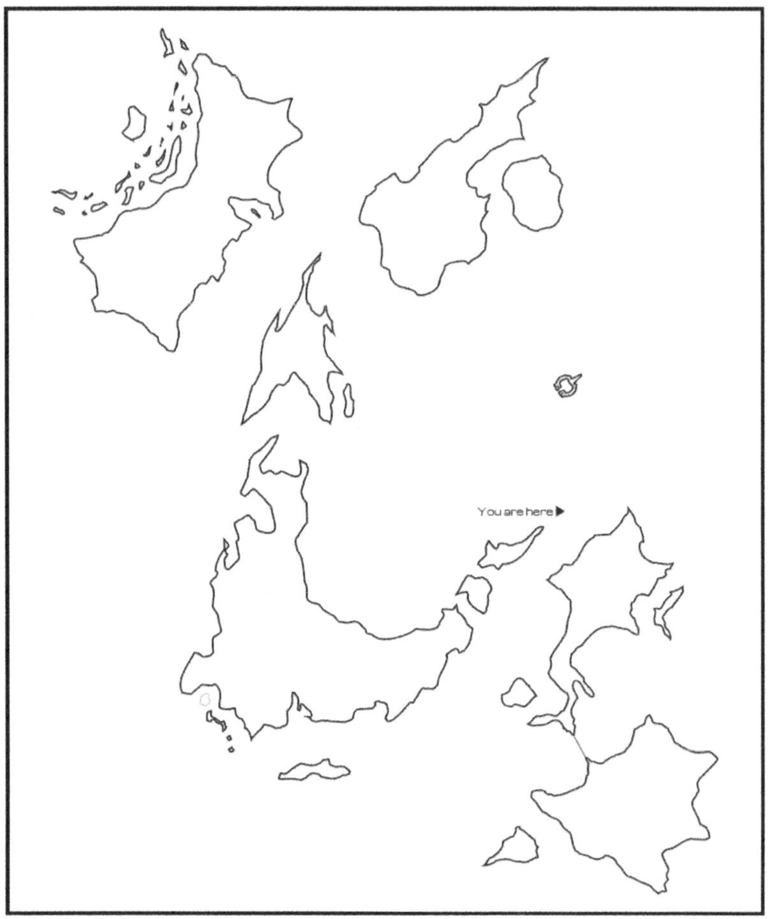

"Lead by example. But leave room for your followers to follow by example."

- General Sasparagu, *The Take-Charge Manual*

Emerging from behind the low bulwark of the ensign's station, Parissah could not help herself taking a few moments to drink in the totally new surroundings. The hazy room made for a nightmarish scene of disaster. Anything sturdy enough to still be standing was caked with spiky bits. The floor was strewn with razor-edged refuse. Suddenly she noted an itchy sort of pain in her wrist. Blinking, she found a five-inch metal shard in it, which she removed with all haste.

Those of the bridge crew who remained alive were in a similar, horrified trance. It was a pitiful sight that ignited her indignation, and she shook herself. Action was needed! *But what to do now?*

She looked to the one who would know – where he had last been. She found him, but he had not got up. Parissah held her breath. He didn't appear to be stirring at all...

She hurried over to Captain Veshinkir. But it was no use. He was gone.

Parissah's eyes flickered as her core sparked an immolating heat. She had known the Captain only a very brief time, but long enough to admire him. The Inquisition had lost another fine leader, when he was most needed...

Fortunately, her reflexive response was also the most prudent course of action. They needed to answer the pirates, blow for blow! They needed to return fire! In between wisps of smoke, she could dimly make out the enemy ship, still looming in front of them, now motionless – undaunted – practically in their crosshairs! But the bridge had halted some critical degrees before the cannons were lined up for a shot. She didn't wait for the chain of command to resolve. She called out herself...

"We must start the ratcheting again! Get the cannons trained on that ship!"

"It can't be done, ma'am," an engineer made report. "There is much debris lodged deep into the turret fitting, which we cannot break loose. Further articulation won't be possible without extensive repairs."

Parissah's breath ran shallow. That one shot from the pirate blunderbuss had ended the battle – a chance worse than any she had guessed. Without the ability to articulate the cannons or maneuver the ship, they had no means whatsoever of returning fire! There was no hope of victory. She reeled trying to think what was left to fall back on...

She considered it all for some time, until she was conscious that the crew was actually waiting on her. She had, after all, essentially taken command, when she attempted to give the first order. And regardless of any chain of succession on the ship itself, she also had the senior rank out of anyone on the bridge...

"What are we to do now, Administrator?" the ensign asked, betraying some fear.

That was a very good question. But after a few moments more of icy, pragmatic consideration, she had a thought...

"We must scuttle the ship," Parissah said. "Above all, we cannot allow this vessel to be commandeered. I'm sure you will agree that such an instrument must never fall into the hands of pirates!"

"Indeed," the range officer nodded. He had some big ugly pieces of shrapnel sticking out of his upper left arm, but Parissah did her best to overlook them, as he had apparently determined to do for the time being. "And there can be no doubt that the pirates *will* take our ship, if we allow it. But how do we scuttle the ship?"

Parissah shook her head. "I know frightfully less than I should about the functionings of our vessels. I am open to suggestions."

"What about the electrical power plant for the drive system?" Baegulgog mused, as he drew in. "Could we overload it?"

"We could," an engineer agreed, clamoring to the elevated walkway from below, brushing aside broken glass. "However, that would not likely cause the sort of explosion we need. If an overload breached containment, we would be far more likely to momentarily electrify the ship and the surrounding water with high voltage. It's worth mentioning, our lifeboats are metal, but their ship is wood. We might only succeed in killing ourselves."

"That would be most piteous," Baegulgog said. "Forget I spoke of it."

"I propose instead that we ignite the gunpowder reserves," the engineer said. "The reserves are stored in widely distributed and heavily insulated parts of the ship. But we could gather them up in one spot where the armor is thin and set them off. That should be effective."

"Are you the senior engineer on deck?" Parissah asked.

"Yes, ma'am."

"Then coordinate with your subordinates here and see that it is arranged. Everyone else is to begin an evacuation effort."

"I fear the lifeboats will have been shredded by the blunderbuss, Administrator," the engineer lamented.

"Most likely, yes, they will be in horrid shape. But we shall have to see about that anyway. If we can coax a few leagues out of them before they sink, it will be worth it," Parissah responded. She looked over all the gathered crewmen with resolution that her mask could not conceal. "We'll swim for it if we must. The fleet is headed our way. If we can get north of the exclusion zone, we might be picked up. If not, it is on each of you to make it back to the Citadel without being eaten by the various ocean fawna. But now we must hurry!" She looked and pointed squarely at the engineer. "And you report back to me when the powder is gathered. I will have the Clerk Baegulgog ignite it for us, if he is willing."

"Quite willing and eager, madam!" the Clerk saluted.

"Very good, Baegulgog. I would prefer not to gamble anyone else's life in the scuttle, if I can help it."

"We can just as easily improvise a fuse," the engineer said. "I can even fire a snail bolt off to give a one-minute warning."

"Alright," Parissah agreed, "we will do it that way. But now let us see it done, with all haste!"

* * *

Skirting more matted debris, Parissah clutched the railing of the ship, restraining herself to a painfully modest pace, to let Baegulgog keep step. The crew was all in an urgent scramble. She found she didn't truly know if things were going well or not, given the circumstances. This was her first nautical command, after all. Wishing to encourage the crewmen and fortify their confidence in her, she went about spouting sailing rhetoric. "Look alive, there!" She might say. "Batten down the hatches!" "Keep a weather eye on the horizon!" And she produced many similar non-sequiturs, as they occurred to her.

All the while, smoke kept rolling in. Most of it was now carried on a frigid wind from the nearby pirate shipwreck, which was smouldering more and more furiously as it slowly sank. But though it no longer filled the air, Parissah noted that vapor still rimmed the edges of the monolithic blunderbuss as well. It was more than a bit unnerving to be under the gun, even now. Another shot like the first, with the crew exposed in their efforts to escape, and there would be little left to them in the way of survivors...

"A question, madam," Baegulgog called to her from some yards behind.

"Yes, Baegulgog?" she called back over her shoulder.

"Do we know what we are doing presently? Or rather, do *you* know what we are doing? I may be sure that *I* don't."

"We must find the Mariner Guards," she answered. "Be on the lookout."

"Would that I could do more than be the first to decry my own ignorance in such matters," the Clerk said. "I doubt very much if I will know them, should I see them."

"Well, never mind, Baegulgog. I expect I know where they are. But so you may have a clue, they will be the ones cradling giant snail guns."

"Ah, jolly good," he extolled.

Sure enough, she found them where she expected. They had congregated on *Radiant's* bow, and were surveying the dark scene before them, and below. It was five in their group – probably the entire ship's compliment. "Ho, there," Parissah greeted them, with some vague sense that she was still pulling from nautical parlance.

"Hello, Administrator," answered the senior Guard. "Have you brought us orders? Is it true that you have taken command?"

"I have. And yes, I regret to say it is true. Captain Veshinkir was among the fallen after the blunderbuss went off."

The Guard nodded solemnly. Evidently they had already known or guessed all that had happened. "We had received only confirmation that the crew was told to evacuate. But it was said the order came from you. Yet, perhaps we still have opportunity to avenge the captain and win the battle." He raised his snail gun, glinting in the dim, ruddy light of the fire still rising off the water. "At least, we ought to be able to cripple the enemy."

Parissah waved dismissively. "No, I don't think that would do. If we provoke them into a second shot now, everyone on deck will likely be killed. But I do have need of your heavy weapons, to complete other critical ends. We must prevent the *Radiant* from being captured. Even now, we are making preparations to scuttle her. I want your team to contribute to that effort."

"What is your order, Administrator?" the Guard asked dutifully.

"I need you to thoroughly destroy our ectodermis tanks. Otherwise, I fear they may keep the ship afloat too long, and leave the pirates an opportunity to plunder. Indeed, we suspect it is primarily ectodermis that they were hoping to loot, since they have mined a Tophtheran trade route. I appreciate your wish to take one more of their ships down with us, if we could. But there may yet be others circling in, and above all we must stop them getting what they are after."

"Yes, ma'am," the Guard confirmed, and they set immediately off to do as they had been instructed.

"Hurry to the lifeboats afterward!" Parissah called after them. "The crew will need all the safety you can afford them!" They did not pause to call back, but she was sure they had heard and understood.

Watching them disappear down-deck into the mists, Parissah remembered unbidden that she was no sea commander. She stood there now with no more orders to give, and no inspired next move, knowing that everything she had done since Veshinkir's demise was little more than a bluff and a gamble. It was only duty and baseless trust that now compelled this fine crew. It was, for her, a moment of humility and doubt, beyond their normal bounds.

"I've never skippered before, Baegulgog," she admitted absently. "Perhaps that is dreadfully obvious. How would you rate my performance?"

Baegulgog huffed. "I am no better schooled in the maritime arts than you. Best that we keep busy, though, I think – rather than take time to doubt. The outcome will be the best judge of your performance."

She nodded. "That is sage advice. Surely there is something we can contribute to the evacuation. Let us find it out!"

* * *

It didn't take long, and Parissah and Baegulgog found themselves helping a small party shoulder a lifeboat to the rear of the ship. The front of the thing was nettled with barbs from the blunderbuss, but it might indeed float a while. There were a number of boats in similar shape. Some had held on by a thread to one of the lines belaying them... others had had both lines totally shredded and been tumbled to the deck. Still more had rolled off into the sea. But any still at hand and in one piece were being taken to the back now, where they could be deployed in relative safety, with the conning tower of the *Radiant* standing as a final barricade between the crew on the deck and the great pirate cannon. The entire length of the ship would provide them cover once the boats started off. But even with the impressive efficiency of the crew, Parissah knew that could take a deal of time...

In the meanwhile, she had to mind her feet. There were enough relatively safe places left to step on the deck, and her scales were tough and unyielding, but she was nonetheless accruing some unpleasant gashes, particularly on the webbing between toes. And certainly, some of the barbs left in the ship's hide were visious enough that she couldn't afford to be totally callous about her footing.

"How are you fairing, madam?" Baegulgog asked. Sometimes she was surprised at how well the floating Clerk seemed to pick up on the locomotive difficulties of bipeds.

"Well enough, Baegulgog," she replied, even as she shifted to better support the lifeboat. "How are you?"

"I'm unaware of any personal difficulty," he said. "Though I grow anxious. Those pirates have been suspiciously quiet since the use of their weapon. I wish I knew what that portended."

"I have been trying to puzzle that out myself," Parissah admitted. This prompted her to decide it might be better to ask a crewman about it. Perhaps a career sailor would know better, as they had already proven in numerous instances throughout the crisis...

"Excuse me," Parissah said, struggling to tap the shoulder of the sailor directly in front of her in the line of laborers carrying the boat.

"Yes, Administrator?" the sailor replied.

"What do you suppose the pirates are up to now?" Parissah asked.

The sailor took a moment to think. "I would say that they are doing what they can to assess our situation, while preparing to board," she posited. "If they know we are evacuating, they will probably give us plenty of time. Meeting us in open battle on our deck would be costly for them."

Parissah was largely relieved that this was her assessment. "You really don't suppose they have anything more devious in mind than simple caution at this point?"

"If they have any more tricks, Administrator, I don't know what they are. But I expect caution will avail them plenty. They will have no trouble taking the ship when we have fled."

"That's what they think," Parissah said. "Or rather, I do *hope* that is what they think."

At once, there was a lurch, a splash, and the ship began to list to the starboard side. The labor party had all it could do to keep the lifeboat from tumbling out of their grip. Parissah heard more commotion as one of the other lifeboats broke away from its attendants, and crashed down into the ocean, some crewmen being taken with it! Before her team could totally recover their balance, the same thing happened on the port side of the ship. The entire rear of the ship was settling into the sea, even as it pitched along its length. This time, there was no saving the lifeboat. Parissah and the rest let go of it, rather than be taken over the edge with it. Everyone did this... except for Baegulgog!

"Whoa, whoa!" he cried, even as he struggled to steady the boat in midair as it rolled and plummeted. Parissah watched with horror as he went overboard. But on the whole, it was not so disasterous. Baegulgog had some strength, after all... and what's more, he had fair reserves of aerial buoyancy. He may well have contributed to the lifeboat landing whole in the water, not more damaged than it already had been. When the Clerk had emerged from the splashdown, she called out her admiration...

"Baegulgog! That was most clever of you!"

She thought she might have heard him mutter something, but he called back up, even as he began lazily floating back skyward to the deck. "I'm sure I don't know what you mean, madam! Unless you are making sport of a very silly oaf in his clumsiness!"

"Not at all!" she reassured him. "From what I can see, you helped the boat to land more gently than it might have! Perhaps you saved it outright from *our* clumsiness!"

Baegulgog flashed bashfully as he alighted over the top of the vessel. "Oh-ho. I think you make a ballad of deeds more suited to a silly jingle." Still, he made a show of clapping and brushing a pair of his tentacles together, as if wiping the dirt from his hands at the end of a weighty task.

"I'm not one to dabble in idle praise, Baegulgog," she indicated. "But I would like you to go over with all of the lifeboats like that, if you don't mind overmuch. Even now that the ship has begun to dip, we should certainly try to set the boats into the water as gently as we possibly can."

"Well, I..." he began, but was cut off by a crewman...

"...But what happened to the ship just now?" he asked. "We seem to be losing buoyancy even as we speak."

Parissah raised her hands up over the nervous sailors. "It is all according to plan!" she assured them. "I have ordered the ectodermis tanks to be destroyed, and the ship scuttled. We must continue to evacuate. But now, we will have Baegulgog help each of you to toss your lifeboats into the water..."

"Well, I..."

"...He will graciously do what he can to ensure the boats survive their plummet."

Baegulgog made a faux throat-clearing sound. "Well, yes. I suppose I shall."

"Very good," Parissah said. "Now all of us, hurry! If the pirates are very observant, they will see that our ship may already be starting to sink. Any plans they have to board will be put into over-drive now!"

They did as she instructed, with Baegulgog doing his best to deliver each boat to the gently rolling waves below. Every tumble he took was rather awkward and inglorious, and no one could say for sure if he achieved anything. But the boats were, to a one, falling without crashing apart, and that was definitely something. The crew itself was leaping in afterward, climbing into the boats in mirrored pairs so the craft wouldn't topple. The evacuation was really taking shape. But Parissah let the balance of her attention be fixed back down the length of the ship. She needed to watch for the Mariner Guards to return from below deck. She needed to watch for the signal shot that would mean a one-minute window before the powder reserves went off. And, perhaps above all, she needed to watch for the pirates. But she did more than just watch...

Parissah turned back to the crew, rounding up a couple of crewmen who weren't too busy and had sidearms. "Come with me," she told them. "The enemy is here."

"You've seen them?" one asked.

"I *smelled* them," she answered.

Rounding the conning tower where the bridge was set, the tumult of mass exodus quickly died away into an echoey distance. It was the dark side of the tower, opposite the wreck, which had by now grown dull anyway, with hardly more than embers still protruding from the watery grave. Above, smoke clung to the bridge. The scent of it helped Parissah feel warmer, for which she was grateful. Of the many discomforts she might welcome in life, cold was not high on her list. It had shaped up to be a truly cold night, with little fingers of mist coiling up over the deck from the ocean, as if it was anticipating the fast-approaching opportunity to swallow their ship.

She stopped up against the tower, and her compatriots behind her. "Whatever our peril, we are going to have to hold fire, until we hear another snail bolt go off. That will be the signal that the ship is one minute away from exploding." She nodded to one of the crewmen. "When we get that signal, you go back and warn the rest of the crew." She nodded at the other one. "You and I will have to hold the pirates at bay to cover the evacuation. And we may have to make good the retreat of some who are still below deck."

"Yes ma'am," they answered.

"Both of you stay behind me," she further instructed, remembering something else. "I will be the vanguard in this maneuver." At this point, she drew out her sword – the one recovered from her arm, where it had been left by the swordsdrone on *Variglew*. "You see, I have a sword."

"What good will that be?" said one of the crewmen, unimpressed.

"I expect it will be plenty of good," she answered, examining the fine weapon, "if I can learn to wield it expertly in the next few minutes."

They slipped quietly around from there to mid-deck – as quietly as could be expected of beings of their size with huge nails treading bare on metal. Then they hunkered down amidst the pigeon cages, which had been evacuated first. A weak and pale light still drawing on the ship's power hung overhead – one of the few on the deck, and needed for scrawling letters at all hours. Parissah sighed. "I should have had the Chief Pigeon Keeper send word to the fleet of *Radiant's* destruction. Some of us will certainly have to survive now, so they do not waste undue time searching for her."

"I wouldn't let it trouble you, Administrator," one of the crewmen said. "The whole area will have to be swept for mines regardless."

"Ah, indeed," Parissah said, consoled.

"Should we be talking like this, Administrator?" the other crewman asked. "I smell the enemy now as well... quite plainly."

"If we draw them in, I welcome it," Parissah said, scanning through the mesh of the cages. "This area is defensible enough." After that, she spoke up, as if emboldened by her own words. "Do you hear that, you buzzards? We are right here! Come and make terms with us! I am a Primary Administrator of the Inquisition, and I appeal to any tradition you may possess by which I am entitled to entreat with your captain, or other ranking officer."

Faintly, she heard some snide laughter, emanating from sources all around, even as more voices joined in. Pirates began to appear at the very edges of what the overhead lamp could reveal. There were plenty of Humans, as the odor on the air had told. But there was also an assortment of Phage shock troops that took Parissah by surprise. They were creatures of unimpressive strength and stature, even next to Humans. But of course, pirates profited little by being choosy about whom they pressganged, and they knew a thing or two about how to turn apparent weaknesses into unexpected strengths. Possibly the Phage had been included in the raid in part because they gave off no discernable scent. Parissah noted that they crawled about quite stealthily on their spindly little legs in their fetching bandanas.

Prominently in the mob, she finally saw a big, strapping Mesomela with a wicked cutlass and a vest of flintlocks. His laugh was the grimmest of them all.

"Arrr," he prefaced, in true pirate form. "Some appeal! We ain't got any such tradition! Why, we'd have to be plain daft t'abide by a rule like that!" He ran a claw along the edge of his sword in sly fashion. "But if it's an officer ye want to gab at, ye got me." Another round of mirth puffed out his imposing chest musculature. "Now what have we got to say t'each other, I wonder?"

"I don't particularly care what we talk about," Parissah answered, "so long as it is something we may discuss at great length."

The Mesomela snorted. "Playin' for time, is ye?"

"Whatever would give you that idea?"

He shook his head disparagingly. "Ye honest folk is so transparent, it turns me gut. Why not appeal to our latent morality next? See if ye can't get us to give up our piratey ways."

"If it is on your conscience, then yes, why not? You all may certainly forswear your dragon master and surrender. I promise that the Inquisition will do everything in its power to return you to your ancestral homelands, or their nearest facsimiles, where you may be properly executed for your crimes."

The Mesomela still had a toothy smile, so sharp and set that he looked as if he had just bit through bone. "Nothin' doin', darlin'. Me morality be a bit more latent than all that."

Parissah strained herself to arrive at more idle talk. So far, her gambit to buy time was working well enough, in spite of its transparency... or rather, because of it. Perhaps she should try to squeeze in some idle threats. She raised her sword to the level with her Jackal foil. He didn't react all at once – she wouldn't have expected him to anyway – but after a moment, something strange happened. His smug expression melted into abhorance and fear. He seemed almost cowed and ready to beg her mercy...

"*Missahr's Bones...*" the Mesomela cursed breathlessly, ears pinned back.

"That's right," Parissah said. "I also have a sword."

He shook his head again, in disbelief. "Ye got some talent for understatement, darlin'. Or did ye hope I wouldn't recognize what ye got in yer hand there?"

Parissah blinked. "I don't know what you're talking about."

"Give up the lies, lass! It ain't yer strong suit. That's a trophy sword of Roemnar, and no mistakin'! Tis awarded only to a master swordsman, trained and certified by the Proconsul hisself!"

Finally, she remembered her theory that the swordsdrones on *Variglew* must have studied with Heron elites. This was a rather funny way of finding out that that was true. In a moment of wonder, she admired the sword herself, in the light of this revelation. To her, it seemed rather plain to be a weapon of such distinction. Even so, she found she felt rather dismal all of a sudden, knowing the thing represented a very high honor that she had done nothing to earn...

"But you don't understand," she admitted. "I never studied under the Proconsul. I am a novice at best when it comes to swordplay."

"Ha!" the Jackal-pirate laughed mirthlessly. "That's the flimsiest lie I heard yet!"

"But it's true, I tell you," she insisted. "You're making a terrible mistake."

"Aye, that I am, assure. Probably the last mistake I'll e'er make." He seemed to be rallying his courage, as best he could. "Even so, we canna go back empty handed! Press the attack, me mateys!"

The skirmishers leapt toward the fray, in spite of their terror, which had obviously caught on. Once they had nearly closed the gap, Parissah and her fellow Inquisitors grappled and hurled pigeon cages, striking some pirates fiercely and obstructing the path of the others. The Human bandits were pressed; they were the swords of the group, and so were kept very much at bay in the opening chaos, able to do little more than watch and hope for an opportunity to dash in and strike. They were not so quick on their feet as Humans might otherwise be, which was a help. They were all wearing armored boots – a smart precaution for such fragile creatures deployed to a battlefield that was tangled with metal debris. Their steps were all a loud crash as they went about hurriedly. But the Phage had flintlocks, and one of them pounced into close range, firing off a round that got Parissah right in the flank of her left thigh. It was a wound highly painful, but not overly crippling. She was fortunate that Phage, being such odd and gangly creatures, were not very aware of the other species' vital areas... and anyway her legs were at a comfortable shooting height for them. She took a cage and winged it at the little gunner, and they both went bouncing out of sight. The agony-inducing shot had the added benefit of enraging her, and she snorted a small stream of fire. But her opponents were deft in their maneuvers at sudden need, and she hardly singed them.

As the mayhem ensued, Parissah found herself trying to scan for that Mesomela officer. He had seemingly withdrawn. Either he was off being devious, or he had fled in erroneous cowardice. She didn't like it much either way.

Another flintlock shot caught her in the back next to her shoulder. She was very fortunate it hadn't got her in the coil of her neck! As it was, there was the sound of a metal ricochet, and she determined that the ball must have been turned back by her shoulder blade. Her considerable pain there seemed to confirm it. She whirled around and caught the offending Phage right below his capsid (where his throat would be, if he had one). Then she sent him overboard like a javelin. Fire whelmed in her core again, but she held it down this time, meaning to keep the deadly flames in reserve.

She saw the battle was going similarly for her comrades. They were having success using the bulk of the pigeon cages to keep the Humans at bay, but the more agile Phage kept taking infuriating pot-shots at close range. Fortunately, they were long in the reloading. One of the Inquisitors did catch a few pirates with his breath, and the scoundrels had to throw themselves from the ship to the mercy of the ocean waters. It was sour business, but for the moment it was going her way. She knew that could all change, however, with nothing more than a few good shots from the Phage or a successful sneak attack by the Humans...

Just then, she noticed as some clever sneaks managed to spirit a few of the cages away. Their improvised buffer zone was being slowly dismantled! She decided to alter the positional tactics.

"Form a 'V' around us, opening on my side, if you can!" she instructed the other Inquisitors. She swung some of the cages out from in front of her herself. It was her hope that the pirates would consider a frontal assault – one that she could with any luck repel with her sword. It invited much danger, but she reasoned that the fear of her supposed skill might be enough to make them hesitate...

"Fight me, if you dare!" she prodded the pirates, even as they did begin to bunch around in front of her, with the other Inquisitors holding a tight hem of stacked pigeon cages behind. To further goad them, she attempted to brandish the sword in a display of martial elegance. In the process, her footing became jumbled and she nearly tripped headlong over her own toes.

"Gadzooks!" a lady pirate gasped. "It's just as Marlin said! She be a proper master in the art of the 'drunken swordsman' form, if e'er I've seen one!"

"*Dianodes*," another pirate cursed in quiet awe.

In a way, it was all too much for her. For a few moments, Parissah could not help feeling torn between her desire to capitalize off of their fear, and her nearly compulsory need to explain how she was unworthy of that fear. The pragmatism won out for the time being. They were probably so certain of her great skill by now that they were beyond reasoning with anyway...

"May it be as you say," she retorted. "Now who will be the first to die by my hand?"

The pirates all exchanged glances. She thought they might actually be trying to decide on an answer to her question. But the Phage gunslingers had congregated too, and they were obviously in on the silent conspiracy...

"Shoot her," one of the pirates said at length.

Parissah gulped. Regardless of their marksmanship, a concentrated round from what amounted to a whole firing squad of little virus folk was bound to hit something important. At the very least, it was going to hurt *a lot*...

Just as some of them were finishing their reload and the locks of their pistols were being drawn back, the whole bunch of buccaneers was rushed from the sides by Inquisitors. There was a lot of chaos and people flying every which way, but in the gloom she managed to identify the reinforcements as the Mariner Guards, who had returned to the deck from their sabotage mission below. It was a very good turn. She couldn't have planned it any better... and in fact, she *hadn't* planned it nearly this well...

Those who were not immediately turned by the overwhelming strength of the Guards settled into awkward stand-offs. The Guards still had their big guns, which were proving effective as improvised shields. She wondered what had kept them using those guns, but she was immeasurably glad of it, since it kept the signal she was still waiting for from getting confused. At any rate, they had defense enough to keep the pirates from committing to many attacks. Getting within arm's length of an Avarican without landing a good hit would essentially mean the death of a Human, and they knew it. But they were deft and clever, and there were still a good many of them, with more joining up from the dark reaches of the deck...

Parissah charged at one of her Guard compatriots, who was becoming encircled. One pirate only just caught sight of her as she reached the fray, and she put the sword to its use. As effective as it was, she didn't care much for the feeling of dispatching an opponent with a weapon of this sort. It was not quite as detached as firing a snail bolt, nor as personal as crushing with one's own hands, nor as elementally primal as breathing fire. It was somewhere unsatisfactorily in the middle of all of those. As a rule, Inquisitors were loath to kill anyway. Once someone was killed, they could no longer be shepherded. It was impossible not to feel guilty after disposing of that much responsibility...

"That was highly unpleasant," she said.

"Behind you!" the Guard she had saved advised.

She whirled to see a number of pirates charging her. She turned them back with the fire she'd been holding in reserve, and they were caught with a wide snort of it, and went and hurled themselves into the sea.

"Now, you were saying something, Administrator?" the Guard asked.

"Well, never mind," she said. "But you have my thanks for coming to our aid; and without firing your snail guns, no less! What inspired that, I wonder?"

"We saw that you were not using your pistols," the Guard explained. "We determined that there must be a reason. So we did not use ours either."

"Most astute," she nodded. "In fact I am waiting on a signal shot. It will mean one minute before the powder explodes. See that the engineer who fires the shot makes it safely to the evacuation, won't you?"

"I will," he agreed. "But what do you intend to do?"

"AAAAAAAUGH!" said a pirate as he rushed them. The Guard batted him down with his big gun.

"I intend to try to keep these pirates busy until the blast," Parissah answered.

"Isn't that needlessly hazardous?" the Guard plied.

"Yes. But that is perhaps why I feel I must do it."

"Right." The Guard nodded, understanding.

Just then, the unsuspecting Guard took a shot from a Phage gunslinger, and he faltered back. The effort was coordinated, and swordsmen came in to further assail them. Parissah swung hard and wide. They gave her a wide berth, but she wasn't able to cover for the Guard, who had already been forced back toward the rest of his group, and the other two sailors. In the midst of this confusion, she finally heard a snail bolt, coupled with a green flash that was impressively dramatic in the near blackness. The engineer had given the signal!

But the Guards hesitated. "Go!" she called out to them. "Escape with the engineer! I can hold these villains."

One pirate rushed her from the right, but she drew and fired her snail pistol, to lethal effect. Their weapons were live now. Immediately more shots went off from the Guards as they covered their own withdrawal to the engineer, and she heard furious cranking to ready the next round as the whole tussle progressed out of sight. In the meantime, she kept swinging, and the rest of the pirates kept their distance. It was still a hopeless charade, but she decided to push it as far as she could with more empty bravado...

"Come, now!" she said. "Is there no one who will challenge me?"

"I will," came a familiar voice. There was a parting in the pirates, and returned was the silhouette of 'Marlin' – the Mesomela officer from the first of her encounter. He worked his muscles, stretching and shaking loose, and he assumed a defensive stance that looked quite practiced. "I am resolved to it now. It be time that I finally measured meself against a true master."

Parissah steadied herself. With an attitude like that, Marlin must have been an adept among his peers. And his great bulk suggested he likely had strength to contend with hers. But she only had roughly forty more seconds to buy, and duels of this sort often involved a long preamble of the two opponents circling each other. Maybe she could ride the circling stage out until the explosion...

Marlin upset these plans by charging straight in with a horrible yell. She misjudged his speed and distance, and swung to deflect his attack much too early. All her muscles locked up reflexively, knowing she had already made her fatal error and was about to be impaled. But Marlin surprised her by faltering too, reacting to her premature swing by stumbling into a desperate defensive stroke that caught only air. With a whimper of effort, he recovered into a ready posture. She gave him a probing jab, but he cleared her blade with accelerating force. She was tossed back, nearly losing her sword and falling all at once.

"Oh, you *are* good!" Marlin said, much to her bewilderment. "Look at ye, feignin' total ignorance of the craft! Lulling me into a false sense of security, is we? It won't work!"

She shook her head, trying to feel out a defensive stance of her own. "I really have no idea what I'm doing."

He ran in for another clash. She timed her first defense right, which was a great moral victory. But the second and third strokes whiffed completely. Evidently, they couldn't compromise on a unified duel, and so were each acting out their own. Marlin tried to guess where Parissah would go next. He dashed toward her right flank, but her sword incidentally fell in his way, and she cut him in the thigh.

"Arrr!" he yelped, spinning away and seizing on his injured leg. "Such guile," he marveled, after a moment of assessing the damage. "Such misdirection! I've ne'er seen the like!"

"It is all in your head, man," she tried to tell him. But of course it was no use… especially now that he was hurt.

After that, he did rally just a bit more courage, and leapt in a third time. This time their blades got crossed, and they simply pushed against each other. Parissah believed this was what was known as a 'hold'. She thought about asking Marlin if that was indeed the correct term, but he seemed to be preoccupied. At this distance she could see that he had a pitiful look on his face. She struggled against his impressive strength, expecting to overcommit and falter, and then be dashed. But after several seconds like this, it became apparent to her that he was too leary of the same potential fate to do anything but keep pushing back…

"Well, what are ye waiting for!?" Marlin demanded in a shaky voice. "Have mercy! Just finish me now!"

"For the last time!" she exclaimed. "I never trained with the Herons! I've never even met Proconsul Zedulon! This sword is not mine! I recovered it from a fallen swordsdrone."

Marlin pulled back out of the hold, aghast. "Ye mean… ye bested one o' those Tophthaeran terrors… without so much as a lick of Heron instruction!?"

"No, I…" she started, but was interrupted by a voice from above…

"Dear me, but what the devil have you got yourself into this time?" asked the voice.

She whirled around and looked up to see the descending interloper. "Baegulgog!" she exclaimed.

"Reporting for duty, madam," he bowed, as he alighted just above the deck of the ship.

"Lands' sake," Marlin gaped. "Here be the swordsdrone now! Answerin' to ye like an indentured servant!"

"I beg your pardon!?" Baegulgog replied. He was probably just about to protest, being mistaken once more for a Berlie Beirel, but Marlin surprised them all by throwing down his sword and falling to his knees.

"O, great master!" he pleaded before Parissah. "I beg o' thee, make me yer apprentice too! I'll renounce all piracy for e'er and e'er, if ye'll but teach me all ye know!"

For a moment, she stood over him with an ironic sort of seriousness. It appeared now completely hopeless that he would ever see her as anything less than the greatest sword fighter of all time. But she could not help speaking the truth. "I already have."

Finally, there was a terrific explosion! A huge shockwave roiled through the whole body of the ship as a fireball ejected much of the forward hull windward into the black ocean. Parissah collected herself, and Baegulgog too. "Abandon ship!" she said, grabbing him by a tentacle and plunging for the open water. But it was not a very urgent splashdown after all. Her weight was hardly sufficient to overcome his buoyancy, and in the end they coasted lethargically down into the waves, which danced brightly in the blasts. Secondary explosions were going off, and the two of them only just managed to dodge incineration. New debris was raining into the sea ahead of them. Splashes overlapping splashes wrought a very thick field of flotsam.

Now swimming, with Baegulgog floating unsteadily nearby, Parissah stole a look back, recoiling as a chunk of ship nearly struck her. The molten carapace of *Radiant* was sinking fast. The pirates would get nothing now. She was much-relieved.

But of course, there were other things to be concerned about. "The lifeboats, Baegulgog! What have you to report?"

"I deployed them one and all, madam," he said, as a few tentacles flung wide while he worked to catch himself in the air. "I should not have felt at liberty to come looking for you otherwise. The crew is on their way back to the Citadel, even now."

"Very good," she sighed.

"How will we be returning? I don't think we shall catch your compatriots now. I suppose I will have to slip and slide all the way..."

"I'm sorry for your plight, Baegulgog," Parissah lamented. "I for one would be content to swim. Though that plan is not without its hazards, what with the many ocean predators. Perhaps we can find some debris to float on. That should be steadier for you and safer for me."

Baegulgog flashed in agreement. "I believe I see something that might serve our need. This way!" he directed, clumsily.

* * *

As *Radiant* submerged to its final rest, and the burning pirate ship finally fizzled its last, the sea became impenetrably dark – just as it had been before the battle. Parissah could see nothing beyond the gentle blue light that Baegulgog was casting roundabout himself. Immersed to her head in the wintering ocean, and with the action now behind her, she began to become horribly cold – a truly miserable state for her kind. But with her metabolism restored, she knew her body would not fail her this time, as it had at the coast. With Baegulgog in the lead, she pawed and stroked through an increasingly dense field of bits and pieces, in search of anything that could serve as a makeshift raft. All the while, Parissah's ears were in overdrive. Her nerves did not easily accept how deadly quiet the world had suddenly become, after so much strife. Every little lapping sound she made as she swam seemed to resonate for miles...

Finally, they found a very big wooden door that was still mostly intact. Parissah did not recall that *Radiant* had had any wooden doors, but she did not intend to look a gift raft in the mouth, and clamored up out of the sea as best she could, with the flighted Clerk's assistance. She was very self-conscious of the racket she made in the effort. If she thought about it, it really was a rather bad spot she was in. In a big group, Avarica could probably fend well for themselves against shark attacks. But with only her and Baegulgog, her odds did not seem so good. It was only marginally safer floating on the door, and she felt much colder in the open air than she had in the water, as the chill breeze wandered past her with a whisper. Being an amphibious creature, she resolved to feel less desperate. But she did not easily arrive at any sense of relief. Just from dimly guessing the things that lurked in the fathoms below, her hunting instincts were set alight. Not the instincts of the predator, of course – but those of the prey. These she tuned out as best she could.

For a short time, she just sat quietly collecting her thoughts, bobbing in the middle of the immeasurably vast, dark plane of the ocean. Once she was fully refocused on the task at hand, it didn't take long to realize propulsion was going to be a problem.

"Do you suppose you could search around for something like an oar, Baegulgog?" she asked.

He sputtered a bit, evidently hesitant. "Mightn't I just as well push us along myself? You needn't always do all the work."

"That would be fine, of course," Parissah answered, "except that you are incredibly slow. I must return to the Citadel or reach the fleet as quickly as may be."

"I suppose I can check around, then," he relented.

"Perhaps the entire idea of floating is ill-founded," she mused aloud. "I could certainly swim faster than I could hope to paddle this thing."

"But would you be able to swim as swift as you suppose, with me in tow?"

Parissah shook her head. "I fear I'm at a loss. I don't know what ought to be done."

Suddenly, she was aware of flashing lights and voices. The pirates were out with lanterns, combing through *Radiant's* debris field!

"Good gracious, th..." Baegulgog began, but she abruptly muffled him. She removed her outer cloak, caught Baegulgog in it, and thrust him into the ocean.

"I'm sorry, Baegulgog," she apologized, "but we mustn't risk them seeing your light. I shall have to hold you under water."

He made some bubbly noises, and flashed thoughtfully under the covering of the dark ocean. She thought he was giving his approval to her action. As she held him under, she certainly hoped that was what he was doing...

* * *

It was a tense episode. All about, pirates were on the prowl – ever in fiercer numbers. At first, there were perhaps a half-dozen boats, searching high and low through the sea surrounding *Radiant's* demise. After an hour, or two, there may have been five times that many. Lanterns swung in all directions just above the oceanic plain, but there were some much higher. Two other pirate ships had arrived late to the battlezone, but were nonetheless eager to join in the search for loot, and for survivors of the failed raid. The sonic environment was the most unnerving of all. The boats had come out quietly at first – the few voices she heard were low and solemn. But as they began to recover some of their buccaneer brethren, the mood picked up, and all sense of caution abated. By now, they were calling back and forth to each other constantly. It seemed to Parissah that every time the voices began to fade to a heartening distance, a new set would call out loud and clear –

and so terrifyingly close that they might as well have been on the door with her! Each time, she would reflexively despair that they had finally found her – and each time, it would turn out that they were pointing out some stupid, worthless trinket...

This continued through the entire third watch of the night. Parissah kept herself coiled tightly down, only daring to snake her head up to look around in rare instances. So soon after she had so thoroughly revived, she was already back on the road to exhaustion. Her cold, wet body quaked as she strained constantly to hold Baegulgog under water. Not that he was being uncooperative – after a short while, she began to see his tentacles fan out rhythmically below the surface. He was swimming downward, as he was able, to contribute what he could to the work of keeping him under. But his bulbous body was exceptionally buoyant, and even with both of them working together, he could hardly stay submerged. The minutes ticked by with incredible lethargy as she tried to manage all of this, with every beam of lantern light that washed over her portending doom.

At great length, she snarled a snarl of general disgust. She had thought better of the whole thing, and she let Baegulgog up...

"Have they gone at last?" he whispered urgently as he splashed into the air. "Good gracious, my papers!" he exclaimed before she had a chance to answer. He checked his satchel. "I shall have to hand-dry each one of them individually. But far better I had them with me, than that they should have gone down with that fine vessel of yours. I can hardly imagine a worse calamity!"

"We are yet in the midst of calamity, Baegulgog," Parissah explained, not bothering to whisper. "The pirates have not gone. We are to be captured; I hope at once."

"Surely not!" Baegulgog flashed in horror. "Surely you don't mean to be taken by those wrongdoers! They have little love for Inquisitors, I am given to understand – and no appreciation for paperwork, besides. It will be very poor company indeed! Help me back under the water, before we are discovered..."

"No, Baegulgog. It must be this way. Their search will go to dawn, at this rate, at which point we will have no hope of escape at all. We have only been forestalling the inevitable. But I have arrived at a gambit that might achieve our ends. You must trust me, Baegulgog."

He nodded his body in the air. "That I shall, madam."

"Good. Now let us be sure and make ourselves known."

It didn't take long at all, with Baegulgog all aglow, and the two of them shouting insults, before the pirates rounded them up. They went without a fight, taken into the very fastness of the huge and wicked ship that had dealt the valorous Captain Veshinkir his death. It was an unhappy meeting. There had always existed very special enmity between pirates and Inquisitors, both professions having sprung from the great, ancient sundering between the few repentant dragons, and the many whose ways remained wicked. As such, Parissah received many leers and jeers from the motley crew, and was directed rather roughly at sword-point past a wide assortment of unscrupulous characters – mostly Humans, but numerous Phage, Mesomelae, some Avarica, and even a few Herons and Meduselda. It was one of the latter which made the greatest stink about the unwelcome visitors…

"Arrr!" said the Meduseldan pirate, brandishing swords enthusiastically, wearing a patch across his body beneath a ruddy bandana, as if he had a missing eye to conceal. "What be the likes o' these here good-nicks doin' on one of our master's ships… all livin' like and what-such?! And one of them a bloomin' Inquisitor, curse us all! Tis sacrilege, I says! In the name of all that be larcenous, let's skewer and gully 'em, and keel-haul the lubbers who brought 'em here!"

Parissah guessed at once that this Meduseldan pirate was a Wuu Gappew. Only the legendary impressionability of a Wuu Gappew would account for his obvious, overreaching zeal for piracy. Anyway, Wuu Gappews were the best-represented Dominion in Idriulthoronta, notwithstanding the resident Berlie Beirels. They had been brought over en masse from the continent in less uncertain times, recruited by the Kaiser of Despotopia, who sought them out to teach Morse Code to the operators of his prototype network of telegraphs. It was not hard to imagine that one of these had been captured by pirates, and had since conformed effortlessly to their lifestyle. Few others among Meduselda would have much cause to fall in with these sorts of pariahs, much less be so excitable about it…

"Stow it, Grumly!" one of the pirate guards who were prodding Parissah and Baegulgog along snipped back. "I reckon the Captain will have other ideas, when he meets our prisoners."

"Will I, now?" called a voice, which was paired with a figure heretofore hidden from view by the darkness, and by the shroud of his very big and impressive hat. But as he began to stride forward, his cape billowed behind him in a sudden and strangely dazzling way, as if it possessed some luminance of its own. An attentive subordinate came up and handed the man a lantern. The warm glow ignited the firey red and gold of his Captain's suit, but did not seem to fall on the cold light of his cape, and was slow in revealing the features of his face. But as he held it forth, Parissah saw a searching eye with a feral aspect – the keen look of a survivor, who had perhaps endured too many close scrapes for his own good. The dark side of his face, closer to the lantern, was evidently encased in some sort of shell, with dark gashes of ruined skin along the edge, hinting at what might be underneath. On his left shoulder there was perched a little Compsognathus, who chirped in the sudden light. He studied them for a fair interval before he said any more. "Well, I've seen the prisoners now, rightly enough. Care to enlighten me what sort of ideas I might be havin'?"

"Cap'n Herringbone!" the pirate guard exclaimed, suddenly alarmed. "I…"

"…Ye was just thinkin' aloud that ye known what I would think, e'en afore I thought it? Ye done made it plain, lad. The machinations of me mind hold no mystery to the likes o' ye."

"Beggin' yer pardon, Cap'n," the pirate guard stammered. "Didn't mean nothin' by what I said… honest I didn't. I be just a simple lout, by me own admission, and surely deficient the profundity o' Captainly circumspection."

Captain Herringbone huffed. "Ye be at that. But even if ye had some sense, I wager Grumly's bleating would be enough t'make ye forget it on occasion. I can excuse ye speakin' out o' turn. But for once I agree with the blue floaty simpleton. These mateys ye brought aboard ain't besuitin' of our fraternity."

"I should say not," Parissah interjected. "But before you reach any senselessly brutal decisions concerning us, you should know you stand to profit handily from our captivity. I am a Primary Administrator of the Inquisition, and you are holding me over from much urgent business that calls for my attention. That puts you in very good standing to demand a substantial ransom."

Herringbone's eye glinted with renewed suspicion. "Pretty words, from an Inquisitor. But would yer people deign to pay the likes o' me? I wonder."

"If the need was great enough," she answered. "Though it pains me to admit it, I am considered nearly indispensable. The safe and speedy return of myself and my associate here could fetch an astronomical fee."

Herringbone stroked his chin. "Astronomical, ye say?"

"Yes," she replied. "Truly an awful lot of money."

For a moment, she was sure she had him right where she wanted him. It seemed simple enough to wave some key words like 'profit', 'ransom', and 'fee' around in his face and let his greedy imagination do the work. But at length, he reared, taking a draught from a mirky bottle (no doubt of spoiled grape juice), and after returning the bottle to the folds of his coat, snapped his fingers with a heavy swallow.

"Mayhaps this be a little rich for me humble blood," he nearly coughed with a mischievous look, speaking loudly as to the gathered crew. "A proposition o' this proportion ought to be run by the Shogun hisself – ain't it so, me hearties?"

The crew agreed in a lively fashion. Their vocalization echoed unsettlingly in her head as a new coldness fell over Parissah's heart... at the mention of a *Shogun*...

Herringbone stepped heavily away with a flash of his cape, and handing off the lantern, clutched the helm of his ship. "Then make ready, ye lubbers! We sail for home, sans delay! I reckon we've fetched the Shogun a worthy prize after all, whether he chooses to redeem them fer a fee, or he has other ideas of a more sinister nature. Take the bilge rats to the brig, and lock 'em up tight! We shan't leave them room for second thoughts now!"

Parissah and Baegulgog were spirited away as the entire ship sprang into full sail, with efficacy that would seem to rival even the strict regimentation of Inquisitor crews, spurred by sadistic delight in the minds of the buccaneers as they pondered the cruelties that their true master might devise for the Inquisitor – and to a much lesser extent, the Clerk...

* * *

Resting on the floor of a small and filthy cell with hardy bars and no light, Parissah despaired that she had made yet another critical error – perhaps the last of her career. Baegulgog was away in his own cell, with other empty cages between them. His faint blue glow was all there was to see by in the creeky confines of the shipboard dungeon. She did not know who or what might be with them in all that abysmal space, lurking in silent vigil. But she decided not to care, and to speak openly with her friend the Clerk...

"I've shown abhorrant judgement once again, Baegulgog," she said. "I should have looked for some clue as to the identity of these pirates, before risking a bargain with them."

"Identity, madam?" Baegulgog inquired. "As in, their clan or band, I suppose? The Captain mentioned a 'Shogun'. I know of only one dragon that goes by that self-styled moniker..."

"As do I," Parissah agreed gravely. "Shogun Shontaulyin. These pirates are Ivory Hyssops, Baegulgog. They are reputed the worst of their kind... as is their master. Our prospect of securing extradition seems impossibly bleak."

"Your omens are ever gloomy, madam... but seldom far from the mark. Yet we have come through many scrapes. Do not abandon all hope!"

She sighed, wearied at the mere mention of hope. "I will certainly try, Baegulgog."

The night passed restlessly. Parissah struggled to get some sleep. Slowly, she was lulled almost to the point of it by the vague echoes of the business on the deck above. But just as she might have fallen into uncomfortable dreams, a waking distress brushed her mind as she heard the crew break out into a chanty – one she found unaccountably dismal, in both melody and verse...

My prison is of flesh and bone
And guilt for which I can't atone
I built it up in younger days
When field and foe I set ablaze
Reckless in my strength and hate
I bought my 'scape from final fate
Hoarding treasures of the earth
And dying to a dark rebirth

Days of plenty and to spare
Our haughty souls were unprepared
    Little did we know
E'er as we gathered to our store
The Makers stood now at the door
    And silently did go!

The lifeless ages since have passed
And countless more this world will last
For no design remains for us
Forever sundered from their trust

So sleep upon your bed of gold
And metal turn your heart to mold!
    Guilded are your chains
Find comfort only in your sorrow
And dread the coming of the morrow
    Knowing naught will change

Plunder still as in your prime
Surrender to your mortal crime
And heedless be to the amount
For better debt than no account

Flight from the Lost City

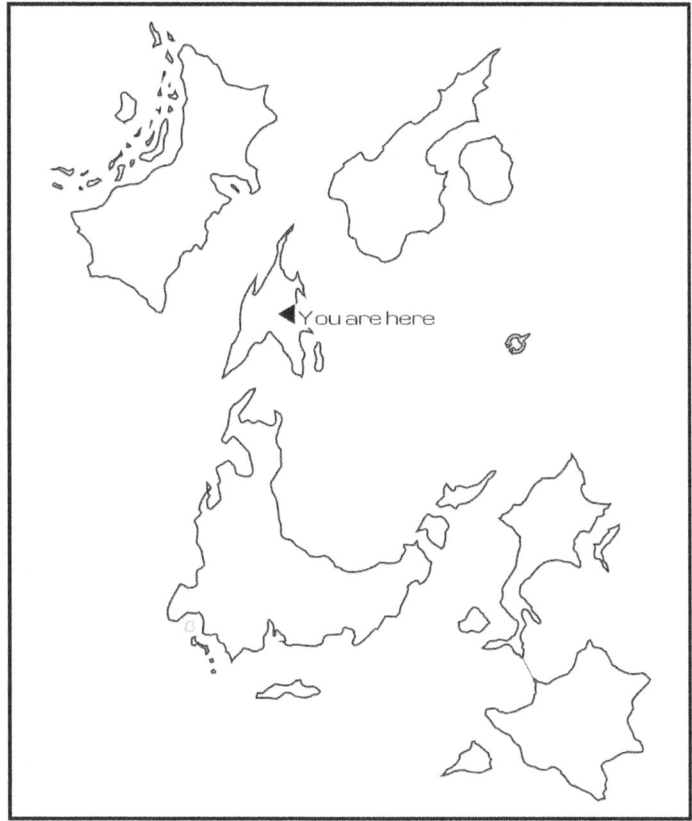

"Not all who flee are being chased. But most are."

- Attributed to some random vagabond

A truly bleak and sulky night had drawn itself up over the capitol city of Roemnar, the likes of which, he felt, were becoming too few and far between in recent times. The sky was clear and motionless, with dismal light raining down from the contours of the Other Worlds. Gasping for air, he found the serene sight above was a remarkable counterpoint to the urgency of the occasion. He knew there would be no sleep for anyone tonight – and least of all for *him*. Emerging silently from the Proconsul's palace, throwing himself to the wall for cover, the sirens blasted in his ears from all quadrants as they marched to the far reaches of the land. Urgent voices echoed round and down from the heights and valleys of hewn stone, while searchlights circled all overhead.

He propped himself up with *Valshaloli* – the storied weapon he held in his talon. He needed a moment's rest. Already his long neck chafed in the rough leather of his Plague Doctor attire, and his breath was thin. He was scarcely in the shape he needed to be for this errand, to say the least. Though it would have been enough to daunt anyone. For all of this commotion – and much to come – was over him. Word was spreading of a national emergency. He had taken the royal spear... and other things, besides...

As he worked to catch his breath in the stifling mask, the thought occurred – he was in need of a travelling alias. Using his right name abroad would certainly tend to raise questions after this episode. He tried to draw inspiration from his vestments. "Doc"? Quite generic, and surely overused. "Bones"? Much better! Yet even as he had nearly decided on it, he felt some sort of extra-cosmic pressure on his mind that foreboded against its use. "Joints"? "Ligaments"? Horrid! He heard the voices of the palace guard drawing closer. At the rate he was considering names, the whole country might find him before he had one he liked. Then another finally dawned on him. *"Marrow?"* he thought. As a squad of centurions rounded the bend in his path, he felt that would have to be good enough...

"There he is!" the centurions said, one to the other. "He has the spear!"

With a powerful beat of his wings, 'Marrow' leapt fearlessly into their midst. There was hardly need of caution; he remembered this fight clearly. Or was it the *other* fight he was remembering? No! As he successfully parried the opening thrusts of the centurions' spearheads, he was assured that this was the fight he thought it was. It was a spectacular battle. His opponents were all preeminently skilled and swift – acting in such a concerted attack that they seemed guided by a collective consciousness. They should certainly have overwhelmed any single opponent. Nevertheless, he beat them all down hard, one by one, permitting them only the indignity of their lives. Between the long, sturdy haft of the royal spear and the unforgiving stone surfaces in that rounded baffle outside the palace, he had all the tools he needed to deliver the five knock-out blows in rapid succession. For among the living fighters of the earth, he had few rivals, and fewer equals. Moreover, Marrow possessed the gift of Heron-kind, rare though it was, even among the members of his race: He could glimpse the future.

When the last of the centurions was neutralized, he darted deeper into the maze of hewn folds and canyons round-about the palace. There was a wide-ranging series of tall dikes and shelves that wound out from all the entrances, hindering and bewildering to any who would come against the Roemnari capitol on foot, but unrestricting to those who could fly. Marrow knew, of course, that he could simply fly out of the labyrinth himself. But the wide-open sky offered little escape. For he also knew that was the *first* place they would look for him...

Clearing a low rise and curling around a rightward bend in the walls, a fell rumor reached his ears. He could hear the snarling of raptors loosed in the maze. Their feral noises were echoing down to him, but whence they really originated he could not guess. Stopping again in his tracks for a moment to collect his bearings, he struggled to remember how he was going to make it to the moat...

"*Left*, then *right*, then *left*!" he chided himself in his sinister voice as he sprung back into a sprint. "You went over all of this already! Or, did you?" He sighed. Looking back, he had probably already turned left, then right, then left. Or anyway, he might have...

At that moment, a lone raptor jumped into the path some yards ahead of him. It shook its snout and clicked its long nails, but did not seem to take immediate notice of him. Marrow nonetheless doubled back, only to have the other route cut off by three more members of the pack, who seemed a bit more alert. They had misled and trapped him in a pincer attack! Springing on one foot and thrusting the spear with the other, he flipped back and caught the lead raptor on the nose as he fled, extracting a horrible, shrieking yelp. The raptor on the other side had since charged in and nearly caught him off-guard, evidently rocketing out of its former air of nonchalance. He scaled the wall in reverse just in time to avoid being pounced on, then leapt off the back of the incredulous raptor itself with a backward swipe of the spear, injuring it. He flew away to a perch upon one of the baffle walls. From there, he scanned the horizon urgently. He had made in the wrong direction, which was only apparent because of the rise of the palace in front of him. Beside that structure, most everything else in sight was either flat, or submerged. The Lost City was built like that – almost everything was carved into the ground, rather than sticking out of it. 'The Lost City', of course, was the rather curious name of Roemnar's capitol. No one knew just why it was called that. People found The Lost City all the time... and seldom even on accident...

Even as the raptors leapt and scratched and clawed at his heels from below, Marrow remembered only just in time another peril. He threw himself back down into the dikes on the opposite side from the raptors, even though it was a step backward for him. As he did so, he narrowly avoided being clipped by a speeding projectile, which blasted away a chunk from the wall. There were cannons round the palace's higher levels, and one had just about got him!

Landing deftly amid tumbling and bouncing rubble, he found himself once again in the midst of a squadron of centurions. He collected himself as they were staggered for a moment by the unexpected rain of debris. This, then, was the *other* fight he remembered he was going to have...

All was a flurry of clangs and clamors for the next few seconds as he was forced to fight his way through this second team of some of his most elite estranged countrymen. He threw off a heavy attack from a pair of them and looked up just in time to behold one of the raptors pouncing down on him from the fresh cleave in the wall. He was forced to skewer it on the spear, and with a colossal effort threw the tumbling body over him on the end of the weapon as he fell to the ground. He had no time to regret dispatching one of the palace's pets, though he had hoped to escape without killing. He harbored no serious ill-will for his country or its inhabitants – particularly not for stupid animals that didn't know any better. Though admittedly he had little love for the Senate...

But it was the designs of the Proconsul himself that truly needed to be foiled – and that need drove Marrow's rogue mission. Zedulon had secret plans that foreboded a great doom and a drastic change in the course of the world. And Marrow was the only one with knowledge of these plans who would dare to expose them before they could be put into calamitous effect. This was his charge – the one he had placed on himself... as only he could...

Marrow found himself unable to quickly retrieve the royal spear and was forced to come to his feet unarmed. He dodged a thrust from one of the centurions and caught the haft in his talon, then wrenched with the force of his body to wrest the weapon free of his opponent's grasp. He followed through with a twist and caught another centurion on the side of his head with the freed end of the spear, then pounced and subdued the one he had taken the weapon from. He had only time enough to recover *Valshaloli* and dash down the path, when the final uninjured raptor came at last into pursuit. He was able to maintain a good lead with his long swift strides, for a while. And with the assistance of his wings he cleared several shelves in the path more effortlessly than the vengeful dinosaur. But finally, the superior velocity of the raptor was winning out. It was nearly on him, and he had to fly to the top of another wall to escape. This time, he found himself on the threshold of the moat he had been searching for. There was a wide, water-filled moat that went all the way around the maze that circled the palace. It was to be another interesting obstacle. For there was more in that moat than just water...

The raptor sprung up some yards to his right. It had leapt from a higher shelf and was able to summit the wall with a bit of quick clambering. It snarled and frothed foul saliva at him. Marrow recoiled, but he had to duck at the last second, nearly having his head bit off from behind. The first raptor, whose nose he had slashed, had stealthily returned to the fight, and closed in on him from the opposite side.

Before he had a chance to make one way or another, a cannon shot rang out again, and the wall gave way beneath the injured raptor. Water from the moat followed the creature down with a crash into the dike. More of the wall felt ready to give way, and he could sense that another shot would be short in coming. He made a leaping dive for it, narrowly traversing ahead of the closing jaws of the remaining raptor...

Splashing into raging water, Marrow righted himself and began the awkward business of swimming. His wings were strong for the task, but the locomotion was unfamiliar to him, and he had to hold his head very high on his strained neck. It became immediately apparent he wasn't ideally costumed for a splashdown. The cold water instantly soaked the cloth stuffed into his plague mask, and he struggled and sputtered against a drowning reflex.

Soon he heard a splash behind him. Marrow flicked a few looks back. The raptor was not dissuaded – and if it experienced any difficulty in swimming, it didn't show. He beat his wings much harder now, coughing and heaving.

There was a strong current to the moat, even without the spillage from the cannon damage to the dam wall. Another shot, and then another, struck the water in his midst. Progressing slowly, he reflexively checked on his pursuer, though he knew better than to look back. The raptor was gaining. His plight began to seem quite desperate...

Still leading the raptor for several more seconds, Marrow noted that the palace's defense cannons had kept silent longer than they needed to. He sensed that the gunners were vesting their trust in the hungry dinosaur nearby, and that they would not risk hitting it with another stray shot.

To be clear, it was not the *raptor* they were afraid of hitting. Looking ahead, Marrow knew that another, considerably larger dinosaur was about to make its presence known...

He felt the spear he had in tow brush something. An angry chittering was now deadly close behind him; the raptor was close enough to bite his feet! He kept pushing. He knew he remembered things turning out alright in the end...

On cue, a loud and violent disturbance exploded out of the water behind him. A huge Spinosaurus snapped the unwary raptor into its oversize crocodilian jaws. The roiling of the struggle sent Marrow tumbling. Between immersions, he caught some of the roaring and the final despairing call of the helpless raptor.

While he was under, he was narrowly missed by the passing sail of another submerged Spinosaurus, which was eager to investigate the catch of its fellow denizen in the moat. There were plenty of Spinosaurus patrolling the water around the palace, and it was Marrow's saving grace that they found the raptor more appealing prey...

He returned to the surface, desperate for air but unable to do better than choke it in a little at a time. He swam and swam with all his strength. At last he reached the outer wall and emerged, rolling over and into the drainage ditch. He seized his mask with great urgency to open it, but only enough to remove the cloths with all haste. He drew some hoarse breaths, and finally had his fill of air again. He lay there for some seconds recovering. But there was a new sound closing in that foreboded considerable danger, if he did not move immediately into lower paths. Too soon, he collected himself and dashed away again, hopping the ditch and risking the cannons to reach the nearest walkways into the City at large...

* * *

Marrow passed few locals as he ran through the broad paths. Many of those he passed were running too, intent to get off the streets and out of the way of the gathering military and police presence. Everything was still under the exasperation of the ongoing alarms throughout the City. He heard some calls and gasps from one or two of the civilians that saw and recognized the spear he was carrying, as he crossed through the lamp-lit crossroads.

And he kept running. He purposed to pass through the wider business sector and into the more remote residential district. It was important to stay ahead of the search parties that were still marshaling, and he knew they would be thinner out there. But he would also be more exposed. And soon, there was going to be more mobilizing to hunt him down than mere policeman on foot and wing...

An airborn patrolman took note of him and swooped down to investigate. "Freeze!" the officer called. The poor dullard had no idea what hit him. Marrow clotheslined him on the run, missing hardly a beat as he flapped and hopped through the blow.

The violence quickly attracted the attention of a whole troop of policemen passing under a streetlamp several yards ahead. They hollered and charged him. Marrow quickly diverted course, and rounding a bend in the street, he ducked into a dark fold of some storefront. The officers passed him by without so much as a thought to check. When they were clear, he doubled back and continued on his original way...

All the while the rumor in the distance was getting close, and indeed sounded to be looming overhead even now. Roemnar had benefit of flying military vehicles, and they had been readied and deployed to the search for the fugitive with admirable swiftness. Their propellors thrummed noisily, shaking everything in sight. Search lamps rained shafts of pale light into the otherwise dim, warm gloom of the streets. Marrow sheltered himself again to observe. He remembered distinctly that there would be bombers on patrol. But as he searched the skies, he saw that fighters had been scrambled too. The air traffic would be thick!

He watched as a bomber passed overhead, and a troop of centurions that had hitched a ride decoupled from their perches on the sides of the hull, beginning independent searches. Marrow knew he was going to have to continue on with great haste – searching eyes in the business district were quickly multiplying. He hugged the buildings and did his best to stay out of the light as he made his way.

* * *

At last, the road he was on sloped up to level ground. He was leaving the commercial district and emerging into the surrounding plains. The residences would be out there, sunken into the ground wherever someone happened to make one. Each was circular and had a narrow trench around it, where the doors to the home emptied out. He could shelter in those trenches as necessary, though they tended only to hug individual homes, and seldom snaked between them, particularly if two adjoining houses' occupants were related. The rest of the time he would have to be out in the open. But he took a deep breath and steeled himself, feeling his bristly feathers smooth out. This was the way out of The Lost City he had determined to take... even if only because it was the way he foresaw himself taking...

The droning of propellers was still close, though he kept his eyes to the path. He needed to remember clearly the way he was going to go, and looking around only tended to distract him.

His blood ran suddenly cold as a search light passed right over him. He knew it would happen at some point, but had hoped that it was going to happen later, rather than sooner. There was no immediate repercussion. But just as he had begun to hope the searchers had overlooked him, two shots came out of the heavens and struck the ground very near to him. He made a tumbling leap into the nearest residential trench, and half-inadvertently ducked and rolled through an open door into the home itself...

The droning passed overhead and the searchlights did not reach beyond the doorway. He landed on his feet, looking into the living room of someone's house. The whole family was there, looking back at him. In a flash, he remembered these people, and their emergency. He went for his medical tape...

"Who are you?" the father asked, putting himself in the gulf between the stranger and his family.

"Do not fret; I'm a doctor!" Marrow responded. He threw the roll of tape to the mother. "Take this and wrap the wound tightly; it will stop the bleeding. It is only a minor cut; he'll be alright." He made quickly for the back door across the long, narrow room.

"What cut?" the mother asked. The hatchlings exchanged a look.

"The one on your husband's left wing," Marrow explained. "I am sorry about the explosion. You will be compensated for all property damage."

"What...?" began yet another question, but at that moment a bomb went off outside, collapsing a part of the roof with much dust and soot. Marrow darted out the door even as he heard the father yell, "My wing!"

Immediately as he left the trench, he took to flight. There would be no evading the bomber without incurring death – either his own or that of one or more civilians. He would have to face the vehicle himself, while it was without close escort...

He flew directly for the craft, narrowly avoiding shots from a swivel gun on its flank. Deftly, he reached the side of the tall vessel, clinging to perch bars along the height where the gun would not reach him. There were centurions still hunkered against higher perch bars, and they took note of him. They jabbed for him with deadly strikes, but he deflected them. One thrust sailed past him and he caught it in his left talon, heaving himself up. The centurion struggled and faltered to hold himself fast, but managed. Still, Marrow advanced upwards, and using the exceptionally honed edge of *Valshaloli*, he made a clearing stroke that cut the bar out from under one of the other centurions, who fell from the craft. He then whirled the royal spear around and plunged it into the side of the bomber, where it held fast. With both talons free, he scaled the length of the other centurion's spear, but narrowly avoided a savage peck from his adversary. In retaliation, he beat the centurion's ears with his wings, stunning him and causing him to tumble free of his perch bar, sending them both into space. But as he fell, Marrow caught the haft of the royal spear in his talons and swung in an under-over pattern as if it were a gymnastic bar. Flung back upward, he grabbed the perch bar. And reaching back, he expertly extracted *Valshaloli* with a flick of his ankle.

Discretely, Marrow clamored up and to the front of the vehicle. He broke through the window of the command cabin, following quickly after the raining glass to the floor behind the control seat. He was quick to subdue the small crew, after which he took the controls himself. This was a major boon for his escape. Veering southeast, now a bomber pilot, he struggled to remember why he had expected to end the journey on foot...

It did not take long to remember. The whole bomber buckled under sudden fire from another vehicle. A moment later, a fighter passed him by on the left. Marrow shook his head in urgent disbelief. How could the fighter know that the bomber had been commandeered? He reasoned that one of the centurions he had flung from the vessel must have made for the nearest fighter and signaled it...

In any case, he was in imminent danger. He set the throttle to full and eased the bomber into a shallow climb. He didn't need more altitude, but he wanted to be sure that he wasn't pointed at the ground for the next minute or so. Then he abandoned the controls and worked his way back to mid-cabin. He took the port gunnery seat, operating a turret. The interface was far from informative. He could only pivot the gun from within the cabin and look out the window at it, making at best a guess as to exactly where it was pointing at any given time. This was no doubt a skill that took years to master. But he was going to have to shoot the agile enemy fighter down *now*, whether he knew what he was doing or not...

Once he had the gun pointed roughly in the direction of the fighter, he opened up. The weapon was sophisticated, offering automatic fire. But there was almost a second between shots, so he was hardly saturating the field. The fighter was about to close a wide arc, and had the bomber almost in its sights. It was Marrow's boon that the fighter had curled back and to the left to attack his flank, because that meant he had the gun pointing almost straight ahead of him, where he could most easily guess its alignment...

The fighter was closing. It fired shots from multiple points, making for a dramatically rapid string of attacks. The bomber was hit at least twice. But Marrow had to ignore the damage incurred and keep up his own shots. He knew he couldn't afford for the fighter to make another pass...

As the fighter nearly did pass him, he scored his shot! The starboard ectodermis tank erupted, and the craft went into a wide spin-dive. Marrow took a moment to recline in his great relief. But even as he did, his stomach lurched. He felt the bomber divert its course, though he did not steer it...

He frantically returned to the controls. He could not assess what had been damaged, but it was obvious that the bomber was in a slow dive now, and he could not seem to right it. He struggled with the controls for several seconds before he was forced to give up all hope of flying any farther. He was going to have to put the craft down the best he could...

The only thing he could do was turn the bomber on its side and try to veer skyward with the rudder. In any case, he would need to land on the craft's side, because it was built tall with a very long stabilizing foil under its body. If that caught the ground first, it would slam the whole bomber to the ground cabin-first like a giant hammer. That would not go well for him.

One engine or other was making a very horrible grinding noise. By now he was mere feet off the ground! A side-foil caught and sent the whole ship into a spinning, skidding lateral roll. Marrow could only hold on for dear life as the bomber took all of its fury out on unforgiving turf, and vice-versa.

After some hundred yards or so, the thing finally came to a stop. The crash had blacked him out for a few moments, and he found himself lodged under the steering column, a bit battered. But he had lived… and what's more, seemed to be whole. He retrieved the spear and fluttered back through the hole he had made in the cabin to begin with… but it took more effort than he'd counted on. Landing a bit awkward, he assessed his right wing. It was bruised – not totally beyond use, but the pain was fresh and sharp, and he wouldn't be able to sustain flight. His long legs were better off. He would run from here. Drawing a deliberate deep breath, he began the last leg of the dangerous escape…

* * *

He had reached the plains beyond the residences and was journeying through uninhabited waste. The ground was still very level and thoroughly purged of trees, shrubbery, and anything else natural that might try to disturb an otherwise nice and flat terrain. Aside from some of the more lazily sprawling farms (which were far west from here), little was allowed to grow above ground on Roemnar. Many generations ago they had gone to great pains to remove unthinkably dense jungle from better than ninety percent of the island. In light of all that work, it simply didn't seem right to let anything grow back up afterward…

But there were some stony hills in the distance to make for – artificial mounds left behind by old mining – and he knew that once he reached them, he could pass the rest of his way undetected to Cape Gulph – his intended destination. Because once among the hills, it would be impossible for anyone to say whether he had made for Gulph, or Port Sanoi, or Yorlar, or Vessingal. Each of those settlements bordered the long-abandoned stone quarries of the hill country. The search for him would be stretched thin indeed beyond this point. But he had yet to reach those hills…

He knew the diligent Roemnari armed forces were not yet done with him. Soon, Marrow felt the approach in the shaking and quaking of the earth, and he heard the thuds and crashes. There was a mechanized infantry base kept to the east, and its vehicles had been dispatched to cut off any possible escape into the hills. They would be sure to have observed the crash of the bomber. They were closing in on him…

Beneath their clouds of dust, he spotted two ahead of him. One to the left; one on the right. Their crashing racket grew loud. These motorized monstrosities were casually referred to as 'tanks' – large, hoop-wheeled vehicles that sped through battlefields trailing iron barbs five feet across on long, loose chains, sowing random destruction behind them everywhere they went. He kept running for them. And they were making directly for him...

Finally, as they all nearly converged, the tank on his right veered off and back, and the left one charged past. Marrow ducked just under a tumbling barb, raked by dirt and small stones that had been flung free from the ground on its last bound. He was very fortunate there were no larger stones mixed in, or even the narrow miss might have injured him critically. That was a grim prospect indeed, now that he was without his medical tape...

Another barb passed a safe distance overhead, tripping into a high side-long spiral. Marrow took a forced bound into flight as the second tank circled back in. Pain shooting in his wing, he narrowly avoided the wheels as they passed, and barely cleared yet another barb. Another pelting by dislodged debris landed fresh hits on his injury. His muscles there faltered and spasmed, and he fell, having only skill enough to land on his feet. Back to running... though the ground was not a good place to be!

A hundred yards more and he would reach the cover of stone. The tanks would not dare give chase there long, for the terrain would become nearly impassable for them, and anyway they would be at much higher risk of getting their barbs stuck fast in immovable earth. He was so nearly escaped! And yet there was no hope at all of reaching the quarried rock before he was overrun again...

His only remaining gambit was to turn back and wade once more into the chaos on his own terms. He peeled away from the wheels only just in time and had to bob and weeve to avoid the fury of the huge flails, but he emerged intact a third time. The tank banked around to line up on him again, but he dashed after it. He meant to find a sweet spot between the two tanks, and try to play their random destructiveness against them. If they could not coordinate very effectively, they might either try to get out of each others' way and leave him a big opening to take off again, or exercise too little caution and possibly catch each other. Charging into the flank of the first tank as it turned, he managed to lead the second tank, and the two were soon in an uncomfortable orbit around him, each lacking the maneuverability or the safe room to run him down. He remained cautiously light on his feet, constantly feeling-out where he needed to be to keep up the deadlock. To an extent, he even began to have some control over the awkward dance. And slowly, he started to make his way back towards the hills as the tanks circled helplessly around him...

At length, it appeared the tank crews caught on to what he was managing. They knew they would need to press their luck, and each decided to do so in disastrous synchronous. The tanks slowed for a tighter turn and revved for a quick passby. Marrow ran for breakaway speed.

Sure enough, the tanks were each other's undoing. As they passed by each other too close, one barb flung wild and wide, and caught the other tank right in the hoop of its wheels. The huge snaking chain went taught in a flash. He had to stop dead in his tracks and duck to avoid being whipped into oblivion by the enormous tense links. The chain held fast to both vehicles, and they were pulled hard to their sides, toppling over and kicking up a great cloud of dirt and stone as all their free barbs bounded for the final time...

* * *

The dust cleared. Marrow strode out from the midst of the ruin. He was quite exhausted, and his footfalls were slow and heavy now. But in the absence of the crashing and buzzing of the tanks, he could now hear the sirens and the propellers of various airships in the distance. With a growl of reluctance, he returned to a jog...

Soon he slipped into a deep ditch – still vaguely square, showing where stone had been dug generations ago. There would be many such havens between the mounds of displaced earth that stretched on for miles, spreading wide into the countryside. Marrow toyed with the idea of marching a mere hour into the old desolation, then stopping for what remained of the night to rest in a sheltered spot. But he thought better of it. By morning, he could be deep into the hills, far from all settlements. There would be plenty of time to rest and heal then. He planned to stay in the wilderness for a week. In doing so, he would all but ensure that the search for him would die down substantially by the time he reached the Cape. It would be assumed by then that he had already slipped all nets, since there were many places along the southeastern leg of the island where a fugitive could sneak onto a ship or boat and be gone... and it would not take a week to reach any of those places.

Anyway, he *had* to wait. He did not plan to simply steal away on his own. His errand to expose the evil plot of the Proconsul would not be his alone. He intended to meet friends at Cape Gulph, few though he had in the world. But he knew they would not even be making landfall on Roemnar for some time to come...

"The fates are now sure," he announced, if only to himself. "I will see you soon, my friends." Though he despised sentiment as a general rule, Marrow had to admit that his heart longed for the meeting. He looked up into the sky, to the Other Worlds as they continued to beam cold, uncaring light onto the wide lands before him. Though he could not truly know it, he felt distinctly that a friend was looking up at the same vista even now, however far away she might be...

The Great Harbor

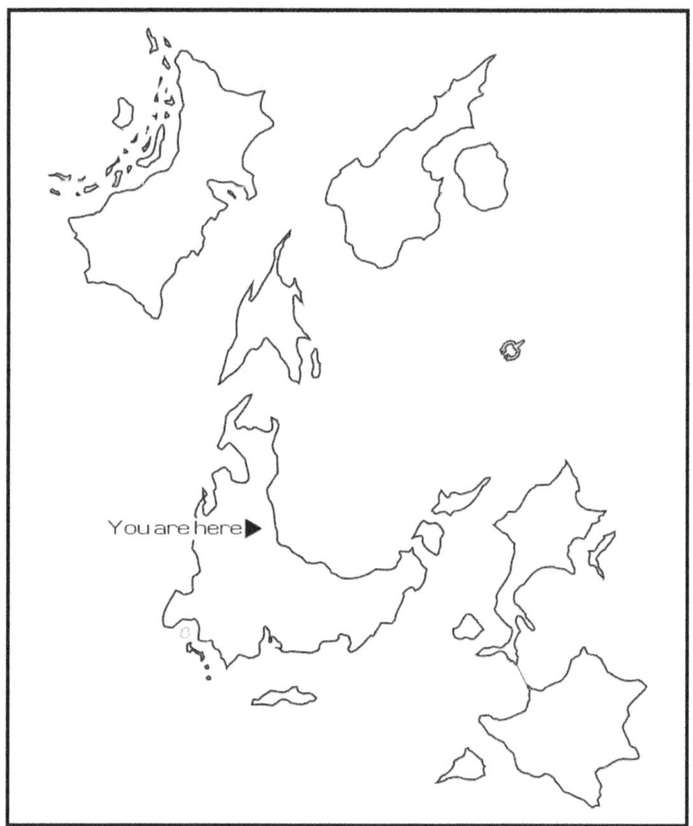

"Any two values eventually form a crossroads."

- Magormissahr, *Referendums on the World, Vol. 725*

Jek awoke in the dark with a start. He had been shook hard, and continued to shake. After the initial shock, he recognized dimly the sights and sounds (and smells) of a night ride in the back of a wagon. He propped himself up and looked out through the front of the canvas cover. Audrey was sitting out there, framed against the dark sky, looking up at the Other Worlds. Beyond her were two other indistinct figures on the driving bench, but he took no note of them.

"Audrey," he called, choking out the words. His throat was dry and disused. "What's happened? Where are we?"

Her eyes flashed to him, and they looked sad. She hesitated, and then came over to his side.

"It's alright, Jek," she told him, though her voice made him doubt. "We got you to a village with a doctor, just in time." She formed a weak smile. "He used *magic* to seal up your leg!"

Jek marveled. He had somehow forgot about his leg! He could tell distinctly now that much time had passed since he was last awake. "Yeah, it... it doesn't hurt so bad now," he replied, daring to move his leg only just a little.

Audrey pursed her lips. "That's wonderful."

Jek's heart still foreboded that something was troubling Audrey. But for the moment, he was satisfied about his health. There were other questions now more pressing. "What are we doing in a wagon? It seems I've missed a lot..."

"We paid for a ride to the coast," Audrey explained. "You were stable, but you needed time to rest and heal. But we couldn't afford to wait. The old man found a cabby that was already planning a trip to St. Argonsburg. We can get a boat from there, and finish our Quest!"

Jek felt some fresh anxiety at the news. "Is it wise to travel this openly? What if the driver gets suspicious?"

"No cause for frettin' about nothin' o' the sort," the old man put in, turning to look back into the wagon. He was evidently one of the two people on the driving bench that Jek had not bothered to try to identify. "I already done told him that we wasn't no kind o' fugitives."

Jek rolled his eyes. He was not reassured, but any further discussion would only tend to incriminate them more. So he let the matter rest, and settled back into the bedding beneath him.

"You really should try to get some more rest, dear," Audrey said, patting him on the shoulder. "The doctor recommended lots of rest. Anyway, things are well taken care of. We should reach Leemograd by morning."

He sighed heavily. It was a lot to take in all at once, and it seemed there was more he ought to know. But he couldn't think what else to ask. And even though he may well have been out for days, in the comfort of the blankets, he still felt very tired. "Alright," he said, shifting for more comfort. He looked Audrey steadily in the eyes for several seconds, while a great gratitude welled up in him. "Thank you so much, Audrey," he said.

She looked puzzled. "For what?"

He laughed, low and hoarse. "For saving my life, of course! You didn't have to. I still wonder if you should have."

She shook her head. "You're ridiculous," she told him, leaning in to tuck the blankets over his shoulders.

"Thanks," he said. And before long, he did sleep again, quite soundly.

* * *

When he woke again, Jek found that he was cold; oddly much colder than he had been in the night, though now it was a bright and clear morning, and harsh yellow light caught him in the face. But cold wind was howling through the flapping canvas cover. It was a coastal wind, he knew. They must be close now to St. Argonsburg, the capitol city – and one of dozens and dozens of distinct burgs that ran along the huge arch in the landscape of Jast-Madiir known as the Great Harbor. In a flash, he sat up to take a look, and if the sudden effort did not make him dizzy, then the sight before him certainly did...

As the wagon faced nearly due north, Jek could see the landscape meet the glistening ocean for trackless miles ahead into unsearchable mists. And all along a high shelf in the coast were countless homes and shockingly enormous buildings, whose numbers were only rivaled by the boats and ships beyond, both moored and in motion. The shore was so densely set with docked vessels that the masts almost appeared to form a great wall of poles and canvas dividing sea from land. The scope of the Great Harbor was quite overwhelming to a simple southerner like Jek. If he had got the full vista all at once, and not just the narrow framing of the wagon, he would have been truly floored.

"Wow," he said to himself.

This got Audrey's attention. He hadn't noticed right off, but she had also bedded down in the wagon since last they spoke. She got up and stretched, looking poorly rested. Her hair was in comical disarray, and she set about pulling it back at once. "Looks like we're here," she said at length.

"Is that all you can say?" Jek asked. "I mean, have you ever seen anything like it?"

"Plenty of times," she said, and at once Jek remembered her merchant past. "Never from this angle though."

At that moment, the old man clamored into the back of the wagon with them. He looked groggy too. He reached at once for a flask of water, and threw it into his face.

"What was that about?" Jek asked.

"Got to look me best fer the business at hand, and have me wits about what's more," the old man answered, rubbing his face with his hands. "Ain't no good passin' yerself off as a bleary-eyed whelp in the refinery o' St. Argonsburg. We're a-gonna do some shoppin' in town afore we figures out about sailin' for Roemnar. Might need to do some hagglin'."

Jek was quite discouraged at the prospect of having to listen to the old man haggle again. "We're practically finished with the Quest," he protested. "All we have to do is sail to Roemnar without being arrested. It's a simple matter of getting from here to a boat and from the boat to Cape Gulph. What could you possibly need to buy so badly that you'd risk blowing our cover now?"

The old man gave him a cross look under his dripping brow. "Well, if ye must knows, I needs a recharge."

Jek blinked. "A recharge?"

"Aye. For me magic. There's a thing what Bronzee didn't tell ye about magic."

"What's that?" Audrey asked.

"It wears off. Ye're '*stuff*' goes back to whate'er it was like afore ya done drank any magic elixir... slowly, over time. I durn near used me powers up fightin' them Revenants. So I gots to get a recharge. T'will serve us well, if'n we needs a fast getaway once we're seabound again."

"*It wears off...*" Audrey repeated to herself. "What about if you, well, you know... take too much elixir? What if you become a Revenant? Do they eventually go back to normal too?"

"Nay," the old man said grimly. "That be past the point o' no return, I'm afeard. So ye needs to be careful how ye goes about rechargin' yerself. Gotta have a good feel for how low ye's gettin', and how much ye done handled in the past. It's a lot o' figgerin' and rithmetic and what-such. Sometimes ye gots to count on yer fingers *and* toes."

"Oh good grief," Jek said. But Audrey looked contemplative.

"Balk if ye like," the old man said. "I'm a-gettin' me recharge, whether ye like it or no. And that's the end o' the matter..."

* * *

Soon, the cab guided them to an alchemist shop. The driver tended the horses and the old man settled up, as Jek gingerly slinked toward the front of the wagon. Audrey watched him all the way, looking very concerned. When he neared the edge of the platform, the old man also took notice, and he too looked concerned. It made Jek feel concerned.

It wasn't until he went to plant his feet on the ground under the wagon that he finally understood what all the concern was about. He nearly collapsed the instant he tried to put any pressure on his injured leg. There was a huge amount of unexpected, shooting pain, and he had to reach back and catch himself. Audrey rushed to help.

"Oh Jek," she whimpered. "We didn't have the heart to tell you! The doctor did the best he could with your leg. But he was afraid you'd never get full use of it back. He could only do so much, even with his magic. He closed the wound and repaired the bone, for the most part. But he said you would probably be hobbled. I hoped he was wrong. How I hoped he was wrong!"

Jek's spirits plummeted to his boots. He had not been spared becoming a permanent liability. More than ever, he couldn't guess what the future held for him, if anything. Even with a pardon for their Quest, he didn't immediately see how he could return to his work at the lighthouse now. What would that leave? Would the state even bother to reassign him to something more manageable, or would he simply fail his next inspection? Would Audrey have to pick up the slack for the rest of their lives? He despaired, feeling he should have just been left to the pit...

But there was no use dwelling on it. He was just going to have to put on a brave face for his wife. He could see that she was hurting deeply for him.

He tried taking some steps. It was very pitiful and gimpy, but he was able. Maybe he could become a hand with a crutch. Maybe he could even get the thing amputated some day, and master a peg-leg. But that wouldn't avail them much for the present. He struggled for something reassuring and gentle to say...

"It's not so bad," he lied. "But I don't think I'd be much good on the run. Guess I'd better stay behind."

The old man surprised him with some tender words. "Ye could still finish the Quest out with us, if ye wanted," he said. "Don't matter much the condition of yer leg, when we's in a boat." He stammered a bit and held his hat in his hands. "Ye been a fair partner in this here affair, despite yer many deficiencies. We'd just as soon ye was with us, when we finds the Knights. We done already decided we'd be willin' to take the risk."

Jek was touched. He had never received such high praise, and it moved him. "Alright. You talked me into it. But we might have to get me a crutch before we go too far."

Audrey smiled through her tears, heartened that he would agree to go on, rather than feel obligated to stay. The old man looked relieved too.

"Right ye are, lad," he said. "We'll get the alchemist to whip ye up one special afore we go... even if she's got to make it out o' me hat!" He waved it around in front of him enthusiastically.

"I don't think that's how alchemy works," Jek said.

"Well shore it is," the old man retorted. "Alchemy be takin' one thing and makin' it inta somethin' else! It be just as simple as that. Now let's not have another word. Get yer maimed hindquarters into that shop! Time's a wastin'! And ye don't get to be the early bird by chasin' worms all day."

* * *

Following Jek into the alchemist shop was a burden of care for Audrey. As much as she was relieved that he didn't sink back into the defeatism he had displayed in the trap, she despaired to see him reduced to such a mean state. She remembered all too well that he had predicted this might be the outcome of his injury. Seeing that unhappy prediction come true was almost too much to bear. It was bad enough to guess how useless and unimportant he felt *before* he was crippled. However brave he was acting now, she knew he was in great pain – emotional as well as physical. She felt it too.

But she wasn't about to accept reality, if she could help it. There was *something*, at least, that she might try to do for him. And she meant to do it. She would, before they left the shop...

"Morning," said the alchemist at the counter, taking note of their arrival. She was an extremely slender older lady in a lab coat with dark goggles, rapping her fingers on the countertop with apparent impatience. "Find everything alright?" she asked.

"Ain't rightly looked yet, ma'am," the old man said, politely and weakly, a bit unbalanced by the strange question.

"Well, try not to take too long," she replied. "I don't have room for loiterers. This is our busy time." They were the only ones in the shop.

Audrey perused the shop on her own for a bit, having not the faintest idea what she was looking at, but looking all the same. There were hundreds and hundreds of bottled liquids on multiple long rows of shelves. She knew what she wanted to find, but as she was still unacquainted with several letters of the alphabet, she had little chance of finding it herself. She was hoping that Jek and the old man would eventually wind up in different parts of the shop, so she could ask the old man to find what she wanted without Jek overhearing. In the meantime, she endeavored to at least appear purposeful as she looked up and down the aisles. "Hmm..." she said thoughtfully.

Suddenly Jek called out from a distant corner of the shop. "Hey, Audrey! They have grape juice on sale in here that's made entirely out of coconut milk and peroxide!"

"That's very novel, dear," Audrey replied.

"And downright appetizin'!" the old man chipped in, from another quadrant. "Pick some up on our way out!"

Audrey rushed silently over to where his voice had come from.

"Old man," she whispered.

"What is it, darlin?" the old man replied, returning her whisper.

She looked around to be very sure Jek was not close by. "See if you can find some Life magic elixir, will you?" she asked.

He bit his lower lip. "Aye, if ye want, lass. But it'll cost us a pertty penny! Tis more expensive than other magics. And they likes to force ye to buy in big quantities, so's they can get even more dough out o' ye. It's a racket, it is."

"Well, I'm sorry about that. But it's very important."

The old man looked sidelong. "I takes it ye don't want Jek to know."

"Not really. He doesn't seem to like magic all that much. And if he knew why I was getting it..."

"...I won't say anything, lass. But I can't very well buy anything in secret. Ain't feelin' that sneaky or clever today, I'm afeared. If he finds out, he finds out."

"That's good enough for me," she said.

Contrary to the expressed wishes of the proprietor, they gave the shop a very good look-over before coming up to check out. They passed on some fish oil made of triceratops spit, a few small flasks of maple syrup made of jellified seaweed, and an especially curious nerve tonic made of potato. It came down to the essentials... the old man's water magic, three bottles of the grape juice Jek had found, and the special item Audrey had requested. They were all in tall, slim green bottles with a wide round bottom. That was the typical container for most everything in the shop.

"Checking out, are we?" the alchemist chimed. "And just when I was beginning to think you might stay forever."

The old man cleared his throat, and it was hardly any wonder why. She had an off-putting way about her. "I take it ye ain't got much love for yer line o' work, eh ma'am?"

"No indeed," she sighed. "I wanted to be a housewife. But oh, no! I was forced to learn alchemy. I could be at home sweeping after grubby little kids right now, but instead I must do advanced science. It is such a bother."

"Maybe ye ought to sweep the shop now and again; see if it don't cheer ye up a bit."

The alchemist actually smiled at his whimsical advice. "I may just do that some time. Anything else before I ring you up?"

"Well, there be one other thing I was wonderin' about," the old man admitted. "We's in sore need of a crutch, and I was wonderin' if ye might make one special. Should be able to make one out o' any old thing, I warrant?"

She pursed her lips, looking quite confused. "I'm sorry; I'm not in the business of solid transmutation. Alchemy is kind of a liquidy thing, I'm afraid."

The old man planted his face in his palm. "I shoulds o' known! Lookin' back, tis all so clear."

"Well, I guess you're never too old to learn something," she said, reaching under the counter and grabbing an abacus. Her fingers deftly set to running numbers. "One Water magic, one Life magic, three grape juice." The old man made hectic gestures to try to stop her totaling aloud, to no avail. "That will be 344 pence."

"*344 pence*?" the old man repeated, seeming at once to forget the indiscretion.

"Life magic?" Jek repeated. "What do we need with that?"

The old man and Audrey exchanged a look. Jek searched back and forth between them. Finally, he settled on Audrey.

"You mean... you wanted... that is, you want to..." he stammered.

"Jek, try to understand..." Audrey replied.

"...Don't be having any second thoughts now," the alchemist butted in. "Store policy – no returns on any items once they've been set on the counter. Especially not very expensive items like Life Magic flasks."

"Durn it," the old man cursed.

Audrey just kept her eyes on Jek. He was immediately troubled and uncomfortable. "I... I think I'll just wait outside," he said, limping away.

"Jek, wait," Audrey said, following him after a few moments' hesitation.

"Ye both go on ahead now," the old man called after. "I'll be just in here a spell, haggling."

"Good luck," the alchemist told him.

* * *

For a cripple, Jek managed to get away in an impressive hurry. Audrey found him around the back of the storefront, huddled down on the first step of a long descending path that ran deeper into the market. He gazed moodily out onto the Harbor in all its exceedingly wide and clear splendor.

"Jek," she appealed, sitting beside him. "I'm sorry if I surprised you. I know you've already had a lot to process today. And I know that you're not exactly crazy about magic."

Jek laughed. "No, not especially. Oh, it was interesting, for sure... until I learned the first thing about it." His attempt at humor was cut short, and he waxed grim. "I don't think it's a good thing, Audrey." He poked around on the ground, trying to reason out how to say what he felt. "Purpose just doesn't strike me as something people should go playing around with. If the *stuff* that's in us is what we need to fulfill our Purpose, who are we to change it up? Are we really wise enough to mess with what we're *supposed* to do in life, on nothing more than a whim? Aren't you worried how wrong the world might get if nobody takes these kinds of things seriously?"

"I'm not *that* worried," she replied. "Think about the old man. He has Water magic. How many different times did we depend on that to get us through? Don't you believe in the importance of our Quest? Could we really have got this far if he hadn't changed his *stuff*?"

"I don't know," Jek mused. "But neither do you. And neither does he. I don't think anyone *can* know for sure. That's what bothers me! We're dealing in things too deep for us to understand. We're gambling, and we don't even know what with."

She searched him, though he avoided her gaze. "I want this, Jek. Purpose is certainly something. But there's Will too. Every time you were hurting, I wanted to know how to fix you. With this, I could do it. It would be easy. And it's not just you, Jek. If I'd had Life magic, maybe I could've helped Bugsley."

Now he did look at her. "Bugsley?"

"Yeah," she stammered. "You know. The poor little Mantid that got blown up."

He grabbed her by the shoulders. "Don't do this to yourself! Don't go naming the dead bug! Besides, his name was Meremoth."

"Whatever!" she argued. "He died because I was careless. The fact that the Revenant died too doesn't excuse it. I want to be a healer! I want to have the power to mend people that are hurting... especially if it's my fault they're hurt. And I want to have the power to heal *you*."

"But how much power would that take?" Jek asked. "The doctor didn't have the power to do it. How much Life magic is enough? How much would you dare to take?" He got all teary and unsteady. "How... how would I ever forgive myself if you took too much?"

She started to feel teary too. "I wish you'd trust me, Jek. It's a chance I want to take. It's okay to want things. Haven't you ever thought it was okay to want something?"

"No," he said flatly. "No I haven't."

Audrey was astonished. "Not ever?"

Jek shook his head. "It's not that I haven't wanted things. It's not that there aren't things I still want. I want to find the Knights. I want to be pardoned. I want to go back to doing what I was supposed to be doing all along and not have to bother about what I want – not ever again. It's so much easier to just keep doing what they tell you to. Why imagine anything more for yourself? You'll only be disappointed in the end."

Audrey considered that for a while. She didn't know exactly what made her think of it, but an important childhood memory sprung to mind. She decided to share it.

"Jek, I want to tell you about something that happened when I was a kid, and it's stuck with me ever since. This was back when I was on board the *Cosigner* – the merchant ship I grew up on. We had just caught a great big load of fish in one of our fishing nets. I was helping gather them up. After a little while, I happened to find this one fish that looked really weird to me. I showed it to one of the older sailors, and his eyes got wide and he said he'd never seen a fish like that before. So he went and showed it to an even older sailor. And he had never seen one like it either! Soon everyone on the ship had seen the fish I found. And not one of them, from youngest to oldest, could say what kind of fish it was. It was new to all of them! I never forgot about that."

Jek gave her a searching look. "Was it a very cool fish?"

She laughed. "No! It was extremely ugly. But still! I found something no one had ever seen before. It made me want to be an explorer. Not for the glory of it… or the fame or the recognition. I just liked finding something new. Is there anything really wrong with that?"

He shrugged. "I guess not. Nothing more wrong than that you'll be sad, when you never get to be an explorer. You know how it is. You're given your job, and that's that." He looked out on the Harbor again, long and hard. And he sighed. "This magic thing is a decision they won't make for you, though. And neither will I, if you want it that bad. But please Audrey, be careful! I really couldn't handle it if you became a Revenant. Especially on my account."

Audrey bit her lip. Somehow, his consent made her unsure of herself. "No, Jek. Maybe you're right. Purpose and *stuff* are pretty cosmic things. I think, at the very least, I should probably give it all a bit more thought… before I rush into anything."

He gave her a rather weak smile. "Thanks, Audrey. I think I'd like some time alone to think myself. Like you said, it's been kind of a rough day."

She patted him on the head. "I'll go check on the old man. You do all the thinking you want." And she left him there on the step.

When she came back around to the front, the old man was grumbling to himself by the horse trough, with the *four* flasks on the ground beside him. Evidently the 'haggling' had gone better than expected. She couldn't imagine what he was stewing about, since he must've saved most of his money not getting the Life magic after all. Probably, he still felt like he had been soaked, paying whatever she had asked for the rest. He seemed about that tight-fisted. But he took notice of her, and became quickly sympathetic.

"What's the matter darlin?" he asked. "Ye look all misty in the face."

She sat dejectedly down by the flasks, and after a moment's study, uncorked one. Some juice was probably just what her nerves needed right now. "Jek and I just had our first fight… I think," she said. "Well, except the one we had about the emu a while back. And the time in the Mantid trap. Oh, who am I kidding – I guess we fight all the time." She took a big draw on the grape juice. It was sour, but she didn't think much of it. Especially considering what it was originally made from…

"Sorry to hear it, luv," the old man sighed. "That be part o' marriage, I's told."

She took another healthy swig. "He was sweet about it, really. Much too sweet, and sensible. I wasn't going to let him talk me out of the magic. But now I don't think I have the nerve to go through with it." She drank some more.

The old man winced. "Would it tend to persuade ye back towards yer original resolution if ye knew that the Life magic cost 250 pence all on its lonesome?"

She guzzled some more juice and gave him an odd look. "Surely you wouldn't think of going back in and buying it then?"

"What d'ye mean, 'go back in'? I already done bought it!"

Audrey blinked. "But there's only four flasks here."

"Aye! I done guzzled me juice same as ye're doin' right after I got outta the shop. Seemed all I could do for me own nerves, bein' taken to the cleaners like that. Anyway, I had no way o' knowin' Jek was going to talk ye down!"

She finished her juice, just as a new uncertainty dawned on her. "Was your juice as sour as mine?"

He looked at her. "Weren't sour at all. Sweet and smooth as the genuine article, it was…"

Audrey looked doubtfully at her bottle. "I was sure I hadn't picked up the Water magic. That starts with 'W', I've heard. I know what a 'W' looks like. I regret to admit, I might have skipped ahead once or twice in Bronzegloom's book…"

The old man's jaw went slack. "Dianodes! I forgot – ye can't read!!!" He jumped up and took her bottle, and reading the label, his look of horror only escalated.

"What is it?" Audrey asked, feeling extremely nervous now herself.

He hesitated to answer. "Looks like ye got yer Life magic after all, lass. And ta spare! Ye downed the whole thing!"

Her whole body began to feel swimmy and she broke into a cold sweat. "I don't feel so good," she said.

The old man leapt straight into panic. "Halp! *Halp*!" he shouted, running back for the alchemist shop.

Audrey got at once very dizzy. For just a moment, she was overwhelmed with panic of her own, and she blacked out…

* * *

She woke up in a cot set up in a storage room. Jek, the old man, and even the alchemist were all leaning over her with ghastly expressions. Quickly remembering all that had happened, she shot up with a gasp. She hugged herself, and felt reassuringly corporeal. She saw her legs and moved them. For the moment, at least, she was still herself, and not a Life spirit!

"Audrey, are you alright?" Jek despaired to ask.

"I don't know," she said, still very afraid. "Am I going to turn into a Revenant?"

"You mean a spirit?" the alchemist asked. "No, that danger has passed. If you were going to turn, you would have done so immediately." She sat back, rubbing her chin thoughtfully. "But I can't begin to understand how you've been so fortunate. The concentration I sold you would have been good for a whole troop of medics! I've never heard of anyone taking that much magic elixir and living to tell of it. Perhaps it was a bad batch. If so, I suppose I could refund you ten percent."

"*Ten percent*!?!" the old man exploded. "After ye bold-faced admit to highway robbery?!"

"Oh never mind that, would you?!" Audrey demanded, a bit surprised at herself. She took a quick internal inventory. "I think I feel magical now. I should at least see what I can do, if anything, before you get into another debate about money..."

She looked intently at Jek, getting off the cot and holding out a hand to his leg. "Can I try?" she asked solemnly.

He gulped. "Yes," he answered.

Audrey tried to exert some magic, not really knowing what she was doing. For a moment she just felt very silly. But a second later, there was pale light coming from her hand. She *had* expected Life magic to be white and glowy. But she had thought it would look warmer somehow...

There wasn't much of a peculiar sensation about the use of the magic. It felt immediately naturalized, like she had done it hundreds of times before. It really was part of her now.

"Ow, ow, ow," Jek said. Audrey winced. She saw that 'ow, ow, ow' was certainly an understatement, as pieces of the spike driven through his leg that the previous healer had not reached were suddenly exorcised from the scabbed-over wound.

"In Heck's name!" the alchemist gaped. "It wasn't a bad batch after all! She really took all of that elixir!"

"Gadzooks," the old man agreed in wonder.

When Jek no longer appeared uncomfortable, Audrey relented her magic. At length, he sprung suddenly to his feet. He took some steps back and forth, and they appeared very smooth and effortless.

"My gosh," Jek gasped, and he immediately broke into laughter. "There's not so much as a hitch! You really did it, Audrey! I mean you really did it!"

The old man jumped up and snapped hardily. "By gum, if that don't beat all! Tis a plumb stack o' miracles!" He ran over to the alchemist, getting mockingly up in her face. "And ye didn't make me pay for so much as a swig of that overpriced rotgut what we didn't use! *Har ha-har*!"

"You people are freaks," the alchemist said. "Please get out of my shop."

* * *

They all did leave the shop, practically skipping down to the trough, arms round each other's shoulders, carrying on merrily like a bunch of morons. They had escaped more than their share of grim consequences that day, and things seemed more hopeful than they had in a long time – even to Audrey, who was not used to worrying much anyway. They were still fugitives, of course, and their Quest was not yet complete. Escaping the Harbor could still prove dangerous. But even Jek appeared quite care-free for the moment. He looked happier to Audrey than she had ever seen him.

"What a turn o' luck this turned out to be!" the old man said. "I feels about like we could go face down the Doom Fleet our own selfs, sans any help from Knights and Inquisitors! Reckon Audrey's got enough magic in her ta cure a cannonball strike, *har ha-har!*"

"Well don't go throwing yourself in the path of any cannonballs, all the same," Audrey replied giddily.

"And this proved something else, too," Jek put in.

She looked at him. "What's that?"

"It proves that you're very important. You would have to be, to have all that *stuff* in you!"

He beamed at her as he said so, but Audrey's heart sank. Being 'very important' still filled her with a vague but strong foreboding about the future – about some unknown destiny she didn't want but couldn't avoid. She smiled weakly, not wanting him to see how much his observation had instantly sobered her.

"Aye, well, one important thing at a time," the old man said, and she was glad for the segue. "We gots to refocus on the Quest. Firstly, I better take me recharge. Then we needs to get scarce! We's already made suspicious characters of ourselfs. Best not to hang around long, I warrant."

"Just be sure you don't drink too much, old man," Jek said. "One Revenant scare is enough for today."

"Can do, lad. I don't want to end up no spook no more than the next lubber."

Hardly had the old man plopped down to uncork his Water elixir when something else unexpected happened. They all heard a peculiar but familiar sound – muffled but synthetic. They each looked in turn at the other, and all seemed to realize in sync what they were hearing. Jek threw down his duffle and started digging. Sure enough, it was the radio! There was someone talking at the other end!

Jek urgently fumbled to operate the device. "Bronzegloom, is that you? Please repeat your message! Over."

There was a bit of static. Finally, something clear came through. "Yes, this is definitely Zeph Bronzegloom," said the radio, sounding a bit strange. "You'll excuse me if I don't sound exactly like Zeph Bronzegloom. I, uh, have a cold." Something struck them funny about all of this, but they decided to take it at face value. "Am I speaking to Jek, Audrey, and an unidentified old man? Over."

"Yes, it's us Bronzee," the old man said.

"Okay, good. Where are you now? Have you reached the Harbor? Over."

"Yes," Jek answered. "We're in St. Argonsburg right now."

There was a beat of silence. "Wow," they heard at last. "No kidding? That is swell news. So listen. I happen to be in town right now myself. I need to meet up with you folks. It's very urgent. Can you be at the old Ecre Point warehouse in two hours? I'll be waiting for you there. Over."

They all hesitated, but no one said so much as a word against it. Bronzegloom hadn't steered them wrong before... and he'd saved their bacon more than once. If he needed their help, they owed it to him... even if the Quest would have to wait...

"Okay. We'll be there. Over."

* * *

It was a job finding this 'old Ecre Point warehouse,' but they managed. It was an old coastal storage building not far from a bend in the railway that had come to disuse. It had simply been built too far from shore... and other, larger warehouses had sprung up closer in years since, making this one obsolete. The place had a disheveled, unwholesome look. But if Bronzegloom was in some kind of trouble, it would make for as good a place as any to hide out. Audrey couldn't imagine any other reason someone would want to go there...

As they opened the door with a rusty heave, they heard the startled cawing of mangey old scavenger birds that were poking around nearby. It recalled unsettlingly their old experiences with the songbirds. They slowly made their way inside, seeing that much of the roof had collapsed. At least it wasn't incredibly dark.

"Bronzee!" the old man called out. "Where the devil are ye!? We's here to halp!"

"Don't shout!" Jek whispered harshly.

"Too late, done already did," the old man said.

They looked all around, and found no sign at all of Bronzegloom, or of anyone. The abandoned warehouse seemed abandoned indeed. At last, Audrey had a thought. "Try the radio again," she suggested. Jek quickly drew it out.

"Bronzegloom, we're at the warehouse... where are you? Over."

"What was that?" the old man gasped.

"What was what?" Audrey asked.

"Don't tell me me old ears was the only ones what heard it! The radio! I heard the other end o' the radio!"

"Where did it come from?"

The old man pointed shakily. "From over there..."

They looked where he pointed, and suddenly someone they hadn't noticed before lowered a newspaper from in front of his face. He was a big, sturdy specimen of the Jackal

People with a distinguished look, his face stern with blanched fur. He folded the newspaper and stuck it in an inner pocket, then tugged his trench coat as he walked their way. He puffed a long series of bubbles from the pipe in his jowl.

"Who are you?" Jek asked, horrified.

"I'm a friend, if you'll believe it," said the Mesomela, retiring his pipe.

"And, iffen we won't?" the old man challenged.

"In that case, I brought this," the big canine man replied, producing a fancy new pistol from his coat. It held them all in motionless fear for some seconds as he approached.

"What do you want with us?" Jek asked at length. "What did you do with Bronzegloom?"

"All I did was talk to him. And that's all I intend to do with you." He gave them a surprisingly sympathetic look. "Although it's really not me that needs to talk to you. I'm just an intermediary."

"Tis mighty tedious, tryin' to keep up with yer yarn!" the old man said defiantly. "We don't even know who ye are, and ye's holdin' us up fer another mystery man! Who is he? Where do we gots to go to talk to him?"

"He's already here," the Mesomela explained. "He keeps a secret office in the basement. I can lead you there."

"Sounds sketchy, I says. But I suppose ye don't intend to give us any choice."

"I'm afraid not. I wouldn't be doing my job if I did. It was a great stroke of luck that I got hold of you when you were already in town. I can't just let you get away now."

"Alright," the old man sighed. "Lead the way."

The Mesomela gestured with the pistol and cocked his head. "You first."

* * *

The big Jackal led them to an obscure doorway that concealed a dark flight of stairs. As they cautiously filed in and down, a haunting but spirited melody echoed up to meet them. At the bottom of the stair was a long hall with many side rooms, all lightless and spooky. But at the very end of the hall was a bright room, starkly white and pristine looking in the distance. The music swelled and raced, even as they grew slower and more hesitant to meet whatever was ahead of them.

"Come on, now," the Mesomela snipped under his breath. They were slowing down so much that it was beginning to make him anxious.

Finally, recognizing the inevitability of it all, Audrey started walking full-clip, and the other two silently reached the same verdict a moment after. So it was they reached the one room in the entire warehouse that was well-kept. The walls were blanched in white light that filtered in from glass paneling high above. The furniture was all chic and modern and white-on-black. The whole room had a synthetic feel about it of harsh monochrome. In one corner, an elegant Mesomela woman sat with her legs crossed, scrawling on paper with a speed and aggression only matched by the hardy tune in the air. And just off-center, about twenty feet from the doorway, they found the source of the music. Another large Mesomela, husky but formidably debonair, was stooped over a grand piano, undaunted as he pushed the instrument to the limits of its performance. He took no notice of them, but kept keying away with effortless abandon. Audrey didn't feel afraid anymore. It seemed impossible to her that anyone who played the piano that well could be a villain.

"Your playing... it's beautiful," Audrey felt compelled to admit.

"It's extraordinary," Jek put in.

"Yes it is," the Mesomela said gravely, his eyes never leaving the keys. After a few more riveting seconds, he brought the whole thing to a thrilling coda, and the music passed at last with a prolonged moment of silence, as if they all mourned its sudden departure.

"*Hmph*," the old man protested at length. "Musical virtuosity aside, I's gettin' plug tired o' all these theatrics. Let's have us some answers. First off, who are ye?"

"No one too objectionable, I hope," the Jackal began. "I'm your attorney. Or rather, I'm Jek and Audrey's attorney." He finally looked at them, and with a sincere aspect he rose and offered them his hand. "Horus Templar; pleased to meet you."

"Charmed, I'm sure," Audrey said, shaking his hand.

"And these are my associates, Artimus Mallard and Miss Deborah Boulevard. Thanks for bringing them, Art. I think we can do without the pistol now."

"Gladly, and gladly," Mallard agreed, concealing the gun.

"Deborah Boulevard?!" Jek asked. "Surely not *the* Deborah Boulevard?! The world's most famous secretary! You're a living legend, ma'am!"

"You're too kind," Deborah laughed.

"Well, I for one ain't tooked in yet by any o' this," the old man said, fists planted on his hips. "If ye're an attorney, then what gives with this secret subterranean office?"

Mr. Templar grinned evasively. "Well, quite often my line of work calls for a fair bit of discretion. It's the rare person who would risk consulting me openly. You see... I'm a public defender."

"*Eulgh*," Jek grimaced, unable to contain his revulsion.

"My *official* office is on a train that swings by every so often," Horus went on, unphased. "But if I see clients at all outside of prison, it tends to be here, away from prying eyes and ears. Do you have any more questions for me? If not, I certainly have plenty for you."

"I'm still trying to wrap my head around how you're our attorney," Audrey admitted. "We aren't on trial. We haven't even been arrested yet."

Horus allowed himself a single, ironic laugh. "Yes, well, ideally the system would work that way. But it doesn't. Not yet. As a matter of fact, you *are* on trial."

Mallard walked up and slipped his rolled-up newssheet out of his jacket to hand to Audrey. "It's in all the papers," he told her.

She waved it off. "No thanks; I can't read... yet."

"Let me see that," Jek said, grabbing and quickly unfurling the paper. Silently, the old man came over and started tussling with Jek for the paper. "Hey," Jek protested, "what are you doing?"

"I wants to see too," the old man whined. "Does it mention anything about *me*, lad? Answer me that much, at least."

"I can answer that," Horus said. "I'm afraid you don't make any of the headlines. The Czarina wants to make an example of Jek and Audrey's case. We've discussed your involvement in open court, but the papers know better than to make any mention of the kidnapping. Though of course it is no excuse, they don't want to risk inspiring any public sympathy."

The old man folded his arms and kicked the ground dejectedly. "Figgers," he said.

"If it helps," Horus went on, "I for one am immensely curious about your part in this story. In fact, if I am to represent these two to the best of my ability, then I'll need you to tell me everything. I must have the whole thread, from start to finish."

At this, the old man seemed suddenly elated. "Well in that case, Mr. fancy-duds, ye better get comfortable and maybe grab a snack, on accounta that's ezactly what ye're gonna get..."

* * *

The old man went through his whole spiel, from his vainglorious escapades out of Meatgrinder Bay all the way up to the present moment. Audrey and Jek butted in more than a few times to moderate for the sake of accuracy, or at least to prevent him taking too much credit for certain things. Horus asked nothing, said nothing, but remained obviously and intensely focused throughout. When it was through, he turned to his secretary.

"Did you get all that, Deborah?" he asked.

"I did," she said, her pen already hanging motionless over the notebook. "But I had to be inventive with the spelling."

Horus grinned and nodded, then returned to his clients. "This has certainly been an eye-opener. I concede that your Quest is indeed noble, if in fact any Doom Fleet is to be found in Meatgrinder Bay, as you say."

"Ye can bet yer boots on it," the old man chimed.

"Yet as luck would have it, I only wear shoes," Horus replied. "In any case, I admit I'm at somewhat of a loss as to how I should advise you. The trial is certainly not going in your favor, as you can well imagine. But regardless of that, as an officer of the court, it is my duty to compel you to turn yourselves in and face arbitration. And I believe, if you care about justice, that is exactly what you should do. Your trial so far has been a sham – a truncation of true due process. Without you present to plead, to confer with me or to accept the judgement passed on you, I would not consider that any final verdict could be fairly reached." He paused, standing and turning to rest a hand on his grand piano. "However... that is only my opinion, and not one that I'm making much headway with in court." He looked back at them. "And there are external matters to consider. Your Quest is not yet complete. I am bound by my oath to implore you to surrender yourselves to the authorities... and now I have done so. But I'll take no action beyond that to hinder you, if you would prefer to press on. And in spite of my duties and obligations, I believe you *should* continue. If what you allege about Despotopia is true, the world may depend on your finding the Knights." He searched each of their faces. "So there you have it. I have advised you both to stay and to go. The choice must be yours. What do you intend to do?"

Audrey and Jek looked at each other, deliberating silently. "We're going to complete the Quest," Jek said.

"Good," Horus smiled. "Then let us see what can be done to that effect. Art, you have a nice little fishing boat tied up in the Harbor, if I'm not mistaken? Why don't you show the old man where it is?"

Art Mallard huffed. "So we're in the business of aiding and abetting fugitives now, are we?"

"*We*?" Horus joshed him. "It's *your* boat you'd be showing him, Art. But you aren't thinking this thing through very clearly. The old man is not on trial for anything. He hasn't even been identified yet. And, if you were to show him where your boat is tied up, you can't very well control what he does with that knowledge. Like, say, come back for Jek and Audrey here so that the three of them can steal it and sail for Roemnar."

"That's one shaky escape clause, in my book," Mallard said. He sighed. "But what the Heck. I'll bite. Come on, old man."

"Works fer me," the old man said, and the two of them departed at once.

But once they were quite gone, Horus Templar looked intensely at Jek and Audrey again. "I do have a few more questions for the two of you. The case resumes tomorrow, and I need all the help I can get." He turned squarely to Audrey. "Firstly, my dear, could you tell me what country you were born in? We've been trying very tirelessly to determine that."

Audrey blanched and pursed her lips. "I don't know," she answered.

Horus smiled and nodded. "That's stupendous," he said. "Better even than I'd hoped."

"How so?" Jek asked.

"Well, it's all a matter of casting shadows of a doubt. If we can't determine anything significant about her identity prior to the citizenship she was granted here, then we cannot be entirely sure that she doesn't have diplomatic immunity."

"*Diplomatic immunity*?" Audrey repeated. "What's that?"

Horus stroked his jowls, searching for a concise explanation. "Its basically a thing that lets you do whatever you want and get away with it, because you're from somewhere else."

"Sounds cool," Audrey replied.

"Yes," Horus snickered. "It will be very good for you indeed. The state may well be forced to turn itself inside-out to determine your nativity before they can rightly execute you for dereliction of duty." He turned to Jek. "No such luck for you. Sorry."

Jek sighed. "That's alright."

"I do have a question for you though," Horus went on. "About the Dronehood Clerk that delivered your inventory the day of the crime."

"About the Clerk?" Jek said, incredulous. "I... I don't remember anything very well... I only saw him for a few seconds. I think his name was Baegulgog. Beside that, I've got nothing."

"Maybe not *nothing*. You might be surprised what I can make use of," Horus said, "at least, in forming some suspicions I already have. Can you remember what his voice sounded like? Was it midtone and indistinct?"

Jek thought for a moment, making a face. "No, not at all. His voice was low, and kind of grumbly, in friendly way... if that makes any sense."

"Did you observe him adjust his hat at any time?" Horus continued.

Jek searched back again. "Not that I recall." He thought some more. "He did sort of bow when I greeted him at the door. If he was going to have to adjust his hat, it would have been then. But it stayed in place well enough on its own, for as much as I can remember..."

"Splendid," Horus said. "Absolutely splendid."

"If you say so," Jek said. "I can't imagine how it helps anything."

"Oh, it does. You may be sure of it."

Horus strode across the room. "It will be some time before Art and the old man return. Perhaps you two would care to join Miss Boulevard and myself in a light repast? We have some mature meat we can share with you."

"Raw and spoiled, you mean," Audrey said. "I know how you guys eat. I think I'll pass, but thank you anyway."

"Same here," Jek was quick to put in.

"Suit yourselves," Horus replied. He had retrieved and filled two glasses, and returned to them. "Have a drink, at least," he said.

"Thank you," they both said, taking the glasses.

As they sipped, he watched them gravely, not at once returning to the kitchenette. "There is one last thing I must impress upon the two of you, now that I have sent the old man away. You should know that he has not been entirely honest with you."

They paused, waiting with bated breath for some further elaboration. "What do you mean?" Jek asked at length.

"I wish I could say," Horus replied. "My instincts tell me that there is something in his story, prior to kidnapping the two of you, which he has altered greatly... though I can't puzzle out exactly what. I must advise that you be cautious of him, going forward. But I'm afraid that is quite the best I can do..."

Legal Gymnastics

"Get in, get your conviction, and get out. Or else."

- Attorney Bernie Samstien of Anubican Barristers International, *Prosecutor's Field Manual*

At the beckoning of Vice-Vizier Senahktenre, order fell over the courtroom like a heavy woolen blanket. "Court is now in session," he announced. So the case of Jek and Audrey vs. the State resumed precisely as prescribed on Monday, the next.

Horus reclined, feeling a sort of resigned sense of serenity. But it was not the resignation of surrender. The days spent out of court had provided him with a strategy at last, and even a providential meeting with his clients-at-large. He had a way forward. Even so, the prosecution's case was ongoing. Hamilton Blackforest still had the prerogative. And as far as Horus could figure from the list of witnesses, he planned to spend a good deal of time introducing testimony that would reveal the actions and movements of the defendants over the past weeks. He knew that Blackforest intended to bring to light the alleged threat of a Despotopian Doom Fleet, as they had discussed the week before. Horus didn't feel that such information could hurt his defense. If anything, it might prove helpful before the end. Especially if Senahktenre were to pick up on Blackforest's ulterior motivations. Horus expected the old Vice-Vizier would be no more tolerant of Blackforest using the case to address side-issues than he had been with Horus on the last court date. Thus, he reasoned that the best thing for him to do through much of the morning testimony was to simply allow Blackforest to proceed unhindered... and maybe damage his own case in the process.

But there was one item for him to address right out of the gate...

"Let Postal Squire Raphael de Lafayette be recalled to the stand for cross examination," Senahktenre declared.

Horus rose. "Your Honor," he began, "in light of further investigation, the defense no longer has any questions for Squire de Lafayette at this time."

The old judge gave Horus an icy squint, and his snout twitched. "Very well," he said at length. "So much for the lengthy cross. The prosecution will call its next witness."

Now Blackforest stood. "I call town cryer Fezwick to the stand."

* * *

Horus sat in silence as Blackforest paraded a score of witnesses – random commoners from the Wading Isle, all. They were brought forward to corroborate each others' testimony that the defendants had made a public address on their island, warning all gathered of the imminent threat of a Doom Fleet. Their testimonies all agreed, and each of them seemed still bound by a spell of great fear, almost as if they had seen the Fleet for themselves. Horus set his jaw and shook his head in bewilderment many times as the prosecution's case unfolded before him. However far afield Hamilton was getting by introducing all of this, the fright in all the witnesses was so oddly genuine and compelling that he was not entirely sure he could have found it within himself to object to Blackforest's line of questioning, even if it were actually in his interest to do so. It *demanded* his attention, though he knew it all already. And it seemed to have the same effect on Senahktenre...

At last, Blackforest moved on to a different breed of witness. "I call Lady Schenburkreiga to the stand," he announced. Horus looked back. He saw a bailiff escort a darkly attired, fierce-looking little woman with a gas mask, tightly pulled-back hair and glasses with loupes to the front of the court. He carefully undid her handcuffs, then attached them to the witness stand, so that she could sit with her hands restrained in front of her.

Blackforest closed in on his witness – a bit more cautiously than usual, it seemed. He declined to rest an arm on the stand with the chains and manacles.

"Now, Ms. Schenburkreiga," he began, "please tell the court your nation of origin."

"I am Despotopian," she said. "Zhis should be obvious." Dark vapor poured from her mask.

"What is your profession?" Hamilton asked.

She was contemptuously loath to answer. "I am employed in international espionage," she finally admitted. There were murmurings among all onlookers.

"Order," Senahktenre cautioned.

"You and your husband were on the Wading Isle, and present for the speech the defendants gave about the Doom Fleet, is that correct?" Blackforest continued.

"Ve vere zhere, yes."

"I understand that you were injured the night before."

"I vas. Zhat does not speak to zee verity of zee defendants' speech, however. It vas not zhey who injured me."

Blackforest permitted himself a sharp smile. "Ah, but you did confront them, didn't you? I have another witness who will testify that an entire skirmish broke out between yourself, your husband and the defendants."

"But you cannot corroborate his testimony. Und you cannot do anyzhing beside insinuate zhat any such fight had to vith my profession, or zhis supposed 'Doom Fleet'." She leaned forward. "Und I know you have no right to question me in zhese vays. Zhese events have no bearing on zee crime of zee defendants vhatsoever."

Blackforest looked at once deflated. He was dealing with a witness that was too savvy of the legal system to be cornered.

"I am afraid she's right, Mr. Blackforest," Senahktenre admitted rather weakly. Horus felt he looked to be in even more feeble shape than he had been a few days ago. And he suspected the judge was very interested in the prosecution's line of questioning – just as everyone present was. He hated to be forced to admit that Blackforest was out of line.

But the prosecutor was a force to be reckoned with. He wouldn't be dissuaded so quickly. "I have yet to hear any objection to this line of questioning from the defense..." he said, shooting Horus a stern look. Horus more or less returned the look.

"The defense has no objection," he said. "As far as I'm concerned, the prosecutor may introduce as much about the exploits of the defendants as he wishes."

Senahktenre pursed his lips under his long jowels. "It seems you have the defense's leave to continue, Mr. Blackforest. But you must try to prove some relevance."

"I intend to, your Honor, with my next witness," Blackforest answered. He turned again to Lady Schenburkreiga. "But let us have this one answer from you, then, and skip all the insinuation and guesswork. *Is there* a secret Despotopian Doom Fleet?"

Silent anticipation drew the breath out of everyone in the court.

"You are inquiring about a state-level conspiracy, are you not?" Lady Schenburkreiga asked in return. "As a Despotopian national, vould I not be incriminating mineself to answer? Vould I not be testifying against mine own husband?" She looked past Blackforest to Oberführer Klinkofhenschmidt, who was seated between two very large bailiffs. He returned her a glinting look of great pride. "I am niezher required to testify against mineself, nor permitted to testify against mine spouse. I refuse to answer."

"But you do not *deny* the existence of such a Fleet?" Blackforest demanded, now clutching the railing between them tightly in both clawed hands.

"Nor do I confirm it," Schenburkreiga said, sitting back. "You vill not learn anyzhing from me."

Blackforest stared icily. Finally, he recoiled, withdrawing to his seat in defeat. "No further questions," he said.

Senahktenre looked quite troubled. "Does the defense wish to cross-examine this witness?" he asked, almost sounding as if he was pleading with Horus to try his own hand at pressing the Despotopian lady for answers.

Horus stood gravely. "No, your Honor," he regretted to admit. "The defense has no questions at this time."

The bailiff began decoupling Schenburkreiga from the stand.

Senahktenre sighed. "The prosecution will call its next witness."

Blackforest came to his feet again, and he and Schenburkreiga exchanged deadly glances as she was escorted past him, back to the deep reaches of the courtroom. "I call Zeph Bronzegloom to the stand," he said.

Horus turned to watch Mr. Bronzegloom rise and come forward. He understood that this was an interesting move for Blackforest. Bronzegloom was, in many ways, a great witness to have on hand for a show-trial, being a controversial celebrity type. However, he had one major flaw that made him a liability to the state's case...

Just as the court officer was about to swear Bronzegloom in, Blackforest unexpectedly stopped them up. "Before we go any further," he said, "do I hear any objections from the defense concerning the calling of this witness? You have been rather mum so far today, Mr. Templar."

Horus stood up. "No objections. But I admit I am surprised at you, Hamilton. It is highly irregular to call a known heretic to give testimony in court."

Zeph Bronzegloom snickered nervously, adjusting his dunce cap.

"It is indeed, Horus," Blackforest agreed, reaching into his suit jacket and retrieving several papers. "That's why I took the time to get these notarized waivers. You will find three separate waivers, each from an Inquisitor, attesting that Mr. Bronzegloom is mentally stable enough to testify."

Horus obliged Hamilton's thoroughness by examining the waivers. "These seem to be in good order," he said. "I see that I have no grounds for objection... even if I had intended to object. Please proceed."

"Thank you," Blackforest grinned, far too pleased with himself.

Bronzegloom was sworn in and took the stand. Blackforest was his tough and confident self again as he circled to the stand. "Now Mr. Bronzegloom, there hardly seems any need in my asking what it is you do for a living."

"Probably not," Bronzegloom nodded. "I do what I do, and most everybody knows it."

"Right you are, sir," Blackforest said. "Could you please begin by explaining, then, your involvement in this case?"

"Well, let's see, how best to put it?" His eyes rolled up to the ceiling as he stroked his chin. "Firstly, I guess I'd better cover my bases and say that the defendants sought *me* out. The old man knew me from when I did what I was doing before I started doing what I do... if you follow me." He waved dismissively with both hands, averting all eyes. "Now I didn't willingly assist them in anything *knowing* that they were fugitives – not at least until I was already in too deep to turn back. I'm already on probation over this whole misunderstanding about the color spectrum, you see, and..."

"...Well, never mind, Mr. Bronzegloom," Blackforest stopped him, and it was well that he did. The witness seemed a very nervous personality, and given to running at the mouth. Horus was left immediately with the impression that Zeph Bronzegloom was the kind of man who would choose to count backward from a thousand to arrive at the number two, if you let him.

"The state has already granted you full immunity for your involvement with the defendants, as I have assured you," Blackforest went on. "There is no need to further excuse yourself. Please confine your answers to my questions."

"Right, right," Bronzegloom agreed.

"Now, please tell the court what the defendants and the unidentified old man approached you about."

Bronzegloom waxed conspicuously thoughtful again. "They wanted to know about magic, at first," he said. "Well, they expected a lot of things, really. I fed them, I put them up for the night, I helped them fight the Despotopians, I..."

"...As to that fight," Blackforest once again interjected. "What did you understand to be the *reason* behind the confrontation between the defendants and the Despotopians?"

"The old man had knowledge of a Doom Fleet that Despotopia was building in secret, as many have already testified. He was onto them... and they were after him because they were onto him about being onto them."

"I take it you were quite convinced by the story the old man gave you about the Doom Fleet, then? You must have been, if you helped them fight."

"My gosh, yes. If I had any room for doubt, the way those Despotopians behaved took care of it in a hurry," Bronzegloom said, pointing repeatedly and accusingly back at Schenburkreiga and Klinkofhenschmidt. "They were absolutely determined to kill the old man and the defendants. They almost killed me too! And they made all kinds of horrible, vague threats that seemed to portend the end of the world as we know it. It was scary."

"Very good, Mr. Bronzegloom," Blackforest commended his witness. "And, what other insight did the defendants seek from you? What else did they ask you about, related to the alleged Doom Fleet?"

"They wanted to know if I knew where the Knights of the Indigo Lodge were holed-up these days," Bronzegloom answered.

There were hushed sounds of astonishment in the court again.

"Order," Senahktenre barked, but with little strength in his voice.

"The defendants were pursuing a Noble Quest, then, is that it?" Blackforest pressed Bronzegloom.

"That's exactly what they were doing. The old man knew nobody would believe his story. Nobody important, anyway... or at least, nobody *more* important than me. He felt the Knights alone would be willing to look into it. Then and only then could something be done about the Fleet itself. He made all of that very clear."

"Thank you, Mr. Bronzegloom," Blackforest said, taking a step back. "I have no further questions."

"But I have one, Mr. Blackforest," Senahktenre announced. "You claimed that you intended to connect relevance to your line of questioning with this witness. But if you have demonstrated *anything* of relevance to this case – with *any* of the witnesses you have called so far today – then I'm afraid it is still lost on me. What have you achieved here?"

"I intended only to firmly establish the *motive* of the defendants, your Honor," Blackforest answered, "and I believe I have done so. It is patently obvious that the defendants are pursuing a Noble Quest to undermine a secret Despotopian conspiracy – a conspiracy that, whether true or not, they honestly believe is at work, as do many residents of the Wading Isle."

Senahktenre sighed and rubbed his temples with his ears pinned back and his eyes shut. His weariness was not just apparent, it was oppressive. "That does seem patently obvious now, yes. Though I remain unsure why we needed endure many hours of testimony to establish *motive*, when you yourself said, on the previous court date, that motive was of little need to the state's case. Let the defense cross-examine this witness," he waved dismissively.

"I have no questions," Horus said, but he resolved to twist the knife, while Senahktenre was weak and Blackforest was in bad standing. "I feel rather as if the prosecution has been doing my job for me. However, in light of the agreed-upon obviousness of the defendants' Quest, I once again urge the court to consider suspending the case until the final fruits of their efforts can be weighed."

Senahktenre surprised everyone by coming to his feet with a snarl. "What is the game here?!" he asked. "Have you all completely lost your minds?" He focused on Horus. "Your insolence astounds me. I cautioned you that your efforts to derail this trial could cost you your life... and still you persist! And *you*!" He turned and pointed at Blackforest. "You were putting on a very fine case indeed, until today dawned! I admit, the testimony of your witnesses thus far has been captivating... even deeply foreboding. But we are *not* here to unravel the mystery of some doomsday plot! You have clouded the issue at hand just as flagrantly as Mr. Templar, though I daresay less boldly. *His* trickery, I could anticipate, at least. But I expected much better from *you*!"

Finally, Senahktenre's rage gave way again to his great fatigue, and he collapsed heavily to his seat. "I have spoken my peace. But I caution you both – do not push me any further! Let us be on with the case, and have at it again with the proper object in mind... lest heads should roll. Am I perfectly clear?"

"Yes, your Honor," Blackforest said.

"Good. Then call your next witness."

Blackforest set his sharp jaw. "I have no other witnesses. The state rests its case, your Honor."

"Very well. Then we are indeed finished with one irrelevance." He turned back to face Horus. "Does council intend to present a defense?"

"I do, your Honor," Horus said.

"Let the defense call its first witness."

Horus looked back over all the folk gathered in the courtroom. "I call Clerk Third Class Wowserchum to the stand." A Dronehood Clerk lofted into the air and floated lazily to the front of the court...

* * *

This was the moment Horus had been waiting for all morning. With this one witness, he would be sure to exasperate the state... and perhaps better yet, the judge too, it seemed. It would take only a few questions...

But as he approached Clerk Wowserchum, he recognized something else – an opportunity to lay groundwork for a point he would render later. Assuming there *would be* a later. There was still the chance, however remote, that the prosecution may be well ahead of him, and that all of this was about to blow up in his face. But that was a chance well worth taking...

"Mr. Wowserchum," Horus addressed his witness, tugging out the cuff of one of his sleeves. "Before we begin, I could not help noticing that your Clerk hat is slightly askew. Perhaps you would care for a moment to adjust it?"

"Oh, yes, thank you," Wowserchum said, patting the hat back and forth into just the right alignment with his tentacles.

"It must be quite the balancing act, trying to keep that little hat atop your body," Horus mused. "Why not use something to fix it in place? Something like... *glue*, perhaps?"

"Aha!" Wowserchum exclaimed. "Hat glue might be just fine for a Sowür Canpattel. But I am of the Berlie Beirel Dominion, and we do not hold with luxuries."

"Suit yourself," Horus said. He could already hear Blackforest shifting in his seat, preparing some sort of objection to this futile conversation he was carrying on with the Clerk. But though no one could yet know it, Horus had already laid his foundation, and was ready to proceed with his actual line of questions...

"Now, could you please tell the court the nature of your association with the defendants?"

"Yes, I can," Wowserchum agreed, flashing brightly behind the stand as he recalled the occasion. "I was the attendant Clerk when the lady defendant – Audrey – was being processed for Jast-Madiiran citizenship."

"Very good," Horus said, whirling to his desk and accepting a few papers from Deborah. He returned to the bench with them in a flash. "Here is a copy of her citizenship papers. Would you please examine them and tell me if they are complete?"

Wowserchum took the papers and rifled through them. "This is her complete certification."

"Now, I notice there is no mention of prior citizenship."

"No, there isn't. But that is to be expected," Wowserchum said, handing the papers back to Horus. "There are no fields for such information."

"I see," Horus said, resting a finger pensively under his snout. "But of course, this certification was filled out only earlier this year. Yet the defendant Audrey is estimated to be around her twentieth year of age. Can a birth certificate be produced?"

"When your investigator approached me about this matter, I checked for such a certificate myself. But there is none."

"Indeed, so you have told me," Horus nodded. "In fact, to your knowledge, there is no record of any kind pertaining to her identity before she became a citizen here?"

"Not that I am aware of. Not, at least, within the records of this country... or *any* in the Archipelago. I have been in correspondence with the central Clerical Dronehood of Berlberi offices across Idriulthoronta concerning this. None have found any record of Audrey."

"Now, think back carefully, Mr. Wowserchum. When you were processing her citizenship, did the defendant ever mention to you where she was from?"

"She did not. In fact, she could not have."

Horus paused, grabbing the railing with both hands. "Why is that?"

"She told me, in no uncertain terms, that she did not *know* where she was from."

Horus withdrew, and began to pace in open court, hands folded behind his back. "Now we come to the defense's point. With the knowledge – or perhaps more bluntly – the *lack* of knowledge available to us, is there any way that we can be sure, beyond any shadow of a doubt, that the defendant Audrey does not have some form or other of diplomatic immunity status?"

"No," Wowserchum answered. "Without knowing anything for certain about her origin prior to coming to this country, I could not swear for or against any such status."

Hubbub prevailed in the court once again.

"That will be all; thank you, Mr. Wowserchum," Horus said, and returned to his seat. He permitted himself only the briefest glimpse of Blackforest, who stood wide-eyed, open-mouthed and seething. "You may cross-examine," he announced.

"Order!" Senahktenre demanded. "The attorneys will approach the bench at once!"

Horus doubled-back quickly. Hamilton came forward only with great reluctance.

"Now, Mr. Blackforest," Senahktenre sputtered, "you see that while you were busy brooding about Despotopia, the defense has not been idle." With much quavering, his very old jowels managed to work up out of the way of his yellow fangs. "The court must concede that, in the case of the woman, we would be out of order to reach any verdict, before we can be assured of proper authorization to pass sentencing. Now you advise me... *how can this matter be resolved*?"

"Your Honor," Blackforest said, in calm but discrete tones. "I will make an appeal to the Czarina's office. I believe she would be most willing to waive any possible claim the defendant might have to diplomatic immunity."

"Wouldn't that leave the Czarina personally accountable for the consequences, if we did execute someone under such protection?" Horus asked.

Blackforest gave him a sharp look. "You know as well as anyone that your client doesn't have any immunity status. We're talking about a shadow of a shadow of a doubt here! The chances are astronomical. I can't believe the Czarina would balk in the least at having to accept that accountability."

"Then see to it you get the Czarina's waiver!" Senahktenre commanded with clenched fists. He breathed most heavily for several seconds, with the attorneys looking on. "We will hear no more today," the judge continued at length. "I tire of all this. And there seems little use in continuing until the prosecution is once again prepared. Let us reconvene in one week. *One week*, Blackforest! There will be no excusing yourself, if the waiver cannot be had by then."

"I will have it, your Honor," Blackforest said, confident.

"Good." With effort, Senahktenre stood. "Court is adjourned. It will reconvene on Monday, the next."

The gavel struck.

* * *

The people filed out of the court, all looking rather shell-shocked. Senahktenre was helped to his study by a bailiff. Blackforest and Templar watched the old judge until the door was shut behind him.

"I think you nearly killed him, Horus," Blackforest said, folding his arms.

"*We* nearly killed him, you mean," Horus replied.

Blackforest snickered venomously. "I suppose you're right."

"It could work in our favor, you know," Horus went on. "I don't think he has much fight left in him."

There was a moment of silence. "Still thinking about that deal we discussed?" Hamilton asked.

"As a matter of fact, yes."

Blackforest gave Horus a very steely look. "Then let me ask you something: do you really think you could blow the lid off this Despotopian conspiracy?"

"I am positive I can," Horus answered, perfectly assured. Though Blackforest didn't seem to take him seriously at once.

"That would sure be something. I gave it everything I had, and came up short."

Horus grinned. "Maybe I know something you don't."

Blackforest appeared quite doubtful, but then he returned the smile and shook his head, sizing his old nemesis up. "You really are a piece of work sometimes. But what the Heck, Horus. Maybe another week will soften ol' Senahktenre a little more. Or maybe he'll feel much better and have both our heads. But if you're *that* sure you can clinch this thing, I'll do what I can to back you up. How can I help you?"

Horus turned, watching as the court recorder packed up his little typewriter. "I'd rather not say as yet," he replied. "But whatever happens, just follow my lead."

The Shogun and the Shadow

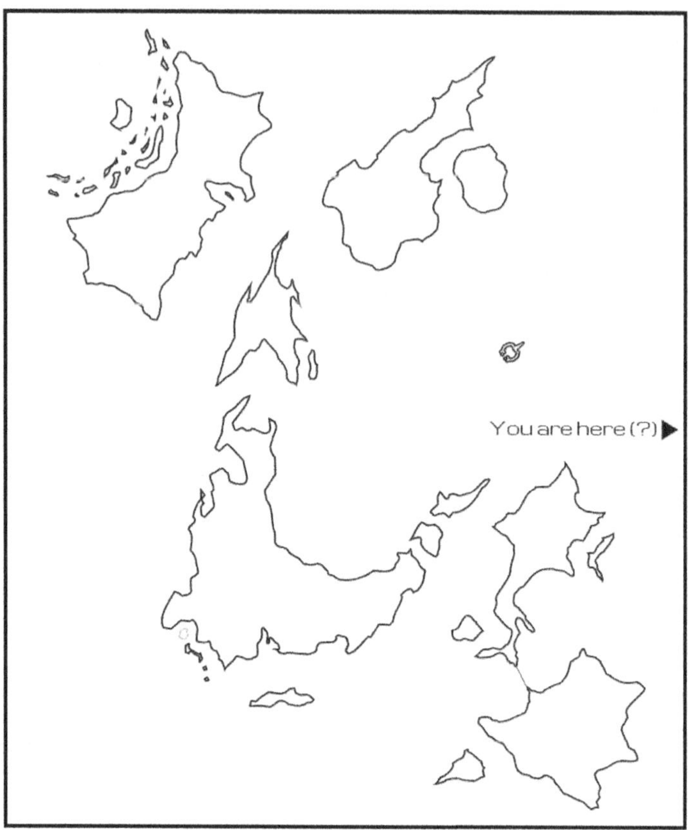

"The Inquisitor is accountable. He is accountable for the world and everyone in it. But above all he is accountable for himself."

- Shaikonnen, *Ascetic Disciplines, 4th Edition*

Baegulgog had to check himself starting to hum aloud again. He had an abundance of nervous energy, there in the dark brig with very little to count. He kept fretting about his poor papers, moldering in his duffle bag. He could lay aside only a few at a time to dry under the overturned cot in his cell. There was nothing else on-hand to apply flattening pressure. Baegulgog hated to think of the papers ending up with permanently curled corners...

After hours of little more than the occasional sound of footfalls on the wooden planking, suddenly he noted a rapid escalation in the tumult above deck. The pirates were agitated about something. It didn't take long to guess what. Calls to furl the sails and cast out mooring lines made it obvious. The scoundrels had reached their secret harbor! Baegulgog and Parissah would soon be taken into the fastness of a pirate base. And not merely a pirate base, but the base of the Ivory Hyssops – a truly infamous Band. They would be brought before the Shogun, just as Captain Herringbone had taunted. It was a grim thought, which he had done all he could to forestall thinking about. But now they were faced with it...

Baegulgog feared for himself. He had never enjoyed dying in an obviously unpleasant way. But the pit he felt in his soul was really for Parissah, his friend. She could come to a *very* bad end here... and a permanent one. That was as unhappy a thought as any he had known...

Unexpectedly, he heard her voice whispering to him weakly. "Oh, Baegulgog," she gasped. "It seems we have reached our doom at last."

"I fear you may be right, madam," Baegulgog replied, finding no words of comfort. He wished he had prepared some.

"I am so very sorry that our association has had to end in this unfortunate way," she continued, sounding very troubled indeed. She sounded quite as sorrowful as she had along the molten paths of Tophthera, when she had confided in him the dark truth about her father's fate, and her part in it. Baegulgog was cut to the quick by her voice. He had already seen her courage in the face of many dangers. It was heartbreaking to hear it fail now.

"Come-come, dear lady!" Baegulgog said, trying to rally some hope as he gripped the bars of his cell in his arm-tentacles. "You are not dead yet!"

"Yet it will not be long now," she sighed. "My heart has boded this for some time."

He tried to cut in with some other appeal, but she began again before he could arrive at anything...

"I am not prepared to die, Baegulgog," she whimpered openly, and it broke his spirit. "I do not fear it. But there is so much more I meant to do before I should face it. So much more I *should* have done, and been through with so very long ago..."

He struggled for something... for *anything* reassuring to say...

"Think not of duties left unfinished, if it grieves you, madam – I beg you! Doubtless you have completed many great tasks in your day. Find solace in them! And do not count yourself among the dead while you yet live, whatever your heart may forebode. You may still find yourself bringing peace to the land of Maenea, and unraveling the threat of the Glowy Lady." He managed a half-hearted chuckle. "Perhaps you shall even catch those silly stewards of yours!"

Now she grabbed the bars between them – he heard the clack of her long nails on the metal. "My friend... you must hear me speak my peace now," she said, her whispering now urgent as well as distressed. "Those errands will fall to others. It is not those that oppress me. I have left something else undone. A burden of guilt I cannot bear to withhold another moment! Someone must know. It falls to you, Baegulgog. You *must* know, before it is found out anyway. It is the only thing I can do to clear my conscience..."

"What is it, madam? Whatever troubles you so?"

Before she could make answer, blinding light flew into the dungeon, and pirates after. They came in sneering droves to extract the prisoners. Whatever it was Parissah meant to say, the opportunity had passed. They were bound and strongarmed back onto the deck. And many precious papers were left behind...

As his sight adjusted to the outside world, Baegulgog beheld the redding sun in the northwest, the calm sky and ocean awash in colors too vibrant. The long dark in the cell, and the harrowing night that led up to it, had made a dim recollection of any color beside his own pale blue luminescence. It was a beautiful evening.

However, the sight was also very grave. A pirate fleet of great strength was marshaled here, with high-masted ships clustered all about. The island – whatever island it was – lay before their ship to the east, rolling in big, regular ridges that overlapped each other for miles. All the flora was very low and appeared to consist only of rows and rows of evenly spaced plants. It was the most peculiar landmass Baegulgog had ever seen. Just a few hundred yards from the shore was a very huge wooden fortress, which rested on immense stilts to account for the curve of the land. A shabby, almost Meduseldan wooden dock rested on much smaller stilts immediately around the ship and several others north and south of them. They were led onto the boardwalks, where ominous creaking made Baegulgog very happy to be flighted.

"It astounds me that an island of this size and proximity to Idriulthoronta has gone undiscovered for so long," Baegulgog admitted, hoping to releave their dread with a bit of cerebral banter. "I believe, if I were to use your numerals, that we have sailed nearly due east for approximately 34 hours. At eight knots, we would have traversed 306 miles in that time."

"I lost all reckoning of time below deck," Parissah admitted. "How can you be sure of the 34 hours?"

"I have counted the seconds," Baegulgog explained. "There was little else to count down there."

"We *are* still close to the Archipelago, then. But it is little surprise to me that this 'island' has not been found, save by these wandering outcasts. This is no island at all, and has rested here for some time less than 100 years, if I do not miss my guess."

Baegulgog flashed with searching thought. "If it is *not* an island, then whatever in the world could it be?"

"It is not of the world at all," Parissah declared. "It is a Moon Moth, making a fabled stopover on its winged journey through the cosmos. They are known to embed themselves in the oceans of the earth sometimes, slumbering for a century or two before they continue on their way. Pirates are notorious for finding dormant Moon Moths and using them as outposts. It has helped them to elude us throughout the ages."

"Terribly clever and resourceful, these pirates. It is a shame that the great Moths should endure them."

"Yet the Moths cannot be blamed, of course. They are incredibly immense, but they are nonetheless simple creatures. And they sleep very deeply. It may be well beyond the capacity of the pirates to rouse one. This Moon Moth is not in the least aware of our presence."

"That is extraordinary," Baegulgog said. But knowing all of this already, she did not share his wonder. They quickly fell back into silence and oppression of heart.

Finally, they came to the very doorway of the fortress. The pirates standing vigil before the door were greatly agitated by the time they arrived, and they sent one of their number ahead to demand an explanation.

"Vhat do you zhink you are doing?" asked the masked pirate, halting Parissah and Baegulgog's entire company of captors. She was Despotopian, by the accent. "Vhy should any Inquisitor be brought here alive?"

"To be put to death, a'course!" a familiar voice called out from behind. Baegulgog perceived backward. It was Captain Herringbone. He had come ashore after them. "But not before she makes a show of appealing for a ransom. Methinks it will amuse the Shogun, and I warrant he could use a good laugh. It'll amuse *me*, at any rate."

The Despotopian pirate shook her head. "Zhis is some extravagance for your sense of humor, Captain," she said. "Vhat of zhis Clerk? Vhat can we do to prevent him reporting zee location of our base, vonce he is a ghost and can go vhere he vill unrestricted?"

"The simplest answer be to let him live," Herringbone retorted. "We made a pirate out o' Grumly handily enough. This here jelly'll come around to our way o' thinkin' too, sans much time."

"I shouldn't stake a penny on it, if I were you!" Baegulgog declared defiantly. "You would lose it. We Sowür Canpattels are not so easily taken-in as your Wuu Gappew compatriot."

"Then ye'll get mighty accustomed to the sights and sounds o' the brig," Herringbone replied. "Tis an easy thing holdin' a Meduseldan captive!" he laughed. "Ain't got to feed ye or water ye or clean up after ye. But maybe once, every few years or so, we'll give ye a chance to reconsider joinin' the Band. If we ain't totally forgot about ye by then, anyway." Now he turned back to the pirate guard. "And as for you, lassy, are we quite through discussin' this?"

"I zhink zhis is foolishness," she replied. "But I suppose zee damage is already done. You may pass."

"Much obliged," Herringbone said, tipping his enormous hat. His little pet Compsognathus chirped indignantly at the guard as they passed. Herringbone slipped it a cracker.

Entering the fortress, they found most of it to be a vast emptiness. There was a great window on the north west, and some passageways recessed under a high shelf with upper terraces along the adjacent side, but otherwise the walls were high and wide and featureless. The floor proved more interesting. There was an enormous pool in the center, with snaking pipes nearly a foot in girth emerging all around, and beside it a long series of huge bellows.

As they took it all in, Herringbone came and stood in front of them, half his face in a menacing grin, the other half still tucked mysteriously away below the dark, ghastly plate he wore over it. The Compsognathus chirped again spiritedly.

"Ah, she's taken a shinin' to ye," Herringbone doted, holding the pet out on his hand in front of them.

"Whyever do you keep that rude little creature?" Baegulgog inquired.

"Sentimental reasons, mostly," Herringbone said, returning the dinosaur to his shoulder. "T'was this little lady and her friends what ate away me face," he explained, tapping on his face plate. "She got me eye herself. Didn't have the heart to part with her after that. Tis an oddity I learned from the master. Ye gots to keep what hurts ye close at hand."

He took a few steps back, pointing to the northeast wall. "Take the jelly up to the holding cells," he said. "He's a defiant one, and I don't want him detractin' from the Inquisitor's meeting with the master. She should be assured o' some quality time without distractions."

At once, sturdy pirates began hauling Baegulgog away. "Madam!" he called out. "Do not lose faith! You will find your way through this! You always do!"

"Do not worry about me, Baegulgog!" she called back. "And do not worry for yourself! I will be sure you are not forsaken here, whatever happens... I promise you!"

As he was taken, Baegulgog had to admit he found no solace in her promise. His own faith had failed him, however he tried to console her. He had known no darker moment – even learning of the Weapon in Tophthera. He would now face many long years' captivity. And his friend would face her doom alone. He could not decide which fate was more unkind...

* * *

Parissah felt a whelming heat rising up in her belly. Her fear for herself was gone, and in its place a steely determination fomented. She had a new mission – the very thing she needed to sustain her – as the pirates gathered at the large string of bellows, pumping out and slowly emptying the pool in the center of the great hall. And her mission was this: she must secure Baegulgog's rescue. To imagine him trapped for the rest of his days in a dark pirate dungeon was too much. She *would* force Shogun Shontaulyin to see wisdom in ransoming them. Failing that – and dying – would not stop her either. It was enough for her to have this one good deed left to do. She would see it done...

The pool roiled more and more vigorously as it drained faster and faster, with more pirates pumping. Before long, the contours of something enormous below the water were revealed – scaly mounds under wet crimson fabric. The creature shivered, and the water began to steam. Soon the whole pool was astir with waking motion. As the huge dragon arighted itself and began to emerge, Parissah was confronted with a sight that disturbed her, if it didn't surprise her much. Shontaulyin's face was uncovered, apart from a long, armored plate he wore between his eyes. For an Avarican to bare so much of his face was a very great shame – the most conspicuous display of unrepentance possible. Even many of the rampaging dragons she had slain throughout her career had at least made some attempt to veil themselves. She remembered bitterly that her father had not been among them.

Shontaulyin's head hung low as he rose. He blinked lazily, and offered a growl like a heavy sigh, though it shook the whole fortress. Parissah was surprised by his manner. He didn't seem angry, or merely groggy. He seemed sad.

"Why am I disturbed?" he asked at length. He sat fully upright in his empty pool now, hundreds of gallons of water still dripping off his huge red cloak and vaulted pauldrons, and his great folded wings. His voice was not harsh, but smooth and grave.

Herringbone removed his hat and knelt before his master. "I bring thee a prize, my Shogun: An Inquisitor we hath captured. She claims that she can fetch thee a mighty ransom." He permitted himself a smile. "I thought her appeal might amuse thee."

At this, Shontaulyin growled again, this time with some real menace. "You should check your honesty before your Shogun, Captain," he replied. "Admit, at least, that you do this for your own amusement, rather than mine."

Herringbone quickly lowered his head. "My apologies, master. But I truly believed thou would relish a chance to scourge thine most ancient and hated adversary."

"You do not know of what you speak," Shontaulyin said. As with many things about this experience, it made Parissah wonder. It seemed to her that Herringbone had spoken well enough.

The great dragon snorted, blowing steaming water from his nostrils as he waxed thoughtful. "Even so, perhaps this is an opportunity to sate my curiosity, in a way you do not expect." He turned to look squarely at Parissah for the first time, and the gravity of his gaze nearly stole away her resolve. "I will hear the Inquisitor's proposition, first of all. You may go, Captain Herringbone."

Herringbone stood and stammered. "But, but I..."

"You may *go*."

And so he did... and all the gathered pirates with him. Within moments, the hall was empty. It was just Parissah, and the Shogun...

* * *

Driven deeper into the fortress, Baegulgog silently came to a series of pragmatic realizations. Firstly, that he must try to escape now, or else never. It was very much as Captain Herringbone had said: Once he was behind bars, the pirates would not have to interact with him ever again, if they did not wish to. But here and now, in these narrow corridors, his captors were within tentacles' reach – perhaps for the last time. And he had certain advantages. They would not expect much fight from a Clerk, for one. For another, he had already discretely slipped out of a pair of his insulated gloves without their notice...

He did, of course, also realize that he would be hopeless to fight his way out. He had never mastered fighting to win. At fighting to *lose*, however, he was unrivaled. And right now, a deadly defeat was exactly what he needed...

As they led him round a corner, he reached out, seizing a pirate with an ungloved tentacle and unleashing enough voltage to send the fiend flying into the wall. The other pirates recoiled in a sudden terror. Baegulgog pounced for the nearest, though of course his pounce was hilariously slow. "Auuuugh!" he cried, trying to put on the most ferocious aspect he could muster. And sure enough, his gambit succeeded. The pirate reflexively cut his way through the Clerk's attack. Baegulgog's clothing flopped empty to the floor, cloven in two, as his physical body evaporated. He was dead... and his momentum carried him right through his killer.

They both turned to face each other, a look of horror on the pirate's face as he realized his fatal error. He gazed helplessly – even pleadingly – at the ghostly prisoner he was now powerless to restrain. Baegulgog inclined himself in the air.

"Many thanks, my good buccaneer," he said. "Too-da-loo."

Then he backed away waving, straight through the wall...

* * *

Parissah studied Shogun Shontaulyin, in her practiced and diplomatic fashion. He was a colossal specimen – many times larger than any dragon she had ever been party to destroying – though still orders of enormity removed from Grand Inquisitor Enscharaulgk. He quickly presented something of an enigma. Having commanded an army of pirates to do his dirty work in his stead for thousands of years, the Shogon's active days were far behind him. And in any case such a huge dragon should have been much harder to wake. She couldn't get a good feel for what drove him. He was no feral raging monster, as many lesser dragons she had encountered were. He didn't swoon at the mere mention of ransom, and he wasn't acutely megalomaniacal, either. He was nothing the book said he should be...

"Now, let us hear your petition," Shogun Shontaulyin told Parissah. He continued to drip morosely, looking cold and miserable.

"I will make you the same proposition I made to your Captain Herringbone," she said, looking up in address. "I am a Primary Administrator. My errands are very urgent and cannot be long delayed. It would be worth a very great ransom if I could be returned to my station forthwith. The Inquisition may well pay you any amount of monetary compensation you demand. Only know this: I was brought here with a Berlberi Clerk. He must also be ransomed. I will not be party to any deal that does not include him."

For a long while, Shontaulyin offered no answer beside oppressive silence. It hung between them until her speech had shrunk to a distant and insignificant memory.

"I see," he said at length. "You would offer the beast his due, and be on your way. A simple matter – like throwing a bone for a raptor to gnaw. It must have seemed a cunning plan. I don't suppose you even considered it might fail?"

Parissah swallowed. It began to sound very much as if her plan *had* failed already. "In fact I did, at great length. Your cruelty is legendary, Shogun. I thought it entirely possible that you might prefer the pleasure of incinerating me, over what must sound an unlikely reward."

"Indeed," Shontaulyin nodded, heavily and absently. "To covet or kill – that is ever the question for one such as *me*... except where we may do both." He cast a searching gaze out the window of his fortress. "You poor unfortunate creature. There is no way that you could guess how my heart has yearned for an opportunity such as this. Indeed, I only now see it myself. For my most outrageous dreams never contrived this chance."

Parissah blinked hard. "You are being very mysterious, Shogun. What sort of chance are you alluding to here?"

Shontaulyin snapped back to her, and seemed to grow before her eyes as his posture waxed stronger. "A chance to see what an Inquisitor – a truly reformed and righteous soul – would do if I returned her offer in kind..."

In a flurry of action, Shontaulyin reached deep into the recesses of his pool and retrieved a very great chest in his maw. He carelessly let it tumble to the floor in front of Parissah, where it spilt out its contents – a trove of gold and precious stones. It was beautiful beyond description.

"Here is *my* ransom," Shontaulyin said. "The entirety of my worth in this world. Would *you* refuse it? Can even the very righteous Avarican deny such wealth, freely offered?"

Parissah was quite overwhelmed. For a trackless while, it was all she could do to remain standing. The treasure was captivating. To have it apparently *offered* to her – the very hoard of the infamous Shogun Shontaulyin – staggered her beyond description. There was no rationalizing it. There was no way to understand how such a dragon could bear to part with even a single, small trinket... to say nothing of spontaneously giving it all away. Yet it seemed... that all she would have to do was say the word... and it would all be *hers*. And she had to admit to herself that she wanted it. It burdened her soul with a cosmic tangle of guilt and bewilderment. Finally, it dawned on her that the Shogun must be toying with her – that his idea of having fun at her expense was something far more sadistic than killing. He wanted to enjoy *corrupting* her...

"This... this is a very hideous game to play at," she said, finally.

"Do not think me playful!" Shontaulyin whispered harshly. "The treasure is yours if you will but take it. Will you?"

It took colossal effort to answer. "I will not. I... I simply *must not*."

And Shontaulyin shrunk again, hanging his enormous head with a quavering sigh. "So ends all doubt," he said. "We are not the same. The desire that long ago destroyed me could not harm you."

More negative feelings assailed Parissah, even as she had hoped to earn some relief, having found the will to refuse his treasure. His words shamed her in a way he could not guess. And she amazed herself, realizing that she felt some sympathy for Shontaulyin now.

"We are not as different as you think," she admitted. "I know the horrible longing. I know very well what it is to covet a treasure for myself."

"You do not," Shontaulyin replied. "Not truly. Not until you have fought and killed for it."

Parissah marveled at all of this. How the course of the whole impossible debate convicted her! "But I *have* killed. I have slain many dragons in my day. Admittedly, not so many as you undoubtedly have... and never alone. But I have slain them nonetheless."

He shook his head, not even looking at her. "Again, I name you an unfortunate creature – you who will not see what glorious innocence you possess."

"And yet you do not guess my guilt."

For a moment, she really felt prepared to reveal everything to him – to a stranger, and what's more, a very hated enemy. But before she could say any more, he went on...

"It matters not," he said. "I offered you everything, and you had the strength to refuse it, astonished as you must have been. Though now, perhaps I will find myself wondering, in the days and years to come, whether it might have been different, if I had only had more to give. It is not such an impressive amount, I suppose – for one who has hoarded for so many ages. You would be surprised, maybe, how hard it can be to keep it all."

She *would* be surprised at that. If there was one thing that a dragon should find quite effortless, it was being adamant to keep every ounce of his treasure, once he had it...

"What is the value, if I may ask?" She surprised herself with the question.

"One hundred talents," Shontaulyin answered. "To the very cent."

Once more, Parissah found herself unsteadied. "You *are* making sport of me," she insisted.

"I do not joke," he told her. "And what would be the humor in my answer, pray tell?"

He did seem serious. If he did not know, then this was perhaps the uncanniest coincidence of all so far. "One hundred talents is the amount set aside for each of the Grand Inquisitors," she answered.

Shontaulyin recoiled, taking heavy steps that shook the fortress. His eyes darted furiously. Now the surprise was his. "I did not know," he said. "I could not have known."

* * *

Baegulgog lingered for a time within a thick wall, trying to decide what to do next. Ultimately, he would have to find the Ocean Citadel and alert the Inquisition as to the whereabouts of this pirate base. But in the meantime, Parissah was in danger. He doubted very much that he could bring help in time for her. But there seemed little he could do to rescue her himself...

He heard the pirates dully through the wall, as word of his escape began to spread. It seemed to cause them very great alarm. Baegulgog was glad. Suddenly it occurred that, if he were to goad them, he might be able to cause enough of a ruckus to make a distraction Parissah could capitalize on. It would depend a great deal on her own cleverness, but after all he did think her clever. And it was worth a try!

As he heard boots echo down the corridor beside him, he ghosted out of the wall behind a group of pirates. "Hullo, there!" he said. "Isn't it me you're looking for? Here I am!" He flew directly at them. The pirates scrambled to try to lay hold of him. It was a spirited effort, but wholly vain and pitiful. Finally, he flew right through the end of the hall, and they were left pressed up against it, and some beat on the wood in frustration. Baegulgog reemerged further round the bend. "Over here, now," he taunted. "You will have to do better than that, I fear." They gave chase again. He resolved that this was to be the pattern. He would round up as many as he could, draw them into the deep corners of the fortress (or even outside if possible), then sneak back to the main hall and see about alerting Parissah.

As he neared a stair, he glided up through the ceiling, and this drove the pirates especially mad. He heard them charge up the steps even as he met more on the second level. His collection of bandits was growing quickly. But still he could only hope it would make some difference, in the end...

* * *

"I wonder if you would tell me, what it was you were taught about the origins of the Grand Inquisitors, and the Pirate Bands," Shontaulyin asked Parissah. Of course, it was a simple story she knew very well. But it was curious to be asked, particularly by one who would know what happened intimately...

"They of course are inextricably linked," she began. "When the Creators departed, Magormissahr came forward, imploring our kind to understand that it was primarily our sins of excess and pride that drove them away. His teachings were very powerful, and spread to the ends of the earth. But in all that vastness, his wisdom convicted the hearts of only six dragons, who came from far and wide to be reformed of all their centuries of bloodthirsty lust for treasure. These Magormissahr adopted as his fellow Grand Inquisitors. But the rest of dragon-kind was unrepentant. The Inquisition formed as the Grand Inquisitors raised a new generation of Avarica to hunt down and destroy the ones who would not give up the Old Way. Many dragons were destroyed, and many others escaped to slumber in dark places forever." She hesitated. "Then there were those like you, who formed bands of raiders, so that your pursuit of treasure might continue, while you yourselves remained safely hidden from the world."

"That is not far from the mark," Shontaulyin nodded solemnly. His face was veiled in heavy shadow, wreathed in the ruddy glint of the waning sun outside. "But there is in this a lie of omission. It is true that Magormissahr declared only six of his fellows truly reformed. They do not tell of the others."

"What do you mean?" Parissah asked, feeling suddenly anxious.

"The conviction in Magormissahr's rebuke was much stronger than history remembers," Shontaulyin explained. "*Many* dragons came forward in repentance, seeking his absolution. Out of these he chose the six. The rest he sent away. The rest, he said... were *false*." The Shogun had great difficulty in choking out the last word.

Parissah shook her head. She felt great sorrow, perceiving at once Shontaulyin's own part in these ancient events. WIthout hesitation, she found herself doing something she had never done before. In that moment she questioned whether Magormissahr had judged aright...

"At last I begin to understand," she said. "I have felt something was amiss, ever since the song..."

Shontaulyin shot her a questioning glance. "The song? What song?"

"Your pirates sang a haunting chanty as we were taken," she recounted. "*My prison is of flesh and bone and guilt for which I can't atone*, they sang... that and many other such dreary things. I could not then account for it."

Shontaulyin turned away, conspicuously embarrassed. "Those are my verses," he admitted. "They are at best a work of adolescent angst. But in all the centuries, I have found no better words."

"I think they are rather beautiful, now that I see the meaning."

The Shogun turned back, with a twinge of a sheepish grin. Then he averted his glance once again to the window. "*Find comfort only in your sorrow, and dread the coming of the morrow, knowing naught will change*," he recited. And the words seemed much more powerful, coming from the one who ordered them. "When we began constructing this fortress, I demanded only the luxury of my pool to sleep in... and this window," he said. "I am cursed with shallow sleep, and only the cold water aids it. But when I am awake, I like to watch the sun grow dim." They both gazed out now, observing that very spectacle. "The sun is a grief to me. Whenever it goes away, it always comes back. The days have worn on so very, very long since the Creators left. But watching the sun diminish never fails to give me a glimmer of hope. Hope that one day, it will not brighten again. Hope for some eventual End to it all. Almost *any* End."

"Why not rather hope that the Creators may one day return?" she asked sheepishly.

He regarded her with narrow eyes. "Do you suppose such a day will ever come, in truth? In their place, would *you* return? Would you find occasion to remember your first universe, if it had only disappointed you... and you had already fashioned a second one, more masterful – more pure and excellent?"

"Do not put me in the place of a Creator," she cautioned him. "Do not imagine that their high thoughts can be understood in terms of our own. It is a great heresy."

"You avoid my question," he plied her. "Do you really think they are ever coming back?"

She *did* wish to avoid his question. "I consider it unlikely, I admit."

He nodded heavily. "Then the End is preferable."

"But that too is a vain hope, I fear," Parissah lamented. "The universe the Creators made is impossibly rugged. I do not believe it shall *ever* end."

"I am sure you speak true," Shontaulyin agreed. "To hold any hope is ever irrational."

Parissah considered a new thought. It was grim, but given all he had said, she doubted she could hurt Shontaulyin much by addressing it. "You could more easily make an end for yourself, you know," she said. "We could destroy you. I regret to make such a suggestion, but I cannot help seeing how it might be beneficial to both of us."

"You are too kind," Shontaulyin said, unironically. "But I have more than myself to think about. These pirates depend on me. Serving me gives their lives meaning. And they are always looking to me for guidance, however I have endeavored to teach them self-sufficience. I fear they would be quite lost if I were gone."

Parissah nearly laughed. The more she talked with Shontaulyin, the more she felt as if she were talking to a Grand Inquisitor. But soon she was grave again. "They seem devoted souls, in their own way," she assured him. "I am sure they could be made to serve a better cause than thievery on the high seas."

"And yet what, in the current order of things, could allow them that second chance?"

Parissah wished to make answer. She deeply wished to believe that Enscharaulgk could be persuaded to give the whole Band his amnesty. But she feared no such assurance would move the Shogun, knowing now that he had already been sent away in disgrace himself. Ultimately, she could offer nothing but silence, which he took as his answer.

"That is what I thought," he sighed, his face still set against the failing sun. "So you see I cannot find my end, wherever I might turn to look for it."

For a few moments, they did and said nothing more, watching the day end moodily...

Then, the sun winked.

Parissah's body was struck suddenly cold. She had *literally* just witnessed the sun darken and draw shut just like a cosmic winking eye!

But this was not some unfamiliar omen... nor was it vague, nor did it leave any room for misinterpretation. If she was robbed wholly of her courage in this moment, it was certainly not because she had no idea what grand events were at work before her eyes. Rather, it was because she knew all too well...

"Did the sun just...?" Shontaulyin began, but she cut in as he hesitated.

"It did," she replied. She looked up at him, and found the fear in her heart mirrored in his look. "Perhaps your end has found *you*."

Shontaulyin looked back out, at last mustering something of a conspicuous fighting spirit. His belly heaved, and with a snarl he let out a great rolling plume of smoke. "Herringbone!!" he bellowed, deafeningly loud.

The front door of the fortress opened immediately. "Yes, my Shogun?" Herringbone supplicated, running in. Parissah did not wonder that he still lingered at the door. Probably, he had spent the whole time listening for her scream as the Shogun immolated her.

"Get everyone into the fortress at once," Shontaulyin commanded. "We will make our defense here."

Herringbone nodded low. "Of course, master," he replied. "But Shogun, art thou quite positive that..."

"Yes," Shontaulyin said. "It is *him*. There is no time to waste. Go now!"

* * *

Baegulgog had a very fine crowd of livid pirates at his beck by this time. He grew more and more irritating in his goading as the whole charade went on. He needed to be sure they did not lose interest. Though he began to worry that he was enjoying himself a little too much...

Just as he was about to lead them all around another bend in the corridors, a shrill voice rang out from far behind, drawing Baegulgog's attention, and that of all the pirates too...

"Come quick!" the shrill pirate insisted. "The Shogun be recallin' everyone to his presence! We's ordered to rally in his chamber immediately!" She led them all back in a new spirited charge. Baegulgog followed after... slowly, and somewhat dejectedly...

* * *

Pirates crowded into the main hall from outside and from deeper in the fort, even as a great stormfront whistled and howled outside, blown in from some unsearchable distance at unnatural speed. The gloom gathered and seemed to expunge all color from the world, leaving only a narrow slit of the horizon still garishly bright. The buccaneers were in a frenzy to arm themselves, and to make what desperate preparations they might. At the Shogun's instructions, even Parissah's own weapons were returned to her.

"You should hide yourself," Shontaulyin told her, over the din. "If you value your errands, you must not be seen."

Parissah was amazed to be so indebted to this unlikely ally. "I will, for I do," she replied, setting her sword into her belt. "Thank you, Shontaulyin. The Inquisition thanks you. I hope your soul finds solace at last."

He smiled at her. "Thank *you*, Parissah," he said. "May our paths never cross again. Be gone!"

Even as she turned to leave, Herringbone returned, dripping wet and frantic. "I am back, my master, but I could not recover everyone! At the last moment, Grumly done mutinied on me! Said he would lead the attack in defense of his Shogun. The fool threw me off me ship, and rallied a third of the crew to his cause!"

They looked out the window. Herringbone's ship was indeed astir, the sails unfurling as it attempted to maneuver into the open water.

"The idiot!" Shontaulyin exclaimed. "They shall all be killed!"

He spoke true. From the roiling clouds stooping down over the Moth, an assortment of dark twisters descended, probing slow and curious toward the ship. Soon they had it in a tangled grip, like the deadly embrace of a kraken, except coming from the wrong direction. Then, the black clouds funneled in through the cannon ports, and in a flash the sky was clear, though still dark in the twilight. A sound like a horrible laugh echoed up to the fort, and the entire ship went up in a huge explosion.

Parissah admonished herelf for standing there dumbly watching as all of this took place. She needed to take the Shogun's advice and hide!

But the parade of horrors didn't relent, and the morbid curiosity proved too much for her. There was a knock at the door to the fort. First a single knock that left everyone breathless.

"Are you sure no more of the crew followed you, Captain?" Shontaulyin asked.

"Nay," Herringbone answered. "I was the last in."

Then there were two knocks at the door, loud and urgent.

"Do not answer it," Shontaulyin commanded. "This is just one of his devious jokes."

Finally there was *pounding* at the door, frantic and unrelenting. The pirates despaired to do everything they could to barricade it.

This went on for some time, until the Shogun chanced to look down at his feet. Through the pipes used to fill and drain his pool, a dark vapor was silently pouring in. Even as he noticed, the trails quickened and moaned, like an endless sigh that drove out all other breath before it.

"The bellows!" Shontaulyin exclaimed, backing out of his pool. "Get to the bellows! He is coming in through the drains!"

The abundance of pirates leapt to action, pumping the bellows with terrified vigor. The vapor lashed out, and it caught some of them. The pirates tried to fight back, slashing with their swords and even firing pistols into the murk. But it was all a useless racket. They couldn't land a single blow, even as the vapor smote them with deadly force.

Still, for a moment things appeared hopeful. The pumping action was not wholly in vain. The vapor was being sucked back out through the drainpipes, and grew thin and impotent. But just as their spirits began to revive, they heard and felt a mighty whirling, and the vapor burst from the cavities of the bellows themselves, rushing in with a curdling scream. The pirates fled to the outskirts of the hall as the clouds broke into the fort with a horrible vengeance. They mounted up black as shadow in Shontaulyin's pool, forming a roiling, fanning pillar that began to resemble folded wings.

The Shogun waxed fierce, burying the claws of his forefeet into the thick foundations of the fort, and rearing his neck as his own black smoke rolled thick for the ceiling. At last, with a great roar he breathed a huge jet of flame over the shadow. For a moment, a hole rolled through the blackness, and it was split in two. But as Shontaulyin's blast failed, the shadow just as quickly regained its shape, and with a thunderclap an entire wall of fire shot out of it, pinning Shontaulyin back into the wall with towering fury.

The Shogun was staggered and hurt, and dozens of shadowy tentacles leapt forward to restrain him before he could muster. He roared and lashed and struggled, but could not wrest loose. It was horrible to watch him fail – too horrible for Parissah to look away or flee, though her cover was only marginal. Time and again he was struck against the wall, which rained splinters and chunks as big around as the tree trunks they had been fashioned from. Shontaulyin was flexed hard against his joints all over as the shadow neared total triumph.

From nowhere in particular, or perhaps everywhere, a voice filled the room. "This is not the Shogun I remember!" the Vile voice declared. "Where is all this weakness coming from? You have *all* lost a step! Am I truly the only one who keeps getting *stronger*!?"

Before Shontaulyin could offer answer, the shadow broke him. Dozens of vertebrae along the neck shattered in concert. The Shogun fell dead.

When the shadow at last shifted again, all watched helpless as its deadly vapors resolved into something clear. Something unmistakable. A manifestation of death as old as anything that yet abode in the universe, save only the Dianodes. The vast murk formed itself silently into the image of a bare skeleton; the ghastly framework of a truly titanic dragon. Last of all, the visage of the creature metastasized, far more bereft of subtlety than any other nightmarish feature. The huge black skull was frozen in a wicked smile, whose potency at once froze the hearts of any who were not already paralyzed with fear. Only Parissah herself proved able to stir at all, though she despaired, knowing there was nowhere to stir to...

The skeletal dragon began to move over the pirates, gazing at each with that infernal grin. There was a low, almost inaudible chuckle. It grew until it could be plainly heard... sloppy cackling, befitting one who had freshly lost his mind. And before she could prepare for it, he reared back, and the laughter burst full-force, like the rapturous anthem of an orchestra too grand for the bounds of the earth. The laughter *was* music, rendering meaning as nothing else could, sweeping the heart into rhythmic syncopation. It was an enslaving melody more perilous than any fire-breath...

It was the laughter of Onyxadon.

For some time after, Parissah was lost in herself. If she had thought the allure of the Shogun's treasure had been a deadly danger for her soul, she certainly should never have expected to face a worse one in the same day. And if she had been mystified by the tragic persona of Shontaulyin, then she was *desperate* now to understand the exultant charisma of Onyxadon, which fueled his power over wills.

But she was kidding herself. Her interest went well beyond the detached, analytical bent she tried to give it. *Understand Onyxadon's power*? A likely excuse! In that moment, she wanted to be *happy* – happy as *he* was. And how could she not? What a compelling, infectious, fresh new feeling it was to her! If she had ever known happiness before, it clearly did not compare with the way *he* knew it. How she wished to share his joy! What she would not have done just to keep an echo of that melody alive in her heart for all her days!

Her only salvation proved to be that she was honest enough with herself to admit as much. With colossal effort, she grounded herself in her training. *There is nothing more evil than happiness for its own sake*, Magormissahr would say. She grew indignant, even enraged, to feel so easily manipulated… until at last she arrived at the gall to resist the sway of Onyxadon's spellbinding laughter. And however long or briefly she fought it, this was certainly the hardest internal battle from which she had ever yet emerged victorious…

As she finally shook herself back to her senses, she found that Onyxadon was now engaged in a very spirited conversation. Rather, he was *directing* a great deal of excitable chatter at the paralyzed pirates – a captive audience in every sense of the word. He went enthusiastically from one thought to another with such abandon that she couldn't make out much of what he was even talking about… except that it naturally pertained to his latest, 'greatest' scheme to conquer the world. The pirates would play some part, small but important. And he made mention of some underground army of plants he seemed endlessly pleased with himself about. But the exposition remained an impossible tangle, especially with her having already missed an unknown amount of it.

From behind the crates she clung to for concealment, she watched as Captain Herringbone slowly began to emerge from his own paralysis. He looked on with blinking horror at first, listening bewildered as Onyxadon rambled ever on. He seemed so terrified that Parissah guessed he had not even heard the music of the *laugh*, having already been quite incapacitated – all but dead on his feet with fear. But at length, he forced himself to smile and nod along, coming to grips with the fact that by default, he had a new dragon-master. After a while he began almost to seem at ease. Perhaps he relished a chance to work for the most diabolical figure in all of history. At any rate, Parissah knew he was a survivor at heart, and would soon acclimate himself to Onyxadon's leadership entirely, if he had not already done so…

A few at a time, other pirates of remarkable constitution began to wake, and they all looked to the Captain as their pattern, reacting to their captor's caperings as he did, if more weakly.

Finally, Herringbone leapt into what he supposed was a segue in Onyxadon's spiel. "O, great O'nyxon!" he said, removing his hat with a flourish. "I, thine humble servant Captain Herringbone, am pleased to hail thee as the new leader of the Ivory Hyssop Band. Our strength is thine to command as thou will. It is thine servant's only regret that our flagship is no more, and shall not be of service to my dread master."

"Oh good gracious!" Onyxadon pulled back, his hypnotic smile shallowly submerged beneath a sarcastic frown. "Was that your flagship? I'm *sooo sorry*! I shall have to be much more careful around your little boats in the future, so we don't have any more unhappy accidents," he said, grinning sickeningly again. He seemed a hand at amusing himself, and his vaporous form pulsated in waves of heat. Herringbone was forced to step back. Parissah guessed that Onyxadon's joy fanned his inner flame the same way that great stress and anger fueled the typical Avarican.

"Think nothing of it, my liege," Herringbone groveled, shielding himself from overwhelming temperatures. Percieving a handy opportunity to please his new lord, he strode around to the front of the pool. Onyxadon wisped and glided ever close behind. Many more pirates suddenly came-to as he passed close, shocked from their stupor by the heat. "Please accept this token of our fealty," Herringbone continued, standing by Shontaulyin's overturned chest and pile of gold. He gestured over it dramatically. "The treasure hoard of the late Shogun Shontaulyin."

Parissah's heart leapt into her throat. Even though she knew this meant the Shogun would have his final peace, she could not help loathing to see his treasure go to the Eternally Most Vile Dark Abomination of Impenetrable Enmity.

For a healthy while, Onyxadon just stooped over the 100 talents, gazing dumbly... as she herself must certainly have done, when it was offered to her. Finally, he craned a great ghostly foreleg over the gold, stretching out his skeletal digits. But just as he appeared ready to sieze it, the fingers curled into a shadowy fist, and he struck the floor with enough force to break through. All of the treasure plunged to the carapace of the Moon Moth below, whence it rolled into the sea, never to be recovered.

Herringbone was the one standing with a dumb look on his face now... he and all the pirates who were alert enough to perceive what had just happened. Onyxadon permitted himself another warm chuckle at their expense. "Let the Shogun keep his baubles," the great enemy declared. "Better that he should face me again someday, and perhaps with a bit more gumption. He *should* be stronger next time, if there is any justice left in the world."

This was all too much for Parissah. She seethed to think that Shontaulyin had come so close to release, only to have Onyxadon spoil it at the last moment, and doom him to eternity in the world, if for nothing more than his own transitive amusement. Shontaulyin could never die now, lest every *single* coin that now lay on the ocean bottom be recovered by someone else. It was a truly terrible doom. She could hardly imagine a worse one...

And if that was not enough to exasperate her, she reeled to know she had witnessed two of the world's worst dragons treat treasure as a triviality within the span of an hour. To call it a surreal experience was not adequate. Reality and all its firm foundations seemed very far away.

Suddenly, she heard a familiar humming behind her. She listened for several seconds to be sure of the unlikely sound. Whatever the tune was, she could tell it was accelerated by nervous energy. She whirled her head around on her snaking neck to face the anomaly...

"Baegulgog!" she exclaimed under her breath. "Whatever are you doing? Why are you *humming*?!"

"I am sorry, madam," Baegulgog lamented. "It is my sneaking music. I have a tune for these odd occasions, when I find I must conceal myself."

"My friend," Parissah said, "I am so very pleased that you escaped and have found me..."

"Madam..." he put in weakly.

"...But you must be silent now. We must not be discovered!"

"*Madam,*" he whimpered, almost too low to hear. Then he pointed over her shoulder with a ghostly tentacle. Parissah followed his gesture... slowly, fearfully...

She leapt back at once, straight through the noncorporeal Clerk. Onyxadon's colossal face hung just before her, rippling in the heat of deadly delight.

This was a paradigm shift in the course of events, she knew. There would be no slipping quietly away now. Any attempt to flee would be a fatal error. He could kill her instantly.

But Parissah did have one card in her arsenal to play.

She was going to have to play it now, or never...

"Hello, grandfather," she said.

* * *

So was revealed another of Parissah's unfortunate family secrets. For it was no empty bluff; she was indeed directly descended from O'nyxon himself. Of course, to call him 'grandfather' could only be considered accurate between Avarica. They were separated by not less than 491 generations. But because you could easily have such ancient relatives still living, and because stringing together the word 'great' hundreds of times was very tedious, Avarica tended to simply refer to each other as 'grandfather' or 'granddaughter' or 'uncle' or 'niece' and drop all other modifiers. Parissah hated to appeal to this regrettable relationship, as if there could be any love lost between her and the Nemesis of all good folk. But she saw she had no other choice...

The eyeholes of Onyxadon's bare skull bulged in sudden recognition, and he gasped. "Why hello, my dear," he doted. "You must be Parissah! At last we meet! It is well that you said something. I admit I did not see the family resemblance all at once." She blinked slow under her mask, unamused. He looked her up and down with an affectionate glint, emanating from somewhere. She could not honestly tell if he meant it. "Bless me, but you do have your grandmother's knuckles," he continued. "What do you hear from your aunt Ya'rari? It seems ages since I've seen her."

"I fear I met her only once, when I was a little girl," Parissah answered. "She went down for a nap during the visit. Presumably she has been asleep ever since."

"Egad!" Baegulgog exclaimed, now behind her again. "You mean Onyxadon is actually your..."

"Quiet now, Baegulgog," Parissah whispered back. "This is family time."

"Who is that?" Onyxadon asked.

"Forgive my manners. This is Berlberi Clerk Second Class Baegulgog," Parissah gestured. "He has proven to be a very trusted and amicable business associate."

Baegulgog was far too frightened to offer a comprehensible hello.

"It is always so nice to meet a friend of the family," Onyxadon nodded. "Now what about your uncle Brekten?"

"Oh, we caught up to him years ago," Parissah answered. "If you catch my meaning."

"I *do*," Onyxadon said. "I couldn't help but notice you're a career woman." Suddenly he pulled out of clear focus, streaking back into a more upright posture. Even as he did, he swept Parissah unbidden up to a high terrace. She did her best not to appear terrified as she was wisked away by a rolling black vapor. He set her down gently, and Baegulgog eventually followed, coming up through the floor.

"Now we can chat more comfortably," Onyxadon explained. "You must tell me all about your job. How is it, working for brother Enscharaulgk? Surely it must be a frightful bore, as he is. Yet I can tell you, he does speak very highly of you. I made a point of asking about your progress... the last time we were murdering each other."

Parissah blinked again, but took the sentiment in stride. "The work is endlessly demanding, and even a small mistake could have lasting worldwide consequences. In short, I like it very much."

"Very good," Onyxadon chuckled. "I have ever been a great proponent of enjoying one's work. And it will be very good for you indeed, in the weeks and months to come. I have much in store for dear old Enscharaulgk, and his whole puritanical fraternity. You are going to be busy."

In a way, Parissah felt she remembered for the first time who it was she was really talking to. There were many great trials afoot in the Archipelago, and Onyxadon could be behind any one or all of them. It was high-time she drilled him about it...

"I should say so. You have certainly been outdoing yourself of late," she said, resting a fist on her hip and pointing accusingly. "No doubt you will make great mischief with your new pirate Band!"

"Yes," Onyxadon agreed venomously.

"And you have some sort of... *plant*... army, if I heard aright..."

"Yes."

"And you probably even masterminded the Free-Dome crisis!"

"Y... wait, what?"

"And I am sure you are behind the ilk of the Glowy Lady!"

"*Glowy Lady*? But who on earth...?"

"Do not try to deny it!" she pressed him.

Suddenly, great black wings mounted up and filled the entire hall with darkness.

"Now you listen to me, young lady," Onyxadon admonished Parissah. "As much as I would dearly love to take credit for all of your troubles, I fear I have no idea what you're talking about! I know nothing of "Free-Dome," nor have I ever heard of this... this *Glowy Lady*."

Parissah was hesitant to accept this news. "Are you quite certain? You would not mislead me in this, would you?"

"I would not! What sort of a grandfather do you take me for?!" He amazed her, seeming truly distraught, averting his head all around in some vain search. "Whatever is your Glowy Lady up to anyway, that you would suspect my involvement?"

"Oh no you don't!" Parissah replied. "You will get no useful tidbits from me! The last thing I need right now is to reveal anything of the Glowy Lady's misdeeds to you, so that you could go and get yourself mixed up in them with her. You will have to look elsewhere for that information."

"Oh, fine then," Onyxadon growled, dejected.

"And now you are going to have to make a decision," Parissah went on. "You must either kill me now, or let me be on my way. I have a great deal to do, and already I've been delayed too long."

Baegulgog whimpered beside her, almost inaudibly. She remembered his great fear of Onyxadon, and no doubt he expected the worst for her. But this was the only thing she could do. Time was indeed short and brutal honesty her only utensil...

But Onyxadon laughed. Not with great potency this time, but it dredged up the anthem fresh in her mind, and she was hard-pressed.

"I suppose we are both very busy people," Onyxadon said as his mirth became manageable again. "Duty calls to each of us! You may go. But I have enjoyed our little visit. We shall have to have another one very soon."

Onyxadon set Parissah back on the ground by the door. He remained gentle, and his skull retained a silly, fawning expression. She didn't doubt for a second that he might incinerate her the instant she stepped through the door.

"Careful in the dark, granddaughter," he said. "It will be quite the shadowy trip to the docks, I fear. This fortress is rather small, you see. I had to leave a good deal of myself outside."

She shook her head at him, unconvinced. "You are a fiend and a villain unlike any the world has ever known, grandfather," she told him. "You will forgive me if I do not much trust you. Are you *really* just going to let me go?"

"Oh yes," he assured her. "For me, it is a simple matter of principle. I never kill anyone who's family." His horrible smile broadened. "...Not unless they kill me first."

* * *

The water sloshed noisily under the small sailboat Parissah had elected to take from the pirates. She had much clumsy trouble trying to get the thing moving in the right direction. Baegulgog understood that she didn't have any sailing experience of her own, and she seemed very agitated besides. Being a ghost, he could only make suggestions, though he too was ignorant in such matters. Finally, they were beginning to sail at appreciable speed with relative ease. Parissah worried that Baegulgog, being immaterial, could not be tethered to the boat, and so might get left behind, but he assured her that as long as he remained over the boat, it counted as being stationary, no matter how fast they were sailing. She was very relieved to know it worked that way.

In the early watch of the night, they looked back and saw the pirate base in a flurry of activity. Seemingly countless torchlights poured from the fortress down to the docks in a mass exodus, even as sails were unfurled darkly against the huge abdomen of the Moth. It seemed that Onyxadon was wasting no time pressing his new fleet into service. With an Inquisitor abroad who knew the location of his base, it made sense to move on. But it must have been quite the nuisance to the pirates to be so suddenly uprooted. Baegulgog almost felt a little sorry for the villains. They were now far out of their league...

"I can scarce believe we have really faced the dread power of Onyxadon," Baegulgog marveled aloud, breaking a long silence.

"You have no idea what an awful trial it was, Baegulgog," Parissah said. She meant it, too. She was still very anxious... even twitchy. Baegulgog only now began to consider what she went through, having been present when he overthrew the Shogun...

"You were with him, then... when he worked the fullness of his might," he said. "I heard what happened. I heard him *laugh*. Though then I was still far away, and I caught but an echo of what you must have endured. Whatever was it like?"

"It was perilous!" she told him. "Much worse than I had ever imagined it would be." She gazed absently at her feet. "He assailed me with the one weapon I could not possibly have prepared for. *Joy*, Baegulgog! Joy beyond a shadow of bitter irony. Joy without reservation. Joy without reason. He invited me – no – he *compelled* me to see life as he sees it – not as a burden, but a blessing. And, if only for one horrible moment, that is exactly what I saw!" She trembled violently. "O, how the echo in my mind still makes my scales to crawl! I fear I will be forever haunted by the sound of it!"

At that very moment, that *laugh* split the air. Baegulgog was lost to terror for a second as he found himself believing that her mental echo had made itself manifest! But the laugh was far off, and as they looked back to the base in the distance, they saw a great jagged shadow rise from the fort, growing ever wider and taller. The sky was filled with flashes like orange lightning, and fire poured over the fort.. and over the Moth as well.

Before long, the 'land' craned up, and it was like watching mountains suddenly grow as the folds of the giant insect carapace rolled skyward. Thousands of tons of dust and debris were ejected like a volcanic eruption, and the silly little fort rolled burning into the sea, where the pirate ships were doing all they could not to founder. Far to the east and west, great tidal surges leapt up and out of the way of what appeared to be glowing bubbles miles in breadth. But these were the wings of the Moon Moth, huge and fantastically beautiful beyond description. With one strong, slow beat, the monolithic beast left the ocean's surface, casting an eclipse beneath its bulk. Then there was a howling that subsumed even the raucous merriment of Onyxadon. It was the howling of a hurricane-force wind, driven out in all directions by the wings!

"Stay over the boat, Baegulgog!" Parissah said. "We are about to be driven along very fast indeed!"

The Safehouse

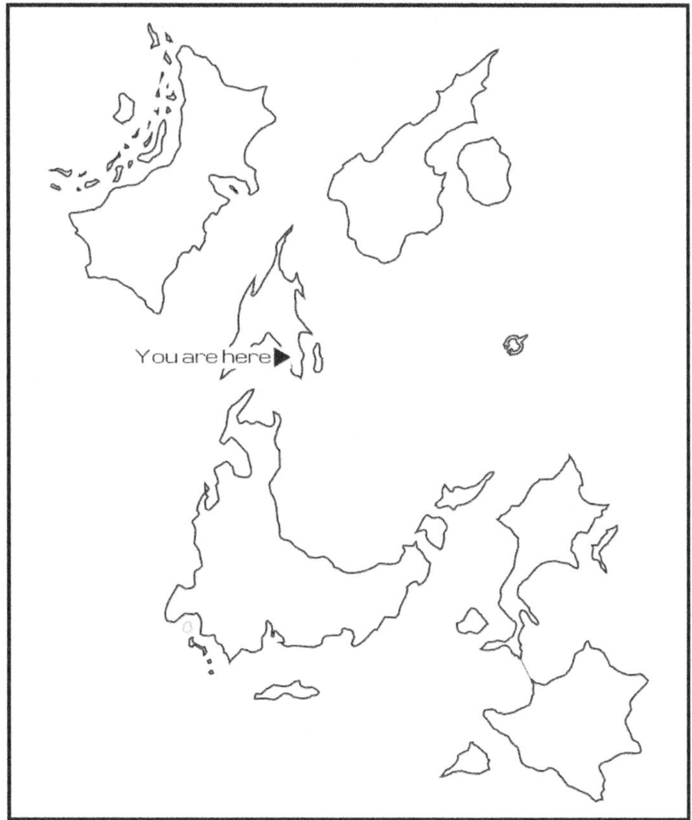

"Nobody enjoys the story of disparate forces coming together to overcome a common challenge of impossible odds. But that's what history sticks you with sometimes."

- Bianca Giovani, *History and Narrative*

Jek was sure he saw a sliver of land now. The sea was calm in the cold morning light, and though the world was still lost in a foggy mist, he had Audrey's assurance that visibility was good for at least two miles all around.

He stroked his face thoughtfully as he squinted at the incredibly narrow strip on the horizon. This did not feel like coming up on the most advanced nation in the Archipelago. It was more like finding a little sandbar in the distance that they were going to have to maneuver around. Even if Roemnar was very flat, there should be things *on* it, at least. Buildings, for one thing. Boats docked along the coast too. He struggled to think what else was missing. Trees. Walls. Maybe some Herons out walking around. But there was none of it. Just a sliver...

"That's not it," Jek said to himself.

"What's not what?" Audrey asked, joining him at the front of detective Mallard's boat.

"That," Jek pointed at the sliver. "You can't tell me that's Roemnar."

Audrey squinted into the distance now. "Yeah, that's it alright."

"But... but there's nothing there! It's just a sliver of land!"

"That's what it looks like," she explained. "Oh, sure, when the sky is clearer and you can see further inland, there are some foothills and things. But that's about it. Beside some low points of light at night, I've never seen anything more, any time we were passing by."

"Well what about the boats and the buildings? What about *anything* you should see from the coast?"

"The buildings are all subterranean, I'm told. And they have networks of deep locks all along their ports, so even their boats are recessed. They like to keep almost all their stuff below ground level."

Jek could not help making a face. "*Why*?"

Audrey shrugged. "I don't know. They just like it."

With an obnoxious loud yawn, the old man emerged from the cabin. "What be the scuttle-butt, ye youngsters?"

"I guess we've just found Roemnar, old man," Jek answered. His voice sounded a little surly, even in his own ears.

"Well, good on ye, lad!" the old man laughed. He came over and slapped a hand on Jek's shoulder. Jek plastered on a weak smile and looked back at him with it. But afterward he gave Audrey a look. He was having a hard time suppressing his distrust for the old man, ever since his attorney had expressed a deep feeling that he was being dishonest about something. Audrey seemed to sense the tension and tried to keep the discussion moving forward.

"How do you plan to get to shore from here?" she asked. "Is it even possible they'd let us into the locks?"

The old man scratched his beard as he looked thoughtfully into the sky. "Hmm. Don't reckon I know. T'was hopin' ye fellers could help me puzzle me way through this here dilemenia..."

Immediately Jek lost all thought of suspicion, and fell back into more familiar old anxieties.

"I don't have any ideas," Audrey said. At once Jek felt even worse.

"This be a pickle, then," the old man said pensively.

Finally, Jek had a thought. It wasn't great, but it beat nothing at all...

"Hey," he said, snapping. "What if we tell them we're refugees from Maenea?"

"That's a durn fool idear!" the old man shook his fists. "They been turnin' away all the refugees... straight to *Despotopia*! Is that where ye'd like to go?"

"Definitely not," Jek shook his head. "But a story like that should at least get us on land. As I understand it, the Despotopian navy has been transporting the refugees itself, from the northern ports. If we tell the Herons that we're Maenean, they'll take us in, process us, ship us up north, and then put us on a ship. Don't you see! Once they have us *on land*, all we have to do is wait until they're not looking and sneak away! Oh sure, it probably won't be easy. But nothing else has been, either. At least it gets us past the locks."

Audrey and the old man looked at each other, mulling it over silently for a few seconds. "I warrant he's startin' to think like a real adventurer," the old man said. "How about ye, lass?"

"I think we should try it," she agreed. "It would be a shame to have to think of something else."

* * *

"Hear ye, hear ye!" the old man shouted out, as they came to a stop outside a Roemnari lock. Jek leaned over the gunwale, looking out in wonder. It was very strange to see something of a 'hole' in the ocean. But sure enough, there were boats behind thin cement walls on water far below – easily dozens of feet. The sight was as ridiculous as it was cool.

In response to the old man's hail, a hatch behind a wall of the lock opened up, and two very official-looking Herons climbed out. They had spears and grim expressions. Jek began not to like his own idea...

"You are Humans," one Heron said, revealing the very obvious with some annoyance. "What do you want?"

"We is Maenean refugees, seekin' whate'er it is what refugees seek!"

"Like *refuge*," Jek added, a bit flustered.

"That's a lie!" the other Heron declared. Jek swallowed hard. "Two of you are wearing Jast-Madiir coats, and your accents are all wrong. What kind of fools do you take us for?"

"Err, I..." the old man stammered, all control of the situation already lost...

"Alright, so we're from Jast-Madiir," Audrey put in. "Would you believe that we're here on a Noble Quest, seeking the Knights of the Indigo Lodge?"

Jek blanched. To fall back on such extreme honesty was quite unnerving. He waited breathlessly to see how they'd react...

"Oooooh," the Herons said, exchanging a knowing look of some kind. "So, you're *those* people," one of them continued. "We were told you might be coming. We'll have you docked in a few minutes. Welcome to Roemnar."

With that, they went back through their hatch. Jek frowned as he thought he heard them snicker a little bit while the iron porthole creaked closed behind them.

* * *

Before they half knew it, they were standing on land. No one gave them any trouble, or even any invasive questions. In fact, the locks workers were downright helpful, going so far as to volunteer good directions. As they took a winding path down into a wide recessed settlement walled with stone – the main street of Port Gulph – the worst thing they came across was a great deal of curious looks from the townsfolk. They knew that being Human made them pretty out-of-place. They tried to appear amicable, smiling and waving at the Heron commoners. This, unfortunately, only fetched them more unpleasant looks.

* * *

"Is there no way at all you can speed up the process?" Parissah asked Baegulgog, hauling him by a tentacle through the deep streets of Cape Gulph.

"No indeed," he answered. "I will be solid by nightfall, and that is that. You must consider yourself fortunate that I lost two tentacles some time earlier, and that *they* are now corporeal. Some of me will serve better than none, I should like to think. But once again, I hope you shall not have to count on me at all in a scuffle. It took every ounce of my skill just to be killed by the pirates."

"We may be able to take the Humans peaceably," she huffed, trying to keep her breath as they dashed. "But they tend to be quite belligerent when they discover they have been hoodwinked." She breathed hard for some seconds, then continued. "Then again we probably won't encounter the fugitives one way or the other. We are already late! I fear they will have come and gone by now."

"I am sorry then, that I was so insistent on picking up a new uniform. It could have waited."

"No, Baegulgog, it is alright. You lost that uniform in your efforts to help me. To remunerate you to the best of my ability is easily as urgent an errand as this business with the lighthouse stewards. Especially considering the loss of all your papers! I know that was a very great sacrifice."

"Indeed. I still mourn them. But let us speak no more of it."

She took some more breaths. "Anyway, we should have been here days ago to give ourselves a proper chance. But I must press my luck. I shall not be satisfied until I have seen the safehouse for myself."

* * *

Jek, Audrey and the old man grew weary as the day wore on. The directions they were provided became the subject of regular, spirited debate. One of them would remember two rights and a left. Another would remember two lefts and a right, and so on. Between the three of them, they must have remembered the route at least four different ways. They tried to stop many Herons to ask which way they should go, but they weren't a responsive lot. When they asked where the Knights of the Indigo Lodge were, they tended to receive more questions than answers. "We don't like living around Humans," a Heron would say. "Why would we be harboring the Knights? And for that matter, what are you doing here?" Evidently, word of the Knights had not got around very much, outside of the locks...

Eventually they found themselves sitting on a bench pole. It was not comfortable – designed for perching rather than sitting. But they needed somewhere to plop down and mope, and this was the best thing they could find for it.

"Maybe we should just go back to the locks, and have them give us the whole thing over again," Jek suggested. "We could write it down and everything."

"That'd be a fine enough idear, iffen there was any hope o' rememberin' which way the locks was," the old man sulked.

"We could ask directions back to the locks," Audrey chipped in. "At least the birds would know that."

"Aye. Except that we's probably about in the middle o' this whole peninsular, and they's about a hunderds o' locks in e'ery direction. We'd ne'er find the same one again, and who's to say if the other locks knows anything?"

"We'll just have to keep wandering until we find the place," Jek sighed, running his fingers through his hair.

"I warrant the Doom Fleet willa done blowed up half the world by the time we finds it *that* way."

So it was they were in the very dregs of their gloom, when suddenly a Heron approached them. As everyone else so far had tried to avoid them, they saw that this was significant, and took immediate notice...

"Excuse me," the young Heron said, in a voice sweet but unsure. "Are you the three Humans who have been wandering around all day, searching for the Knights of the Indigo Lodge?"

All their eyes bugged at once. "That we is, darlin'," the old man answered her.

"I thought so," she said. "I've never seen a Human before, but you three are about the sad specimens I expected."

"Thank you?" Jek said.

"Anyway, a plague doctor stopped me a few minutes ago and told me you would be needing some direction. He said the place you're looking for is right down the street behind you, up over a fork to the left that comes to level ground. Just keep going straight for a few hundred yards after that, and you'll find a wide depression with waterfalls all around flowing down into a garden. The safehouse is in the middle of that."

The old man slapped his knee and sprung to his feet. "Well, if that don't beat all! Bless ye, young lady, and yer random plague doctor besides! Can I shake yer talon?"

"If it's customary, I guess," the young Heron said.

"It is, it is! But ne'ermind! I'll just pat ye on the beak and we'll be off!" So he did, but she did not appear to like it any better than a handshake. "Thank ye a zillion times over!" he called back "Ye don't guess it, I warrant, but ye done saved the world today!"

"Whatever you say!" she called back, unconvinced.

* * *

Jek could scant believe his eyes. There beneath them, in the warm, muggy shadows of the late afternoon, was a wide bowl-shaped depression, with artificial waterfalls at regular intervals around the perimeter. They flowed in bubbling streams past great wedges of low crops, converging eventually in a central, swirling pool. Over this pool were many bridges leading to an overgrown building at the very epicenter of it all, hardly visible amid vast fruit trees and vines. It was just like the young Heron had told them! Jek knew that he should wonder why the answer to their search had come to them so providentially, after they had long labored for it in vain. But he couldn't bring himself to puzzle it out – not now. He could do nothing but bask in this special moment – the moment before they climbed down into the secret fastness of the Indigo Knights and fulfiiled their destiny! He still struggled to believe that he had really survived to this point. He felt very honored and humbled to get to see the whole thing through to the very end... and if his eyes were a little moist right now, then he just hoped that Audrey and the old man didn't notice...

The time came. They took the nearest flight of stairs down into the garden. But just as they reached the bottom, there was a low rumble behind them. They whirled and saw the stairs retract into a seamless wall. In fact, each and every staircase around the whole garden drew itself back in the same way. When the rumbling stopped, they all looked at each other in uncomfortable silence. There was currently no way back out of the garden...

"That's kind of ominous," Jek said at last.

The old man snickered nervously. "Ain't nothin' to worry about, I'm asure. Knights gots ta have their booby traps, is all. Only, maybe get yer muskets ready, just the same."

They did. Afterward, they proceeded very cautiously...

Slower and slower they approached the safehouse as the warm light in the sky turned to grey. They didn't want to go *in* the safehouse... lest they find more 'booby traps'. The unspoken consensus seemed to be to linger outside and hope a Knight might just come out to get a kumquat or something. Then they could hail him from a safe distance...

As if in answer to their hope, a shadow stirred in the doorway beneath the cover of the fruit trees, even as they continued their sheepish advance. Audrey pointed. "Look!" she said.

The shrouded figure seemed very large, yet hunched. He must have been a *very* big guy. If they were honest, the form didn't even look Human. But there was a sword on the belt, and that allayed their fears for the moment.

"Hey! Knight! Over here!" Audrey called, waving emphatically. It was hardly needed. The shadow was already striding for them. Jek focused on the heavy-falling feet of the Knight's silhouette. There was a cape or cloak that ran all the way to the ground, but every now and again it stirred away, and he could see that something was horribly amiss. The feet were not in steel boots. They weren't even shaped like feet. Not *Human* feet, at any rate...

"*Dianodes*," Jek cursed. "That's no Knight! That's an Inquisitor!"

At that moment, the Inquisitor revealed herself, throwing aside her cloak as she emerged from the shadows. "And you are the fugitives, Jek and Audrey," she said. "At last, we meet again. You have done well to make it this far. I regret to end your Quest this way, but it is my sworn duty to place you under arrest. You will be extradited and face your trial, if it is not already concluded. And your old man will be processed. Each of you will receive the justice that is your due. I can promise no more."

Jek marveled as he recognized the voice. "By golly! You're the one from our house! You were there on inspection day!"

"Yes," she said.

"How did you know we'd be here?" Audrey asked. "Where are the Knights? Can't we at least talk to them first?"

"There are no Knights here," the Inquisitor explained. "This was all a trap set for you. As fugitives, I deduced that you would seek the Knights. I sent carrier pigeons ahead of you to the Fish Islands, and the Wading Isle, instructing the local Inquisitors to spread word that the Knights were here. It is a ruse we have nearly perfected, after generations of runaway Humans. It pains me to use deception, but it is a trespass for which I have already made my penance. Now please, I urge you to come peaceably. Let this not end in an ugly way."

"RUN!" the old man exclaimed.

"You are trapped," said a voice from behind. A Meduseldan had flanked them! He barred the way back across the bridge. "There is nowhere to run."

"ATTACK!" the old man exclaimed.

"Oh, bother," Parissah said, drawing her sword...

* * *

They all charged the Inquisitor in unison. At least, for the first few steps... when the old man suddenly doubled back for the Meduseldan. He probably hoped Jek and Audrey wouldn't notice. They did, but by now they were dedicated to their own charge, and kept going. Another call rang out behind them, as the Meduseldan lazily floated to draw battle against them. The Inquisitor strode into the fray...

Audrey and Jek's muskets met with Parissah's sword. She was still hopelessly inexperienced. But they seemed not to know what they were doing, either, and couldn't concert their attacks. They were tripping over each other, even as she was tripping over herself. So the battle was closely pitted for some time.

For the old man's part, he met the Meduseldan head on. He tried to dodge one way or the other and get around the primordial creature, but its tentacles were out wide, and there just wasn't room enough on the bridge. Finally, with the Meduseldan's body exposed, the old man simply heaved his sword up and brought it down to cleave his opponent in two. But to his shock, his blade met no resistance. It simply went right through harmlessly! The Medusledan was already a ghost!

But it was the ghost's turn to act now. Inexplicably, its arm tentacles were solid, and grabbed hold of the old man's arms, overpowering and immobilizing him. He struggled for all he was worth, but could accomplish nothing. They circled round and round on the bridge for a while as he despaired to get free. Then he remembered his magic. He brought a great wave up out of the stream ahead of him, and doused himself and the creature. It had little effect, as naturally the water was as insubstantial to a ghost as anything. But now, with the pavement slicked with water, the Meduseldan suddenly lost his balance in the air, and his tentacles flew out again in an effort to steady himself. The old man was loose, and he charged right through the Meduseldan's phantasmal body, leaving it utterly flummoxed...

Further up the bridge, the battle between the stewards and the Inquisitor raged on. Finally, the woman overcommitted, and Parissah seized her in one hand, lifting her from the ground. The little Human beat and flailed for all she was worth, and Parissah had to give her credit. The blows were at least uncomfortable. But she could not hope to break her hold.

The man was greatly distressed, and he leapt for Parissah's outstretched arm. She blew a jet of flame in his path to stop him up, and he threw himself back against the ground. But he lowered his musket and took an expert shot, getting her in the arm anyway. Her muscles failed her in the pain, and she lost her grip on the woman, who fell back to her feet. But Parissah was relentless, and forced herself through the pain to sieze her again before she could escape.

Just as she was turning her attention back to the male steward, she saw a flash of pale light. The woman worked some sort of power on Parissah's musket wound, and it eschewed the musket ball and sealed itself. The pain coming out was easily equal to going in, and Parissah lost her grip a second time. This time the woman hit the ground running, and Parissah was forced to draw her pistol on her, to her great regret. But as she swung her arm to line up a shot, the loop of a rope slipped over her wrist, and she was yanked back, pulling the trigger erroneously. The man, still laid out on his back, had expertly lassoed her! He got up and hauled for all he could, desperate to at least restrain her. But she pulled back with overwhelming force, yanking him into the air, and he careened into one of the streams.

Audrey watched in horror as the Inquisitor reached into the stream, extracted Jek and began wrapping him up in his own rope. She took her shot, getting her Avarican nemesis right in the back of the calf. The Inquistor roared and staggered, and her mask glowed orange-hot, but she didn't lose her grip or falter in restraining Jek. Audrey charged, bayonette leveled. But before she could reach her target, a huge surge of raging water leapt out of the stream and threw the Inquisitor down. The old man was still at work! But the Meduseldan was closing in on her now. Audrey was a bit overwhelmed by the rapidly unfolding situation. There were a lot of moving pieces. But the Inquisitor still had Jek! So Audrey knew she must continue her charge. As she came just over her opponent lying on the ground, the Inquisitor hoisted one great powerful leg and caught Audrey with her long toes. Audrey's musket missed its mark and skittered off the ground, kicking up sparks. She lost her grip on it, and seized the toes over her shoulders, trying fruitlessly to peel them away...

"Grab her, Baegulgog!" the Inquisitor shouted. The Meduseldan arrived and caught Audrey in two coily tentacles. She was restrained helplessly in the air again, this time without recourse. Jek was soon very thoroughly hogtied...

That left the old man alone against the Inquisitor...

Amid her struggle, Audrey saw him now, at the end of the bridge, sword swung out in challenge.

"Save yourself, old man!" she called out. This drew the attention of the Inquisitor to him.

"Can't hardly, lass," he said. "I gots some honor left, I like ta think. And anyway, all the steps is still gone."

The Inquisitor stood and started for him, hardly limping. "You can still come peaceably," she said, though she drew her sword again.

"Can't do that neither," the old man said, slowly closing the distance. "Our Quest be too important. We all either lives by it, or dies for it. Ain't no other way."

They drew closer and closer together on the bridge. Audrey and Jek both strained in desperation. There seemed only one way this could end. With all their being they strove, unable to accept that they had failed at last so disasterously, after so many impossible victories. But they were helpless. Helpless to do anything but watch and wait for the last fight to commence...

Suddenly, the Inquisitor stopped in her tracks. Her body waved, unbalanced on her feet. With great effort, she willed herself through half a step more, but faultered and fell flat to the ground. She tried to heave herself up, but her arms were impotent, and clawed in vain. Finally, she collapsed... motionless...

All was silent and speechless, save for the sound of a great flutter of large wings from above and behind them, which no one looked back to observe. No one could take their eyes off the fallen Inquisitor. Audrey gaped. So did the old man.

"Madam!" the Meduseldan cried, letting go of Audrey at once. He floated to her side and rolled her over. Suddenly, she produced a crocodilian sound. It was a snore.

"Oh, madam!" Baegulgog lamented. "What have they done to you?"

"It wasn't us!" Jek protested. "That is, I don't think it was us. Was it us, old man?"

"Nay, not hardly!" the old man insisted. "I ain't got no power to make nobody fall sleep-stricken like that! Like as not, she has some sorta sleep disorder, or somesuch."

Baegulgog remained suspicious, shaking his fallen friend with his extant tentacles, taking little heed of the Humans, against whom he was now practically powerless. But he could not long ignore them. Soon, the old man came up, and held his sword over Parissah...

"We can do a lot worse to her though, I warrant, unless this here jelly makes hisself cooperative," the old man said, low and menacing. Baegulgog was abhorred.

"I don't like this," Jek said, Audrey releasing him from the coils of the rope. "I don't like this one bit. What are you thinking of doing?"

"Thinkin' a turnin' this whole hostage sitiation on its head," the old man answered. He turned to Baegulgog. "And ye's gonna help us. Or else."

Baegulgog let go of Parissah gently, rising back into the air. "I will do what you ask," he said. "Only do not hurt my friend."

* * *

Parissah flopped. She roused herself and came-to, shooting into an upright seated position. It was night now – another bright clear night with the Other Worlds shining overhead – and she found she was in a very nice fishing boat, tied hand and foot, with her arms behind her. She didn't at once struggle against her restraints. Rather, she strained to understand what had happened. She had fallen suddenly unconscious. *Why had she done that*? A great exhaustion still lingered. She must have been poisoned. But she couldn't figure when or how those fugitives could have managed such an infernal trick!

Craning her head around on her neck, she examined the scene, suddenly aware of distant chatter. It was Baegulgog's voice she heard, coming from the bow...

"You mean, you have never heard the tale of Chordonoto?!" he asked. "He who is the very inventor of music... my most famous forerunner?"

"There's a lot of stories I've never heard," the fugitive Audrey replied. "I'd be glad to hear it now."

"Oh, jolly good!" Baegulgog laughed merrily. "Scant would give me more pleasure than to tell it!"

"Baegulgog!" Parissah exclaimed, feeling very confused, and rather betrayed. "Whatever are you doing, consorting with these criminals?"

"Madam!" Baegulgog cried, forgetting at once his story. "It is so very good to see you have awoken!" He floated into her midst. The fugitives followed, cautiously.

"I am awake," she replied, "but horribly confused. What has happened?"

Baegulgog flashed uncomfortably. "It is a rather unpleasant story, I fear. But all is mended now... by my reckoning."

She was quite unconvinced. "You must tell me."

"Well, after you fell asleep, these fine folk here threatened deadly force against you. I was compelled to help them in order to spare your life. I lifted each of them from the garden, and I bore you wheresoever they went. They concealed you in your cloak, as if you were merely some big sack of stuff! And a rather convincing pack of traveling gear you made, if I daresay. In this way they hoped to take us hostage back to their boat."

"It wasn't easy," Audrey put in. "We couldn't remember where we were parked. But some Heron came up and told us that a plague doctor had left us directions. It was really weird! All the weirder since the very same thing happened earlier, when we were looking for the safehouse."

"I didn't ask *you*," Parissah admonished Audrey… who pursed her lips and clammed up. She turned back to the Clerk. "Please continue, Baegulgog."

"There is little left to tell, anyway," he went on. "We came at last back to their boat. The operators at the locks were more than a little surprised to see the Humans return. But they had no cause to hold them, and at any rate, they preferred to see the strangers go. So they filled the lock and let us sail away."

"But Baegulgog," Parissah said, "it is past nightfall and you are still a ghost! How can this be?"

He hesitated. "Oh my, yes," he chuckled nervously. "About that. I'm afraid I became rather foolhardy, after I regained my substance. I tried to overpower our captors and carry you back to safety. My efforts were quite spirited. Regrettably… I forced them to kill me."

"*Murderers*!" Parissah exclaimed, fierce with sudden outrage. Her mask sizzled and glowed.

"Now, now, don't be hasty," Baegulgog consoled her, waving her down with lethargic tentacles. "Much has transpired since my latest demise. I was left with no recourse but to hear them out, and I have come to believe that they are very good at heart, and well-meaning. I have quite forgiven them for killing me, and I implore you to do the same."

Parissah seethed silently for a few moments, but her mask cooled, and she relented. "Very well. But that does not excuse their other crimes. They must still be arrested."

"*Har ha-har*!" the old man laughed. "I'd like to see ye try! Ye're *our* prisoner, now… and there's nothin' ye can do about it!"

Parissah stood and broke her binding effortlessly.

"*Oh fiddly sticks*," the old man whimpered, cowering.

"I am commandeering this boat in the name of the Inquisition," she said, striding to the rudder control. "We will make for Maenea, where I have another errand. With any luck, I may relinquish you into the custody of Countess Jengadocea, where you will remain until the mission is finished. Then I will secure your extradition."

"But, madam," Baegulgog stammered, "perhaps we could…"

"…Please, Baegulgog, do not side with them. You know this was always the plan. Well… close to the plan, anyway."

"At least hear us out," Audrey pleaded with her. "We really are on a Noble Quest."

"*Noble*?" Parissah repeated, indignant. "You have killed a Clerk, and you have poisoned me. What pretense of nobility can you attach to your Quest?"

"We didn't poison you!" Jek was quick to claim. "We didn't do anything to you!"

"You shot me twice," she reminded him. "I count that as something."

"But I already healed you of both those shots," Audrey said, and Parissah realized with some surprise that her leg was indeed totally mended. Audrey herself held the musket ball out for her to see. "And if you were poisoned, it wasn't by us. We didn't get any poison when we went to the alchemist shop. I'm practically sure of it."

Parissah crossed her arms, still unconvinced. "Well, *someone* poisoned me. It is not my habit to just fall asleep for no reason. If it was not you, then who?"

"It was I," a very frightening and authoritative voice rained down on them from above. Parissah and the others looked up. Against the framing of the Other Worlds, the dark shape of a Heron alighted on the top of the boat's cabin, folding his wings gingerly as he landed. He carried some long, inscrutable object wrapped in cloth, and he wore the outfitting of a plague doctor. The bristly feathers of his wings and tail fanned-out and caught the pale sky-light, glistening like thousands of thin knives waving in the gentle wind. He stooped over the cabin's edge, his bone-white mask and perfectly reflective goggles piercing each of them with a fearful aspect. They all stood spellbound by the presence of the stranger for a long while, until he leapt down to their level. Then, at last, it seemed the talking could resume...

"Who are you?" Parissah asked.

"I am called Marrow," the Heron answered.

She was unsure. "What an odd answer. Who calls you that?"

"I do," he said. Parissah wasn't immediately sure where to go from there.

"You're a doctor!" Audrey exclaimed. "Are you the same one that kept sending us directions all day?"

"Princess Aaliyah!" Marrow exclaimed in an awed voice, turning and bowing to her at once. "*How* I have missed you, oh dearest of friends!"

Audrey blanched. She was quite befuddled and embarrassed. "There must be some mistake. I... I don't believe we've ever met."

"But of course we haven't, my dear!" Marrow laughed. It was a rather tyrannical sort of laugh, if truth be told.

"This is gettin' mighty peculiar," the old man muttered.

"And you, master Jek!" Marrow said, turning to Jek. "Brave, *brave* master Jek! My dark heart is happy to see you as well." Jek was even more flummoxed, hearing the stranger use his right name, as well as the name he had always attributed erroneously to Audrey. And if the rest were not enough, now he was being called 'brave'...

"Hi," Jek said, trying to smile and wave.

"You know these criminals?" Parissah asked. "I suppose that is a foolish question. You are in league with them! You helped them by poisoning me."

"I *do* know them," the Heron confessed, not at all impressed by an Inquisitor. "Though they do not know me. Yet. But I know you as well... *Parissah*. You and your silly Clerk Baegulgog."

"Silly!?" Baegulgog protested.

"Enough with all this mystery!" Parissah demanded. "What is your part in all of this?"

"What part I will play in your various tasks is yet to be seen," Marrow answered. "I am come now on my own errand. I have something that your eyes must see."

Parissah looked around, wondering at being suddenly singled out this way. "My eyes?" she asked.

"*Yes*," Marrow replied, sounding impatient. "And why should you wonder? Yours are the eyes of a Primary Administrator. What I have to reveal is of grave importance to your order."

She felt a strong foreboding at once. There was something oddly compelling about this Marrow. And after all, she did revere the uncanny perception that she knew some Herons possessed. She knew she must entertain whatever it was that he meant to show her. "Then let us have it now."

He reached into his coat and produced large, heavy documents, unrolling them on the ground in their midst. The etchings were very technical and detailed, and the information overwhelming. Parissah had to admit she had no idea what she was looking at. "What is this?"

"They are battle-plans," Baegulgog gasped, able to absorb paperwork at a breakneck pace. "Official and classified... drawn up by Roemnari Fleet Admirals for the eyes of the Proconsul himself!"

"Battle plans?" she repeated, still feeling clueless. "I don't understand. Why do these concern *me*?"

Marrow looked and gestured to Baegulgog. "Go ahead," his powerful voice implored. "Tell her."

Baegulgog hesitated, all eyes on him anxiously. "I'm afraid the plans are to deploy the Roemnari Fleet to the Inquisition Citadel."

Parissah recoiled, utterly shocked. "Surely not! Proconsul Zedulon would never!"

"Do not presume to tell *me* what the Proconsul would and would not do!" Marrow barked. "I brought these plans forth from his very chambers, at incredible risk to myself."

"I cannot believe it," Parissah said all the same. "It is a betrayal almost beyond precedent! True, Zedulon is an eccentric recluse, perhaps. But he has had long friendship with Grand Inquisitor Enscharaulgk. And anyway it is madness! He cannot hope to succeed against our navy."

"You would value more proof, I assume?" Marrow asked.

"I would," she agreed.

Marrow returned to the roof of the cabin, retrieved his parcel, and brought it back down. In an expert whisking motion, he removed the cloth covering. Parissah's eyes nearly bugged from her head. She stooped and retrieved the object to study it for herself.

"This is *Valshaloli*," she named it. "The royal spear of the Proconsuls!"

"...Retrieved along with the plans from the royal chambers," Marrow continued. "Are you now satisfied?"

She studied very carefully, hoping against hope to find some seam or flaw that would reveal the weapon as a fake. But she could find none. "This is an ill omen indeed," she said, absently handing *Valshaloli* to Marrow. "One among an ever-increasing number. I do not know if I could possibly accept one more bit of bad news."

"Ye mean the Roemnari is plannin' naval mischief too!?" the old man exclaimed. "We hasn't even got to the part where we done mentioned the Despotopian Doom Fleet yet!"

"Oh good gracious," Parissah said with a hot sigh, sitting in a heap. "I think I need a moment."

To everyone's surprise, the old man came over to Parissah, and patted her on the shoulder. "There, there, m'lady," he said. "It can't be all bad."

She looked up at him. "Can't it? I begin to wonder. Do you half realize all the things that are going wrong out there? The Tophthaeran Isles are vying for technology that could spell the end of the entire Meduseldan race. Maenea is falling to insurrection. Magic is spreading and we have no idea what should be done about it. And in our time of greatest need we've lost most of our best diplomats on failed outreach missions to the Mantid tribes."

"That sounds pretty bad," Jek sympathized.

"Those are only the maladies from a week ago, or longer," she went on. "I have since learned that Onyxadon is abroad again, and he has the entire Ivory Hyssop Band backing him. Now you bring me tidings of an attack against the Inquisition by Roemnar! And if this old man is to be believed, Despotopia – who has been our only staunch ally in all these troubles – is planning havoc as well. And all of this must be faced in Enscharaulgk's absence! He still has not revived. Nor can we seek the counsel of the other Grand Inquisitors. All attempts to reach the continent have failed – and we do not even know why."

"That is really, really bad," Jek despaired.

"You're forgetting the *other* ill omen," Baegulgog pointed out. "You might as well have it out too, while you are dratting all the rest."

"But we don't even know anything about *her* yet," Parissah argued. "It will mean nothing if I speak of the Glowy Lady."

"*Glowy Lady*?!" Marrow exclaimed, stepping forth urgently. "What do you know of the *Glowy Lady*?"

Parissah blinked. "As I said… nothing, I fear. Except that she has offered the Twin Queens the horrible technology I earlier mentioned." She suddenly sprang to her feet. "But for pity's sake, what do *you* know of her!?"

"Perhaps less even than you," Marrow lamented. "I know… that is… the Proconsul described her to me, once."

"Go on," Parissah insisted. "What did Zedulon tell you? Is she the one from his Chocolate Prophecy?"

Marrow nodded gravely. "She is."

Parissah sat again in a slump. "Then it is as I feared. The Prophecy chooses a most inconvenient time to fulfill itself."

The old man at once sat beside her in his own slump. She eyed him uncomfortably. "But I was so asure that the Doom Fleet were the fulfillment o' the Chocolate Prophecy," he sighed.

"That doesn't even make sense," Parissah said.

"It made sense ta me," the old man replied weakly. Jek and Audrey felt for him. He was so dispirited, he looked at once like a *very* old man.

"But whatever do we do *now*?" Baegulgog asked. "We seem to be a boat full of people at cross purposes."

"I am still sailing for Maenea," Parissah declared. "That was my next mission, and so it remains. The Inquisition is advised of Onyxadon, and aware of the mystery of the Glowy Lady, at least. And I can send pigeon from Maenea to warn of the impending attack of Roemnar. Were the battle-plans dated, Baegulgog?"

"They are set for Novtober 14th," he answered.

"*7/14/21*," Parissah nearly whispered to herself. "I might have known."

"The date means something to you?" Marrow asked.

"Yes, but there is no use explaining it now. Are we settled on Maenea as our destination?"

"We most certainly isn't!" the old man snapped. "This here boat is fer finding the Knights o' the Indigo Lodge!"

"On whose authority?" Parissah asked.

"On *mine*, since it be *my* boat!"

"But this is Artimus Mallard's boat," Jek reminded him.

"Finders-keepers, lad! Ye's supposed ta be backin' me up here anywho! Whose side is ye on?!"

"Well if it's going to be about choosing sides, I'm all for cooperating with the Inquisitor," Jek admitted. "I certainly wanted to find the Knights, but there's no chance of that now. We have no idea where to look. Ultimately, it's Enscharaulgk's pardon we need anyway. It was always the Inquisition we needed good graces with, in the end."

"But this ain't the *Quest*, lad! Our only hope was to finish the *Quest*! Ye can't just run oft and then change yer objective half-way through! I never heard o' nobody what got pardoned for somethin' like that."

"He might be right, Jek," Audrey said. "This Inquisitor has maintained all along that she was going to arrest us. Helping her won't change her mind. She might not even *let* us help her."

"I doubt very much that she would," Baegulgog concurred.

"Baegulgog!" Parissah said, shocked. "You are still siding with *them*!?"

"I am very sorry, madam," the Clerk replied. "Remember that I have already heard their story at length. I fear I am quite convinced that they have legitimate business, trying to check into this Despotopian thing. I wish we would."

"That's three against two, *har ha-har*!" the old man capered. "Ye's outnumbered, m'lady. The search fer the Knights goes on!"

"No!" Marrow beckoned... and the matter was put to rest at once. Still he deigned to explain himself for their benefit. "We *will* go to Maenea first. For that is where I have foreseen that we shall go. The future is immutable!"

"You do possess the gift of foresight, then?" Parissah asked.

"Indeed I do... in grievous proportion," Marrow admitted sullenly.

"Well, I guess that settles that," Jek said. "But what will become of us when we get there, I wonder?" He looked searchingly at Parissah. "Will you let us help you? Will you give us a chance to prove that we really do have noble intentions? And if we do prove reliable, will you check into the Doom Fleet for us? It would mean an awful lot."

Parissah looked to Audrey, and her face had the same pleading look. But the old man was disgusted, and stormed to the cabin with a grunt.

"If you wish to be of aid, I'll not refuse it," Parissah answered at length. "Goodness knows I need any help I can get. And I trust my friend Baegulgog. If he thinks there is stock in your Despotopian Doom Fleet, then I am willing to look into it. Only we must try to heal the nation of Maenea first. My schedule will not allow otherwise."

"So it begins," Marrow announced, as if to himself, holding out and clutching a deadly talon tightly in a gesture of fiendish elation. "A partnership that will shape the course of history."

"...By keeping it in the same shape as always, I should hope," Parissah added.

"We shall see..." Marrow boded.

* * *

The night became chilly, and they all removed to the front of the boat around a lantern, having set course to a favorable wind. Even the old man eventually rejoined them, though he remained quiet and conspicuously grumpy, arms folded. Jek and Audrey huddled together with a blanket over their shoulders. Parissah recovered her cloak. The cold bothered her most of all.

"Let's have that story about Chloronatio now, Baegulgog," Audrey suggested.

Baegulgog laughed. "I'm sure you mean 'Chordonoto,' dear lady," he corrected her.

"Right, sorry," she said.

"No trouble at all. I am only glad you remembered, and still insisted on hearing the tale."

His ghosty form flashed brightly as he recalled the narrative to the forefront of his mind. "Here, then, is the story of the invention of music. I shall first set the stage. It is very near to the middle of the Meduseldan Era – the year 5,700, by your reckoning. It was a dark time. The clouds were ever thick and spouting the first rains, for Water had only recently been created, and it took millennia for the oceans to fill. Light and Dark had yet to be split into their seven varieties, and so the world was colorless. And, of course, there was nothing at all living upon the land – not plant or animal – nothing at all besides the Seven Dominions, who were ever at war.

"It was into this dim and featureless world that a Sowür Canpattel named Chordonoto one day poofed into existence, as is our wont. He was not a warrior. The Queens did not consider it proper that all of their drones should be warriors at once... for even then, long before the Inquisition or the Avarica themselves, they valued moderation. However, in that time we had thought of nothing else to do, except to mill around aimlessly. I do not say 'pace'... for pacing as an art and a pastime had yet to be invented – or in any case perfected – by the Angus Dei Dominion. But now we are getting off subject...

"The fateful day came at last. It was a day quite like any other for Chordonoto. Every so often he would float this way or that for a few feet, just as all his fellow non-warriors were accustomed to doing."

Audrey pursed her lips. "This definitely isn't how I would have expected the story to go," she said. "Chordonoto's life sounds really dull. What in the world could have inspired him to sing?"

"Ah, well! That is perhaps the most miraculous element of the tale," Baegulgog expounded dramatically. "You might consider that the whole thing happened rather haphazardly. For on this momentous day, in the company of numerous of his compatriots, Chordonoto, feeling so moved, simply burst forth into song. There really was *nothing* in particular which so moved him, a Meduseldan – neither love, nor lost-love, nor tragedy, nor beauty, nor doubt, nor hope... nor any vexation. And so, having nothing really to sing about, he simply reared back, turned his tentacles to the sky, and sang:

'Ooooooooooooooooooooooooooooo...'

"And that was the first song!"

"Wow," Audrey replied at length, if only politely.

"Yes!" Baegulgog agreed most fervently through his jolly laughter. "It really was an historic moment! Though I confess its full significance dawned rather slowly. The other Sowür Canpattels who were present for this spectacle weren't immediately sure what they thought of it. But later they decided that it was alright.

"While of course, music has become somewhat more complex over the ages, the *Refrain of Chordonoto* is still much-studied, and many great volumes of musical and philosophical theory have been written about it. And all music has its origins in the *Refrain*, for the note that Chordonoto struck in his performance of the first song has since become "the middle-C" – the most elemental note in the musical spectrum!"

"Huh," Audrey replied to all of this. "It's crazy how history is made sometimes." She looked at Jek. "Have you ever read any of those books about Chordonoto's song?"

"I tried one once, but it made my head swim," Jek admitted. "Far too technical and complicated."

The conversation quickly died after that. Baegulgog flickered contentedly, having got the chance to tell the story that was dearest to the hearts and heritage of all Sowür Canpattels.

The rest sat in a comfortable quiet, listening to the gentle lapping of the water outside the boat...

"Well," Marrow said after a few peaceful moments, stirring. "I believe that will prove an important bit of exposition. But now we must move on to other pressing business." He took up the royal spear with a flourish. "I must train Jek and Audrey to fight."

"Ye needn't do no such thing," the old man said. "I already done it!"

"I mean *really* fight," Marrow replied. "Do not forget that I was there in secret today, when you all confronted each other." He looked to Parissah thoughtfully for a second. "And on that note, please remind me to get my poison dart back from you some time."

Parissah didn't respond with words, but started immediately craning her head around in crazy contortions and feeling at her back, checking herself for the poison dart...

"Anyway, the battle was pitiful beyond description," Marrow went on. "Maenea shall prove to be a harrowing warzone, and you will need to learn all I can teach you before we make landfall."

"But it will take us a few days at most to reach Maenea," Audrey said. "What can we hope to learn by then?"

"Very little, I admit, my dear friend," Marrow lamented. "With so short a time, I can give you the skill to face four, perhaps five opponents at once. But nothing more!" He seemed truly downcast. Jek and Audrey exchanged a look.

"Can you teach me too?" Parissah asked. "I have a sword."

"Yes you *do*," Marrow said, his voice sharp with accusation. "And a sword which you do not merit, I daresay. Not by many fathoms. That is a sword which rightly belongs to one of my pupils."

Parissah was astonished. "*You* trained the swordsdrones? But I was told that the Proconsul himself..."

"I have already cautioned you not to expound to *me* the Proconsul's dealings," Marrow admonished. "I know what he has done and what I have done. Now if you want to learn something, then take up the sword and follow along! But I do not give priority to you. You have many virtues that will serve you well enough in Maenea already. And I fear your whole species is incurably clumsy. But you may certainly try to prove me wrong... if you dare."

"I will try," Parissah said, drawing the sword.

The old man brushed his hands together noisily, walking back to the cabin again in dejection. "I washes me hands at this whole affair," he said. "I already taught ye fellers. But if ye thinks the bird can teach ye any better, more power to ye." Jek and Audrey's hearts sank again. In spite of failing to find the Knights, there did seem some hope now. They sorely wished the old man would see it too...

"Don't fret about him," Marrow said when the old man had gone, apparently seeing that Jek and Audrey were distraught. "He is an obstinate creature, and we will have more trouble with him yet. But I expect all will be mended between you... before the *end*."

They didn't know what he meant, nor did they dare ask.

"Come now," Marrow continued, holding the spear out. "Let your training commence."

*   *   *

Audrey collapsed, sitting and struggling to catch her breath. "That's all I can do for tonight," she gasped.

"Yeah, I'll go along with that," Jek said, collapsing too. "We can train some more in the morning. Maybe."

"Very well," Marrow said, leaning on his spear. "You have learned next to nothing. But it is a start."

"I could go on," Parissah said, gesturing out with her sword. "I'm not tired."

"No," Marrow replied in belittling tone.

Parissah let her sword down, and put it away at length.

"We should all retire," Marrow went on.

"Even me?" Baegulgog asked.

"Of coure not *you*," Marrow snapped as he re-wrapped *Valshaloli*. He and Parissah removed to the rear of the boat. They didn't bother investigating the lodging in the cabin, giving the moody old man his space. Rather, Parissah went back to the bench beside the gunwale where she had earlier been unconscious. Marrow finally flew up to the crow's nest and perched to sleep. As he was incapable of resting anyway, Baegulgog was to monitor their progress. If the boat began to pitch one way or the other, though, he would have to wake someone else to deal with it. He was a ghost, after all, and couldn't very well steer the ship, even if he had ever been instructed how to pilot one.

That left Jek and Audrey alone at the front of the boat…

Jek looked over at his wife. He could not help noting how the light from the Other Worlds fell very beautifully upon her cheek bone. And not even the left cheek bone – he was looking at her *right*. He surprised himself, feeling a sudden wish to plant a little kiss on that cheek. But he fought it back at once. In the weeks of terror and danger they'd shared, he had come to care for her very deeply. But *this*… this was new. And at present, he felt very unsure whether she would appreciate such a gesture. He wondered how a man was ever supposed to know. So he abandoned the idea, looking down past his feet a bit dejectedly.

It proved a bad time for such feelings anyway, because in the next moment, Audrey drummed-up a serious discussion. "You think we should just sleep up here?" she asked Jek. "I don't feel like moving anyway. And I don't want to bother the old man right now."

Jek sighed as he was reminded of the old man. "I don't know what we're going to do about him," he lamented. "He's stubborn and he's not taking this change in plans well at all. And I can't help thinking about Horus Templar's warning."

"You shouldn't read too much into that, I don't think," Audrey said. "After all we've been through, I can't believe the old man is intentionally deceiving us."

Jek shifted uncomfortably. "I'm not sure I really believe it either. But now I wonder if… maybe… he might be *unintentionally* deceiving us."

"What do you mean?"

"Well, he is very old, you know. People that make it to that age can get things mixed up in their head sometimes. Maybe things aren't quite the way he remembers."

Audrey was shocked. "You think he might be wrong about the Doom Fleet? After everything we've been through? After those Despotopians nearly killed us on the Wading Isle? And the *birds*, Jek! Think of the birds!"

Jek shook his head. "I'm not saying Despotopia is off the hook, exactly. But we have to consider what Marrow brought to light. Really, what are the odds that both Despotopia *and* Roemnar are plotting some kind of diabolical naval action at the same time? I mean, I don't know... maybe they're in cahoots somehow. The Despotopian navy has been making stops at Roemnar around the clock for months. Maybe Hienrechenshlagen is complicit with Zedulon. But the more I think about it, a secret Roemnari fleet makes a *lot* more sense than a secret Despotopian one. They have their locks – they're already very practiced at hiding their things. But the whole Despotopian Doom Fleet hinges on the idea that they could somehow calm the waters in Meatgrinder Bay. How many people with Water magic would *that* take? We still don't even know if it's possible."

Audrey considered everything that Jek said at length. "It sounds like a lot of guess-work to me," she finally said. "Though I have to admit you're making sense. But I'm not about to just rule-out everything the old man told us. Not until we *know* for ourselves... one way or the other."

Jek nodded. "And I'm not saying you should. You're right. We're going to have to find out about Despotopia for sure. Because right now, if we're honest with ourselves, we simply don't *know*..."

Case Closed

"Never underestimate the power of an idea. Especially a very stupid idea."

- Zeph Bronzegloom, *What if Galahadron Mucolyptus was Wrong?*

Another Monday in court began. Horus was quick to make a study of Senahktenre. It didn't take much sleuthing to see that his condition had not improved much in the intervening week. The old vice-Vizier didn't even bother to stand when he convened the court. Horus could not help feeling a little relieved.

At this point though, there was really no use trying to gauge his odds. There were fateful actions he had taken earlier that morning that were now impossible to take back. He had already gambled everything. The die was already cast...

"Our first order of business must be to introduce special permissions, granted us by the office of the Czarina," Senahktenre announced. He turned his head toward Hamilton Blackforest with a slight tremor. "Does the state indeed possess these permissions?" He had a cautionary tone in his voice.

"It does, your Honor," Blackforest said, rising and producing papers. "I have here a waiver, which relieves the court of any accountability in the case of Jek and Audrey vs. the State, in the event that it is one day learned that we passed sentencing on a citizen with diplomatic immunity status."

He brought the papers forward to be stamped by the court officer, who processed them with marked efficiency.

"Let the record show that the court has authenticated its special permissions," Senahktenre declared.

For a moment, everything seemed to be going quite as normal. But something happened then that proved no minor disruption...

A muttering quickly escalated among the people in attendance, as was wont to happen whenever something scandalous occurred in the court. Horus knew exactly what the hubbub was about. He sat very calmly with his arms folded, suppressing a mischievous grin, while he watched Blackforest and Senahktenre squirm.

"Order!" Senahktenre barked, backing himself up with the gavel. "What is the meaning of this outburst!?"

"Your Honor," Blackforest began, hesitant even to explain the calamity. "The court recorder is *missing*."

"*WHAT*?!" Senahktenre exploded. "Inconceivable! This is an affront far in excess of anything I have known in all my years of legal practice! We must find the recorder at once!"

"Your Honor," Horus said, standing. "The defense remains ready to go forward with its case. May we proceed, despite the absence of a recorder?"

"Are you *mad*?!" Senahktenre replied. "Even now, every word we are saying goes without memorandum! The court recorder is absolutely integral to the proper carriage of this trial."

"That is interesting," Horus said bobbing his head, pacing toward the bench pensively. "Is it the court's contention that this trial is, in some way – shall we say – incomplete or inauthentic, if all of its actors are not present to fulfill their function?"

"That is precisely what..." Senahktenre began, but then cut himself off. Now, with effort, he *did* stand. He pointed his gavel at Horus. "This is *your* doing!" he shouted. "You are still on about *In Absentia*! You would have me admit, would you, that we cannot proceed without certain integral figures in this case? Very well! I admit the obvious! But by law, your clients are *not* integral here! This is a most futile maneuver, and the final straw! What gives you the audacity to do something so foolish? At least explain yourself, before I have Blackforest object, and rule you in contempt of court!"

Horus stood tall and undaunted. "I am sorry, your Honor. I understand that what I did was incredibly foolhardy. But after all, I had to try something. My conscience would not have allowed otherwise." Horus looked solemnly over at Blackforest. "A very admirable man once told me that it's important to have strong convictions, but it's much more important for those convictions to be right," he said. Blackforest returned the look, grinning and shaking his head. He knew very well who had handed Horus that line, long years ago. "It is my firm conviction, your Honor, that *In Absentia* is *not* right, and never has been. For a trial to be a trial, all parties must be present. And, if we are giving these people – Jek and Audrey – anything less than a trial, then we must also be giving them something less than justice. I, for one, do not believe in cutting corners when it comes to justice." Now Horus looked back at Deborah, imploring her to understand with his eyes. She smiled in just the way that let him know she did. "That is a belief I know I must stick to, whether I live or die by it."

"And die you shall, Mr. Templar," Senahktenre responded in an icy voice. "The prosecution will now object to the defense's filibuster, which is entirely out of order."

Hamilton said nothing.

"I'm waiting, Mr. Blackforest," Senahktenre warned.

Finally, Blackforest shifted in his chair. "There is no objection from the prosecution."

Senahktenre sputtered and wheezed in malice. "You coward!" he at last struck out at Blackforest. "You would not dirty your hands in this? Very well! I rule Mr. Templar in contempt of court anyway!" The gavel struck.

Now, Blackforest stood, a sharp smile on his face. "You'll forgive me, your Honor, but you can't do that."

Senahktenre burned holes in Blackforest with his scowl. "What did you say?"

"I believe you heard me, your Honor. Just as I heard you say only moments earlier that the trial could not continue in the absence of the court recorder. I'm afraid you can't rule Horus in contempt of *anything*... since, by your own determination, court has not truly been brought to order. My esteemed colleague here is guilty of nothing more than speaking his mind... on his own time."

With that, Senahktenre collapsed back to his chair, a broken old Jackal. "The two of you are in league against me," he said, cradling his head in his hands with his elbows on the bench. "What have I done to deserve such impudence? I have only done my duty! I have only tried to keep all of this moving towards a proper conviction! But it is obvious now that the two of you will not allow it. Whatever is a weary old man to do?"

"Would you care for a suggestion?" Horus asked boldly.

After a bit of stunned silence, Senahktenre laughed weakly. "Why not? There seems little use trying to prevent you saying whatever suits you."

"Then I suggest you grant me audience with the Czarina. Let me present my misgivings about *In Absentia* to her. Ultimately, the legality of it is hers to decide, and hers alone. If she cannot be moved on the matter, then I will finally have to be content that there is nothing more for me to do. But until I have done *everything* I can do, I will never relent."

"I will arrange it," Senahktenre replied quietly, after a long fitfull hesitance. "What more, Mr. Templar? Shall I dismiss this case? Will you then leave me in peace?"

"I wouldn't go so far as to dismiss the case just yet, your Honor," Horus answered.

Senahktenre's ears perked up, one after the other, and he looked quizzically at Horus. "You actually wish to continue, when I have offered you a dismissal?"

"Surprisingly, yes," Horus said. "There is one final witness I would like to recall. His answers to my questions should be entered into record, at least, before the case is dismissed."

"That will prove problematic," the judge responded, "since, as you know, we are without a court recorder."

Horus turned. He gave a nod to Artimus Mallard, who was standing in the back by a closet. Mallard nodded back, and he opened the closet. From within, the court recorder stumbled out, wild-eyed.

"The court recorder has been found, your Honor," Horus said. "Apparently, he was here all along. Now isn't that something."

"Very witty, Mr. Templar," Senahktenre growled. "Now please, call your *final* witness."

Horus eyed the room with a gaze that froze all hearts. "I recall Clerk Second Class Baegulgog to the stand."

* * *

The Clerk flashed vibrantly as he was called, Horus could not help but note. Doubtless he was quite bewildered to be recalled. And that was fair enough, in many ways. To be *re*called tended to be much more unexpected and stressful than giving initial testimony. But by now, Horus knew that this 'Baegulgog' had special reason for anxiety. A great doom hinged on his ability now to expose that reason. With just a few simple questions, he knew he could...

"The Clerk Baegulgog has already been sworn-in," Senahktenre said. "Let him remember that he is under oath."

"Baegulgog will tell no lies here, your Honor," the Clerk said quizzically, as he floated to the stand.

Horus checked his inner pockets, then adjusted his coat as he stood. He approached the stand – slowly, deliberately – even casually. He leaned right on it when he got there.

"Now, Mr. Baegulgog," he began at length. "You will forgive me if I indulge a personal curiosity for a moment. I confess I have always fancied the hats that Dronehood Clerks wear. May I examine yours?"

"Certainly," the Clerk answered, removing his hat and handing it to Horus. He took it and admired it thoroughly.

"Extraordinary, isn't it?" Horus asked.

"I guess I don't share your appreciation," the Clerk answered. "It is rather plain in my estimation."

Horus nodded. "To each their own. Yet, perhaps the hat itself is not so extraordinary as the fact that you have just handed it to me." He let his curious statement hang, and handed the hat back to the Clerk, resting both elbows on the bench now.

A few tense moments of silence intervened. He studied his witness. "You look tired, Mr. Clerk, if I may say so." he said at length.

More silence. The Clerk flashed with bewilderment. "That is quite impossible. Surely council knows that Meduselda do not sleep. There is no rest for me to be behind in."

"Hm, yes," Horus said, tapping his chin. "Perhaps I am merely attributing my own fatigue to you. I confess last Thursday was quite an ordeal for me. I have not yet fully recovered."

"I'm sorry to hear it," the Clerk answered, unsure.

"How was your Thursday?" Horus asked.

"It was alright."

"Any trouble with the shedding?"

"No, it went quite as usual."

"That's terrific," Horus answered, drumming on the bench and standing up straight. He reached into his jacket and retrieved a small parcel with a ruffle and a crinkle. He held it out to the Clerk.

"I show you now this candy bar," he said. "Would you like to eat it?"

"You're too kind," the Clerk said. "But I can no sooner eat than I could sleep. It simply isn't possible."

"Ah, of course, you're so right," Horus answered, replacing the candy bar and taking out a paper in its place. "I shall now read you a statement; I ask that you convey its meaning to the court." He snapped the paper crisply in his grasp, and with an intense look began to read. "Dot-dash-dash, dot-dot-dot-dot, dot-dash, dash... dot-dot-dot-dot, dot-dash, dash, dot..."

"...Your Honor," Blackforest cut in. Though he stood uncomfortably for some moments, not even sure what to say. "...I... I am hesitant to object to the defense's line of questioning. Though I feel I disgrace myself to even call what he's doing a line of questioning. Do I at *least* have the defense's assurance that he hasn't completely run amok? Is there any possible relevance to what you're doing here?"

"There is," Horus assured him. "Much in every way."

"Let me see that," the Clerk said, taking the statement from Horus and reading it himself. "Ah, yes, it is as I suspected. It says: 'What have the Creators wrought?' It is a famous statement."

"Very interesting that you would know that," Horus said, taking on a sterner aspect at once. "Would you care to tell the court what coding that message is written in?"

"It is Morse code," the Clerk answered. "I know it well."

"And why is that, 'Mr. Baegulgog'?" Horus pressed him. "Could it be that you have done work in Despotopia in the past, helping them set up their telegraph lines?"

"Well yes, I…" then the Clerk fell silent.

"You *did* work on Despotopian telegraph lines? You are consummate at Morse code, and in fact were contracted for your fluency? Isn't that highly irregular – even unheard of – for a Sowür Canpattel? That is your Dominion of origin, according to all your paperwork. Yet it is Wuu Gappews – and Wuu Gappews *alone* – whom the former Kaiser coveted for their knowledge of Morse code, is that not so?"

"They must have made an exception in my case," the Clerk answered nervously.

Horus gave him a hard stare. "I don't believe they did. In fact I do not at all believe you are a Sowür Canpattel."

"But I am!" the Clerk replied. "Really, really, I am!"

"Are you?" Horus demanded. "Then why, when I asked you about your shedding on Thursday, did you not correct me and say that you shed on *Tuesday*? For that is the day when Sowür Canpattels shed their ectodermis! It is the *Wuu Gappews* who shed on Thursdays."

"I… I must have misheard you. Tuesday and Thursday do sound alike, after all."

"You still maintain then, that you are a Sowür Canpattel?"

"I do."

"Then how do you account for your *hat*?!"

The Clerk faltered, patting his hat in place absently. "My hat?" he asked. "I don't understand."

"Of course you don't. Only a true Sowür Canpattel would. It is their convention to fix their hats to the tops of their bodies with hat glue. Yet you handed me yours effortlessly!"

Recalling the bit about hat glue, which Horus had established the previous week, the people in the court began to murmur. Senahktenre did not bother to stop them this time. Indeed, he seemed intent enough on the sudden turn in the questioning, he may not have even noticed. The Clerk flashed desperately. "I… I ran out of hat glue months ago," he said. "I've been forgetting to get more. That's all, I swear!"

"*You* swear," Horus replied. "And just who might *you* be, really? You told the judge earlier, that Baegulgog would tell no lies here in this court. But that is scarcely any wonder or assurance, since the real Baegulgog has never been *in* this court."

"But I am the real Baegulgog," the Clerk insisted. "You cannot prove otherwise."

"Can't I? Or, have you forgotten about this?" Horus held out the candy he had earlier offered the Clerk. "Yes… and now we come to it. The smoking candy bar."

"I'm afraid I don't follow," the Clerk admitted.

Horus spun and made for his table. Deborah handed him a folder. Horus returned with it.

"Behold, defense exhibit-A," Horus said, holding the folder up to the Clerk. "Medical records from a specialist in Roemnar."

"Whatever does that have to do with me?"

"They're *your* medical records," Horus answered. "Or rather, they are Baegulgog's medical records. He has been seeing a specialist on occasion about a very peculiar, personal abnormality. You see, the *real* Baegulgog suffers from an eating disorder. Which is, to say, he *eats*. The real Baegulgog, then, would not have refused this candy bar as you did."

The shock in the crowd escalated. The Clerk was utterly beside himself. "My goodness! I'm cured!" he said. "It's a miracle!"

"A miracle," Horus repeated, beaming with confidence. This was the perfect lead-in to his final, clinching point. "If that is so, it's not the only miracle you're tied up in... and indeed not even the biggest one. No, Mr. Clerk... I daresay the greater miracle is that you've managed to be in two places at once these last few weeks in court. For if, as you continue to insist, you are indeed Baegulgog, then you are both here and abroad."

"That's preposterous!" the Clerk exclaimed. "On what do you base the idea that I am currently someplace else, as well as here?"

"On your personal excusal from appearing to give testimony in court."

The Clerk flared with hard thought. "But I have no personal excusal. I did not fill out any such document."

"Of course you didn't," Horus agreed. "For, I daresay as much as you Clerks love your paperwork, you do not tend to indulge yourselves in it to the point of utter redundance. There was never any need for you to fill out your own excusal. Doubtless, the real Baegulgog knew that."

"What in the world are you talking about?"

"I'm talking about the other eyewitness. The one who *did* fill out a personal excusal. I'm talking about the Inquisitor... Primary Administrator Parissah."

"But what about her? How do you connect her with me?"

"She made the connection herself." Now Horus went and retrieved the excusal from Deborah. "Here is the waiver she filled out. As a Clerk I'm sure you will applaud her thorough approach. She filled out every single field. Importantly, she filled out *this* field," he said, holding out the document and pointing. "It is the field for requesting additional allowances. I ask that you read the contents of that field aloud to the court at this time."

He set the paper on the bench. The Clerk retrieved it, reading it to himself. He pulsated with hesitation. "Must I read this?" he asked the judge at length.

"The witness *will* read the statement aloud, as instructed by counsel," Senahktenre answered.

The Clerk held the paper up in front of him, reading it to the court in a trembling voice. "In addition to my own absence I beg the indulgence of the court to excuse the appearance of Clerk Second Class Baegulgog. I have need of his assistance in several of my ongoing affairs, and I have already approved all of this with his office. He will be abroad with me and quite unavailable for several weeks." He set the paper down at last. The court hung on a tenuous silence.

"The defense has only one remaining question for this witness," Horus said, building the suspense to its zenith. "Are you, in fact, *not* the Sowür Canpattel Baegulgog, but rather a Wuu Gappew and a Despotopian spy?"

The Clerk flashed no more. He did not even lightly blink. All his pretenses of misdirection and subterfuge came abruptly to their end.

"*Yes*," he all-but whispered.

"Let's have it louder," Horus demanded. "So the court can hear you."

The Clerk floated high behind the bench, like a sudden-hoisted banner of scornful defiance. "Yes!" he shouted. "Yes, yes, *yes*! I am an agent of his Highness, the Kaiser... by whose whim you will *all* soon perish!" He gestured wide with his tentacles over the shocked onlookers in a deep and patriotic exultation. "Long live Despotopia!"

Jengadocea's Bluff

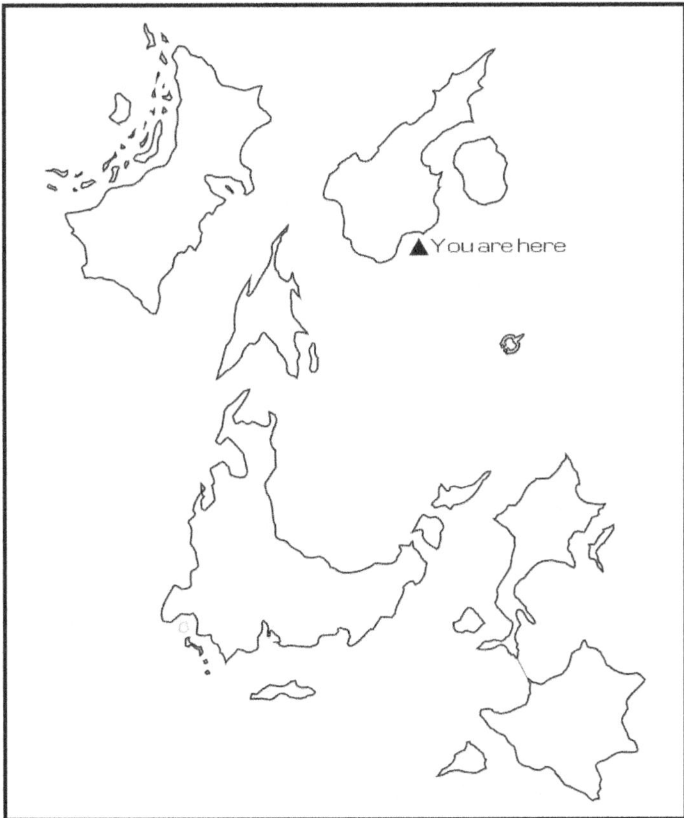

"Let us demystify progress. *What is progress, in truth? It is a conceit of the young. Would they have me believe they are wiser than their ancestors? I knew their ancestors. I have seen uncounted generations, and not one has improved on the state of affairs left over from the previous. The heart still yearns, the spirit still tires, the wit still fails. Brother still turns against brother. Show me anything,* anything *at all that has got better, and I will as soon show you that which has got worse."*

- Magormissahr, *Referendums on the World, Vol. 754*

The reality of the monumental task ahead of them only really began to dawn on Jek as his boots struck the muddy shore of Maenea. He blanched thinking back to that moment, only a few nights ago, when he had rather casually volunteered to help heal a failed state in which a madman and his army of revolutionary zealots now roved, unchecked by the powers of civilization. The Inquistor – Parissah – had made it sound like it was all in a day's work. As Jek's eyes roamed over the vast lands before him, that conceit was glaring. If his first impression of Roemnar had seemed underwhelming, Maenea could not have been more the opposite. Not far from the sandy coast, the land marched down into a sprawling, grassy valley, with dense forest barring the eastern expanse. Stately, snow-capped mountains could be dimly espied beyond, cloaked in a misty distance. He could see for many miles all around, with no sign of settlement in view, though he knew Maenea was well-settled – or at least had been prior to the Free-Dome crisis. It was immediately obvious that this was a *huge* country. Not quite as huge as his native Jast-Madiir, but certainly a much, *much* larger region than he felt any ability whatsoever to affect the fortunes of, whether for better or worse...

"Is this really where we meant to come ashore?" Jek asked, as Parissah deboarded next to him. "There doesn't seem to be anything here. Or even anywhere near here."

"There was no mistake," Parissah said. "Your wife guided us expertly. This is precisely where I hoped to make landfall."

"Do you mind if I ask why?"

"Not at all." She pointed along the edge of the forest, finally banking her hand toward the east. "We are making for a fortification on the north-east of that jungle," she said. Jek was immediately troubled.

"*Jungle*," he repeated before she had a chance to continue. "That forest *did* look unsettlingly like a jungle. I hoped against hope it wasn't."

"Oh, it is very much a jungle," Parissah nodded, assuring him. "Within it lies a host of killer Mantids, who have claimed a great many of the envoys that we could sorely have used for this mission. And yet, the Mantid jungle has its use for our current purposes. None have dared to settle in this valley because of them. That means that our long trek to Jengadocea's Bluff is unlikely to meet with many of Herz Bravado's patrols. There simply isn't anything out here to patrol."

"Jengadocea's Bluff?" he asked.

"Yes, it is the name of the fort we are making for. It cannot be seen from here, but there is a cliff that rises up out of the jungle on the north side, and a fort is built into the sheer face. It is the only settlement that borders the jungle, and one of the last remaining holdouts of the loyalist forces. Even New Miranthar, the capitol, is now besieged by Bravado. But I fear we shall have to go there eventually."

"What exactly is our mission here?" Jek asked. "What can just the six of us hope to do against this whole army of Free-Dome fighters that are running amok out there?"

"Hopefully we will not have to do anything against them. My mission is to rendezvous with a delegation of my peers at Jengadocea's Bluff. Unfortunately, Herz Bravado's movement now controls enough of the country that we must recognize him diplomatically, and attempt to mediate between him and the Countess, Jengadocea herself."

Jek made a face. "You mean, the Inquisition is just going to give Free-Dome its blessing? I thought his ideas were way too controversial for that!"

"All of that remains undetermined," Parissah explained. "The Inquisition has not had direct dealings with Bravado yet. We had long hoped Jengadocea would crush his insurrection. But it has gone quite the other way. Now we must hear him out, and see whether we can possibly accept his seemingly vulgar new idea of governance by popular sovereignty, and the idealism that underpins it.

"But there is much danger. We have no assurance that he will recognize our delegation. That is why we are taking the long road. We could have made landfall around the coast to the north-east, and been considerably closer to our destination. But that approach would have meant putting-in at a coastal city. We cannot be sure of the safety of such an approach, since Bravado now controls nearly the entire navy, and his forces rove about besieging the coastal holdings."

Jek shook his head. "Your job is very complicated," he said.

"Yes," she agreed.

"So, what do we do first?"

"I planned to scout ahead for a while, and look for signs that my fellow Inquisitors have passed this way. They will have left me some clue." She looked at him appraisingly. "Do you wish to accompany me?"

Jek pursed his lips, shrugging. "Okay," he answered. He almost surprised himself with his willingness. But after all, it seemed easier to be brave now. *Especially* now... in the presence of a travelling companion who actually came across as knowing what she was doing...

* * *

Back on Mallard's boat, Audrey set about mooring. She was unassisted by the old man, who was weaving another long yarn on the Clerk Baegulgog – of all their new companions, the only one the old man seemed to take to. After all, the Clerk had backed him up, and proven a good audience for his account of the Doom Fleet... and many other tales since. She felt rather bad for Baegulgog, knowing that the old man didn't like to let go of an ear, once he'd bent it. But it did her good to see that the old man was in higher spirits than he had been the last few days...

When the boat was secure, she went into the cabin to retrieve her own pack and provisions. It was dim and moody below deck, with the light that came from the windows flaring uncomfortably in her eyes, and yet seeming hardly to fall on anything in the room. Marrow was down there, facing away from her. He appeared to be looking for something. She felt some uncanny impression, just then, that he did not know for what...

"It was all for you, you know," Marrow said, still turned away. Then he laughed, low and grim. "But perhaps that is too prescriptive. I do not deny that this is what I wanted. More than anything. Or, *nearly* anything. And yet, you must believe. You must *know* that I did it for you."

Audrey shook her head, quite perplexed. "What are you talking about, Marrow?" she asked.

"*Marrow*," he repeated quietly, almost as a question. The gaze of his mirrored goggles snapped back to her as in sudden surprise. "When are we?" he asked urgently. It was a curious question.

"We... we just reached Maenea," she answered meekly.

"Oh dear," he replied, waxing distant again for a moment. "I quite lost my place, just then."

"But goodness, whatever were you talking about?" she asked, feeling a tender sort of sympathy behind her confusion.

Marrow hesitated. "Something I have no cause to say yet. Though something, I fear, I shall never have the proper chance to say..."

Audrey was very affected by all of this. Marrow's words revealed nothing, but the feeling in them spoke volumes. She had watched Marrow behave quite callously toward most of the others in the days they had traveled together. But always with her he was specially gentle. She wondered at it. "You're seeing the future again, is that it?" she inquired.

He sighed, nodding. "That is ever my curse."

She shook her head. "I can't imagine what it's like to see the future. I would have thought it would be awesome. But it sounds like you hate it."

He laughed with a heavy heart again. "Even I must admit, it is not *all* bad. I have always cherished my memories of you, my dear."

"I take it we come to be very good friends," she said, marveling at the strange nature of this whole conversation.

He nodded. "Yes we do."

Now she suppressed a nervous snicker. "I can't imagine why. You seem so wise and proud – and domineering and strong. I'm really none of those things."

"Then perhaps it should be no mystery," he replied.

She ran her fingers through her hair in exasperation. "Practically everything you say is a mystery," she said. "Like with this other thing that's been bothering me."

"Oh?"

"Well, that first night, you said the future is immutable and that we would go to Maenea first."

"And so we have."

"But the only reason we ultimately decided to go to Maenea is because that's where you told us we would go!"

Marrow gave a long, slow nod. "Ah! You begin to understand Time."

"No," she disagreed at once. "Just the opposite – I feel very confused about it now."

"That is exactly what I mean," he explained. "You understand Time only once you understand that you do not understand it... because Time is weird."

Audrey was left speechless for a spell, stricken with a dopey smile of exasperation. Marrow was endlessly bewildering… in an endearing way, of course. And he exuded some sort of regal tragedy like a thick slime. For her part, she did begin to see how they could be friends…

"Now let us ready ourselves for the task at hand," Marrow went on at length, taking up *Valshaloli* and striding purposefully past her.

"That *is* what I came down here to do in the first place," Audrey said, grabbing her pack and following…

* * *

Soon they were all prepared. Jek and Parissah returned from their scouting, bringing good tidings.

"The other Inquisitors have gone ahead of us," Parissah reported. "It does not guarantee that they ever reached Jengadocea's Bluff, but it is a better omen than none. If they do not make the fort, then hopefully we will. And, of course, vice-versa."

"N'there's a bit o' optimism," the old man muttered.

"I fear our progress will be slow," Parissah went on. "Baelgulgog can only float so fast, and we can do nothing to speed him along in his ghostly form. But we cannot afford to leave him behind. If all of us die, it falls to him to return to the Citadel and report everything that he has witnessed here."

"Another mighty hopeful thought," the old man retorted.

"We certainly cannot reach the fort before nightfall," she continued, ignoring the peanut gallery. "You must be prepared to travel through the night. There is no time to set aside for sleeping. So let us be on our way now. And keep your eyes open for enemies. Bravado's men may still traverse this valley to make war in the western reaches. We must also be wary of the jungle, for as I have told Jek, it is fraught with Mantids."

"But Mantids won't leave the jungle willingly," Audrey said. "Not even to ambush stupid passers-by, I wouldn't think."

"Well, do not take that for granted," Parissah warned. "I have not forgotten your remarkable encounter with Mantids native to your land. But one tribe may not be quite as the next. So we should not fail to exercise caution. Still, we must skirt the jungle, because it is the fastest way, short of cutting through, which is too great a risk. And hopefully it will make us hard to spot, if Free-Dome fighters do enter the valley." Without further delay, she put a shoulder to her pack and started walking. "Come now," she said. "Anything more can be discussed on the way."

* * *

They journeyed for hours, risking no sound beyond the pitter-patter of their feet. Even armed with considerable new training from Marrow, Audrey's healing powers and the greatly increased strength of the Questing Party at large, Jek couldn't help feeling rather anxious in the shadow of another Mantid jungle. And the happy sounds of little birdies up in the branches certainly did nothing to ease his mind. He noticed Audrey cast many glances under the trees. He could little know that she was remembering Chief Katydid and the Dyeus Tribe... entertaining a curious hope, however distant, that they might have come here, and were now living happily at war just beyond her sight...

It was early afternoon before Marrow finally spoke up, breaking the long silence. "We will not make Jengadocea's Bluff without a fight," he said.

Parissah stopped in her tracks and turned to regard him. "Have you had a premonition?" she asked.

"No," he answered. "I simply happened to look to the west, just now..."

They all looked now. Sure enough, a sizeable troop – around 30 to 40 – had come into view, advancing eastward across the valley at an aggressive march.

"It seems the opposite of what you feared has happened," Marrow went on. "The Free-Dome fighters are not marshalling against the west. Rather, they are returning from it. Perhaps victorious. Or perhaps because they have been recalled to a more decisive battle."

"Oh come now!" Baegulgog exclaimed. "Let us not be needlessly pessimistic. Is it not at all possible that they are returning in defeat?"

"Pessimism is never needless," Marrow retorted. "And I deem that chance exceptionally remote."

"Maybe we oughts ta shelter in the trees," the old man suggested. "Can't be Mantids behind e'ery one o' them. I warrant we gots a better chance a few rows in than we gots in the open."

"I concur," Parissah said. "The five of you should shelter. But I am going to remain here."

"You're what!?" Jek asked. "What about making the fort? Why gamble your life here and now?"

She regarged him. "It occurs to me now: If these are Free-Dome fighters, then this affords me an important opportunity to gauge their regard for the authority of the Inquisition. To learn where we stand with them now will be invaluable going forward. I do not believe I should let that pass."

"But what if they try to kill you?" Jek pressed her.

"Then we stop them," Marrow said. "They number only 35." Jek was not encouraged.

"Baegulgog, you go ahead and scout into the trees," Parissah instructed. "If there are any Mantids here, they will hopefully reveal themselves in a vain effort to kill you. The rest of you follow at a safe distance."

"It will be done, madam!" Baegulgog saluted, before lofting lazily into the jungle.

Jek watched tensely through the brush. He could see Parissah, and vaguely glimpse the distant troop of Free-Dome fighters. It was a very long, anxious wait. It honestly did not appear that the troop had taken any notice of Parissah, and may well pass beyond the valley and the jungle northward, without ever being the wiser. Jek became hopeful...

It was about then that Parissah drew her snail pistol, wound it up, and fired at the troop! Her electromagnetically-accelerated slug hit the ground in their midst with sufficient force to dislodge a plume of dirt and debris hardly dissimilar from the strike of a cannon ball. Needless to say, it got their attention. After some moments of confusion, they began to advance in Parissah's direction. She wound another shot, then holstered her pistol. Jek and Audrey readied their muskets. Marrow was no where to be seen...

There were several more uncomfortable minutes, waiting for the insurgents to reach the jungle's edge. The clatter of their heavy plate armor heralded their approach with a healthy lead. Jek was honestly rather mystified by the pace they could sustain on foot, outfitted as they were. Grueling discipline was one thing. He felt distinctly that there was more at work here. Namely, dark fanaticism.

"Hail!" Parissah called out at length. "Greetings to the people of Maenea. You are Free-Dome fighters, is that right?"

The ironclad soldiers hesitated, exchanging looks under scary helmets. "We are Free-Dome fighters," answered one, in a cold voice. "Who are you?"

Now Parissah hesitated. "I can give you my name, if it will mean something to you," she said. "I am Parissah, Primary Administrator of the Inquisition."

The soldiers continued to seem perplexed. "We know nothing of this *Inquisition*," the one said. "Perhaps you are a new regiment?"

Jek marveled. They hadn't heard of the Inquisition? He had never heard of anyone who hadn't heard of the Inquisition...

"A new *regiment*?!" Parissah replied, not much able to suppress her own astonishment. "What an incongruous question! My Order is as old as any principality yet upon the earth, save the Seven Dominions. It is known to everyone. And you ask if it is a new *regiment*? Surely you jest, though I can't imagine why."

"We make no jokes," the insurgent answered, rather annoyed. "Nor do we care for your self-important boasting. There was nothing before Free-Dome, and there will be nothing after. So now answer for yourself: You attacked us! Was this in error? Is your 'Inquisition' for Free-Dome, or against it?"

Parissah shook her head. "I don't know yet. Presently we are a neutral third party."

The insurgent drew a heavy broadsword, and his troop did likewise. "We recognize no neutrality," he said, grimly. "If you are not for Free-Dome, then you are an enemy."

Parissah drew on him. "I am here to speak with Herz Bravado," she replied. "Take me to him. Let your master decide whether I am to be treated as an enemy or not."

The insurgent shook his head. "Your words betray you. You *are* an enemy indeed. I do not need Herz Bravado to make this decision for me."

"And why is that?"

"Because he told me so."

Jek managed not to notice that Audrey was already running to Parissah's aid, until she was nearly at the tree line. Seeing this, he charged after her urgently. All three humans soon joined Parissah in the standoff, with Baegulgog making the best time he could.

"It's no use," Audrey declared, leveling her musket against the troops. "You'll have to kill us all."

The 35 insurgents regarded their four opponents. "I think we'll manage," one said. "Charge, men!"

Jek's heart leapt to his ears. He didn't even hear the first strikes of the heavy plated boots as they charged for him. Parissah fired, and two enemies fell. Jek and Audrey fired next. But their shots did little more than stagger the thickly armored Insurgents. Not less than ten of them were mere steps away!

It was at this moment that a dark shape descended from the sky amid the Free-Dome fighters in a deadly wrath. Even the vanguard of their attack stopped short, hearing the distress of their brethren from behind. Marrow had loosed himself into their ranks, wading through the enemies with the easy grace of a dance he had performed hundreds of times.

Jek looked on mesmerized, as did the insurgents who were near enough at hand to strike him down. Watching Marrow fight was visually baffling. It was a spectacle as well as a puzzle. Marrow had one leg to maneuver on, and one to hold the spear... yet it seemed no handicap. And he defied the old man's principle of 'be faster'. His success didn't come from getting twice as many moves in, but rather, from getting five times the result out of every one move. And even the unyielding steel of the Maeneans could not seem to hinder the keen edge of *Valshaloli*. It was the perfect weapon for the perfect fighter.

As Marrow worked deeper into the ranks, and so farther away, it seemed everyone at the front remembered at once that they were in a melee. Two Free-Dome fighters turned their broadswords against Jek with impressive strength as well as finesse...

But to his own amazement, Jek navigated every overlapping attack with exhilarating clarity. Despite their skill and their zeal, the Free-Dome fighters were undeniably hindered by their heavy gear. Jek not only had superior agility, but now – thanks to the few days of grueling regimentation under Marrow – he had real expertise to take advantage of it. Of course, to call the fight *easy* would have been conceit. The blows were too heavy for him to do better than lead them a few critical degrees out of the way. Each slash was a close shave, and one mistake would have been fatal...

But he was *able*.

Harder still was finding a vulnerable spot on his opponents. The armor turned his bayonette away time and again. Finally, he found success slashing at the back of the knees. Jek was in such an acute mindset of survival that the cold pragmatism of the fight brought shame he only felt distantly and dimly at the time. But there was a corner of his mind that lamented what a horrible sort of a thrill it all was...

Finally, relieved of his own engagements, Jek rushed to Audrey's aid, although she was wrapping-up at nearly the same time. The two of them assisted Parissah and the old man, who were still embattled. By now Baegulgog was loose on the battlefield, floating in a fret, wishing to contribute something.

But he needn't have worried. The four of them defeated the ten in their midst. Marrow took the rest.

Even after the fight was won, it did not altogether end. The injured Free-Dome fighters did not relent, though they could do nothing beyond crawl after their adversaries. It was a very piteous sight. Now the guilt came, and it hit hard. Jek was no soldier – and even if he had been, this was not truly his fight. He didn't know anything – rightly – about Free-Dome, beside frightening rumors. He felt sympathy he could not help for the troops they had just slain or maimed. And if he had any prejudices against their cause going into the battle, he could not feel sure of them now...

Audrey was clearly troubled too. "Oh, this is awful," she said. "Can I heal them?"

"Regrettably, no," Parissah answered. "It is clear they would only repay your kindness by trying to kill us again."

Marrow returned to them, leaning on the spear. "There is another way to relieve their suffering," he said darkly.

"I'll not have that either," Parissah replied, pointing cautioningly. "We have acted in justifiable defense of ourselves. But to execute these fighters now would be in breach of my neutrality."

"But how can we just leave them here?" Audrey asked. "That's almost worse than killing them."

Parissah sighed. "If they are returning from the west, it stands to reason others will pass by the same way. Surely they can enlist the help of their fellows. That will have to be good enough. I believe we should leave this place immediately, and take counsel on the road."

She began walking away at once. It weighed on the Humans, and Baegulgog flashed with some remorse. But eventually, they all followed silently.

* * *

They walked on moodily for some minutes, before the old man piped up. "I think we's far enough away," he said. "So how is it them Free-Dome fighters ain't never heard o' the Inquisition? 'Less they was born yesterday, can't rightly wrap me head around it."

"That is a grievous puzzle," Parissah replied. "It is true, the Inquisition's influence here has indeed waned in the crisis. But for them to be utterly ignorant of us? It defies explanation!" She snaked a look back over her shoulder. "What do you make of it, Marrow?"

"I too have more questions than answers," Marrow said. "I had heard that Herz Bravado has made all manner of the Countess' soldiers into turncoats. Even some of her most loyal and elite Colonial Guard are said to be working for him now. I was loath to believe it, before today. But some of those I fought were not atrocious. A few had real skill... and I fear they bore the mark of the Countess on their armor."

"Just what *is* the deal with Herz Bravado?!" Audrey asked, exasperated. "I know he's in charge of this whole Free-Dome cult or whatever that's turned the country upside-down. But surely you know something more than that! Where did he come from? What's his background?"

"Little is known for certain," Parissah admitted. "In our attempts to learn such things, we have only unearthed folk legends. They say he is some sort of wild man. That he grew up in the hills, only dimly aware of the civilized world through much of his youth. And those are only the more believable tales." She pointed out east, past the covering of the jungle, to reaches they could not see. "Many claim that he wandered long in the mists of *Thasagral*... the only mortal ever to return from its eternal shroud. Perhaps it is this mystique that allows him to command such zeal among his men. Yet that is only a guess."

"I ain't in no mood for such mysteries," the old man declared. "Me old brain is fer simple problems, with simple solutions."

"That's half-true, anyway," Jek retorted. "Our old matter of the Doom Fleet might be a comparably simple problem... but does it really have a simple solution?"

"Ye know well enough, lad," the old man admonished. "The simple solution was ta find the Indigo Knights."

"But that is no solution at all," Parissah argued. "That is just bringing a problem to someone else's attention, and then expecting them to solve it for you."

"Aye," the old man agreed. "That be the very definition of a simple solution."

"In any case, I suppose we shall have to hope to learn something from the loyalists, when we reach Jengadocea's Bluff," Baegulgog put in. "But it is a shame that we cannot avail ourselves of our Heron friend's foresight in this. A statistician hates a puzzle."

"As does the Heron fortune-teller," Marrow retorted. "But my foresight tells me this much: We will have the answers to our questions, ere long. For good or ill."

It was well past nightfall when they reached the lip of the valley, and turning east as the trees allowed, began to march down into another lowland, even as the jungle to their right started to mount up higher in the distance.

It was a tireless cross-country adventure. For many hours it had seemed no exertion at all, being kept to a shuffling pace so that Baegulgog would not fall behind. But the skirmish demanded much strength, and now Jek was feeling his exhaustion catching up with him. He looked at his Human companions, and they were in a slump. The poor old man was panting through his jagged teeth. Even Marrow seemed to show signs of weariness, if Jek could interpret anything of bird posture. Parissah, on the other hand, was upright and alert. Jek began to suspect she could maintain this pace for weeks without stopping. Baegulgog, of course, could not tire.

It was nearly dawn when Parissah spoke next. "There it is," she said. "I can see at last the pinnacle of the Bluff around the bend in the jungle."

"Praise be," the old man wheezed, not even bothering to look up. "Me legs can't bear me no further."

"That is a conundrum," Parissah replied. "I can *see* the Bluff, but it is still leagues distant."

"Well darn it all ta Heck," the old man said, collapsing to his knees. "I shore ain't got stanima enough left fer that! Ye all go on without me. This be as fine a spot to take me dirt nap as any, I warrant."

Parissah regarded him. "You really are quite exhausted?" she asked. "This is not just more of your drama?"

"Nay. I is true, plug tuckered out," the old man sighed. "And I resents the implication."

Parissah strode over to him. He hardly had time to look up and go wide-eyed before she had snatched him from the ground and slung him over her shoulder. "There you are," she said with a reassuring pat. "You may rest now." She turned and continued on the way. Jek smiled weakly at the comical look of shock and embarrassment on the old man's face.

The march scarcely got easier as the fort drew closer. The morning light – pink and orange – the mists over the dewy grass, and the thicker fog weaving through the mountains was altogether enervating to Jek. Still at whiles his body seemed to recall its rhythms at the lighthouse, where morning meant bed time. Privately he began to mentally stake-out Parissah's other shoulder. It was at this point that he felt a small hand on his own shoulder, and suddenly a shocking wave of restoration swept over him. He was refreshed, as if he had just had some heavy-duty sleep. He looked back and saw Audrey beside him. She smiled, and seemed quite vital herself.

"Was that your Life magic?" Jek asked.

"Well yeah," she chortled. "It just occurred to me I could probably use it this way."

Jek made a face. *"Life magic,"* he whispered, as if to himself. "I don't mean to complain... but sometimes, it feels like a cheat."

"Oh well," she shrugged.

"A cheat it may seem," Marrow cut in, a bit startling. "But do not be fooled. Your powers are great, my dear, but they are not infinite. There are limits to the magic you may exercise without resting it... even if you use the magic to refresh yourself. Take care that you never push those limits! You may come, hard and fast, to an exhaustion too great to remedy."

Jek showed immediate concern. "Is she in any danger of that now?"

"Gracious, no," Marrow replied. "To grant the semblance of rest to the two of you is a small enough deed. She could do much more today. I merely wish her to understand that her Life magic is not inexhaustible, no matter how cleverly she may use it. Eventually she would have to sleep, for her reserves of magic cannot be used to replenish themselves. And she must be very conscious of the condition of those she tries to heal. The closer the patient is to death, the more her strength will be taxed – at an exponential rate." He looked directly at Audrey now. "Push yourself too far, and you may just find you are dying along with them."

"Good to know," Audrey said, hardly sounding phased by Marrow's grave warnings.

Grimacing, Jek chanced to look directly at the old man, his upper body still draped limply behind Parissah. "You should really help him out too," he suggested.

"Nah, not yet," Audrey argued. "When we reach the fort. For now, I'll let him sleep. I'd just hate to disturb him when he looks so comfortable."

Jek blinked. 'Comfortable' was not the word he would choose for the old man's current state – being doubled over and swaying like a wet noodle with a scaly shoulder to his gut.

"I think if he was *comfortable*, he'd be snoring," Jek said. But Audrey just shrugged again.

* * *

Finally, around midday, they reached Jengadocea's Bluff. It was an oddity. The fort was indeed built into a sheer rock face, but its construction was wooden. The people of Maenea had felled hundreds of trees, stripped their branches, and then stuck them in the ground in an overlapping fence pattern. The stone they had chiseled out of the cliff face had then been unceremoniously piled up against the walls in sloping heeps. Above, something of finer workmanship revealed itself. There was a barbed wire running in strands from the tops of the walls up to the overhang of the cliff in many places. Audrey surmised that, due to the fort's close proximity to the Mantid jungle, this was probably a contingency against enemies that could perform flying leaps. At any rate, it was an ugly fort, and unrefined. But it looked somewhat defensible.

"So this is Jengadocea's Bluff," Jek said. "It looked pretty bad a ways off. It doesn't look any better from here."

"Kind of rough, huh?" Audrey commiserated.

Jek set his jaw. "I guess I just wasn't expecting something so... so *primitive*, for lack of a better word."

"Maenea is a bit backwater compared to Jast-Madiir," Audrey told him. "They do a lot of things more old-fashioned in this country. They have a very long and proud colonial history, which they've never really let go of, even though they were disowned by their parent state many generations ago."

"I know the tale," Jek said. "To some extent, anyway. Maenea was just a fiefdom under the Ganzerburken Empire, which controlled them from the continent. They used to levy a huge tea crop from Maenea year after year. But after losing hundreds of trade ships to Meatgrinder Bay, and with the rise in the popularity of coffee, Ganzerburk eventually decided it was too expensive to maintain Maenea as a colony, and basically told them to start ruling themselves. The local line of Counts and Countesses has been in charge ever since. But I think they've never given up trying to reclaim their colonial status with Ganzerburk. Evidently they haven't moved on."

"I couldn't have put it any better," Audrey agreed. "From all I've ever heard, they're very stuck in the past. All kinds of things reflect that. They've hardly advanced anything about themselves since they were a colony – except where it was absolutely necessary. I doubt if we'll see any firearms while we're here. But they do have cannons."

"That doesn't bode well in a wooden fort," Jek said.

"No, but I bet they built this fort mostly with Mantids in mind," Audrey replied.

"You are correct," Parissah chimed in, overhearing their discussion. "This fort went up early in Jengadocea's reign, as an initial effort to start settling closer to the jungle. Maenea's population was booming at that time, and it seemed very practical to start making new towns and villages and to claim more territory for agriculture. She could not have guessed then that most of her country's inhabitants would be driven out by this mad insurrection...

nor that she would have to defend her new fort against a radical element of her own subjects. It is a pitiless irony."

"I guess so," Jek nodded.

"Still, this fort proves better than none," Parissah went on. "It *is* one of the Countess' few remaining bastions. In that sense I am sure she does not regret building it."

As they drew toward the foot of the front wall, well under the shadow of the Bluff, a voice at last called down to them. "Hoy, there!" came the voice of a soldier, stooping over the wall's edge. "What's your business?"

"We are on an errand of the Inquisition," Parissah called back. "Myself and my associates were to rendezvous with a larger delegation here. Have the others arrived safely?"

"Aye, that they have," the soldier replied, sounding at once satisfied by her answer, but also dismayed. "Only I'm afraid they up and left without ye already."

Parissah stood flummoxed for a few beats. "That leaves me in an odd spot," she said at last. "Why have they gone?"

"Pray ye come in and hear the whole thing more comfortably," the soldier answered, and the small door of the fort swung open beneath him. "The Countess herself is waitin' for ye. They told her there would be another."

"The Countess is *here*?" Parissah asked. "That is more strange tidings."

"Aye, well, these be strange times. But we'll take ye to her straight away. She'll explain it all."

Another soldier in heavy armor entered the doorway and waved them forward. Audrey suddenly felt hesitant, and even a little fearful. The rest of the party seemed to have tangible reservation. Maenea was pretty topsy-turvy at the moment. Being invited into this fastness, without the reassuring presence of the other Inquisitor delegates, felt uncannily like walking into a trap. She exchanged a nervous look with Jek.

But Parissah turned to Marrow. "Do we go in?"

"Yes," he said.

Baegulgog made a noise like clearing his throat. "Perhaps you should unload your baggage first," he indicated to Parissah.

"Oh my, yes," Parissah said setting the old man down. "I had nearly forgot about him." He didn't straighten out much, being set on the ground. He stirred and groaned and cursed under his breath.

"Did you sleep well, old man?" Audrey asked.

"Nay," he answered through clenched teeth. "But it were much better than bein' awake now! Me back's been pinched into a horseshoe! Can't straighten it out for the life o' me!"

Audrey knelt over him with a healy hand. There were audible pops, and a few more carefully-chosen oaths. But after a few seconds, the old man limbered up, and he stood, testing his flexibility, and seeming quite pleased with the results.

"Thank ye, darlin'," he said solemnly. "Ye saved me goin' through life like an inchworm with a hernia. I's much obliged."

"You're very welcome," Audrey said.

Just as everyone began shuffling for the door, Parissah stepped up to Audrey. She didn't speak right off, and seemed almost a bit embarrassed. "While you're exercising your magic," she finally began, tapping her long fingers together, "I wonder if you might help me with a flesh wound I incurred during the battle with the Free-Dome fighters. It is relatively minor; I hesitate even to mention it."

"Let me see," Audrey replied. Parissah turned, and there was an enormous gash in her side, from which a great deal of flesh was hanging loose. It was one of the grossest things Audrey had ever seen.

"My gosh," she said, recoiling. Then she set immediately to work, both hands glowing bright with magical radiance. "Say something next time!"

Passing into the fort proved to be a morose spectacle. The shody walls concealed unexpected crowds of people, looking to be in equally rough shape. There were many dispirited-looking soldiers, but they were vastly outnumbered by women, children, and the elderly. All had made a hard living – as Humans were wont to do – but it seemed a lifetime of labor was not sufficient to give them the ruggedness they needed in the present crisis. They were dirty and their eyes were dull and vacant, and they looked malnourished.

Audrey hurt for them. And she was unpleasantly surprised. For many that she was paraded by looked up from the dirt, and they met her gaze intensely. And their aspect changed as they did. Those that looked to her were no longer empty husks of people. They appeared suddenly expectant. Perhaps even hopeful. This troubled Audrey even more.

"Who are all these people?" Audrey asked, too distressed to let the subject lie unbroached.

"They're all that remains of the citizenry loyal to the Countess," their soldier-guide answered. "The rest have either fled the country, or been absorbed by Bravado's dark crusade," he continued. "Most of these escaped from the capitol, as the Countess herself did. We made use o' the old underground passageways that lead out o' the city. But most of our forts have secret escape routes o' that sort, and some of these came here from elsewhere in like fashion."

"It is miraculous that any escaped that way," Parissah said, "let alone the Countess herself. The passageways should have been no secret to the Colonial Guard that Bravado has swayed."

"Nevertheless, the ways were not watched," the soldier recounted. "We canna imagine why not. But it is a good turn we'll accept, sans questions."

They came at last to gates that opened into the rock face at the back of the fort, and within was a hall, bright and ornate. It was no palace hall, but it was far cozier and more refined than anything else they had seen within Jengadocea's Bluff. Natural water from the deep, dense stone was collected into gentle streams flowing down into several small fountains. Brilliant sconses reinforced severe shafts of light, captured from outside and cleverly redirected by a series of mirrors into the chamber. The light fell on some impressive art installations along the walls – mostly colored-pencil depictions of important battles for the fate of the world from all across history. Audrey regarded them rather absently for a few seconds. They seemed a fitting muse, given the situation. The country's fate hung by a thread, and would soon be decided once and for all. The certainty of that doom was palpable.

At the end of the hall, beneath a trio of hydra skulls, there was a modest seat of power. And on that seat was a woman – well-dressed, but not extravagant. There was no crown on her head, nor even a circlet... though her rich hair was braided within a great silvered clasp. Beside that, the stateliest element of her attire was a very splendid cape, held over her shoulders by a silver chain. A furrowed brow stooped above keen, bright eyes as she rested the side of her head on long fingers, regarding her new guests. It was just as the soldier had said. This was the Countess – Jengadocea herself. She *had* to be... for only Counts and Countesses, among the sprawling spectrum of the uppercrust, could exude such taste, refinement, charisma, and wisdom... even without doing or saying anything. Or, so Audrey had been told...

"Hope alive, here be the final Inquisitor at last!" Jengadocea said, standing to receive them, clasping her hands together. Almost immediately, her gaze fell directly on Audrey. It was a disarming moment. Because, for whatever reason, the Countess was looking at her in exactly the same way all the commoners had. "And is it not just as I guessed?" Jengadocea went on. "You have brought her with you! She with the cheekbone! The one from the Prophecy!"

Now Parissah turned to look at Audrey. Her look was not so hopeful. More like perplexed and accusatory (from what could be told behind her mask, anyway). But quickly she returned to face forward...

"Greetings, Countess, and well-met," Parissah said, kneeling. Everyone else followed her example, except Marrow, who deigned nothing more than a nod. "I only hope that my presence here will be of some service, even in this exceptionally late hour." She looked back at Audrey again. "But you make it sound as if I have already done something for you quite unintentionally. What Prophecy are you referring to? Surely not... the *Chocolate* Prophecy!"

"Ah, surely nay!" Jengadocea exclaimed. "But it be another of Zedulon's prophecies that I spake of. One that he delivered in my grandfather's days. The Visitation Prophecy."

"You will have to forgive me, and refresh my memory, Countess," Parissah said.

Jengadocea strode forward, her unseen shoes clipping crisply on the stone floor. "You know our history, at least, I assume? Maenea is in truth but a colony. Nay, indeed we are a deal more humble than that. We are a *forgotten* colony – long-since disowned. Many generations of our folk have come and gone, hoping that one day we would be remembered by our rightful lords away on the continent, and be ruled again from afar as of old. And each generation has lost a little bit more of this hope in the turning o' the years. But in the Visitation Prophecy, we took heart. Zedulon foretold that a monarch from the continent would once again walk in our midst and command our respect... at the very time of our land's greatest need! I have no doubt that time is *now*... for ne'er have we faced such a black fate as what Herz Bravado has in store." Now she rested a hand on Audrey's shoulder. "And so I have no doubt that you have brought forth the fulfillment of that very Prophecy. This is Princess Aaliyah!"

Audrey was incredulous. *'Aaliyah'* indeed! What had begun as a perfectly innocent time where her husband forgot her name had since grown into a very unfortunate serial. Now it seemed just about *everybody* was calling her Aaliyah... and what's worse, *Princess*!"

"Thou artest mistakeneth, your Countessliness," Audrey replied, in her best high-falootin' grammar. "I ameth just Audrey."

"Gracious! Don't go using that grammar for the likes o' me, m'lady!" Jengadocea recoiled, covering her mouth as she laughed nervously. "Tis bad enough you've knelt. Please stand! I am only a Countess, and you owe me no sign of reverence, whether this be my land or no."

Audrey did stand, and she dropped the grammar, for it was a struggle to render anyway. "But I'm really not a Princess," she insisted, almost in a childish pout. "You must believe that."

Jengadocea shook her head. "Sorry, m'lady, but I can't. Zedulon's description of you left no margin for error. I do apologize if you find your own royalty inconvenient, but the fact of it remains. And I canna help but be grateful! You've finally come to save us!"

Marrow took a step forward, clearing his throat with some conspicuous discomfort. "I fear you are misrepresenting the Prophecy, Countess. Zedulon's words were that Aaliyah would come, 'At the very time of your land's greatest need,' as you yourself have just recounted. He said nothing at all about her actually saving you."

Jengadocea blanched. "Well, even so, I'll take whatever providence I can get at this point. We're in deep, ye might say."

"I gather that," Parissah said, standing. "I hope you will explain your situation, and what urgency has caused my brethren to go ahead without me."

"It's a host of things," Jengadocea began. "I ne'er got around to conscripting homesteaders for this area. The fort went up and then the project got shelved. But we canna very well plant any crops now and expect to reap them before we starve! We've had to raid our own nearest settlements. It is a wonder that Bravado has not yet discovered our whereabouts and crushed us. But as it is, my latest scouting report reveals that he is still besieging the capitol. He's waitin' there to starve us out. He doesn't realize that we're *already* out... and now we're starving elsewhere. We don't have the power to challenge him. The best I could do was to let him go on believing I was still within the walls of New Miranthar, and hope and wait for outside help to come."

"Interesting," Parissah mused. "This *Jengadocea's Bluff* is aptly named, then."

"Quite so," Jengadocea nodded. "Anyway, your other Inquisitors left to try to begin negotiations before we ran out of food and I was forced to surrender from here. I don't believe your Order wants to see this whole country fall to Free-Dome any more than I do."

"We do not," Parissah agreed. "Not based on what we have so far learned and heard. Is it very true that Herz Bravado intends to create a social system where the people may choose their own vocations? Where they even make their own state-level decisions by majority rule?"

"I fear all of these troubling things are true, and many more besides," Jengadocea lamented. "Why do ya think my constituents have been fleeing the country in droves? His ideas are radical!" She got a sad, distant look in her eyes. "My people have long yearned for *more* authority in their lives – not less. They just canna take anything so unorthodox. So new and untried."

"It would seem your people do not much care for new things," Baegulgog commented.

"That they don't," Jengadocea answered. Suddenly she turned, and crossed over to one of her art installations. "There was a time, long ago, when new things abounded," she said. "A time when ideas flowed like a mighty river, and all knowledge and power was within mortal reach. You know the Time. For we all recount it – not as the greatest chapter in history, but the darkest. A calamity so vast it is a wonder that the universe endures to the present day." She reached for the drawing, nearly touching it. Her guests gathered round her, admiring the artwork.

"The Great Regression," Parissah said, as if obligated to complete the thought. "This is a remarkable illustration of it."

Audrey studied the drawing intently. The ground was charred and ruined, but the sky was all a tangle of vibrant color – a violently erupting abstraction. Only the twilit horizon made it identifiable as a sky. In the foreground was a host of Inquisitors, forming two arms of a vanguard before five colossal armored dragons – one of which was so huge that he extended beyond the top of the frame. Below these, at the epicenter of the entire drawing, there was a very strange figure, like a man with a falcon head, whose elegant hands spouted long, sharp talons, and cradled bluish energies. His visage was inscruitable – neither fierce nor benevolent, but utterly disarming and dreadful, with eyes aglow. Even more unnatural, he led a train of free-floating shadows that stretched up, out, and back beyond the atmospheric veil, into infinity. Audrey didn't know what to make of it all…

"It captures the likeness of the Grand Inquisitors well," Marrow commented. "The six of them that emerged from that time, anyway."

"*Six*?" Baegulgog repeated, flummoxed. "If we are going by those numerals, I count only five ancient dragons."

"That is because you do not know Magormissahr," Parissah explained. She pointed to a small Inquisitor, easily overlooked amid his towering fellows. He wore more armor than the rest, and a full robe beneath it, and his mask gleamed like a mirror.

"You're saying *that's* one of the Grand Inquisitors?" Audrey asked. "He's so tiny!"

"Yes," Parissah nodded. "He is no larger than I, even to the present time. But his deeds that day were enormous, and in his wrath he was unequaled by any of his fellows. Or so it is maintained." Audrey blinked, having a difficult time imagining how that could be true.

"And yet, the true hero was Ethon himself," Jengadocea said. "In those days, mortal-kind had gathered all secrets from the far corners o' the cosmos. But that *knowledge* now is lost. It was Ethon's coming alone that taught us *wisdom,* which has endured."

"But, how could'st we have learn-ed wisdom from he who is-eth the opposite of knowledge? Doth that even maketh sense?" Jek asked the Countess. It seemed a fair question, recalling Ethon's nature as a Dianode – and the elemental force diametrically opposed to Knowledge.

"Never conflate knowledge and wisdom, lad," Jengadocea answered. "Wisdom is about more than knowing things. It's about understanding what you *don't* know, and what you *shouldn't* know – and respecting those limits." She looked back at the drawing. "This be my most prized possession," she remarked absently, still absorbed by it, as if she too were seeing it only for the first time. "Ethon is much-revered in this land. It is believed he holds special power here... and there are many local folk-tales of people encountering him in his harbinger form. They may hold some stock. A Dianode's harbinger must reside somewhere, after all. I, for one, do not dismiss the stories off-hand."

"That is strange," Parissah said. "Of all the Dianodes, I would consider Ethon the very last that one should have any idea where to find." She, too, was again taken by the drawing. "But in any case, I applaud the workmanship that went into this drawing. It is a masterful homage to the heroes of the Great Regression."

"Truly," Marrow agreed. "Yet something tells me it would have been much more enlightening to see the villains instead." They all eyed him, not at all sure what he meant.

After a few moments, Parissah stepped down and away from the wall, back into the wide central path. "It suddenly occurs that I have no idea what to do now," she said. "My mission has gone ahead without me."

"The other Inquisitors left days ago," Jengadocea told her. "It would be pointless to try to catch them, if that is your mind. Best to stay here and wait."

"But to what end?" Parissah asked. "Do I serve any function by staying? It is a conundrum. If my fellows fail, I must learn of it. But if I am detained here, I shan't likely escape to bring word of our failure back to the Citadel."

"Don't forget, that is what you brought *me* for, madam," Baegulgog assured her.

"You're right Baegulgog," she nodded. "It is plain, then. I must stay. Though I deplore to sit on my hands for any length of time."

"If it's work you want, I can put you to it," Jengadocea said. "Most of my soldiers have just returned from a bold raid. None expected them to return, let alone with provisions. But so they have – thank the Creators! – and there be many wagon-loads to curate and distribute. You can help with that, if ya wish."

"Jolly good!" Baegulgog exclaimed, reacting with great enthusiasm before anyone else could half consider the proposal. "If there is something that needs curating, madam Countess, then you may certainly count on me to do it whole-heartedly. Show me to these wagons!"

* * *

Parissah set a barrel on the ground and pealed the lid off, allowing Baegulgog to take stock of the contents. Just as she turned to unload another, she paused to observe the Human Audrey struggling under the weight of a wooden crate. Parissah marveled at the sight. She knew that Humans, and particularly Human women, were physically weak creatures. But the real extent of that weakness still amazed her at times. The load Audrey was carrying could not possibly have been over 200 pounds! The sight moved her, and she decided that this was a good opportunity to start to build some friendly familiarity with her new travelling associate...

"I see you are struggling with that burthen," Parissah called out to Audrey.

"Yeah," Audrey grunted.

"I must say, I have always admired your people for their extreme physical weakness. It seems to me a very fine inadequacy to have to overcome."

"Okay," Audrey grunted.

"Tell me, do you find that it keeps you humble?"

"I... guess so," Audrey said, setting the crate down with a final heaving effort.

"That is splendid," Parissah nodded, patting Audrey on the shoulder affirmingly. "Well, keep up the good work."

"Thanks," Audrey said, hunched and breathing hard.

"HARK!" called a soldier from above, keeping watch from atop a catwalk behind the walls. "Hark! Hark! Enemies on the horizon!"

* * *

After an interval of confusion, the Countess was brought forward from her chamber. She bade the travelers join her atop the wall to assess the situation. They all joined Parissah, who had gone straight up at the announcement.

Audrey's eyes danced up and down the open country before the fort now. Little had she considered open warfare, or its scope, before today – and her imagination did not approach the reality. The enemy was silent and small and distant, but the shadow of their threat loomed large as the host continued to multiply. More and more and more Free-Dome Fighters were spilling over the horizon into the valley. It was a great and glistening army, whose armor caught the rays of daylight, prematurely harsh and red. The inter-tribal conflict between the Dyeus and the Mantids of Despotopia waned small in Audrey's memory. Here, arrayed before her eyes, was the mounting might of an entire island nation, about to be loosed against the pitiful walls she stood upon. It was kind of scary.

"Our time of greatest need indeed," Jengadocea said at length. "We're outnumbered ten-to-one already, and still they keep coming."

"It never fails to bewilder me," Parissah commiserated, shaking her head. "I cannot rationalize the power Bravado holds over these masses. His speeches we know of are neither persuasive nor eloquent. He is not profound or even educated. If I were to judge him from only what I know, I would deem him an ignoramus."

"That is the key to all his great success, if I may venture a guess," Jengadocea replied. "And guess I must, unfortunately... for e'en after all these years of strife against him, I still do not *know* how he has beaten me! Yet remember – if there is power in knowledge, then there is equal power in the absence of knowledge. I canna say why, but I believe this is where Herz Bravado draws his strength from. It is the strength of Ethon himself Bravado wields – the power to confuse all counsel – to utterly exasperate the fragility of the mind."

"Let me be sure I understands, m'lady," the old man said. "Ye says he's powerful, on accounta he's so dumb?"

"That be perhaps too prejudicial, old man," Jengadocea answered. "It's true, he hasn't proven very tactical or observant... or subtle or persuasive. Indeed, I think he knows very little. But the few things he knows, he knows all too well. He can win wars. He can turn stout and loyal hearts to sludge. Those be better tricks than I know."

"Well, what in the world are we going to do now?" Audrey asked, still mesmerized by the huge gathering of enemy soldiers. Suddenly, she had a thought, and turned to Marrow. "Hold on... what about *you*? *You're* really good at fighting! Do you think you could just take this whole army yourself?"

Marrow laughed, long and venomously. "Ah, perhaps in my younger days, my dear," he said. Then he looked out over the wall again. "No, never mind... not even then. Certainly, you may rest assured I will put my skill to use. But you cannot count on that alone to sway the battle in our favor!"

"Do not be mysterious," Parissah cautioned him. "This is no time for vague portents! Do we win the battle, or don't we? Surely you would remember something like that!"

"I do not," Marrow replied. "And even if I did, I have found there are some things whose outcome should not be foretold. If you care for an opinion, I *suspect* we will lose. Yet even in defeat, there is Purpose. It is a worthy fight, and we shall rightly play our part in it."

"There is a part I would like you to play *before* the fight, if yer willing," Jengadocea interjected. She looked at Audrey, and it caused her all the old, increasingly familiar anxiety... the anxiety of being important. "The very moment of prophecy is at hand, Princess Aaliyah. Will you speak to my people? Will ya lend them some inspiring words in the face of this doom? It would mean so much to me... and e'en more to them!"

Audrey turned and looked down on all the frightened loyalists, and the sight froze her heart as much as the army on the other side of the wall, if not more. They were still looking at her expectantly. She wanted them to be comforted. She wanted for them to find courage now, in their darkest hour. But she didn't want to be the one to do it. She didn't think she *could* do it...

"I... I don't know," Audrey said, feeling faint. She ran a hand down her face, as if to wipe away the abundance of trepidation.

"Please, m'lady," Jengadocea implored her. "I don't think there is much hope either way. But I'd rather they faced Bravado with some fire still in their hearts."

"But these are *your* people," Audrey reminded her. "Wouldn't some words from you mean more to them?"

Jengadocea laughed. "Nay, I'm afraid not. They are *loyal* to me, it is true. But I'm afraid their *respect* only runs so deep. I have made the mistake of being quite lenient with them over my rule. They think me rather soft, and my failure against Bravado has only deepened that suspicion. And in the end, I be only a humble steward – an interim ruler in their long wait for the authority of the continent to once again guide their lives. *You* have that authority! And they know it! Please honor their wishes and command them. It may well be their *final* wish."

Audrey still wavered. She felt she must do this thing – that much, the Countess had convinced her of. But how to do it? It was horrible to be put on the spot this way!

"Alright," she answered at length. "But I need some time. Can I have some time to think?"

"Of course, m'lady," the Countess assured her. "Take all the time ya need!" She laughed. "As long as ya don't wait till after the battle."

* * *

Audrey withdrew to a quiet corner of the fort to puzzle through the whole thing, and to try to wind herself up for it. For several minutes, she accomplished little besides running her fingers through her hair and grunting occasionally in frustration. She didn't know how to write speeches. Maybe if she knew how to write *at all*, it would have helped.

Finally, when she had become totally dispirited, she heard a great fluttering sound. Marrow alighted in her midst, folding his wings, slow and cautious. She surprised herself, how glad she was to see him. Already she began to value his wisdom... and now she knew she needed it. Perhaps they would become friends even faster than she thought...

"Hi, Marrow," she said.

"Hello, dear friend," he nodded. "How are you feeling?"

"I'm alright," she lied.

"That was a rhetorical question," he replied. "I know you are feeling terrible."

She laughed. "Yeah kinda."

"Your destiny is not an easy one, child," Marrow sighed, with sorrow in his voice.

Audrey groaned. "Please, Marrow, this is a hard enough ordeal as it is. Don't make it about anything as big and terrible as destiny."

He paced in a brooding discomfort. "I'm afraid that is exactly what it's about. I can do nothing to spare you from it, friend Audrey. But I *will* do what I can to prepare you for it. That is why I have come. I'm going to tell you a story that may enlighten you in this moment of uncertainty."

Audrey nodded. "Alright," she said.

"Once long ago there was a very wise Empress. Her name was Upsilonna. She came one day to the city of Grevaughn, and found it completely overgrown with lobstergrass, to her great displeasure."

"Is lobstergrass a lot like crabgrass?" she asked.

"Yes. Very much so, but far worse. Anyway, like all great wise rulers, the Empress decided to take this displeasing discovery and turn it into a social experiment. She had the west side of the city gathered to her, and told them that she would personally hold each of them responsible for the removal of all the lobstergrass from their properties within the span of a week. If they failed to remove it, she warned that she would have their tail feathers plucked."

Audrey made a face. "You mean, she didn't threaten them with execution? She must have been a lenient Empress!"

"Yes, well, everyone has their faults. But you are getting almost ahead of the story, for there was the other half of the city left – the *eastern* half – which she gathered into her presence after dismissing the western half. This time, she rendered the ultimatum differently. To these citizens, she explained that *Bill* would hold them responsible for the removal of their lobstergrass. And, if they failed, she revealed that *Bill* would have *all* of their feathers plucked, and also their wings snipped."

"*Bill*?" Audrey repeated, shaking her head. "But..."

"...So, after the week had passed, the Empress returned to survey the City once again. She found that every property in the western side of Grevaughn – the side she had *personally* threatened – had been picked clean of lobstergrass. But, on the eastern side – which was under only the dubious threat of *Bill* – less than half of the properties had been cleared!" Marrow snickered to himself, low and dark. "I will tell you, Bill was a busy man, plucking all of those feathers, and snipping all of those wings."

"But who the Heck was 'Bill'?!" Audrey demanded.

Marrow leaned in with a theatrical flair, ready to make his point. "Precisely."

Audrey pursed her lips and rolled her eyes skyward, trying very hard to make sense of it all. "That's definitely not like any fable I've ever heard," she said.

"*Fable*?" Marrow repeated. "It is not a fable! It really happened!" But he suddenly stopped... and raised a talon to his beak pensively. "But if you'd like to hear a Heron fable, I'll be glad to share with you my very favorite."

"Okay, sure."

Marrow's goggles stared up past her, deep into the annals of narrative folklore, as he waved a talon before him. "Once upon a time, there was a village of arctic giraffes that lived by a hill."

"Wait, what?" Audrey replied. "You've lost me again already. Arctic giraffes don't live in villages! They're just dumb animals... right?"

"They are. Indeed, if they were actually intelligent creatures, this would be a parable, and not a fable."

"Oh!" Audrey exclaimed. "I never knew it worked that way."

"It does. At any rate, there was a village of artic giraffes that lived by a hill. The villagers ate the foliage that grew on the north side of the hill. But no one ever, ***ever*** ate the foliage that grew on the *south* side of the hill! This convention stretched back into the very most unsearchable depths of time. Not a soul dared question it.

"Then one day, a very special arctic giraffe was born to the village. His coat was totally white and without spot. They named him Snowflake. Years later, when Snowflake grew to manhood, he decided to start eating foliage from the south side of the hill. Everyone was quite shocked by his irreverent behavior, and purposed to shun him at once...

"But Snowflake soon chanced to save the town from some unforeseen peril, and also had occasion to render copious incontrovertible scientific proofs that the foliage on the south side of the hill was absolutely identical to the foliage on the north side of the hill in every way.

"That night, there was great rejoicing as the village mayor declared the south-side foliage fit for giraffe consumption. They were all overjoyed at having been liberated from their antiquated presumptions. Then, the next morning, they all died."

Audrey gaped. "Oh, that is a very sad fable!"

Marrow nodded. "Yes. And that is how you may be sure there is a lesson in it."

Audrey sighed. "I'm afraid all your lessons are lost on me, Marrow. I'm still trying to understand the point of your first story."

Marrow took another step forward. "The point of that story is this: When the Empress invoked Bill, few were impressed. The threats that carried weight were those she promised to enforce herself."

"Are you saying I should threaten these people?" Audrey asked.

"If you wish," Marrow replied. "But that is still not my point. I will put it plainly: Do not go up there and extol Jengadocea. It is *your* mandate the people crave. Give it to them! Assert your own authority. Then, and only then, will these men and women be inspired!"

Audrey shook her head with a disapproving grin. "If *that's* the point you wanted to make, your story was all wrong. Jengadocea is like the Empress. She's the one the people know. I'm the stranger here. I'm the Bill."

"A fair point," Marrow conceded. "But they all know the Prophecy. They are all expecting a Princess from the continent. Do not let them down! Give them the one they are expecting! Simply *be* the Empress of the story! You can live up to that, even if you think you can't."

"But what will I do? What will I *say*?"

"The words are immaterial," Marrow answered. "Say whatever you will, and do not concern yourself about it. Only say it with *authority*. The authority that is yours, and no other's."

"But what authority do I have, in truth?" She hesitated even to ask her next question. "Am I really a Princess?"

Marrow nodded gravely. "You are."

Audrey slumped. Those were the words she dreaded to hear. She truly felt crushed. "I don't want to be a Princess," she said. "I can hardly think of anything I'd want to be less."

Marrow came to her side, and rested a talon gently on her shoulder. "There, there," he said, his voice sympathetic, and yet carrying all the gravity of cold, careless fate. She waited in vain for him to say something more...

* * *

Audrey stood upon the wall again, looking down into the fort as all the loyalists were gathered to her. She looked over at Jek, wishing to draw some strength from him... or at least some sympathy. He gave her a weak grin and a shrug. It was enough for her. She knew that he knew she was miserable...

It was Jengadocea who addressed the crowd first. "My good and faithful subjects," she began, in a clear and authentic voice. From the first, her speech carried impact and strength. Audrey had no idea what she could add to it. "Today is the day you have dreaded. Herz Bravado's forces have found us at last."

The crowd murmured uncomfortably, though by now most had already heard.

"You have all remained loyal to the very end. I could not be more proud of your courage and steadfastness!" She turned, indicating Audrey with her glance. "And yet, I know the reward for your faith does not come from me, as indeed I am not its object. Always you were hoping and waiting for a true monarch to return to you. Here, then, is the one you have been waiting for!" Now she gestured to Audrey. "May her words sustain you through all the darkness to come!"

The crowd cheered. Audrey's blood ran cold. But she stepped up anyway.

"Hello there," she began weakly... waving a weak wave. She swallowed, trying to think what more there could be to say. "So, they tell me I'm a Princess," she continued. "That's what I keep hearing... seemingly from everyone. And, to be honest, I don't know any better than to believe they could be right. I hope they're wrong. But for your sakes, let's just agree to say I really am a Princess for the time being."

Audrey felt insufferably stupid, hearing her own words echo back to her in her head. But to her bewilderment, the crowd still looked on with unflinching admiration. So she willed herself on, finally recalling Marrow's advice...

"Yes indeed... I am a Princess. And you'd all better respect me. Or... else." She looked over at Marrow, who gave her an affirming nod. "That's right, people. You'd better tow the line! Because this is it. This is the battle that's going to decide the fate of your country. You don't want the forces of Free-Dome to prevail, do you?"

"No!" they all chanted with one voice.

"You don't want to have to make decisions for yourselves, do you?"

No!!" they chanted all the more.

"You want to be told what to do... just as your fathers were, and their fathers, stretching all the way back really, really far in the past. That's what you want, isn't it?"

"Aye!"

"Good. Because that's what's at stake here. You're not only fighting for your lives, and the lives of your loved ones. You're fighting for your right to *be ruled*! Your right to have people that are more important than you, who can tell you what to do, and then hold you to it! And that, my dear Maeneans, is the one right that no amount of Free-Dome can give you!"

The throng shouted their agreement. It kind of disgusted her, really. In Audrey's own estimation, she'd given them a meager earful of obvious rhetorical nonsense; nothing to deserve such enthusiasm. For their own dignity, she wanted to give them something more. She looked through the crowd, hoping to find inspiration. Her eyes settled on some random guy in the front. She held a hand out to indicate him to the masses...

"If this man should fall..."

She froze midsentence. Brain block! *If this man should fall...* what??? She needed some profound clincher, and she needed it now...

"...pick him up!" she said.

They all cheered with great abandon. She had to stop herself rolling her eyes...

When the ovation died down sufficiently, Audrey stepped back at last, bewildered and emotionally exhausted. Little did she know, this was only the beginning. She was forced to maintain an air of confidence and congeniality as some of Jengadocea's Colonial Guard led her in broad arcs through the crowd for an interminable episode of smiling, waving and nodding. She took some measure of cold comfort in the knowledge that her efforts, feeble though they were, had done wonders for the loyalists' morale. But it was a very great bother to her. She didn't enjoy her first swing at princessing at all...

Finally, after what seemed hours, she was led back to Jengadocea's hall. As she might have guessed, Marrow was there to meet her.

"You did very well, my friend," he assuaged her immediately. "It was a mighty deed. These folk have endured great hardship, hoping only for the attention of one of your stature. And you did not disappoint them."

"But it was a horrible speech!" Audrey exclaimed. "I can hardly bear the embarrassment of it. Every sentence – every word I used was dumb!"

"That is true," Marrow nodded. "But you needn't worry. I can guarantee that, for as long as their memory endures, they will always remember it as a stirring and masterful oration."

Audrey gave him a quizzical look. "*They* will. I'm sure of that. I could see it in their faces. I've seen it once or twice before. But *you*... you know it was bad? You weren't affected by it, the way all the others were?"

Marrow laughed, waxing once again fearful and terrible. "Of course not! I am not as they. I am beholden to no authority in this world. Indeed, you will never meet anyone with more earthly authority than I am destined to command."

She shook her head. "I'm sure I don't know what you mean... as usual. But even *you* once answered to Zedulon, your Proconsul. Is that not so?"

"That is a very good question," Marrow answered. "Would you care for a straight answer?"

"Sure," she shrugged.

Just as he was about to speak, the door opened behind them. "Princess," a Colonial Guard interjected, bowing. "Our enemies art advancing! The siege of the fort doth commenceth!"

The Devil You Don't Know

"Victory is a process, not an outcome."

- Shaikonnen, *Ascetic Disciplines, 4th Edition*

A war council was hastily assembled in Jengadocea's hall, even as the field before the Bluff teemed with Herz Bravado's legions of Free-Dome Fighters. The people were already prepared to fight... even to the bitter end. But a little strategy to go with all the gritty, diehard sentiments couldn't hurt.

Jek sat at a long table that servants of the Countess had set up for the council. He felt very out-of-place, being neither tactically savvy, nor possessing any kind of authority whatsoever. Nevertheless, there he was. Apparently being the dubious travelling partner of an Inquisitor-delegate was status enough...

Except now, he knew he was more than that. He was also the husband of a Princess. That, too, seemed somewhat dubious. Jek wasn't sure, but it seemed like there would be some kind of rule against a commoner being married to royalty. Maybe it depended on the country. He really didn't know...

And, to his surprise... he really wasn't worried about it. He made a firm decision not to be intimidated by Audrey's importance anymore. And right now he was proud... *very* proud of what she'd done... of her eloquent speech, which had been so inspiring. Truly, it had been a very regal oration. The fact of her royalty was now undeniable... and Jek was more sure than ever of his own role as her protector. Whatever premature fate awaited him as such, he was becoming more confident of his ability to steel himself and accept it. Even such a grim Purpose was not without its rewards. After all, he did believe she cared about him very much. That belief was paradoxically the most humbling feeling he had ever known, and perhaps the only thing about himself he had ever been truly proud of...

He smiled as she sat down next to him. With Audrey at his side now, he didn't feel so out-of-place. He was just glad to be there, whether he belonged or not. It was easy... far *too* easy... to forget that they were seated at the table only because they were about to be totally overrun by belligerent rebel forces. But as the meeting convened, that fact was soon enough recalled...

"We're about to be totally overrun by belligerent rebel forces," Jengadocea began, rising from the table. She laughed mirthlessly. "Though who am I joshin'? At this point, *we're* the rebels."

"Speak no such abuse against yourself, Countess," Parissah said. "Yours is still the legitimate government, as far as the Inquisition is concerned, however many or few of your people are behind these walls. I do not deny Bravado's strength will almost certainly win him his war against you. But it will avail him nothing in the end, if he cannot ultimately assuage our doubts about the character of the state he means to set up in your place. Even if we all die, the Clerk Baegulgog will report to the Ocean Citadel, and return with an entire army of Inquisitors, if necessary."

"That, at least, is a silver lining," Jengadocea replied, furrowing her brow. "Tis more hopeful than any strategy we're likely to contrive here, I'm afraid."

"I fear you are right," Parissah agreed. "But perhaps we should suspend all such judgment until your general staff is convened with us."

A loud clanging met Parissah's appeal as an armored man stood from the table. He was yoked with a short flagstaff on his back that flew the Countess' mark, and the plated suit beneath his beard was very heavy. Still, his greatest burden was clearly internal. He looked very dispirited, if not totally exhausted. "But the general staff *is* convened," the man said. "Here I am."

"Oh dear," Parissah replied. "When last we were advised, you still had five generals. But I take it this is your chief of staff, the Viscount Backgammemnon?"

The armored man sputtered nervously. "I... I regret to say I'm not, madam Inquisitor. It... it seems the Viscount... that is..."

"It's alright, Valtetris," Jengadocea interjected. She looked at Parissah. "Ye'll have to excuse his stammering, but he does like to protect me from mention of the Viscount... my son..."

"He has perished in battle," Parissah lamented. "I am sorry."

With the clatter, no one could help noticing Valtetris suddenly bury his face in his gauntlet.

"Nay, nothing so quixotic, I'm afraid," the Countess replied, her voice reduced to a sigh. "We thought for a time that he'd perished. But it was not so. He turned up again one day... among Bravado's ranks..."

A horrified silence constricted the company. None could think of a word to say. What *could* be said, to begin to allay such a betrayal?

Finally, the Countess was obliged to get things going again herself, even managing a diplomatic smile. "Anyway, ye're still owed a proper introduction. This is Lord Valtetris, my only remaining general. Lord Valtetris, meet Primary Administrator Parissah and her delegation, including her Royal Highness the Princess, Aaliyah."

"Well met," Valtetris nodded, and Parissah returned the nod. He turned and bowed to Audrey, who gave him a weak wave in return when he had risen again.

"If you are somewhat underwhelmed by my staff, he must shoulder some of the blame," the Countess continued. "I did tell him he could promote some of his better men into generals along with him."

"That ya did," Valtetris agreed. "And yet we have few enough left in our ranks that a colonel could command them all." He shook his head. "I am sorry, m'lady... but if I canna do anything to make yer army any bigger, then at least I can try to keep it properly proportioned." He sat back down heavily.

"Fergive me sayin' so, General," the old man interjected. "But e'er since we gots in here, ye seems about as cheery as if ye just stepped in a pile o' poop... face-first. How comes, I wonder? Didn't Audrey's speech stir yer blood?"

"I'm afraid I missed it," Valtetris sighed.

"The General has just returned from the bold raid he led against Port Mauraisa," the Countess explained. "Whence he set immediately to plannin' his next raid. He is tired, and finds no time for reprieve." She gave him a look. "Which would seem good enough reason to me to elect another general or two..."

Valtetris gave one weak laugh. "Very well, m'lady. I'll be sure to double your staff... if any of us survives this battle."

"Aye," the Countess nodded. "And how will we do that, I wonder? Bravado has discovered our whereabouts. The army outside is great, but I warrant there are many more he can yet rally."

"We observed first-hand the muster of Free-Dome Fighters from across your land," Parissah nodded. "It seems doubtful we encountered the last of the stragglers."

"We're already too outnumbered to succeed," Valtetris sighed. "I should have made the tunnels more of a priority. But I've been careless. I began to believe Bravado was too thick to pinpoint us."

"There aren't any escape tunnels out of the fort, then?" Audrey asked.

"No indeed, Princess," the Countess answered. "Our advantage here was all in the Bluff's obscurity. The fort is unfinished, and in pitiful shape. Now that we are discovered, we're in very deep."

"And I have no ideas," Valtetris said. "I may have used up the last of my wits in Port Mauraisa. But that was a surprise attack, and against fewer enemies than we guessed. I have no idea what to do now, with the fortunes so reversed. We have no edge."

"But perhaps we *do* have one," Parissah suggested. "Bravado cannot see past the walls. And after all, this *is* Jengadocea's Bluff, is it not?!"

The Countess waxed thoughtful. "You think we can deceive him? Make him believe we are stronger than we are?"

"Or weaker!" Baegulgog chimed. "Perhaps if we could sell the illusion that the fort is empty, he will move on!"

"But the tracks of my troops and the laden wagons won't allow that," Valtetris said. "Anyway, Bravado's just spent months besieging an empty capitol. I don't think he'll be satisfied to make a snap-judgment about the population density of the Bluff from the outside. He can hew his way in with relative ease, if we don't resist him. These walls are little better than a fence."

"And a fence be always greener when ye's on someone else's grass," the old man expounded.

"Sure, sure," Valtetris agreed doubtfully.

"Rather, I think we must do the opposite," Parissah said at last. "I am still here to negotiate, and that is what I intend to do. But I shan't be very successful if we let on how depleted we are."

"But how do we exaggerate our strength?" Valtetris asked. "Anything we try to do now will be observed. It be too late for any clever deception."

"Which is why I will attempt a more desperate gambit," Parissah answered.

"And what might that be?"

"I will lie through my teeth."

Jengadocea nodded. "Very well. Yet that leaves still unanswered the question of what we will do, in the likely case the negotiations fail."

"We can defend the walls with burning pitch for a time," Valtetris said. "But we risk burning our own walls down, if the wind doesn't favor us. It's a shame we don't have any more precise means of using fire to our advantage."

"Are there no sorcerers in your ranks?" Marrow asked.

Jengadocea laughed. "Not in *this* country!" She exclaimed. "I don't curry with the likes of magic. It's too new and edgy... and more than a little reminiscent of the fearful powers from the Great Regression. I have a standing ban against it."

"And that is a judgment I have always given you much credit for," Parissah said. "Though I admit, magic would be handy in this pinch."

"In such need, I agree with you," Jengadocea said.

"I gots magic!" the old man was quick and boisterous to volunteer.

"Well that is some boon, at least," Valtetris said. "I'll put you up on the wall, where your powers can be put to use at once."

"I have magic too," Audrey said. "I can heal stuff."

"Very good!" Jengadocea exclaimed. "We will certainly have need of that."

"Yes. I'll take a pair of sorcerers over none," Valtetris continued. "But I canna say how that will rate against Bravado. Doubtless, he does not share our qualms about magic. Indeed, I suspect he'd be friendly with any eldritch powers he could call on."

"I'm sure you're right," Jengadocea agreed. "But after all, we are little better now, thankful as we are to have some access to magic in our final stand."

Marrow stood from the table, hoisting up *Valshaloli*. "No more of this talk will avail us," he said, and all took heed. "The battle calls. We must face it such as we are."

* * *

The entire group returned to the catwalk behind the front fort wall. Jek looked out on the same sight he had glimpsed a dozen (or perhaps a few dozen) times since clamoring back up. The Free-Dome Fighters were close – nearly close enough for archers to engage some of their forward ranks. But they were motionless... planted stalwartly in place. It was unnerving. Jek could only dimly guess what they were waiting for. Perhaps they meant to starve them all out. Evidently Herz Bravado had tried that when he still believed the Countess was in New Miranthar. Or maybe they were waiting for reinforcements... or even Bravado himself, who had yet to make his presence known, if indeed he was there at all. In any case, they were waiting. More than the fighting itself, Jek hated the suspense.

Suddenly, he was aware of Marrow, who stood next to him, peering out. Nothing in his posture or his mask betrayed any great alarm at the size of the enemy force. Jek, by contrast, was visibly shaken. He was increasingly disappointed in himself, having already bled much of the seemingly adamant confidence Audrey's speech had inspired. But rather than let his doubt continue to build, he decided to consult the Heron...

"Marrow," Jek whispered hoarsely.

"Yes, Jek?" Marrow replied, not bothering to be hush.

Jek checked around. No one was standing within a few yards. He continued in his own discrete tones. "Well, listen. I know we've only known each other a few days..."

"I suppose you would see it that way, yes."

"...And even though you've taught me much in that short time, I'm not sure whether you would deign to consider yourself my master or not..."

"I would."

"Okay, good. Well, as your student, I must say I don't honestly believe that you haven't seen the outcome of all this."

"And you would be correct," Marrow nodded.

Jek double-checked the area was clear of attuned ears. Then he returned his gaze to Marrow with a pleading intensity. "So how does it go? Can't you at least tell *me*?"

Marrow cast his goggled eyes down upon the field. "If you mean, 'How does the battle go?' I'm afraid we lose very badly. The war, however, does not come to such a grim end."

Jek blinked. "But this is the *final* battle. I don't see how we can ultimately win if we lose today."

"And yet no victory won on the battlefield – *any* battlefield – is ever *final*. The Grand Inquisitors are not without wisdom. Shaikonnen, in particular, has much to say concerning the ephemeral nature of all victory. Gains must always be guarded, and no matter may ever be considered closed."

"That does sound like wisdom," Jek nodded. "But you're talking in pretty broad strokes. I still want to know what happens to *us*."

Marrow sighed and shook his head. "You have much growing left to do, brave master Jek. But I will remind you of this much: I did say we would go to Maenea *first*. Our journey does not end here. Bravado's, on the other hand, may well be cut shorter than he suspects."

"I guess that's a comforting thought," Jek said, looking out absently. "From all portents, he's a maniac."

"He is. But you will know sympathy for him, before the end."

Jek shook his head. "You seem to always be talking about things that will happen 'before the end'."

"Yes. And that should be a comforting thought, too."

* * *

Parissah surveyed all before her with tireless, unmoving vigilance. If the legions of Free-Dome could stand to wait motionlessly for some unknown development, then so could she.

But that dogged patience was not universal. "Whatever are they waiting for?" Baegulgog asked as he floated at her side.

"I'm sure I don't know," Parissah admitted. "Perhaps there is siege equipment on the way. That is one thing worth waiting for, even against a fort such as this."

Baegulgog considered her thought silently for a brief time, before lazily pointing a tentacle nearly due north. "There is some stirring on the horizon," he said.

Parissah's eyes snapped about to find the spot. Finally, she made out movement among the enemy. "Good eye, Baegulgog… if you will accept the expression," she commended him.

"Yet not good enough to discern what is causing the commotion," he replied. "Not siege equipment, I think."

She watched silently for a long while. Baegulgog was quite right – whatever was passing through the ranks was not nearly big enough to be some tower or ramp with which to win over the walls of Jengadocea's Bluff. But there *were* dark shapes making their way toward the front – figures perhaps a foot or two taller than the armored soldiers. With sudden shocking recognition, Parissah finally placed these larger phantoms…

"*My goodness*," she gasped.

"What is it, madam?" Baegulgog asked.

"It is the delegation," she answered. "The other Inquisitors sent to negotiate between Bravado and the Countess." She looked directly at her friend the Clerk. "Perhaps there is yet hope for diplomacy, Baegulgog! Bravado seems to have recognized the Inquisition after all."

"Jolly good!" Baegulgog exclaimed. "Fortune smiles on us in a most surprising way."

"Indeed," she agreed. "The way we were received by the troop on the plains, this is a good turn I had not dared to expect."

"What's going on?" Audrey asked, noticing Parissah and Baegulgog's excitement. She and the old man, as well as General Valtetris, came over at once.

"My brethren have returned," Parissah explained. "They approach the fort as we speak!"

The Humans looked out at once. "What about Herz Bravado? Is he with them?" Audrey asked, even as Jek and Marrow drew near as well.

Parissah studied for some seconds, trying to make out any Human advancing with the group. "It does not appear so," she answered at length.

"Well ye better hope he's mixed in there someplace," the old man said. "Can't very well negotiate without him."

"Aye," Valtetris mused. "More likely your fellows have returned to issue an ultimatum."

Parissah had to mull that over for a moment. "That is an unhappy thought. But these are very experienced envoys, whom I know and trust. Whatever they mean to do, you may be sure it is the prudent thing. I must be allowed to hear them out."

Valtetris nodded. "Of course. Not an arrow will fly from the wall without your say-so."

At that moment, there was a great clamor. All eyes flew back out onto the plain. The Inquisitors had reached the front, and the army was advancing with them. That was an omen Parissah couldn't qualify…

"Almost looks like they're leading the Free-Dome Fighters now," Audrey remarked aloud. "Did you expect that?"

"Not at all," Parissah said. "And I don't like it. It certainly puts an unwelcome strain on our discussion."

"Aye, don't seem at all forth-right," the old man agreed. "They can set straight away to workin' us woe, iffen ye says somethin' they don't like."

"And more than likely, she will," Baegulgog said. Parissah gave him a look. "Sorry madam, but that is your way."

"No, you're right. It is," she agreed.

Valtetris' eyes were wide with the terror of the vast army arraying itself at their very feet. "Well, please try not to be unduly provocative," he said over the thundering drone of footsteps below.

"Very well," Parissah nodded.

Moments later, the Free-Dome Fighters stopped, their front rank even with the wall. It could not have been mere irony that the first few rows of soldiers were handling big, meaty axes... each of the sort that looked utterly ravenous for tree-flesh. But at the center of the front wall, the soldiers were parted in a wide semi-circle. The Inquisitor delegation occupied this otherwise empty space. Parissah waited for their hail. But seconds ebbed by in enervating silence. Finally, she called out to them herself...

"Hail!" she cried.

"Who hails us?" one of the Inquisitors answered. The question staggered her.

"Up here!" she replied. "It is I, Parissah, Primary Administrator."

"Do you represent the war criminal, the Countess Jengadocea?" they asked.

"Whatever do you mean?" she asked, utterly bewildered. "I represent the Inquisition only, the same as you! That has not changed. How have your negotiations with Bravado faired? I deem not well, by your manner."

"You speak in riddles, stranger," the Inquisitor answered. "We are here to negotiate *for* Bravado. If you do not represent the Countess, bring forth one who would... or else bring forth the Countess herself, so that we may accept her unconditional surrender."

Parissah was stricken temporarily speechless. She looked back at her companions.

"They seems to have made their choice," the old man said. "They's thrown in their lot with Bravado! Yer Inquisition don't recognize the Countess no more."

"No, it is worse than that," Parissah boded. "It is like unto our talk with the Free-Dome Fighters on the plains." With a dry swallow, she reached her determination. "They have *forgot*... somehow. They have been made to forget."

"*Forget* what?" the old man pressed her. "What is it they's forgetted?"

"*Everything*," she answered breathlessly. "Their mission. Their neutrality. Their own identity. The very cause they have dedicated their entire lives to. They have forgotten everything."

"They did call you a stranger just now, didn't they?" Audrey said.

"But how could they be made to forget?" Valtetris demanded. "What power would allow it, save Ethon's own?"

"I don't know," Parissah admitted. "But there is no other answer."

"I don't believe it!" Valtetris shook his head.

"Then I will make proof," Parissah resolved...

"The Countess will come forth in her own time," she called out to her former compatriots. "In the meantime, I have identified myself. To whom am I speaking? If you have any pretense as diplomats, you will answer."

The Inquisitor below hesitated, even conferring briefly with his fellows before continuing. "We are the army of Free-Dome."

"That is no answer!" Parissah contended.

"It is the only answer," the Inquisitor replied. "Now let the Countess face her accusers."

Again, Parissah withdrew, turning to those in her midst. "You see – somehow or other, they have lost themselves entirely."

"But maybe it is only a ruse," Baegulgog posited. "You Inquisitors are not without your cleverness."

"It is no ruse," Parissah lamented. "They would have ways of letting me know."

Audrey came over and set a hand up on her shoulder, offering a deeply sympathetic look. "I'm sorry your friends are Free-Dome zombies."

Parissah slumped. "As am I. They were incomparable professionals, one and all." She focused on Valtetris. "But there is no time for me to grieve. We must consult the Countess."

"Nay," Valtetris said, his face twisted with defiance. "No more dancing around the inevitable. They said they would accept the word of one who would speak on her behalf. And I say we will fight to the last before we would acknowledge their Free-Dome!"

"Very well," Parissah nodded. "We will fight. But let me make one final appeal first."

"As I said before," Valtetris inclined himself, "my men wait on your word."

"Thank you," she replied. And she threw her voice down. "Now hear this. You have not honored the spirit of this parley. If you wish to have words with the Countess, then let *your* leader be brought forth! Let us have Herz Bravado! You are in no position to make such bold demands, without at least acting in like faith. These fort walls conceal a force many, many times stronger than yours."

"You lie!" the Inquisitor called back. "But mark this: Bravado *is* coming. And when he arrives, he will not find walls, nor enemies fit for fighting." With that final threat, the Inquisitor and his fellows drew their snail pistols, and fired splintering rounds into the wall. The whole army cried a deafening, bone-chilling chant – "FREE-DOME!" – and as one the front ranks hewed into Jengadocea's Bluff with terrible strokes of their axes...

"Return fire!" Parissah ordered, and the archers on the walls loosed a weak trickle of arrows down on the axemen. Their armor turned most of the shafts, and few were even staggered. Valtetris was already busy waving up the cauldrons of pitch.

Without warning, an enemy arrow landed in Parissah's shoulder. She studied it for a second, even as she began to hear other missiles whiz by. "Take cover!" she told the men on the walls. Drawing and cradling her snail pistol, she hunkered over to Jek and Audrey. "Those axemen must be foiled," she told them. "Train your muskets on them." Even as she said so, she dared to stand and took a shot over the wall. Arrows from below now filled the air in alternating clusters, like blasts of rain in a hurricane. Covering again, she noted that Jek and Audrey seemed hesitant.

"Is it really safe?" Jek asked.

"Of course not," Parissah answered. "But the arrows are not so thick. I have been hit only once."

"Twice," Audrey corrected her, pointing. "There's one in your back now."

Parissah snaked a look behind her. "Even so," she said, winding another shot. "We need to buy time for the pitch."

Jek and Audrey forced themselves to uncover and take shots. They snapped back down, whole and uninjured, and set to reloading. Parissah soon fired again. A random hail of snail-bolts from the Inquisitors below blew super-sonic chunks out of the wall, sowing chaos and flinging some of the loyalist archers into space at great speed.

At last, some of the pitch was cabled to the summit of the wall, and feverishly the cauldrons were overturned onto the enemies below. Valtetris turned to the old man. "Now or never!" he exclaimed. "Ignite the pitch!"

The old man looked around in a mad fluster. "*Me*?!" he asked.

"Aye, *you*!!" Valtetris shouted. "Ya said ya had magic!"

"*Water* magic!" the old man corrected.

Valtetris was livid. "*Water* magic!? What good be that!? I thought ya had *Fire* magic!!!"

"Ye *assumed* I had Fire magic!" the old man shouted in kind. "And Water magic be plenty o' good... 'cept maybe not in this here instance."

Valtetris shook his head and moved on, shuffling on hands and knees to the edge of the catwalk. "Bring up torches!" he commanded.

"But perhaps I can help," Parissah called after him.

Valtetris looked back with wild eyes as another cluster of arrows whined nigh overhead. "Aye, yer a fire-breather! No need to ask my leave!"

She took a very deep breath, thinking the angriest thoughts she could conjure, and snorted a stream down at the pitch. Just as she did, she was struck with an ineffectual arrow to the chest. Ineffectual, that is, in that it managed not to reach anything vital. But the blow staggered her in mid-breath. Her range failed her, and tongues of flame reached wide, catching the wall...

"Oops," Parissah said, nearly waiting too long to cover again.

"Oops?" Valtetris repeated. "What is, 'Oops'? Did ya not quite reach the pitch?"

"I did not," Parissah replied. "However, the flames may yet reach their mark, as they burn down the outer wall..."

"Oh, great!" Valtetris lamented, face-palming.

Over the din of the battle, they heard a great protest of snapping as some of the logs of the outer wall were felled. It created a temporary confusion among the Free-Dome Fighters. The bulk of their force was over-eager, and had not given the axemen room to fell the logs. But they backed off, and soon the hewing resumed. Small orange tendrils of flame began to reach silently up over the walls. Fresh hails of arrows filled the air. Snail bolts fragmented posts. A random bolt caught one of the pulleys hoisting a cauldron of pitch, and the cauldron swung wild, spilling the stuff disasterously over friendly ground. The situation was already desperate...

Finally, Parissah remembered the one thing they had left in their arsenal. "Marrow!" she called. "Can you go down there and stop those axemen?"

He stood upright with proud elegance – the picture of avian confidence. "Yes," he answered.

"Then by all means, do it!" she implored him.

He nodded, and took to wing, slashing all of the wire out of his way with a swift stroke of the spear and descending to the unsuspecting axemen. It was not long before cries of great distress reached back up to their ears.

"What should *we* do now?" Audrey asked, even as she healed the projectiles out of Parissah's hide.

"We should abandon the wall," Parissah answered. "Its ruin is now inevitable. Let us join the soldiers on the ground."

By the time they had all climbed down, the outer wall was ablaze. In essence, the failing wooden wall was, for the moment, shrouded in a third, firey layer. If it could have lasted, it would have been ample protection. But compromise was indeed inevitable. Water was being carted out into the open yard, with no thought to conservation. They were bringing it *all*. It would be needed, to keep the flames from spreading inward. Posts of the inner wall would more likely fall inward than out. The air was hot and thin. Smoke was gathering thick under the shelf of the cliff above, shrouding the fort in unnatural dark, even with plenty of hours' daylight left. Jek was ill at ease.

Another round of snail bolts flung burning chips into a wagon of still-unloaded foodstuff, rending the wheel and starting the wagon itself on fire. The old man hurled water over the crates, extinguishing them...

"Told ye Water magic weren't without its use," he goaded Valtetris.

"A fine way to prove it," Valtetris snipped back. "Now the food will be soggy, rather than cooked. Though either way, soon none will be left but Free-Dome Fighters to eat it."

Suddenly, the small door to the fort gave way unexpectedly, severed from its hinges with savage speed. All weapons turned against the open way as the loyalists waited breathlessly to see what would come through. Finally, a small form rolled in amidst encircling flames. When the fast-moving shape resolved, it turned out to be Marrow, his tail feathers singed and smoking. His students, Jek and Audrey, rushed to him...

"Are you hurt?" Audrey asked, not bothering to wait for an answer before casting Life magic over him.

Marrow struggled to catch his breath. "A bit scorched..." he managed at last, still choking for air. At length, he sighed with some relief. "I thank you for your aid, my friend."

A stream of Free-Dome Fighters charged in then, heedless of the flames in their zeal. Jek and Audrey, nearest the door, reflexively fought their way through the whole sprawling group as they came.

With weaving, swirling excellence, the stewards guided their muskets through strokes so efficient that they achieved equal distinction in offense and defense. It wasn't until a dozen or more fighters were defeated that the two of them realized they were fighting alone. All enemies fallen for the moment, they looked back at the loyalist soldiers, who all returned their look, rather awestruck.

"That was some really good fighting," Valtetris commended them, unblinking. "Who trained you?"

"I did," Marrow and the old man answered in unison. Each looked flummoxed at the other.

A fresh, thick pelting of arrows struck among the back ranks of loyalists. They were dismayed, and a few badly hurt. Few were sporting the kind of armor the Free-Dome Fighters boasted. Maintaining such armor, and carrying it through many hastened retreats, had not been very practical over the long, sad trajectory of the war.

"We must hunker closer to the wall," Parissah said. "They are aiming their shots higher now."

"But the wall's ablaze, m'lady," Valtetris protested. "Some of us will be cooked if we try to make room for everyone."

"We would do better to part our forces, left and right," Marrow instructed. "Nowhere is now more perilous than the middle."

"How do ya figure?" Valtetris demanded.

"Never mind," Parissah answered for Marrow. "If he says it, we had better listen."

Hardly had Valtetris cleared the middle when chaos struck with overwhelming force. A huge volley of field cannons fragmented a wide swath of wall posts at their bases. At last, the wall was breached by the enemy. Smoldering posts crashed to bits with disastrous randomness. The old man was beside himself, trying to douse all the fires in some sensible sequence as they worked to spread into the fort. Audrey, too, was magically backlogged, overwhelmed by the burns and wounds being sown. Jek stood ready to fire on whatever would first come through the gaping new hole in their defenses...

Sooner than any would have guessed, enemies encroached, even as the ruined posts strewn out in the gap remained blazing. The Inquisitors came in, snail guns cutting vectors of death. Jek drew on them before he could give himself the opportunity to think twice. Whatever they were before, they were too deadly to be given any quarter now. He hurt one with a good shot. But Avarican resilience was such that no one musket shot was likely ever good enough. Jek hurriedly reloaded. His heart was beating in his ears again, and he had to coach his shaky hands to be less urgent. By the time he was ready for another shot, the Inquisitors were still advancing, arrows sticking from their hides in many places. They began to spurt fire from their masks. At first it was all ineffectual, as if the were only just learning of their own ability to breathe fire – a likely case, since they had had their memories erased. But they got the hang of it soon enough, streaming fire disasterously into loyalist forces.

Jek took another shot, and this one proved enough to stop an Inquisitor in his tracks. A few more fell to excessive arrows… virtual walking pin-cushions by their end. But by the time the last two were subdued, Jek made a horrible discovery. The five attackers were merely a diversion. The other five Inquisitors had snuck in behind, dousing the base of the wall with great barrel-fulls of water, making the way safe for the whole army to follow. Jek tried to shout this to the attention of the loyalists, but it was already too late. Free-Dome Fighters crowded into the fort in droves. The two armies rushed each other with horrible, desperate shouts. Jek charged in with them…

Jek fought until he was utterly exhausted, and then he kept fighting. The relative bottleneck of the gap in the wall kept the Free-Dome Fighters from quickly overwhelming the Countess' meager army. Rather, they were being slowly, *excruciatingly* overwhelmed instead. Victory was impossible. It was only a matter of how long they could hold out…

Jek expended a bunch more strength (more than he thought he still had) grappling with a strong, fresh Free-Dome Fighter. An over-eager and wearied loyalist clove Jek's embattled adversary, but gave Jek a nasty gash in the process. They were all bunched-in to a horribly tight cluster. It was like being the sand at the bottom of an hourglass, ever-more buried under the unrelenting stream of new granules. Shoving and trampling were becoming as commonplace as actual fighting, if not more.

More of the wall collapsed in on itself, smashing heroes and villains alike. Shouts and metal clattering congealed into a droning racket. Confusion reigned over all else. Only one other feeling prevailed in Jek's mind. He felt very alone. He was cut off from Audrey, and from the old man, and Parissah and Marrow. Wherever Baegulgog was, Jek knew he was safe, at least. But he feared for all his other companions, not able to recall Marrow's reassurances in all the madness. He was really afraid again. Whether it was his own death he feared most, or theirs, or just that horrible sense of isolation, he could not say. But on he fought, without comfort and without hope…

"ENOUGH!" a feminine voice cried out over all the insanity, and it proved enough to prevail. The fighting ceased, and all sought the source of the cry. Jek's eyes turned up to the top of a wooden lodging. Standing at the precipice of the roof was Countess Jengadocea. "Enough of this killing!" she continued. "I surrender, if that will sate yer bloodlust! It is authority you Free-Dome Fighters scourge, so let your wrath fall on authority… not on those who would prefer to cling to it. Let them go, if you value liberty, as you claim! But I will have no more die in my name. It is useless. I am finished." She drew a sword, a horrible defiant scowl darkening her countenance. But after a moment she simply let the sword fall to the ground, clattering unceremoniously in the dust. Yet the scowl remained.

Gasping for air, Jek's heart slowly sank, as it gradually dawned on him that they had indeed failed. He and all he knew had fought for all they were worth, and still evil had won the day. *Won the day,* he reflected. Finally he remembered Marrow's words – about the impermanence of victory. Maybe he should have found solace in them, assured as he had been that Bravado's crusade was actually destined for some future failure. But that was cold comfort now, at best... if indeed it was any comfort at all...

Meanwhile, Jengadocea was still standing unanswered. Unresolved silence held all the fort in suspense. "Well?!" she demanded at length. "How does the host of Free-Dome answer? I have surrendered, and I have named only one condition, which ought to be in line with yer ideology... at least as I understand it. Do you accept my terms, or don't you?"

"We don't," one of the remaining Inquisitors answered. "You still speak as if you had charge of something. Autocrat! Let it not be said that the armies of Free-Dome ever entertained the conditions of one such as you."

"Very well," Jengadocea replied, lips curled and quaky as she addressed her pitiless adversaries. She seemed almost ready to crack in spite of herself. "Then do whatever you will. I canna restrain you. Nothing now can, apart from your own hesitance. But what in the world are ya waiting for?"

"They wait for me!" announced a voice, boisterous and manly. All eyes turned to the front of the fort. Wisps of smoke curled out of the way of a great muscular man in a worn leather vest, his hair frizzled and wild like his eyes. Sauntering from the ruined wall into the parting midst of the Free-Dome Fighters, he strode just a little too confidently and smiled just a little too broadly, resting the blunt of a huge sword against his shoulder. Jek blinked in bewilderment. The man was hard to focus on, currently treading both sides of the fine line between abundantly charismatic and delusionally grandiose. Something in his whole aura was unstable. Looking steadily at him was like watching a hummingbird's wing or a stricken tuning fork. And for some unknown reason the top half of his face was painted green...

That's him, Jek marveled privately. *That's Bravado.*

Bravado

"FREE-DOME!!!"

- The war-cry of Herz Bravado

–

That's Bravado, Parissah thought to herself. And, of course, she was right. As he lived and breathed, so now he walked through the ruins of Jengadocea's Bluff – the last outpost in all of Maenea not deferential to his radicalism – freshly fallen.

But even as he was coming in, many of his own men filed out. Those that remained formed a perimeter as close to the outer edges of the fort as the heat from the smoldering timber would permit. They herded the loyalists in toward the center. Parissah marked it very strange. If anything, the Free-Dome Fighters should have been forming some sort of buffer zone around their beloved magnate. But as he passed unguarded ever closer to the Countess, his own men hemmed armed adversaries in around him, before they themselves withdrew, as if to some safe distance. Only the threat of their arrows and the honor of the loyalists seemed to sustain the odd tension. But Herz Bravado showed no fear. Rather, he beamed with a stupid sort of confidence.

"So comes at last the revolutionary," Jengadocea addressed him. "Herz Bravado, I presume?"

"That's right," Bravado nodded, still strutting. "This is a meeting a long time in the making. But you don't seem all that happy to see me."

"If you had come a little sooner, perhaps we might have been spared all this bloodshed," Jengadocea retorted.

He pursed his lips and shrugged, boyish in his various mannerisms. "I wasn't the one who waited too long to surrender."

"Well, yer here now, whoever is at fault. What do you want?"

"I'm here to finish what I started. Bringing Free-Dome to your people. All of them." His smile changed from egomaniacal to mischievous. "Even to you."

"I think you'll find me rather disinterested."

"Most are. At first." Bravado turned, raising his voice to address his men. "Bring the civilians," he called.

"Let me call on them maself," Jengadocea said. "No need to involve yer ruffians."

"Very well," Bravado nodded. "You have ten minutes."

Jengadocea, Valtetris and other officers were allowed to pass deeper into the fort. Parissah observed this all intently. She knew the further unraveling of much mystery was nigh at hand. And she intuited that she was powerless to affect the outcome of anything about to happen. There was only one thing she needed to do now, and she hoped ten minutes would be enough...

"Madam," Baegulgog's voice met her weakly from behind, even as her thought turned to him. "We seem to have found ourselves in another dratted spot."

"Yes," she agreed. "But you also seem to have found *me*, and that is a good turn. We must retrieve all our traveling associates, and remove ourselves to some distance from Bravado!"

"Have you learned something, madam? Something of import?"

"Only what observation and instinct may reveal," Parissah replied. "They are rounding us all into Bravado's midst. So I would prefer to be as far away as we can be. But in any event, we should be together."

"I believe I can handle that much myself," Baegulgog said, and immediately he floated high into the air, waving his tentacles in a silly, flamboyant fashion. Many took note, and there were abundant quizzical looks. But Parissah nodded, confident that her friend had found an expedient way to draw the rest of the party forward...

* * *

"We got your signal," Jek said, circling in behind Parissah. He and Audrey arrived in unison. Marrow and the old man had been even closer at hand and were already rallied by this time.

"Very good," Parissah nodded. "Now let us pick a distant spot from which to observe."

"You mean, you're not going to butt-in?" Audrey asked.

"No," she answered. "This is between the Maeneans now. It is plain that Free-Dome does not respect the authority of the Inquisition, any more than the authority of the Countess. What happens now is out of my hands." She twisted her head quizzically. "Do you not agree?"

"Oh yes, I don't think there's anything you can do at all," Audrey answered. "I'm just sort of surprised you see it that way too."

"Well at least we are of one accord then," Parissah said. But she turned to regard Marrow. "Unless you would bode otherwise."

"No indeed," Marrow replied. "I believe your instincts will carry the day."

She nodded again. "In that case, all of you follow my lead. Closely."

* * *

The ten minutes were up. Commoners continued to shuffle in closer. It was a piteous sight. The reality of being brought before their most feared nemesis had sapped the last dregs of their spirits, such that they all already looked like zombies. Most alarming was the sight of all the women with little children in tow. Parissah felt great guilt that she had been unable to prevent this calamity, even as she and her associates struggled upstream against the current of gathering folk, discretely as they were able. It was then that Herz Bravado began his speech in a strong, clear voice...

"Maeneans, countrymen – brothers and sisters – the last of my kindred that have been estranged from me. I'm very glad to have you all here today. And I think, very soon, you'll be glad too. Because my friends, I'm not a crazy person. And I'm not here to kill you. I've come to share with you a beautiful vision... the most beautiful vision of all. *My* vision. You already know it by name..." and he looked up, casting a shade at Jengadocea, "...though I hear that some rather shifty characters have been conditioning you not to like it very much. But once you know the *truth* about Free-Dome – the honest-to-goodness truth – I promise you will think better of it...

"So, what is Free-Dome, really? I'll tell you what it is. Free-Dome is doing what you want to do. What*ever* you want to do... whenever you want to do it. Free-Dome takes everything you're used to and flips it on its head! In a society of Free-Dome, you don't exist to serve the government. The government exists to serve *you*! In fact, you *are* the government... and so you exist to serve yourself.

"What else is Free-Dome? Free-Dome is the life of ease – the life that has been denied you through all the generations, up to the very present day. Because Free-Dome rejects responsibilities, in favor of entitlements. It venerates what you *can* do, and eliminates what you can't do. Free-Dome is contributing whatever you feel like, and nothing more. Free-Dome is demanding, 'Give me, give me, give me!' until you get. And Free-Dome is *not* asking permission... it's not asking forgiveness. Free-Dome is not asking at all. Free-Dome is saying, 'You know what you want, and I know what I want, and anything beyond that is too complicated.'

"So I hope now you see, my vision is not so profound, and not so sinister. I'm just trying to build a world where everything you want is all that really matters. And I'd like you all to share in that vision! What say you?" He paused, surveying the silent onlookers. "Are there any questions?" He continued to look over them, until he spied a hand raise, weakly and warily. "Yes, you in the back..." he indicated.

"What do ya want from us, master?" the timid elderly fellow asked. The crowd murmured as in accord with the question.

Bravado's smile fluctuated and faltered a bit as he blinked a long series of blinks. He seemed rather floored by the question. "What do I want from you? Why, nothing at all! And I'm not your master!" He spoke with strained amiability. "I'm sure I just explained it all very clearly. Didn't you understand me? Surely you all must have understood me..." He raised his own hand now. "Let's have a show of hands... who feels he understood my speech?"

He waited a long time, but the only hand ever raised was his own.

Bravado sighed, cupping a hand over his brow. "Okay, so no one got it. That's okay! There're plenty of other ways of getting this across." He walked right up to a nearby loyalist. "Here's a demonstration," he said. "Watch this." Then he grabbed the loyalist by the shoulders and head-butted him full-force. "Huaah!" he shouted, even as the young man fell unconscious to the ground.

"See!" Bravado commended the crowd. "That's *Free-Dome* in action!"

The crowd *was* moved... but with concern, and certainly not any sudden epiphany. There were many suppressed cries. "Why did ya head-butt that man?" someone asked.

"Because I felt like it!" Bravado explained. "That's the law of Free-Dome!"

There was another confused silence. "Ya made it a law to head-butt people?" another Maenean asked.

"No, no, no," Bravado chuckled. "I don't make the laws. *You* would make the law to head-butt people, if you wanted to."

"But why would we want a law like that?"

"Fine! It's *fine* if you don't want a law like that. You can make a law *against* head-butting, if it really bothers you that much."

"Very well, master," another commoner spoke. "Let us have that law, if yer willing."

"No!" Bravado exclaimed. "You're still not getting it. I don't tell you what the laws are, and I'm not your master. Don't you see? It's all up to *you*!"

"But I don't understand!" another commoner pleaded. "Is there head-butting, or isn't there!?" The murmering escalated to open debate.

"Look, *forget* about the head-butting!" Bravado replied, his confident and friendly demeanor crumbling. "It was just a demonstration. Let me give you another example – hopefully something more enlightening. I'm going to tell you about the day I got married. One day, I came down out of the hills, right? And I saw this lady, and I really liked her. And she liked me. So, we got married. That's Free-Dome! Does that make any more sense?"

More murmuring. Bravado began to appear downright dispirited.

"That can't be the whole story!" some loyalist finally asserted. "What about the bureau? And the paperwork? And how did ya arrange to be in the right part of the queues together?"

"There was no bureau and no paperwork and no waiting in line," Bravado answered. "I *did* tell you the whole story. I saw her, I liked her, she liked me, we got married."

"I think I'm gonna be sick!" a peasant exclaimed.

"And that's just the tip of the iceberg," Bravado continued, undeterred. "You'll get to make all kinds of choices like that. You can choose where to live. You can choose your job. You can choose what to do when you're *not* doing your job. Oh yes, there will be time spent not working! *Free*-time, it will be called."

"What is the purpose of this 'Free-time'?"

"There is no purpose at all! Except what *you* intend," Bravado explained. "That's true not only of Free-*time*, but of Free-Dome as a whole! You get to make your *own* purpose in life!"

The murmuring catapulted into outrage. "HERETIC!" one peasant shouted. Many other such shouts and accusations rang out, building one upon the other.

But Bravado himself just stood there, a small island in a tumultuous sea of angry people, a displeased look on his face. It may have been a scowl, or it may have been a pout. Parissah was not quite sure. But so he brooded. And brooded, and brooded. Until finally, he acted...

Bravado raised his sword to the sky. Bluish energy caught the blade for one brief moment before the blinding flash, and then the shockwave. All within the sapphire blast stood stricken suddenly silent and motionless. Everyone beyond its reach was flung into a horrible panic, and they began to flee with cries of terror...

But not Parissah. She remained firmly anchored. She heard her associates stir, but she raised a hand at the same moment. "Do not move," she said, only barely audible above the chaos. But they heeded her. They all stood dumbstruck, just as those who had been reached by Bravado's eldritch energies.

"What the Heck was *that*?" Audrey asked. "What did he do?!"

"This is the answer to the riddle of Bravado," Parissah replied. "He has *magic*. But not ordinary magic. Not Fire, or Life, or Water, or any of those common varieties. He has *Ethon's* magic. He has the power to cause to *forget*."

"But how in tarnation did he get his filthy mits on that kind o' magic?" the old man demanded. "I ain't ne'er heard o' anyone discovering the secret of *Ethon*-magic afore!"

"Indeed, that is the one sort of magic I would expect to be absolutely beyond discovery," Marrow concurred.

"That is the next riddle," Parissah said. "And I am duty-bound to unravel it as well."

"How do you propose to do that?" Jek asked.

Parissah looked at him solemnly. "We will allow ourselves to be duped," she answered. "To be taken-in by his philosophies."

"Surely not!" Jek objected.

"Yes, I'm afraid we must. It will be difficult. Truly, at the moment I can hardly imagine a greater challenge. But we *must* pretend to find his ideas compelling. Even wise. That is the only way we walk out of here with our memories and our purposes intact. And that is the only way we can get close enough to discover the truth..."

Even as she spoke, the circle of Maeneans ahead of them began to stir. Each was looking around wide-eyed and blinking, their freshly wiped minds doubtless stumbling over manifold questions, trying to decide which most needed answering. *Where am I? Who am I? What is going on?* And so forth. But before they could get too worked-up, Bravado stepped in...

"Good afternoon, my countrymen," he announced. "Right now, you all have a lot of questions. Fortunately for you, I have the answers you're looking for. What would you like to know?"

At length, someone spoke up. "I... I'd like to know my name, please," he said.

"You don't have a name," Bravado answered. "But you will some day. Right now, you are simply a part of the army of Free-Dome. You *all* are... every one of you!"

"But what is a Free-Dome?" another asked.

"I'm so glad you asked that," Bravado replied. "Free-Dome is your calling! It's your sacred cause. It's your whole life! There is nothing you wouldn't do for Free-Dome."

"That sounds very proper, I suppose," someone said. "So what must we do in the name of Free-Dome?"

"Each of you will have to decide that on your own, in time. But for now, you should all report to my men – the armored guys standing all around you. They will tell you what most needs done. They will direct you, until such time as you no longer need direction." He allowed himself a troubled sigh. "I hope that day will come."

The oblivious new Free-Dome zealots began to disperse immediately at Herz Bravado's instruction, seeking out his men as he bade them. Perhaps most troubling of all, Parissah saw as Jengadocea began to climb down from the rooftop she had stood on, seeking guidance with all the rest. But in the shuffle, Parissah lost sight of Bravado himself. She tried to crane her head to find him again. But it wasn't until nearly everyone had cleared the way that she found him, stooped to the ground, cradling his brow. Whether he was wearied by exertion in the use of his magic, or he was under emotional strain of some sort, she could not say for sure. But she and her associates did not observe him long, before he noticed them in return...

For a time, he was motionless... even mesmerized. He looked at them as if they were from one of the Other Worlds. Finally he stood, pointing at them with his sword.

"*You*," he said. "My powers didn't reach you. Why did you not run, like all the rest?"

"Because," Parissah began, "we have been seduced by your profane ideology."

The other associates silently nodded.

Bravado made no response at first. Then suddenly he began to approach them. His stride was powerful and deliberate. Tension reached a palpable viscosity. Parissah feared he might somehow see through her deception. From this range, he could easily wipe their minds. And he drew ever nearer, with a clear visage of skepticism...

Finally, he reached them. He studied them up and down with narrow eyes. Then he gave a mighty sniff. Parissah wasn't sure about the sniff, knowing that Human olfactory senses were pitiful... but she let it pass. "What did you say?" he asked at length.

"She said we like yer idear," the old man translated. "Yer whole yarn about Free-Dome and what-like sounded good to us. Mighty, mighty good." His interlaced teeth were drawn wide in a strained, plastered-on smile.

"Verily," Marrow nodded, backing him up.

Parissah tensed all the more as she waited for Bravado's reaction. This was the critical moment...

But fortune proved kind. His skeptical look started to melt. His lower lip began to quiver. The big, conquering man appeared ready to cry. "Do you really mean that?" he asked.

"Yes," Parissah lied.

Before she even knew what was happening, Bravado seized her. But it was no attack. It was an embrace. He was hugging her, immense gratitude radiating from his arms. "Finally," he sighed. "Someone who understands."

Parissah patted him on the back, hoping he would let go soon.

When eventually he did, Bravado leapt back and started to wave in a spirited fashion. "Hey Murtaugh!" he shouted. "Murtaugh! Come here! You have to meet these people!"

The travelling associates waited uncomfortably as Bravado waved Murtaugh over. He was a man in full armor and helm, all painted with loud colors that evoked no inspiration beyond total abandon. And he seemed to take his sweet time reaching them. Beyond that, Parissah could form no immediate impression...

"Murtaugh," Bravado said, "I want you to meet my new best friends in the whole world!"

"I thought I was your best friend," Murtaugh said, totally matter-of-fact.

"Not anymore," Bravado explained, with a great warm joy in his voice. "Would you believe these guys heard my speech, and were actually moved by it?! These are true believers, Murtaugh! The first willing converts to Free-Dome!"

"That would seem to make them distinct," Murtaugh nodded. If he really found the news interesting, it wasn't very obvious.

Bravado laughed, loud and hard. "Oh, Murtaugh, you're such a card," he said at length, slapping his knee with amusement. "But forgive my manners," he went on, addressing his 'converts'. "This is Murtaugh. He's the first person whose memory I wiped. I admit, he was pretty dull for a long time, after I brainwashed him." He started laughing again. "But he sure makes up for it now! His personality just keeps getting zanier by the day… doesn't it, Murtaugh?"

"I am out of control," Murtaugh said.

"Ha-ha! You sure are, buddy." Bravado slapped him hard on the shoulder plate. After no further response from Murtaugh, he turned back to his new friends. "So! The speech! Pretty good, eh? Much better than any of the other ones I've done! I admit, I got some outside help this time. Really, I had hoped it would make a bit more of a difference. But then, Maeneans are pretty stubborn by nature. Looks like you folks are from out-of-town. Maybe that accounts for something. Man, I'm just so glad that someone finally sees Free-Dome for what it is! Someone besides *me*! You have no idea how much this means. What was your favorite part of the speech? Huh? What really came across?"

They were all silent for an uncomfortable interval.

Finally, Marrow piped-up. "I enjoyed the head-butt most," he answered. "It was delightfully violent."

"As for the speech itself," Parissah began, rendering some answer as best she could, "its total disregard for conventional wisdom was quite uniform. I find I cannot choose a favorite part."

"Wonderful!" Bravado exulted. "You loved the whole thing!" He hugged her again, but fortunately only for a moment this time.

Meanwhile, Murtaugh was performing a series of gestures, his attention drawn away toward where the front wall of the fort now lay in smoldering ruin. Bravado took note of it. "What news, Murtaugh?" he asked.

"The men have finished rounding up all of the stragglers, just beyond the wall," Murtaugh reported.

Bravado turned to Parissah and her companions, clapping his hands together. "Duty calls," he said. "Things are about wrapped-up here. I'm going to be moving on very soon. But I hope you'll join me in the next phase of this crusade! The journey ahead will take some time – time we could all spend getting to know each other – true compatriots in Free-Dome!"

"We will come," Parissah answered. "We certainly intend to learn all about you. And what's more, I should very much like to learn what you mean by the 'next phase'. It seems to me you have already achieved your end. Jengadocea is defeated. Maenea has fallen wholesale."

"But this is about so much more than just Maenea," Bravado explained, low and solemn, but with a dauntless smile, his aura aglow with ambition. "This campaign was only the first step. Free-Dome can know no boundaries. It must be brought to every corner of every land."

Parissah's heart froze. "But surely that is too great an undertaking," she said. Bravado hardly flinched.

"It's a big job, I know. And I think it'll require a lot more power to achieve. But now I know where to get that power. I have to go back to the source. That's where I'm going next."

"And where, pray tell, is the source you speak of?" Parissah inquired.

Bravado turned west. "I must return home – to the hills of Magna Koepna... and beyond." After a few moments' reverent pause, he started to walk away, striding powerfully as ever. "But back to the business at hand," he called back. "This won't be but a moment."

They watched him disappear behind the veil of smoke. Then they heard cries of fear, escalating quickly to panic. Then the blue flash. And silence.

"What have we just got ourselves into?" Audrey asked.

"Another wide bend of the road, fraught with weirdness," Marrow answered.

* * *

Less than an hour later, they had taken their last leave of Jengadocea's Bluff, voyaging on with Bravado, Murtaugh, and a small escort of former Colonial Guards. Any time Jek looked back, the smoke was still rising from under the sheer face of the slope, rolling up in a vast column, like a monument to the dark victory that day had known. Finally, he resolved to stop looking back.

The following hours of plodding over the countryside were nervous and tiresome. Having fought a grueling battle, whether on one side or the other, most of the travelers drew near the point of exhaustion. Audrey leant a hand, but she had used much magic during the fight. Evidently the consistent exertion of such power could take a toll. Her Life magic was drained to a trickle, and she had to ration it out among many (she gave some restoration to the Free-Dome fighters as well). Most of the power went into wounds.

The only one in the bunch who was truly refreshed was Bravado. At times he was literally walking circles around the others, engaging with each of his new 'best friends in the whole world' with great exuberance. Jek stuck close to Audrey. More than anyone in the party, he dreaded being singled-out by Bravado. He didn't trust himself to behave like a true believer in Free-Dome at need, and deeply worried that his insincerity toward the cause would be patently obvious. Even Parissah at least had her unflappable sense of duty to fuel her false front. Jek just wasn't deceptive by nature, and had no framework for dealing with the clinically insane.

There was a bad turn in the weather just as the last glimmers of evening light came out of the sun. First came rogue gusts of wind. But before long, the bluster was unrelenting, with powerful bursts punctuating the droning whistle of the air through the waves of whipping grass to the south of the road, and the eerie creaking of trees to the north. Cold, spitting rain heralded a frigid deluge. The weather had only just got Jek's mind off the strange company they were keeping, when at last Bravado turned to Audrey and him...

"Hello, friends!" he said, utterly oblivious to the storm.

"Hi there... Herz Bravado," Jek replied, making only a feeble attempt to look his 'friend' in the eye. He felt at once a torrent of pressure to initiate some sort of ice-breaking small-talk. "Nice weather we're having."

"Ha-ha-ha!" Bravado guffawed. "Yes, it is wonderful! Any weather is good weather, when you actually have real friends!"

"Yeah," Jek nodded.

"So, you must be Jek and Audrey, is that right?" Bravado went on.

"That's us," Jek said.

"And the two of you are from Jast-Madiir? That's what the old man told me. Honestly, I don't know all that much about your country... except that it's... it's north of here, right?"

"South," Jek answered.

"Ah, south! That's even better! What else can you tell me about your land? Is it very much in need of Free-Dome?"

Jek's eyes bugged. This was the test! He'd better not choke...

"Um, sure, I mean yeah, definitely..." he answered.

"Well don't you worry," Bravado assuaged him, clapping a firm hand on his shoulder. "We'll bring it to them." Then he took that same hand and held it out in front of Jek – clearly signaling for a handshake. "Brothers for life?" he asked.

Jek blinked, but again played along. "Yup," he nodded. Bravado's handshake nearly ripped his noodly arm off. Then he turned to Audrey...

"And you, my dear," he said, taking Audrey's hand in his hands and stopping to kneel. "It is very nice to meet you." Jek found he didn't appreciate the attention she got any more than he had liked his own.

"Nice to meet you too," she replied, patting his hands with her free hand. Bravado kept kneeling. He stayed like that well past the point of awkwardness.

Finally, he cleared his throat and stood," I also heard the two of you are married," he said.

Audrey nodded. "That's very true."

"Jek's a lucky man," Bravado said, as all began to walk on again. "You have a very beautiful cheek bone. And your heart must be equally beautiful, to have been persuaded of Free-Dome." Jek was surprised, as he realized Bravado's seemingly boundless joy had evaporated. "I hope some day I'll meet another lady, very much like yourself."

She gave him a searching look. "But aren't you already married?" she asked. "You shared the story of your marriage..."

"So I did," Bravado laughed ungenuinely. "I forget that you would remember that. The story was true... up to a point. I did meet a lady once, when I came down out of the hills. And we liked each other. But I'm afraid I change the ending in the telling... for demonstrative purposes, of course." He fell silent, his eyes downcast. "I couldn't convince her to marry me. 'That's not how marriage works,' she said. I told her that's how it *should* work. I told her all about Free-Dome." He made another mirthless laugh. "I don't even remember how much I knew about Free-Dome myself, before I started telling it to her. But she wouldn't be persuaded."

He said no more, until Audrey asked, "What ever became of her?"

"I wiped her memory, perhaps a year or two later," Bravado admitted. "But only as an incidental part of the crowd. I was taking her village, just as you saw me take the fort... just as I've taken every settlement throughout this land. It's always the same routine. I try to make them see first. I've tried so many, many times." He knocked a fist to his head. "You don't know what it's like to have a brilliant idea – maybe the most brilliant idea of all time – and to have it trapped in your own head. Free-Dome really is everything to me. It's the most beautiful vision I could possibly imagine. But no matter how I try, I've never been able to make anyone *see* it." Finally, he offered them a weak smile. "Not until the six of you came along, anyway," he said.

"But what about the lady?" Jek asked, eager to keep the focus off them. "You didn't just tell her she was your wife, after you wiped her memory?"

Bravado recoiled. "You think I would do something like that?" he said, and his look of revulsion was quite genuine. "Never! That's not why I wipe people's minds!" They dared say nothing more to him after that. But at length he sighed, and spoke again. "Perhaps, in time, I can find her again. Some time in the future, after she's found herself. Maybe then I can see if she likes me, as she did before. But she was someone else then. I don't know who she is today. It might not be any of my business to know." He shook his head. "It's all very hard to figure out. If only I could have shown her Free-Dome, that first day. If only I could have got her to see it..."

Jek's heart sank into his squeaking boots. Another of Marrow's premonitions had come true. He *did* know sympathy for Herz Bravado...

* * *

They splashed and trampled on late into the night. The wind lost some of its gusto, but the rain never let up for a moment. Tired, soaked, and numb with the cold, they came at last to Port Mauraisa, spying dimly the peaks of the secondary island, Magna Koepna, many many leagues in the distance, marching up into the utter blackness of the rainclouds. The warm light of the few lanterns in the port ahead kindled much-needed relief. That was, until Jek discovered that Bravado intended to go straight through the Port without stopping – and worse yet, that Parissah was very much in support of this course. She was every bit as eager as Bravado himself to reach whatever the end of this new quest might entail. She had even improvised a sled for Baegulgog to float over, so that his ghostly form could be transported with greater speed.

Fortunately, a spirited debate broke out. The old man made plenty of appeals to being old, and thus needing rest. Marrow had similar sentiments, adding that he had felled dozens of adversaries during the battle, and thus had earned a respite. Even Murtaugh voiced against going on. It took a good deal of argument, and more than a little whining, but eventually the matter was settled, in favor of staying the rest of the night in the Port.

Thus persuaded, Bravado was handily able to secure them rooms in the finest inn Port Mauraisa had to offer. It wasn't much, with Maenea's buildings being simple, humble and earthen. But after such a draining journey, no accommodations could have seemed more lavish.

They were each taken to a bath room, where tubs of hot water had been drawn, and towels and night gowns had been set aside. Jek found it marvelous, soaking in the soothing heat. But as his body relaxed, his mind grew troubled. The day had brought many horrors, and at last there was nothing to divert him from grim reflection. He didn't tarry long, drying off and resolving to get some sleep, if he could...

Audrey and he hung their traveling gear over the fireplace in their room. Soon the sound of dripping, sizzling moisture over the hot clay bricks met the driving patter of the cold rain raging outside. The nurturing light from the fire mingled with the meager, pallid rays from the window. It seemed to Jek that this modest room was a sanctum of comfort, not the less because of the intrusive reminders of the squalor just beyond the walls...

And he was in good company. This was perhaps a natural environment for him to be reminded that his feelings for his wife had been more abundant lately. He would have dearly liked to admit as much. But as she continued drying her already-dry hair absently, Audrey seemed rather distant, and in any case very tired. He resolved to talk to her about it later. It was easier just to recline by her in silence, and hardly less comforting.

But after a while, when he was nearly asleep, she spoke. "Jek?" she called quietly.

"Yes, Audrey?" he replied.

"Do you ever worry about the future?" she asked.

Jek laughed. "Sometimes. In the past I've usually been too busy worrying about the present." He turned to regard her. "But even that's been easier lately. I've started to notice: Things tend to work themselves out."

She didn't look consoled. "But do you ever wonder what things are working themselves out *towards*? Does that ever give you pause?"

He furrowed his brow. "I'm not sure I know what you mean," he admitted.

She sighed. "It's hard to explain. I keep thinking about this conversation I had with Marrow."

"His conversations seem to have that effect."

She laughed. "Yeah, they do. But he said something at one point that really troubled me. He said I had a destiny."

Jek offered her a smile of affirmation. "I'm sure he's right."

"So am I. That's what bothers me." She paused, but Jek remained silent, finding no words for his befuddled sympathy. "I don't think I want a destiny, Jek," she explained at length. "I've tried to explain that all along. But no one seems to listen, and nothing can seem to slow down whatever's coming."

"Oh, Audrey, I hate to see you worry!" Jek replied. "It's not like you. And anyway, I'm sure your destiny is nothing to worry about. You're a Princess! That's a good thing. Maybe the attention daunts you right now, but I have no doubt you'll get used to it. And I know you'll be a great leader some day. Just think of that speech you gave to the Maeneans!"

"I'd rather not," she blanched. "And being a Princess isn't the great thing you think it is. Oh, sure, it sounds simple... until you realize you are one. If I'm honest, I don't know the first thing about princessing. And apparently I'm not *just* a Princess... I'm a Princess from the continent, of all places. I've never been there and I don't know anything about it! How am I supposed to princess a country properly when I've never even heard of it? When I don't even know which country is mine?"

Jek smiled again, daring to brush a bit of her hair out of her face. "There's no reason to fret about any of that now," he said. "Destiny is destiny. If there's one thing you can be sure will work itself out, it's that." He rolled over and settled back into a comfortable spot. "Get some sleep, dear, and don't worry. Whatever comes, I'll be with you till the end."

Quickly, Jek fell into sleep, consoled as he was by his own words. It never entered his tranquil mind that she may not have shared that consolation...

They woke some time still in the dead of night to the sound of pounding on their door. Jek leapt with a start and fumbled in the dark for his musket, the embers of the fire having died down to a dull shimmer. He flung the door open with his bayonette affixed. But at the first sight of their visitor, he immediately retired his weapon. It was the old man.

"Get yer stuff," the old man said. "We's leavin' now, while the leavin's good."

Jek's face crumpled up. "What?" he demanded in a hoarse whisper. "What are you talking about?"

"I's talkin' about the Quest, lad! The *real* Quest! Or did ye really forget it already? We still gots to find the Knights, and warn the world o' the Doom Fleet. Ain't nothin' more important than that. So get yer stuff like I says... chop-chop and on the double!"

Jek grabbed the old man under the arm and hauled him into the room, shutting the door. There was going to be some debate to come, and it didn't need to break out in the hall for all to hear...

"What in tarnation are ye thinkin', yankin' an old man around like that? What's come over ye, Jek? Y'aint hardly yerself lately. If I didn't know no better, I'd think ye'd really thrown in yer lot with this Inquisitor!"

"I have," Jek said. "And so should you! We have a firm ally in Parissah. If we leave her now, we'll ruin everything that we've been so fortunate to gain. Her trust is all we need! She already agreed to check into the Doom Fleet. All we have to do is see this Maenea thing through to her satisfaction, and we'll be off the hook! We don't need the Knights anymore. Why in Heck would we go looking for them now, when we don't have the first idea where they are, and we already have a sure thing here? We'd have to be crazy to do that!"

"We'd be even more crazier to go any further with Parissah!" the old man argued. "See this through to her satisfaction, ye says? How long will that take, I wonders? We was just 'aposed to be along for her negotiations. That ship done sailed, lad. And now we's roped into another mystery. Where will that lead us? To another one? And another? I warn ye, boy, we's on the edge of a rabbit hole, and ye's about to leap in head-first... with a madman to lead ye, no less!"

"Granted," Jek nodded. "But even Bravado's not as crazy as he seems. There's actually a bit of normal Humanity in him, I think."

The old man recoiled, aghast. "Ye's persuaded to his Free-Dome?!"

"No way!" Jek replied, laughing nervously. "Not even close. I'm still hoping we can find a way to undo the damage he's done. But I think he's leading us the way we need to go to do that. In any case, we can't afford to ignore him, any more than the Fleet. I don't know what he said to you, but he told Audrey and me that he means to bring Free-Dome to the whole world! We can't let that happen either!"

"So let yer precious Parissah handle Bravado. Ye seems to think she knows what she's doin'. I wonder, meself. She seems a mite disposed to hurl herself frivolously into danger. But that Baegulgog's a fine enough feller. And the bird... well, he gots some skill, I admits. They can prevail, I warrant. What does they need us for? We gots our own mission! Tis high-time we got back to it!"

"I'm not going," Jek shook his head. "I'm sorry, but I'm not."

Silence fell between them. The old man looked crushed. But he soon hid his real pain under a veneer of anger. "So that's it then. Ye's just gonna walk out on the silly old man, after all he done for ye? Big man in the night gown gonna turn away his mentor. In his hour o' need, no less."

"No," Jek said, reaching out and resting his hand on the old man's shoulder. "I don't want to send you away at all. I want you to come with us. It doesn't have to be the hard thing you're making it. We can still blow the whistle on the Doom Fleet. We're just going to have to be a little more patient and do a little more work than we planned."

The old man softened a bit. But he didn't quite relent. He looked past Jek to Audrey. "Audrey lass, what do ye say t'all this? I'd value yer insight. Especially if ye agrees with me."

She looked between the both of them, hesitant to arbitrate. She began with a heavy sigh. "Sorry, old man, but I think Jek's right. It would be faithless to abandon the others now. I trust them, and I think they trust us. That's not something I really want to throw away."

The old man shook his head. "Alright, darlin', if that's what ye wants. But ye used to trust me, too." He went sullenly to the door.

"We'll see you in the morning, then?" Jek asked after him.

"Ye will, surely enough," the old man replied. "I ain't about to bolt on ye. Not yet." He had nearly shut the door behind him, when suddenly he leaned back in to make one last point. "We came real close, didn't we? Ta makin' a name fer ourselves, I means. We woulda been remembered, assure. We was gonna be world-savers."

"We still will," Jek said. "We'll save the world yet, I think. And people will remember what we did."

"Aye," the old man sighed. "But what share o' the rememberin' will we get, I wonder? Now that we gots to split it with an Inquisitor, and a Heron warrior-doctor? I sure do wonder about that."

He closed the door.

* * *

In the morning, they were greeted by another knock at the door. This time it was their friend the Clerk, Baegulgog. It was the first time they had seen him solid and in his uniform. He invited them to breakfast, for which he expressed some unexpected interest. Jek and Audrey were rather incredulous. They understood that Meduselda do not eat. He explained that he had acquired it as an unfortunate habit. That might have accounted for his uncommon girth, but it still didn't make any sense.

The morning repast proved a bit awkward. The old man was quiet and grumpy again. Parissah and Marrow had already eaten privately, citing some sort of concerns about modesty, and so just sat and watched everyone else eat. Jek and Audrey passed on attempting to engage with Murtaugh or the Guardsmen, who fed in silence. Bravado gorged himself. He had an aggressive case of unaddressed bed-head.

Suddenly, Parissah started. "Baegulgog!" she exclaimed. "Whatever are you doing?"

He paused, and set down the food in front of him, flashing with embarrassment. "I am sorry to indulge my bad habit, madam. I am often most hungry after I have just returned to life, and I did not wish to be distracted during the journey by thoughts of eating."

"But you *aren't* eating!" Parissah insisted. "You have just been holding food up to your front side and saying, 'Nom, nom, nom'!"

Baegulgog pulsated thoughtfully. "I thought that's what eating was," he explained.

* * *

The sky that morning was dark but impotent. Thunder rumbled in the distance, and there was lightning round the heads of the mountains of Magna Koepna – their apparent destination. But they encountered no rain that day.

First they crossed the channel – an uneventful, silent affair. Bravado was not so clingy today. He was looking ever ahead, apparently too lost in the object of the journey to engage in the present. But once they made landfall on the great secondary isle, he proved time and again on the road and in the wilderness beyond that his attention was unnecessary. This was his true home – the part of Maenea from which he hailed – the cradle of Free-Dome. He knew intrinsically where he was going, leading them past brambles and thorns, pits and sheer clefts, over canyons and raging rivers, never wasting a step.

After ascending from such perilous wilderness, they emerged into a rolling hill country – steeper than the miles behind, but otherwise tame and grassy. They stopped to camp one night at the foot of Scotzimbasha – the nearest mountain – one of three in a cluster at the center of Magna Koepna. Only then did Bravado begin to seem as he had the first day – almost so eager to talk that he suffered for want of a faster mouth. He shared many stories of his younger days, roaming the very hills they had crossed as they looked back down upon them. He spoke of his parents – rangers charged with watching this remote, wide stretch of country – who had evidently been forgotten by the colonial government shortly after their assignment. Perhaps it accounted somewhat for his irreverent ways. Bravado did not truly know civilization... but neither had civilization known him.

That second morning, Bravado was agitated on a whole new level. He rushed breakfast, he rushed the breaking of camp, he rushed up the mountain... and it was all anyone could do to keep up with him. As on the first night, Parissah melded effortlessly with his mindset of urgency, becoming almost an assistant slave-driver. Jek and Audrey found it a little tiresome, but mostly understood what drove her. Doubtless she was very anxious to learn something meaningful, and so salvage at least a tiny measure of success for her mission, and for her fallen comrades. But caught between Bravado charging ahead and Parissah cracking the whip behind, tension and anticipation were palpable to all.

At last, they summited a wide arm of Scotzimbasha. The air was stagnant and moldering, and the sight of the land beyond robbed Jek of what breath he could manage. The three peaks joined arms to form a wide, misty valley, wreathed in rounded steps of dense jungle. All below, and even above, was drenched in a strikingly rich and deep bluish-green hue, as if all other colors were suddenly sapped from the world. Truth be told, it felt like they had left the world behind, and stepped into some uncanny abstraction of it...

Jek kept studying all the great bowl of the land before them, hoping to find comfort in some sight that did not seem so alien. It was a vain search, because the details proved even stranger than the larger first impression. He saw huge constructs of some sort, resting on stilted mounts – sticking out of the trees or clinging to the encircling slopes – pointing like enormous, eldritch cannons into the very heart of the valley. Their purpose or origin, he could not hope to guess. But even from a great distance, he could tell they were very ancient, and disused. Bravado spoke no word about them, and Jek and all the others were content not to ask...

Down they marched, into the alien jungles. So mystifying was the landscape, it was only after they had ventured deep within that Jek considered the possible implications. "Are there Mantids in these jungles?" he asked. His voice was unexpectedly loud.

"No," Bravado answered. "Nothing lives here."

Jek blanched as he realized for the first time just how complete the silence had been, ever since the summit...

"You should all watch out for the Sentries, though," Bravado continued, as sort of an afterthought.

"But you just said nothing lives here," Audrey retorted.

"Yeah," Bravado replied.

Coming to some shear shelves in the landscape, Bravado reluctantly began to lead them on winding paths. At times he hesitated, and it was clear that this was not an area he was quite so familiar with. Occasionally they passed craters, wide and deep, filled with scorched earth that had never grown back over. And the ground was strewn in places with big chunks of metallic flotsam – some of which looked distressingly like limbs. Jek's nerves began to fray. He didn't care for this eerie place, and grew ever more conscious of the fact that he didn't know where they were going, or why.

At length, he fell back to Parissah.

"You must keep up the pace, Jek," she cautioned him. "This is no time for Human frailty."

"I'm just here to talk," he explained. "What do you know about this place? Surely an Inquisitor would have heard something about all this weirdness."

"We are approaching *Thasagral* – the valley of eternal mists. It is indeed among the world's strangest places, but its secrets are little known to the Inquisition. We once considered proscribing this entire region. However, that proved unnecessary. Its reputation alone has been enough to deter most interest. No one that has entered *Thasagral* itself ever found their way back out. None, except, allegedly, our own Herz Bravado... as I explained near the beginning of our mission here."

"Do you really believe that story?"

"I do now. He spoke of returning to the 'source' – and this is where he has led us. I know that he has much mental instability. But even *he* is not capable of such delusions of grandeur as to believe he has been to *Thasagral* and back, when indeed he has not."

"Are you absolutely sure of that?"

"I am reasonably confident. That will have to suffice, if we are to learn anything."

Jek's mind was little eased by Parissah's words. In fact, he began to think the old man's assessment of her character might have been too true for comfort...

Later, they came to another shear drop, which they could not circumnavigate. But Bravado found a narrow outcropping that led down the face in a rough, ramp-like path. It was so narrow, in fact, that they dared only shuffle with their backs to the wall. Murtaugh and the Guard went first, with Bravado bringing up the rear this time. He reasoned that if the path came to a dead end, it would be most expedient to have him in the back, where he could return to the top and start searching for another way down. Jek shuffled just ahead of him. Baegulgog floated heedlessly to the ground.

"We can make it to the bottom," Murtaugh called up the path, after an interminable time. Jek sighed in relief. The shuffle down was bad enough without having to wonder if they might have to shuffle back up...

Still perhaps twelve feet off the ground in front of him, Jek came to some more metal debris, right in the path. He winced at it in disgust. It was shaped exactly like a severed arm. There wasn't enough room to go around it – he had to step right over it. One foot went over fine. But to his great dismay, his balance faltered and he roughly kicked the arm with his other foot. To his even *greater* dismay, the arm retaliated, grabbing him by the ankle!

"AHK!" he cried, and nearly panicked... before Bravado's broadsword impaled the arm, effectively severing it at the wrist with sparks and smoke. The hand quickly lost its strength, and Jek kicked it away into the abyss.

"Beware the Sentries," Bravado recited.

"Oh I will now, don't you worry," Jek huffed. "I won't be kicking any more metal arms if I can help it."

Bravado stopped him and gave him a look. "Some of them are a lot more than just an arm."

Jek gulped.

Finally at the bottom, the group was able to advance more freely, the ground receding before them at a gentler angle. Perhaps a half-hour went by without further event or obstruction. And then, at last, they reached the edge of the mist...

Bravado paused just before its wake. He looked vacantly into the unsearchable fog for a long time. After a while, Audrey walked right up to him, and Jek followed. It was a strange sight. Bravado did not appear to be gathering strength or resolution. He wasn't steeling himself against some great peril. It was just a purely empty stare... and getting emptier. Audrey waved a hand in front of his face. It took seconds before Bravado came out of his apparent trance, blinking wildly.

"What was that about?" Audrey asked him.

"What was what about?" Bravado asked in return.

"You were really tuned out there. It looked like you didn't have a thought in your head!"

"Right," Bravado nodded. He turned his back to the mist, preparing to address his whole group. "Thank you all for seeing me this far. But I'm afraid I'll have to go the rest of the way myself." He held out his hand, as if to avert an outburst. "Now now, I know your deep loyalty would compel you to follow me to the very end. I know that wild stegosaurs couldn't drag even one of you from my side. But you *must* let me go on alone. The danger to the rest of you would be too great. For I am the only one who ever ventured beyond this point and returned to the world as you know it. I, and one other. So please, stay behind. Please, *please* do this for me... even if it breaks your hearts."

"Okay," Murtaugh agreed.

"I'll return soon," he assured them. "And I will have with me the Power to bring Free-Dome to the world at large."

Parissah strode up to him, holding out a trinket. "*Thasagral* is indeed perilous," she said. "Even if you have navigated it once, you should make no presumptions about succeeding again. You must not lose your way! At least bring a compass."

Bravado took the compass from her. He examined it for a moment, then threw it on the ground, busting it into a million pieces, and stomping the ruin with a crunch. Parissah gasped. But before she could protest, he explained himself...

"If I had even the slightest idea where I was going, I'd never get there," he admonished her. And with that, he turned and vanished into the depths of *Thasagral.*

* * *

Everyone stood mystified for a while. They hadn't known what to expect going into this journey. But to suddenly be left high and dry by Bravado, with no answers, or even shadows of answers, had certainly not entered their minds. It was very hollowing.

"What do you think he meant by that?" Audrey asked at length.

Parissah did not answer at once. "I think..." she began, but stopped. Then she turned to them. "I think it is a clue," she said. "Certainly, it means *something*. Perhaps it is the key to navigating *Thasagral*." She grew rather excited, even as she said this. Jek felt his heart sink. Her excitement could mean only one thing.

"You're going in after him, aren't you?" he asked. "With only the most oblique guess about how to come back? After he very specifically warned us not to follow him!"

"Yes," she said. "Who will come with me?"

"I will come, madam!" Baegulgog said, sailing on the air to her side.

"I almost wish you wouldn't, Baegulgog," she said. "Your immunity to death will not avail you, if we are to be lost forever in an unnatural fog."

"Yet I will chance it, if you allow me," he answered solemnly. "I should not forgive myself, if I let you alone to such peril."

"Thank you, Baegulgog," she nodded. "You may come."

"I too will accept the danger," Marrow said, striding with *Valshaloli*. "And do not ask me if we shall return! It becomes tedious."

"Yet you encourage me," Parissah replied. "I doubt you would come, if you did not expect return was likely."

"That is a fair assessment," Marrow nodded.

Parissah regarded the Humans. "What of you three?"

"We'll be along in a jiffy," the old man answered for them all, to Jek's immediate surprise.

"Very good," she said. Then last of all, she turned to Murtaugh and the Guard. "I know well enough I am about to defy your master's wishes," she addressed them. "You are within your right to try to restrain me. But I caution you! I will not be deterred. Any attempt on your part to stop us will prompt an overwhelming response."

"Okay," Murtaugh agreed.

Parissah nodded to him. "Farewell, then. And if I never return, then may sanity and propriety grow up anew in this fertile land of Maenea." Then she too vanished, and Baegulgog and Marrow behind her.

That left Jek, Audrey, the old man... and the totally disinterested men of Free-Dome.

"Alright, old man, what is it now?" Jek sighed. "Why did you hold us up?"

"Me argument's the same as afore," he answered. "She's leadin' us to ruin, I tell ye! This is just the kind o' death wish I was tryin' to warn ye about! We oughts to vamoose now, while we gots one last chance."

"I won't," Jek answered flatly. He turned to face the mists himself. "For once, I'm not afraid."

"Ye're not?"

He was hesitant to answer. "Okay, I am still afraid. But not as much as I used to be. You can leave if you really want to, old man. But I'm going to see this through."

"So am I," Audrey said, joining him at the very threshold of *Thasagral*. "We've already been through one place no one ever returns from, anyway."

"Ah, crimedy," the old man protested, slapping his knee. "Fine. *Fine*! We'll take one more gamble on the Inquisitor. But I warn ye! This be the last time! If this turn don't pay all, I's strikin' out on me own! I done it afore, and I can do it again!" Then he joined them too.

They all stood gathering courage for a while. Though really, the longer he stared into utter, wispy nothingness, the less courage Jek felt. So he resolved to go now, before it became any harder...

"Are you two ready?" he asked.

"Sure," Audrey shrugged.

"Aye," the old man said.

"Okay." Jek shut his eyes, and took one great big step forward...

The Harbinger

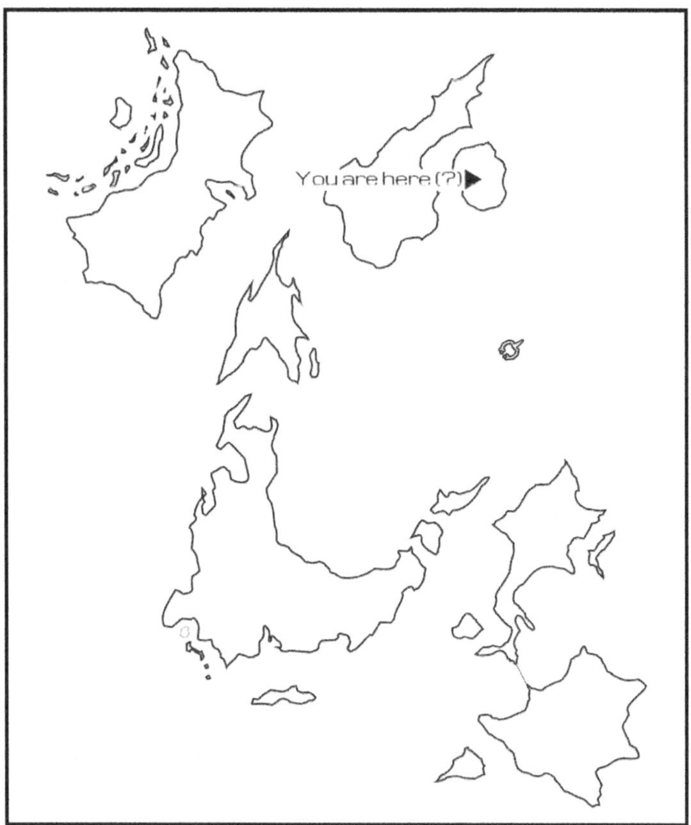

"There are many questions about the universe that it is not healthy to ask. Chief among them is, 'why'?"

- Zeph Bronzegloom, *What if I Was Wrong?*

Baegulgog turned to regard the bungling sound behind him as Jek emerged into the fog of *Thasagral*, slamming right into Parissah's back. All the clatter and the fumbling made for only a very dull commotion in the enigmatic, featureless mist. Sound *could* be made here... but it was obvious that it did not belong, and was quick to dissipate. Even Baegulgog's internal music was stymied. He had immediately wished to craft some mysterious anthem for all of this, of course. But no matter how he tried, he found he could not string two notes together! Such direction and structure seemed totally lost on him in this strange place...

"Sorry," Jek apologized to Parissah, still composing himself from the collision.

"Do not be," Parissah told him. "I meant to cut you off, so that we could precisely mark our starting place."

"I could be more precise than that, if you wish," Baegulgog volunteered, whisking back whence he came. "I floated exactly two seconds past the threshold at a speed of approximately 1.32379 feet per second, meaning the exact starting point should be... here." He held a tentacle over the threshold.

"Very good, Baegulgog," Parissah nodded, most pleased with his accuracy. "Now Jek, would you oblige me and step past Baegulgog's mark?"

Jek hesitated briefly, but took a step beyond the point that Baegulgog held his tentacle over. In theory, he should have taken one step back into the surrounding valley. But he was still standing in fog.

"Do you see the real world from where you are?" Parissah asked him.

"No," Jek said, rather aghast. "It doesn't seem to be back here anymore..."

"Take a few paces more, just to be sure," she instructed him.

He took nine more steps. "Still nothing," he said. "Nothing but more of this fog."

"Excellent," Parissah said.

"Nay, but it *AIN'T* excellent!" the old man protested. "Farthest thing from *excellent*, I warrant! We gets here, and afore anything else, we finds out fer dead certain we can't go back!"

"Not the way we came, at any rate," Parissah replied. "But this is just one experiment I mean to try, in order to confirm my theory about this place." She turned to Baegulgog. "To that end, I wonder if you might oblige me with more of your impressive mathematics, my friend," she implored him. Baegulgog flashed with excitement. He was nothing if not eager to accommodate...

"Certainly! What would you have me to calculate, madam?"

"I need a reliable estimate of the breadth of *Thasagral*, if that is within your ability."

"Indeed it is! From our initial vantage point at the zenith of Scotzimbasha, it appeared that these mists ran 2.1287 miles across, give or take."

"Wonderful. Let us proceed ahead, then, in precisely the direction we were pointed when we entered the mist..." She turned and strode forth, and all the others fell in behind...

*   *   *

10228, 10229, 10230... Baegulgog counted the seconds, and thus he came to exactly 72 minutes – 10/13ths of an hour. That would put them at 13921.2871 feet from the starting point, with 31981.7128 feet to go until they reached the other side. All of that, perhaps, went quite without saying. But all their venturing continued to be utterly featureless. There was naught to be seen anywhere. The senses could not penetrate the perfectly uniform bluish haze, rising into an overhead darkness, where there should still have been daylight. Thus, Baegulgog tried to make the most of any math at all he could keep track of. There was simply nothing else to think about – an unnerving prospect, even for an easy-going fellow like himself...

"The ground here is so incredibly smooth," Audrey commented, at length. They had walked in anxious silence until this point. "Has anyone else noticed that?"

"I admit I had not noticed," Marrow said. "That is a very keen observation on your part, my dear... in this place where there is seemingly nothing to observe."

"It *is* very smooth... whatever it is," Parissah agreed quizzically. "Yet I cannot help wondering whether there *is* ground in here at all."

"Well, we's walkin' on *somethin'*, isn't we?" the old man demanded.

"That is a very good question. Yes, perhaps one of the essential questions. I wonder..." Parissah trailed off, scratching the chin of her mask, saying nothing more.

Jek squinted nervously down towards his feet. "I sure hope there's ground," he said. "The idea of walking on nothing doesn't sit well with me."

"Aye," the old man concurred. "T'ain't natural. Downright spooky, I deems it."

"Sorry I brought it up," Audrey said.

* * *

Parissah continued to lead them for some time. Baegulgog kept his running tally of the seconds and the feet, but did not speak of them. He was powerless to prevent his internal glow pulsating with a growing anxiety as the counts continued to run and run, with no change in their surroundings.

"We have gone some ways, if I do not miss my guess," Parissah said finally. "What of it, Baegulgog? What do your calculations tell you?"

"I regret to say we should have come out the other side of *Thasagral* quite a while ago, even by the most conservative estimates," he answered. "2.1287 miles across, I made it. 2.3172 miles at most. Yet, upon the very moment of your first utterance just now, we would have made the 3.8313-mile mark!"

"Good," Parissah answered. "Then there is no room for doubt. We have overshot any end we should have found to this fog."

"What part of that is good?" Jek asked. "We weren't able to go back, and we gained nothing by traveling right through the heart of this place. Now we can't even find the far side!" Jek was wide-eyed, appearing a bit shell-shocked. "I know we discussed the possibility of getting lost in here forever, but I was really hoping against it."

"Don't despair yet," Parissah told him. "We have merely performed the second in a series of experiments. And I daresay, the results are heartening to me, because they are precisely as I expected."

"How many more o' these 'experiments' is we gonna have ta do?" the old man asked. "And be there any hope whatever that we can put what ye learn ta good use? Or is eternity in this here mirk the price what must be paid ta sate yer scientastic curioscity?"

"Believe me old man, I don't wish to be trapped in here forever any more than you do," she answered. "In fact, it would be more disagreeable for me than any of you, who would simply die after a while. But I would be forced to endure, thinking endlessly about all the work I should be doing outside. Rest assured these experiments are for more than my curiosity – they are eminently purposeful. I think that, in order to effectively navigate *Thasagral*, we must first firmly understand how we can *not* effectively navigate *Thasagral*. And that should require only one additional experiment. Yet be warned, this is the most perilous of all the experiments, and may lead to some unpleasantness."

"I don't like the sound of that," Jek brooded.

"Everyone gather closely round Baegulgog," Parissah instructed. "We will form here a tight circle." They did as she asked, all five of them forming a ring around the Clerk, like some sort of big group hug. Baegulgog was a bit incredulous, not sure why he had been singled out in this peculiar manner...

"Well here you all are," he said, looking around at them. "Yet the significance of this formation eludes me. What next, madam?"

"Now we must split up," she answered. "We must each back away until we do not see any of the others. Our whole intention must be to go our separate ways."

"Surely not!" Jek protested, gripped with sudden terror. "All we have in here is each other! Asking us to split up is too much! I can't take it!"

"Come now!" Parissah commanded. "Do not make a spectacle of yourself! This is no time for extreme cowardice. We must try this! Each of you is to back away from all the others... all but you, Baegulgog. You are to float upward. Yet keep your focus on the ground beneath you! All are to remain focused behind, *not* ahead! You are all to be mindful of your growing distance, each from all the others. Only in this way can we confirm the dynamics of three-dimensional space within *Thasagral*."

"But..." Jek began to levy again, but was cut off.

"...Jek, you must desist," Marrow said. "Do as she says, if only because I say so."

Jek sighed. "Alright."

"Very good," Parissah nodded. "Now let us all begin."

Baegulgog coasted up into the air, watching all of his companions back away from one another. It was an unnerving sight. He did not appreciate the thought of sundering the group any more than Jek did. Yet without protest, he was now floating high and away, watching all of his friends become small, and faint... and at last, quite invisible in the blue nothingness. He floated and floated. But bereft of any reference point, he could not even say with certainty that he was moving anymore. A tiny fleck of panic sparked within him, and it began to spread like wildfire. He nearly called out in distress...

...when suddenly he was aware of a series of impacts...

Five different objects ran into him at once, all from different directions. He stopped directing all of his vision down, scanning around himself in a flurry to determine what had happened. To his astonishment, he had been run into by his friends! They had all backed into him, just as he had come up into their midst from below!

"What the devil?" the old man cursed, whirling around. "How did? What did?" But no matter how he tried, he couldn't spit out a complete question.

"Ah yes, very very good!" Parissah said, clapping her hands together. "This experiment has also gone just as I hoped."

"But... we all backed away," Audrey stammered. "If there was one thing we should have been sure of, it's that we were getting farther apart..."

"Precisely," Parissah agreed. "In this we find the essence of *Thasagral*."

"Do enlighten us," Marrow implored her. "You have had some theory all along. What is it? What have you learned from all your tinkering?"

"I have learned that I do not *know* how to navigate *Thasagral*," Parissah explained, "and that, indeed, I *cannot* know."

The old man leapt at her, and it was all Jek and Audrey could do to restrain him. "I knowed it! I knowed all along ye was gonna lead us to ruin, ye..."

"Silence, Human!" Marrow demanded in a grave voice, and it stilled the old man. "Let her continue."

Parissah began to pace thoughtfully, arms folded behind her back. "So far, all of our attempts to navigate this place have been based on our knowledge of physical space... where we came in, where we should have been able to come out again, and where each of us is relative to the other. Yet *Thasagral* has supplanted our expectations at every turn. That is because we have come to the place where no *knowledge* can avail us. For if it is not already quite obvious, this is not an earthly place at all. We have come to the very dwelling of Ethon. Of that, I now have little doubt."

"That makes sense," Audrey said. "If Bravado came here, and found Ethon, it could explain how he has his power."

"It is a long way from truly explaining all that," Parissah replied, waving a hand dismissively. "I do not understand how encountering a Dianode would result in attaining a measure of its elemental essence. But it is a start. Bravado spoke of this place as the source of his power. And we have already learned that his magic is Ethon's magic. Therefore, I believe Ethon dwells here. And I also believe that, if this is his dwelling, we cannot hope to find our way – whether deeper in or back out again – by any force of reasoning. This place defies knowing."

"Then we *is* lost forever!" the old man despaired.

"In a way, yes," Parissah nodded. "But that is to our advantage. I believe that all who came here before, and never returned, failed to do so because they never gave up trying to reason their way back out."

"So you're saying that we should just throw ourselves into a panic and run in any old direction," Jek said, suddenly appearing rather confident with himself. "That sounds easy enough!"

"That is not what I'm saying," Parissah shook her head. "Even panic has a form of rudimentary logic about it. You reason that if you flee hard enough, long enough, you can find some escape. Even to do that much will not grant us any success. I have little doubt that all who came before resorted to panic quickly enough. But that did not serve them, and it will not serve us."

"What in the name o' Heck is we to do, then?" the old man asked.

"We must walk around erratically," Parissah explained. "Totally without consistent direction or aim – not meaning to go forward nor back – trackless of whither we go. I believe that is the only way we will happen across anything of significance in this place."

"Let's do it then," Audrey said. "It's worth a try."

"Aye," the old man sighed. "Prit-near anythin' is, when ye's in a pickle like this."

"Very well," Parissah said. "Only understand this: I think we must each choose our own route. If one should try to follow another, then the follower will be trying to conform to some intelligible pattern. Such an approach would not be in the spirit of this place, and I do not think it would be rewarded."

"So we have to split up again?" Jek asked, disturbed.

"Yes," she answered. "But we have done that before, and it was not so disastrous. So take courage, Jek! The sooner we lose track of one another, perhaps the sooner we will all find each other again."

And with that, Parissah started taking random steps – some to the side, some backward, turning this way and that, so that it appeared that she was trying to do some dance – surely, the clumsiest dance that had ever been seen. One by one, they all began to do likewise, solemn expressions on each visible face – every one of them knowing that their lives depended on infusing their course with as much nonsensical abandon as they could muster...

This was particularly hard for poor Baegulgog. He veered to the left and right, forward and back – even up and down – but no matter how he tried, he could scarcely divorce his movements from some sort of mathematical precision. *30 degrees left, 1.1882 feet per second, 0.8 seconds, 93 degrees right, 0.9819 feet per second...* he found himself thinking. "Oh, drat!" he exclaimed to himself. He tried much harder to block out the numbers. But his mind was just so frightfully orderly that it seemed impossible.

Pressure built steadily as Baegulgog continued to veer all about, when he became conscious that some of his companions had been lost in the shuffle! It seemed Parissah was right after all. Those whose steps had been the silliest were already gone – with any good fortune, to some more significant spot – perhaps into the very presence of Ethon himself. But Baegulgog was still quite where he had been. He struggled and sputtered and despaired to be random enough, but the numbers would not relent. He threw his tentacles in a wiggling display of absurdity, but it seemed not to help at all.

Finally, he was alone.

Baegulgog stopped moving, lost for a spell in a sudden, crushing despair. He was not accustomed to such moments of doubt, and it proved too much for him. His bulbous body deflated as his spirits sank. "That is it for the Clerk Baegulgog, then," he lamented to himself. "O, what grim fate! To be lost in the nothingness by myself until my 140 years are passed!"

His glow flashed like a singularity with sudden befuddlement. "What did I say? *140*? Ha! That is *their* numerals..." He shook himself with whimsical mirth. "4 and 5 and 6!" he laughed. "What silly, silly numbers they are! Yet you are onto something, Baegulgog old chap. If you cannot keep the numbers out, why not confuse them instead?"

He began to wander again. "15, 62, 94, 57, 640, 513, 42..." he chanted to himself, exerting all his mathematical thought into coming up with a random string of numbers, each including digits from the Human system to ensure maximum silliness. "85, 449, 76, 34..."

...He was cut off as he unexpectedly smooshed up against an unyielding surface. Backing away reflexively, he worked to take stock of this strange discovery. It proved quite a lot to take in. Before him was a tower – rough and grey and monolithic like cement, but glossy like stained glass. He looked up, and though the tower did not seem the least obscured by the supernatural fog of *Thasagral*, it reached to absolutely unsearchable heights. He looked down, and found that ran also into unsearchable depths, as if he now floated just above the surface of a mirror that reflected only the tower. He lofted further back and back, trying to see more of this obelisk, until he was aware that he was not alone. Marrow was there with him.

"Ah, Marrow! Well met, sir! I admit I despaired there for a time to think whether I should ever be silly enough to catch up with the rest of you."

"And yet, of all of us, I would still deem you the silliest," Marrow said. "Yet I am glad to see you as well. Bravado is a peculiar man indeed, to have endured this weird place alone. It is unnerving. But how fortunate we are! I no longer have any doubt that Parissah was correct in all her deductions. This is the ethereal sanctum of Ethon's harbinger form. Here is his tower – the unsearchable heart of all this thoughtless silence." Marrow took a step forward, and pointed to a spot a ways off to the right of the tower. "And there is Bravado, entering through the front gate."

Baegulgog watched in great wonder as the big man with the curly locks and the half-green face walked straight into the tower... an intense, inscrutably absent look on his face.

"By Jove!" he exclaimed. "That *is* Bravado! However did we arrive ahead of him?"

"We have already learned that Space does not behave itself here," Marrow replied. "Perhaps Time is just as nebulous. But come now! He would have words with Ethon. We must eavesdrop, if we can..."

* * *

Jek found himself wedged into some cramped shelf with a wide, thick viewport overlooking a dark chamber. He was there with Audrey, and Parissah too, who, though Jek could hardly make her out in the gloom, appeared especially uncomfortable in this narrow spot. Jek could not discern the purpose of their overlook, nor even remember clearly how they'd reached it, or what had caused them to duck into it. Right now, they were simply looking down on an empty chamber, dim with streaks of blue light that came from no where. The more he thought about it, the more it disgusted him that he couldn't reconcile any of these things. He resolved to ask, hoping one of the others would know...

"Where are we?" he whispered.

"We are in Ethon's lair," Parissah answered.

"Yeah, I knew *that*," Jek said, but then fell uncertain. "I think I knew that, anyway. But what is this shelf we're hunkered in? What are we watching for?"

"I don't know about the shelf," she answered. "It is certainly a convenient vantage point... whatever it is, and however we reached it. But as for what we are here to observe, I suppose that will become apparent, once we begin to observe it..."

"This is so much nonsense," Audrey said.

"Indubitably," Parissah agreed.

Just then, Jek saw a shadow pass into view. From beneath them, a lone figure emerged, resting a big sword on his shoulder, until finally he stopped, set the sword down carefully, and knelt to the ground.

"That's Herz Bravado!" Jek whispered. "We found him!"

"By golly, you're right," Audrey replied. "We're just where we need to be to watch him kneeling in an empty room. What do you suppose he's doing?"

"He is paying homage to his master – to the one he knows as the source. He is kneeling in deference to Ethon."

Just then – perhaps at the very invocation of the name – there was a roiling sensation on Jek's palette that made his eyes want to roll back in their sockets. His mind was set at once struggling through a vast fluff – soft and springy and vaguely course. The intervals between one thought and the next were not demarked – perhaps hours at a time, perhaps only a moment. Gentle, soothing oblivion caressed every contour of his brain.

He tried to recall something simple...

What am I doing here?

...For that matter, who am I?

It was hard to remember...

What was hard to remember?

He slapped himself, and his mind came humming back to life. He slapped his compatriots. His wife looked cross. The Inquisitor whispered, "Thank you."

Thus, they were all at least passably conscious to watch as other shadows marshaled into the room below. Long shadows, paired and mirrored, converging – coming toward Bravado's stooped form. Then another figure emerged into view, hardly larger than Bravado himself. From him came the shadows, and more shadows yet were in his train... some cast to the ground, others floating into the air and onto the walls behind. The entity had the body of a man, but the head of a falcon – with piercing, glowing eyes that obfuscated the mind. Jek tore his gaze away from those eyes, wisely fearing to lose all that he had ever known if he long endured the sight of them. So it was that he, a humble mortal man – perhaps as humble a specimen as they come – beheld a Dianode in its harbinger form. And not just *any* Dianode, but the most mysterious and infamous of them all. Jek saw Ethon.

"You return, my disciple," Ethon spoke, and the voice filled all the boundless space of *Thasagral*, for the very plane of existence was but an extension of Ethon himself. "I see that you have done a great work since our last meeting. Much that was once known is now forgotten in your lands. This pleases me." As he stood before Bravado, who did not rise, Ethon crossed his arms, with his long talons rolling gently over the folds of his elbows. "Your purposes in returning here, however, are not so pleasing. Yet I bid you… speak for yourself! State your wish, that I may judge you by your own words."

"Master," Bravado implored, not moving, eyes to the ground. "Your servant has indeed done much. He has liberated all the wide country of Maenea with the power you granted him." He paused, perhaps too polite to start forming his request straight away. It was very strange indeed to see Bravado, of all people, in such a grovel. "But he has much work left to do, and time is of the essence. It's a big world out there, and your servant won't live forever." He raised his head, if only a few degrees – enough to look at Ethon's feet. "So I ask for more strength to do my work. Share with me the secret of the Power that was known of old! The Power my folk knew in the Great Regression – the total mastery of all the elements. Let me wield it, so that I may bring Free-Dome to all the lands."

Ethon stood unmoved. Bravado fidgeted under the colossal weight of his silence, appearing to be in pain. But finally, Ethon came forward, and rested a claw upon Bravado's shoulder, until he rose to his feet, still looking down. Ethon began to stride slowly around his disciple, his train of shadows raking the chamber as he passed. "Do you think I care about the fortunes of your crusade?" the great being asked. "Or am I a teacher, that I would wish for someone to learn from me? Yet this is just the sort of ignorance that once endeared me to you. When first you came here, you succeeded in finding your way… not because you had any way in mind when you came, but because you were content to wander. Only one other before you ever ventured to *Thasagral* in this spirit. And when you found me, little did you understand who I was, or what I was. And in this, too, I was greatly pleased. Your mind seemed content in its emptiness. I allowed myself to believe that you were worthy of doing my work, and so it was I shared with you a measure of my Purpose." He stopped, standing indignant before Bravado again. "But I see now that you defrauded me… just as she who came before you. Even if you were in earnest the first time, now you come again seeking not to conform yourself to my Purpose, but to poach the secrets that have been trusted to my keeping."

He reached out his hand again, this time laying hold of the top of Bravado's head, several inches worth of clawed nails hanging perilously down. "This mind is no different from all the others. It is *ravenous* to learn whatever it foolishly believes it can turn to its advantage. It is a maw, whose self-serving cravings can never be sated! How I find all minds abhorrent! Even Knowledge – my adversary – I do not hate. There is a place for Knowledge in this universe, or there should have been no place for me. That is Balance – a principle you mortals make pretense to cherish. And yet you would eschew Balance, sans all hesitance or remorse, if only you could find a way to tip the scales in your favor! How each of you fritters in vain to learn a way you might reshape all things to your liking! A curse be on you *all*!" He withdrew his hand quickly, and Bravado cowered, expecting to be struck. But instead, Ethon reached within his flowing raiment – deep within the vest of it, like there was nothing beneath – and slowly, with a tremor... he produced a pamphlet. "Even *this* curse... the greatest I can bestow..."

Bravado regarded the sheet of paper in front of him, incredulous. "What is this?" he asked.

"The object of the mind, if anything be," Ethon answered. "You came here begging the secrets to bend the cosmos – even to break it, if you would. Now I freely give them to you... the very secrets that she who came before you stole in ages past – those that above all else it is my charge to keep. They are yours. I grant your wish! I can do nothing greater to spite you. For regardless of the way you intend to use this Knowledge, it will only bring the End, as it nearly did before. When that happens, you will all look to me for help. You will wait and pray and beg and despair for my return to set things right again. But I will not come." Ethon cast the pamphlet at Bravado's feet. "Go now and take your prize! And know that whatever doom comes of it, it comes with my blessing."

Ethon's retinue of shadows collapsed in on him, and he withdrew in a swift and silent shroud. Bravado held out a hand as if to stay him or beg his pardon. But it was too little, too late. Ethon was gone. Only the Pamphlet remained.

Bravado stooped again, now bent with sorrow. It was clear that he did not understand what he had done to so displease his master. Jek was aware of feeling rather sorry for him again, even amidst his own swirling confusion. What sort of craziness had he just witnessed? There were seemingly endless questions, and his mind stumbled over itself trying to sort them all out, or even articulate what they were.

It was then that Jek heard a curious sound...

"Hmm hmm, hm-hm" hummed the humming sound.

"Baegulgog!" Parissah exclaimed in a terse whisper. "When did you get here? But never mind! Silence yourself – this is no time for your sneaking music!"

"Sorry, madam," Baegulgog whispered very quietly. "My nerves got the better of me. But come now! I have been here all along. When did *you* get here?" Marrow was also there, and nodded as in agreement that they had been the whole time.

"There's no way you've been here all along because *we've* been here all along!" Audrey put in.

"Shut up!" Parissah whispered over them all. "Do any of you dimly understand the implications of what has just transpired before our very eyes?"

"Hardly," Baegulgog admitted. "Though it does distress me greatly. It seemed that Ethon behaved rather crossly."

"Yes!" Parissah exclaimed. "That alone should be cause for unbridled alarm. Ethon *behaved*. Cross or joyful or sad... it does not matter. He should not have been capable of such emotion... of *any* emotion. That is a characteristic of Will. Dianodes do not have Will! But it is apparent that *he* has one! That is a grave distortion of nature I should never have imagined, unless I had witnessed it for myself. And worse... worse by far! Worse than any foreboding I have ever known... his Will is expressly to abandon his Purpose! He could not have been any clearer about that, in word or deed. Do you realize what he has given to Bravado?"

"It looked like a brochure," Audrey commented.

Parissah shook her head grimly. "That is *no* brochure. It is a *pamphlet*. *The* Pamphlet. None other than the hallowed Pamphlet of Unknowable Things."

"*Holy moley*," Jek reeled. Then he blanched. "...Pardon my language."

"Certainly," Parissah nodded. "Indeed, if ever there was a time for gross explitives, it may be now. There is an elemental force of the universe who has vowed not to intervene in future calamities... and if that were not enough, he has delivered into mortal hands the sure means to such calamity! The system of Balance on which all depends is now destabilized. Indeed, it may be long since there has been *true* Balance... perhaps many centuries. Who can say how long Ethon has been in this unnatural state?" She sighed. "Things have gone steadily from bad to worse... and now, to worst of all. Too long have we been without Enscharaulgk's direction. Yet now, I fear even his wisdom will not avail."

"Don't despair, madam," Baegulgog comforted her. "I think we must focus on what we can yet control. Bravado must not be allowed to escape with that Pamphlet!"

"Too late," Jek said, checking back out into the now-empty chamber. "He's already gone. And the Pamphlet with him."

"Then we must follow," Parissah said. "Baegulgog is right. The secrets of the Pamphlet cannot be left in Bravado's hands! All other concerns will have to wait."

* * *

After a while, the party found themselves back in the mists. Once again, as Jek tried to look back, he found he did not recall the route that connected his current spot with the cramped little space they had been hunkered in. It was some comfort that they were already this far back. But he felt sudden doubt. Parissah had discovered the key to finding the epicenter of *Thasagral*. Would the same trick really work now to send them back?

"Well, we're back in the fog," he said. "What's the trick now?"

"The same as before," Parissah answered. "I hope." She started dancing around again like a buffoon. All the rest did too. Dimly, Jek heard Baegulgog grumbling some numbers to himself. He wondered about it, but only for a moment. Soon he didn't even hear it anymore. He looked up and turned his head as he continued to shuffle in odd directions, but he could not find the Clerk. Turning back, he no longer saw Audrey. They were all vanishing again... to where, he did not know, but would soon enough find out...

Abruptly, Jek stumbled over his own feet. He fell backwards – perhaps a full turn, perhaps more – and then emerged into temporarily blinding brightness. Hard, real ground met his back, and it was most unpleasant, but also reassuring. He felt the rough crunch of twigs and gravel. Looking up and around, he saw again the creepy blue-green jungle that encircled *Thasagral*. It amazed him how comforting the sight of that horrible place was! Soon others of his party were tumbling out of the mist beside him, until each of them was laid out, except for Baegulgog, who caught himself in the air.

Finally, Herz Bravado emerged, striding out quite undaunted, but still grim and troubled. He looked down at all the travelling associates, his brow slowly drawing up. "What are you guys doing?" he asked.

"We were just taking a nap," Audrey covered.

"Oh," Bravado answered. He sunk his sword into the ground and gave both Audrey and Jek a hand up, followed by the old man.

"So..." Audrey continued, brushing the gunk from the ground off of herself, "Anything interesting happen in there?"

"You could say that," Bravado replied. He said no more, even as they all waited.

"Well?" Parissah insisted. "Have you indeed returned with the power you sought? The power to advance the cause of Free-Dome to the reaches of the world?"

"No," Bravado shook his head, extracting his sword and slinging it over his shoulder, starting to walk his manly walk. "I return with nothing. Nothing but a bone to chew."

Jek winced. It was a curious response. Even knowing what he knew, he didn't get the feeling that Bravado had lied. Continuing his strong one-man march, he didn't seem evasive. He seemed *angry*.

"But what do you mean?" Parissah asked after him, grabbing Baegulgog by a tentacle and starting after Bravado. "And where are you going now?"

"I'm going south," Bravado said. "To the docks of Jairenbarl, where the bulk of the navy is moored. I have another visit to pay." He didn't slow, and was getting already out of earshot of those still on the threshold of *Thasagral*. Jek and the rest charged forward to catch up.

"Well I hope you are not planning anything rash," Parissah said.

"That is all I ever plan," he replied.

"But perhaps you should consider your next course of action when you are not so flustered. You seem very mad, Mr. Bravado."

"I should be," he spat. "She lied to me! She told me my master would be happy to share his secrets. Happy indeed! Well, I can be 'happy' too, when I see her next."

Parissah overtook him at once, grabbing him by the shoulder, stopping him dead in his tracks. "*Her*? Whom do you speak of? Who sent you to consult your master?"

Bravado gave her a quizzical look, unprepared for her insistence. "She doesn't have any name I know."

Now she had him by both shoulders. "Describe her."

His eyes rolled up to the sky as he searched for words. "Tall hat, busted-up armor… a really nice halberd…"

"…Does she *glow*?!" Marrow demanded.

Bravado still looked rather incredulous. "Yeah." His eyes swept from face to face. "Do you guys know her too?"

"No," Parissah answered. "But I have been meaning to meet her for a long time. Can you take us to her?"

Bravado nodded. "That *is* where I'm going." He rested a hand on Parissah's shoulder, and another on Jek's. "You guys are my friends. You can come if you want." He turned and shouted. "Hey Murtaugh! We're going to see the Glowy Lady. You wanna come?"

"Nope," Murtaugh called back, not looking up from some whittling he was doing.

"Okay, good," Bravado replied. "It's really great that you're exercising some free-will, buddy." He turned back to the rest. "Let's go."

"The sooner the better," Marrow said.

They were off. But only a few steps into the new journey, Jek was stopped in his own tracks from behind.

"What did I tell ye?" the old man asked him. Jek's heart skipped a beat. He hadn't seen the old man since the first round of the mists… and hadn't had occasion to think about him in all that time, either. "Always another link in the chain with that Inquisitor! We's still on *her* quest; couldn't be no further from our own."

Jek shook his head. "Are you really still on about that? After where we've just been and what we've seen? We're mixed up in a lot bigger stuff than just some plot by the Kaiser now. We've been to another plane of existence for crying out loud! This thing with Ethon isn't just some regional problem… it's not even a *world* problem. This is serious paranormal stuff!"

The old man worked his jaw under his scraggly beard, unimpressed. "Don't make the Doom Fleet any less real, lad. Ours is a job what still gots ta be done."

Jek groaned. "Look, we still need to climb out of this valley. Better to do it with Bravado and Parissah and Marrow than without. There are still those 'Sentries' out there. And anyway, we're headed for another port. We can part ways there, if we have to. But I wish you'd stop being so stubborn! Frankly, I can't even figure out how none of this interests you."

There was an odd glint in the old man's eye just then. "There been one thing in all this foolscap what interested me." His eyes flitted around in a paranoid sort of scan, and he leaned in with a hushed voice. "It's that *Pamphlet*, lad. That be the key ta everythin', mayhaps. Think about it! All the greatest secrets o' the universe… in one little folded up piece o' paper! We could use it to find the Knights, I warrant. But one way or a'tother, there be a way ta find a name for meself in there. That much I's sure of!"

Jek was a bit disturbed. More and more, the old man's characterization of their Quest seemed to be taking on a selfish undertow he hadn't noticed before. But he couldn't focus on the matter now. They were lagging behind, with Bravado in a hurry. "Maybe so," he replied, "but this isn't the time or place to stand around and talk. Look! Audrey's already gone way ahead with them. At least let us all decide what we're going to do together!"

The old man shouldered his pack crossly. "So be it, lad. But ye can't kick the can down the road ferever! We's comin' sure as shoot ta the final debate. Mark me words, t'will be soon. Real soon."

* * *

Southbound out of the eldritch heart of Magna Koepna, there was little initial reprieve from the wild weirdness they had known. The march up from the valley proved more eventful than the trip in. The Sentries were in somewhat better condition in the south quarter. Jek spied not a few mechanical torsos dragging themselves back and forth through the woods on some eternal patrol. Some were even still on shambling feet. All were rusty and worn, but showed obvious determination to kill them. Bravado hewed many, fierce in his rage. Any time battle was drawn, his signature war-cry would rend the air. "FREE-DOME!" he cried, chopping the Sentries to pieces, and then chopping those still-squirming pieces to pieces. They were each so pitiful but so determined, Jek actually began to pity the creepy machines. Time and time again they assailed them, turning the last leg of the climb into a parade of metallic carnage. And Bravado filled every brief interlude with silent, toxic brooding.

Jek's other companions were in little better mood. The old man kept looking all around with a vexed expression, as if he might bolt and leave them all then and there, if he could only spy a way that looked pleasant enough to him. Parissah and Marrow were as grim as Bravado, if not moreso. They really had some beef about this 'Glowy Lady'. Jek didn't understand it, but dared not ask. Marrow *had* claimed that she was the evil Zedulon foretold in his Chocolate Prophecy. That was perhaps tidings enough...

Night had once again fallen over Maenea when they reached Jairenbarl. This time there was no debate. Bravado boarded a ship at once, leaving the poor unsuspecting captain quite beside himself. His orders proved rather weighty. It was not enough for Bravado to set sail immediately. He declared the whole fleet was to follow. Jek's eyes may have been as wide as the captain's. Bravado was not a subtle man...

It was somewhere in the second watch of the night when the final confrontation broke out. They were all set up with cots in the captain's cabin, each laying restless, when a whistle rang out on the deck. Bravado sprung up to investigate, and the rest followed, unlikely to sleep anyway.

When they got to the source of the commotion, it turned out to be the old man, cornered by the crew near one of the life boats, which had been partially deployed. An officer was there with him, and had probably been the first to raise the alarm. But now the old man himself had the officer's whistle, and was tooting it obnoxiously. Everyone was incredulous. Jek was surprised himself. He knew all along this was going to happen. He had just expected a little more discretion…

"What's going on here?" Bravado asked. "What are you up to, old buddy?"

"Now ye cut that out!" the old man snapped. "Ye's a crazy person, and I ain't yer buddy! And as fer what's goin' on, I's takin' a boat and leavin'! I wash me hands o' this whole weirdness!"

Bravado held his hands out and backed away. "Alright, alright! If that's what you really want. I hate for it to end this way. But if you mean to leave, I won't hinder you." The attendant officer started to protest, but Bravado stopped him. "This man is my friend. Let him have the boat, if he wants it." Then he turned and left. The officer looked on for a moment, before he left too, shaking his head.

The old man harrumphed. "Well, guess he weren't all bad after all." Then he started lowering the boat again straight away. "As fer the rest o' ye, I wish ye well on all yer travels. Really, I do. The work ye's doin' is probly important enough in its own right. But I gots ta finish what I started. I gots ta find the Knights and lead 'em to the Doom Fleet." He halted what he was doing and turned for a moment to regard them. "Jek and Audrey is still welcome to come with me, if they wants, and share the glory o' me Quest. But if nothin' else, I hope ye'll all help me get this here boat in the water, at least."

Unexpectedly, Parissah started helping, as best she could reason how. That, more than anything, really surprised Jek. "You're helping him?" he asked her. "You're really willing to just let him go?"

"I am," she answered. "I see that I have subjected him to a longer and more perilous mission than he bargained for. Yet through it all, he proved trustworthy enough. It may be that his Quest has merit – I cannot say. But I would repay his faith by allowing him to complete his own errand, and suspend all judgment until then."

"But we're fugitives!" Jek insisted.

"You and your wife are fugitives," Parissah corrected him. "You fled from your duties in Jast-Madiir. But as for this old man, I do not know where he is from, or if any would hold him liable for such desertion. I do not even know *who* he is."

"Aye, ye speak well at the last, m'lady," the old man said, still busy. "Ye don't know who I is. Ain't nobody what does. But ye *all* will, when me job is done. Then ev'rybody ev'rywhere will remember the old man."

"There you go again!" Jek exclaimed. "Cheapening our old Quest by making it sound like a hunt for glory. I mean, for goodness' sake, what's really important to you, anyway? Saving the world or making a name for yourself?"

"Both!" he answered. "Ain't no use makin' a name for yerself if there ain't no world ta remember it. Now come along, Jek! If this is to be our partin', I wish ye wouldn't hound me so. Lend a hand if ye would."

Audrey set silently to work, mostly helping Parissah figure out how to lower her end. But in his heart, Jek still resisted this whole turn. He couldn't bring himself to help see the old man off. But neither could he imagine leaving with him now. The new Quest far outweighed the old. There was no other way to see it...

"You really will leave without us, then? If we refuse to go, that won't stop you either?"

The old man sighed. "It'll be a sore loss. But I started this Quest in a boat like this, with two companions. And that's just how I woulda finished it, if I'd had me druthers. But I *will* lead the Indigo Knights back ta Meatgrinder Bay alone if need be. That weren't no bluff!"

Audrey stopped suddenly, coming over to the old man. "But what about your ship? I thought you left Meatgrinder Bay in your *ship*... the *Sadie Hawkins*..."

Now the old man really started to break down, taking his hat in his hands and folding it around with a downcast look. "Aye, that I did, lass. But things ain't quite like I told ye. *Sadie Hawkins* weren't no ship. T'was the dhingy we was travelin' in from the onset. And I ain't ne'er had charge o' no bigger vessel. The ship I was on outta Meatgrinder Bay weren't my command. These here duds belonged ta the *real* captain. He died some time after the pirate attack off Tophthaera. T'was just a happy coincidence that his un-ee-form fit me like it do." He rested his hands on Audrey's shoulders. "But it weren't all lies, lass! Me Water magic t'was the savin' grace what got us out o' the Bay ahead o' those Despotopian ships! I didn't invent that!" His eyes shifted again to the deck. "But I ne'er made Captain. Not in all me many, many year's o' sailin'." A long, quavering sigh escaped his lips. "They is loath to give command to a man without a name."

At last, Jek felt he understood, and his heart went out to the old man. "No wonder, then, you want to make a name for yourself so bad. I might too, if I'd never had one."

"That's it ezactly, lad," the old man sniffed. "Now will ye help me go?"

"Do it, Jek," Marrow said, and it surprised them all. "This is a hard parting, but it is a crucial one. It is important that we grant the old man his wish... and do it now. Part ways while the goodwill lasts!"

Jek searched the old man's face. The old man searched back, and it seemed to Jek that his eyes pleaded just to be let go. Finally, though he still felt sadness, and much guilt, he reached out to shake the old man's hand. Then, as they shook, he pulled him into a hug. "Good luck, old man," he said. "Save the world. Make a name for yourself." He laughed. "And don't be a stranger! You'll always be welcome, back at Brighamok's Lighthouse... if ever Audrey and I return."

"Thank ye, lad," the old man replied warmly. "Ye sure has gotten braver since we met. Keep at it! I warrant some day, there won't be no wimpiness left in ye at all!"

"Thanks," Jek nodded, and he tried really hard to mean it.

Audrey gave the old man a big hug next. "I hope we meet again soon," she said. "And I'm so sorry we're not going with you! We owe you more than we could ever repay for kidnapping us."

"Ye're so welcome, lass," he replied. "I's mighty glad I kidnapped ye crazy kids too. And no hard feelin's! All's good what comes to an end o' things."

Then the old man went over and hugged Baegulgog. "Been nice ta meet ye, Baegulgog. Ye's about the best listener I done e'er knowed, and a real fine feller besides. Good luck with whate'er it is ye do."

"Thank you, my good man," Baegulgog inclined himself in the air. "May all good fortune speed your journey."

Finally, the old man looked at Parissah and Marrow. "I didn't like neither o' ye very much, but I's wrong about people sometimes." He waved. "Have yerselfs a nice day."

"You too," Marrow said.

"Yes," Parissah agreed. "And if your search for the Knights proves vain, I bid you come to the Ocean Citadel. I would still honor our agreement to look into the Doom Fleet you allege. But it will be a little while before our naval resources are freed up. We will need our ships for our defense against Zedulon's 7/14/21 attack. But after that, I believe I could oblige you."

"I'll keep that in me mind," the old man said, beginning to climb down the side of the ship's hull to the waiting boat. "But I hope to find the Knights ere then! The Quest done already waited long enough. Goodbye to ye all!"

"Goodbye," they replied, watching first him and then his waving hand disappear below the gunwale, down into the darkness...

"So begins the breaking of the Traveling Associates," Parissah brooded. "Who will be next to leave us, I wonder?"

"I think you know," Marrow answered.

Parissah stood thoughtful for a moment. "Yes... I fear I do."

Audrey was lost on this exchange, and put forth her own question.

"Will we ever see him again?" she asked.

"Yes, child," Marrow nodded. "You will."

* * *

They sailed two days – dispirited, anxious, and struggling to rest, ahead of whatever the coming encounter with the Glowy Lady might demand of them. They spent much time below deck, despairing to think of something to do. Bravado was still in his moody traveling mode, and did not often regale them with tales or other nonsense. Parissah ate much and often, and as a rule no one saw her when she ate. Audrey spent a lot of time catching up on reading Zeph Bronzegloom's book. She and Jek were drilled by Marrow some more, and for these occasions only, Parissah joined them. Baegulgog found various things around the ship to count and re-count and re-re-count – be it rungs in the rope ladder to the crow's nest, nails in the deck boards, or the total number of buttons on all the crew's shirts – and he kept close record of it all.

Meanwhile, Jek made repeat trips to the ship's bow, spending long minutes looking ahead. All the first day, the fleet hugged the contours of Maenea, keeping their homeland on the starboard side. For a while Jek assumed the Glowy Lady must reside somewhere on the western board of Maenea. It would make sense enough, since there had been dealings between her and Bravado. But on the second day, after sailing almost due north in this fashion for a while, they veered *west*, and held a straight course. The dark shadow of a grim irony began to grow in Jek as he considered their vector...

Finally, on the third morning, he gathered all the remaining Traveling Associates to the bow with him. He gestured out to the horizon, rich orange with the rumor of the new day.

"We've been sailing this way since yesterday," he told the others. "Our course took us around Maenea for a long time. I had really thought we'd put in somewhere along the coast. But now we're headed into open ocean, still at full speed."

"Yes," Parissah nodded. "The ship has not slowed, that I have noticed. Surely we will reach the Glowy Lady soon. Then at last, I hope, we may have a reckoning."

"I know *who* we're going to see," Jek replied. "But has anyone stopped to think *where* we're going?"

"You say we've held this course since yesterday?" Audrey asked. "Why, we're headed nearly due west." Jek watched the horrible realization take hold of his wife. "But that would mean we're sailing straight for..." she trailed off, and said no more.

"Go ahead," Jek said. "Please, Audrey... you're the mariner in the group. I need to hear *you* say it. Where are we sailing?"

She blanched. "We're sailing straight for Despotopia."

The Glowy Lady

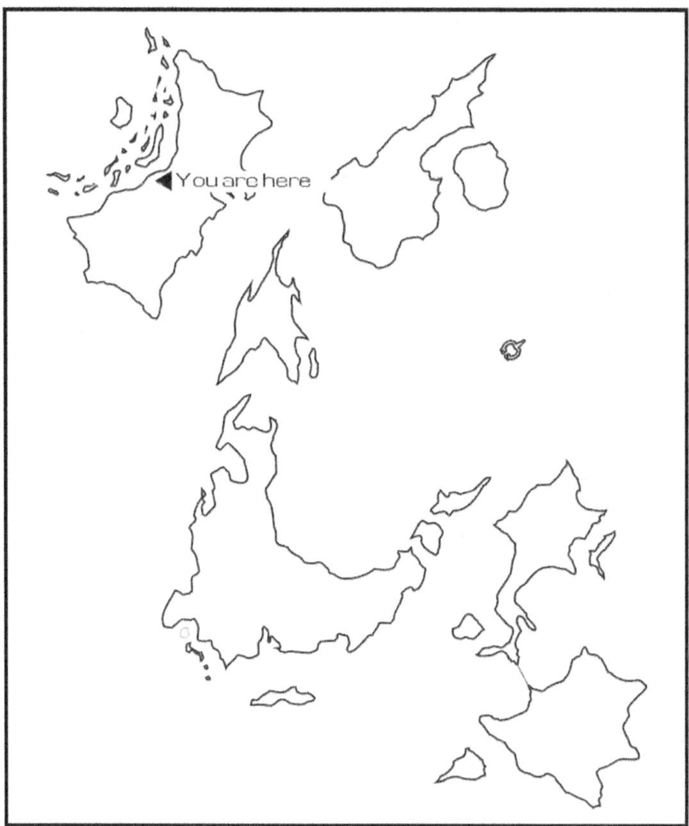

"There are plenty of differences between one sentient being and another. But the qualities that would make a hero are common to all."

- Enscharaulgk, *Zenithyst Inquisitor: A Compendium of Wise Anecdotes (Curated by Warren Liefletson)*

Trackless miles worth of smoke and steam rolled up from the land ahead, holding back the fall of twilight over Despotopia, leaving the gathering dusk naught to do but try to hem the country in from the sides. At Bravado's direction, the Maenean navy fanned out across the mouth of Gzeigharkzt Harbor, forming an effective blockade of Despotopia's primary commercial docks. Even Marrow seemed ill at ease to consider the implications of this blatant act of aggression. Bravado was living up to his namesake.

But when his ship moored, they were greeted by the harbormaster cordially. He welcomed Bravado and said that his coming had long been looked for. The fact that he had arrived with a fleet in tow did not seem to trouble the harbormaster, if indeed he even noticed. Bravado appeared rather stymied by this reaction... or perhaps more accurately, by the lack of a reaction. The mood of the Traveling Associates did not brighten.

Of those she considered her real companions, Jek's was the only face left in the party that Audrey could read, all other faces either masked or non-existent. In spite of their increasingly long and impressive series of travels, each new environment seemed to overwhelm her husband with wonder, and Despotopia was certainly no exception. Audrey couldn't help feeling pretty overwhelmed herself as they were escorted from the coast, and into the sprawling, sooty concrete jungle. She had seen Despotopia from the *Cosigner* plenty of times. But in every observable way, the country had greatly intensified since last she'd looked upon it, for lack of a better word. The rich hues of the evening sky reflected down from the heady pillars of ten thousand smokestacks. Countless electric lights blinked to life in snaking patterns through the unsearchable reaches of the urban complex, readying the night shifts for their share in the unending pursuit of dizzying new industrious heights. All the while, the amplified voice of Kaiser Hienrechenshlagen echoed off every exposed surface, filling the stuffy, scratchy air with the quickening energy of his impassioned shouting. Locals passed them by on every side – confident, upright, supremely focused. If they came across somewhat mechanical, the country itself made up for them, enjoying an abundance of life all its own.

Jek covered his ears as they walked under a blasting megaphone. "They sure make the radios bigger in their homeland," he said, when there was acoustic space for talking again. "Maybe a little too big."

"These amplifiers are indeed paired with radio transmitters," Marrow began to explain. "But it was not always so. They invented the amplifiers first. Even in those early days, the Kaiser had an abundance of desire to share lengthy patriotic anecdotes with all the people of his country. But at that time, the only way to transmit his speeches to the masses was through telegraph lines – a nearly instantaneous medium for a simple binary code. Marrying this technology with the amplifiers proved a strange coupling... but for a time, the dots and dashes of his eloquent propaganda were to be heard echoing in every corner of Despotopia. Particularly strange it was, since very few Despotopians ever knew Morse code. But now, with the emergence of radio, the Kaiser's verbosity is redoubled, and his transmissions never cease."

"Evidently you've been to Despotopia before, then," Jek commented.

"Several times, over the course of my long life, yes," Marrow answered. They all passed near to another megaphone... not so deafeningly loud this time, but making a firm impression, nonetheless.

"I wish I knew Despotopian," Audrey said. "I have no idea what he's saying, but it sounds magnificent."

"It is," Marrow admitted. "Hienrechenshlagen is as formidable a wordsmith and orator as they come. His voice has reforged this land. Prior to his rise to power, the people of Despotopia didn't think they were all that great of a nation. But the Kaiser has spoken at considerable length to the effect that they really, really are a *very* great nation, and so now they feel much better. And indeed, his boasts have proven true. Even much truer than when last I beheld this place. I remember when, not so very long ago, this whole country was just a hovel for impoverished coal miners and kidney bean farmers. The change is remarkable, and it gives me pause to consider it now. I knew one day they would attain to such heights. But I did not imagine it would happen so quickly..."

"I wonder what the Kaiser is like in person." Audrey mused. "Have you ever seen him?"

"Suffice it to say, we have met," Marrow told her. "And we will meet again. It is not an encounter I look forward to."

"Why is that?"

"The Kaiser is formidable in more than just his public speaking. He is a consummate fighter... and that is to say the very least. He is fit as a bull-moose and ready for a fight! Among the living members of your race, he has no rival that I know of." Marrow regarded his companions. "Have you ever chanced to hear about his private army of royal assassins?"

"No," Jek answered. "But that sounds very dangerous."

"Yes," Marrow said. "Dangerous to the *Kaiser*, in theory. For these royal assassins were not hired to assassinate other people *for* the Kaiser. They are hired to assassinate the Kaiser *himself*... or at any rate, to try as best they may. But none of them have ever yet out-fought or out-foxed him. And if he were not already dangerous enough, cunning warrior that he is, he has also availed himself of Fire magic! An unnecessary advantage, if I may say so – rather like giving the gift of broad daylight to one whose eyes are already keen enough to spot a black beetle at 200 yards in the dead of a cloudy night."

Audrey laughed. "It's strange to hear you talk this way about a Human, Marrow. It almost sounds like you're afraid of him."

"I have a healthy regard for his talents," Marrow qualified. "And you may be sure – the day is coming when I will be measured against them. The Kaiser and I will meet on the field of battle, ere all is finished... and who shall claim the victory, I have not seen. Perhaps it is odd, or at any rate unusual, that a Heron should be wary of a Human. We *are* more skilled, more beautiful and more wise than Humans. But skill fails, beauty is feather-deep, and wisdom only teaches misery in the end."

Neither Audrey nor Jek had any answer for that last encouraging bit of rhetoric. But now they overheard Baegulgog talking spiritedly at Parissah, and all hurried ahead to catch the yarn, if they could.

"What are you guys talking about up here?" Audrey jumped in, the first place she found an opening.

"Baegulgog was just sharing a vast assortment of statistical figures concerning the growth rate of Despotopian industry," Parissah answered.

"Quite so," Baegulgog said. "I was just coming to some deforestation values. Less than 10 full years ago, the Dronehood maintained that there were 21813 square miles of jungle along the feet of the Forbidden Mountains – their northwestern range adjacent to the coast of Meatgrinder Bay – considered unreachable by land and sea alike since the island's founding. But with great difficulty they cleft a path through the jungle to the range, so as to expand their coal mining. I have already given Parissah the figures for their rate of coal consumption, and they are most impressive. But as for the jungle, the Despotopians were evidently not satisfied to have their road. When last it was surveyed, the total square mileage of the northwestern jungle was reduced all the way to 910! It is near the point where the Dronehood would consider counting the trees."

"Well, we could have told you they were cutting their jungles down," Audrey said.

"Never mind," Parissah waved dismissively. "I am very alarmed by all of this expansion! Particularly that word of it was not heretofore conveyed from Clerk mouth to Inquisitor ear. It is bad enough that our agents in this country have not raised any red flags of their own. Perhaps they can be excused, somewhat, for being so close to the situation that the growth seemed gradual. But all these numbers would seem to reveal an aggressive ambition, which we should have been monitoring more closely. Why were we not warned, Baegulgog?"

"There are many reasons I can think of," the Clerk responded evenly. "Not all of the indicators we look at suggested that Despotopia is dangerously on the rise. Their military, in particular, has been trending down. It took a heavy toll on the Kaiser's army, clearing those jungles of enemy Mantids – and those lost men have not been wholly replaced. And they have invested nothing in their navy for many years, beyond simple maintenance expenses. The fleet Bravado brought here could perhaps contend with theirs. And most bewildering of all, none of this industrial expansion has made any impact on their net exports. Whatever they are producing at such rates, it is not being bought. Despotopia is still poor."

"Everywhere I turn, more mystery ensues," Parissah lamented.

"And there is one other reason the Dronehood has overlooked some of these trends. Our focus in this country has largely been on trying to account for the influx of Maenean refugees of late. The office of the Kaiser has been quite insistent on handling the records internally. But whenever we sue for new census data, we receive only small regional reports, and at a trickling speed. And few of the regions we have up-to-date information about have had notable population spikes. Where they are settling the bulk of their new citizens, we do not yet know. We have eagerly awaited figures that would begin to reflect the sort of growth we estimated."

"That, too, alarms me," Parissah said.

"It should," Jek put in. "The old man maintained that Despotopia was using all its refugees to pad its labor pool, in the construction of its secret Doom Fleet. I don't think he had any evidence, of course. But if you accept the idea of a secret Doom Fleet, it makes a lot of sense."

"It does indeed," Parissah nodded. "And I daresay, it would little surprise me now to learn that there really is a Doom Fleet in Meatgrinder Bay. Especially now that we know the Glowy Lady has taken up residence here."

"Yes," Marrow concurred. "In fact I would suggest that only these questions truly remain: Who is she, and what is the true scope and nature of her designs?"

"We will learn the answers," Parissah resolved, "even if it kills me."

Marrow nodded. "Well said."

Even as they brooded, the errand-runner of the harbormaster led them past other curiousities, on their way to Heck only knew where. If Despotopia was a bit proud of the coal-burning steam power they had pioneered, then it certainly showed in the seemingly endless applications they had already found for it. In equal wonder and fancy, Audrey pointed out to Jek a steam-powered horse-drawn carriage she spied. It was a remarkable artifice – nothing quite as uncanny as the Sentries they had run afowl of in the valley of *Thasagral*, but so much the better, in her opinion. There was nothing at all unusual about the carriage itself. It was the *horse* that was extraordinary – or rather, the engine that resembled a horse. The whole thing was essentially a big metal boiler fashioned into a roughly equine shape, with four piston-type legs that spouted straight down out of the body of the engine. The pistons each struck the ground with approximately the speed and force of a jack-hammer, and this flurry of impacts propelled the engine that pulled the carriage. The mechanical horse bounced and wobbled and skipped and sputtered in apparent rhythmic chaos over its chattering legs, but somehow or other the carriage seemed always to progress in a straight course. It was really cool.

But there were other vapors rising from Despotopia, beyond those of the innumerable industrial engines. Further down the road, they encountered several wagon-loads of books that were being hurled by the armful into a large, raging fire pit. Audrey didn't know what to make of it.

"Bronzegloom did say they burn books here now, didn't he?" she said.

"Yeah, I remember that," Jek replied. "It makes me wish I had thought to ask him why. Not that I would question a thinker, mind you, but if I hadn't seen it for myself just now, I might have never really believed they would do something like this. It's so... so strange."

Audrey took the matter up with the other Associates. "Do any of you know why Despotopia is burning all their books?" she asked.

"They were instructed to do so, with an edict from the Kaiser," Baegulgog answered. "That is, I seem to vaguely recall coming by record of such an edict one day at the office, when I was rummaging through some of the filing cabinets for little more than my own amusement. What the Kaiser's reasons for this policy are, I could not guess. Perhaps it is just one of those cultural things that cannot be wholly explained to an outsider."

Even as they considered this, a very old book crumbled away from its binding as it was lifted from a wagon. The wind took hold of the pages, and they were swiftly whisked by Audrey and the others. But one page caught Jek squarely on the face, and there it stuck until he finally removed it. Jek looked rather cross. Audrey was amused.

"More flying debris sticking to you, dear?" she joshed him. "You remember what Chief Katydid said... you have the perfect face for it."

"I do not know who this Chief Katydid person is, but she spoke true," Marrow said. "Never before has a face been more perfectly designed for the capture of windswept refuse, and never again shall we see its like."

Audrey gave Jek a goofy smile.

"Well, I guess that's something to be remembered for," Jek sighed.

At last, they came to a train stop, and here they halted. The errand-runner promptly excused himself and left them waiting for a train to come. It was by no means a long wait. Almost in tandem with their own arrival, a train with two engine cars (both steam-powered, with one at the front and one directly in front of the caboose) pulled into station, pouring hot gas from the midst of its wheels as they bled excess pressure. Bravado took them around to the caboose at once, but before they were able to reach it, they had to swim upstream through many cars' worth of deboarding Despotopians. Audrey wondered about his choice. No one deboarded from the caboose. And when they climbed aboard, no one was there to meet them...

After some blasts from the whistle and a few powerful lurches, the train was soon off again, hurdling westward with great speed. Audrey and Jek found themselves pressed against the windows for some time, astonished by the pace that the countryside passed them by. Baegulgog was also impressed, and almost childishly delighted. But the other three were not to be moved from their funk. Their mood eventually prevailed, and for a long time they all sat as if on their way to a funeral. Perhaps their own.

Finally, it was Bravado – the moodiest of them all – who broke the silence. "I have a question for you guys," he said. "There's a shadow of doubt that's been looming over me, almost ever since we met. It's been particularly heavy on my mind since the old man left. His parting words seemed to belie any fondness he ever claimed to have for Free-Dome." He looked at every one of them in turn, his eyes flicking in a horribly effective searching pattern. "What about you guys? What do you think about Free-Dome? What do you really, honestly think of it?"

The Associates all exchanged troubled glances. In their mutual attempts to gauge each other's opinions about whether or not to actually tell Bravado the truth, it quickly became clear that the truth was already obvious.

"Sorry, Mr. Bravado," Jek said at last, "but to tell you the truth, your ideas all scare the daylights out of me."

Bravado betrayed no immediate change. He looked past Jek. "The rest of you feel that way?"

"Essentially, yes," Marrow replied. The rest nodded.

Finally, Bravado heaved a great sigh. "That's what I was afraid of. After all this time trying to convince even *one* other person... I guess I knew all along it was too good to be true." He rested his troubled, green-painted brow in his hands, as lights in the dusk whizzed across the top of his wild hair from outside the train car. "But I thank you for your honesty, even if it comes in the twentieth hour. It seems, even in taking over all of Maenea, I've ultimately failed. Oh, the countless minds I've erased! I thought, in time, they would all come to value their Free-Dome. But they all still seem so lost, so eager for outside direction. They continue to look to me when they ought to be figuring things out for themselves. Sure, out of the gate they're zealous. But only because I told them to be. Even Murtaugh – he's had more time than any of them to develop some sort of autonomy. And to an extent, he has... I suppose. But I can tell his heart isn't in it. In the end, he doesn't love his Free-Dome. At best, he accepts it." He was silent for a while, all choosing not to fumble for comforting words, but merely to stay attentive. Finally, he went on. "All my life I just wanted to have an idea... just *one* idea that would change the world. Is that such a wrong thing to want?"

"I can hardly think of anything more wrong," Parissah answered. "Those who had the right to change the world have long since gone out of it. Yet, if it will be of any comfort, I no longer believe that you yourself are wholly evil, Herz Bravado. I see that there is earnesty and selflessness bound up in your dangerous ambition. And that is some slight redemption."

"Thanks," Bravado said. He sighed again, staring into space. At length he shook his head. "What in the world am I doing here? I begin to think this was a horrible mistake. Ever since we made landfall... I haven't been able to shake the feeling that Free-Dome is about to die with me."

"I have felt much the same, these past few days," Parissah said. Audrey wondered what she meant. "If I were you, I would not continue your path of aggression. So far, the Despotopians seem to have overlooked your blockade. But you are alone now, deep in a strange land. Further acts of provocation may bring the end you fear. Do not press your luck!"

Bravado nodded. "Alright," he said. "Any other suggestions?"

"No suggestions," she replied. "But there is one other course I must insist on. The Pamphlet, Bravado. You must relinquish the Pamphlet now. Above all else, that document cannot be permitted to fall into the hands of the Glowy Lady."

Bravado stared blankly. "Pamphlet?" he repeated. "What Pamphlet? What are you talking about?"

"The one from *Thasagral*!" Baegulgog explained suddenly. "The piece of paper your master cast at your feet!"

"It is of universal import," Parissah continued. "You should give it to Baegulgog for safe keeping. Surely a Clerk may conceal a piece of paper if he means to."

"Like a needle in a haystack, madam," Baegulgog saluted.

Bravado shook his head. "But I don't have that piece of paper!" he lamented. "I left it right where my master threw it. Whatever it was, I felt no desire at all to accept it. I felt only shame for so angering my master… and I could think of no other way to apologize but to leave his gift behind." His eyes narrowed accusingly. "You guys saw all that?"

"Yeah, we were there," Audrey admitted. "Sorry we lied to you. Again."

Bravado pursed his lips thoughtfully. "It's alright, I suppose. Mostly I'm just surprised. It used to be kind of an exclusive thing… journeying to *Thasagral* and back."

"Well, never mind," Parissah interrupted. "We must reconstruct what transpired. There was only a brief time you were out of our sight. When we looked down again, we saw that both you and the Pamphlet had gone. If you did not take it, then where did it go?"

Jek snapped his fingers. "The old man!" he exclaimed. "He wasn't with us above the chamber! He must have slipped in and took the Pamphlet, after Mr. Bravado left without it."

"I think the boy's onto something," Baegulgog flashed with agreement.

"He is," Marrow concurred. "You may be sure of it."

"That is rather distressing," Parissah said. "And yet for the moment it is a boon. At least that means the Pamphlet is quite safe from the Glowy Lady. We do not have it with us, nor do we even know where it is. We couldn't possibly reveal its whereabouts, no matter how she might torture us for the answers."

Jek laughed nervously at the mention of torture.

Parissah turned back to Bravado. "Well then, what say you, Herz Bravado? We may not all be for Free-Dome, but our alliance persists in this much: We are both here to demand answers of the Glowy Lady – our mutual adversary."

"That's good enough for now," Bravado said, reaching out to shake her hand, and she took it. "Let's get what we came for." There was a jerking motion in the car at that moment – strong enough to cause Jek a scare. He opened a window, leaning out to search ahead…

"We just decoupled from the rest of the train!" he said, hair blowing in the rushing air.

"Then it won't be long now," Bravado said.

Soon, the engine ahead of them not only decoupled, but diverged – the track shifted between the two segments of the train, sending Bravado and the Traveling Associates on a northward bend, straight towards the very Forbidden Mountains they had earlier discussed. Dimly they could make out a very great vapor beyond and about the heads of those mountains. But it was not the smog of industry they saw. It was a horrible storm-cloud, miles and miles high and across, absolutely gorged with torrential rain that refused to pour. Audrey knew well enough what lay on the other side of the mountains, under the cloud. The Mausoleum Peaks of Meatgrinder Bay. And the Doom Fleet.

*   *   *

A few more anxious hours passed. Their short train climbed through and up the mountains in a hopelessly bizarre pattern. They came to expect something around every bend and at the end of every tunnel… ever more-so, even as they left countless bends and tunnels behind. Finally, the brakes of the train shrieked. Outside their windows they saw nothing, however breathlessly they searched. They came to a stop right in the middle of a dark tunnel. Their doors opened autonomously with an affirming, electronic beeping sound, bidding them step into the black. Bravado led the way.

Once they all stood on the ground, the train huffed and puffed back to life, only too eager to leave them behind. Its whistle moaned eerily away, and the echoes of the faraway wheels on the tracks made them shiver. They stood in brooding dark, forsaken. But at last, an unseen door in the tunnel opened wide, revealing the bleak reception hall of a howling cement compound. Two guards were standing just beyond the threshold. One approached Bravado.

"Glutentöffen," he said. "I extend zee Lady's greetings." He surveyed all present. "She vill be most pleased to see you all at vonce."

"That may be," Bravado answered. "For my part, I didn't intend for this to be a pleasant visit."

"Zhat is too bad," the guard said. "Still, vhatever your manner, it is enough for her Ladyship zhat you have come, visiting."

He gestured for them to enter. Bravado slung his big sword to his shoulder and walked on by. The others followed.

They had not yet passed beyond the reception hall when Bravado stopped and turned to them. "Before we go any further," he said, "it bares mentioning that you might get sick. You might even throw up. But whatever happens, don't worry about the walls. It seems like they will sometimes, but they won't ever close in on you."

They exchanged more glances.

It didn't take long before they had some idea what he was talking about. The way to the Glowy Lady through the compound was as mercilessly winding as the train ride had been. And every new room and hall induced a constricting claustrophobia. It really did seem like the walls, the ceiling and the floor were all pressing in upon them. Audrey tried to grope her way through the converging space, feeling like a giant trying to thread herself through a needle's eye. But her pawing hands seldom reached anything. And it seemed to take hours just to cross from one room to another.

And she did throw up. Twice.

Exhausted, they slowly began to feel normal again. Or else, they got accustomed to whatever Space was doing in that horrible bunker...

* * *

It was at this time that they reached the final room. Marrow *knew* it was the final room. He had seen it before. It was quite unlike all the others. Rather than feeling too small, it was *wide*, arcing out into a formidable semicircle. But from *there*... from there on it broadened and deepened into an unimaginable vastness... into the very furthest reaches of space itself. Marrow felt his body and mind being drawn out in front of him, stretched along trillions of miles of the empty void. It was discomforting. Even as he reeled and swooned and nearly lost himself, he suddenly experienced a springing-back sensation. Space was normalizing. He was coming back fully into the room… and whatever it was out there, lurking at the end of space, was coming back with him…

Finally, the portal knit itself back into the concrete fabric of the compound, completing the circle of the chamber. Standing, or perhaps floating, in the midst of the resolving real-space was the one he had seen in his horrific vision. A neon phantasm of empty, ghoulish armor with a high conical helm, clutching an adamant halberd. At her appearing, a fluttering erupted from all around. Tiny little songbirds encircled their Lady, then dashed angrily through the air at Jek and Audrey, chirping up a vengeful rebuke, before vanishing as quickly as they'd come. And in this moment, Marrow knew fear, as he had known it only once before. This was not the exact moment he had foreseen. But that moment was now deadly close…

* * *

When the last of the songbirds passed, Jek almost immediately forgot his shock and terror at their sudden return, mesmerized as he was in the presence of the Glowy Lady. The furious tweeting of ten thousand birds could not have long drowned her soft, entrancing music. The very air around her tingled with celestial secrets, maddeningly and melodiously whispering one over another in an unending torrent. At whiles, a clearer voice would nip at his mind from some rogue vector, leaving a piercing sensation, as if the secrets were probing for some weak spot in his psyche, so to crowd their way in. Eventually even these louder, pricking voices formed a harmony. Terrified, Jek struggled against it all, and the secrets remained indistinct. But he could not help beginning to glimpse the vastly intricate structure in the way that each truth and fact related to the other – a swirling, syncopated pattern that continued growing in his mind in layers and orders of complexity. It came to the point that he even began to anticipate the melody as it wound ever on. He found that he knew it by heart, and it disturbed him. What *was* this music? Where and when had he heard it before? He *had* heard it before! Many times. *Countless* times…

Finally, the music of the cosmos diminished, decrescendoing down to an endurable, incredibly distant chanting. The Glowy Lady, though unmoved, must have taken notice of the discomfiture of her guests. From a low elevated dais she looked down on them, short cape and elbow-length shawl rippling gently, weightlessly…

As Jek's mind regressed to its familiar, scrappy shape, he had an astonishing revelation about the identity of their host. After all, he had his peculiar talent for guessing a person's name, if their face was in plain sight. She had no face… or head, or body. But it was enough that her face, if she'd had one, was not covered…

* * *

Parissah, freed from her trance, took stock of the room, and of the guards, who came forward and knelt in two arcs at the foot of the dais.

"Mine Lady," a bowed guard entreated. "Zhine distinguished guests have cometh to call."

"So I see," a young, fair voice replied as she surveyed her guests. "And how delighted I am to have you all here, at last." She extended an incandescent gauntlet, open palmed, toward Bravado. "But to each in his turn. Hail Herz Bravado, lord of Maenea!"

"I don't find that very funny," Bravado said, resting his sword on the ground. "No funnier than the little quest you sent me on."

"Ah, yes," the Glowy Lady nodded, her floating earrings bobbing. "You return from *Thasagral* once again! For news of this, I have waited most eagerly. Step forward, my good man, for I would hear it all."

Bravado did not stir, except to fidget rather anxiously.

"You hesitate?" the Glowy Lady inquired. "Come now, Bravado! You have no more cause to fear me than have I to fear you."

At length, Bravado did cautiously step up onto the dais. The Glowy Lady folded her arms behind her back and began to pace, floating silently through the air, the ghostly toe of her boot gliding along the ground.

"You do not seem yourself today," she went on, as Bravado continued to stand in silence. "It is a curious change. You left this place exultant and grateful. Now you return to me sulking." She paused to regard the Traveling Associates. "Could it be the company you are keeping these days? Doubtless some of them would be quick to vilify me with vague rumors of misdeeds. Do you entertain the slander of such false friends?"

"I gather they have some grievance with you. But whatever it is, they haven't shared it with me," Bravado answered. "I have my own to speak for. You lied to me!"

"Oh, what a pity," the Glowy Lady lamented, floating back in his direction. "The idealist feels I have deceived him. Yet how should I answer for myself? You have yet to share with me the outcome of your quest. Did your master give you the power you asked of him?"

"He gave me a folded piece of paper. Perhaps there was power in that. Perhaps it's the paper you've wanted all along. Well, you won't get it from me! I left it where he cast it."

At this, the Glowy Lady laughed. The laughter drove with a sweet, childish timbre, but left a trail of malice. Bravado was perplexed, and more than a little unsettled by her outburst. They all were. "Clever fool," she said. "Do you think you stymied my plans by leaving the Pamphlet in the bowels of *Thasagral*? No. In fact, this is a more expedient outcome than any I'd dared to imagine. The Pamphlet remains safely out of reach. Yet he *gave* it to you! Tell me, what was the manner of his gift-giving?"

"He was outraged," Bravado answered.

"*Outraged*?" the Glowy Lady repeated, a venomous eagerness in her voice as she stalked forward. "Do go on, Bravado..."

"He said many curious things in his anger. He said the Pamphlet would bring the End. He said he wouldn't intervene this time, even if the whole world begged him."

"Did he *really* say all of that?" the Glowy Lady despaired to know. "Was he really so explicit? O, what kind fortune! The centuries of waiting and searching have given their blessing! Now there is nothing to keep the plans going forward. *All* the plans." For a moment, she absently studied her dreadful halberd. "Except for this final small matter. There is one being left in this world who still poses a threat to me."

"Who is that?" Bravado asked, in a final irony. It was the last thing he ever said. She impaled him on the end of her halberd. Bravado sunk to his knees – silent, surprised – gasping in vain.

"Don't let it concern you," the Lady answered. "For now there are none." And then Bravado died in a heap. The Associates were horrified. Even Parissah felt remorse, witnessing his brutal passing.

Satisfied that he was dead, the Glowy Lady turned again to the Associates. "Now to you, my other friends. What shall we discuss, now that Bravado has left us? You have many questions, I deem. Gladly would I answer all your minds crave to know. Indeed, my very nature all but compels me to." She raised a hand in signal. "But first, you will forgive me if I explore the veracity of Bravado's claims." She spoke now to the guards, who returned to their kneeling spot. "Search the body and the prisoners for the Pamphlet," she instructed them. "We must be sure he did not come up with some superficial gambit to withhold it from me. And do relieve the Clerk of his duffle!"

The guards set to the search. They took Baegulgog's bag, which caused him obvious alarm and grief, and searched everyone else's pockets and accessories. In a moment of clumsiness, Zeph Bronzegloom's advance copy of *Literacy for Knuckleheads* came tumbling out of Audrey's bag, falling open-faced onto the ground. All were shocked by a green flash like lightning, and the Glowy Lady gave a choked call as her radiance wavered. But then the book burst into flames – incinerated in an instant.

Slowly, the clumsy guard turned to his Lady. After a moment of shared looks, he fell to his knees, making some impassioned plea in his native tongue. But there was a horrible crash, and he fell silent. In a dash of eyes, the Associates found the source of the clamor as its haft waved to and fro – the Lady's halberd was now lodged two feet into the wall behind the offending guard. He, too, fell dying. But as he did, there was an eerie whisper, and his whole body grew black – blacker than black, so that no light reached it. And then he disappeared. All, including the guards, looked back at the Lady, mesmerized by another great show of brutality.

"Continue the search," she said, sounding suddenly weary. But she steadied herself, and her halberd suddenly reappeared in her hand. "And perhaps be more cautious."

They rummaged for a while more with no further incidents. "Zee Pamphlet is not here," one said, "unless it be in zee Clerk's bag. Zhat will taketh more time to examine."

"You may go," the Lady excused the guard. "And take this with you," she said, indicating Bravado's body. "Show it to the Maenean fleet. Explain to them that their new supreme commander is the Kaiser."

The guard bowed, and did according to her wishes. The others remained.

"Twice today Bravado's brash defiance has turned in my favor," the Glowy Lady said. "Perhaps the rest of you will learn from his example, and be less feisty." She floated into their midst. It was a tense proximity, but they knew well enough by now that there was no sense trying to flee. Gently she passed in front of each in turn.

"What a remarkable group of visitors have I today," she said. "Parissah, Primary Administrator – a de-facto lord of the Inquisition, in your own lord's long, convenient absence. Aaliyah – continental Princess, final hope of Maenea, gifted healer. Much more still could have been said of you, if you had chosen a longer path. Even the Clerk Baegulgog is not without his accolades – unpretentious champion of the horse tracks. And *you*.." she paused in front of Marrow. "Perhaps you would prefer to remain anonymous?"

"I would," he answered.

"Very well," she said. "It suits my designs well enough. But know that I *could* name you, if I chose."

"And I can name *you*," said Jek, unbidden. "You're Bellanchora! I can see it plain as day in your lack of a face."

Now she paused in front of him, and he did all he could do not to shrink under her unseen gaze. "But who is this that steals my thunder?" she asked. "Did I not say I would happily answer all your questions? You pay me greater injury than you know, denying me the chance. *You* – the only one in the group who is nothing at all." She held her fingers under his chin, tipping his head up on the sharp ends of a gauntlet that felt much realer than it looked. His bared neck felt deadly exposed, and he struggled not to flinch. "Your only merit is your weak Will. And even that has of late grown too strong to be choice."

"But he cannot have spoken right!" Parissah declared. "You cannot be *the* Bellanchora... the Princess of Great Regression infamy. She is long, *long* dead!"

"Do I look alive to you?" Bellanchora retorted.

"She's a Revenant," Audrey chipped in. "That's what the Mantids called it. She's an elemental spirit, like the ones we faced in the jungle. Only she's not made of Fire or Water... or any obvious element like that."

Bellanchora cast Audrey a look, displeased. "Again I am thwarted. That is another fine mystery I should have liked to explain myself."

"Then oblige yourself and explain it," Parissah bid her. "For I still do not understand."

"Don't you? Have you not watched anxiously from your Ocean Citadel as the world turned to *magic*, wondering if these new elemental powers might be a steppingstone toward a second Great Regression? I tell you now: We *did* discover magic first! It was a power soon cast aside, as we learned *true* power – the mastery of the elements themselves, rather than the meager emulation. But I saw that magic had other distinctions – even *merits* – which still deserved consideration. It offered a contingency – an escape from death. For this reason, I kept an elixir always with me, even after I learned to bend all the Dianodes to my will... save the one."

"But the Revenants we saw couldn't do anything, except burn stuff," Jek puzzled. "How could you be a Revenant? You don't seem to have any restrictions."

"If one is to become an elemental spirit, one should choose her element wisely," Bellanchora began. "A Fire spirit may burn things. A Water spirit may wet things. I am a *Knowledge* spirit. A Knowledge spirit may do whatever can be learned. I learned to speak, and so speak I still may. I learned mastery of the elements, and now as before they do my bidding." She cradled her halberd. "I learned to interact with what has substance, even though I have no substance of my own. Yet I knew it *could* be learned, for Onyxadon has long possessed this ability – and so learn it I did. So you are both correct. I *am* a Revenant... if Revenant you call it. Yet I know no earthly limits. Or if I do know such limits, they are very few."

So that was it. The Glowy Lady was Bellanchora, returned as a magical Knowledge spirit. Parissah reeled to consider it. All along, Bravado had had Ethon's power – the very elemental force that could have cancelled Bellanchora out. Besides Ethon alone, he was the *only* one with access to this power. But none of them had known, or could have even guessed, just how important to the fate of the world Bravado might have been. Now that it was plain, he was already dead...

"That answers one of my questions, to my satisfaction," Marrow said. "We now know who you are, and what. But what are your plans? That, too, I know something about. You will assault the Inquisition at its heart – the Ocean Citadel! But to what end, I wonder? What is the true scope of your designs?"

Bellanchora sighed. "How much you all know, and guess, before I may expound." She glided to the back of the wide room, and even as she did, a deep mechanical sound thrummed and grinded, and a wide viewport opened up before her. The blinding light of day showed beyond, hindered though it was by the stopped-up storm clouds. And the Associates came forward, shielding their eyes, to see what lay below the overlook. Breathlessly, they gazed out on Meatgrinder Bay – shrowded in unnatural gloom, yet in a serene state of suspension. Stretching out in all directions, there were great peaks and horrible – jagged rocks in the water, strewn with the bones of thousands of ships. But amidst all of this were *other* ships. Whole ships. New ships. Great steaming metal contraptions covered in big, bright guns. Against their backdrop of death and destruction, they appeared invincible. There were hundreds of such ships. It was, unequivocally, a Doom Fleet.

"This is what most of you are here to see, I gather," Bellanchora narrated, reduced merely to a voice as their eyes were fastened to the Bay. "What do you think? I suppose it might seem quite impressive to you. Bravado's fleet will make for a laughable extension to the Kaiser's armada." The viewport closed again, leaving them all in darkness. "But then, it is *all* rather pitiful, anyway. To think that the doom of a world could hinge on a few little metal boats. This is because the world, too, is pitiful."

"Not so pitiful that you would not deign to conquer it," Marrow contended.

Bellanchora shook her head. "This is not about conquest. Not for *me*. Perhaps the Kaiser will be content to enjoy it as such. I care not for the fortunes of the world. They are of utter inconsequence."

"Proud words, for one so engaged in meddling in those fortunes," Parissah said. "You are behind the Tophthaeran Civil War, and the Maenean Insurrection!"

"Not *behind* them," Bellanchora corrected. "Those problems caused themselves. I merely invested in them as convenient distractions, to keep you Inquisitors jumping through hoops, while your real doom was prepared in secret. You see, it is not the world I care about. It is *you*. Your whole stupid order is much too proud of itself. Enscharaulgk, in particular, has earned my vehemence."

"I should say so," Parissah nodded. "It was he who killed you at the Battle of Ethon."

"You mistake me again," Bellanchora said. "I do not mourn the loss of my flesh, nor seek to avenge it." She looked at her own ghostly hands. "This new form is but a very small step in the right direction. Yet it is *some* improvement. Moreover, I could have allowed myself to simply die at his hand that day, and perhaps then I might have started my greater journey much sooner. No. If this was about what he did to my body, I should have thanked him. It was my *plans* he should not have foiled. You understand, it could have Ended then. It all should have Ended that very day! But Ethon and Enscharaulgk and the Inquisition prevailed. The universe was spared, and in my dying moments I was left to wonder *why*. Why had I failed? Why was mastery of all the elements but one not enough? Why were all things doomed to go on just as they had before, as if I had achieved nothing? As if I had not learned the true meaning of Destiny. I saw no reason I should not have attained it.

"But do not think me entirely beyond admonishment. Always I have understood the value of correction to the studious. After I imbibed the Knowledge elixir, I withdrew into the depths of space. I spent long centuries searching the cosmos from one end to the other, looking for something – for *anything* – that would make me understand why my plans had to suffer delay and defeat. It seemed the least I could do to reflect upon my failure. It was a very great quest for enlightenment – long and wide and deep and perilous – turning inwards as well as out. And in all that time, do you know what I found?"

They all stood silent, having no framework with which to venture an answer.

"I'll show you," she said at length.

A loud, sonorous howl engulfed them as Space opened wide before their eyes once again. But this time, it was not stretched out in a fixed direction, but in countless directions, and the distance between objects in the void was compressed, and they were subjected to dozens of wide vistas at a time, each careening past them to the next, and the next, and the next, so that they were given the whole universe in brief. They experienced many hundreds of beauties and wonders and sights and sounds and smells so sublime that they required only the fraction of an instant they were given to pierce the soul.

Parissah was moved. She was moved very far. There was so much *more* than she would have ever dared to imagine. Never had she even vaguely guessed what a small, insignificant flake of the Creators' work she had spent the last century trying to steward. Life and Death in boundless variety suffused these numberless worlds. Soon it proved too much. Within seconds she despaired for it to be over. But on and on the cosmos unfolded in front of her...

"Do you see now?" the voice of Bellanchora softly explained, somehow prevailing over all the din. "Look at it. Just a few simple ingredients, iterated over and over again ad nauseum, with no meaningful distinctions between one mixture and the next. Long did our ancestors search for the reason that the Creators left this universe. But if you simply look at the universe for what it is, the mystery vanishes at once. They were not satisfied with what they made. And how could they be? It is no more than the thoughtless regurgitation of what they themselves had known in eternities past. It is at best a sketch – a first draft – a mockery of greater works... well intended, perhaps, but a mockery, nonetheless.

"One question, then, remains. Why did they leave without first completing the universe? That is to say, without *Ending* it? But I know the answer to that too. I have always known. They brought the Beginning. It is for us to bring the End."

At once they were returned to her dark sanctum. Those in the party of Associates who breathe were suddenly aware of breathing very hard. It had been quite an ordeal, and they were staggered, even as Bellanchora levitated calmly in front of them, eager to continue the conversation.

"Are there any more questions?" she asked.

Parissah struggled to arrive at a question, having had all her senses totally overwhelmed. But Audrey composed herself first...

"Why do you want to bring the End?" she asked. "Why is it so important to you? If you don't like the universe all that much, that's one thing. But to *End* it all? How does that make for a desirable outcome?"

"It is *not* the outcome," Bellanchora explained. "The End is not *THE END*. There is much more afterwards. So very, *very* much more..."

"You do not know that," Parissah said. "You cannot know that. The Creators never revealed anything about the interplay between eternity and the soul."

"They did not have to. Yet it *is* revealed, in their very nature."

Parissah grew indignant... righteously so. "What could someone as wicked as you presume to know about the nature of the Creators?"

"Much more than *you*, or any of your order of righteous pretenders, I daresay," Bellanchora snapped. "Heed my words, for I speak now of things Unknowable. Bravado meant to keep the Pamphlet from me, but he did not know that it has already been in my keeping – once long ago, in life. Its secrets are mine. Here, then, is the answer to all the riddles. Here is the Truth about your dearly departed Creators:

"They are not all your imagination makes them. They were once just like *us*."

The words froze Parissah's heart. It was not merely the shock of such blasphemy. Bellanchora's words resonated with a horrible power, as if all of creation had become a sounding board, echoing back what she had said – concentrating it – *confirming* it! And at once her music rose and became oppressive again, and the structure of the song was made plain. Parissah *had* heard it before, as she'd earlier felt. They *all* had. It was the rhythm of the Grand Design – creation out of destruction out of creation – all in an endless, open-ended progression...

"No," Parissah forced herself to answer, out of zeal alone, with no real vestige of disbelief. "It cannot be." Though she knew it was true.

"You only harm yourself by denying it," Bellanchora replied. "This is the Design. Souls populate a universe, until they learn to Destroy it. Then, in the absence of all diversion, the soul Changes – it *grows* – it germinates in the Utter Void. And when, after many eternities, it is mature, it Creates... and the cycle begins again. Our Creators were once created themselves, and their Creators before them, ever back and back uncountable times. Even the Pamphlet of Unknowable Things does not reveal how many times this has happened, or what the *True* beginning of it all was – if indeed there is such a thing.

"But it matters little. What we must do now is implicit. It is obvious, and undeniable. More than that, it is eminently desirable. There is only one Power worth coveting, and it is not to be realized in this existence. I should know, for I have wielded every power in the universe to its utmost, save one. They are all but meager utensils of Destruction... and Destruction is banal – necessary, but surely the least of the powers. Change, I would more glady endure. But it is the Power of Creation I long to attain! There is no greater mark of supremacy, no loftier achievement, no more exclusive priviledge, and surely no substitute. I will create a universe of my own! And O! what a universe it will be! Even if I have to remake it a thousand, thousand times! I will make it such a universe as has never been before, filled with truly unspeakable wonders. Things greater than love, more terrible than pain, more permanent than death, more binding than fate. I cannot wait to imagine them!"

By the unhinged urgency of Bellanchora's aspirations, Parissah was again greatly dismayed. She tried to imagine the kind of universe the ancient Princess would create. Even though she had no framework with which to conceive of it, she knew at once it would be a truly horrible place. And if in all things Bellanchora spoke true, Parissah was powerless to stop her...

But perhaps she could be delayed again. It was a hollow consolation. But at this point, anything seemed preferable to simply letting her have her way...

* * *

"...Yet wait I will," Bellanchora continued. "Had I known I should receive such permissiveness from Ethon, perhaps I would never have concocted this whole matter of the Doom Fleet and my revenge on Enscharaulgk. But concoct it I did, and now I must own it. It is only due diligence to see a plan through. And the delay will be short. The Fleet is ready. So I will send forth the Kaiser and his little metal boats, and his soot-stained peasants and his arsenal of fleeing cowards, and I will throw down the unchallengable might of the Zenethyst Inquisitor – the grandeur of his navy, the fastness of his Ocean Citadel, and the old dragon himself. I'll show the peoples of this world that his victory over me was false – a long, meaningless detour from the true course of fate. I would have them know it, before I bring the End. Inasmuch as there is memory beyond death, it will prove a valuable lesson."

Jek was truly astonished. If he thought that the Quest had taken a whopper of a cosmic detour with the journey to *Thasagral* and the encounter with Ethon, now he knew for sure he had stepped right into the deep end. Saving the world was one thing. Even that seemed out of the question now. But saving the universe was *way* out of his league! He stood there fidgeting, despairing to think of some meaningful way to resist. There was none. It was horrible! They had enjoyed so many narrow escapes and unlikely victories, and now there was absolutely *nothing* left to do...

Then Jek heard a curious sound. It made him wince. This wasn't some aural trick of Bellanchora. The sound was not supernatural. It was just plain *un*natural...

Jek heard Parissah laugh. She laughed long, and hard, and spitefully. It was really weird.

"So you think you'll get the better of Enscharaulgk this time, do you?" Parissah mocked. "I would like to see you try! It should prove twice as embarrassing as before!" She laughed again. "Oh, not that I'm entirely unimpressed by your travels and your heavy reading, Princess. But for all your study, there are two things you have not fathomed: humility and a gentle heart. Enscharaulgk knows these things, and by them his wisdom is proved greater than yours. He will stop you again. It is inevitable. Your plans will suffer a second delay!"

There was a very tense silence. Jek did not breathe. He was not sure there was air in the room...

"Curious," Bellanchora said at length, low and calm, but still with a shade of seething. "It is not often one hears a brazen appeal to the virtue of humility. Tell me, *Inquisitor*: What do you know of humility?"

"Much, if you would care to be instructed," Parissah said, drawing herself up very tall and straight.

Bellanchora's phantom boots met the ground with a loud clang. She no longer seemed a small Human. She was at once tall and mighty, and yet still substanceless. She raised her halberd. "You intrigue me. I see you have a sword," she said.

"You did not have the foresight to take it from me," Parissah continued to goad her.

"Happily, I did not. If you think you could use it to give me a lesson in humility, I welcome you to try."

Parissah took up the sword. "So be it."

"Wait!" Jek said, turning urgently to Parissah. "Don't do this! Do you know what you're..."

Marrow set a talon on him, staring into his eyes, cutting him off. "She knows."

With no discernable fear, Parissah strode forward to meet her nemesis. Watching, Jek recalled the dinosaur – all her huge body and long arms were tense with feral strength. But Bellanchora strode still more heavily. The compound trembled beneath her boots...

After overcoming their own incredulity, the guards still in the room came forward to intervene. Parissah drew her pistol with her free hand, ready to fight her way to Bellanchora if necessary. But the Princess raised a hand.

"Do not interfere with this!" she commanded them. "Restrain her comrades, if you feel you must do something. My fight may be with Ehscharaulgk… but I believe I can spare a few centuries of grievances to share with this upstart Inquisitor."

"Just you try," Parissah retorted, still unaccountably eager to twist the knife. The guards did as they were told, holding the Associates firmly in place, a captive audience to the duel. At present, Jek could think of nothing he would care to see less. The course of the battle was a foregone conclusion…

As they met, there was no immediate confrontation. There was circling and assessing. Parissah betrayed some uncertainty by trying out a few different defensive postures. Just waiting for the fight to start took a toll on Jek. It was so senseless. Nothing good could come of it…

"Well, we seem to have found each other," Parissah said at length. "Do you intend to do anything about it today?"

"I'm waiting for you," Bellanchora replied. "Let the instructor lead the lesson."

Parissah came in swinging. Fingers of her long hand curled up and around the cross-guard, limiting the range of movement in her wrist but fortifying her grip. It was a point of technique which she and Marrow had debated more than once, until the old Heron got sick of trying to figure out how a dragon-hand should hold a weapon, rather grumpily resolving to drop the subject once and for all. But the piecemeal training he had given her was nonetheless on display here. Her footing was sure, and her attacks smooth and efficient. But more than anything, there was strength in her blows – terrifying strength, so that Jek could imagine her felling trees in one swipe. She had mastered only the basics of swordplay, perhaps. But Jek was proud – and very glad – that she was on his side.

Even so, Bellanchora made little show of mounting a successful defense. Her counter moves were too easy and too quick, so that after a while Parissah began to seem slow and ungainly again, as she had in the earliest lessons she and Jek shared.

"You fight well enough for one of your kind," Bellanchora conceded. "But I am the Knowledge spirit here. Let me share a bit of what I know…"

The volume and pace of the fight doubled in the blink of an eye as the Princess took the offensive. If there had been a clamor before, it was deafening now. Bellanchora's attacks were infused with her abundance of spiritual potency; she unleashed blows that would have shattered any lesser weapons. Parissah could not help giving ground, and each counter grew more desperate. She had to exert so much force just to block or redirect the attacks coming her way that even in her successful parries, she looked like she was being beaten with a stick. As the Princess' assault stretched on, Jek felt more and more distinctly that she would *have* to relent soon. Then at last he realized it was a false hope. He was thinking of her as a mortal fighter, whose stamina was exhaustible. And so she continued to hew away at Parissah, ever with as much speed and impossible strength as she'd shown from the first strike…

Finally, it was obvious that Parissah's defense had totally failed. The Princess allowed her time for one heavy gasp of air, then struck her savagely with the haft of her halberd… first once, then twice, then three and four times. The impacts made a gut-wrenching sound, pulverizing thick-scaled flesh, cracking ribs hard as steel. Jek swore he could feel a faint aftershock of every blow himself. Parissah fell.

"I grant Enscharaulgk this," Bellanchora gloated, "he has done marvelously at keeping his Inquisition just as I left it. You are every bit as stubborn and stupid as your forebears. I revealed the truth about the Creators, but still you cling to Magormissahr's lies. We could all have been perfect saints like he is, and still they would have left us. You could keep this world in its unhappy state forever and ever and ever, and even so they would never return. Your hope is empty, and your foundation is false. But by all means, hold fast to them! You make good sport."

Parissah got back up, bold and fierce again, so that Jek forgot all her injuries at once. Bellanchora let her drive her back almost to the wall. But it was a feint – the Princess made one riposte and wrenched the sword free of Parissah's hand. Then she struck Parissah again, staggering her while she went for a flanking maneuver. Parissah turned to face her, but as she did the Princess lunged through her, passing substanceless. But her halberd was still solid, and the Princess lifted the haft of it to Parissah's throat, hauling her up and back. Bellanchora was now behind her, choking her with the long handle of her weapon, dragging her along. Parissah stumbled back, giving way to the throttling action, until she reached the wall. Bellanchora ghosted right into the wall, only her hands still visible, clutching the halberd, strangling Parissah between the haft and the concrete. Jek gaped. It was even more horrific than watching his friend be beaten senseless. She struggled mightily to push the halberd back from her neck, gasping and suffocating, her huge chest heaving in vain.

All appeared lost, and Jek floundered in the horror of wondering how long an Avarican could hold on without air. But suddenly, from Heck only knew where, Parissah found more strength – strength enough to bend the haft of the Princess' adamant weapon! Slowly but surely it bowed out, creaking with an aural immensity, like the sound of one of the Kaiser's battleships being twisted in half. Finally, Parissah threw it down – and Bellanchora came with it, tumbling out of the wall...

The Princess was on the ground now, sitting and looking up at her opponent. Jek's heart soared, as did all the Associates'. This was a chance beyond hope. For Bellanchora to have known even one moment of doubt in this fight exceeded optimism at its most reckless...

But it was only a moment. The Princess glided back to her feet. She held her halberd fast in one hand and ran her other along its haft, straightening it in one fluid, effortless motion. Her strength and rage were multiplied. Parissah had only time to recover her sword. Their weapons clashed again a few more times, but Bellanchora got ahead of Parissah very fast, and let loose on her with more furious blows, careful only not to kill her outright. She endured punishment that would have ended a dozen Humans, and the Princess was swift to reward her superior resilience in a seemingly endless variety of painful new ways. Parissah recoiled, wheezing and reeling, desperate to form some distance and keep the fight up...

It was at this time that Jek heard an odd cry – not from Parissah, but from next to him. The sound rubbed his mind, but it couldn't wrench his attention away from the grisly spectacle before him. Parissah would block one blow, then suffer another, over and over in a nearly unbroken pattern.

Sudden despair and weakness finally drove Jek's eyes away. But what he saw was no comfort. He looked to Audrey, who stood silently looking on, bleary-eyed and weeping – a sight, he realized, was glimpsed through the haze of his own tears.

But then he noticed a stir – a guard springing up from the ground – and he noticed then that Baegulgog was gone...

"NO!" the Clerk cried, hurling down from the air, lightning all in his tentacles as he careened for Bellanchora. She dashed him with her halberd without skipping a beat. Then, lest he meddle further, even as a ghost, she trapped him in a portal and he vanished.

But Baegulgog's demise filled Parissah with a vengeance. Finally, with a gurgling breath, she roared and expelled a powerful jet of flame at the Princess, so that all in the room felt the heat. Bellanchora let the fires roll over her, second after long second. At last, Parissah relented, utterly spent. The Princess' phantom armor steamed and sizzled, but she stood totally unharmed.

Then she swung her halberd and struck again. She whisked Parissah's feet out from under her and beat her on the ground. Truly heart-rending sounds were extracted from the Inquisitor – like the death throes of a brachiosaur. The Princess was unmoved. Her onslaught continued unbroken. If anything, she was getting *more* angry, swing by swing...

Finally, she drove the blade end of her halberd through Parissah's thigh. She gave a horrible roar, and the Princess twisted the blade. "Beg, you obstinant creature! Beg for mercy!"

"No," Parissah replied.

Bellanchora sunk her halberd into her shoulder. "*Beg*!"

"No!"

Her halberd fell a third time.

Parissah made no more sound.

* * *

Why?

In his abject grief, Jek surprised himself with the question.

But after all, what could Parissah have hoped to gain? Why had she invited such a horrific death? Why had she forced the rest of them to bear helpless witness? Wouldn't it have been just as well – far better, in fact – if they had all died together? Jek couldn't understand *why*...

Audrey attempted to dart forward, but she couldn't break free from the grasp of the guards. They were more attentive now, since of all people, the Clerk had freed himself. Bellanchora took notice of the little scuffle...

"Do not let the healer near!" the Princess commanded, pointing an admonishing finger. She left her halberd behind, stuck fast in Parissah's dead body.

"Vhat art ve to do with zhese ozhers, mine Lady?" a guard asked.

"Give them to the Kaiser," she answered. "Two of them are prior enemies of the state. Let him make a show of their death. Someone should enjoy it. As for me, I've had my fun, it seems." Though she behaved rather disappointed.

"And vhat of zee Clerk?" the guard continued.

"Ah yes, I'd nearly forgot..." Bellanchora replied, and at once a portal opened and expelled the ghostly Baegulgog. "Let him be executed as well."

"But... how art ve to execute a ghost, mine Lady?"

"That is no concern of mine. Only see that the Kaiser makes quick work of it. His Fleet will be set in motion very soon. It would be most embarrassing if it were to sail to glory without him."

"Yaevogel," the guard saluted. And so they began herding the few remaining Associates away. They struggled and they looked back, and Jek beheld Baegulgog as he stooped in the air over Parissah.

"O, madam," he lamented, flashing with deep sorrow. "You have gone far before your time! Perhaps all of creation will soon follow you. But however short or long the Clerk Baegulgog endures, he shall not cease to mourn you, my good friend."

"Baegulgog!" Audrey called back, even as they were all driven from the room.

"Mercy!" the Clerk cried out. "Must I leave my fallen friend, only to see an end of those I have left? O! I suppose I must! Goodbye, my friend Parissah! Goodbye!"

Public Execution

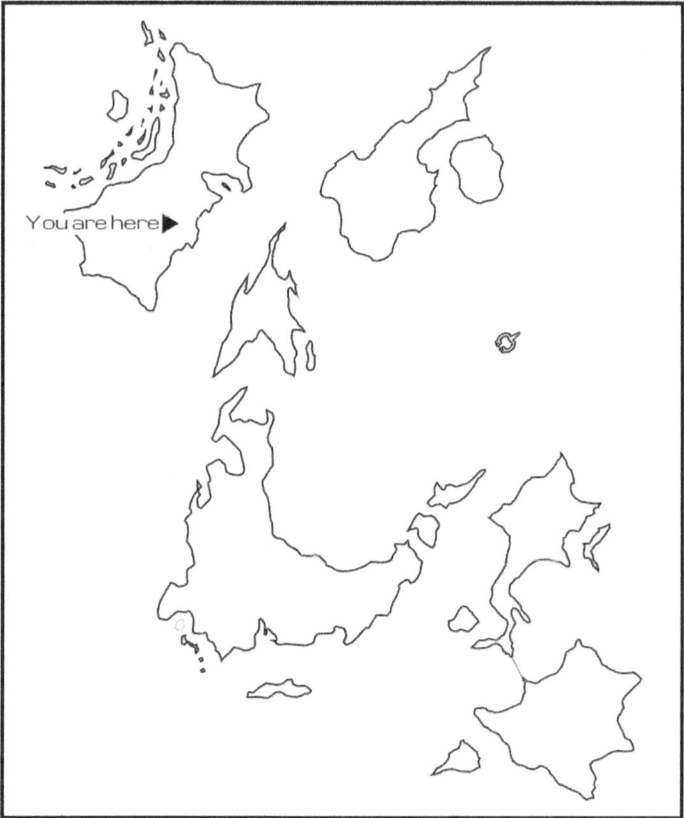

"But just how loud should I have to blow the whistle? What will it take for you people to finally wake up and realize that it's all an illusion? It's all THEIR illusion! They control the world and everything in it. They have for thousands of years. And the worst part is, it's obvious. It's SO obvious! Still want proof? Then try this out: Name one great calamity in the history of the world where they didn't make an appearance. Name JUST ONE! You know darn well, you can't."

- Chippley Spencer, *Wxldlr's Death Cult: Knights of the Indigo Lodge Unmasked*

Jek stood with his hands bound upon the gallows, watching hundreds of Despotopians crowd into the square, eager for the spectacle. Today was a day to be remembered. The denizens of Autocratropolis had no job to report to at present, for all the factories and foundries had been closed, and every man and woman given a short reprieve. And why not? Their great work was finished, and the Kaiser was nothing if not a man of the people. He wanted all the country to share in the joy of their coming glory. And, true to form, he meant to kick off the revelry with a little tasteful showmanship. Jek, Audrey, Marrow, and Baegulgog – all that remained of the Traveling Associates – were to be the star attractions...

And the show was already in full swing. Smokestacks near the square eschewed their usual vapors in favor of steady streams of confetti. Ceremonious music echoed behind the cheerful voices of the sea of spectators. The air was filled with potent, refreshing fragrance; undoubtedly the Despotopians needed pretty powerful perfumes to overcome the smell of coal. Jek felt a bit like a spectator himself, having never seen so much pomp and fanfare. He watched as vendors carrying towers of confections weaved in and out of the crowds, calling for customers, handing out treats. He started as a series of fireworks went off nearby without warning – not the most comforting surprise while standing in front of a firing squad. He heard a little kid say, "Look, mozher! Zhey are going to die!"

Jek looked at Audrey. She looked back, shrugging. Jek nodded grimly. That pretty much summed up their plight...

It was at this point that the chanting started. It was distant at first and hard to hear over the general din. But when it caught, it spread like wildfire, until the entire crowd was united in it. The sudden change was dramatic, and rather terrifying. One moment they were all a lot of Despotopians milling around and enjoying themselves... and the next, they were *Despotopia* – one nation calling with one voice. Jek didn't understand their tongue, but he intuited who it was they were calling for. They called for their Kaiser.

The chanting grew feverish, never breaking perfect syncopation. From within an adjoining wing of the palace, the Kaiser emerged, one gloved hand tucked into the chest of his heavy grey coat, the other waving to the masses. They broke the chanting and cheered. They cheered as if graced by the presence of a Creator, suddenly returned from the long centuries spent on the other side of the Undervoid.

Seeing Kaiser Hienrechenshlagen for himself, Jek too had a hard time accepting that the great specimen was merely Human. If Oberführer Klinkofhenschmidt had seemed huge, hulking and muscle-bound, it was obvious now that he had modelled himself into a mere forgery of his lord. The Kaiser's muscles seemed to have muscles, perhaps to the third or fourth degree. Strength he clearly had to call on... and if his confident, suave stride was any indication, then his movements were subtle and skillful as well. Jek could hear his footfalls as he came up to the gallows, even despite the still-deafening cheering. Especially up close, it was little wonder that Marrow feared he may have met a match in Hienrechenshlagen. And it was little wonder that the nation of Despotopia so loved their Kaiser – a perfect avatar for their own swollen strength. As he began to speak, it was obvious that that love was mutual...

"Mine beautiful laborers," began Hienrechenshlagen, his voice resonant, triumphant, and absurdly charismatic. "Today is zee dawn of a new age. *Our* age. A gilded age of glory und ascendancy, vhen our people vill be revarded vith all zee riches of an hundred generations vorth of sveat and toil. You, mine peasants, have sveat zhis sveat, und toiled zhis toil! You have taken a pauper's inheritance und forged it into *strength* – strength enough to avail against zee greatest und most ancient powers in all zee vorld! Very soon, ve vill begin zhis age vith a due demonstration of zhis strength. An short season of reckoning vill secure for us a zhousand years of peace, prosperity, und growth unrestrained!" After allowing a healthy interlude of applause, he gestured to the Associates, and continued. "Let zhat reckoning begin, here und now, vith zhese fugitives. Appropriately enough, zhree citizens of Jast-Madiir, our rivals of old… und zheir Heron accomplice here. Let zheir grisly death fill you vith all zee joy zhat you are due! Long live Despotopia!"

"Long live Despotopia!" the crowd replied.

The Kaiser turned to stand over his victims, face all inscuitable in gas-mask, goggles, and military visor cap. "Judgment has been passed on zee four of you," he said, his voice still inexplicably echoing as if amplified. "You are to be hung by zee neck und shot until dead."

"What about me?" the ghost of Baegulgog asked.

The Kaiser hesitated. "Ve vill do our best vith you," he said at length. He walked down the platform.

Baegulgog sighed. "I wish Parissah was here to see this," he said. "It is all rather exhilarating." He cleared his throat as the rest of the party gave him a look. "Oh, it is quite a horrible turn, of course. But if you all must die, at least it will have been an occasion. And I, for one, am very proud to float here beside you now."

"Thanks, Baegulgog," Audrey said, and she seemed to mean it.

"Zee condemned vill now commence vith zee making of zheir last vords," the Kaiser announced. "Who vould be zee first to speak?"

"I would!" came a voice – harsh, terrible, and utterly domineering – familiar to Jek and yet unfamiliar. He winced and looked round to see who had just spoken…

"This entire execution is a farce! It is unlawful! To continue would be to invite unimaginable retribution." It was Marrow who spoke, and all of Despotopia cowered before his voice, just as they had exulted for the Kaiser's. "*You*, Hienrechenshlagen, have no authority to put another head of state to death in this fashion!"

The Kaiser appeared unmoved. But as he spoke, he betrayed some uncertainty. "Who are you zhat speaks vith such forcefulness? Declare yourself, criminal!"

Marrow removed his plague doctor's mask, revealing a face of old, blighted feathers, and a false eye that shown with a tangerine brilliance. "I am Proconsul Zedulon, supreme lord of Roemnar!"

Jek blanched.

Looking back, the very fact that he had had a Dire Heron friend and mentor of any stripe was passing unlikely. But as it turned out, 'Marrow' was an assumed identity for none other than Zedulon – sovereign of Roemnar since before Jek's grandfather's grandfather was born – the very originator of the Chocolate Prophecy they had just unraveled, and dozens of prophecies besides. It was a little surprising. He probably wouldn't have even believed it. But with the mask off, the truth of Marrow's claim was as plain to Jek as the face on his face. Besides that, the legendary glowing false eye was some clue...

The reaction of the Kaiser was also some clue. He was livid, waving up some minister or adviser, diving headlong into a hushed but very animated debate. Jek didn't know exactly who she was, but she looked very evil. It fit, though... since as a rule, all royal advisers ought to be conspicuously evil. Meanwhile, everyone else held their breath... Jek not the least among them.

Finally, the Kaiser spoke up. "Very vell. Despotopia has no immediate vish to compromise its good relations vith zee sovereignty of Roemnar." He nodded solemnly. "I recognize und pardon you, most esteemed Proconsul Zedulon."

Guards came and unbound Zedulon. Rather embarrassed and nervous they seemed, and a bit clumsy for it.

"What about my companions?" Zedulon demanded. "I extend my diplomatic immunity to them."

"In zhis, ve regret ve cannot oblige you, Proconsul," Hienrechenshlagen answered. "Zhey are not your subjects, und so zhey cannot share in your immunity. Unless zhey too are secretly heads of state, zhey must still be executed."

"Oh, *oh*! I'm a head of state!" Audrey said. "And this is my husband," she continued, indicating Jek. "That should count for something, I would think."

The crowd murmured in bewilderment.

The Kaiser turned back to his adviser for some more terse words. Then he turned back. "Pray tell! Vhat state are you zee head of?"

Audrey hesitated. "I don't know."

The Kaiser shook his head. "Zhen zhere is nozhing I can do for you. Mine apologies, but you vould have to be more specific zhen zhat."

"Darn," Audrey lamented.

Jek took dim notice of all of this. Not that it shouldn't have demanded his full attention, of course, since his life basically hung in the balance. But even as the debate wore on, a light had flashed repeatedly in Jek's face. It was blinding and very annoying, and he determined to find the source. It did not take long. He looked to the rooftop of one of the tall buildings in the square, and lo, the flashing came from the exposed blade of a sword, held aloft by a shadowy figure, catching the light of the sun. Jek squinted, trying to determine something of this cloaked swordsman. But it seemed that discovering the one swordsman had the odd, nearly instantaneous effect of seeing through a magician's trick. Suddenly he spied a second bright sword and dark cloak on a rooftop. And a third. And a fourth. A quick scan of the skyline revealed roughly a dozen phantom swordsmen, all on the move, darting deftly from roof to roof...

Well, I'll be, Jek thought to himself. *Wonders never cease*!

Of course, he couldn't say with absolute certainty who the men were. But he had a notion. And a hope...

"Let us be getting on vith zee last vords," the Kaiser said. "Who vould go next?"

"I will," Jek said, stepping forward. "I have a little speech I'd like to give. So here goes...

"If, upon the Great Looking-Back of all things, we are found to have done good, then let us have doneth the most greatest good that we could do..." Jek recited.

"Vhat is he doing?" the Kaiser asked his adviser.

"He doth recite zee pledge of zee Knights of zee Indigo Lodge, mine Kaiser," she answered.

"If we are found to have done bad, then let us have doneth the least worstest bad that we could do..." Jek continued.

"Stop him!" the Kaiser ordered. "He pays us insult! As if zee Knights would sympathize vith zheir plight!"

"If we pursued the good, may it have been..." Jek was cut off, a noose put round his neck, already tight enough to strangle...

"...May it have been so to attaineth it!" a clear, joyful voice continued for him, even as a cloaked figure leapt down to the gallows. The crowd cried with new doubt.

"And if we pursued the bad, may it have been so to destroyeth it!" another such voice called, completing the Pledge. The figures cast aside their cloaks, revealing beautiful suits of polished armor, all silver and iridescent indigo. Jek nearly shed tears of joy, even as he continued to choke.

"Zee Indigo Knights!" the Kaiser exclaimed. "Stop zhem!"

The Kaiser's men stormed the platform. The Knights held their ground. There was a brief, tense standoff...

"Ha-ha!" another Indigo Knight called, swinging into the action on a long rope, importantly bowling down the firing squad. Soon two or three more arrived in similar high spirits and like fashion. "Ho-ho!" they called... and "tallyho!" and many such exultant nothings. The clash between the Despotopians and the Knights broke out. With a few swift sword-swipes, the Associates were freed in the rising confusion. Jek quickly recovered his breath, even as they were all spirited away, directly into the royal palace, of all places.

Jek stole a look back into the square, taking a moment to marvel at the exploits of the Knights. A merry bunch they were, and effortless fighters, having much fun at the expense of their Despotopian opponents, whom they made appear quite hapless. It was a page right out of his childhood dreams. He was beside himself with wonder.

Suddenly, Marrow – that is, *Zedulon* – tackled him. Hardly a fraction of an instant later, a fireball hurled through the space he had just been standing in. Collecting himself, Jek looked back out, and found himself under the steely gaze of the Kaiser. He was on a personal warpath straight for them...

"We cannot linger here, Jek," Zedulon said. "Not even for a moment."

"Sorry, thou sir Proconsul... sir," he apologized awkwardly, getting back up.

"Do not patronize me now!" Zedulon snapped back. "You must continue to think of me as your unquestionable sage master, and nothing more. Get you gone! Our peril is still deadly dire."

They fled for all they were worth...

The palace did not prove an easy place to withdraw to. They may not have had to wade through the crowds this way, but a steady inflow of guards met their advance with more armed resistance than they might have found outside. Jek, Audrey, and even Zedulon were almost totally dependant on their escort of Indigo Knights for protection, being without weapons. Four Knights in total were with them. The fate of the rest was uncertain, but with the Kaiser electing to nip at the Associates' heels, it seemed hopeful they could win their own escape. Meanwhile, the streets were alive again with the sound of loudspeakers – word of the getaway was already echoing through the reaches of Despotopia.

"What a jailbreak!" Baegulgog exclaimed, being carted along on a little sled the Knights had produced. "What a fine, merry swashbuckler we've found ourselves in! But wherever are we going, I wonder?"

"Thine escape is made for thee, on the palace's south side," an Indigo Knight replied, grappling with and subduing a palace guard. Jek was a bit surprised. Their use of the high-falootin' grammar was not so classically archaic. It seemed rather updated and streamlined. He didn't fancy it much. But after all, they were the *real*, genuine Indigo Knights, and he certainly wasn't about to debate grammar with them... especially given present circumstances...

"What about weapons?" Audrey asked, all of them still shuffling deeper into the palace even as they were continually assailed.

An Indigo Knight wrenched a sword from the hand of a guard, caught it in the air and tossed it to Audrey. "Your right weapons hath been recovered, and await you," he said. "But please accept this in the meantime, fair lady."

Free of pursuers for a moment, they charged down a hall. The high, elegant walls of the palace were bright with light from the outside world, streaming through tall, lofted windows. The pathways of the Kaiser's home were not adorned with many treasures, but were nonetheless stately and elegantly built. And the palace was large – large enough so that here and there, the Knights seemed to hesitate, as if trying to remember their way through a labyrinth.

They came to a door that was barred. The Knights tried to hew it, but it proved a thick and sturdy door, and an unfortunately loud one to hack at with swords. They were sure to draw attention.

"Verily, we must get past this door," a Knight said.

Zedulon turned to Audrey. "Give me your sword," he told her. She did, and at once he flew to a high window and smashed his way through.

Just as they watched him flutter out of view, they heard the ominous advance of heavy boots. Suddenly the shadow of the Kaiser filled the hall behind them. He was slow in his approach, but inexorable – armed with no weapon but himself. The Knights looked one to the other in doubt.

From the other side of the door, sounds of unlatching reached their ears. Zedulon flung the door open. But the Kaiser was near...

"Fly!" the Knights said. "Thou wilt go with brother Zavion. We three shall entertain the Kaiser."

"Come!" Zedulon waved them forward, allowing no time for protest. He stood in the doorway as Audrey passed, then Jek, who now had Baegulgog's sled in tow. After they had all gone, and the Knight Zavion with them, he looked back down the hall. The Kaiser returned the look of the old bird. It was a knowing look. A look of open challenge. His hands and forearms glowed like embers, covered in magical flame.

"Not now, you old fool," Zedulon told himself. "But soon enough. Yes, soon enough..."

Then Zedulon dashed away as well. The three Knights, remaining behind to confront Hienrechenshlagen, did what they could bravely, and with distinction. They came never back to the Indigo Lodge...

That one close shave with the Kaiser proved their most desperate moment in the flight through the palace, but guards continued to dog them all the same. The Knight Zavion fended for them well, but Audrey had to hold her own on a few occasions. She struggled, but mostly because the sword was an unfamiliar weapon. Zedulon also claimed a sword and was naturally brilliant with it. Jek focused primarily on towing Baegulgog.

At last, they came to a door that led into a small sheltered court – a garden of some kind, though the plants were dull and looked neglected. Zavion waved them round a brown hedge, and there waiting for them was one of those crazy mechanical horse contraptions Audrey had pointed out to Jek on their way into the country.

"Get thee into yon carriage, my good fellows!" Zavion instructed.

Jek did as he was told, but not without misgivings. "I feel a bit unsure about this," he admitted. "How do these things handle?"

"Alas! I could not say," Zavion lamented. "T'was brother Palintar who didst steer the thing before. But concern thyself not! The burden falls to me now, and I will bear it."

"I'll be only too glad to instruct you, if you're unsure," Baegulgog volunteered, flashing eagerly. "How I wish I were whole! Then I would surely take the reigns myself, and let any Despotopian horseman, living or dead, try to run us down!"

"You've piloted one of these before, Baegulgog?" Audrey asked, as they all piled into the carriage.

"Technically, no," Baegulgog answered. "I have only worked with living horses. But surely the differences are marginal..."

Zavion pulled a cord with a hard yank and the thing sputtered and spat three great dark plumes before the motor hit something of a cadence, and the piston-legs sprung to chattering life. Then he leapt to the driver's bench, took up the reigns, and floored the acceleration pedal. Off they went, mechanical horse fuming and bouncing like mad on the ends of its flurried pistons...

"Hey, here's our weapons!" Audrey said, finding them all in a rattling bundle under the frontmost passenger bench in the carriage. Jek and Zedulon stooped over the package, eager to have their hardware back.

"Indeed!" Zavion called back to them over the racket of the horse-engine. "Bless me; I forgot to tell thee that they were back there with thee! How fortunate thou foundest them thineselves."

They let Zedulon have his spear (which, it turned out, really *was* his spear all along). But when it came to the muskets, Audrey held a hand over them both. Jek gave her a quizzical look.

"What is it?" he asked.

"I want to be sure I have my own musket back," Audrey said.

Jek kind of huffed a little laugh and tried to grab one of the muskets, but she stopped him again. "Surely it doesn't make any difference which is which," he insisted. "They're both the same."

"No, they're a little different," Audrey shook her head. "Mine has this funny thing with the hammer now."

Jek blinked. "What kind of a thing?"

Audrey shrugged. "How should I know? It's some kind of a thing, like the spring catches a little bit when you pull the hammer back. It's a little internal 'twang' or 'twing' thing that happens."

Jek smiled. "And you were afraid I might not pull the hammer back far enough if I wasn't expecting the thing?"

"Not really," Audrey admitted. "I just kind of like that little catch. It's a quirk that grows on you, I guess."

Suddenly a few arrows whizzed into the carriage. Jek and Audrey blanched.

"We art beset!" Zavion called.

"By all that is dreary and forlorn, argue about little hammer things some other time!" Zedulon commanded them. They abruptly filled their hands with muskets and started loading.

Outside the carriage, four similar carriages full of Despotopian soldiers had caught up to them, with two already immediately on either side.

"This doth bode ill," Zavion said.

Baegulgog laughed. "Tis childsplay, my good man!" the Clerk replied. "Here, allow me." Baegulgog floated into the same space as Zavion, reaching out ghostly tentacles to where the Knight held the reigns.

"How is your response time, dear Knight?"

"Quite good, as ought to be," Zavion responded. "Pray, what art thou doing?"

"I will pretend to steer the craft – you must mimic my movements," Baegulgog answered.

Zavion was a bit unsettled, hearing the responding voice emanate from within his own chest. "This is passing strange," he admitted. "My internal organs doth feel rather twitchy."

"Yes, perhaps they would," Baegulgog replied politely. "Now for goodness' sake, get a higher grip on those reigns! There's far too much slack in the line."

Audrey fumbled with the powder as the shadows of many buildings passed over her hands from the fast-retreating cityscape outside. This business of reloading was not a skill Zedulon had honed with them, and not one she had worked on much herself. But finally, she forced down the musket ball and her shot was ready. More arrows flew into the carriage from behind her. After they relented, she uncovered over the door and took a shot. An archer fell in the adjoining carriage. Jek went through a similar routine on the other side seconds later, even as she was back in the reload.

Up front, the enemy carriage to their left sped ahead, and an archer drew a bead on Zavion. The Knight took up his shield just in time to deflect a series of arrows from the repeating crossbow.

But it was a coordinated attack. A Despotopian skirmisher leapt into the front of the carriage from the other side, forcing Zavion into a very tight duel. Baegulgog sat still at the reigns, incredulous. There was now no pilot for him to direct, and he was helpless as he watched the mechanical horse bound on its reciprocating feet wheresoever it would. The path proved straightforward enough, but began to wind side-to-side in slowly broadening arcs. Worse yet, there was a bend in the road up ahead, coming up very fast!

"Hurry up with the swashbuckling!" Baegulgog exclaimed. "We are careening to our doom!"

Zavion slashed and brought both their swords hard down to the floor, then deftly ran along the railing to flank the Despotopian. With a bash of his shield, he sent the enemy stumbling back in time to catch several arrows from the other carriage before he fell into the street. Zavion took a knife out from behind his shield and pitched it at the archer. The throw was quite accurate, and another enemy fell. Finally, and only just in time, he sat back through Baegulgog and took up the reigns, diverting the speeding horse-engine round the bend in the road. The other carriages had pulled back a moment earlier to avoid the collision themselves, but were soon closing back in...

"Concentrate, Jek!" Zedulon instructed his pupil. "You must concentrate *much* harder! This is no time for sloth or sloppy work!"

Jek was engaged in reloading, his hands fumbling more and more as Zedulon's instructions multiplied. He finished with the powder and went for the bag of shot...

"Yes, get the shot out, Jek!" Zedulon told him. "Hurry with the shot!"

The bag of shot came open unexpectedly. All the little balls scattered along the bottom of the carriage with a crisp marbly sound. Jek shut his eyes and pursed his lips, holding back internal combustion.

"Well, now look what you did," Zedulon admonished at length.

Jek got an uncharacteristic feisty look about him. "And how about you?" he demanded. "What have *you* been contributing to all this? Did you leave most of your fighting genius behind with your mask?"

Zedulon stared him down for a moment, then chucked *Valshaloli* out the window. The spear lanced straight through an enemy horse-engine, and the whole contraption immediately went up in a big, violent explosion, even as Zedulon returned to his staring contest with Jek.

"That was just a lucky throw, wasn't it?" Jek asked at length.

"Of course not," Zedulon replied. "And even if it was, I would never admit it. Now take that bayonette and cut me a hole in the roof! I must retrieve *Valshaloli*..."

Jek did as instructed. Audrey covered for them on the other side. Taking another good shot, she leaned out of the carriage and stole a look behind them. "Better hurry," she said. "Another carriage is pulling up in place of the one you blew up!"

Jek completed a hole, and Zedulon leapt up and out.

The carriage on their left closed in, smacking them sidelong. Audrey faltered, but came back lancing at the archer opposite her. The limbs of his crossbow folded back, and a pair of saw blades leapt out. In a swipe, the archer took the end of Audrey's musket clean off! She looked aghast.

"Um..." she called, looking back at Jek, "...I can't shoot!"

"Duck!" Jek said, turning to face her. She did, even as the crossbow of the enemy archer went off. Jek's musket went off almost in synchronous. Uncovering and turning back, she learned the archer was no more. But when she returned to face Jek, her smile was rent away, seeing he'd been caught in the shoulder with an arrow. She tackled him with glowing hands in her reckless eagerness to make him well. The Life magic worked its wonders, and the arrow came out of his shoulder, leaving no mark but the new hole in his frock coat.

Somewhat tenderly, he smiled up at her. "Thanks," he said.

"Sure," she smiled back.

They lingered like that a little too long, then sprung back to action. They both started reloading, until a moment passed and Audrey realized with a groan how pointless it was to try to load a cleft musket...

Zavion took a moment to survey the scene, getting his bearings and assessing the danger. "We art again surrounded," he said. "It is not a good spot to be."

"Au contraire!" Baegulgog exulted. "We have them right where we want them! Now we know how this thing corners, let us put that knowledge to use. Pay close heed now, and follow my movements exactly..."

Just before an intersection, Baegulgog directed Zavion to pull back and corner hard. They flew back from between the carriages on either side, and their own carriage grazed the horse-engine to their rear, diverting its course disastrously. Then, almost before Zavion could react, Baegulgog motioned to divert hard the other way and slam on the breaks. They were pulled into a grinding, drifting spin. The carriage's wheels skidded and sparked and their horse engine stumbled and tumbled, spinning sideways end-over-end in a deafening, clumsy clatter. Those split seconds of utter twirling chaos seemed to last forever, and the sound of one of the other carriages smashing into a building won over all, another explosion showering them with gears and springs. Then, whether by happenstance or sheer skill, their horse-engine landed back on its feet just as the carriage straightened out behind it. Baegulgog motioned for all speed, and Zavion hit the accelerator and tugged the reigns. The carriage went speeding down a side street, leaving what pursuing enemies were left outmaneuvered, charging in the wrong direction.

But this was far from a real end to their troubles. There was a major obstacle which even Baegulgog had not anticipated...

"Oh dear," he said.

"Verily," Zavion agreed.

The carriage went charging full-speed through a street-side kidney bean market, sending unsuspecting citizens dashing out of the way, nudging and side-swiping carts and stands full of Despotopia's signature crop. They were pelted with fiercely-clucking chickens as they flew headlong through a whole meandering flock of them.

"So much for my budding aspirations as a street racer," Baegulgog lamented. "Tracks seldom have such flotsam."

"Still I would say that thou hast done well, on the whole," Zavion replied to the voice in his chest. "But we must veer again east, as soon as may be. I am in danger of losing my way in these side-streets."

"Say no more," Baegulgog said, and directed him through another sharp turn, sending them east again through an even more narrow alley, but fortunately one more devoid of people and stuff.

"It is some comfort to know that you have a path in mind," Baegulgog went on calmly, even as Zavion's palms and brow were slicked from the sweat of such death-defying maneuvers. "But where is it we are off to, if you don't mind my asking?"

"Why, we make for the Indigo Lodge, of course," Zavion explained.

"Indeed?" Baegulgog asked. "I should never have guessed the Lodge was in Despotopia..."

"It is where we need it to be." Baegulgog wondered at the response, but didn't press it. "Let us return to the main road, if we may," Zavion went on.

"Indubitably," Baegulgog agreed, and led him through another pair of turns...

It was at this point that Zedulon returned, his shadow filling the hole in the roof even as Audrey was just getting around to wondering where he'd been. His old wings folded, every scraggly old feather whipping in the wind. He looked rough.

"You were gone a while," Audrey told him as he carefully reentered the carriage.

"Are you in a mood to criticize me as well, my friend?" Zedulon replied. He sighed, sitting as best the wide bench allowed him. "This has not been a good day for me."

"Sorry," Audrey said. "It just seemed like a long time. If you'd been gone any longer, I would have worried."

"In that case, I thank you," Zedulon said, and he seemed to perk up a bit, if only momentarily. "Your concern would not be without merit. I am feeling my age, at times, on this demanding journey. And I begin to second-guess myself. Third-guess myself, even." He looked around, eye distant with reflection. "I could have confronted the Kaiser, there and then, in the palace. What stopped me? Did I really know the proper time had not yet come? Or was I just a frightened old bird, whose wisdom has turned to folly?" He shook his head in doubt.

Audrey pined for him. She didn't have firsthand experience with the complexities of foresight or the toll of advanced age, of course, but he certainly made them sound sad. She went over to him, brushing down his fluffed-out neck feathers tenderly. "In all the days I've known you, you've never once been wrong," Audrey assured him. "I don't know why it's so important that you fight the Kaiser. But if you thought today wasn't the day, then I'm sure you were right."

"Thank you again, dear friend," Zedulon said, his false eye losing nearly all its luster as he calmed down.

"That still doesn't explain why you were gone so long," Jek said. They both looked back at him, rather surprised, but he had a sarcastic grin. "Are you going to pin that on old age too? Maybe you *are* losing a step..."

"Well, if you *must* know," Zedulon answered, "I needed to stop and eat some rocks."

Jek's face scrunched all funny. "*Rocks*?"

"Yes," Zedulon replied. "They're for my gizzard."

"Herons have gizzards?"

"Dire Herons do."

"What do rocks taste like?" Audrey asked.

"Why, they are extremely delicious, of course!" Zedulon exclaimed. The Humans sat with puzzled looks. After a few seconds, Zedulon began to laugh his diabolical laugh. Then, in a cheesy sort of way, they all shared a big, long laugh together...

* * *

It was nearly dusk when the carriage came to a halt, the horse-engine sputtering and popping as it falteringly powered down. Audrey was more than half asleep, but the change in motion and the sound of the backfiring was enough to wake her. They all got out of the carriage. Behind them, the land of Despotopia fumed again. Ahead of them, just below a sandy ridge, was the ocean.

"Ah, the Indigo Lodge," Zedulon said. "What a place of distinction that I have never yet ventured to, save in dim memory of today."

"I don't see it," Jek said, and Audrey shared his sentiment. "I don't see *anything*."

"Yet our lord the Proconsul speaks aright," Zavion said, nodding solemnly to Zedulon, before pointing to the sea. "The Lodge lieth thither! Let us away on foot now. The metal beast will serve no more." He walked up to the crest of the ridge, Knightly cape waving heroically in the sea breeze. Then he gestured out again. "Behold," he said.

As Audrey and Jek joined him at the summit, they looked down into a small gulf, and there was a ship – an *indigo* ship – not at all dissimilar from an Inquisition vessel – smooth, metal, enclosed, light in the water – without any conspicuous means of propulsion. And Audrey realized at once how fitting it was. In an island chain, what headquarters for justice and do-goodery would serve better than a ship? And how else could it be that, after many centuries, the location of the Lodge had remained still unknown? Yes, it all made sense now.

"We shall give the others till the second watch of the night to return," Zavion explained. "Then we must make with all haste for the Inquisition Citadel. They must learn of this Despotopian plot that thou hast unmasked, if they have not already."

"But how did *you* know about the plot?" Audrey asked. "And how did you know we needed your help? We spent a long time looking for you; I never expected you guys to find us instead!"

"The answers thou seeketh awaiteth thee within the Lodge," Zavion replied. "An old ally of yours, I believe, doth tarry yon. I shall give him the honor of explaining."

Jek and Audrey exchanged a gleeful look. "The old man!" Jek said. "He must've found them somehow – bless that wily old pirate!"

"Let's go see him!" Audrey replied. And they all made their way carefully down the dune, the sands whisking whimsically away behind their feet...

Within minutes, they had stepped once again out of the waking world and into myth. The Lodge was ornate and elegant in its construction, its rooms and corridors arching, walls criss-crossed with carefully inlaid, sloping wooden shelves, seamless and smooth as polished marble. And the farther into the Lodge they ventured, the more treasures adorned these odd shelves – trinkets and mementos of so many secret crusades. Audrey did not know and could not guess the history or significance of any of them. She was even pretty sure one of the displays she passed was just a regular old paperclip tied to the end of some string. She certainly didn't know what that was about. But everything she saw seemed to radiate history, so that a tangible sense of importance was in the air everywhere she turned. She felt important herself, just by being there. It was not a comfortable feeling, as ever.

Finally, they reached a room of obvious, particular importance. It was great and oval-shaped, with a lofted ceiling. Covering a great deal of that ceiling was a huge dragon skull, hung upside-down... and from its cavities emanated the light that filled the room. On the back bend of the wall, there was one sloping shelf that stood out – studded with huge zenithysts. Audrey spied many trophies along this and the lesser shelves of the room, more mysterious and alluring than all the rest. But most of all, she studied Jek – his face beaming with boyish wonder. She knew this experience meant a lot to him, and she basked in vicarious awe that far exceeded what she could have mustered on her own.

At length, Jek zeroed-in on the crest of the great shelf. He walked over to it, with Audrey close behind. She was a bit mystified. It was just a simple plaque he had crossed the room to look at.

"This *really* is the Indigo Lodge," Jek whispered to himself.

"Obviously," Audrey said, easily overhearing him. "What's with the plaque?"

"This the plaque that famously hangs in the Lodge, dedicated to Carlos Washoe."

"What does it say?" she asked him.

"The Heck I can't."

She squinted. "The Heck you can't what?"

"No, that's what it says... 'The Heck I can't.' Remember, I told you those were his words, as he walked out of the Baja Inn."

"Oh, right," Audrey replied. "I remember that story." She examined the plaque for herself – unable to read it, but not so unable to appreciate it. She touched the emblazoned letters, as if to absorb their deeper meaning. "It seemed kind of dumb to me then. But standing here, with all this history just lying around, somehow it seems less dumb now."

Zavion returned to the room with three other Knights. They hadn't even noticed he'd gone. But now that he was back, he spoke to them again...

"Thine acquaintance doth come hither," he said. Jek and Audrey turned to the side entrance, their legs wound to pounce on the old man the moment he entered the room, whence they would hug him, whether he wanted it or not...

But their visitor emerged, and his appearing stopped them dead. It was not at all who they expected...

"Horus Templar?" Jek asked, incredulous.

"By jove, who is this?" Baegulgog asked.

"Why, I'm their attorney, of course," Templar replied, grinning mischievously. "Who were you expecting?"

They all stood flummoxed for a few tense seconds.

"Hm, it seems you really *were* expecting someone else," Templar continued at length. "Sorry to disappoint."

"No, don't be sorry," Audrey said. "It's not that we're not glad to see you. We just thought you were the old man."

Horus' ears perked. "He's not with you?" He looked around and sniffed the air. "No, apparently he isn't. I suppose there is quite a bit for us to catch up on..."

"Yes," Zavion agreed. "Tis the proper time and place for council – even here, where council for the fate of the world hath been taken many times before. This is the very hall of meeting for the Indigo Knights, if that was not already plain."

"Yeah, with the Plaque and everything!" Jek said. "It's awesome to be here."

"Awesome it may be," Zedulon retorted, "but let us dote about it later. The time has indeed come for council – and I would start by knowing what Mr. Templar's part in all this is. I had not expected to meet him so soon."

Templar nodded to Zedulon. "Your majesty," he said. "For what it's worth, I'm equally surprised to learn of your involvement. But you did ask me first. Very well. Here's what I have to say for myself..."

* * *

"...So, when the Wuu Gappew spy realized he had been thoroughly found out, he did what Wuu Gappews do best..." Templar continued, coming to the tail end of his account of the Case of the Stolen Stewards, "...he got a little too excited. And in one, big, patriotic rant, he spilled the whole plan – or all he knew of it, anyway." Horus grinned to himself, recalling it. "He went well out of his way to let us know just how doomed we all are."

"Yet if he had managed to in any way impress the true extent of the Doom we face, you would not make light of it," Zedulon admonished him.

"Hmph!" Baegulgog hmphed. "To think a Wuu Gappew would have the gall to try to pass himself off as a Sowür Canpattel! And that he almost succeeded! It is unconscionable. You have my sincere thanks, Mr. Templar, for exposing my double!"

"You're very welcome," Templar replied. "And may I say, it's something of an honor to have finally met the *real* Mr. Baegulgog. The imposter is certainly no substitute for the genuine issue." The attorney's eyes went suddenly aflutter, as he searchingly reached a realization. "The only honor I would have liked better was to meet the Inquisitor. It was her thorough paperwork that made the whole crucial discovery possible. Where is Parissah? She *is* an elusive one, it seems."

Silence prevailed, with no one particularly wishing to be the one to answer.

"I've struck a nerve again, haven't I?" Templar asked.

"Yes," Audrey answered. "I'm afraid we've lost her... very recently." Jek hung his head. The Indigo Knights presently did likewise.

"I am truly sorry," Templar replied solemnly. "But I hope it brings you some solace... that you have come to a successful end of your Quest, seemingly against all odds."

"But the Quest *isn't* finished," Jek said, and all regarded him. "Don't get me wrong, I couldn't be more thrilled to have found the Knights of the Indigo Lodge... er, to have them find *me*, anyway. But knowing what's out there – what's *really* out there – I can't just walk away now. I don't want to speak for Audrey, but I need to see this thing through, whatever the outcome."

"You speak for me well enough," Audrey said. "I feel the same."

"That is well," Zedulon interjected. "For you will both be present for the battle. We all shall be. But we get ahead of ourselves. Horus Templar has yet to answer my question to my satisfaction!" He turned to the Mesomela. "The case was solved, and that might have been an end of it for you. Why are you *here*? How did *you* find the Knights?"

"They sought *me* out," Templar replied.

"Indeed," Zavion nodded. "Thine court case was quite high-profile. It was thus that we learned of thine Quest. But O! the irony! We could no sooner find thee than thou could'st find us! That is why we didst seek Mr. Templar – to see if we might glean some clue as to thine whereabouts. Thence did we learn that thou hadst taken a one Mr. Mallard's boat in search of us, and that there was rumor of a Safehouse in Roemnar that was in our keeping. We didst track thee there, but thou hadst already gone – to the north, said the Herons of the locks – but where north, they could not say. We feared that thou hadst for some cause returned unto the very belly of the beast – to Despotopia! For weeks, we did watch, and listen, for some sign of thine comings and goings. And lo! Just as we prepared to abandon all hope, we did hear word of a most momentous forthcoming execution: Two Jast-Madiiran fugitives, an Heron, and a Meduseldan. We knew naught of the Heron and Meduseldan, but the two Jast-Madiirans fit well enough! And now, perhaps, thou understandeth fully how we came to be here, and so, how thou came'st to be here thineselves."

"*You*, and *us*, yes," Zedulon agreed, but he cast an orange-hot gaze at Horus. "But not *him*!"

Templar laughed subsumedly. "You're making a grander mystery of this than it merits. Who would pass up a chance to travel with the Knights of the Indigo Lodge? Carlos Washoe is a hero of mine, as much as anyone." He looked at Audrey and Jek. "Anyway, I meant to thank you, if you could be found. If it hadn't been for your case, the odds are very good I would never have secured audience with the Czarina, to redress the legality of *In Absentia*. It's essentially the opportunity I've worked for all my life. I cannot thank the two of you enough."

"We can't thank you enough for winning our case!" Audrey replied.

Horus smiled and shook his head. "But I *didn't* win your case. I merely had it dismissed. There's an important distinction." He took a bubble pipe out of his suit jacket and soaped up. "Still, I wouldn't worry much about your legal position now, if I were you. The Knights, I think, will petition for your pardon quite energetically, when we reach the Citadel."

"That we shall," Zavion agreed. "We are persuaded of the Despotopian Doom Fleet. We did spy it out, even as we searched for thee. It is a grievous oversight on our part that this has gone undiscovered. And yet, the fiends doth wax far too clever! For verily, to enter into Meatgrinder Bay intentionally doth never occur to the mind of any sane person. How they hath mastered the Peaks, I cannot fathom. But perhaps this is where we should have thine account in full, most honored guests! Pray thou wouldst reveal all that thou knowest concerning the crooked dealings of the Kaiser."

"If you would know all," Zedulon began, "then prepare yourselves! For the tale I am about to tell will astonish you. An evil far beyond the Kaiser is at work here – the very evil I spoke of in the Chocolate Prophecy. Perhaps that will begin to explain my involvement. The mystery of the Prophecy has ever been on my mind, since the very day I spoke it. Now, at last, I have found my answers. And what I have learned, I share with you..."

* * *

And so Zedulon related his own tale, which was quite an eye-opener at the beginning for Audrey and Jek, and Baegulgog too. The rest of the story had them spellbound too, for even though they knew that part, he sure had a way of retelling it with authority. They relived afresh the terrors of Bellanchora's compound – the window on the Doom Fleet, the dizzying folding and unfolding of space, the enthralling music of the cosmos, and not the least, the Ghost-Princess herself.

"...Our Associate Parissah made a gallant effort to subdue Bellanchora," Zedulon continued. "I'm afraid that is how she met her doom. The rest of us were sent to the Kaiser, which brings us to our present crisis. We are left now with this question: How are we to defeat the Princess? That is, if there be any way to defeat her at all..."

"I have another question first," Jek said. "I listened all through your story about going undercover and your flight from The Lost City, hoping I could eventually make some sense of it. But now you've told us everything, and I'm still completely lost! *Why* in the wide, wide world did you pose as one of your attendants – implicating yourself in your own disappearance! – just to have to flee for your life across a country you could have left any time you wanted to?"

"And what about the phony battle-plans?" Audrey chipped in. "If you knew about a forthcoming attack on the Inquisition, why didn't you just warn them about *that*? Why bother to make your own attack plans, and then make them suspicious of you instead of the real bad guys?"

"Yeah," Jek agreed. "That doesn't make any sense either."

"You are not considering the bind I was in very carefully," Zedulon explained calmly. "I could *forebode* an attack on the Ocean Citadel, but I did not yet know who was going to make the attack, or why. I only knew *when*. The only way I could think of to render tangible, timely proofs of such an attack was to arrange to make one myself, so I could produce the plans to Parissah, whom I intended to meet on our journey. But it would not have done to appear as myself – as Zedulon – and say, 'I am going to attack your silly Citadel, here are all the plans.' No! I had to pose as a concerned bystander, or else the plans would have been meaningless. Parissah would have thought I had gone utterly batty to expose my own secret plot!"

Audrey and Jek hesitated. "Okay," Jek said at length, "that makes *some* sense. But still, it shouldn't have had to be that complicated. You're a respected head-of-state! You're a long-time friend of Enscharaulgk, or so I've heard. I still think you could have just gone to the Inquisition and told them what you knew, and that would have been enough."

"And say what?" Zedulon insisted. "Do you have any notion how ridiculous I would have felt if, one day, I arrived at their doorstep, only to tell them, 'You are all going to be attacked on 7/14/21, and yet I have no idea by who, or from where, or for what purpose, except that it involves a mysterious Glowy Lady'? That I would not have endured."

Jek blinked and shook his head. "You're saying you went to all that trouble, risked your safety, your life, and possibly the fate of the world just to avoid feeling ridiculous?"

Zedulon raised his head proudly. "I believe that *is* what I said."

"There's one other thing that bothers me about all that," Audrey said. "All that time we were in Roemnar, walking around in your ditches – if you'll excuse the term..."

"Not at all – the term is fitting," Zedulon did excuse her. "We do like being down in the ditches. It tends to reflect our mood."

"Okay," Audrey replied. "So yeah, we spent all that time walking around in your ditches, and yet we never once heard that you were missing! That seems like it would be big news."

"It was, you may be sure. But it is not the kind of news we would happily share with outsiders. It is rather embarrassing, to misplace one's supreme leader."

"And Herons are apparently really against any kind of embarrassment," Jek commented.

"That we are," Zedulon nodded.

"We're getting rather far-afield with this," Horus Templar said, trying to rope them back into more meaningful debate. "There's still the matter of the Ghost-Princess threatening the universe."

"Forsooth," Zavion agreed. "That is no small tidings. Bellanchora was positively a terror of old! And she doth return e'en more deadly dangerous."

"And we cannot depend on Ethon's help this time," Zedulon said. "Indeed, from what we heard, we can be quite sure he will *not* help. That leaves us in a terrible bind. She could begin to tear the universe asunder any time she chooses! Only her crusade for vengeance on Enscharaulgk now stays her hand. That, I think, will provide us an opportunity to face her again. She *will* come forward, to witness her revenge. But what will we do with that opportunity? With what weapon could we hope to assail her?"

"Books!" Audrey exclaimed. "We could use books against her!" Everyone gave her a questioning look. She returned it. "Don't you guys remember? She got really upset when that guard dropped Bronzegloom's book in her presence. And then she blew it up! I could have sworn she seemed weaker for a while after that..."

Templar nodded, deep in thought. "Perhaps you have something there," he conceded. "Books contain knowledge, and she *is* a Knowledge spirit. Perhaps she cannot help being drawn into an open book."

"It makes sense to me," Audrey nodded. "The old man may have had Water magic, but he used real water to douse the Fire Revenants in the jungle. She *is* a Knowledge spirit; she has knowledge's weaknesses. *All* its weaknesses! We could trap her in a book!"

"But what book would be daunting enough to entrap her?" Zedulon rebutted. "To contain all her great secrets? Or how many books would it take? Should we open a whole library in her presence? I'm sorry, my friend, but it is not very efficient..."

"If we only had the Pamphlet of Unknowable Things," Jek lamented. "I bet that could hold her. We need the old man back! But what chance do we have of finding him before 7/14/21?"

"Our search for him is ongoing," Zavion said. "We hath many agents still afield." But he sighed and hung his head. "However, I doth admit there is little hope of finding the elderly fellow in time. Tis a hard thing, to inquire as to the whereabouts of one who has no name."

"Is there no chance that Enscharaulgk could defeat Bellanchora, as he did before?" Horus asked. "I know she is a spirit now. But Enscharaulgk has long since learned the secret to striking a blow against what is substanceless. His many duels with Onyxadon reveal as much."

"Yet there may be many types of substancelessness – some, perhaps, more difficult to hit than others," Zedulon argued.

"Enscharaulgk probably won't even be awake for the battle," Jek pointed out. "He's been dead for generations. It would be a pretty big coincidence if he happened to wake up in the next few days."

"*Coincidence*?" Zedulon repeated. "I think not, master Jek. Remember that Bellanchora plans to take her revenge on Enscharaulgk. That it is the whole motive for this great Despotopian armament. If she has scheduled the attack for 7/14/21, then you may be sure that Enscharaulgk will awaken in time to see his Inquisition crumble. How she might predict such a chance, I cannot say. But my own heart forebodes his return is imminent."

"Then maybe we do have some hope," Audrey said.

"It is a hope in need of shoring up, then, for it is extremely remote. Her vehemence for Enscharaulgk and her single-minded focus are paramount – you may be sure she will never let him get too close. It is not as if a creature his size could sneak up on her! Not, I think, a *second* time, at any rate. No. If Bellanchora is to be dealt a fatal blow, it must be done with somewhat more discretion. *We* could handle that, perhaps – a small band in a very large battle. But still we are in need of a weapon that would serve!"

"Say no more," Zavion said, raising an ironclad hand. "The alternatives, I doth think, have been thoroughly explored. It is plain to me now – we must furnish the instrument that thou requireth. Come hither!"

He led them all to the back of the room – to the very Plaque that Jek had shown to Audrey. But when he reached the Plaque, it retracted, revealing a recessed compartment. From within, a small shelf emerged. And on it a single, dark object. A spot of light shone down in a beaming ray – the source of which, none could be sure. It bathed the black object with a celestial splendor. At once, Audrey perceived the form of this hidden relic. Deeply moved, she spoke what was on her heart…

"It's a boot," she said.

"Thou speaketh true!" Zavion said, his voice exultant. "But tis *more* than a boot! Tis the *left* Boot, of the pair that did once belong to brother Carlos Washoe – chiefest and greatest of our order! And of all the many relics in our keeping, tis the most powerful by far!"

"*My gosh...*" Jek marveled. "To be *this close* to something Carlos Washoe wore on his feet! Someone pinch me!"

"But it's just a boot," Audrey insisted.

"Nay, thou dost not understandeth, fair lady," Zavion explained, with the other Knights gathered round him solemnly. "With his kicks did brother Washoe cure the world... and seldom did he ever deliver a kick which did not first passeth through his boots. An hundred times or more, this Boot thou seeth before thee was the very instrument of our fair earth's salvation. But this is no mere remembrance! For ere he entrusted this Boot unto our keeping, brother Washoe did store within it one more of his great kicks! He did this, so that in the time of our greatest need, we should not be forsaken. I believe the hour has now come, when the world's only hope of redemption is another kick from Carlos Washoe!" It all began to seem very hopeful, until, at this juncture, Zavion fell into a slouch. "Yet alas! Even this solution hath its flaw. I fear that we, the Knights of the Indigo Lodge, are quite unable to wield this Boot against Bellanchora."

"But why?" Audrey asked.

"Because, spirit or no, and incomparable villain or no, Bellanchora *is* a lady – and our strict code of chivalry most assuredly doth not permit us to kick a lady! Tis near the very first rule of the chivalrous credo..."

"Well, darn," Audrey lamented.

"Even so, I have something of an expedient solution in mind, if thou art willing to entertain it," Zavion continued. "Doest thee, Audrey and Jek, truly mean to see thine Quest through unto the very end?"

They looked at each other, eyes searching deep, and finding firm conviction. They joined hands, adopting a mushy quality to the moment. "We do," they answered.

"Then, if thou art also willing, it is within the scope of my authority to initiate thee into the ranks of the Indigo Knights." Jek beamed, and Audrey smiled back. "Thine exploits reveal two people of stalwart character, and that is one requirement. However, there is another! Thou hast to be good at fighting."

"I trained them myself!" Zedulon interjected. "They have much to learn, but they are worthy pupils. Already they can handle themselves in a pinch."

"That doth suffice," Zavion replied. "Worthy indeed are any students of the Proconsul." He turned back to Audrey and Jek. "Would thou becomest Knights of the Indigo Lodge?"

"We would."

"Raise thine right hands."

They raised their hands.

"Huzzah! Thou art now auxiliary members of the Lodge! Welcome brother Jek, and sister Audrey!"

"Brother Jek, sister Audrey," the other Knights present hailed them, kneeling to each.

"Cool!" Audrey said. "I get to be the first woman Knight of the Indigo Lodge."

Now, the Knights all exchanged looks. "Begging thine pardon, sister Audrey, but that is not so."

She couldn't help looking a little disappointed. "It's not?"

"No!" Jek laughed suddenly. "Not even close!"

"Thou art the twenty-first woman to attain Knighthood, sister."

"Well, gosh!" Audrey said. "Why haven't I ever heard about any of these others?"

"I could not say," Zavion replied. "There art a number of books in which some of them appear."

"That would be why, then," Audrey sighed.

"A book or two may be written of thee, sister, if we are successful in our gambit," Zavion continued. "For now that thou art member, it is to thee that we intend to entrust the Boot." Zavion took the Boot from its shelf, and kneeling with head bowed, presented it to Audrey.

"For real?" she asked, her face cringing somewhat. To accept some guy's centuries-old boot didn't immediately appeal to her.

"Verily," Zavion said. "Tis the perfect remedy to our quandary. We, as chivalrous men, cannot kick the evil Princess. But as thou art woman, thou art bound by no such restrictions."

She took the Boot doubtfully. "I guess that makes sense," she said, holding it at arm's length at first. Then, mustering courage, she brought it in close for a sniff.

"*Wow,*" she said, suddenly overwhelmed by an extremely impressive fragrance.

"Ah," Zavion said. "Thou hast smelt of the Boot."

"I thought it would be really gross," she replied, examining the leathery footwear. "Some old sweaty boot festering in a locker for who-knows-how-long. But it smells great!"

"It is by no means a sweaty boot! Only once in all his life didst brother Washoe begrudge a bead of sweat; unfortunately that relic is not to be found here. Tis the odor of pure manliness that thou detects! Tis pleasant to a lady, but on other men it hath a powerful humbling effect." Audrey continued to smile at the Boot, even as the other Knights and Jek started to slump from the fumes.

"I suppose I should just put it on then..." Audrey said, setting the Boot down and reaching to unlace her own...

"Nay!" Zavion stopped her urgently. "Not until the final hour shouldst thou weareth the Boot, sister. It doth contain one kick of Carlos Washoe – and *only* one! Even once thy foot doth wear the Boot, thou must taketh the greatest care! Thou must not falter or stumble! For if the kick be unleashed, whatsoever it kicketh will surely come to ruin! And the kick will then be lost, and all hope of defeating Bellanchora shall go with it."

"Yikes," Audrey said, and she took the Boot back up. "Maybe you should take this back for now, then." She handed it to Zavion.

"We shall keep it, sister," he nodded, and put the Boot back on its shelf, whence it retracted back behind the Plaque.

"This is a hopeful turn," Zedulon said, giving his weighty approval to all that had transpired. "There is some destiny in it. Though perhaps less destiny than we would wish." He closed his eye, concentrating. "Alas, I can *see* the battle, in all its rolling fury! But it's shape, and its *outcome*... those I cannot now perceive." He opened his eye, and seemed to cheer up somewhat. "Yet I believe there *is* hope for the future, after all! I foresee that we Associates shall all be reunited, upon a private investigator's fishing boat!"

"You mean Art's fishing boat?" Horus asked. "I already gave that to Jek and Audrey..."

"Yeah," Audrey agreed. "All that already happened."

"Hm," Zedulon said. "That is regrettable."

"At any rate, I think we have done our best to address the threat of the Princess herself," Baegulgog suddenly chimed in. "But we are neglecting the Doom Fleet! That is a matter of no small consideration. From our vantage alone, I spied 272 able warships. That is 272 in *Human* numerals, mind you! A grand armament, indeed."

"That does sound substantial," Horus remarked. "And I foresee another problem. Jast-Madiir is responding to the threat by gathering its whole navy to St. Argonsburg. The Czarina expects the Kaiser's vengeance to fall on *her*. And to that end, she has been petitioning the Inquisition for warships to back her up."

"That is grievous!" Zedulon exclaimed. "After I went to such lengths to be sure the Inquisition's strength would be in the proper place! Your Czarina has confused their council."

"I am very sorry about that," Horus lamented. "In a way, it's my fault. I exposed the plot of the Doom Fleet... but I could learn nothing about who it was directed at. I am as guilty of presuming that Despotopia would come for Jast-Madiir as anyone."

"Take heart, gathered friends," Zavion encouraged them. "There is still time to sort this matter out ahead of ourselves. We hath pigeons."

"Then let us send messages to the Czarina and the Citadel at once!" Zedulon commanded.

*   *   *

They all rushed topside to the place where the pigeons were kept, Zavion scrawling messages even as he speed-walked. Then he stamped them with a signet – the mark of the Indigo Lodge – a curious shape, which looked nearly the same if you rotated it 180 degrees – a fact that had long made the Knights suspect in some of the more backwater places of the world. Audrey felt an odd frantic feeling – a sort of desperateness – like no amount of haste would now suffice to complete this simple errand. Something sinister was about to happen, or else was already happening, though they could not perceive it yet...

Halfway across the deck, they heard calls from behind. All turned in sudden alarm. But the voice was friendly.

"Hark!" called the voice. Audrey squinted. In the gathering cascade of dusky colors, she spied the glint of armor as first one man, then many others, came running up the ramp and onto the deck. "Hark, brethren! We must put to sea at once! Our location will soon be made!" The other Indigo Knights had returned.

"Calm thyself, brother Orellius!" Zavion replied. "Declare yourself plainly. What doth transpire? Where art brothers Jarod, Palintar, Reginald, Gilgamesh, Sorenson and Bartimus?"

Orellius and his company ran to a halt, and they hung their heads. "They come never back," he answered solemnly, if breathlessly. "But our own fate doth remain uncertain! Spies of the enemy are fast on our heels!"

As if on cue, Audrey heard the echo of distant birdsong. She looked into the twilit sky over Despotopia, and lo, an enormous host of little tweety birds filled the air! The Princess had evidently learned of their escape from the Kaiser...

"What is this devilry?" Zavion asked.

"It is the work of Bellanchora!" Zedulon explained. "By nature, a Princess enjoys fellowship with birds such as these. But she has corrupted them to ill use, enthralling them as unwilling spies!"

"He's right," Jek said. "She's used them against us before... but never in such numbers!"

"We must send the pigeons at once!" Zavion said, but Zedulon stopped him.

"It is useless now," he said. "These birds will surely intercept any message we try to send. The pigeons would be overwhelmed at once." He sighed. "We have already failed."

"But we must leave at once!" Orellius reminded them. "The birds are but the vanguard – surely leading the Kaiser's army towards us. This coast is no longer any place for the Lodge!"

Zavion paused in a moment of doubt. But looking to Zedulon, he at last decided that there was nothing more for it. "Then let us away," he said, and they all withdrew back below deck, just as quickly as they'd come...

* * *

Later, as the Lodge was speeding away, Audrey and Jek found themselves in lodging of their own – the room previously belonging to brother Palintar. It was more than a little morose, knowing that they had taken the room of one who had given his life to save them. Despotopia had fallen to evil and needed to be resisted, it was true. But Audrey couldn't rationalize the cost – six lives lost to save four. *Three*, not counting Baegulgog, who was likely in no lasting danger.

Then, there was the other life that had been lost. Parissah's horrific death was still fresh in Audrey's mind. Jek was sullen and withdrawn, and she knew at once that he was remembering her too.

She sat next to him, running her fingers through his hair. She looked right at him. He was slow in returning her look, and often his eyes flitted away.

"You're taking this pretty hard, aren't you?" Audrey asked openly.

"What do you mean?" Jek asked. "I just became an Indigo Knight. Never in my wildest dreams, Audrey... I mean, it's still surreal that we're even here, among them! Things are great, for the moment. Everything should be great..."

"But you miss her," Audrey insisted.

He nodded silently, wrapping his arms around his legs, nearly resting his chin on his knees. "It's sort of ridiculous, really. I barely knew her. She was all business, and she was overbearing and impatient. But she was a lot of other things too. She was diligent, strong, full of conviction. And everything we did with her seemed so important. I feel like I could've gone on forever like that, Audrey. Just us Traveling Associates, solving one mystery after another together, with her leading the way."

"You admired her," Audrey said. "I understand. There's something of a special friendship between me and Marrow... that is, between me and Zedulon. I can't really explain it either. We're very different people, just like you and Parissah were very different. But I think that's part of what made us such fast friends."

Jek sighed. "If she considered me a friend, I wouldn't know. But you're right – I did admire her. I wish I'd had the opportunity to say so, before..." and he trailed off.

"I'm sorry, Jek," she said, hugging his neck. He returned the hug, holding her in a firm embrace.

Then he kissed her right cheek...

She blushed, and pulled back, searching his eyes.

"I guess that's one thing that's been on my mind a lot since she passed – the important things left unsaid in life," Jek lamented, teary-eyed. "I love you, Audrey. Carrying on without Parissah is going to be hard. But I would never make it without you. Looking back on all those months we ran that lighthouse together – an eternity ago, it seems – I can't shake the awe of it. If it hadn't been for... for all this... I might've gone through the rest of my life never knowing that the whole time, I was sharing it with the most amazing person in the world. And nothing – not the honor of Knighthood, not the thrills of adventure, not all the wonders of the universe paraded before my very eyes compares with that.

"I know I don't give you much reason to love me back, Audrey. You should've had a proper Prince for a husband – a man of real distinction and courage. But the universe might be about to end... and even if it doesn't, I don't really expect to survive. It's still just as clear to me as it ever was – what my part in this Quest is. I'm a one-time redemption for you, Audrey. Sooner or later, one way or another, I'm going to have to give my all, so that you can go on to your destiny. But before I die, I just wanted you to know how I felt."

Audrey began to tear up herself. She felt ashamed. She didn't know what to say.

Just as she might've tried, there was a knock at the door. Jek sighed and closed his eyes. Audrey called out in a cracking voice. "Come in," she said.

It was Zavion. "Begging thine pardon, brother Jek and sister Audrey. We art presently holding a vigil for our fallen brethren, to which thou art invited. Thou may, if it is thine wish, light a candle for thine fallen friend the Inquisitor as well. We did e'en offer to light a candle for the Clerk Baegulgog, since he be currently deceased, but he politely declined. Wilt thou come forth?"

Audrey looked at Jek, deferring to him.

"Yes," he said. "It's the least we can do. For her... and for all of them."

* * *

The vigil was indeed a solemn spectacle. The Knights, who had seemed so jolly at the start of the day, were now slow and silent in their grief. The lights were low, so that each newly lit candle appeared to shine very bright. Six in all the Knights lit, one after the other in a solemn procession. But they had set one final candle for Parissah...

"So we honor brothers Jarod, Palintar, Reginald, Gilgamesh, Sorenson, and Bartimus – brave Knights, whose gallantry we knew in life didst confirm itself in death. And now, we would also like to honor the passing of Parissah – an Inquisitor true. Long hath fellowship endured between the Lodge and the Inquisition... and may that fellowship continue ever on, unto the Great Looking-Back of all Things." Zavion gestured to Jek. "Thou may lighteth the candle, brother Jek."

As ceremoniously as he could, Jek lit the candle for Parissah. He basked in its soft, warm glow a few seconds, feeling some affirmation, however slight in all the sorrow.

But then, to his amazement, the candle started to flicker, as if caught by some rogue wind. His heart leapt. And then it froze entirely. He watched helplessly as the flame was snuffed out before him, going up in an uncaring thin grey line of smoke...

Jek was mortified. It felt as if the universe itself had denied them the dignity of their grief for a worthy friend. There were not words for his horror.

"*Egad*," Zavion said softly. Jek was hardly comforted by this gentle outburst. "This is a strange omen, indeed," he continued. "I doth wonder what it portends..."

Sins of the Father

"Be very thankful you live in a world of many strict rules. Without such a foundation, all things we find valuable and virtuous quickly become meaningless. Even mercy means nothing apart from rules. Yes, perhaps mercy most of all."

- Magormissahr, *Referendums on the World, Vol. 5*

The first thing she was aware of was a smell like vinyl. Her nostrils flared reflexively, followed by a tingling sensation. That sensation quickly flourished intensely, like an electric shock that passed through her snout before convulsing the whole length of her body.

Her body. But was it? An uncanny sense of displacement struck her at once, like she didn't belong... an invader – or a prisoner – in her own flesh! Every single jump-started nerve ending was alien to her. The feeling was immediately severe and nightmarish. She gasped in a fit of terrible anxiety as it gripped her heart. This, too, proved overwhelming. That first gasp of air was sharp and piercing, and those first frenzied beats of the heart were hard and fresh.

It all felt new.

It all felt different.

She was nearly lost to the terror...

Fortunately, some orderly corner of her mind imposed itself on the fright reflex, wrestling it quickly into a semblance of moderation. *Peace, creature*, she seemed to tell herself. *You will make sense of this. Keep taking stock.*

The determination to investigate rationally met some swift resistance, for one of the first things she noticed was that her supply of air was quickly growing very thin and hot. Suddenly she realized that she was bound up in some thick, leathery substance. Remembering her arms, she swatted furiously to free herself. The leather disappeared in an instant, filling all her sight with blinding light. *Her sight*! This, too, she had forgot... before this dramatic reminder...

Slowly, the vision of a room resolved. It was the first thing that felt familiar to her at all, even if the colors seemed a bit off – a little more vibrant, a little more violet-tinted, and perhaps a bit smaller than she remembered. But this was *her* room. There was her wardrobe, her feeding tray, her washboard, her armory – everything she owned exactly where she always kept it.

As her eyesight returned to the full, she looked down where she sat, still gasping with strong lungs. She thought she had freed herself from the leather with her arms. But now – to her great surprise – seeing her limbs sprawled in front of her, she realized the leather and her arms had been one and the same...

And they weren't *arms* anymore...

Those are new, she thought.

Checking around a bit more, it turned out she *did* still have arms, too... which came as somewhat of a relief. She racked her brain trying to move them – limp things hanging from her sides. Finally she strained the right set of neurons, and her arms came twitching and fidgeting to life. For some moments, she studied these limbs, puzzling out the dynamics of using a new part of her brain for old motor skills.

As she clumsily and shakily tumbled her hands in front of her – strange, mere three-digited things – it all started to come back, albeit rather slowly. Who she was, what had happened, and how she had arrived in this present predicament. Her head craned on its long neck, and she peered under her bed, seeing the very stuff that had made this doom possible as it shimmered faintly in the shadows. Her breath relaxed, and she heaved a hollowing sigh. She was no longer terrified. But this was a moment she had dreaded for ages – the prelude to a long walk of shame and disgrace. The reckoning for her long trespass was upon her...

Best to get on with it.

She stood on wobbly legs, climbing off the bed, retrieving a black sheet for a shroud. It was immediately plain her clothes would no longer fit. Though it would hardly lessen her dishonor, she certainly did not intend to make the journey in her bare scales. And she was particularly careful to conceal her face...

Just willing herself to open the door proved perhaps the hardest part. But in her first fluid motion, she opened it... and began the long march. The high paths of the Citadel glistened in the bright shafts and rays of day – a veritable cascade of light soaked each nook and cranny. There was no concealing her passing. The timeless light of four hundred generations filled those halls. Many Inquisitors she passed, each stopped dead in their purposeful tracks, looking up with surprise and dismay at the trespasser in their midst. Most eventually turned their backs to her, as was proper. But a few were particularly troubled – suddenly bewildered and bereaved – so that they hesitated, gazing on with sorrow in their hearts.

"Do not forget your duty!" she told them. "I am disgraced. You must turn away."

The parade through that bend of the Citadel went on for ages. Haste might have been in order. But she took the walk slow. Why, she didn't know. It was just too solemn, too fateful, and too long in the coming for her to willingly expediate this final journey she was making. There could be no quick relief for her. Nor should there be.

Looking out to her left, she passed countless windows on the sea, and she spied many of the Inquisition's warships, deployed beyond the embrace of the Citadel's wide, curling arms. To her right were other windows, overlooking the vast and deep racks of the artificial harbor, where many more warships were still berthed, layer upon layer. She took heart, seeing that the bulk of the fleet had indeed returned from the Tophthaeran blockade.

But even as she watched, she saw that the great pumps were being primed, and the ships themselves made ready to be flushed into the harbor. It was cause for alarm. She did not know the day, or how long she had been gone. Perhaps Doom was already upon them. Or perhaps the fleet was about to be drawn away by some diversion – whether by one she could guess at, or some other unforeseen calamity or ruse, she did not know. But such a massed deployment did not bode well, the more she considered it...

Finally, she reached the Citadel's tower. The stories-high walls of the main path withdrew as she entered a vaulted space that climbed up to the reaches of the sky, and dove down on either side into a bright abyss. It was a colossal enclosure, and on all sides of the walkways frantic bands rolled over countless guide-wheels, with hundreds of thousands of feet worth of tape passing through the great hollows of the tower every few minutes. The endless droning of the speeding data tape was very loud at first (especially in her newer, wider earholes), but its sonic power retreated very quickly after she reached and rounded the edge of the Wide Path. A new sound echoed down from a sunbathed vista so high above as to be nearly out of sight. The Pi Chorus was even now singing forth the day's new digit. Reverent and beautiful... even surreal were their voices, as they extoled the latest in the unending series of values comprising the Circular Infinity – Pi – the hallowed wonder of the Creators.

In her mind's eye, she could see the splendor of that high chamber – the whole sky caught in a panoramic shaft of stained tiles, ivory arches and burnished brasswork, with the whole allegoric history of the earth splayed out overhead in brilliant frescos centuries in the drawing – the Glass Chapel. It was the lofty perch of *Pharonomagnus*. Supreme reigned this instrument in all the world – the pipe organ to end all pipe organs – a true behemoth, whose voice could shake the very foundations of the Citadel, when it chose...

Today, the thing was silent. She strained to hear some shadow of a melody in the pipes so high above, just as she should have, for it always had partaken of the Pi Chorus' daily ritual. For a moment, she almost had herself convinced that she heard such music faintly, even if it was coming from a universe away. But her deepest powers of imagination could not belie the plain indifference of *Pharonomagnus* today.

Not a note would it grudge.

Rather than worry overmuch about it, she focused on the Chorus instead. *Seven*, she said, translating the daily digit to herself. *Somehow, I suppose there is poetry in that...*

The Wide Path led deeper, into the utmost fastness of the great oceanic outpost. For a stretch in that enormous, yawning hall, there was little light. For here the superstructure was thickest, and the weight of the miles-high tower rested on forked supports, forming a sort of huge, dark tunnel between them. Still unsure on her new legs, she fumbled and faltered in that dim expanse, surely looking the part of a proper spook, as she continued to seed dismay among her former comrades wherever she went – a grief deep and sharp and unspoken.

But the shadow passed, and again the rays of the blinding world outside rained down on her. Just a few hundred more yards, and she would be at the threshold. At the *door*.

Ahead, she saw Guards – Inquisitors with huge snail guns, keeping watch over the last chamber. Entering their midst proved a moment of uncertainty. For a guilty one to approach this place was unheard of. She considered they would be within their right to shoot her on the spot. But of course, she would only try again...

Perhaps they knew that. Or perhaps they showed some partiality, where they should not. But whatever the case, the Guards simply turned away from her. Unresisted, she reached the very final steps before the door...

Then she stopped.

And there she fell to her knees in a broken stoop, resting the backs of her hands on the ground, her new limbs sprawled flat behind her.

And there, like that, she would stay.

She would stay until someone was forced to make her move. Either back, to the exile she had earned. Or else forward, into his presence...

She knew, of course, there was no telling how long she might have to wait there, in a slump on the ground. Time was pressing and much might yet be done... but there was no other audience to be had for her now. Her former peers would be obliged not to heed a word she might try to tell them. He alone *might* listen... and even that, she deemed unlikely. And with the time that was left, and he still asleep, perhaps she would achieve nothing here but to wait for the End...

And, even if somehow the world were to endure the coming storm, she knew he may yet sleep for years... or *decades*... to come...

But it was absurd to imagine it turning out that way. Doom hinged on what happened here. Everything came down to this. Either Enscharaulgk would revive just in time to save the world... the very way he had already done hundreds of times throughout history. Or, he would at last sleep *too* long... and all hope would fail forever...

So there she knelt. And there, having already forfeit all honor, she dared a final heresy. She appealed to the Creators, that Enscharaulgk should awaken. It was a silent petition – one they could not hear across the Undervoid, and one they should never have heeded if they could...

Long she knelt, until grief and despair overtook her, and she could not any longer endure the sight of the closed door. But still she would not be moved. She simply hung her head. She hung it until the pure, convicting light that bathed the floor around her proved unendurable too, leaving her only to close her eyes. The Guard changed, and the white light of the Path began to yellow. And still she knelt. She endured some crowds of silent gawkers – pardonable on their part, perhaps, since few had ever beheld a trespasser... and certainly never one who would willingly submit herself to the judgment of Enscharaulgk. And still she knelt. The day gave way entirely to a pitch-black night, which turned again to pallid day. And *still* she knelt. She knelt alone, hopeless and forsaken, feeling ever more foolish for it, knowing certainly that the Grand Inquisitor – should he wake – would only send her away. She knelt in utter defeat, surrendering at last to a viral fatalism, wishing that the End would simply come...

Then... and *only* then... the door parted.

Ruddy, golden light spilled out into the Wide Path. The Guards turned, gazing within. But she kept her head down. The door resounded – its enormous halves lurching to a halt, now fully open. Silence slowly returned. And still she did not stir nor peak.

Finally, a warm, rich, nearly omnipresent voice arose. "*Why*, young one?" the voice asked her, full of sorrow. She tried to prepare some apology, though of course it would redeem nothing. But she only had a moment to stammer before he spoke again...

"Why do you sit so downcast? Get up! Come here and talk a while with me...

"...Parissah."

The Grand Reunion

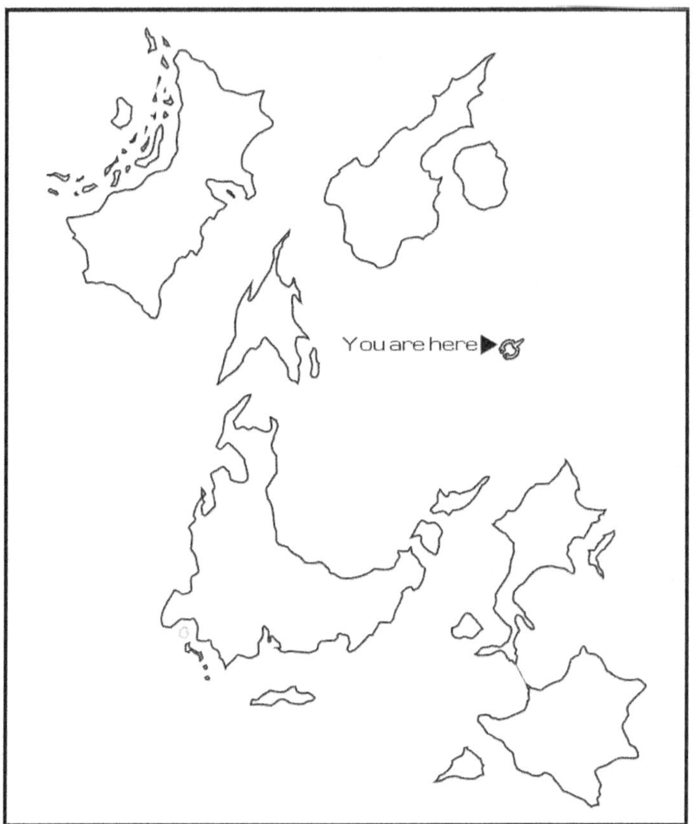

"I love long goodbyes. Why? Because every long goodbye forebodes a long hello."

- Charlize Monophli, *Mushy Stuff*

It's too big, Jek kept thinking to himself. *It's just way too big!*

And really, he was right. The scale of the Ocean Citadel was absolutely bananas. At present, the top of its tower was not to be seen. It was veiled in clouds – and not especially low clouds, it seemed. Still reaching hundreds of feet above the water level, the tower cast out great, scooping arms, forming a sanctuary harbor. As the Lodge drew closer and closer to the arms, the station's proportions became baffling. The turreted ends of the harbor now seemed to reach the heavens – clear and dark metal monoliths. But the *real* tower was still very far off... and all that far side of the Citadel was light and blueish behind the haze of the atmosphere, so that it looked as if it had been painted into the sky.

And still they had not yet reached the harbor. Even at the impressive pace the Lodge could set, that might yet take some minutes...

Presently, Audrey and Baegulgog joined Jek – he sitting down above deck, towards the bow of the Lodge. There was little use standing here – the top of the ship was not railed nor guarded against people falling overboard, since there were no duties to perform on the top surface, and no real reason to be up there. Only the whimsical desire to see the Citadel as they approached it had drawn Jek out. But even if standing on the deck had been a steady and sure experience, he might just as well have been floored by what he saw...

"Have you been here before too, Audrey?" he asked.

"A few times," she answered. "Even Inquisitors need supplies and stuff."

He looked at her, more puzzled than ever by the evenness of her response. "Is that all you have to say? I suppose even this... *all* of this... doesn't daunt you."

"Are you kidding?" she said, sitting down next to him. "Of course it does! The Inquisition Citadel is ridiculous! It's *way* too big!"

"That's just what I was thinking," he nodded.

"It is two miles in diameter, all round the arc of the arms," Baegulgog told them. "If you wish to know just *how* too big it is. Few earthly structures even approach the scope of *Variglew* Bridge and the sprawling Archives of Berlberi. But even they are dwarfed for mass, next to this."

Jek smiled back at their friend the Clerk. He had dawned a fresh Berlberi uniform, having recently solidified. It was nice to see him alive. Jek decided to say as much. "You're looking well, Baegulgog," he said.

"Yes, once again I am whole... and not since my cavalry days have I found myself saying that nearly so often! But perhaps after this next great battle, I can be done with death for a spell. It becomes rather a nuisance."

Jek snickered a bit. "We should all have such a problem."

Baegulgog flashed brightly, seeming a bit embarrassed. "I am sorry if I seem to make light of such things. Rest assured, whatever I may say concerning myself, I do not think of death quite so trivially as I used to..." He was sullen then, drooping in the air, and they heard an ocean-swell pass under the bow before he continued. "It has taken from me the two greatest friends I have ever known... and ever wish to know." Unexpectedly, he pointed a tentacle at each of them accusingly. "So it is on the two of you to survive this battle with the

Doom Fleet! For as much as I love to tally things, I would prefer not to add to my list of dead friends, if it may be helped. It is the only list I have which I count already much too long."

"We'll try, Baegulgog," Jek said, feeling rather daunted as he considered his own response. "We'll certainly try."

Finally, they passed within the arms of the Citadel's harbor. Even as they did so, Jek was again overcome. He'd briefly been shown countless alien planets, and had even stepped out of the known universe for a time. But this new experience was surreal to him in an entirely different way. The Ocean Citadel was not other-worldly. Rather, it was the opposite extreme. To behold the Citadel was like being shown the protruding end of some cosmic pillar that the whole earth rested on – a fulcrum or focal point of reality as they knew it, and as it had been known by hundreds of generations that came before. It was the fortress to begin and end all fortresses – the cornerstone and dwelling of peace and order given adamant, ironclad form. Presently, strength was issuing from its many sheltered berths – dozens or hundreds of advanced warships were deploying, or had just been deployed.

And so, if only for a passing time, Jek was relieved of his worry, seeing plainly that Princess Bellanchora's intent to throw this grand place down was a fool's dream and an impossible errand. Surely a bastion such as this could endure a hundred Doom Fleets!

So it seemed to Jek, just then, in the stark shadows of the Citadel, under the full light of day, when trouble and doubt were still out of sight... if only just over the horizon...

They sailed long and slow through the harbor, until at last they were approached. No warships troubled them, for the Inquisitors knew the Knights and their Lodge. Rather, it was a pair of tugboats that greeted them, helping to guide and moor the Indigo Lodge against a long , enormous ramp that extended out and down from the Citadel's principle tower.

Soon enough, they stood on that ramp, and were greeted by Inquisitors. Some doubt returned to Jek, as he remembered that Audrey and he were still considered fugitives in Jast-Madiir. He turned to Horus Templar, who had come forward with them.

"So, how exactly *do* we stand after the dismissal of our case?" he asked the big Mesomela. "Can we be quite sure they won't arrest us here and now?"

"I'll make sure of it," Horus assured him. "And if not I, then doubltess Zavion and the Knights can persuade them. And you also have the Heron Proconsul's voucher. I wouldn't worry."

Jek nodded. That sounded adequate.

"Hail, Knights of the Indigo Lodge, and assorted guests, including his Highness the Proconsul," an Inquisitor greeted them. "Your appearance here was not anticipated. But it is little wonder, with the present state of affairs. Always the Knights have come unlooked-for, in the hour of the world's greatest need. We welcome you now. Enscharaulgk himself welcomes you."

"Enscharaulgk doth wake? That is happy tidings!" Zavion declared. "And, I gather from thine speech, he is made aware, to some degree, of the coming of Doom. Pray, good Inquisitor, what has Enshcaraulgk been apprised of?"

"Everything," the Inquisitor replied. "Unless you bring some new word. He knows that Bellanchora comes, bent on vengeance against him."

"Then he knows what we would tell him," Zavion marveled. "I call it strange indeed. The devices of the enemy prevented us from sending timely word." Jek frowned as his thought was momentarily directed back at the host of birds circling above. "Yet word has reached our good Grand Inquisitor all the same! How may this be?"

"Enscharaulgk himself will answer for that. He comes forward."

"He doth?" Zavion asked. Then there was a heavy tremor throughout the ramp. "*Oh*! Indeed he doth..."

The tremors continued in a steady cadence. Jek looked back and saw ripples on the ocean where the ramp went down to meet it. He gulped. Enscharaulgk, the Zenithyst Inquisitor, a colossus left over from the world's youth, caretaker of the Archipelago since before the founding of the Citadel itself, and unrivaled guardian of all good things through the ages, was drawing near...

But from the very moment he first beheld Ensharaulgk, Jek was not afraid. Though the ancient dragon was indeed much larger than Jek's wildest imagining, not unlike his great Citadel. He was *enormous* – swelled with the size of his countless lives. Many he had spent, in the feral treasure-hunting days of his youth. And many more still he had *given,* in defense of the world against Onyxadon, Bellanchora, and so many other, nameless terrors. His body had grown so incredibly huge that it didn't even seem to know how to manage itself anymore. He had an excess of limbs, with an extra set of forearms protruding from his front legs, and his wings numbered three-pair. And all this vast bulk was clad in thick steel. A stately suit of armor indeed he wore, befitting a champion who had hurled himself to the front lines of a thousand cataclysms. He looked absolutely unassailable – shining as a bright paragon even in the deep shade of his Citadel, like shadows could not easily fall on him. His every long breath was scalding, so that his guests were greatly discomforted, until he craned his great head into the sky, and they could breathe easily again. His last step shook Jek from the surface of the ramp, and he nearly stumbled. But even so, Jek didn't know a moment of fear. Through all the armor and the heat and the strength and the mass, there beat a gentle heart that was plain for all to see. No, Jek was not afraid, standing before the biggest, mightiest, most deadly creature on the face of the earth. He was overjoyed.

Long did the Grand Inquisitor regard his guests from the top of his high neck. At length, he deigned to speak, and his voice was like the rolling of the sea, or the echo of space... or else the unfolding of some other, greater frontier, yet unimagined...

"Hi there," he said.

"*Wow*," Jek whispered to himself.

"Hello, friend Enscharaulgk," Zedulon replied, and Jek was amazed at how the voice of the small Heron did not shrink next to the greatness of the one he answered. "You have tarried long in slumber. But again, you awaken, only just in time to meet the trial."

"Oh, it's you, Zedulon!" Enscharaulgk exclaimed in sudden realization. "What a wonderful surprise! How have you been, old buddy?"

"Terrible," Zedulon replied.

"That is good to hear," Enscharaulgk nodded warmly. "And what of these others with you? The Humans, Jek and Audrey, trusty Sowür Canpattel Clerk Baegulgog, the Knights of the Indigo Lodge, and this other Mesomela I was not advised of..."

"Horus Templar," Horus introduced himself. "Pleased to meet you."

"The pleasure is mine, I'm sure," Enscharaulgk replied. "I admit I do not know of you. But you would have to be a really good guy, to stand in the midst of ones such as these."

Jek was quite embarrassed. Enscharaulgk spoke as if he knew little old him... by *name*, no less! And not only that – he seemed to reckon he had some appreciable measure of character! It was all too much...

"But how in the world did you know my name, and Jek's?" Audrey asked before Jek could collect his own thoughts.

"I know all that a friend of yours could tell me, young Audrey," Enscharaulgk assured her. "*Two* friends, in fact. Dear little lady, I have known about *you* for hundreds of years! You shouldn't wonder about it. Zedulon has always cherished the friendship you now share." Audrey looked back at Zedulon, who also seemed embarrassed now. "It is from him that I first heard your name. He has told me your *right* name as well. Though I understand you don't prefer that name, so I won't use it here. Not now."

"But you said *two* friends," Audrey counted back to him. "Who is the other?"

A heightened warmth and eagerness came over the Grand Inquisitor just then. "I'm so glad you asked! It just so happens I have a very special surprise for the ones known as the Traveling Associates. Trust me – this will really make your day!"

His huge head turned on his huge neck, and he gazed back to the mouth of the Citadel that opened on the ramp. Apparently on cue, someone came out from the deeper shadows. Another Inquisitor – a very large one, Jek soon realized... though it had been hard to tell at first, all things looking quite tiny next to Enscharaulgk. This puzzled Jek to no end. Again, he had expected the old man to suddenly appear... or perhaps Zeph Bronzegloom. Though even *he* would not have known to refer to them as the Traveling Associates...

Who was this Inquisitor? This strange, eight-foot-tall Inquisitor he had never met? He had known only one Inquisitor in his life, really...

But surely, it couldn't be...

"Parissah?" Baegulgog was the first to ask, as the large one reached their midst. "Is that you, madam?"

"Hello, Baegulgog," the Inquisitor replied, in an uncannily familiar voice.

"Bless my desk drawers, it *is* you! Dear, dear friend Parissah!" Baegulgog exclaimed, floating lazily up to embrace her, tentacles flung wide. Soon he had her coiled up as he bawled incoherently, quite beside himself with unexpected joy.

"It is wonderful to see you, Baegulgog," Parissah said gruffly, sounding rather uncomfortable. "But please let go. You are both constricting and electrocuting me."

"Oh dear, how clumsy," Baegulgog replied, recoiling. "Please forgive my outburst! But I am so very relieved! I thought never to see you again!"

"There is nothing to forgive on your part, my friend," she assured him. "Though unpleasant, it was a far happier greeting than I merit. Of course, you did not expect me. But how relieved I am to see you! When last I knew, Bellanchora had hurled you into space! I feared you would be lost there forever." She looked over all the Associates. "Indeed, I counted all of you lost. It is a joy beyond hope that you have returned safely! How ever did you manage?"

"It was the Knights," Audrey explained. "They heard we were looking for them, so they came looking for us. And it seems they found us just in time."

"Then this is thine friend, the lost Inquisitor?" Zavion asked in wonder. "Zounds! What a merry chance!"

"Truly remarkable," Horus Templar shook his head, and he walked up to Parissah straight away. "So this is the elusive Parissah I gave up all hope of ever meeting." He held a hand out to her. "May I shake your hand?"

"Why?" Parissah asked, naturally not knowing him from her elbow.

"I'll explain some other time," Horus replied, still holding his hand out with an eager look.

"Alright," she said. And they shook hands.

Without a thought, Jek came up and shook her hand too. "I'm so glad you're back," he said, rather emotional... and still lost in disbelief. "But how? How did you survive?"

"Is that not quite apparent?" she asked. "I am a trespasser. All along, I have had a treasure."

Jek was shocked! Now it made perfect sense that she was alive again. It was the very nature of the Avarica – the dragon-folk. But he had never imagined that Parissah of all people would break the very strictest rule of her order! Even now, hearing her speak the very words, he couldn't believe it...

"Then that was *your* Zenithyst!" Audrey exclaimed suddenly. Jek shot her a questioning look, struggling to think what she was talking about. "You remember, Jek," she assured him. "The one you gave Faucette, when we negotiated with her. The one you thought was *mine*."

Jek marveled, being reminded of the great quandary of that Zenithyst, which seemed lifetimes ago now. "Is that true?" he asked, searching up at Parissah for an answer, even as he thought it through himself. "But of course! It *must* be true! You were the last one to handle my dad's bowl-vase-thing!"

"Yes, it is so," Parissah lamented. "I had long been attempting to divest myself of my earthly wealth. And to you came the Zenithyst... far and away the greatest treasure I possessed... and the hardest to part with." She paused for a moment, reflecting morosely.

"But I am very surprised you had time to find it," she continued at last. "I believed it would go unnoticed there for weeks, if not months."

"You have no idea what a good thing it was he found it when he did," Audrey told her. "You saved our lives with it!"

"That is another story I shall have to have later, if there is time," Parissah said.

"But now something else begins to make sense," Jek said. "I couldn't imagine why you goaded Bellanchora the way you did! But you got her to kill you on purpose! So you could make it back to the Citadel in time to warn about her attack!"

"That was my intention, yes," Parissah nodded. "It was not without risk, of course. I had no reason to expect that anything I said would be heeded. You do not understand, perhaps, the sheer magnitude of the disgrace I returned in. There is no greater trespass than for an Inquisitor to keep a treasure. But it seemed the only chance. I had to take it. And it has turned out well. Much preparation has been made, since last we saw one another."

"But what will happen to you now, since you broke the biggest rule of all?" Audrey asked. Jek looked on her anxiously, unable to anticipate a happy answer...

"That has yet to be decided," Parissah replied. "For now, with regard to the pending crisis, I have been reinstated... temporarily."

"I hope you will let *me* decide whether your reinstatement is to be temporary or not," Enscharaulgk interjected.

Parissah looked up at him. "We have been arguing about this for some time," she told them. "He wishes to pardon me entirely, I believe. But I am vehemently against any special treatment."

"And yet yours is a special *case,*" Enscharaulgk said. "You are being far from forthright with your friends, Parissah. You're all like, 'I have a treasure'... but you don't bother to explain how you came by that treasure!"

"Indeed I don't," Parissah retorted, folding her arms. "It does not matter how. The guilt is the same."

"It matters to *me,*" Enscharaulgk replied. "And I think your friends deserve to know the truth. And since you will not tell them, I will."

He paused dramatically before beginning, and all gathered – even Parissah herself – waited on his tale with bated breath...

"You see, Parissah's father was not an Inquisitor. He was a civilian, and a treasure-hunter."

"By Jove, yes!" Baegulgog exclaimed suddenly. "He was a nacre-whale tickler, and a generous soul – in the early years, at least. *Ninety percent,* she said... ninety percent of the money he made from the first nacre-whale pearl, he gave away! She did tell me all of this once."

"That's good," Enscharaulgk nodded. "I'm very glad she found someone to confide in about these matters. Though I expect even you didn't get the whole story, Baegulgog. Suffice it to say, it was not until many years later, after her father died, that she found out who that first ninety percent had gone to. He did not give it away to just anyone. He gave it to *her*...

"Yes, his last will bequeathed her the ninety percent, which he had set aside, collecting interest, unbeknownst to our dear Parissah all those years. He couldn't have guessed what a pickle he would be getting her into! She was only a child when he put the gold and gems on deposit... but by the time she got her inheritance in the mail, she had already been an Inquisitor a long time. It was a tragic irony, if I may say."

"It is both far more ironic and far more tragic than you begin to hint at, Grand Inquisitor," Parissah interjected, quite downcast. "Baegulgog alone would understand in the full."

"Yes, I begin to see it now," Baegulgog lamented. "And I am very sorry."

They shared some moment of knowing, but Jek scantily had time to guess what sort of grief passed between them. Parissah turned back to her master. "But you, Enscharaulgk! How ever did you know all these things!? I am sure I never told you..."

"Young one, I have known all along you had a treasure. I knew from the day it was delivered."

She was aghast. "But how?"

"Well, think about it. Do you suppose that a few crate-loads of treasure could be mailed to my Citadel, and I not learn of it? I am a *dragon*! What's more, I am the greatest treasure-hunter of all time, which I may say with all possible modesty... and remorse. I could smell the gold from miles off! So, I ordered a discrete inspection of the Citadel, enlisting the help of Berlberi technicians. When this treasure turned up, and turned out to be *yours*, I was shocked! But I was patient, and had the matter investigated further. It did not take long for the whole truth to be unearthed."

Parissah marveled. "I am quite overcome with embarrassment," she said. "And I am moved by your graciousness, Enscharaulgk. You never once treated me any different, even in the weeks and months you may well have thought that I intentionally betrayed your trust."

Enscharaulgk sighed. "In a way, my dear, I knew all along you would not let me down. And this is not the first time that something such as this has happened. Other Inquisitors throughout history have secretly taken treasures of their own. But always I gave them the chance to think better of it... to repent and give it away. Those that never did fled from me in fear and humiliation when they knew they would be found out. But others redeemed themselves... and they did it on their own... without my ever having to confront them."

"That is what *I* meant to do," Parissah nodded solemnly. "But I admit, it was a sore trial. I was left with quite a great hoard! I could not very well have smuggled it all out of my room at once... even if I had the willpower...

"Indeed, it was a greatly humbling experience. I had thought I would be immune to the allures of treasure, if ever I was tempted with it. I thought my conviction ran all the way. But I turned out much weaker than I supposed. The best I could do was to divest myself of it a little at a time. On occasions, I was strong, and I gave much. Other times proved harder, and I could grudge no more than a single coin. This went on for many years. And it would have taken many more, at the rate I was going, before I could have rid myself of it all." She hung her head. "But now it is too late. I have failed."

"You didn't fail," Enscharaulgk assured her. "Not in my book. You were doing the right thing. You simply ran out of time. And what's more, when the need arose, you sacrificed yourself, even knowing what it would cost you. You endured the disgrace and presented yourself to me, when all others before you had fled. And now you would have me be *ashamed* of you! Young one, I could not be more proud."

"Thank you, Enscharaulgk," Parissah nodded. "Indeed, no thanks are adequate. Your understanding lightens my heart beyond words."

"Really, this *is* a good thing," Audrey suddenly chipped in. "You're not just back... you're bigger and tougher now! That should come in handy."

"And that's not all!" Enscharaulgk exulted. "Show them now, Parissah! You simply must show them!"

"Oh, I do wish you would stop doting about those," Parissah replied, mask-palming.

"I won't. Now let them see! Check this out, guys!"

Parissah groaned, but then she did as instructed. Strange, doubled-over limbs at her back came unfurled with a leathery snap, and everyone jumped back as she revealed an impressive new set of wings!

"Wings!" Baegulgog exclaimed. "Good gracious!"

"Those are really nice," Audrey nodded.

"*Nice*?" Baegulgog demanded. "Dear Audrey, they are much more than nice! It is exceptionally rare for an Avarican to develop wings on only their second life! Indeed, the odds are astronomical!"

"Yes," Enscharaulgk doted. "That is what makes it so cool."

"Oh, this is splendid!" Baegulgog continued. "Happily, I do welcome you to the world of flighted creatures, madam! Perhaps the two of us may float up in the air together some time."

Parissah folded her wings back up, avoiding eye-contact. "You do get carried away, Baegulgog. They are wings, yes. But I am not sure they are proportionate. Even to glide might be beyond my capability."

"Perhaps we will see," Zedulon boded. "But time runs short. Today is the thirteenth! Indeed, there may be no Time ever again, after tomorrow."

Enscharaulgk cleared his long, long throat. "Yes, perhaps it is about time we focused-up here. But where to begin? What business is closest at hand?"

"I may report the fleet is nearly all out of dry dock," the other Inquisitor informed his master. "But *Carroccio* waits for me. I will away and oversee the deployment, if you deem, Grand Inquisitor."

"In a minute," Enscharaulgk replied. "I have forgotten my manners. Let me introduce you to the Knights and the Traveling Associates. This is Captain Taurnuren, my most distinguished naval officer... and Parissah's boyfriend."

At once Taurnuren and Parissah both appeared embarrassed.

"But surely you don't intend to betroth us now!" Parissah insisted. "Not after all that has happened."

"Would it bother you, Captain?" Enscharaulgk asked Taurnuren.

"I don't believe it would," he answered evenly.

"Very well." The dragon turned to Parissah. "Then since your true feelings in the matter are already well known to me, I see no reason that the engagement can't go on. I am an old-fashioned romantic that way, I suppose."

"Yet again, this is better discussed later... if there is to *be* a later," Zedulon commanded. "We must make long use of short time!"

"But much is already done," Parissah began to explain. "I was given autonomy to oversee preparations myself, some days ago now. I have reached out to the neighboring lands. Jast-Madiir is sending us a fleet, though it shall be far from their full strength. The Czarina maintains that Despotopia will likely come for her... if not first, then certainly second. So she would not part with the bulk of her defenses... and for those she *would* part with, she levied a heavy fee.

Fortunately, I believe we can depend on yet more help, after a fashion. I also reached out to the Twin Queens."

"But why would they help?" Zedulon asked. "They would not appreciate the desperation of this hour. They know only their own petty squabble."

"Indeed, you are right," Parissah nodded. "And it is in that manner that I appealed to them. I took the liberty of perpetrating another deception. I told them that the technology they have sought has been secured by the Inquisition! Each comes forth now, believing we will grant her the means to destroy the other." She itched at one of her ankles.

"*Twin Queens*?" Enscharaulgk repeated, bewildered.

"Oh my. I forgot, you do not yet know about that," Parissah blanched.

"So you *have* contrived a way to lure them into the fight, have you?" Zedulon continued, unabashed about leaving Enscharaulgk out of the war council for the moment. "That, I grant, was very clever work on your part! The Queens may be some help, even if their navies are quite pitiful. But Jast-Madiir, I fear, will not stack up against the modern Despotopian war machine. At best, they might screen the Maenean annex of the Kaiser's fleet."

"Yes," Parissah agreed. "It is a small thing, but I hoped they could offset Bravado's Free-Dome Fighter ships. Every little bit counts in such a crisis."

"Bravado?" Enscharaulgk puzzled. "Free-Dome Fighters?"

"At any rate, *Marrow*," Parissah went on, "it would also help immensely if I could have your assurances that your own fleet is not coming to crush us."

"The Roemnari fleet, mustered against *me*?" Enscharaulgk was at a loss. "Good grief! What else have I missed?"

"Quite a great deal," Zedulon rebuked him. "That is what happens when you do not revive for seventy-five years."

Enscharaulgk craned his head. "I suppose I deserve that. You are always tough but fair, Zedulon old pal. You'd have made a good Inquisitor. And you've been a very good friend."

"Yes I have," Zedulon agreed proudly. "And as your friend, I think I know what you intend to do next. I would say do it! With all haste!"

"I will at that," Enscharaulgk nodded. "It's time I got my head in the game..."

His many huge wings opened up with a rolling like thunder – unfurling canvas enough for a whole extended family of galleons. Jek and all the others had to throw themselves forward to stop being swept back by the raging rush of wind.

"Wait!" Parissah said. "Where are you going, Enscharaulgk?"

"I will scout out the enemy Fleet," he answered. "You admitted yourself you could not give me a full account of their strength. I think we could learn a lot, and advance our strategy very far, if I could just get one good look before the battle..."

"Well do be careful," she cautioned him. "You mustn't forget that Bellanchora intends your death before all else."

"Don't worry. I'll fly much too high for their little guns," Enscharaulgk assured her.

"One last thing before you go," another voice intruded. It was Horus Templar – a largely forgotten accessory to the meeting. "As legal council for the Humans Jek and Audrey, I feel obliged to remind you of their current dubious standing with the law." He grinned back at them. "They themselves seem to have forgotten it for the moment!" He returned to face Enscharaulgk. "At any rate, it is only your pardon they need now, to be free of any future recrimination. Do you grant them that pardon?"

"Yup," Enscharaulgk said. Jek felt sudden, incredible relief. "You guys have done a really good job," the Grand Inquisitor went on. "I am only too happy to pardon you. And I will do all I can to make sure you live to enjoy that pardon... starting now..."

"But what of your fleet, my liege?" Taurnuren asked.

"Wait for my return, Captain," Enscharaulgk called, climbing up the ramp, and then the tower itself. "We can array our ships tonight, or even tomorrow morning, if need be. But let us have some intel first! I am going to see what is up with the Doom Fleet..."

At last he took to the sky. They all hunkered for what seemed the longest time, the torrent of air from his wings buffeting them so that they were robbed of their very breath. But even though he must have weighed something like a zillion tons, once Enscharaulgk got going, he flew with an effortless elegance that made him appear quite weightless.

At first, Jek delighted at the sight of him wheeling over the Citadel, displacing all the tiny tweeting scouts of Bellanchora like a kraken careening heedless through a cloud of krill. But as he slowly disappeared below the shroud of the arms, Jek's heart began to sink. He had felt quite courageous up until this point – almost eager to confront the coming evil. He did not guess how much of that courage might have been borrowed, just from being in the midst of Enscharaulgk, the world's oldest hero...

* * *

The hours that followed were anxious ones. There was some joy and levity, as they continued to catch up with Parissah. It was remarkable how much there was to say, after being apart only a few days. They told her about their rescue by the Knights. Baegulgog, in particular, was in high spirits, as he spun the tale of 'driving' the horse-engine. And per Parissah's request, Jek and Audrey recounted the fateful meeting with Faucette – at least, in part. Horus Templar expounded on his courtroom antics again, eager to let Parissah know how she had made his unlikely victory possible. She shared her own account of coming back to life – a phenomenon the Humans were quite curious about.

But invariably, everything that was said returned back somehow to the coming of the Doom Fleet… or else prompted some future plan, only to remind them that the future was in question. And the further into the chatting they got, the more distracted they all became… trying at whiles to hear the flapping of titanic wings wheeling back to them…

They got other visitors first. A very small ship of Jast-Madiir make came sailing up to the ramp. Jek was not at all sure what to make of it at first. He hoped this wasn't the 'fleet' from his country that the Inquisition had paid a huge bill for…

But Parissah seemed to have some idea what was going on. She approached the ship and hailed them.

"Grosdrev Trockelov!" she called. "I am so grateful you answered my summons!"

"Came as soon as I heard," one particularly scarred-over man replied – apparently Trockelov. Jek was a bit mystified. These didn't look like Parissah's sort of people. They looked like ruffians and scoundrels, and perhaps even brutes. *Mercenaries*, Jek thought. What a controversial profession! He was very glad that *he* had never been conscripted to be one…

"It is well that you did. I'll gladly reward you for your speed, Trockelov," Parissah replied, as they all met on the ramp. "Our need is very urgent! If you had arrived tomorrow, it may have been too late."

Trockelov looked around a bit incredulous. "Things seem fine to me," he said. "Miles-wide fortress, hundreds of fancy warships. I don't know what you expect Guppy Troop to add to all this." He laughed a hoarse laugh. "Guess we made a good impression on the last job. But of course we jumped at the chance to work for your reward again! 'Big Spender…' that's the name we take up in our toasts! 'Here's to Big Spender,' we say." Suddenly, he winced, as if he had finally got a good look at her. "What's with the new digs?" he asked.

She looked down at herself, then suddenly remembered. "Ah yes, my new body. I have trespassed. I had a treasure all along, and I died and regenerated."

"No foolin'?" Now he really laughed. "Hear that, boys? Big Spender's got a bad side!" He turned back to Parissah. "I knew I liked you."

"Personalities aside, I am forming a new strike team," she went on. "It was to consist of myself, numerous Inquisitors, Guppy Troop – if you came in time – and whoever else you could round up."

Trockelov rubbed the back of his neck, looking down. "Couldn't get many volunteers, I regret to say. You know mercs don't come runnin' when the Inquisition calls. That goes double when you're bein' summoned to their big Citadel. Sounded like some lousy trap to the other Troops. We did get four guys – mostly folks whose Troops had gone to pieces and had nothing else... and one rather peculiar bloke we met on the road not far from here. No one I could swear by."

"Three guys now, boss," Ivan spoke up. "Don't know where that last one ended up. Now we're here, we can't find him."

Trockelov looked back, quite miffed and puzzled. "There's no figurin' that codger! First he's all uptight to join us, then he jumps ship!"

"Well, never mind," Parissah said. "We have a great deal more strength to call on than I had dared to hope. The Knights of the Indigo Lodge are here! And what's more, they come bearing my Traveling Associates! That is not a group you would know of, but they are as formidable and capable a team as I have ever had the privilege of working with."

"Sounds good to me!" Trockelov replied. "Teaming up with Indigo Knights!? That's a dandy of an accolade! Should look real good on the resume!" His scarry face crumpled up, betraying sudden doubt. "But that is a lot of heat for a strike team, isn't it? What are we going to be striking, I wonder?"

"We must try to contrive a way to kill Bellanchora," Parissah answered.

"Bellanchora?" Trockelov repeated. "Who's Bellanchora?"

"She's a Ghost-Princess who can call on unlimited elemental power at will."

At length, Trockelov nodded and pursed his lips. "This is big boy stuff, then. No wonder the Knights are here."

"Verily," Zavion put in. "And ne'er let it be said the Knights cometh unprepared. We bringeth a weapon, which doth possess full measure of the power this grave task demandeth."

"Do you?" Parissah asked urgently. "That is by far the best news yet! Explain about this weapon... its nature and how it may be wielded."

"They gave me an old boot," Audrey explained.

There was an awkward silence.

"A boot, eh?" Trockelov asked at length.

"Do not make light of the Boot!" Zedulon's imperious voice beckoned, captivating all present. His false eye flashed with a fury. "This venture may succeed, if only you are all steadfast in protecting the Boot-bearer. But be warned! Do not any of you falter! The fate of all creation hangs in the balance!"

"Who's the scary bird?" Trockelov asked, when he had recovered his wits.

"That's Proconsul Zedulon of Roemnar," Parissah answered. She looked back at Zedulon. "He will join us in the strike team, if he deigns."

"For as long as we are headed in the same direction, I will go with you," Zedulon said. "But our errands may diverge for a time."

Parissah nodded. "That is good enough for me." Then she looked doubtfully up into the sky. "The day grows old. We should away and eat. Anyway, it will be better for us if we are not standing here when Enscharaulgk returns."

"I'll go along with that," Jek said. "His takeoff was nearly the end of us."

"Enscharaulgk?" Trockelov asked. "The big beastie's awake, eh?"

"That he is," Parissah nodded. "And not a moment too soon."

They started up the ramp. As they went, Trockelov came up with yet another inquiry for Parissah. "So where's that sword of yours? I thought sure you were going to hold on to that..."

"I would certainly have liked to, if I could have," she replied. "I lost it when I caught my death. Most likely it is still in the depths of Bellanchora's compound."

"Then here," Trockelov said. "Have the other one." He went to hand her the other sword from the swordsdrone they had fought.

She eyed him questioningly. "It is a most excellent weapon. Are you sure you wish to part with it?"

"Sure I'm sure... or else I wouldn't offer it. Figure they both belong to you. It was your hide they were stuck in. Anyway, it sounds like you'll be needin' it."

She took the sword. "Thank you, Trockelov. I am once again in your debt."

"Not hardly," Trockelov laughed. "And if you are, a debt to a mercenary is easy to square. As long as you still got money... Big Spender."

They all picked at food for something like hours. It was hard to be hungry, and not just because of all the constricting doubt. The dining experience in the Citadel was more than a little exotic. It wasn't that the menu was so strange: Inquisitor food consisted mostly of a very healthy balance of all different kinds of meat. It was the dining hall itself that was bizarre. There were private booths for eating, rather than tables. Finally, Jek remembered that Avarica had a taboo about uncovering their faces. It wasn't something he really understood, nor did he feel inclined to ask at the moment.

But the Inquisitors were accommodating, setting up a table for their assorted guests. There were few enough social gaffes during the meal, all things considered. Horus Templar made a special request for his food to be uncooked. The mercenary Trockelov asked some leading questions about something stronger to 'wash it down with'. Jek huffed. If the man really thought there would be grape juice on the Citadel, he must not have been very bright. Baegulgog refused to eat – now that he knew he had never actually *been* eating from the first, he was cured. But now that Zedulon was making no further effort to conceal his identity, he ate with them. When Jek wasn't pushing things around with his own fork, he mostly watched absently as the Heron pecked his plate.

And he worried. He worried about Enscharaulgk. He worried about everything. He worried about nothing at all.

* * *

Later, near dusk, some of those concerns abated, even if they proved valid. They returned to what Parissah called 'the Wide Path,' and she made some stink about the patrols being out of whack somehow. But it was soon enough forgotten – hardly had they returned to the great big door that led out to the ramp when Enscharaulgk appeared again at last. He had a rough landing (an experience they all shared). Jek looked on with sorrow, seeing that the Grand Inquisitor's wings were peppered with little holes. The battle had yet to be, and already, their titan seemed hurt and exhausted. In his heart, Jek maligned the black souls who could open fire on such a noble creature.

"I could not fly so high as I planned," Enscharaulgk explained, gasping metric tons of air. "The vapors of their ships were obstructing my view. I had to get closer... indeed, too close for comfort!"

"Are you okay?" Audrey asked him.

"It hurts real bad," Enscharaulgk answered. "But I'll be fine."

She didn't merely take his assurances. Rather, she did what she could for the huge dragon with her magic healy hands. Jek marveled as he watched what seemed an acre of shorn wing-flesh fill back in.

"Thank you, young Audrey," Enscharaulgk sighed. His body was largely mended. But some weariness clung to him still...

For the next several hours, they all talked strategy. It was a war council that far exceeded what Jek had experienced in Jengadocea's Bluff. Enscharaulgk expressed some hope of victory, where the naval battle was concerned. The Doom Fleet appeared large and strong, but not so overwhelming as he had expected. And he did not believe there was anything in the Despotopian arsenal that would negate their range advantage – the gift of their electromagnetically-propelled ordnance, which could reach for leagues beyond traditional gunpowder cannons. He and Taurnuren hashed out a formation that would concentrate their Coup-de-Grâce battlecruisers behind mobile barricade ships – something Taurnuren claimed the Inquisition navy drilled all the time. They would cover the flanks of the formation with their battleships and destroyers... and the fleet from Jast-Madiir, if it arrived in time. No mention was given to coordinating efforts with the Twin Queens, whose timely arrival was also in doubt. Since they had been lured on a false pretense, their cooperation was dubious. But it would still be better to have their strength at hand, and to gamble that they would take up the plight of the Inquisition, in hopes of getting their Weapon...

Finally, they turned to the principle issue – how to kill Bellanchora. Winning the ship battle would count for nothing, if she endured. It was still understood that without the intervention of Ethon, she could probably end the universe on a whim. Enscharaulgk assured them that the universe was big and robust, and even for her the Destruction might take some time. But it seemed little encouragement, imagining all of creation crumbling slowly, rather than all at once...

"Well, we have the Boot," Audrey said. "And we have the team of fighters to take on the mission. I don't know about war stuff, but it seems to me the only thing missing is some way to actually *get* to Bellanchora."

"I've got an idea about that," Enscharaulgk said. "Among Despotopia's hundreds of vessels was a flat-topped troop ship. I can think of only one use for such a ship in this battle. They mean to raid the Citadel, and abscond with my treasure."

"Undoubtedly," Taurnuren agreed. "To kill you is not the victory Bellanchora craves. She has killed you before. To kill you *permanently* – that must be her aim."

"Right," Enscharaulgk nodded. "And we must let her have what she wants."

They were all horrified.

"I hope you will explain yourself..." Parissah said at length.

"Of course I will," Enscharaulgk replied. "You see, it is our chance at a covert counter-strike. If her men are successful at taking my treasure, they will return with it to the Flagship. I am sure she would want to see it, and claim it for her own. That is what I would want to do, in her place. So, this is my plan: we allow the troop ship to board the Citadel, then all of you guys sneak onto their ship. And when they return to the Flagship with my treasure, you launch your attack! You fight your way to Bellanchora, and then you kick her, and all is mended! What do you think?"

"It is a bold gambit," Zedulon said. "I, for one, support it." He looked menacingly round the gathered councilors. "Who, then, would dare to think otherwise?"

"I don't like the risk," Parissah admitted. "But I certainly have no better ideas. It may work."

"Then it is settled," Enscharaulgk declared.

Taurnuren had reservations. "The chief difficulty will be to keep the battle going long enough to let the troop ship pass by – twice. It will appear suspicious, if we shell all the rest of the Doom Fleet into oblivion, only to let the objective ship go about its business."

"You are that confident in your battlecruisers, Captain?" Enscharaulgk asked.

"If Despotopia cannot match us for range, I would deem their victory very unlikely, even if they outnumbered us five to one."

"Well, see you don't let them catch you off-guard," the Grand Inquisitor cautioned him. "Bellanchora is subtle and clever. She is *no* dummy."

Taurnuren nodded. "I'll keep my eyes open, my liege."

"But there's one other, *other* problem," Audrey said. "We have to fight our way to Bellanchora. But I can only use the Boot once... and my musket's broke."

"We hath already attended to that, sister Audrey," Zavion told her, producing a big long thing rolled up in cloth that no one had taken any notice of. "Thine musket is reforged! *Both* of thine muskets!"

Audrey and Jek took the parcel and opened it to find their muskets. They looked much Knightlier than they had before, but felt and handled just as always.

"They are improvèd, so that now they wilt surely turn away e'en the vile oscilations of the enemy's blades. And lo! Thou mayest fire not once, but *twice*, with each reload."

"How did you manage that?" Jek asked, absently admiring the Knights' wonderful handiwork.

"There, I tell no tale," Zavion replied. "T'was not I who did make with the reforging. And time draweth too short for unnecessary technical banter."

"Well gee, thanks a lot!" Audrey said. "This is really nice!"

"Thou art welcome, sister Audrey, brother Jek."

"Very good," Enscharaulgk approved. "Now, I think we should dissolve this council, and concentrate on getting some shuteye. Is there anything more that ought to be discussed first? I can think of nothing..."

"I still think we should bring some books," Audrey said. "If something goes wrong with the Boot, then at least we can try to suck up Bellanchora."

"But I'm afraid Zedulon is probably right," Jek lamented. "There may be no book short of the Pamphlet itself that can contain her. She's just too powerful of a Knowledge spirit."

At once, they all thought they heard a clatter, somewhere off the edge of the ramp. Everyone turned suddenly to look. But they saw nothing. And they heard nothing more. Finally, they dismissed it, and returned to the debate...

"Never balk at contingencies," Parissah admonished Jek. "I will gladly bear the load of numerous books into battle. It will be much better to have them at hand, if all else fails, rather than to feel foolish that we left behind even a shadow of a hope."

"And I will do likewise!" Baegulgog soared with enthusiasm. "It will be a good role for me, I think. I can open three books at once, at need!"

"Not so fast," Enscharaulgk said. "I don't intend for you to go with the strike team, Baegulgog. But it's a good thing you spoke up. I had a job for you in mind, which I had nearly forgot."

Baegulgog made an unsure low grumbly sound. "Very well, Grand Inquisitor. What would you have a humble Sowür Canpattel do?"

"It is precisely the fact of your Sowür Canpatteliness that compels me to ask of you what I am about to," the dragon replied. "The propaganda of the Kaiser is loud and compelling, and Bellanchora retains her power to sway wills with her music. We are in need of sonic warfare! And for that we have the perfect weapon – *Pharonomagnus*, the Great Pipe Organ. But I understand it has gone silent for some weeks. It refuses to play, and none dare to touch its keys. We need some way to rouse it! I think you, as a Sowür Canpattel, could do so. Yours is the legacy of all earthly music."

Baegulgog hesitated, flashing with internal consternation. "I am greatly honored. In fact I can think of no higher honor than collaboration with *Pharonomagnus* – chiefest of all instruments! But you mistake me. I have no musical talent. I am disgraced among all my Dominion."

"You are the one who is mistaken, Baegulgog," Enscharaulgk assured him warmly, "if you believe you are without your rightful gift. Surely, some granule of the spirit of Chordonoto lives on in you, as in all Sowür Canpattels...

"...I think."

"Thank you, sir," Baegulgog said solemnly, inclining himself in the air. "If there is any truth in what you say, then I will discover it."

"Thank *you*, good Clerk," Enscharaulgk replied. "And now, if there are no more objections, I dissolve the council." He looked over them all, but no one spoke a word against it. "Then good night to all you people," the Grand Inquisitor said, ducking and plodding into the Wide Path toward his sanctum.

* * *

All the rest went their separate ways. The Knights to the Lodge, the mercs to their ship. But the Traveling Associates were put up in the Citadel, near to the Path.

Jek and Audrey only just reached their room when Audrey was unexpectedly called away – alone – into the presence of Enscharaulgk. Jek was mystified, but made no objection. He and Audrey simply waved goodbye. Jek bedded down, troubled, intuiting that something heavy was on the heart of Enscharaulgk. But he was left without a clue what it might be, and how it could possibly relate to Audrey. He agonized over it for some time, trying in vain to make himself rest, when there suddenly came a knock on his chamber door. Eagerly he rushed to open it – flinging it wide with a sloppy abandon, hoping Audrey was in some mood to share what she had talked to Enscharaulgk about... even prepared to insist on it...

But it was not Audrey at the door. It was Parissah standing there, in the bright, underlit halls and great dark windows of the Citadel.

"Hello, Jek," she said.

"Oh, hi, Parissah," Jek replied.

"That was some door-opening, just then."

Jek cleared his throat. "Yeah. I thought you were Audrey. She's been called to confer with Enscharaulgk, for some reason. It has me a little worried, I guess. I've gotten used to being in the loop."

"Well, don't fret," she assured him. "I'm sure whatever it is, Enscharaulgk simply doesn't wish to trouble you with it at present."

They both stood at the door for a long second.

"What was it you wanted to talk about?" Jek asked at length.

"I'm glad you asked," Parissah replied. "It is proving difficult. I came not to speak, but to give you something." She held out a shaky hand, and in it was a really superb amethyst.

Jek suppressed a laugh. "What's this?"

"It is the best of what remains of my treasure," Parissah answered. "I am very glad the Zenithyst proved a redemption for you and Audrey, and for your friend the old man. But I am rather distraught that you were forced to part with it so quickly." She looked down at her gem. "This, of course, falls well short of replacing the stone you lost. But as I say, it is the finest article I have left to give. Please accept it."

Jek was deeply moved. He wanted to refuse, feeling that he didn't merit such a gift by any means. But he quickly realized it was better to accept. The amethyst was only a curse to her, even if she loved it. He held out his hand.

Parissah extended her own hand... slowly, hesitantly. Finally with great effort she slapped the amethyst into Jek's palm.

"Ow," Jek said.

"Sorry," she replied.

"No, no... thank you very much," he said. "I'll treasure this forever. Unless I spend it. But goodness, Parissah, you don't owe me and Audrey anything!"

"Perhaps I do, and perhaps I don't. But I am glad to make time for one last good deed before... before whatever is coming. And beside Baegulgog, whom I am not sure could fully appreciate a gift like this, I thought most of rewarding you. You have a wonderfully contrite heart, Jek. That I knew from the day I came to smash your belongings."

Jek laughed again nervously, embarrassed. "If I'm contrite, it's only because I'm afraid of everything."

"That may have been so at one time. But you have grown since your days at the lighthouse. That is plain to me as well. You have a bravery about you now. *Real* bravery, which stems from a sense of duty, rather than foolhardy bravado." She paused, and rested a hand on his shoulder. "To have a heart that is at once courageous and contrite. I do not think a Human can do much better."

"Thanks," Jek said, holding in tears of gratitude.

"You are most welcome, Jek," she nodded. "Have a restful night, and do not fear."

Jek nodded back. "Good night, Parissah."

He shut the door, got into bed, and set the amethyst on the nightstand next to him. He admired it until a shallow sleep came over him...

Finally, Audrey returned, and it woke Jek straight away, though he did not let on. He watched her through the narrowest possible slits in his eyelids, trying to appear still asleep. He couldn't make out her face – she a dark silhouette in the doorway. But she lingered there, looking at him, and he could tell that she was troubled. It troubled *him*.

At length, she carefully crawled into bed, trying not to disturb him. He listened to her toss a few times, not easily finding comfort. He heard nothing more for a while. But just as he thought that perhaps she had fallen asleep herself, he felt her hand gently rubbing his back. It was at once reassuring and most distressing. The last council of Enscharaulgk was weighing on her, keeping her restless. *What had they talked about*? He despaired to know. But with much effort, he decided to honor the Grand Inquisitor's discretion. He didn't ask.

Some time later, her hand fell, and he was satisfied she was asleep. He knew he had better try to get to sleep himself...

But his attempts were disturbed. They were disturbed by the sound – real or imagined – of the Kaiser's avid speech, amplified and echoing long leagues through the night. And behind it, a music... sweet, soft – indeed, inaudible – and absolutely inexorable...

7/14/21

"Keep hope alive, even if it kills you."

- Enscharaulgk, *Zenithyst Inquisitor: A Compendium of Wise Anecdotes (Curated by Warren Liefletson)*

The wide door of the Citadel opened into a raging tempest. The Traveling Associates, sheltered just within, were immediately soaked just by the gushing dregs rolling down from the shallow metal eaves. Marching out into the squall, under the churning of a dark and greenish sky rimmed in pale purple, Jek immediately felt like a drowned deinonychus, gasping just to find some drops of air somewhere in the rain...

"This is quite a storm," he understated, needing to speak up just to be heard.

"Any storm would be quite the storm on the Ocean Citadel," Zedulon told him. "It never rains here."

He squinted down at the Heron, blinking much water out of his eyes. "Never?"

"Not once. Ever."

That was an omen Jek found odd. But obviously, it was bad.

The Knights and mercenaries came up the ramp to meet them, scrambling through the downpour as if they were running for cover, even though there was none. Jek watched as both their ships pulled away, rushing against the swells to join the Inquisition fleet.

"Hail, Traveling Associates, brother Jek and sister Audrey!" Zavion called.

"Hi Zavion," Audrey called back. "Welcome to the big day!"

Jek winced. To call this 'day' seemed an empty boast. He pushed away a distressing thought – he may have already seen the sun for the last time ever... yesterday.

His attention was quickly diverted, as he noticed Horus Templar striding into their midst.

"Horus?" Jek called. "What are you doing here? Surely you don't mean to join the strike team!"

"Don't I?" Horus replied, and Jek saw he was shouldering a huge war-hammer in the likeness of a gavel. "I wonder why I shouldn't. I *am* retained as your defense attorney, after all." Now he cradled the hammer in both hands. "And if ever you were in need of defending, I would say it's now."

Audrey smiled. "Thanks, Horus. But I thought your people were pacifists!"

"It's true, we don't care much for warfare. It's not as purely cerebral as is our taste. But I, for one, don't shy away from the important battles. What battle could be more important than The Final Battle?"

"Name it not, 'The Final Battle'!" Zedulon commanded. "For if it *is* The Final Battle, none shall endure to remember it as such. But if it is *not* The Final Battle, then it shall certainly have to be called something else later. Name it not at all! Only let us *fight* it."

"Sounds like wisdom to me," Horus shrugged. His sharp ears folded back against his head, and he looked around with a grimace. "Too bad about all this rain."

As if on cue, the rain relented – or seemed to – over the strike team, anyway. Jek turned curiously to the sky. High overhead, Enscharaulgk clung fast to the Citadel tower, scanning the horizon. A great lightning bolt was mirrored on his bright armor as it flashed. One wing he held out, shielding the strike team from the deluge as he kept his lofty vigil.

"Ah, Enscharaulgk!" Parissah cried. "What have you to report?"

"Good morning, young one," the Grand Inquisitor replied, his huge voice cutting through the rain and wind. "I have news that should please you. Jast-Madiir's fleet arrived some hours ago, and Taurnuren and I have wrangled them successfully into formation. The money you promised the Czarina was well invested! They brought a bunch of ships." He turned in a wide arc. "I spy the Queens as well, sailing up out of the far south! They are slow in coming, as Meduselda are wont to be. And their ships do appear to be skirmishing, each with the other... as they are able. No surprises there. I hope they can see past each other, when the time comes."

"That *is* good news, on the whole," Parissah replied. "Yet I am troubled, Enscharaulgk. It seems like we forget something, but I cannot think what..."

"Good grief!" Enscharaulgk gasped. "The Citadel! We ought to realign it!"

"Dear me, yes," Parissah agreed. "Please do!" Jek didn't know what they were talking about...

Enscharaulgk climbed yet higher along the tower, and he splayed his wings in some sort of signal pattern, even as he seemed to look through a window in the Citadel itself.

"Realign?" Jek asked. "What does that...?"

But as he spoke, a great roiling in the ocean churned up all along the arms of the Citadel. Jek felt his stomach twist, and all but Parissah nearly lost their footing. Disheveled and momentarily sick, he was not immediately conscious of anything else. But soon, he could see for himself what was happening. The whole Citadel was pivoting! He marveled as the gap in the arms revealed the Inquisition fleet and its militia from Jast-Madiir – a greater gathering of naval strength than his wildest imagining. All the slicked-down little hairs on the back of his neck stood on end as his mind was filled with one grave certainty: This was going to be a really, *really* big battle...

Tense minutes passed. Jek struggled not to be totally overwhelmed by the enormity of the whole thing – the number of moving pieces, the scale of the board, and the stakes on the table. He looked over at Audrey, and drew what strength he could from the look she gave him in return. Suddenly things closed in, resolving into focus. The entire ocean – to the very ends of the earth – could fill up with war and chaos, and it wouldn't matter. His mission was simple. It had always been simple.

Finally, Enscharaulgk beckoned down to them again. "We have our first rumor of the enemy!" he declared. "Our alignment is good! They come headlong, straight into our teeth!"

Jek strained his eyes to see what the old dragon was talking about. Then he saw, as it were, a low cloud, darker than all the rest, bisecting the horizon. His ears pricked with a phantasmal voice – sharp and strong, but incredibly far away. As both the cloud and the voice grew, Jek began to hear a great multitude answer. Soon, he could make out the form of the speech, though the words were still alien to him. The Kaiser was leading some sort of chant or war cry, with all his men shouting their replies to each prompt in frightening unison, so that the ocean might have quaked at the sound of their feverish zeal, if it were not already up in its own tossing fit. Only after Jek's heart was frozen in his chest by the forcefulness of the distant sound did the ships themselves actually begin to appear – a wide and thick array of glistening points on the skyline. He watched those points grow to silver shapes still far away. Uncouth they were – grim, pale and soulless – a shrewd marriage of guns and armor, blotting out the sky with their smoke. What they lacked in the elegance and refinement of Inquisition warships, they made up for in their bombastic spite of all subtlety. They were cold instruments of death, efficient and unceremonious, and absolutely loaded down with firepower.

In the thick of this, Jek spied the troop ship –their first objective. It was indeed largely flat at the top, but seemed to consist of multiple tiers, each reaching wide in all directions from the main hull beneath. It looked large enough for a whole army! He sincerely hoped they could sneak aboard unnoticed, rather than have to fight their way to the ultimate objective...

As in thought, his eyes turned to what lay behind the troop carrier. There, with all the rest of the entire Doom Fleet arrayed about it in one grand, miles-wide wedge, was the Flagship. It was a colossal behemoth, mounting up with cannons like towers crowding each other for space upon the bulging masses of superstructure, all caked in a gratuitous slathering of steal, belching enough smoke to shame an erupting volcano. It was tethered to huge zeppelins, which berthed yet more huge guns. By itself, the ship was probably as massive as half the fleet, utterly grotesque in all its unspeakable excesses of impunity and might. There, he knew, they would find the Kaiser... and the Ghost-Princess herself...

Jek's eyes were strained quite hard to see all this, still miles off. He rubbed them, hoping to peel away some layers of morbid imagination. But the sight remained just as nightmarish, no matter how he tried to look at it.

"That's some Flagship," Jek admitted aloud.

"We have a term for such things in court," Horus Templar said quizzically.

Jek gave him a searching look. "You do? What on earth would that be?"

"*Malum In Se*."

Jek waited in vain for some clarification. "*Malum In Se*? What does it mean?"

"Trust me, it's not good," Horus replied. Jek was content to leave it at that.

"Hey, what's that?" Audrey asked, pointing just off to the left of the Doom Fleet.

Jek squinted again, and soon saw something very strange. Just as the Fleet was crowding all the sky above it with soot, it appeared rather like the sky was answering in kind, suddenly dropping a shaft of white cloud to the ocean floor. Jek watched as this shaft, fine and straight but dense, grew longer, marching along a diagonal path in front of and across the Despotopian armada. Then he noticed the same phenomenon closing from the opposite direction, with little air ships at the head of each plume. Finally, it was apparent what was happening. The Despotopians were shrouding themselves behind a drawn curtain of smoke half a mile high! He gazed in horror as the outermost ships began to disappear in the converging veils...

"A smokescreen!" Enscharaulgk called from above. "That's no good! Captain Taurnuren needs his effective range! I will have to dash those little planes, if I can..."

Near the end of this short statement, the dragon's words began to fade – subsumed in the sudden onset of a gentle music. Jek felt one moment of fear before something else came over him. It was *Bellanchora's* music, he knew. But this was different than what he'd experienced back in Despotopia – some other insidious tune of hers– not overwhelming to the mind, but compelling to the heart. Jek blinked heavily. Even as he watched Doom encroach, for the first time in days, he felt truly restful – at ease. The music filled him with an aggressive serenity, so that he was no longer an elite strike team member, or auxiliary Knight of the Indigo Lodge. He was just a little fly, swaddled in the warm and secure cords of a web's embrace, while the old spider herself softly whispered in his ear, 'Let it be.'

Internally, Jek fought. He fought just for the will to fight… and in moments of strength, he found it. But this was to be a long and arduous battle, and his part in it would not come for some time. He hoped that his Will could hold out until then…

"*The music*," Enscharaulgk gasped. "It is as I feared! Now is the time for *Pharonomagnus* to get up off its duff!" He climbed and climbed, incredibly high up the tower – into the very thunderstorm – struggling against the weaponized peace tugging at his own heart. Finally, his face reached the Glass Chapel. He nodded within, signaling to the Clerk, whose role in the battle (strange but important) must now be played…

* * *

Baegulgog hummed to himself, combatting anxiety with his feverish but ineffectual grunty little notes. Soon, he would be expected to rouse this incredible colossus – *Pharonomagnus* – an instrument that dwarfed and daunted him, filling the contours of this high vault with its thick, brassy pipes strewn in rows through, above, and below dozens of arches. So intimidated he was by the thing that he could not even tally the arches and the pipes – a simple chore for a Clerk, but beyond his capability in his current state.

Suddenly, a very huge dragon face appeared in a stained window and nodded at him, lightning catching the glazed contours of its dense armor. Baegulgog flashed with fresh fright. That was his cue! And still he did not know how he would get the thing to play, if it did not wish to…

Master yourself, Baegulgog old chum, he thought to himself. *At least try what you may…*

Cautiously, he reached out a tentacle for *Pharonomagnus'* keys. Just as he nearly touched one, he recoiled, spooked by a horrific sound: The great pipes hissed at him! He floated there, fazed, until the only sound left in the room was the rolling pitter-patter of the gushing rain outside.

Well, you got a response, he assured himself. *Not a musical one, regrettably. But at least you may be sure the thing is paying attention…*

He made a noise like clearing his throat and tried various snatches of song to see if the Organ would play along. It did not respond to any of them. Baegulgog was unsurprised. His tone-deafness was grimly on display here. Probably, he could not have inspired even a humble, self-aware little triangle to ding along with him, let alone this *great* instrument, world-renowned.

"Oh fiddlesticks!" Baegulgog at last cursed aloud. "Some Sowür Canpattel you turned out to be, Baegulgog! The spirit of Chordonoto is very far from you!"

His own words sparked sudden inspiriation.

"Chordonoto," he reflected to himself, tapping his front end with a thoughtful tentacle. "Eureka! If that will not do to stir this great Organ, then nothing will!"

Baegulgog removed to the choir loft of the Chapel, a platform on an arch some distance away from the Organ's heart, in the epicenter of all the pipes. Spreading his arm-tentacles to the heavens, he focused all his Sowür Canpattely essence into channeling one note – one *song* – the elemental legacy of Chordonoto at its most basic and powerful...

"Oooooooooooooooooooooooooooooo"

Even as he reached near the end of his count, he perceived a low response, the pitch so bass that it nearly dropped off the audible spectrum. But from there, the voice of *Pharanomagnus* grew, winding and twisting into a frenzied cascade, crescendoing exponentially in magnitude. The mindset of the Organ was clear... if Chordonoto had started music, then now *Pharonomagnus* meant to *finish* it. It would prove its unrivaled musical genius by here and now improvising a whole sprawling symphony fit to answer that *one* note, and answer it for good...

Baegulgog exulted. He had done his bit! He had thrown down the gauntlet at *Pharonomagnus*. And now, with all its fell voice, it was answering. It was doing *everything* it could do to answer...

* * *

Enscharaulgk himself recoiled at the unexpected strength and energy in the sudden burst of music emanating from the Glass Chapel. Louder and more vengeful notes had never been voiced in all the world! He was greatly pleased that his faith in the Clerk was proven right... and indeed, far more than right.

Below, Jek blinked fully out of his trance, his hot blood surging, carried along on an anthem too proud and domineering (or at any rate, much too *loud*) for even Bellanchora to contend with. And if that were not enough to stir all hearts, Enscharaulgk punctuated the song by lending his own, larger-than-life voice. Jek nearly hit the ground. The sound of his roar was as earthy and immense as two molten worlds crashing into each other. The sonic impact momentarily stilled the sea and split the sky, so that the sun blinked forth through all the clouds and smoke, if only to do so for the very last time...

Jek was indeed quite cured. Never had he been so ready for a fight!

But he would *still* have to wait, of course – wait on the Despotopians to come to *him*. For now, he could do naught with his gumption but stand there and fume in it, and watch as the grandest naval battle in history began to unfold before his very eyes...

This is the account of that battle – as he saw it, and as he could not see it...

Enscharaulgk threw himself down from the dark tower, sweeping his wings out into a low glide over his fleet, quickened on the electric melody of *Pharonomagnus*, even as the opening shots of Taurnuren's battlecruiser division carved paths in the seas, the hundred-score magnetic catapults big as city buildings firing blindly into the enemy shroud. He passed row after row of these great warships, while they hurled implosive charges between the openings in their wall of mobile barricades at impossible velocities, each payload erupting so brilliantly that a faint flash shown through the curtain. Dimly behind *Pharonomagnus'* symphony, he could hear the unaccountably gentle chirp of the guns going off, creating the truly magnificent, hazy fireworks display that lay still leagues before him...

But whether those guns were actually hitting anything was a very anxious mystery. Enscharaulgk purposed to do what he could about it. He would interdict the planes that were responsible for dropping the smokescreen. Without another pass or two by the planes, it was quite likely the Doom Fleet would be forced to sail beyond the protection of the shroud while they were still out of range to return fire. Already the Inquisition's fleet had been cheated out of a considerable window of opportunity, and the Grand Inquisitor had to be sure that trend did not continue, lest the Despotopians neutralize their range advantage entirely...

It was then that Enscharaulgk heard something else... something unaccountable: A series of explosions behind him. It alarmed him, and almost without thinking he whirled back around. There seemed to be bombs going off in the midst of his battlecruisers! He wheeled skywards, and finally understood what was happening. The Despotopians were *already* returning fire... not directly, but from the *sky*! Evidently they had long-range strike capability of their own. Not in the form of cannons, mind you... but rocket-propelled artillery. Enscharaulgk gazed into the sky and saw the long fuel trails of a continuous stream of such missiles, arcing miles through open space to land among his most valuable warships! He signaled with a free pair of his wings that the battlecruisers should fan out, to get free of the barrage zone. Not a moment too soon did he give the signal, for they were already taking casualties. Most of the rockets were falling harmlessly into the water, kicking up tall sprays. But too many caught some quadrant of a battlecruiser's hull, and those that scored hits often proved quite devastating.

Watching his ships begin to strafe and break formation even as they kept up the firing, Enscharaulgk was quickly reassured they had at least responded with all possible speed. And with all *his* speed, he doubled-back in a tight aerial maneuver, resuming his hunt for the planes...

Little did he realize that he, too, was being hunted. Even as he neared the next spot where the planes would cross paths, there was a *huge* splash... indeed, *two* huge splashes. And barreling out of the water up into the sky at him, he was suddenly savaged by a pair of sea serpents – long-time denizens of Meatgrinder Bay, where they had looted many thousands of derelict ships over the course of centuries. In all that time, the two had been rivals – greedy scavengers each trying to stake the same turf – and had often killed each other. This perhaps accounted for their *incredible* size. It was a simple enough matter for

Bellanchora to seek out these serpents early in the commissioning of the Doom Fleet, and to bribe them with considerable promised wealth if they would both lend their strength to the battle she had planned. The creatures, once Avarica, proved they could still be reasoned with...

Perhaps neither of these pouncing foes quite reached the mark they were aiming for on Enscharaulgk as he flew over them. But after all, he was much too big to miss entirely. They grabbed hold with their huge maws, and kicking up metric tons of water, they worked to curl their long, constricting bodies around him, their attacks fueled by the enmity that only the most wicked could know for the reformed. Suddenly and disasterously beset, Enscharaulgk pushed his wings to the limit and struggled into a steep climb. But it was a flight he couldn't sustain, and try though he may, he could not break free of the serpents. Seemingly in slow motion, the three titanic Avarica began to fall out of the sky, plunging into the waiting sea below...

Captain Taurnuren observed all of this with grave disquiet. From his ship, he signaled for corvettes to move forward, to support their Grand Inquisitor and harry the terrible sea serpents. And to shoot down the planes, if possible...

Unfortunately, whether by virtue of confusing the signals or ignoring them entirely in favor of other cues, the ships of Jast-Madiir, which were clustered in with the corvettes and other support ships, advanced as well. Taurnuren's signal men tried their best to wave the allied fleet back into their place, but to no avail. The commanders of Jast-Madiir were proud men – self-assuredly the latest links in the chain of their country's great naval tradition, which included no shortage of past victories against poor little Despotopia. They were itching to show the upstarts what-for, just as their ancestors had done throughout the history of the Archipelago. Their vainglorious galleons sailed straight past the Inquisition corvettes and into the shroud.

Far away, this vanguard action did not escape the view of Kaiser Hienrechenshlagen. With keen eyes and binoculars of great virtue, he surveyed all that was before him from the fastness of *Malum In Se*'s command deck, missing nothing of relevance. He could scarcely keep from laughing when he spied the little wooden sailboats emerge from the other side of the shroud on their brave raid against his huge metal cruisers. Admittedly, they were spectacular works of craftsmanship, and truly exceptional vessels of their sort. But they were the same ships Jast-Madiir had thrown at them for generations. And here they were now, pitting themselves against a whole new make of warship, apparently none the wiser as to just how severely they were outclassed. The Kaiser, like any true Despotopian, relished the chance to pay Jast-Madiir the due penalty for their arrogance...

"Ah-ha. An attack from old Jast-Madiir," he mused. "Zhey purpose to make fools of us just like an hundred times before. Maybe zhey will not find it so easy zhis time. Do you watch, mine Lady?"

"I see," a youthful, disinterested voice behind him answered. It was Bellanchora, who tarried in deeper shadows, floating with her hands folded behind her. The Kaiser, as usual, was having a hard time unpacking her true manner. Her faceless countenance seemed equal parts vigilant and aloof. Hienrechenshlagen had to admit to being somewhat stymied. Today was the culmination of their long conspiracy – a single decisive victory that would make Despotopia unchallengable in the Archipelago! And so far, even though their attack had ultimately been anticipated, it was going over without a hitch. He had hoped she would seem more pleased...

Returning to his study of the battle, he watched gleefully as rows of cannons on two of his battleships swiveled and fired, shredding a pair of Jast-Madiir galleons in an instant, sending the rest into flight. The flash of all those huge guns going off proved a gorgeous display of overkill. His heart soared... only to crash and burn a moment later, when a volley of electromagnetic projectiles from the Inquisition battlecruisers punched a series of gaping holes in his battleships...

"Zhose diabolical lizards!" he exclaimed. "Zhey homed in on our muzzle-flashes zhrough zee fog!"

"And so old Jast-Madiir embarrasses you once again," Bellanchora retorted. "Tell your ships to save their shot. The Maenean fleet can screen Jast-Madiir if someone must. But do not let your men forget who the *real* target is here."

"Yaevogel, mine Lady," the Kaiser replied, very stymied indeed...

Meanwhile, Enscharaulgk's wrestling match with the sea serpents raged on. The long-time adversaries knew each other's every move, which seemed to lend them a devastating knack for coordinating their efforts against the dragon now. The Grand Inquisitor was hard put to it indeed, tossing and squirming furiously as the three of them continuously displaced enough ocean water to quench a desert island. He roared and threw his head and beat with his wings, but the limbs he really needed were all coiled up. He tried at least to free more of his neck, which was doubled over under the constricting grip of one of the serpents. It would have been no trouble breathing under water, but he was slowly suffocating in such a choke hold...

The Inquisition corvettes had by now reached the scene, and were firing desperately into the grudge match. Their gunners were expert, but such was the confusion that they could not always help but miss entirely, or even occasionally strike their own Grand Inquisitor. He could tell that the serpents were not enjoying the pelting they were getting. Indeed, their vexation was clear, because they seemed to be taking it out that much more on *him*. Savagely they bit at him and worked their bone-crushing embrace. But Enscharaulgk's armor was thick, and his constitution far thicker. He was sure he could ride this out somehow...

But time was not permissive. His head tumbling briefly out from under the covering of the sea, he caught a glimpe of the planes as they drew in, weaving the next layer of the smokescreen together. Enscharaulgk knew at once he must get away, and stop those planes! The water around him boiled as he began to draw on his vast reserves of enraged willpower. With one powerful twist he righted himself in the water, revealing his back to the sky, and he beat again with all his wings, calling on strength enough to topple a mountain. Slowly but surely, he emerged again from the sea... he and the two serpents with him. Now airborn, they had no leverage left to toss him this way or that, and they were exposed targets for the corvettes. The field of fire intensified, and Enscharaulgk at last muscled free with all his might while the serpents wavered. He threw them off and breathed down on them a torrent of indigo fire. Hurt and dismayed, they retreated to the depths, if only for a time. Enscharaulgk mounted up and made with all speed for the planes...

Seeing that it would be intercepted, the first plane broke its path. But Enscharaulgk was too swift for the little propeller-powered toy, and he was on it in no time. He let his body crash into it heedlessly, and the plane fell smashed out of the sky.

The second plane was more elusive. But it could not long avoid its fate. Taurnuren was greatly relieved, seeing that the threat of the smokescreen was now controlled. The Despotopians would be forced to take some direct hits now, before they could get close enough to return fire themselves. And his battlecruisers were now clear of the bombardment zone, even as Despotopia's missile barrage continued, unaware as they were that their artillery was being wasted. He had the cruisers clustered in two groups on either side of the artillery field, and their barricades still sailing back and forth in front of them. With ammunition plentiful, the cruisers continued to fire wildly... and again with greater abandon, now that the Jast-Madiir fleet had retreated back to their side of the screen. Things seemed at last to be going well...

Little did anyone notice that more trouble was coming to call, unexpected and unbidden by either side. Another fleet was inbound, approaching from the east, carried on the wind of the very blackest cloud. It did not truly rival the Inquisition or the Doom Fleet in strength or scope, but it was a large fleet nonetheless, possessed of shrewd and devious devices... not the least its racks of mines, and its huge, shrapnel-belching blunderbuss cannons...

With his one remaining eye pressed tight into the glass of his scope, Captain Herringbone grimaced as he took stock of all the commotion ahead of him. Here they had come a-spoiling at the behest of their new dread master, expecting at least to catch the Inquisition at unawares. But there was some enormous battle already in progress! It appeared the whole Inquisition navy was martialed out against an eldritch wall of smoke miles across. He didn't have a clue what to make of it all, except that it seemed to exasperate a mission that already felt like suicide. The sight was altogether surreal. Yet his eye didn't lie... the distant echo of continuously imploding ordnance confirmed as much. His pet Compsognathus chirped an uneasy chirp in his ear.

Chewing moodily at his lower lip, Herringbone handed his scope off, at a total loss for words or orders. He could think of only one rational explanation for so much chaos. But the very one he thought about was even now taking shape right behind him, equally flummoxed...

"We draweth nigh unto the enemy Citadel, O dread master," Herringbone reported. "Evidently we are not the first to do so. What do thou make of it? Is this some other arm of thine ingenius plot for revenge, O Most Vile?"

"No," Onyxadon answered, greatly bewildered, to the point of not even smiling a little. "No it isn't. Much as I would joyfully accept blame for... for whatever this is." Herringbone stood silent, letting Onyxadon study the field just as he had – brooding and full of doubt. "Would you just look at this," the vaporous elder dragon lamented at length. "I'm gone for a little while, and they go and cook up all sorts of mischief on their own! What ever is the world coming to?"

"It's rather a lot to take in," Herringbone replied. "What shall we doeth now?" He asked in full hope that Onyxadon would call off the raid, given all the unforeseen strife that was already afoot. Or, at the least, surely he would give the order to hold, and let whatever disparate forces were at work wear each other down, hopefully to something manageable...

Onyxadon's skullish eyeholes were narrow with monstrous gall. "I am very unhappy about all of this. Shoot everything."

Herringbone gulped. Too quick he had forgot who it was he was working for now. "Ye heard the master!" he called in a cracking voice to the Ivory Hyssops. "Onward!" None too quickly, the ships of the great pirate Band started drifting for the fray...

Still surveying the field, Onyxadon caught sight of something at length – a huge form wheeling through the sky, swooping like a great bird of prey at some writhing coils disturbing the ocean's surface as they maligned a troop of smaller Inquisition ships.

"There you are, brother," O'nyxon spat to himself. "At the front as always, I see. So predictable!"

"Did thou say something, my liege?" Herringbone asked.

"Never you mind. This is between me and him. Just as it has ever been."

"Him who, O dread master?"

"*Enscharaulgk*, you simple sycophant!" Onyxadon barked, heat roiling his visage. "I don't know what the trouble here is about, and I don't care. This mystery smoke should have left well enough alone! It is *my* wrath that brother Enscharaulgk is owed before all others. And it is my wrath he will have!"

Onyxadon roared, and proved every bit as fell and horrible in the height of his rage as at the pinnacle of his fiendish delight. His own pirates threw themselves down, overcome with heart-stopping dread as great mirky wings drew up in toxic streaks over their ships. So it was that the terror of the ages hurled himself headlong into the battle of 7/14/21, more hungry for vengeance than ever, having been upstaged by these unknown usurpers. Whatever they were here to prove, he would prove it first...

"Did you hear zhat?" the Kaiser asked, perplexed by the intrusion of some new, distant roar. "It vas not zee sound of Enscharaulgk, nor one of our own serpents." He turned to Bellanchora. "Vhat vas it?"

The Ghost-Princess opened a small portal through space with which to spy beyond the veil of their own smokescreen. It was some sort of convex distortion which revealed a very wide panorama of the battle in all directions. Though Bellanchora had promised to stay her strange arsenal of supernatural powers and let Despotopia claim victory in a fair fight, the

Kaiser had not been displeased to let her rob the Inquisitors of their courage at the first with her music (an advantage now offset by the great Organ anyway), nor did he begrudge her making so small a window now, only to satisfy his curiosity.

She quickly homed-in on what it was she sought. A huge black vapor was careening into the battle like a comet.

"Oh," she said. "Onyxadon is here."

"Zee Eternally Most Vile!" the Kaiser exclaimed. "Here? Now? Vhat are zee odds of zhat?"

"Quite good, if you know aught of Onyxadon," Bellanchora answered. "I hope he doesn't spoil all our fun..."

Enscharaulgk swooped again, trying to nab one of the sea serpents, but again it slipped his grip. Now that the airplanes had been taken out, this was the next logical threat for him to tackle. These fallen members of his race were grown too large and deadly, and they posed a serious danger to his ships. In his brief time away, they had come back and nearly devastated the corvettes which had aided his escape. Now they were protecting each other...

The Grand Inquisitor tried yet again, only to come up empty-handed. If he could get just *one* of the serpents, the threat could be managed. He could surely defeat them individually. Together, though, they were perilously strong.

He made another pass, and this nearly proved disastrous. The two serpents caught him again instead. And he may have gone under, too, if not for what happened next...

In all the ruckus, Enscharaulgk had missed that one sound he knew better than any – the roar of Onyxadon. He paid for that oversight with a furious gut-check. His ancient arch-nemesis swept over him like a gale, wrenching him instantly from the death-grip of the serpents, hurling them both skyward, back toward the Citadel. Enscharaulgk struggled valiantly, but he was much too caught at unawares. And Onyxadon was in rare form, possessed by an uncharacteristic rage. He slammed Enscharaulgk against his own tower, crumpling steel siding yards thick and buckling the very foundations of the whole titanic structure.

Below, Jek and the strike team faltered, shook like dust mites on a rung bell. Shielding themselves, they looked up with horror at the sight. Here was that elemental battle – the contest of all contests, which had stretched on for more than ninety centuries – playing out once again before their very eyes. Brother versus brother. Enscharaulgk versus Onyxadon!

"O great calamity!" Parissah lamented. "Onyxadon is come unlooked for, at the very time we should have looked for him!"

"Let's shoot him!" Audrey exclaimed, more than ready to start contributing to all this mayhem.

But Zedulon laid a talon on her musket. "It will do no good. You cannot harm O'nyxon. You will only waste shots if you try."

Audrey groaned. "There are too many things in this world you can't shoot," she said.

"Fie!" Zavion exclaimed. "If only brother Washoe could have managed to stow *two* kicks in the Boot! Then we would'st have an answer for this old villain too! Alas that we must spend all the great power of our relic on Bellanchora alone."

"But that is precisely what we must do," Zedulon said. "Enscharaulgk assuredly would not wish otherwise. Do not fear for him! This is the fight he knows best. Far be it from any of us to imagine how long he has been fighting it! And he succeeds as often as he fails."

"But his *treasure*, Zedulon," Parissah protested. "The mission depends on the Despotopians absconding with his treasure! If Enscharaulgk fails this time, he shall never live to win or lose again!"

The crashing and roaring overhead caused them all another jolt as the two great dragons dueled up and down the Citadel tower.

"You know as well as I that is a risk he would accept," Zedulon answered Parissah.

Conceding the point, she sighed and nodded. "You're right, of course. He would."

Back at the front, the corvettes went into full retreat, now at the mercy of the sea serpents. Taurnuren signaled the battlecruisers to cover their retreat, and their electromagnetic guns were leveled into the midst of the monsters, kicking up a huge squall in the sea with their supersonic projectiles. After a hearty barrage, the cruisers were waved back into their original firing pattern. When the whitecapped water began to settle, there was no sign of the serpents anymore. They may have been dashed. Or they had just as likely withdrawn once again to the depths, waiting for another chance to surprise the Inquisitors. All the sea commanders would have to remain vigilant.

Meanwhile, the two layers of the smokescreen were beginning to fail. Mostly, they had come to tattered, wandering edges at the top. But slowly – *painfully* slowly, perhaps – the fraying of the smoke was intensifying, marching its way down to the ocean-floor. Whatever might seem to be going against them, the Inquisition fleet would soon have its chance to take unobstructed shots...

As if in response to the heightening peril of the Doom Fleet's plight, the Maenean navy came charging through the mist, much as Jast-Madiir had done mere minutes ago. Captain Taurnuren didn't entertain the bait, keeping the main guns of his division fixed forward. The smaller cannons could effectively screen the Maenean galleons, once they were in range. He knew he needed to keep the real pressure on their bigger, metal cousins...

And he was right. As the press-ganged sailboats swept through the ocean swells into range, it very quickly turned into a rout. The Maenean volley was well-synchronized, with the ships all in a row, at last turning their broadside cannons and marching in single file down the front of the Inquisition line. But hundreds of their cannonballs were screened by the mobile barricades, and the Coup-de-Grâce battlecruisers returned fire with their point-defense guns much more expertly. Some Maenean ships were shredded in a single shot by the spinal guns, when a battlecruiser simply failed to shoot around them. All remaining raiders turned back in flight. The ever-eager commanders of Jast-Madiir gave chase as far as the shroud – another hinderance to Taurnuren's division, which was forced to take special care not to blast their own allies again. But on the whole, morale for the Inquisition-alligned forces was on the rise. The Maenean raid seemed to betray some desperation in the enemy camp.

Yet not all was well, even then. The serpents returned to harry some of the Inquistion's Destroyers. They were large enough monsters to wrestle a proper capital ship into a watery grave, and had deigned to prove so. The sudden attack threw the whole port-side fleet of support ships into confusion.

At the same time, the missile bombardment from the *Malum In Se* intensified and broadened, and a few of the battlecruisers didn't notice in time enough to dodge the encroaching field of fire. Some were lost, and the rest were forced further outward. The shuffling to make more room disrupted the whole systemic firing pattern. But the Inquisitors were intensely drilled and disciplined, and the paired formations of battlecruisers were soon in stride again. So the battle raged on, even as the shroud began to fray and fade more and more. Anticipation and anxiety grew as the time for the two navies to truly meet drew near...

Dodging a snap of phantom jaws as he clung desperately to the side of the Citadel tower, Enscharaulgk reached out and grabbed Onyxadon by the throat. For just a moment, the evil dragon gaped in distress – a firey breath choked back by the throttling action. But then his face melted into its horrible smile. And then it melted entirely. Enscharaulgk was left holding nothing, even as four grinning heads on four craning necks ghosted suddenly in around him, bathing him in scorching heat from all sides. His armor glowed orange-hot by the end, and the Grand Inquisitor coughed and sputtered, stifled in his mask so that his gills temporarily failed him. Onyxadon's heads converged, snickering at his enemy's expense. But Enscharaulgk was not long staggered, and he forced in a great breath... then forced it back out ablaze. Onyxadon was washed into a swirling plume before Enscharaulgk's fire stream, and all his mighty essence seemed no more than the smoke rolling off the flame.

When finally Enscharaulgk relented, he could see nothing of his foe besides distant, fading black ribbons of ghostly murk. This was not unlike he had seen Onyxadon perish countless times before, but he intuited well enough that the old fiend was just playing dead – one of his many favored simple tricks, with which he never failed to amuse himself. But Enscharaulgk was glad, and sighed in relief. It gave him time enough to catch his breath, and to check on more global concerns. Already tired, he climbed higher, up and around the tower, surveying the battle through the dense water rolling down his visored helmet. There was no new devilry that he could espy, and it looked like the smokescreen was thinning in the rain and wind.

On the surface, things appeared good. But the old dragon felt a sudden weight on his heart – a foreboding... or, something. But what exactly was it he felt? It was dreadful, whatever it was. More than the battle itself, he found himself trying to unpack his own *feeling*. It wasn't just a fear. It felt more like an emptiness... as if an integral part of himself had abruptly gone missing. He had never felt anything like it before. But it grew more acute and oppressive even as he considered it...

At last, he understood. It was impossible, but he was nonetheless sure of it. It was his *treasure*! It had already been *taken* from him!

Phantom claws rent his armor from behind. He roared in pain, even as a second swipe overpowered him and threw him down. He rolled and crashed, leaving huge dents in his Citadel, his armor, and his hide alike. Finally, he landed in a heap on the roof of his own Wide Path behind the tower, with sadistic laughter echoing down on him from on high. He rolled over with a groan and picked himself up. Even in a fresh new body, which should have been good for hours of a contest such as this, he already felt ruined. On tender legs, it was as if his armor – a glorified rough, rattling sack – was the only thing holding his jellified bones together...

"Did you think the fun was over so soon, brother?" Onyxadon asked as his terrible blackness gathered.

"Nope," Enscharaulgk lamented. "Certainly not before a few more tricks. You have never relented your devious ways, brother. Not in all the ages. Though long I held out hope you would reform."

"That is part of what makes you a dunce," Onyxadon replied, marching down the tower. "You are become so good that you look for virtue where there is none. And you are a muscle-head with an insufferable humility complex. You're the only one besides me who keeps growing grander and stronger, and yet still you willingly play the stooge for brother Magormissahr." His grin grew more venomous as he closed in for his final point. "But you know what it is that bothers me most about you?"

"It escapes me," Enscharaulgk answered.

"In all these millennia, you never developed a sense of humor."

Enscharaulgk huffed defiantly. "I could say the same about you."

Onyxadon recoiled, then nodded with venomous appreciation. "Ahh... petty insults. Well, that's a start."

With a growl, he rejoined the duel...

Aboard the *Carroccio*, Taurnuren closed the last few feet of distance between himself and the shimmering, rain-streaked viewport. At last, as he watched, real Despotopian muscle was emerging from the screen – hulking battleships charging sidelong for their flanks. They came out guns blazing, though Taurnuren couldn't be sure off-hand whether they were truly in effective range, or if the enemy was taking its own wild shots. But it mattered little. With a pointing gesture, he gave the order to turn and fire on the nearest battleship. Within moments, the whole division was immolating enemy ships-of-the-line with their lightning-fast implosive shells. The affray quickly reached a fever pitch. Victory seemed at hand...

Jek winced, his gaze drawn to the water at the foot of the ramp. The sea was still roiling in the storm, but there were bubbles all of a sudden. Some other sort of disruption was at work here before his eyes. Even as he wondered whether he ought to say something, the bubbling grew furious, and marched back into deeper water perhaps some hundred feet or more...

"What is that?" Jek asked.

"We must find cover!" Zedulon answered, and all heeded him, sure of some sudden insight into the immediate future.

"There is a narrow catwalk beside the ramp," Parissah explained, leading the way at once. "We can hide there."

"Hide?" Jek said, even as he followed them down the ramp urgently. "But what the Heck are we hiding from?"

The answer began to reveal itself in the next moment as untold gallons of water rolled off a great flat surface that peaked up from below. Jek was incredulous as he rounded the base of the ramp onto the catwalk, waved on by Parissah. It was a ship – submerged – bursting from the sea! And not just *any* ship. By all appearances, it fit the profile of one particularly crucial mission asset...

"Is that the troop ship?" Audrey asked, reaching the same conclusion Jek had.

"It is!" Parissah marveled. "But how can that be? We had eyes on the troop ship just before the screens went up..."

Jek looked out into the harbor, and beyond, to the battle. It had picked up steam, with the screen now failing, and the Despotopian ships resolving into view. Straining his eyes, the mystery deepened...

"There it is now! It's still in the middle of their formation!" he exclaimed.

"A decoy..." Parissah realized. "They have *two* troop ships. One for our guns, and one submerged to slip our nets!" She shook her head. "Submersible ships – what a vile trick!"

At once, they heard a clamor behind them – snail guns going off, fighting and slaying. They grew very quiet, even as the chaos approached them... from *higher* up the ramp, not lower! A whole special forces unit of Despotopian insurgents came tromping down from the Citadel, some carrying huge casks.

"Those villains," Parissah whispered. "They have been here since before the battle!"

"What?!" Audrey asked in amazement.

"A ship like this could have come at any time unlooked-for!" Parissah explained. "They infiltrated, they waited, and now the ship has returned for them, and they make their speedy getaway with Enscharaulgk's treasure!"

"This is no time to puzzle out every detail," Zedulon said. "They board with their prize, even as we speak! We too must sneak aboard, or fail in our mission!"

Quickly but discretely, they all rushed ahead for the Despotopian troop ship. Jek didn't know what made him do it, but at the last second he stole a look back, into the furthest shadowy reaches of the catwalk. There, he could swear he saw the outline of some strange figure... but only for a moment. An ocean swell broke over the walk between them, and the figure was gone. He blinked in disbelief, then hurried after his comrades...

The screen was no more. Taurnuren himself felt a little overwhelmed at the size of the enemy navy – still too close for comfort – even as his division continued to disembowel the huge ships in small groups, unanswered by effective return fire. Though the enemy was very great, and drawing near, on the whole their situation remained seemingly ideal…

But Taurnuren was ever grave and vigilant. So it was that he noticed a couple strange things happen in synchronous. Things that boded a sudden, disastrous change in the course of the fight. Barely half a moment he spared in hesitation as he contemplated their danger. Then he gave the order…

"Breakaway speed!" he called. "Signal all ships into full flight!"

Sheltering around the bend in a low level of the troop ship, ready to break through an access hole if the ship suddenly submerged, the strike team caught another glimpse of the fleet battle. The other troop ship was going under now, in full view of the Inquisition navy! Incredibly, the Despotopians seemed to be tipping their hat, letting their enemies in on the ruse…

"Did you see that?" Jek asked. "The other troop ship just went under!"

"That is not what I noticed," Parissah said, in a voice of disquiet. "I noticed the missile barrage. It has ceased!"

"And now the fancy battlecruisers are splitting off," Trockelov observed.

"What doth it all portend?" Zavion asked.

Parissah ignored the question, throwing herself up against the railing for the best possible view.

"The *missiles*," she said. "Of course! The bombardment was never any blind swing. They split Tarnuren's ranks! Don't you see? They have cleared a spot!"

"*Cleared a spot*?" Jek asked. "Cleared a spot for what?"

"For more of the same," Parissah explained breathlessly. "More submersibles."

Her conclusion was only too true. Hardly did the words pass her mask, and the first few spikes of the enemy's secret weapons split the surface of the water far away, between the Inquisition's lines. A pair of destroyer-sized protrusions followed, waterfalls cascading off the ends of long, huge cannons, which tore into the nearby battlecruisers with sudden, savage might. A half dozen were claimed at once in a blinding plume of gunpowder. More were quickly targeted and blasted.

But this proved only the beginning. The two new assets on the field, emerging from the depths, continued to mount up ever higher. Another layer of cannons, greater and longer than the first, bubbled up out of the sea, unleashing a torrent of new fire, even as the higher guns continued to acquire new targets. Another layer followed. And another, ever larger.

Taurnuren's division tried to punch its way through the spread wings of the rest of the Despotopian Fleet, desperate to escape the sudden rout of the submarine-dreadnaughts. But now those enemy battleships were in range too, and the Inquisitors were being savaged from all sides. Even smoldering battleships they had thought wholly derelict somehow found vehemence enough to bite the vanishing ranks of the Inquisition as they passed in mad flight. To make matters worse, the barricades hindered their retreat, staggering and even crashing into some of the ships they were meant to protect. And yet more guns came up from the depths, seemingly in an endless stack. The paired dreadnaughts, tall and terrible, cast a shadow of death over the field all about. The guns of Despotopia had an insatiable appetite, mowing with deafening clamor, like an entire army of thunderstorms thrown into a sudden fratricidal confusion.

At the skirt of the battle, the ships of the Twin Medulseldan Queens – all but forgot about – wandered a bit too close, and were quickly turned into target practice, effortlessly sunk by the ample leftovers of the Despotopian arsenal before they could contribute aught to anything. What little remained of the Inquisition navy had not opportunity to take any notice of the sudden failure of their unlikely allies. Their plight was far too grim, and their own total failure nigh at hand...

Enscharaulgk's duel raged on all the while, back and ever up the side of the tower again. The Grand Inquisitor grew very weary indeed, and was succumbing to his wounds.

It was in this manner that he looked out again over his fleet, suddenly decimated before his eyes, horrible towers of the enemy now standing over a burning sea of utter ruin. He was horrified – horrified as he had not been in many an age, if indeed he had ever witnessed such a moment of despair. Desperately he climbed, fending off weightless attacks from Onyxadon as he worked to coax his incredible bulk skyward...

It was a slow climb... painful, and without hope. Until at last, the Grand Inquisitor was satisfied that he was high and prominent enough. He spread his wings and roared, signaling total retreat. He hoped against hope to coax more speed out of the remnants of his forces. He hoped against hope the display might attract some Despotopian guns to him, if only to draw even the slightest malice away from his fleet. Beyond all else, his heart railed against the sure doom of all who had depended on him, even as the awful jaws of fate swung shut...

Jek and the strike team looked back to the Citadel, hearing the call of Enscharaulgk, strong but dire. His wings waved wildly, filling the sky. But even as he signaled, the team feared they may be the only ones left to observe it, their carrier ship now passing heedlessly between the shadows of the terrible dreadnaughts, on its way to deliver Bellanchora's prize.

In a final, culminating moment of defeat, Onyxadon seized on the Grand Inquisitor from behind, finding him careless in the wild abandon of his call...

And Enscharaulgk fell then, perhaps never to rise again...

Coda

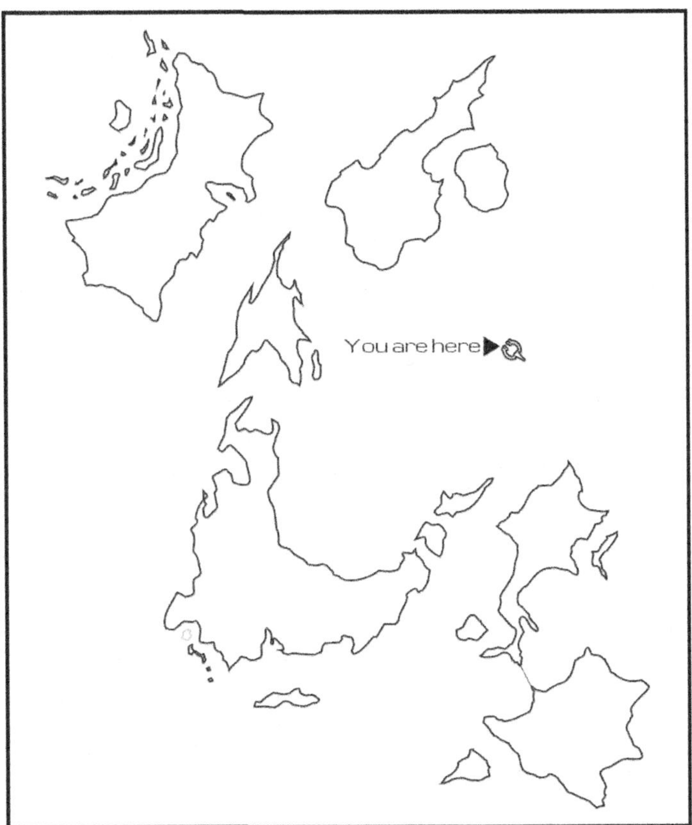

"I have been asked many times about the End. When will it happen? What will it be like? Should we even expect an End *to begin with? In any case, I do not know. Nor could any of the Heron monarchs I've spoken to over the ages seem to shed any light on the subject. But if, ultimately, the universe does go on forever, I would say it is no meaner fate than it deserves."*

- Magormissahr, *Referendums on the World, Vol. 254*

"Now the battle may begin in earnest," Zedulon said.

The rain rolled loud off the deck above. The ocean roared. *Pharonomagnus* began yet another movement of its wild, brilliant sonata. But from the party, there was silence…

"*What*?" Jek demanded at length. "Is that supposed to be some kind of joke? The battle is *over*!"

There was a strange light in Zedulon's false eye. If anything, the old bird looked disgustingly pleased with himself in this, the hour when evil claimed its final victory.

"You forget many things, brave master Jek," Zedulon replied. "First, the battle is most assuredly *not* over for us. Our mission parameters have not changed. Bellanchora must still be kicked, and for that there is yet hope. If you pine for the loss of so many good Inquisitors, I understand… it turned into a horrible rout! But even the Doom Fleet, I would not yet count victorious. They still have much to contend with." He flitted up to the railing, and craned his head out, as if listening on the winds. "I think the reinforcements are arriving, even now."

"Reinforcements?" Parissah asked. "Of what nature?"

"*My* nature, of course!" Zedulon laughed, whirling back. "Did you truly think I had those battle plans drawn for nothing? No indeed! The Fleet Admirals of Roemnar come to attack this very place! And with my royal spear, I shall lead them – not against *your* people, few of them that are left – but against the *Princess*… the enemy of us all."

Even as he spoke, a new sound came thrumming from far off – a droning noise in the sky, like the flurried beat of ten thousand giant insect wings. Jek's heart suddenly elated, and he was left with a dopey smile for his enigmatic master, the Heron Proconsul.

"This is where we part ways, for a time, my friends and associates," Zedulon continued. "I have other business. But we shall all meet again on the *Malum In Se*, soon enough."

"Is that a premonition, Proconsul?" Parissah asked, also sounding much more pleased now.

"That, young Parissah, is a *fact*." And with a rolling backward leap, Zedulon took to the sky on swift wings, soaring with his spear glistening behind him as his false eye shined bright to lead the way…

As he flew with great haste, Zedulon found the western corner of the sky thick with his fighters and bombers, plodding but inexorable. They were making straight for the Citadel tower. And they may have made quite a nice burning husk of it, too. But Zedulon interdicted them, rounding a narrow arc to fly at their head. If the hundreds of pilots did not at once notice his spear, they could not very well have missed the great orange glow of his eye. So it was they saw that, against any expectation, their sovereign – long-missing – was leading them into battle. And when, after some seconds of holding course in front of them, he veered to the left, choosing a new course that led them directly over alien ships, tall and horrible to behold, it was only too natural that they dutifully followed, one and all…

On the dreadnaughts below, sirens wailed. Heavy guns swiveled for the great wave of airplanes – but they were clumsy things and slow. The crews were too late in their response.

And for all their sloth and bulk, the Despotopian behemoths made themselves ideal targets for the hailstorm of bombs that hurled down from above, rolling over the sea...

Yet such great peaks of steel would not be quickly flattened. Below the carpet of blasts, the dreadnaughts remained standing. Willful and robust was Despotopian armor, and their weaponry shrewd and cunning. Smaller guns, spitting deadly flak, began to bite back at the bombers overhead – roused slowly as from deep slumber, but able to chip away at the daunting air raid. Even with so many aircraft at his beck, Zedulon saw that it would indeed take time to whittle down the Doom Fleet...

"What is this now?" Bellanchora demanded, seeing and hearing the batte reignite far off, much to her sudden chagrin. "*Herons*?! Outrageous! You elected not to kill their Proconsul, and yet still he accosts us!"

The Kaiser barked an order through his loudspeaker. At once the *Malum In Se* itself was loud with sirens, the deck creaking and buckling as a huge space before the artillery batteries began to open up and extrude long ramps, sloping skyward.

The Princess sighed. "It is well we prepared for the possibility of enemy aircraft. But what a nuisance! Our business is with Enscharaulgk alone. Must all the other powers in Idriulthoronta rush to his aid?"

"Perhaps, mine Lady... perhaps," the Kaiser answered, pointing slowly out toward another, south-easterly point. "Ve appear to have even more uninvited guests."

Bellanchora floated past Hienrechenshlagen, silent for a moment as she looked on. "My word. What are *those* things doing here?"

In that far corner of the battlefield, keenly espied by the Kaiser and the Princess, a dense multitude of pale blue lights began to bubble up out of the ocean. From the floundering ruin of their ships, the armies of the Twin Queens had broken forth, and were now swarming in great droves to the surface. Little did the Despotopians realize that by sinking the rough barges of the Queens, they had effectively knocked a pair of beehives to the ground with a stick – and none too long a stick at that. Soon there was a great and growing blot of drones washing over the sea, lethargic as ever, but driven and powered from afar by the magnetic force of their Queens' rage. And this might have proven problematic enough, but it was only the first of the Despotopians' woes to emerge from the derelicts. Larger, faster, and far more terrible drones suddenly burst skyward and out towards the unsuspecting Doom Fleet...

Then came the *real* terror. The ocean flashed a deep red for many hundreds of yards round about. It was a furious light show, reflected in synchronous by the bluish glow of the Berlie Beirel armies above. After breathless moments of this, two great roilings in the sea gave way to the enormous, angular forms of Irisa and Asiri themselves. Rare indeed in living memory was the sight of a Queen of the Meduselda to any but attendant drones. Now there were *two* of them hovering over the battlefield – livid, thrumming – like living storms of red crystal wreathed in lightnings as potent as any the sky could produce – each of them so huge that it seemed impossible that any ship had borne them forth. It was a moment out of history. For the first time, the Twin Queens, who had been at war with each other since their inception, found they had a common enemy. And with single purpose, they and their grand armies advanced together into battle...

Enscharaulgk lay where he had been cast, performing what seemed a vain search for the will to move. His great body was alight with searing pain. He'd known far worse, in many past battles. And of course, the incarnation of himself he now commanded was the largest, the toughest, and the mightiest he'd ever had. No, the problem was not his body. It was his spirit that was broken at the last – the one thing that should never have failed him...

"What are you doing?" Onyxadon demanded impatiently. "Get up!"

Enscharaulgk sighed. His towering neck flopped ineffectually. "No, brother. It is no use. I am beat."

"Not yet, you're not!" Onyxadon snapped. "What is happening to you people, anyway? The ones I used to call brother and sister? Where is your old strength? Let alone your *new* strength?"

Enscharaulgk growled in exasperation. "What are you complaining about? The victory is yours, brother. Just take it."

"Oh, I intend to. Make no mistake, I'm going to kill you this time, Enscharaulgk. But not yet! If I have to wait nigh on a hundred years again for our next battle, then you must oblige me with a better contest than *this*!"

Enscharaulgk turned to look at him. "You would wait in vain. This is to be our last fight. I will not return. She's come back for me, brother. She has come and taken my treasure! I am finished. All things are finished..."

Onyxadon looked on in staggered astonishment. "Taken?" he asked at last. "Taken your..." and he faltered. "*She*? *She* who!? Who the devil is behind all of today's nonsense?"

"It is Bellanchora," Enscharaulgk sighed. "She has spent years engineering my downfall. Now it comes to you to complete her work. So why hesitate? You have won at last... forever."

For a while, there was silence between them, filled only with rain and thunder, and the Organ far overhead. But as the moment wore on, blairing sirens and the sound of distant explosions came echoing round the Citadel tower. To the east, surging red flashes bathed the sky in a flurry of flashing twilights, and a thrumming sound beat their eardrums. Enscharaulgk's head finally craned up, his wonder at these new developments lancing through his heaviness of heart.

"It doesn't sound like your fight is finished to me," Onyxadon said finally. "Someone remains to face this enemy of yours. *Bellanchora*, did you say? We've not met. Isn't she the one that cooked up that other big cataclysm a while ago? The one I missed out on completely?"

"Yup. That's her," Enscharaulgk answered.

Onyxadon growled, looking out toward the battle at large. "I think I should like to make her regret such a slight."

At last, Enscharaulgk came to his feet, sending Onyxadon a look of great resolution through his mask. "Then let us for once in history mess stuff up together!"

The smile of Onyxadon grew wide and villainous indeed, his whole essence roiling with deadly intense heat. "Oh, but I do like the sound of that..."

And with that, the two dragons took at once to wing...

"*Holy moley*," Jek gasped. "What are those huge terrifying red things in the sky?"

Parissah tore her gaze away from the air battle, scanning the ocean. "Ah, good," she said, finding what he had indicated. "The Queens are taking hand, at last. And it looks like they brought their entire defense battalions. That is excellent."

"Boy, this is actually starting to work out good," Audrey said. "The Doom Fleet's in trouble, and we made it aboard the troop ship without being seen."

"Yeah, that was lucky," Jek agreed. "If we just stay here out of sight, we'll have nothing to worry about till we dock with the Flagship."

As soon as he finished talking, new alarms went off – klaxons from the troop ship itself. The hatch they were hunkered by quickly flew open, and a Despotopian death squad leapt out at them. Jek groaned. The strike team's part in the fight had come now too, ready or not...

Zedulon stole a look back under his wings as his bombers unleashed another torrential downpour of explosive fury. From the very first pass, there was a terrible fire in all layers of the dreadnaughts. But after many passes, the burning skeletons refused to yield! The old Proconsul was a little incredulous. Hardly in time did he notice the latest Despotopian trick...

Sweeping out of the north, a whole new wing of airplanes was moving to intercept them – fast and smokey planes with many wings. The *Malum In Se*, it turned out, had a considerable bank of aircraft, and had set about slinging them into the sky from tall ramps, like arrows in great ballistas. If he had not spotted them then, they may well have maneuvered into the flank of his airforce and decimated them. But Zedulon had time left to react. He angled his spear behind him to point, and within a few moments, his fighters started to peel out of formation, plotting a new course to engage. Then Zedulon led his bombers in a wide arc away, to keep some distance while the gunners in the bombers made ready...

Very soon, he heard the guns of his fighters open up, with enemy guns answering in kind. The huge dogfight ensued. But he stayed focused, lining his bombers up for another run on the dreadnaughts. He had to break them soon! Many Despotopian support ships were drawing near, surely with more flak guns...

Suddenly, Zedulon heard a loud roar, that was answered by another loud roar. Just beneath him, Enscharaulgk flew by with a powerful gust of wind from his wings, hurtling toward the encroaching Despotopian ships. The Proconsul blinked in redoubled surprise, when he spied Onyxadon's shadowy essence close in from the other side of the dreadnaughts, as if the two dragons had coordinated a pincer attack. Indeed, they had done precisely that. *And why ever not*? Zedulon wondered to himself, amused. It was, after all, a bit of weird day...

"Looks like we're coming up on the battle now, sir," a Phage pirate lackey said.

"Aye, and fortunate it turned back into a proper battle just before we got here," Herringbone replied, still mulling rather absently how they could possibly come out of this.

"What are our orders, sir?" the lackey continued.

"We do just as the dread master told us. Shoot everything." He tried his best to sound personally convicted of the course.

Presently they heard a roar, and saw the dread master himself, swooping down into the fray ahead of them. Herringbone was a little surprised to see both him and Enscharaulgk filling the sky, wreaking mayhem on the ships, rather than each other.

"Looks like the master's set his sights on the grey ships," the lackey pointed out meekly.

"Aye," Herringbone agreed. "Then those be the ones we'll do the most shootin' at."

Jek parried a stroke from an oscilating blade, proving the virtue of the Indigo Knights' forging. A quick remise and he felled the last of their enemies to present themselves in that first assault.

"Well, they know we're here," Grosdrev Trockelov pointed out. "That could cause a ruffle in the plans."

"And they have radios too," Audrey explained. "They can warn the Princess that we're coming."

"If indeed we continue to come," Parissah said. "They may also stop the ship until they have overwhelmed us. We will have to reach the control room. Hopefully the radio will also be there, and we can signal an all-clear, so the Flagship may still be caught at unawares."

"There's bound to be an army between us and the command room," Trockelov said. "How are we goin' to make it?"

"They have already made us at this location, and I would say you have a dandy choke-point," Parissah strategized. "Can Guppy Troop keep the pressure up here?"

"Sure thing. Where are you goin'?"

Parissah went to the railing, stumbled up, and reached the overhanging floor of the deck above. "We are going to climb for the top deck. Hopefully they will not be expecting an attack coming from a different level."

"That's crazy!" Audrey exclaimed. "The rest of us can't reach up there!"

Parissah drew herself up over the lip of the deck, then hung back down, extending a hand. "I'll bring those of you that can't climb up one at a time," she said. "Come now! We shall have to hurry!"

"Let the Boot-bearer go first," Zavion announced. They helped Audrey up, careful that she wouldn't stumble, and Parissah hoisted her to the next level.

"Best none of the smokey mouth-breathers see this," Trockelov mused. "Let's get just inside here, shall we, Guppy Troop? Head 'em off, before they get a glimpse of our plan."

The Guppy Troopers nodded, and taking their weapons up, they infiltrated the hatch, cautious and discrete. The other Inquisitors present did as Parissah had done, if with a bit more effort for their somewhat smaller bodies, and soon they were helping the Knights and Associates up and over. Horus Templar may have been tall enough to reach himself, but slinging his warhammer across his back, he accepted help from two Inquisitors.

In this manner they quickly ascended to the top deck. Jek was the last to shimmy up that final layer – a rather harrowing experience in the slippery rain. As he sat for a moment on the deck, recovering his breath, it was taken again as he looked out over the surrounding insanity. Not far off, pirate ships and surviving stragglers of the Inquisition and Jast-Madiir navies were mixing it up with Despotopian battleships, while further back the terrible aerial battle ensued above and about the smoldering dreadnaughts. He watched as Enscharaulgk and Onyxadon dived down and toppled enemy destroyers, while the sea serpents made desperate lunges after their flighted counterparts. Even further away, the Berlie Beirels swept over a whole Despotopian flotilla in a great and ghostly tide, while their towering Queens raced overhead with larger, abominable drones in formation, singeing whole small ships out of existence with single lightning bolts.

Next to all that, he saw a *huge hand*! He recoiled... then realized it was just Parissah giving him a hand up. He took it.

"So far so good," Parissah said, panting a bit as she helped him to his feet. "We are unresisted. Let's make for the front! Surely the control room will be that way."

Hardly had the group begun to jog for the bow of the ship when another hatch opened a ways in front of them, swinging up from the deck to reveal a wide stair, with Despotopian regulars leaping out! Even as the Knights, Inquisitors and Associates ground to an unsure halt, their swift enemies formed a firing line with their crossbows. Jek and Audrey blanched. There was nowhere to go...

Parissah leapt into the gulf in front of them, curling her wings before herself just in time to catch a slew of Despotopian arrows in the thick leathery folds. Jek and Audrey slid out from behind her on a knee, taking two shots (each) with their muskets. The remaining Despotopians reacquired their targets to return fire. But Parissah's wings swung out to shield them again, and as they did she breathed an immolating stream of orange flame. By that time, Zavion and the Knights closed in to harry the skirmishers, and Jek and Audrey made use of the free moments, with Jek reloading, and Audrey bathing Parissah's wings in Life energy, eschewing the arrows as she went. Amid the fray, a rogue Despotopian archer sprung out of the crowd to line up a shot, but Parissah was faster on the draw with her snail pistol. Beginning to reload her sidearm in sync with Audrey as Jek finished readying his own musket, she also drew her sword with the claw of her wing. So the strike team took its first few wading steps into what was sure to be an epic fight...

We must crack these dreadnaughts at once, or there will be no bombs left for the rest of the Doom Fleet... and no bombers to drop them anyway, Zedulon thought. As if in answer, one of the dreadnaughts suddenly burst – erupting with blinding magnificence from some sort of internal calamity. The scalding blow of the shockwave staggered Zedulon. He blacked out, but caught himself in the air a moment later. *That was nearly a disaster*, he mused. *I should know well enough to mind what I wish for by now...*

Even so, he was going to have to keep the pressure on the other dreadnaught until it was neutralized as well. He led the bombers lazily around for another run.

His ears suddenly popped and rang, and he hit a wall of intense turbulence, all-but shook into free-fall. A round of flak went off too close for comfort! And another soon followed, fortunately more wide than the first. He was being targeted! He flew an evasive pattern, but it took nearly all his nerve just to stay the course. One wrong move or specially good shot, and he would be shredded. But he couldn't turn aside...

Finally, the dreadnaught was just under him. He found himself staring down into the utter blackness of four or five flak gun barrels. It was not a hopeful sight. This might indeed be his final pass...

That turned out to be so. But not for the morbid reasons he feared. Just before he might have been dashed, huge projectiles smashed through the side of the dreadnaught lightning-fast, igniting fierce implosions. The already badly-wounded superstructure gave way at last to sheering force, and all the highest layers began to buckle and topple over the sea. Zedulon looked up into the distance, searching for the source of the timely shots. Taurnuren had formed a new line of battlecruisers far off – gravely depleted in ranks, but still deadly! He grunted his approval, even as the bombers spent one last round of ammunition on the ruin of the second dreadnaught, blasting its smoldering remnants into the waiting abyss.

The Proconsul gestured a command to fire at will, releasing the bombers from his charge to do as they would with the rest of the Doom Fleet. He had led the charge long enough, and feared now for his friends, still trapped on a huge ship that was lowsy with some of the Kaiser's best fighting men...

Just as he turned to leave the aerial theatre, he found someone he did not expect, and it comforted him...

"Baegulgog!" Zedulon exclaimed, nearly running into the Clerk in midair. "What *are* you doing here?!"

"Good show, old boy!" Baegulgog replied. "I was hoping you'd find me – or anyway that someone would. But this is indeed a chance meeting!"

"Aren't you supposed to be in the Glass Chapel? How have you managed to wander so far from the tower in so short a time?"

The Clerk flashed as with some embarrassment. "I suppose I have abandoned my post, yes. But my work was done, and I grew anxious. I had an Inquisitor rush me down to meet you, but you had all already gone. I floated high aloft to see if I could discern where you'd got to, only to be swept up in this great black cloud and whisked very far afield. And so, here I am! Do you know, I think that cloud may have been *Onyxadon*!?"

"It was," Zedulon said. "But let us get you to the troop ship, with the other Associates. If you mean to contribute something more to the battle, I daresay you'll have your chance there!"

"Dear me, yes," Baegulgog lamented. "They are embattled!"

Zedulon turned and looked down at the troop ship, watching as small figures and distant rushed out into some sort of tussle on the top deck. There were many, and the situation appeared critical. But not far off, he found something else – something that might avail greatly in such a large melee...

"Don't be alarmed, Baegulgog," Zedulon said, reassuring himself as well as the Clerk. "We'll reach them in plenty of time. But we must round up some of our allies first."

He grabbed hold of Baegulgog and tugged him earthwards...

"Zee dreadnaughts are no more," Hienrechenshlagen announced in a haunted voice. "I vill recall zee Fleet at vonce. Zhey will be safer under our guns."

"Are you having doubts now?" Bellanchora upbraided him. "Is the strength of your devices less than you supposed? Remember that I offered you more. *Much* more." Her empty helm looked down at her ghostly gauntlet. "Even now, you could call on the power to destroy all your enemies, if you wished."

"Zhat vas not zee agreement!" the Kaiser objected. "Und surely you boast."

"You will see for yourself soon enough," the Princess replied. "For the time is fast approaching when I will exercise my power to the full – with your leave, or without."

Before he had time to consider her boding, a radio operator removed his earmuffs and turned and stood before the Kaiser. "Report from zee troop ship, mine Kaiser. Zhere has been an insurgency! Zhey are under attack by enemy stowaways."

"Order zhem to hold until zee situation is controlled," the Kaiser replied.

"No," Bellanchora commanded. "I would not have the delivery of Enscharaulgk's treasure be forestalled. Surely your men can handle a few saboteurs. And if not them... then you yourself."

Hienrechenshlagen looked to his evil adviser, who had also recently weaseled her way into becoming his war minister. "You take zee con. I am going to mine armory."

"Yaevogel, mine Kaiser," the minister said.

"Perhaps it is time we both stepped out for a bit of fresh air," the Princess told the Kaiser. She floated to the very front viewport, and ghosted straight through it, out into the raging storm. The Kaiser shook his head, then retired to his armory.

Jek and Audrey swirled around each other in a perfect series of tandem attacks, fending off the ever-more-numerous Despotopian skirmishers. They ducked, just in time for Parissah's wing to pass over them, sword-in-claw, with a wide clearing stroke.

"Watch out!" Jek cried, seeing that a new wave was charging in directly behind Parissah. But a moment before they might have been doused with arrows, a huge warhammer knocked all the soldiers' feet out from under them.

"Thanks, Horus," Audrey said.

"Just doing my job," the attorney replied, swinging mighty swings.

"This isn't exactly the battlefield you're used to, I'm sure," Jek said, dueling a swordsman, "but you seem to be doing well."

Horus grinned, clubbing down another archer. "Plenty of transferrable skills between legal work and this," he said. "You have to be shrewd, heavy-handed, and perhaps even a bit devious."

More hatches opened farther up the deck. A whole legion of Despotopian troops was storming onto the flat.

Parissah sighed, cutting down one trooper with her wing, firing through a line of enemies with her pistol in opposite hand. "Our hope fades," she lamented. "I fear there are simply too many."

"Speak thou not of faded hope!" Zavion called, pointing out. "Look thou yonder!"

A great multitude of Berlie-Beirels (whether from north, south, or from both, they could not say), rose up over the side of the ship, spilling onto the deck in a forking assault. Into the midst of their diverging forces, Zedulon returned from the sky, and Baegulgog with him. A pair of swordsdrones – the Proconsul's own former students – rallied behind him, and the three of them cut a furious path to the Knights and Associates, with Baegulgog following, holding up his dukes as if to protect their flank.

"You've come back, Zedulon!" Parissah said, still fending off enemies, if thinner in rank. "I'm grateful for your intervention! Though I am a bit perplexed. I thought you said we would meet on the *Malum In Se*..."

"I didn't say we would not meet again before," the Proconsul retorted, expertly brandishing *Valshaloli* as ever.

"And Baegulgog!" Parissah continued. "I did not think to see you at all!"

"Even the majesty of the Glass Chapel could not long hold me, knowing my friends were in peril," the Clerk said, tapping an unsuspecting Despotopian troop on the back with extreme voltage. "I too owe our good Zedulon a debt of gratitude for bearing me hence."

"It is a happy meeting all around," Parissah agreed. "But we must not relent our vigilance. These Berlie Beirels are poor fighters – their tide may only buy us a short diversion."

"Yet my students will prove stalwart defenders," Zedulon replied. "And they will continue to guard you, after I have departed once more."

"Why leave?" Audrey asked, hunkered down to reload as Jek covered for her.

"A trial long in the coming waits for me on the *Malum In Se*," the Proconsul answered. "It will be well for you if I rush to face it before you arrive."

"That's only half an answer," Jek retorted, switching with Audrey.

"Don't you know me by now?" Zedulon replied. "Why should you expect any more?"

Jek fumbled with his ammunition bag, his fingers cold and slick in the rain. "I'm going to need a few more seconds," he warned Audrey.

"No problem," she said, musket clashing.

At that moment, Jek felt all his hairs drawn tinglingly upwards, and he was aware of a universal pause in the clamor. They *all* felt it. He looked up into the sky, watching in stupefied awe as a Berlie Beirel Queen passed overhead, carrying the dead husk of an enemy cruiser in its long, merciless tentacles.

Shaking himself back to urgency, he finished his reload and came up swinging. A battleship exploded off the port bow. Bombers went whizzing by, barely missing the troop ship with heavy ordnance. Suddenly death seemed freshly close. As he fought by Audrey's side, he was not unmoved by it...

"Audrey!" he called, warding off a pair of soldiers.

"Yes, Jek?" she replied, risking half a look back over her shoulder as she fought.

"It occurs to me these might be my last moments. And if they are, I just want to tell you one more time that I love you, and to let you know that it's okay."

"Thanks, Jek," she said, twisting the sword loose from an opponent's grasp. But she hesitated. "What's okay?"

"It's okay that you don't love me back," Jek replied, repelling a hardy downward chop.

"What?!" Audrey demanded, riposting with the full length of her musket. "What do you mean I don't love you back?!"

"Like I said, it's okay. But it's not like I couldn't put two and two together, Audrey. I told you how I felt some time ago. If you felt anything like what I did, I'm sure you would have found a way to say so by now... what with the universe probably ending and all."

"Find a way to say so?" Audrey repeated. The two of them backed past each other and traded opponents. "You mean, you didn't read it?"

Jek winced, and not from nearly taking a sword to the gut. "Read it? Read *what*?"

"The note I wrote you this morning! I packed it in the same bag with your lunch... and dinner... and desert." She twisted round and hamstrung another soldier. "I can't believe you didn't read it!"

"Well, knowing today might be doomsday hasn't exactly left me much of an appetite," Jek argued, growing somewhat impatient. "I'm sorry! I haven't even looked in my pack! I didn't know about your note!"

There were a few seconds they filled only with fighting. But at length, Audrey returned to their debate. "Read it now," she said simply.

"What?!" Jek demanded. "Like, *now*-now? Are you nuts!?"

"No," Audrey grunted. "I just want you to read it! You said yourself, any moment could be the last. So it might be now or never. I can cover for you for a bit. Think of it as just another reload! Only instead of reloading your gun, you'll be reloading your feelings."

"I'm not going to read a note in the middle of a battle!!" Jek insisted. "This is completely ridiculous!" He looked to see that his friends were nearby. "Parissah, tell her she's being rediciulous."

"No, Jek!" Parissah replied, much to his sudden consternation. "I believe it would be well for you to do as she asks." She raked a pair of soldiers down with a feral swipe of her wing. "I do not speak from experience, but I understand that it takes work for a marriage to be successful. So read it, Jek! Do it for the health of your marriage!"

"That's not the health I'm most worried about right now!" Jek said, backing away as three soldiers all closed in on him together.

"Please, read the note, master Jek!" Zedulon put in urgently, suddenly repelling the three soldiers, and more besides. "It is said that at times we must do crazy things for love!"

"Surely they can't have meant anything like this!" Jek said, growing utterly exasperated. "Baegulgog, back me up here!"

"Don't involve me!" Baegulgog laughed nervously. "I cannot judge in such matters! Romance has no purchase in my nature."

"That's exactly why you're the only one I'd trust to be rational right now," Jek argued.

Baegulgog turned thoughtfully to Audrey. "How long is the note?" he asked.

"Just one side of one page," Audrey answered, smashing somebody with the butt end of her musket.

"Ha!" Baegulgog laughed. "Then what ever have we been arguing about!? By all means, go ahead and read it, Jek! Surely you can spare the fraction of a second it would take to read a single page!"

Jek groaned. "Fine," he said, removing his knapsack.

"We shall all cover for you, Jek," Zedulon announced, prompting the whole group to form a defensive ring.

With a bit of rummaging, Jek found the note. He surprised himself, smiling with sad eyes. Now it was in his hand, he really did begin to feel touched, all sense of being blindsided and pestered melting away in an instant...

But as he unfolded the note to read it, the warm fuzzies disappeared just as quickly. He squinted, hard and repeatedly, eyes dancing bewilderedly over the note...

"A, B, B, A, D, C, E, G, I, E...?" he read aloud. "I can't read *this*!" he exclaimed. "Half of it isn't even letters! Just squiggles!"

"Well I'm sorry I didn't get around to learning the whole alphabet in time!" Audrey replied. "But every one of those letters and squiggles is straight from the heart, Jek!"

Jek pursed his lips and frowned a bit, taking another, more sympathetic look at his note. "Well, that's very nice, I suppose. But what does it *mean*?"

Audrey groaned then, and she turned to him, heedless of danger, while Zedulon and Parissah closed to take up the slack. "It means, you drive me bonkers, Jek. Out of everybody that's been making too big a deal about me, you're by far the worst. But I love you anyway. You're a good man, Jek. That is, you always care about what's good. And I know you would do it, no matter the cost. I love that you're my conscience. I love watching the sense of wonder on your face every time we venture someplace new. I love your tender heart and I love getting to laugh at you every time you embarrass yourself." That last comment furrowed his brow. But she drew very close, and her earnesty in her searching gaze blotted out all else. "But you know what it is I *really* love about you?" she asked at last...

"No," he replied.

She put her arms around his neck. "Neither do I."

They smooched.

"Ah, young love," Zedulon doted. "I suppose this is as good a juncture as any for me to race ahead to the Flagship... before I grow nauseous." Unheeded, he took to wing...

There was certainly more room for him to maneuver in the air than on the surface of the troop ship, but the chaos was hardly less tense. Everything that remained on the field seemed to be converging toward one point. The *Malum In Se* was drawing all lesser ships to it, friend and foe alike. In the thick of it all, Zedulon chanced across Enscharaulgk.

"Friend Enscharaulgk," he called. "Heed my words!"

"I hear you, old buddy," the great dragon replied. "What's up?"

"You must try to lead the allies as far from the Citadel as you can!"

Enscharaulgk flapped his ecliptic wings. "We're pretty far away already, don't you think?"

"Not nearly far enough! You must trust me, old friend."

"Still seeing the future, even now, I take it?"

"Ever less and less... the closer we get."

"I'll lead them past the Flagship. It won't do to leave such a terrible ship wholly intact."

"Do as you see fit. But to trade fire with the *Malum In Se* is another deadly danger!"

Seeing that his talk with Enscharaulgk had led him off his course, Zedulon quickly diverted after his parting words of warning.

Enscharaulgk circled the other way to find his brother. "Brother Onyxadon," he called. "I have just received an omen. If you value the lives of your pirates, you must lead them far away, at once."

"I don't value their lives," Onyxadon replied. "I had expected to lose them all in today's diversionary attack anyway." He sighed. "But I suppose there is little use just wasting them now. Very well, brother. I'll lead them to safety."

"I'm glad," Enscharaulgk nodded. "You're doing the right thing."

"You make me regret it all the more by reminding me."

They parted ways.

Meanwhile, Guppy Troop, having met with almost no resistance since they entered the bowels of the troop ship, had made their way to the command deck, and overthrown the administration handily. They had sent radio messages to the Flagship indicating an all-clear, and were now reclining in the seats of officers after a job well-done.

"Good show today, mates," Trockelov said, arms folded behind his head. "Nothin' to stop us dockin' with the *Malum In Se* now."

After a brief moment of shared basking in admiration of themselves, Ivan shot up straight with sudden angst. "Nothing to stop us, alright!" he said. "More like, *nobody* to stop us... or even slow us down! Do you know how to dock one of these things? I sure don't!"

They all looked stupidly at one another.

"Abandon ship!" Trockelov ordered. All leapt for the nearest door...

"Ve have zee all-clear from zee troop-ship, mine Minister," a Despotopian radio operator reported on the command deck of the *Malum In Se*.

The Minister huffed, not taking her evil eyes off the view straight ahead. "All clear mine foot! You can see from here, zee whole top deck is still embattled!"

The command crew hesitated.

"Should ve still allow zhem to dock, as zee Lady commanded?" one officer asked meekly.

"It may be too late to stop zhem," another replied. "Zhey seem to be coming razher quickly."

The Minister took a few steps forward in sudden fear and disbelief. "Full reverse! Give zee order to fire on zee troop ship! Hurry! Ve must stop zhem at vonce!"

Bellanchora levitated in her usual pensive fashion, observing as enormous cannons swiveled just overhead. The gun crews covered their ears and hunkered down. Deafening, devastating firepower was unleashed on an Inquisition battleship as it passed by. The concussion wave of recoiling muzzles within arm's reach tugged at the Princess' phantom drapery while she strained herself to find any enjoyment at all in the destruction. Another thunder of guns rent the enemy warship in half. Bellanchora seethed in silence, feeling farther from revenge the longer the battle droned on...

Unamused, she turned to the fore, to see that the troop ship was on final approach. She would have Enscharaulgk's treasure very soon. That, at least, served to please her...

Then, alight with new orders, the guns overhead swiveled out to match her gaze. At once it occurred – the troop ship was not on course to dock... but rather, to *ram*...

More antics, she thought darkly to herself.

Zedulon darted between elevated gun decks and huge exhaust pipes, infiltrating *Malum In Se* with deadly secrecy. It was a truly huge ship, and all of it aflutter with activity, its super-heavy mass drivers pulverizing anything foolish enough to get close. It was carnage out there. But that made the perfect environment for his subterfuge...

He took a stair in the shadows up to a higher loft between more guns. Toward the top, he peeked over the edge of the stairwell. Seeing that both the big turrets were swung wide outward at passing targets, he ran the gauntlet between them, taking another stair that led directly toward the stern.

The Proconsul didn't exercise any additional caution as he reached the top of the flight. Nor did it turn out to be necessary. Surmounting the next highest deck, he found what he was looking for... or rather, *who*...

He found the Kaiser.

The great hulking man plodded forward with a heavy swagger, all decked-out for mortal combat, betraying no surprise whatever at the sight of his fellow sovereign. He was not armed at all, except with immense bracers of thick metal shaped into beveled capsules – one pair on his forearms, and another on his shins – each piece looking to weigh thirty pounds or more. And on the ends of the bracers he wore on his arms, there were heavy chains, perfect for entrapping a weapon or bludgeoning an enemy. They clinked menacingly in the rain as the Kaiser drew near. For armor, he had a great grey chest piece, striped on one side with his various decorations for excellence in war and statesmanship. Zedulon could see that this was not the same impervious stuff as the bracers, but still likely enough to turn a glancing blow, even from a weapon as honed as *Valshaloli*.

As for Zedulon himself, he had his spear and his skill – the same tools as always. Privately, he felt daunted – small, and getting smaller with each pounding step the Despotopian juggernaut took toward him. But the fear only served to inflame his inner tyrant – his desire to assert himself over all mortal powers that would presume to rival him. He dropped *Valshaloli* from wing to talon with a flourish and a flash of his eye, and with a sudden leaping attack, he denied the Kaiser even one more unresisted step...

The two fought. And throughout all the long ages, no closer contest nor finer exhibition of martial skill was ever to be seen... among the ranks of the living, the dead, or otherwise. It was a spectacle befitting the grandest possible audience – a fight to end all fights. Yet as they dueled, only one looked on from above... and she was far from impressed. Her gaze wandered once again up to the troop ship, and the imminent collision...

"We're going to crash!" Audrey exclaimed, even as they all continued to fend off the Kaiser's legion.

"We're not going to crash!" Jek insisted. "They got Enscharaulgk's treasure, and they beat the Inquisition fleet without a hitch. I'm pretty sure these Despotopians know what they're doing."

"I'm telling you, we should have slowed down ages ago! We're going to crash!"

Jek chanced a look out past the front of the ship. His knees buckled as some overwhelming awareness of the speed and mass of the huge thing he was standing on suddenly swept over him. "We *are* going to crash!" he agreed.

At once, huge explosions erupted on the stern. *Malum In Se* was firing on its own troop ship, desperate to prevent the collision! Before they could even gather themselves, another wave of deadly fire blasted more chunks of the ship away.

"Run!" Parissah commanded. "Run for the bow!"

They all did immediately, spurring themselves in their unenviable plight, caught between a crash and explosions...

Audrey felt all the muscles in her neck tense up as she braced against the moment of impact. She misjudged it slightly, but all the lead time in the world would not have helped. They were all thrown ten feet or more, and it was all Audrey could do to duck and roll at the end, and not to strike the toe of the Boot against the deck. The tumbling continued ad nauseum, until it became clear... the whole troop ship was pitching skyward, its nose driven into the impervious hull of *Malum In Se*, but its rear being far too heavy to simply stop. She scrambled to her feet while the incline was still shallow, only just in time before such a feat would have been impossible. So they all continued to run, and run at an ever steeper gauge as the deck kept rising and crumpling. On the way they dodged Berlie Beirels and tumbling

Despotopians. And behind them, more explosions – heavy guns fulfilling their orders too late, blasting huge holes as they ran...

Audrey was quite overcome. The pitch was too steep, and getting worse by the second. She couldn't possibly maintain her cadence, practically careening into open space step-by-step...

"I'm going to trip! I'm going to trip!" she despaired.

At the last moment, an incredibly strong arm scooped her up from behind, her legs dangling free over retreating ground. She turned, and first saw Jek, caught up next to her. A big masked face craned in between them, hooded and stifling.

"Parissah!" Audrey beamed. "You're flying! We're all flying!"

"Don't be silly," Parissah replied. "This is a glide, at best."

Flying or gliding, the three of them passed over the ruin of the troop ship, alighting on the bow of *Malum In Se*, much to the wonder and sudden bad luck of the ubiquitous gun crews. The Associates were at once embattled again, but their attackers were no match. They won the bow, taking a moment to look back into the squall whence they came. They feared the worst for Horus, and the Knights and Inquisitors and mercenaries they had been traveling with. But many of their fears were quickly assuaged. Baegulgog came floating up behind with Horus in tow, and the Knights and Inquisitors had grabbed hold of Berlie Beirel soldiers, and they too were soon enough deposited on the nose of M*alum In Se*.

"Well done, strike team!" Parissah congratulated them all. "That was passing adequate!"

"Almost like we planned it," Audrey said.

"Now, to the Princess..."

Maligned by plenty more of Despotopia's finest, they began to hew a path to the heights of that horrible machine...

Phased by the crash for only a scant few moments, the Kaiser and the Proconsul rejoined their epic duel. Zedulon was indeed tested to his very limits – forced to discover depths of his own skill that he had never known. He had to be utterly flawless, every fraction of every moment. A contest with Hienrechenshlagen demanded no less of one of his stature. The Kaiser had strength that his lean but lanky features could not begin to rival. If that strength caught him even once, he would be broken. Only through superior agility could Zedulon hope to prevail. Yet even in agility, the Kaiser proved able to match him at his best.

Spear and bracer met time and again. The thunder of the storm and the guns punctuated move after move, like an earth-shaking applause. Zedulon had more than a few close shaves. The wicked chains of the Kaiser's bracers were eager to entrap his spear, and to leave him defenseless. After barely avoiding such calamity several times, it finally dawned on Zedulon. The Kaiser's whole stratagem was to first catch *Valshaloli* in his coils, then finish him off. He decided then on his *own* stratagem – essentially the same one they were in the middle of enacting against the Princess. He would play into the Kaiser's hand. He would let him have his way...

Leaping up, Zedulon swung round with his spear – a dramatic move, and quite containable. Hienrechenshlagen easily caught the weapon in his hands, not even needing the help of his weaponized chains. But Zedulon was close now, and not at all caught off-guard. He swiped at Hienrechenshlagen with his large talons.

The Kaiser was quick-witted, though, and Zedulon was flung back, spear and all, with a great heave. He righted himself in the air with his wings, landing deftly on the ground, rebounding and flying directly into a second, stabbing lunge. Only in midair did he see that the Kaiser had indeed been staggered, caught in the face with the talon-swipe. He turned too late to see the Proconsul hurling back at him like a missile...

One more instant, and *Valshaloli* would have been sticking deep in Hienrechenshlagen's chest. But something else came between them just in time to save the fiend. A window in space opened, and Zedulon passed whole through the Kaiser, emerging behind him ineffectually. He staggered for only a split-second, disoriented by the bending of reality. But it was enough. A heavy, fire-engorged bracer clubbed him down...

Zedulon fell, broken...

The Kaiser looked down upon his fallen foe. The pitiable creature stirred a little, still clinging to life. Then, the Kaiser looked up. There on the deck above was the Lady, stooping over them. He stared at her for some seconds, until at last she simply floated away.

Hienrechenshlagen blinked in the rain. He had a distinct feeling he knew where she was going. At length, he hunkered down, grabbed hold of one of Zedulon's feet, and stood and strode with him in tow, dragging his limp body behind him – a bone for him to chew with the Princess...

Fighting down a path on the *Malum In Se*'s starboard, Audrey gazed out over the surrounding oceanscape, greatly alarmed as she caught just a moment of the horrible Flagship's onslaught. It was making mincemeat of everything that came into its considerable range. Nothing seemed able to slip this one-ship blockade, nor bite back to any effect.

"We need to hurry," she said. "We're losing a lot of good people."

"Here is a cross-roads," Zavion said. In fact, they had come to a stair on their right that led up to higher decks, while a large troop advanced on them from further aft upon the same level they now stood. "Go thou up yon steps, and we shall hold the way behind thee."

The Associates did as instructed, while the Knights and Inquisitors held the line. They did advance more quickly now, meeting lighter resistance as they climbed. Stair after stair they ascended, the *Malum In Se* marching ever skywards as they drew towards its utter fastness in the rear...

Kaiser Hienrechenshlagen threw Zedulon's crumpled form at Bellanchora's feet, meeting her upon the height of the rear deck – a place of special, high prominence, from which all that yet transpired could be easily espied below. A wide stair led up to it from mid-ship, and narrower arcing ones on either side, with a final stair leading up from lower decks farther back, covered over by a short cabin. All else was flat and scenic up there at the top, placidly removed from the conflict all around. But now, here too was strife. The Kaiser had brought it with him...

"Restore him, if you have zee power," the Kaiser demanded flatly. "You had no right to meddle in zhat contest. It is zee bird who should be standing here now, confronting you. But you spoiled zee rightful outcome. Now we must have it all over again from zee start."

The Ghost-Princess sighed. "You continue to disappoint me, Kaiser. You, the distant progeny of my brother. I had hoped that of all people, there might be some kinship between your spirit and mine. But I see now beyond question that you lack true ambition. You have no higher aspirations than *he* has!" she pointed at Zedulon. "Would it truly be enough for you, Hienrechenshlagen? To be the lord and champion of but one earth? Are you so small that you could find content in that?"

"Vhat more is zhere?" the Kaiser demanded. "Vould you have me master all zee vorlds for you?"

She shook her head. "Your questions reveal all that answers might tell. Indeed, I had a mind – for a time – to set you up as lord of many worlds... yes, of *all*, if necessary. For perhaps then, the spirit I had looked for in you may have made manifest. And if not in you, then in some future heir of yours, I thought. But now I have no patience left for such an eventuality, nor any further need of delay. You are no kin of mine."

"Bring back zee bird," Hienrechenshlagen insisted.

"No," she answered. "But look around you, Kaiser. You may enjoy these last moments of your Fleet's victory over all the island powers. That is the final courtesy I extend to you."

A radio operator on the command deck turned again to the War Minister. Even as the guns continued to chew up the rag-tag remnants of all the enemy fleets in their desperate counter-attack, *Malum In Se* was acquiring even more distant targets...

"Report from zee artillery stations, Minister," the radio operator said. "Zhey have acquired zee enemies' long-range battlecruisers, und zee aircraft carriers of zee Herons, as vell."

"Give zee order to fire," the Minister replied, pleased with her evil self. "Zhis shall prove zheir final ruin."

Within moments, the missile tubes opened and pivoted, cycling projectiles, making ready the killing strike...

Swiping off one more assailant, Audrey breathlessly coaxed herself into another mad flight up yet another stairway, waved on by Jek. They were making all haste for her, the Boot-bearer, seeing that time was indeed short, and that every second they lost was costing more lives – an incalculable sacrifice to the insatiable bloodlust of the Despotopian Flagship. She raced with all her strength to save whomever she may...

Then, the unthinkable happened.

The toe of the Boot caught on one of the steps!

Audrey had faltered. Audrey had *tripped*!

At once, the various mechanisms of the *Malum In Se*, from greatest to least, stem to stern, seized up in an explosive fury. The heavy guns were atomized. The zeppelins went up in fireballs and ash. The missiles backfired in their tubes. Circuitry overloaded and all the great crank shafts of the engine room were thrown down with a terrible crash. The last and greatest of Despotopia's war machines failed utterly, a ruined husk...

But, if the nation's pride was reduced at all by this sudden calamity, it should not have been so. For, even after suffering the full wrath of one of Carlos Washoe's kicks, *Malum In Se* – though inoperative – floated still. There could be no more ultimate testament to the magnificence of their engineering than that...

But O! the greatness of her failure! The entire universe had depended on Audrey to kick the Princess. Now, the kick was spent. She groped around on the stairway, as if madly scrambling to somehow scoop the kick back up. But it was, of course, irrecoverable. It was a mistake for which there could be no remedy – the crowning error that would seal the doom of all...

"What have I done?" Audrey lamented. "I lost the kick! It's gone! O! It's gone!"

Her companions looked on, every bit as hopeless, but even more acutely broken-hearted for her. Any of them could just as easily have miscarried all mortal hope in such a moment. But the responsibility was hers to live with, while there was living left to do. How could any of them possibly comfort her now?

Parissah made a despairing attempt first. "Do not fret, Audrey!" she called with unexpected conviction. "The ruin of *Malum In Se* has spared many worthy folk. And you forget... we still have your contingency! The books! That idea of yours may redeem us yet..."

She went for her pack... only to realize then and there that it had been slashed some time in all the fighting, and its contents spilled. The books were lost... just as the kick was lost. They stood now nearly at the height of *Malum In Se*, as all its once-great strength lay burning and crumbling below them. They had done the impossible. They had reached the summit. And yet at the last, they had come up still short. There was no further recourse for them...

They all gazed in horror at the empty sack. Parissah clawed all through it. She turned it inside-out. But there was nothing left. Not so much as a tiny stack of sticky notes.

Baegulgog flashed, ghostly-pale with grief. "O! black and miserable day! What shall we do now?"

A short interlude of silence ensued. "We will complete the mission," Parissah answered finally, gravely. "We will confront the Princess."

"With what!?" Audrey demanded. She dully kicked the steps repeatedly. "It's gone! It's *all* gone! We have nothing to confront her with!"

"Then we confront her with nothing, if that is all that remains for us to do."

All the Traveling Associates looked one to the other, a fatalistic resolution passing between them. And in that moment of solidarity, they began again up the long stair... slower now, but no less adamant...

The Kaiser dived out of the way as debris from his own Flagship, hurled up by fantastic explosion, nearly landed on him before rolling off the deck. He looked down on the ruin below, utterly baffled by this sudden, inexplicable failure. His precious Doom Fleet had crumbled before his very eyes. His heart pounded in his chest, and he breathed in heavy draughts, but neither the smell nor the sensation of the coal that stoked his lungs could allay him now.

A roar overhead snapped him out of his trance of horror. He watched as Enscharaulgk wheeled in the sky, leading the remnants of his Inquisitor fleet and its allies to the waters beyond, passing *Malum In Se* by, like it was refuse on the street. There were no words for his bewilderment in that moment. For Despotopia to claim its ultimate victory had come down to the point of mere formality only seconds ago. And now, for no reason that he knew, the Kaiser was just a powerless little man again, watching the great dragon fly over unscathed...

If this served to humiliate Hienrechenshlagen, that was nothing next to the effect it had on Bellanchora.

"There he goes," she said in whimsical tone, as she too watched Enscharaulgk pass. "Unfettered, undaunted... unreached. None the worse for wear, for all my long scheming. He will go and get a new treasure, I suppose. He will reclaim his Citadel and build another fleet. By and by, he will right every wrong. He will steer the course of the whole world back into its endless path to nowhere. Yes, it could not be more plain what he will do now..." Her words for Enscharaulgk were empty and mechanical. But then she turned, sudden and sharp, toward Hienrechenshlagen, her halberd appearing in her hand...

"And *you*!" she snapped at the Kaiser, he still on the ground in his grief. "How would you answer for your part in this comedy of errors?! I would have made for you a feast of all the universe's secrets, but in your pride and your smallness you would accept only *crumbs*!"

Hienrechenshlagen had had enough of her scolding at that point. He hurled his hand, unleashing a potent fireball at her. But a moment before it might have struck her, the fireball leapt outward, exploding into a great wall of flame some hundreds of feet across. The Kaiser looked incredulous at his own firey hand.

Bellanchora emerged unharmed through the wall, and it dissipated in a flash. "*Fire*," she mused. "The tool of a mind bereft of cunning. At least, you might have learned to truly wield it. But you refused that secret also." She looked past him – miles beyond – her gaze falling on Enscharaulgk's Citadel. "Yet perhaps you might have been inclined to learn something, if you'd ever had a proper demonstration. Turn now and see what Fire's opposite may do..."

The Kaiser, even in his moment of willfulness, found he did as she bade. And as he watched he saw a narrow shaft of water draw itself straight up in the very midst of the Citadel's arms, almost too slight to see from such a distance. He watched as this pillar of raging ocean began to grow, widening in all directions, until it became a great beam, perhaps hundreds of feet across. At any moment, he expected her to turn the beam on the Citadel's tower in her wrath. But ever the pillar kept racing straight upwards, all the while growing... and *growing*. Now he could faintly hear the roiling across all the wide leagues. Surely, he thought, she wouldn't be able to sustain any more growth. He had the same thought, over and over, until the pillar was clearly a mile wide. And *still* it grew. It grew to the diameter of the great Citadel itself. He watched in unspeakable, horrible wonder as the waters boiled over its arms, dissolving fathomless tons of steel superstructure...

Behind the pillar, well beyond the perception of the Kaiser, the tower itself – the heaviest and grandest structure – began to crack and crumble. Thin beams lanced through floor after floor, slicing into the highest heights, until the vault of the Glass Chapel itself was embattled. *Pharonomagnus*, having faded into a brooding dirge, leapt to life again suddenly as doom raged into its midst. Never before and never again was such a fearful melody wrought into the waking world, nor even into the very darkest of nightmares. The arches of the Chapel cracked and split, and the ages of history in the guise of a thousand brilliant frescos overhead were dashed into crumbling oblivion as the sea leapt up to wash away the old world and all its firm foundations. The great pipes stopped up with water, but still the notes sprang out in a ghostly vengeance, until at last the Organ made a final overwhelming cry – whether out of defiance or despair, or a thousand other urgent feelings at once, none ever knew. But such was that final defeaning stroke that it seemed as if the phantasmal force that drove *Pharonomagnus* had fallen to unwaking slumber upon the keys, from first to last, making one note of all notes...

So it was that the Ocean Citadel met its ruin, swept entire into the sky by the sea...

And *still*, the pillar grew!

It heaved the clouds out of the way, rolling them back in all directions with lightning raging in the mounting folds. And it continued to grow. The Kaiser was mesmerized – plunged to the depths of instinctual dread. Only seconds ago, power far beyond his wildest imagining was unleashed before his eyes. In the time since, this great beam of rushing ocean had grown tenfold. It was many miles across, and still growing. It would reach and engulf *Malum In Se* in moments. His mammoth constitution failed him. He fell to his knees and cowered, unable to endure the sight any longer...

"Behold a fraction of a single Dianode's power," Bellanchora said. "I could have given you mastery over them all. *All*... save one. And then you might have learned that this power does not sate. It cannot satisfy. Not even close."

"Holy Heck," Jek whimpered, seeing that the whole ocean was being drawn at breakneck speed into the sky behind him.

"No time for terror or expletives!" Parissah spurred her Associates. "Onward! We must confront Bellanchora while she's still getting warmed up!"

Zedulon sputtered, struggling for the strength just to cough. Likely as not, his lungs were crushed. He could not say. He was aware of nothing but a gathering numbness, and a droning, rumbling sound. With a great impulse of will, he forced his eye open. But all was a rolling haze. He swooned, ready to shut his eye again for good. Until, at the last moment, he saw dark figures leap up before his sight...

Jek and Audrey reached the top of the last stair, leveling their muskets. Jek quickly acquired a living target – a huge man, hunched over on the ground, turned away from the raging sea. He was slow in realizing this was the Kaiser, appearing a broken man.

"Get up!" he said, holding his musket on the villain.

Hienrechenshalgen stirred, and then stood with deliberate, slow action. It was as if the sound of Jek's voice rekindled at least a pretense of his old domineering self, unwilling as he was that he should appear so timid before an enemy and a peasant. He turned to Jek, not bothering to raise his hands. Yet something in his goggled eyes assured Jek that he did not mean to try anything – that he was a willing bystander in whatever might be about to transpire, with no love lost for the Ghost-Princess. Still Jek held him at gunpoint. There was no sense covering Bellanchora with his musket, anyway.

Suddenly he was aware that Audrey dashed ahead, and he saw in her path a smaller shape, prone and apparently lifeless. He gasped as he realized it was Zedulon.

Audrey reached her friend with hands already glowing. Passing as much Life magic to him as she could, she had no immediate awareness of any such energy left in him. Agonizing moments passed between them, and still she felt nothing. She exerted herself to the limits, but the magic seemed unable to cling to the old Proconsul...

Audrey very nearly gave up, exhausted and utterly broken-hearted. But then she saw Zedulon's chest move – inflated by mending power, and then by air. At last, he was healing! She could feel her own strength wittling down to nothing. But she kept pushing herself. And finally, as she collapsed, Zedulon's eye gleamed open. He was still weak, as she was, but in his eye was warmth and knowing, and he drew a wing over her arm as the two of them lay there, no better than a stone's throw from death's door.

"Thank you, my dear friend," Zedulon said, his voice weak, but less horrible than she'd ever heard it.

"Sure thing," she replied.

"Ah, the whole merry band of adventurers," Bellanchora mused. "You have replenished your ranks since last we met," she continued, evidently indicating Horus Templar. "Which will be first to challenge me in single-combat this time, I wonder?" Even as she spoke, the raging water broke around them, drawn up in perfect walls all round *Malum In Se*. "Or, you meant to use the Boot, I suppose?" she laughed. "But it appears you have misspent your kick. I suspect you'll have a bit of trouble, trying to get a refill from old Carlos Washoe in this pinch."

"Yes, our gambit seems to have failed," Parissah said, arriving at last at the top of the stair herself, towing Baegulgog. She let him go and drew her sword. "But I *am* game for a rematch, if you are."

"Now what have we here?" Bellanchora mocked, an amalgam of venom and amusement in her voice. "The Inquisitor turned infidel, come back from the dead just in time to watch me bring a happy ending."

Prompted by her voice, tears in the very fabric of reality began to molt the air around them, revealing an invisible nothingness behind – neither dark nor light. There was a dizzying, whirling feeling, while she twisted the universe in a rending action, straining its every seam. The silencing melody of the Grand Design spilled into their midst through the cracks...

Jek and Baegulgog worked through their terror, helping Audrey and Zedulon to their feet, if only to defy the Princess with some outward courage. "Only *you* could characterize this as a happy ending!" Jek exclaimed. "This is horrible!"

"You think it so because you do not understand the nature of a happy ending," their nemesis retorted. "A happy ending... is any Ending at all..."

"Nay!" a voice called out from behind, within the shelter of the small cabin over the last stair. Bellanchora hesitated, turning finally toward the intruding sound. "Tis only a status-quo ending what be a happy one!" A figure stepped out of the shadows, veiled below a big, awesome hat.

"Old man!" Jek cried. He and Audrey elated. "You've come back! But how?!"

"Ain't no time fer stupid questions, lad!" the old man snapped at him. "Suffuse it ta say, I done some sneakin'. And here I is, when ye needs me most... like ye shoulda 'spected all along." It was indeed a triumphant reunion – a warm ember before the cold, eternal night...

"The ancient mariner," Bellanchora gasped. "The first to slip our nets... and now the last as well. As in all things, symmetry. But no more! I am bringing the old order to rest forever... and when I am finished there won't be dust left to settle. What would you, of all people, do to stop me?"

"This!" the old man replied.

In an expert action, he whipped the Pamphlet of Unknowable Things out of his jacket, opening its celestial, papery folds before the Princess. At once there was a tremendous drain on her power, with green ghoulish essence leaping from her, weaving itself onto the leaflet. She groaned, and all were transfixed...

But Bellanchora, even so ambushed, would not go quietly...

In a flash she hurled her halberd! They all watched in horror as the old man was struck, and his strength gave way, and in his surprise and anguish the Pamphlet flew free of his grasp...

It floated, wafting ineffectually through the air, no more than a single eddie in the wind away from being caught up into the skyward torrent, or slipping through a tear into the empty infinities of the Undervoid...

Breathlessly they watched as this last, extraneous hope readied to fly away with all the rest...

...Then... the fates swung the other way, one final time...

The Pamphlet whisked this way and that, tither, and yon... until at last it came to rest... plastered wide open against Jek's face!

The Princess faltered again, all her deepest Knowledge being drawn back into the very document of its extra-cosmic origin. She struggled mightily against it, but to no further avail. She tried to drag herself away, but more and more of her form was vanishing. The fabric of reality buckled suddenly, growing terrifyingly thin in a moment of paranormal silence, as she made one last titanic effort to simply end it all before she could be foiled. But the moment passed, and as she grew weak the space around them gradually began to fill itself back in. At last, the withering strands of her glowing silhouette showed no more sign of resistance...

Bellanchora sighed, exasperated. "Another delay," she lamented...

And then the last of her had passed, absorbed whole into the Pamphlet...

"Old man!" Audrey cried, rushing to his aid. Jek, after a moment of sheer incredulity, having had the most evil villain in the history of the universe drawn into a sheet of paper on his face, removed said sheet and rushed in to help... or at least be close in these critical moments – perhaps the old man's last...

But other things were afoot. Horus Templar was the first to take note. "Well, that was a providential moment," he began. "But now what are we going to do about *this*?"

"About what?" Parissah asked.

"About the trillions of gallons of water in free-fall..."

Horus was right, of course. Without Bellanchora around to will otherwise, the ocean was tumbling straight back down. Suddenly aware of it, the polarity of the rumbling they felt and heard seemed to reverse. Those that had stomachs endured a nauseating lurch as the *Malum In Se* began to be displaced upwards by the mad rush of fathomless mass.

"This is going to kill us," Jek said. "I don't know exactly how, but this is definitely going to kill us."

"But the sky is still clear directly overhead!" Baegulgog pointed out. "I can fly two, perhaps three of you out. Parissah, you grab the rest."

"But I cannot truly fly!" Parissah protested. "Save whom you may, Baegulgog! I will return. And Zedulon, you must try to fly as well!"

"There is no need," Zedulon said. "Look!"

Directly above, far overhead, they spied a bright singularity. It shone like the sun, but at intervals in its blinding brightness it appeared to have form... perhaps like a Human or a Meduseldan, though not quite like either. But as they studied it through narrow eyes, they perceived a mind. It was an entity of some sort, and no mistake. A shimmering, incandescent entity...

No sooner had they noticed it, and the creature filled all the visible sky with a raging fire – an inferno that they felt from far off. So intense was the blaze that the walls of water were cut short, all their height rent in twain by the great floating carpet of fire, which boiled away the abundance as it fell, round about for miles on end. Through the great flame they could see (and hear) the sky protest, swirling and swollen with rolling vapors. Thunder and hissing filled their ears so that they had to cover them. Their guts were wrenched as *Malum In Se* crested, all of them laid out flat on their backs by the skyward race, so that they did not see the many miles of raging squall all around as the displaced sea struggled once again to find its level. They were tossed hard, both low and then high again, over immense distances, watching the sky above burn all the while. At last, the fires receded, and the entity withdrew to the obscurity whence it came. But still, they were tossed, and ever their peril seemed to grow, rather than fade, as the *Malum In Se* began to rock and pitch violently in the confused tempest. The rain redoubled. The air-breathers in the group had to lie on their bellies, clinging with desperation to any falt or seem in the deck they could find...

The strain proved too much for Jek, and after enduring all his body could take, he blacked out, just as an enormous shadow swept down over everything in sight...

The Great Looking-Back

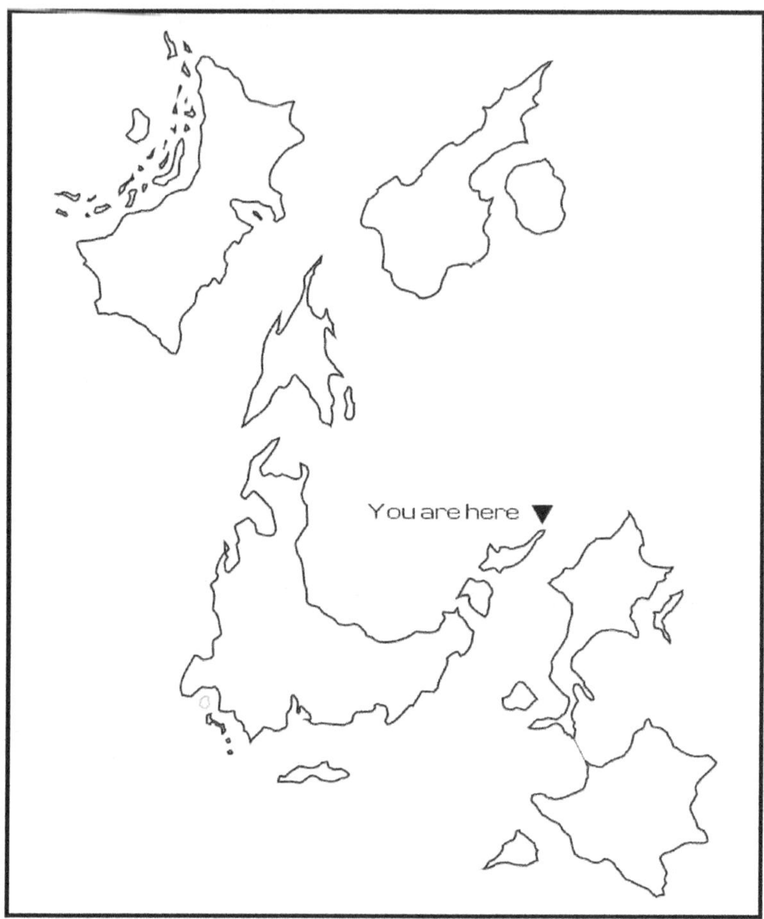

"If you want to know where you're going in life, think about where you've been. That's as good a guess as any."

- Zeph Bronzegloom, *What if Galahadron Mucolyptus was Wrong?*

"Wake up, master Jek!" Zedulon called to him, shaking his mind hazily to consciousness. "You must wake! Your old mentor is not long for this world, I fear..."

Jek blinked a great deal. The rain was still oppressive – probably worse than it had been before he blacked out – and his brain was in a fog. "You're not?" Jek asked. Then, and only then, he remembered... and at once he shot up straight...

"The old man!" he exclaimed.

His boots trudged through the mud of some small island – hardly more than a sandbar in the middle of the sea, really – more than likely a feature that had spent millennia submerged, only to be exposed for the first time today by the raising of the ocean. In fact, that was precisely the case, and many surviving ships narrowly passed them by, still driven perhaps by the terror of what they had so narrowly escaped, and hardly expecting to encounter such obstacles in the open sea.

But in the moment, Jek was not conscious of these comings and goings. He homed in on the spot where the old man was splayed, Bellanchora's terrible halberd still stuck in him. Audrey was stooped there already. She would have been weak with grief anyway, but she was far beyond that now, spending energy she didn't have in vain effort to heal him. Jek ground to a halt on his knees in their midst, and she took slow notice of him.

"It's no use," she lamented. "I used up too much magic too fast when I healed Zedulon. And it seems like this weapon is fighting me somehow. It would take real rest for me to be able to heal this. But I don't think I can even buy him that much time..."

"Just leave it be, darlin'," the old man said. Jek teared up just hearing his voice. They were reunited only a few short moments, and now they were already saying goodbye again, this time for good...

"This ain't quite how I done pictured meself kickin' the bucket," the old man continued, eyes gazing up blankly at the sky. "But I's at peace with it." He managed a weak laugh, stifled by a cough. "Shore came close, didn't I? Ta savin' the world, I means. Dang close."

"But you *did* save the world," Jek assured him. "This one and all the rest. We could never have beat Bellanchora without you! The Pamphlet was the only hope we had left. And you brought it just in the nick of time, after we were sure we'd already lost." He marveled for a moment. "How in the Heck did you manage that anyway?"

The old man coughed again. "Tis a strange tale. Ever and anon I was a-lookin' for the Knights. Didn't have no luck findin' them, a-course." He looked to Jek and Audrey, weakly lifting his head. "But I got rumor o' ye folks, after a spell. T'was headin' back for Roemnar, thinkin' them Herons might have some other ideas 'bout where the Knights might be. That was when I done seen the sky filled with them horrible little tweety birds again! I thought sure they was on me a second time! But they flew right by. Then I thought-a *ye*! I figgered them birdies had to be after Jek and Audrey, if they wasn't after me. And when I saw they was headed straight fer the Ocean Citadel, I gots ta thinkin' about 7/14/21, and how it were nearly here! So's I followed after the birds, shore as frog's hair that ye musta been the ones goin' on ahead o' me. I met some mercenaries, done said they was headed for the Citadel too, and I joined up with their lot.

"But when I gots there, and I sees ye had found the Knights... well... guess I had all manner o' second thoughts. Ye'd already completed the Quest without me! But I still had that there Pamphlet, and a chance ta make a name fer me own self with it, mayhaps. But I stucks around, eaves-droppin' – heard yer whole talk with Enscharaulgk, hunkered down as I was on that catwalk by that big ol' ramp. When ye said the Pamphlet might be the key to savin' the world, I decided right there, I was gonna do the same thing ye was gonna do, only I was gonna get there ahead o' ye and do all the savin' meself!" He coughed. "It were a selfish plan, I admits... and I's ashamed o' meself now. Guess I done got what I had comin' to me, fer bein' such a louse."

"We understand," Audrey reassured him, holding one of his cold hands. "You always wanted to make a name for yourself. And now you have! Jek's right – we could never have won without you. But I guess you could never have won either... without Jek's face." She sighed. "Everything must have turned out the way it was supposed to." Her eyes searched him for a while, growing quizzical. "But how did you get there, anyway? We didn't notice your coming or going from the Citadel to the troop ship, or from the troop ship to the Flagship..."

"There were a fair bit o' tricks and gimmicks with me Water magic involved," he answered. Then he coughed again. "But this ain't quite the chitchat I were picturin' fer me final words. I had half a mind ta diverge meself of a few partin' sentimentalisms, and a fair haul o' much-needed wise anecdotes besides... 'steada hashin' out all these 'splanations about how I done did all this here stuff." He was seized with a sickening convulsion. "But I don't think there be time for it now! I's fadin' fast." His voice was very weak now, and his breaths shallow and stunted. But he managed to fix a kindly glint in his gaze at last. "So stuck I was on findin' them Knights... turns out I done had a pair o' them with me all the while! Ye was good people, both o' ye, and I's glad I gots to know ye. Please remember me... that's all I asks! Be kind and remember an old man, once in a spell."

Jek clapped his hand on the old man's shoulder, feeling a strange assurance he had just the right thing to say in this moment, even when all words would seem to fail. "But you're not just an old man," he said, shaking his head. "You're *The* Old Man!"

With that, the old man's face curled up in one final, snaggle-toothed smile. His eyes welt up with pride and gratitude. And then they closed forever. Jek wept softly over him. Audrey laid a shaky hand on his shoulder, too weak to cry her own tears.

"I am sorry that you have lost your old friend," a gigantic voice said, emanating from above. Jek looked up to see Enscharaulgk's head craning down over them on the end of his long neck.

"Thanks, Enscharaulgk," Jek replied. "I'm glad you're safe. When did you get here? I didn't even notice you... somehow..."

"Same time as you," the Grand Inquisitor said. "I helped retrieve you and all your strike team buddies from *Malum In Se*. But now, I fear, we must all be off again! The ocean is refilling, and this little island begins to vanish more quickly than I thought it would..."

"But the old man!" Jek insisted, some peculiar urgency overwhelming him. "We can't just leave him here like this!"

"A sea burial is fitting for a sailor," Enscharaulgk replied. "But if that is not how you wish to honor his remains, I'll gladly bear him forth again. Indeed, even were he a zillion times heavier, I would consider the burden worth bearing. But we must go!"

At his insistence, Jek finally began to notice the rapid receding of the shoreline. Water was lapping in from all sides. He came to his feet, but blinked hard, not knowing where to go from there...

"But how... how do we get on your back, Enscharaulgk? You're so huge!" He looked around him. "Do you have like a rope ladder hanging down from you somewhere?"

"Oh, right," Enscharaulgk answered with a bit of embarrassment. Suddenly, he looked up into the clouds. "A little help again, brother?"

A great sigh burst on them from nowhere in particular. "Must I?"

"I wish you would," another voice called up. It was Parissah. Jek hardly saw her, already seated atop Enscharaulgk, looking quite small.

"Oh, very well," the scary voice relented, as dark tendrils of vapor descended from the sky. "Anything for my beloved little granddaughter," it doted.

Jek blanched as he was engulfed in black cloud, which began to convey him upright in a nice straight line through the sky onto Enscharaulgk's back. "Is... is this...?"

"Yes! It is brother Onyxadon," Enscharaulgk nodded. "Isn't it marvelous what a good sport he can be? I always knew he had it in him."

"Shut up," snapped Onyxadon, Eternally Most Vile, terror of the ages, even as he continued to gently queue Jek, Audrey, Zedulon, and the old man's body back up to their former perch. "Helping out with an enormous battle is one thing. But I should have known you'd rope me into just these kinds of tedious little acts of do-goodery afterwards."

He let them go, and not too soon for Jek's taste. They all walked into a depression in Enscharaulgk's armor where Knights and Inquisitors were already gathered, avoiding the sharpest edges. It was kind of a huge dent... probably also furnished by Onyxadon. He laid the old man's form in their midst, and his vapors relented back into the sky. Enscharaulgk wasted no time beating his many wings, making a dramatic departure from the vanishing ground below.

"Where-to now, I wonder?" Onyxadon asked, streaking into his familiar, terrifying form.

"I make for Jast-Madiir," Enscharaulgk answered, still struggling into a climb. "For that is where most of Parissah's Associates belong... and I do not presently know where else to go. But I wish you would do one more thing for me, brother."

"Only if it is not too dull. What would you ask?"

"Seek the Twin Queens. It should be a small favor, for they are big and easy to find. Send them to meet me on Jast-Madiir's eastern tip. I will have to find some way of officiating between their claims."

"But Parissah has already come to a solution, which might be viable," Baegulgog called out, floating forth from beside Parissah.

Enscharaulgk craned his head around to look back, which unsteadied his takeoff efforts. "Do you feel able to articulate it to them, my good Clerk?"

Baegulgog flashed with hesitation. "Erm, well, yes... erm..."

"That's terrific!" Enscharaulgk exulted. "Take him with you, brother!"

Before Baegulgog could construct an intelligible protest, Onyxadon had swept him up in a whirlwind.

"Fair well, Baegulgog!" Parissah called out. "And do not fret! Only consider the great task you are undertaking!"

"Goodbye, madam!" the Clerk called back. "I hope I may return to you soon! I do so hope that... very, very much..."

All the while, they continued to climb, the wind under Enscharaulgk's wings rushing over them like a gale. It was a lot to take in, as usual. But as they settled into flight, Jek soon enough leaned back and relaxed... and let go the white-knuckled death-grip he realized he had on Audrey's hand.

"Ow," she said.

"Sorry," he replied.

"It's okay, Jek." She settled in next to him, with her head resting on his shoulder. She sighed, exhausted. "Some day we've had, huh?"

"Yeah," he chortled, putting an arm around her. "We've had a few of those, haven't we? But none like this one." His head swam at the merest reflection on it all. "I can't even begin to process everything that just happened. Everything that *almost* happened..."

"Don't try," Audrey told him. She looked up into his eyes. "Why not sleep some more? I think we're in for a long flight."

He smiled down at her, as his mind fixed on one thing he was only too glad to recall. He remembered their smooch. "Always looking after me. You really do love me, don't you?"

She brushed a hand along his cheek. "I do. Very much." She gave him a little peck on the other cheek. "Now rest, dear. You've earned it. You saved the universe."

She settled back into their embrace. Jek watched contentedly as the little island shrank into the sea behind. Holding the one dearest to him, he let his mind empty of everything... everything beside these two assurances. First, that they *had* saved the universe... against all hope and expectation. And second, that it had been very well worth all the trouble it took to save, all along...

* * *

'Rest now,' she had advised him, just then. *'You've earned it. You saved the universe.'* And now, already, he was asleep. It still surprised Audrey sometimes how quickly her assurances could ease the heart and mind of her husband... and how slow she was to find any comfort in them herself. Bones aching with total exhaustion, she was nonetheless utterly lost in private reflection. Yes, they *had* saved the universe. But what part had she played in that,

ultimately? She couldn't help wondering whether they might have succeeded without her... or, even, in *spite* of her...

Audrey took a deep, strained breath, not even bothering to try to push away her misgivings in the present moment. The fact could hardly be helped that whenever she looked back on her own deeds, all she saw was failure... one betrayal of fate after another.

The pattern had started hard enough, when a simple mistake of hers had cost an innocent Mantid its life. Uncertainty over the fate of the Dyeus in general still plagued her at whiles. Knowing now that they were indeed destined all along to triumph over Despotopia, she shrank at the thought that that victory could never have come in time to help the Tribe...

And then there was all that business in Maenea. A whole country had looked to her for its deliverance. Her – their apparent prophesied hero. But in their time of greatest need she had proffered only empty morale in the form of a lot of bumbling rhetoric. And after that laughable little episode they had lost everything. Their hopes, their nation... their own identities...

She looked down at the boot on her left foot. Carlos' Boot. The greatest relic ever laid aside for world-saving... as far as she knew... entrusted to her, for that very paramount purpose. And once again, when the stakes could not possibly have been higher, she faltered. Fortunately, providence had come through for them anyway. But what if it hadn't? What if everything really had come down to her wielding the boot against Bellanchora? She shook her head. The whole question was irrelevant. But it managed to haunt her all the same...

She settled further back into Jek's arm, trying to find some sleep to surrender to. But her restless eyes fell next on the old man. The sight leeched even more of her strength, if it were possible. His lifeless face was still curled up in content... which formed a ghoulish contrast with the halberd sticking out of him. She wanted very badly to remove it, but hadn't the heart nor the power at present. She felt very much that she had failed him too... a mentor and a friend. Certainly, she didn't regret saving Zedulon. Nor could she have known that as she did, she was making something of an impossible choice... to redeem his life, at the expense of the old man's. Could she have navigated the whole thing differently? No. Finally, her tired mind was resolved on that. She'd had just enough magic to save one of them. But why? Why couldn't she have had enough to save them both? It *was* Purpose that fueled her magic. And evidently she did have an exceptional amount of Purpose in her. Even so, in light of all these shortcomings, it seemed more than possible she didn't have enough...

Braving the rushing air and the rain, Audrey suddenly noticed Horus Templar had come to call, his tall ears tucked underneath a billowing hood, or some other improvised head covering. He set down his huge warhammer and sat on his haunches next to her and Jek.

"Now what have we here?" Horus asked. "A rather dissatisfied client, by all appearances." He grinned sarcastically. "Why so glum, Audrey? We won the day... if you hadn't noticed."

She quickly dismissed any thought of trying to pretend she wasn't rather distressed. Horus was an attorney, after all, and could surely see through any half-hearted insistence that she was alright. "I failed, Horus," she admitted sheepishly. "And not for the first time. I've failed a lot of people in the last few weeks. Only today, I failed everybody. Absolutely everybody... everywhere." She looked weakly at the old man. "And I failed him."

He reached out and carefully set a clawed hand on her shoulder. "You came up a little short, is all. Any one of us would have, alone. No sense in dwelling on it. Your Quest has redeemed more than you know. Certainly, more than you're considering."

She grinned back a bit. "You mean about your case, don't you? About your getting to repeal the In Ablatia."

"*In Absentia*," he corrected, suppressing a laugh. "Maybe that example doesn't resonate so well as I'd like. But all the same, your crusade sparked others, which have turned out favorably. A great justice long overdue has been accomplished in your country. And who knows if my own courtroom battle is the only example? I seriously doubt it is. We can never know the true extent of the part we play. Not until the Great Looking-Back of All Things."

She pursed her lips. "I guess that helps a little. But I still feel bad. I still wonder why I couldn't have been able to save the old man."

"But think of the one you did save," Horus affirmed her. "Audrey, the old man's death shouldn't weigh on your conscience."

"But he *is* dead because I couldn't save him," Audrey replied. "That's a fact I can't seem to get over."

Horus sat fully and leaned against the bowl of the depression. "Sometimes you have to look past the outcomes and assess your intentions. You would have saved them both if you could. That alone should free you from any sense of guilt. You didn't save Zedulon to condemn the old man. Don't make it out like you did. You had nothing but the best intentions."

"Bevare good intentions," a resonant voice said, intruding into the quiet privacy of their counsel. Horus and Audrey's glances snapped to the source. Kaiser Hienrechenshlagen was in their midst, standing over the old man. After just a moment of mutual staring, he reached down...

"Don't you touch...!" Audrey began, but was cut off. The Kaiser had plucked Bellanchora's halberd from the old man's body before she could finish her thought.

For a few tense seconds, Horus and Audrey were silent, Hienrechenshlagen armed and imposing. But then, he slowly and carefully set the halberd down beside Audrey. Then he crouched, further inviting himself into the conversation.

"It seems you vere just counseling zee lady about zee virtues of good intentions. So I say again... *bevare*. Zheir are few zhings so dangerous."

"What would you know about it?" Audrey asked, low but defiant.

The Kaiser averted her gaze, even with benefit of his goggles between them. He did not answer at once. But after a while, he spoke. "For many long years, I have carried zee hopes and adoration of mine people. Alvays zhey looked to me as zheir champion, long before I had done aught to earn such love. Zhey vere poor und hungry. Zhey vere bound by a history of constant defeat. None of mine predecessors had ever given zhem a victory vorthy of note.

But still zhey had loved zhem, even as zhey loved me." He shook his head, and after it hung even lower between his huge shoulders. "For zhat, I vould have become zee champion zhey made me to be. I vould have given zhem victory beyond zheir vildest imaginings. But in zhis I erred. Yes, I erred fatally. I courted powers I did not understand. Und it has cost us all."

Audrey surprised herself – not for the first time – feeling a pang of sympathy for a mortal enemy. And his words confronted her with a different anxiety... not born of reflection, but looking ahead. Princesshood still hung over her future like a sky full of bricks. Soon enough, she might be making her questionable decisions for a whole country...

"Sorry, Kaiser," she said, really meaning it a little bit. "I guess it's been kind of a hard day for everybody."

"Yaevogel, it has," he nodded. "Und I do not know vhat is to come. I hope zhat I may be permitted to accept zee responsibility for zhis. I hope zhat Enscharaulgk's judgment vill not fall too heavy on mine people."

"I wouldn't worry about that, if I were you," Horus assured him. "Even so, I am an attorney. I can mediate on your people's behalf, if you like. Though I doubt it will be necessary."

"I vould zhank you to do zhat, stranger. Und I zhank you for your reassurances. Maybe zee Grand Inquisitor vill be quite satisfied to let zee blame lay on zee figureheads. Vone tyrant you have ensnared. Anozher throws himself at your mercy." And suddenly he searched, his gaze settling on a point across from them. "But perhaps zee greatest tyrant of all is zee vone zhat now sleeps among us."

Horus and Audrey followed his look. They all beheld a rather sad heap of matted feathers as it slumbered restlessly.

"Zedulon, you mean?" Horus almost laughed. "That wouldn't have been my read."

"Do not underestimate him," the Kaiser cautioned him. "He bested me in single combat. Und no doubt, it vas in no small part his vision vhich dismantled Bellanchora's plot. Who can say vhat more he has seen? Vhat plans of his may still lay in our future? I am left to vonder."

"He has a formidable personality, I grant," Horus went on, "and powers of foresight to match. But don't overplay your hand, Kaiser. Casting shades at Zedulon isn't going to earn you any more sympathy in this company."

"That's right," Audrey backed him up. "He's my friend."

"You misunderstand me," the Kaiser gestured. "I hold zee Proconsul in zee highest regard. He has von zee mastery. Und my allegiance... vhile it lasts..."

Audrey watched as Zedulon tossed in his sleep. He *was* her friend. But what more might he be? There was a lot she didn't know about him yet. Not that she was too worried. She determined that if there was one uncertainty she didn't feel like entertaining now, it was the character of her friends and associates. She needed them. All of them. And Zedulon not the least. She snuggled again in the arm of the only one she needed more, as she watched the Proconsul's feathers ruffle. He was clearly dreaming. She wondered what the dreams of an expansive mind like his would be like...

Trying to imagine such visions was the first thought that really allowed her to begin to feel drowsy. Her eyelids were getting heavy, at last, as pure fatigue won out over all other concerns. She mindlessly watched the horizon recede endlessly before her eyes. She knew she was looking almost due north... toward the greater old world. But she felt some comfort, knowing she was currently flying south... toward the unknown frontier that had always been her fancy. In one last whimsical flourish, she pictured Enscharaulgk just flying on and on, past all the shores they knew. And finally sleep took her...

* * *

Jek woke once in the first watch of the night, when Enscharaulgk reached his mark, on the far east of his own homeland, Jast-Madiir. It was another hairy experience. Without Onyxadon there to help them down off of Enscharaulgk's back, the only expedience seemed to be for the old dragon to put down in the water, and let them swim to shore. This was explained with somewhat less notice than Jek might have liked. But after a doozy of a splash-down and a very chilly swim, things quickly normalized again. It was dark and everyone was still exhausted... not least the Grand Inquisitor himself, who had flown for hours after a very great fight. He gathered everyone under the fold of one of his wings, where he hid his own head. His hot breath quickly made them all feel warm and dry, and before long, they were sleeping quite soundly under their great leather canopy...

The morning brought refreshment. Jek stretched, feeling almost fit for another calamity. Beyond the covering of Enscharaulgk's wing, he could still hear the rain gushing. As the dragon began to stir, Jek intuited they were in for another great debate. Much had transpired, after all. Huge fleets were decimated. The Ocean Citadel had been razed to total ruin. The future could happen now, but whether things would ever be the same again was still very much in question. Doubtless counsel was badly needed.

Jek looked over at Audrey, still asleep. He deplored to wake her, remembering how she had exerted herself the day before. But he felt a little nudge from him would be more civil than a sudden dousing from the sky when Enscharaulgk inevitably returned upright. So he gave her a gentle shake, and when she came-to, he at least tried to help her get her hair in order...

It didn't take long before everyone was up and about. Many of the Indigo Knights and Inquisitors from the larger strike team disbursed in order to grant the council relief from a sizeable crowd of gawkers that had come from farther inland. After all, it wasn't every day a Grand Inquisitor crashed into your island... particularly not one who had been dead for longer than perhaps any of them had been alive. It took a lot of work to turn them all back toward their homes...

When at last they had some respectable elbow room, Enscharaulgk began the meeting.

"Seems we have a lot to talk about," he said, stooping over them all. "Where to even begin? I don't suppose I know."

"Perhaps we ought to start with the enemy in the camp," Horus Templar put in, leaning on his warhammer. "We have a rather prominent personality here who probably should have gone down with his ship, by all rights. But I'm one to talk! I'm the last person who should convict someone before their trial..."

Jek gave Horus a strange look. "But what *are* you talking about, Horus?"

"Zee Jackal speaks of me," a scary, echoey voice said. Jek turned, recoiling reflexively. Kaiser Hienrechenshlagen was standing nearby, still terrifying and larger-than-life, even in defeat. Jek jumped slightly. He didn't have the foggiest clue that he had slept through a whole conversation between his wife and the Kaiser the day before. "Und he is right. I have entertained vulgar ambitions, und I have played zee fool for a terrible villainess. I should not have been saved from zee *Malum In Se*. Vhatever punishment avaits me now is vell-earned."

Horus grinned up at the Grand Inquisitor. "What do you think, Enscharaulgk? I'd say his fate is yours to decide. The Kaiser himself seems to believe as much. I think he'd willingly accept any penance, provided it falls on him alone, and not his people."

Enscharaulgk drew in very close to the Kaiser, who seemed suddenly to shrink next to one so much greater in stature than himself. The dragon's breath was oppressive – like endless gusts of blazing wind. "I *am* held qualified to be both judge and jury... and other things, besides," Enscharaulgk boded. Jek gulped. There was almost a bit of menace in his voice, which was quite fearful indeed, coming from the old dragon – the greatest of all his kind. But at once his head drew back to a less threatening distance. "Yet I would let the Kaiser speak in his own defense, before I rule. So, what of it, Kaiser? Have you learned your lesson?"

"Yaevogel... most certainly!" the Kaiser assured him. "I vould not so quickly take up vith a Ghost-Princess again. Nor do I seek to build any more Doom Fleets to conquer zee vorld."

Enscharaulgk looked back at Horus Templar. "That's good enough for me," he said. "Anyway, he is a head-of-state, so I suppose I should cut him some slack. Very well. You are pardoned, Kaiser Hienrechenshlagen. But you *will* be on parole, unto the seventh generation."

"Zhank you, mine Grand Inquisitor," the Kaiser nodded solemnly, slumping a bit in his relief. "You are too kind."

"You might be right about that," Jek muttered to himself.

The Kaiser heard his soft bit of derision. "But mine change of heart is auzhentic. You vill remember, vhen you came to call against Bellanchora, I did nozhing to resist you. Until zhen, I had not vaguely guessed zee kind of company I had been keeping. Great vas her knowledge and power, I knew – but I had no idea *how* great. I vas as shocked and dismayed as anyvone, vhen she revealed herself openly. I am only too relieved zhat you vere able to entrap her."

Jek blanched, reaching into a fold of his frock coat. It seemed almost dreamlike to look back on that final deed... the capture of Bellanchora. But as he drew it out with trembling hands, sure enough, there it was...

The Pamphlet of Unknowable Things. And imprisoned within it, their deadliest adversary. Both were still in his keeping...

"Her power *was* terrifying," Jek agreed, in a mesmerized sort of voice. "Even after I was warned about it a dozen times or more, I didn't find myself prepared." He examined that great leaflet – a hallow of the Dianodes – filled with wonder about it, and the cosmic threat they had endured. Finally, he looked up questioningly at Enscharaulgk. "How did she ever get all that power, Enscharaulgk? What could make it possible for her to direct the elements, as if she were the Dianodes themselves, all rolled into one? When I really think about it, no one has explained that yet. Not so I understood it, anyway."

"That is a big question, young man," Enscharaulgk sighed. "If you haven't learned the answer elsewhere, I'm afraid you certainly won't hear it from me."

"But surely you would know," Audrey piped up. "By what Zeph Bronzegloom told us, you Grand Inquisitors might be the only ones who came out of the Great Regression with your memories intact. Besides Bellanchora, apparently."

The dragon nodded. "I should like to believe that is true."

"Well come on then, Enscharaulgk!" Audrey demanded. "We faced her for you. She would've raised the entire ocean out from under us! And the universe was coming unraveled before our very eyes, near the end of it all. Can't you even hint around at how she did it?"

"Look," Enscharaulgk answered, dismay in his voice, "I'd like to tell you guys, really. But I promised Ethon I would never reveal the matters which he shrouded in forgetfulness. And I just feel like a Grand Inquisitor's word ought to count for something. Not the less if I gave it to a Dianode. Even a fallen Dianode."

"*Fallen*, you say?" Parissah asked, even as she plucked an arrow from one of her wings that had heretofore gone unnoticed. "But how could a Dianode be *fallen*? How could Ethon stand by and give his blessing to this entire catastrophe? That, more than anything, still puzzles and deeply troubles me. Can you cast any light on that, Enscharaulgk?"

He shook his absolutely huge head. "I dare say nothing more than that these questions are far more closely related than you all guess..." he stooped in close again, his voice falling low, "...and that the answers you seek are in *there*." He indicated the Pamphlet. "That, of course, is where Bellanchora first unearthed them. And now, she is ensnared with the secrets she so coveted... for all time, it is to be hoped. Learn well from her example, you keepers of the Pamphlet! Don't be too eager to know the Unknowable!"

Jek blanched again, and tried urgently to pass the Pamphlet on to Audrey. She looked a bit cross, but ultimately she took it.

"But surely you don't expect us to *keep* this thing," Audrey said, holding it out with obvious disgust. "Shouldn't we take it back to Maenea, and dump it in *Thasagral*? That's where it belongs anyway."

"But we can no longer trust it to Ethon's keeping," Parissah pointed out. "He discarded it once, and there is nothing to indicate he would not do so again. Another like Bravado, who might brave the mists, could arise in time. Or, if Ethon is as wroth as he seems, he may even cast it out of *Thasagral*, back to the waking world, for anyone to find. No, I think to return the Pamphlet would be careless under the circumstances. We must think of something else to do with it."

As Jek watched, Audrey suddenly rent the Pamphlet with both hands. She tried to rip it! But she couldn't. And all her crumpling action didn't leave so much as a crease...

"This is tough paper," she said through clenched teeth, and with a groan, she relented. "Or I'm just much too weak right now to tear it up."

"You would be really, really strong indeed, if you could damage the Pamphlet," Enscharaulgk said. "It is as indestructible as the knowledge it contains."

"Is there no way to destroy it at all?" Audrey asked. "I think we should, if we can. Wouldn't we be much safer if we could get rid of it forever, and Bellanchora with it?"

The Grand Inquisitor did not answer right away. He craned around on his neck, gazing deep, deep into the north. Though none could see his eyes, still they were all struck by how far away he looked, just then...

"There may be a way to dispose of this thing... on the *continent*," he replied finally, his voice sounding at once very troubled. Jek was moved to immediate distress, unable to guess what weight might be on Enscharaulgk's heart in that peaceful moment. "Perhaps, Princess Aaliyah, you of all people are not surprised to hear me speak of that faraway land. My thought is ever drawn there... and beyond..."

"Something vexes you sorely, Enscharaulgk," Parissah lamented. "What ever could it be? All is well, for the moment."

Enscharaulgk hung his head. "It is. But for how long, I wonder? The peaceful years go ever faster! I lengthen them only by tarrying in between one life and another, when I should not. It is a dreadful habit, and growing worse! How I kept you all waiting for my return! And I was little enough help, when I finally came back..."

He sighed again – a sonorous heave of so much air. "But I don't intend to go on like this anymore. I don't believe I can! The world has waited on me long enough."

Parissah was horrified. "What are you saying, Grand Inquisitor?"

"Tell her, Enscharaulgk," Audrey put in. "Tell her everything you told me, and be done with it." Jek was astonished, but remembered at once her private conference with the dragon, two nights before.

"Yes, for goodness' sake," Parissah agreed urgently. "If you have something to tell me, then please, do not leave both of us in agony! What troubles you? What is on your heart?"

Enscharaulgk was not quick in his response. "I..." he started, faltering. "That is, I have been thinking..." They all looked at him with blank, frightened expressions. That probably didn't help his articulation. "...Well, for some centuries, I had thought... perhaps... I might... *retire*."

Parissah gasped. "*Retire*?! Surely not! Is such a thing even possible for a Grand Inquisitor?!"

"I don't know," Enscharaulgk admitted, in slow despair. "Though I'm sure it never entered into the scope of Magormissahr's plans. Nor would I lightly consider it, I hope you know. But, I admit, the last 9021 years have been *harrowing*... even if I spent more of them than I should have resting. The strain of *so many* lives... it wearies me! Every time I come back, the urge grows stronger – the consuming wish to sleep upon a bed of gold through all the ages to come. Please believe me! Beyond all else, I had hoped to avoid making an excuse of that imperative. But many are the times past now, when I thought I could no longer bear up against it. And it is only harder since. If only I could shoulder the load with my great body, I would! But it is my *mind* that must endure the burden. My *mind*, which keeps growing weaker. It is a wretched fate. But it is one I must face now with honesty, lest the world should continue to look to me as its champion, only for me to fail it suddenly... *disastrously*... as I nearly did yesterday. Even now, without a treasure, I fear that sudden failure! All the more, in fact, if I am compelled to claim a new treasure, and so faced with yet another insufferable distraction. So you see, I *must* retire! I *need* to *chill out*!"

Parissah studied him, then looked down to Audrey. "He told you all this?"

"And more," Audrey nodded. "He has plans for his retirement. Very particular plans."

"Oh, this is so frightfully embarrassing," Enscharaulgk lamented, collapsing to his hanches.

Parissah strode over to him, resting a hand on the roll of his elbow. "Do not feel too bad, Enscharaulgk," she comforted him. "Great is my dismay at learning about this. Our material losses can be recovered, in time. Even the Citadel could in theory be rebuilt... though centuries it would take. But I cannot imagine how to mend the weariness that is in your heart. I see now, for the first time, the weight of the expectation we have all placed on you: To make of yourself an eternal fixture – unmoving forever – as if you were one of the Dianodes. In truth, that is how I have always considered you, if I am honest with myself. But you are *not* a Dianode, whatever any of us may think. You have a will – a *strong* will – which you have suppressed through many long ages."

"I thank you for trying to understand, young one," Enscharaulgk replied. "Yet you make for me the same excuses I have fumbled with privately for centuries. And they sound little better in your voice than in my own."

"I know you'll only disagree with me again," Audrey commented, "but I still think you're being way too hard on yourself. How many times have you saved the world, anyway?"

"I lost count," Enscharaulgk answered.

"Exactly," Audrey continued. "If anyone has earned a retirement, it's you. Even dragons get older... in a way. What you want is perfectly natural."

Enscharaulgk stooped urgently. "*Natural*, yes. But you must never make an excuse out of nature, dear Aaliyah. After all, what is nature, in truth? Have you ever considered it? Nature is scarcity craving excess. Nature blurs the line between needs and vices. It shows us the proper path even as it invites us astray at every step. It is our only success and all our failings. It is, for us, at once both good and evil – Purpose and Will. *Nature* is the greatest peril of all."

Zedulon sniffled. "That was beautiful, my friend. Magormissahr himself could have said it no better."

"Beautiful?" Jek pursed his lips. "I thought it was terribly discouraging."

"Yes," Zedulon agreed, as if with sudden realization. "I believe that is it, exactly."

"But now let us have the rest," Parissah interjected, still distraught and eager to know all that her liege would say. "How do you wish to retire, Enscharaulgk?"

He returned his gaze to that first distant point, beyond all horizons. "I would seek Galahadron's Gate… and join the war against the Second Universe."

Parissah was staggered. "Hmm…" she said at length. "Your idea of a final rest from your labors differs somewhat from mine."

"Rest is but one of my wishes," Enscharaulgk explained, "and the one I consider least noble. But I would see the Creators at work again, Parissah! Them… and Opepci, too."

"Opepci?" Jek asked. "Of course! The Dark Inquisitor! The one who joined Galahadron's crusade. She's another first-generation dragon, isn't she? Basically, she's your sister."

"Opepci is *not* my sister," Enscharaulgk explained, quite resolved on the point.

Audrey smiled up at him. "You loved her," she reasoned. "Oh, that is so sweet! You didn't mention anything about that the other night! Won't you tell us about it now? I've never heard a dragon love-story before."

"Well, alright," Enscharaulgk replied. "But bear in mind, this was way back in the unscrupulous days before arranged marriages. We had no elders or administrations in place for it… none besides the Meduselda, and they were naturally quite ignorant of such matters. Each of us had to go out and find their own mate. It may sound ridiculous, but there was no other way. The system was fraught with failure and disappointment. As a general rule, especially among your folk in the age to come, the males were always trying to impress the females, and never succeeding. Conversely, the females were never trying to allure the males, and yet always succeeding. It was an epoch of much rejection and uncertainty."

"That sounds awful!" Audrey exclaimed.

"It was. That is… except when a pair actually requited one another's affections. In such cases, the love was very strong and special – a chance as rare and cosmic as an alignment of the Other Worlds! So it came to be between Opepci and myself. But that is getting far ahead of the story…

"For many lifetimes, each of us sought gold. We were on totally separate quests to amass a fortune. And we each faired well! But when we were quite secure in our own wealth, we began to covet the hoards of rival dragons. Every victory expanded our treasure, and our ambition; every defeat multiplied our might. She and I were catapulted to the very front ranks of our race, and it is thus that we first became aware of each other. Legends of her great ferocity and inaccessible wealth reached my ears, and began to fill all my imagination; and for her it was the same concerning me. We sought one another out, and the battle was fiercer than any the world had known! This happened many times. For centuries, all we longed for was each other's treasure. But, as time went on, we realized that what we *really* longed for… was each other's heart…

"When at last there was love between us, we pillaged together, and we quickly learned that with our strengths combined, there was nothing we could not destroy."

Enscharaulgk nodded to himself, his nostalgia wrapping all gathered like the swaddle of a warm blanket, even in the hard, cold rain. "These were good times. That was, until the Supreme Exodus… when we realized they were actually *bad* times. The departure of the Creators, and the weave of Magormissahr's teachings, convicted our hearts, and showed us the error of our ways. We worked very hard to reform each other from our avarice. And as the Inquisition began to take shape, we committed ourselves wholly to its advancement – to the reformation of our people, and later, of all peoples. Our love had been a salvation; we long held each other accountable to a life that was no longer centered on the pursuit of more gold…

"And yet, that same love was also an acute memento of our glory days. We found ourselves too often reminiscing about our conquests together. The joy we found in each other's company took on the twisted guise of all our past guilt. It was a mingling of the best feelings and the worst – all in a tangle we couldn't right – and our hearts were not strong enough to endure it forever. Finally, I resigned myself to the exile of sole stewardship here in the Idriulthorontan Archipelago. To create some distance seemed the only thing I could do to spare us this anguish.

"But though our love failed in sadness, it never perished. We would see each other, now and again, during summits of the Grand Inquisitors. And for a time, I firmly believe that we were on the verge of patching things up. That was, until the orthodoxy of Galahadron Mucolyptus came between us. His belligerent plans to win back the attention of the Creators rekindled her old ferocity, which was never deeply submerged. There was nothing I could say – whether privately or in open summits – that would convince her to stay, once she was satisfied that the Second Universe could be reached. She urged all of us to the cause. She claimed we were fools to believe we could simply hold the world together indefinitely, with nothing to sustain us but an ever-diminishing hope that the Creators might return of their own volition someday.

"Then she built her Gate.

"And she was gone.

"Thousands of years later, and I can't help feeling she may have been right all along. I, for one, have not weathered the time well. I am discouraged. I am *tired*. But above all, I have been too long sundered from my love! We are, and have been, universes apart. Literally."

Jek wiped away a single tear. It was positively the most beautiful and tragic love story he had ever heard… which perhaps bespoke the few and poor love stories he'd known in his day. But if nothing else, it was certainly distinct: Besides Bravado's tale, it was the only love story he'd ever come across that didn't begin with the words, 'We got married.'

"Oh, Enscharaulgk," Parissah sympathized. "The more I am convinced… the burden you accepted was too heavy for any sentient shoulders to bear forever… even yours. And yet, how shall we *ever* replace you!? Short of Carlos Washoe himself, I do not believe anyone could do better than merely succeed you. And there is little hope of finding *him*…"

Enscharaulgk looked down at Audrey. She nodded back at him. "You'd better tell her that, too," she said.

"Tell her what?" Jek asked, a childish excitement suddenly welling up in him. "Don't tell me he knows something about the fate of Carlos Washoe!"

"No, indeed!" Enscharaulgk blanched. "Nothing like that. But I did have a different replacement for myself in mind..."

"Who?" Parissah asked. "Who do you propose?"

The old dragon hesitated. "Well... I thought first... of *you*, Parissah."

At this news, Parissah sat down flat. "Good gracious," she reeled. "I need to sit down." She checked around herself. "I'm already sitting down."

"I'm sure you don't feel up to it," Enscharaulgk began. "And in many ways, you're not. Not yet. But as for the administration of the Archipelago, I believe that you could fill my shoes. The truth is, you already *have* been filling them. Many are the years now that the islands have been under the de facto stewardship of yourself and the other Primary Administrators."

"That is so," Parissah said. "And you may note that the whole place very nearly crumbled under our leadership – and the universe along with it!"

"A fair point," Enscharaulgk nodded. "But that comes with the job. The world almost ended plenty of times on my watch. You must learn to let that kind of thing roll off your back and simply resolve to do better next time."

"But..." she began, until Enscharaulgk cut her off.

"...I know you will have many reasons why you shouldn't be considered. But believe me, this is not a conclusion I have arrived at lightly. You should take a moment to examine the reasons that, I think, you would make a splendid candidate. For one thing, your various merits. For another, as far as I can make out, you're probably the only Primary Administrator left to me... and that certainly narrows it down. But perhaps most of all, you are a *treasured* dragon now... and so, I fear, you are doomed to remain. Who can say what has become of your treasure, Parissah? Was it hurled into space? Has it fallen to the bottom of the ocean? Is it in the very air around us, incinerated by the Dianode of Fire? For it was *he* that created the great flaming net, which cushioned the fall of the sea – you may be sure. But in any case, your treasure is out there – lost in some unsearchable fathom, or atomized – but still extant. For nothing is ever truly destroyed, until *all* is. And so you will persist, young one... whether you want to or not. And you will *grow*. You will grow until the day arrives when you must either be a paragon or a plague... or else find a place to hide yourself forever. That is the fate of all dragons. I know the path that you would choose. Choose it! And do not doubt yourself."

Parissah was deeply moved, if not quite convinced. "You encourage me, Enscharaulgk... even as you remind me of my awful doom. But however great I may become, there is one essential trait of yours that I can never boast. Indeed, the most essential trait of all. I have no memory of the Creators."

Enscharaulgk sighed. "That is a pickle. But I'm afraid there's nothing for it. No other successor I could choose would have such memories. Not even Carlos, if he were to return." He seemed to grow very droopy and downcast once again. "Yet perhaps it is not as impeaching as you think. After so long a time, my own memory of the Creators is all but lost! I can barely recall them, though I try! It is millennia since I witnessed their gentle comings and goings, and the miraculous weave of new things in their wake. Only vaguely do I remember the way they glistened – like the strands of a spider's web in the sunshine just after a rain. For so they appeared, as nearly as can be described with any worldly analogue. Perfect, shimmering lines, without either width or breadth... and yet containing many infinities. So slight, as to inspire wonder at the very tiniest of things... but stretching beyond the outermost reaches of the universe, passing all grandness. And so, you were content, knowing that they created all things great and small with equal care."

"Sounds like you remember them alright to me," Audrey chimed, giving him a verbal nudge in the ribs.

"I'm sure it does, to one that has never seen a Creator," he rebutted. "But the other Grand Inquisitors would deride me, if they heard such a poor recount. They were way cooler than I know how to explain."

"Yet even a faded memory is better than none at all," Parissah said. "You must face this, Enscharaulgk. I will never be a Grand Inquisitor."

"No," Enscharaulgk admitted, drawing in close to her with a gentle voice. "Nor do I ask you to. I *cannot* ask that of you, if only for the very reason you just brought to light. I know that you can never be a *Grand* Inquisitor. I only ask that you continue to build on that which you already are... a *Pretty Great* Inquisitor."

Parissah sighed. "I will consider it... for my part. But surely all of this will require the blessing of the other Grand Inquisitors."

"Yes," Enscharaulgk nodded. "But that is why I chose to discuss all this with Aaliyah. She is a Princess of the continent. And I believe she is bound to return there. In time, when all is prepared, she will come with us both, if she is willing."

"Can I come too?!" Jek asked urgently.

"Yes, of course, Jek," Enscharaulgk answered. "As far as I'm concerned, anyway. But I await the final word of the Princess."

Everyone looked at Audrey with great expectation. Her eyes darted from one face and mask to another, seeming a bit unsure. "Okay," she said at last – it seemed, to Jek, a bit weakly, given the remarkable occasion. "I'll go."

"*Yes*," Zedulon said slyly. "We shall *all* go forth, unto the continent. For you may be sure, that is where each of our destinies now lies in wait for us. And not altogether good destinies, I fear. Many are the things doomed to fall which have long stood. Yes, more legacies beside your own are ripe for the ending, Enscharaulgk. I have said it many times... I will be the last of the Proconsuls."

"You have never said that," Enscharaulgk replied.

Zedulon's false eye flashed with some annoyance. "Well then, I remember saying it many times to come."

"I take it your foresight is coming back to you, then?" Jek asked.

"It is. An End that might have been was not. Now that some future lies ahead of us, I can once again discern a bit of its shape."

Jek blinked. "But you said before that Time..."

"Never mind what I said about Time!" Zedulon barked. "We are going to go to the continent, and that's that. We will *all* be going."

"*All* of us?" The Kaiser asked, suddenly engaged again. "But surely zhat does not include me!"

"Nope," Enscharaulgk answered. "I have other plans for you, Kaiser. You must do for me one of the very things you swore never to do again. You must build another Doom Fleet."

"Enscharaulgk!" Parissah protested.

"Now, follow me on this, Parissah," the dragon replied. "Our fleet is crushed, and we don't have the Citadel to rebuild it, nor the manpower. But the Kaiser has the full might of industry still at his beck! The Archipelago needs a peace-keeping armada, and he is just the man to build one for us, as quickly as may be. At least as an interim fleet, as we slowly amass more of our own ships."

"It vill be done, mine Grand Inquisitor," the Kaiser said solemnly. "Mine people vill be proud to provide zee strength to uphold your cause. Perhaps just as proud as zhey vould have been to produce zee strength to destroy you."

"Great," the Grand Inquisitor replied, seeming to wink beneath his inscrutable visor.

"And my navy can act as an interim for the interim," Zedulon put in. "You forget, my ships were untouched. Though the airforce is thinned, and that is a considerable loss to us."

"Thanks, Zedulon," Enscharaulgk said.

"Oh, there are *so* many things to do before we may depart," Parissah said, resting a hand on her helmet. "We will need to resurrect a provisional government in Maenea. And I think we will have to spare some manner of a fleet to set out with, if we can manage. Whatever is going on on the continent may demand it."

"*Going on* on the continent?" Enscharaulgk repeated. "What do you mean?"

"Oh dear," Parissah gasped. "I don't suppose anyone has thought to tell you. We have not had any word from there in the last fifty years."

"Well that figures," Enscharaulgk stewed. "This is what I get for trying to retire."

"And here comes one of our other big problems," Parissah pointed.

All turned to look where she indicated. A great cloud, blacker than all the rest of the swollen sky, rushed down upon them, weaving into the guise of a fire-drake skeleton. Onyxadon alighted. He looked around shiftily, as if surprised that everyone was a bit unsettled at his appearing. Then, perhaps in token of his continued truce, he promptly held out a claw, and released a small glowing figure...

"Ah, Baegulgog," Parissah greeted the tagalong. "How did the negotiations with the Twin Queens go?"

"Poorly, as may be expected," the Clerk replied. "They were quite wroth at first, to learn how you had deceived them. It is fortunate that the *Malum In Se* blasted them both into oblivion, for if they had not been ghosts, the scene would have turned ugly. But after their initial outburst, it seemed for a brief spell that they would be more pliant. We pitched your idea to Asiri, as we had to Irisa, about one of them claiming their ancestral homeland of Berlberi, and the other remaining lord of Tophthaera. She saw merit in the idea. And Irisa – not to be thought less reasonable – went along with it. But soon it came to the debate of which would go where. That squabble wages on, even as we speak."

"It was insufferable," Onyxadon spat. "How disagreeable sisters can be!"

"About like brothers," Enscharaulgk said. "But what am I saying? You have proven very agreeable for once, brother. I am still grateful, and rather amazed, how much help you have been in my time of need."

"You might have tried *asking*," Onyxadon replied. "You never know what I may have been liable to do! But at any rate, I was not about to share the credit for your demise, brother. Especially not with the likes of this Bellanchora."

As the dragons spoke, Baegulgog floated into the company of the Associates. He stooped over the old man, his glow pulsating with sudden sorrow.

"I never did relay my condolences," he began, speaking to Jek and Audrey. "I did not know him well, but he seemed a stout fellow... and he was one of our Associates. His loss is grievous. Though I might have expected far worse. It is remarkable that we should all have come out of such a scrape with our lives. All but one of us, that is."

Jek smiled weakly. "Even *you* survived this time, Baegulgog! That's really something!"

"Indeed!" the Clerk laughed. "Even the mildest of scuffles tends to result in my death. Certainly, I had never thought to endure the *Final Battle*!"

"Don't call it that in front of Zedulon," Horus warned him. "You'll get an earful."

"Rightly so," Zedulon went along. "There will be other battles now. To call this one 'Final' is inherently inaccurate. We shall have to contrive another name for it, at once."

"I have just the thing," Enscharaulgk announced. "It shall be remembered as: 'The Battle of the Five Navies.'"

They were all dubiously silent.

"Well?" Enscharaulgk demanded, as if having expected his name to meet universal praise. "Don't you guys approve? Is it not a fetching name for a battle?"

"I'm still trying to make the total come out right," Audrey said, squinting up in the air and counting on her fingers. "There was your navy, and Despotopia's. And Jast-Madiir's and Maenea's..."

"The Indigo Lodge was there," Jek reminded her.

"Yeah, that's kind of its own, I guess." She went on calculating. "Then Onyxadon's pirates showed up. And the Berlie Beirels – though they were really more like armies. And finally Roemnar, but they mostly used planes. So, it's more like The Battle of the Eight or Nine Navies, Plus Two Armies and an Airforce." She threw her hands down. "I don't know, Enscharaulgk, but however I count it, it never comes to Five!"

"That's too bad," the Grand Inquisitor said, unmoved. "I am the wise old dragon. And I say it will be called The Battle of the Five Navies."

"Well, I can't argue with that," Audrey shrugged.

"But we must return to our plans and preparations," Parissah interjected. "The fate of nations hangs in the balance as we speak."

"What are we planning and preparing for?" Onyxadon asked.

"We're going to the continent," Enscharaulgk summarized. "Want to come?"

"I *do*," Onyxadon grinned horribly. "It is much too long since I caused any trouble there."

Enscharaulgk growled. "You will have to behave! Or I will uninvite you."

"But I think he must come in any case," Parissah suggested. "Surely we can't leave him behind to make his mischief in the Islands."

"That's thinking like a Pretty Great Inquisitor," Enscharaulgk nodded.

"But we're not just going to pick up and leave, are we?" Audrey asked, apparently a bit exasperated. "Haven't we earned a little bit of down time for saving the universe?"

"We can ill-afford much 'down-time,' I'm afraid," Parissah answered. "Indeed, we have saved the universe, and perhaps you should all take a moment to congratulate yourselves for that, if it seems appropriate. But you are mixed up in Inquisition business now, which is an ever-ongoing ordeal. Even so, as I said, there is much work to do here in the Archipelago before we may seriously consider departing. I doubt if we could leave within a year. Perhaps we may be fortunate even to set out before two years have passed. But we should have a respite from war and battle, I expect, if that is any assurance... and many sea-voyages between the isles."

Audrey was a bit dubious, but shrugged it off. "I guess that doesn't sound so bad."

"That *is* the way it goes," Enscharaulgk explained. "One Quest is over, and the next begins. Soon enough, we will seek the Gate, and the homeland of Princess Aaliyah. But yes, many things must first be addressed." Enscharaulgk then drew himself upright on his many feet, stately and official-looking. "For starters, let us reform your group, Parissah. I extend to them ongoing status as envoys, one and all. Baegulgog – Clerk Second Class, Horsedrone Extraordinaire, and Herald of Chordonoto. Zedulon – Last Proconsul of the Dire Heron state of Roemnar. Parissah – Martyr of the war against Bellanchora, Once and Future Administrator of the Archipelago, and First of the Great Inquisitors. Aaliyah – Bane of *Malum In Se*, Boot-Bearer, Healer and Princess in exile. Jek – Squire of the Proconsul, Auxiliary Knight of the Indigo Lodge, and He Whose Face Did Save the Universe. And let us not forget, The Old Man – once a Traveling Associate, Water Mage, Keeper of the Pamphlet... the Nameless Hero." Suddenly, Enscharaulgk shuddered, coming to an unpleasant revelation. "But that is only *six* Associates! Surely there cannot be only six! It is unheard of!"

"What about Horus?" Audrey asked. "He traveled with us a bit. And he was working really hard as our attorney long before that."

"Yes, we cannot forget about Mr. Templar," Zedulon agreed. "There will be need of his legal expertise, where we are going."

"Very well," Enscharaulgk solemnly declared. "And Horus Templar, Attorney at Law. Your part in this Quest shall be remembered along with all the rest."

"Why, thank you," Horus said, his ears perking. "It's not every day a public defender is named in the company of heroes."

"Yet so I name you," the dragon said. "The Seven Traveling Associates."

"I am glad of the formalities," Parissah said. 'But we must get to work. Yet where to even begin?"

"I think we need to take care of the old man first," Audrey answered. "He should have a proper memorial. But I admit, I don't know what we could do that would be fitting..."

"I may have just the idea in mind!" Baegulgog elated.

Before he could elaborate, they heard a strange metallic sound behind them. As they turned, sand was flung in the air as a hidden hatchway burst open. From within came an odd sight – familiar to some, alien to others. A handful of Flytraps emerged, surveying the scene, until all their faces converged in Onyxadon's general direction. It seemed then that they smiled quite exaggeratedly, pale and blighted plants in the dim light of day.

"O Dread Master!" one of them chimed. They waved with their spindly forelegs.

Onyxadon stared back at them rather blankly. He shook his head at length. The Flytraps, suddenly seeming dejected, returned underground, closing the hatch behind them...

"What was that about?" Enscharaulgk asked, after a prolonged and uncomfortable silence.

"Wouldn't you like to know..." Onyxadon goaded him.

Everything New...

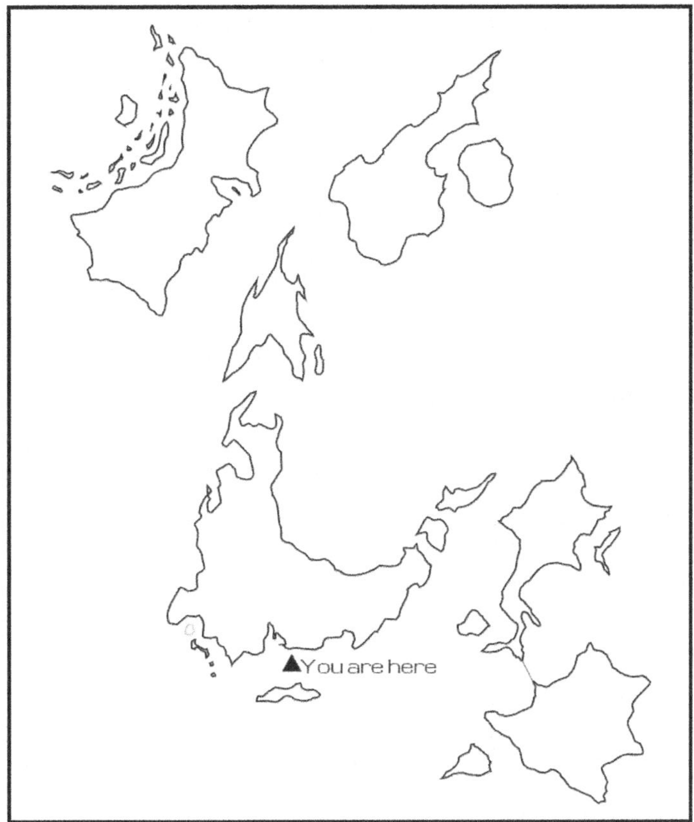

"...is old."

- The Old Man

AAAAAAAAAAAAAAAAAAAA...

On and on, the foghorn blared in the distance, while the pleasant aroma of three or four different meals wafted from a pot on the stove. For all its bluster, the horn could not quite drown-out the patter of heavy rain on the roof, still raging after a week straight. But the storm held no anxiety. He knew it would pass, when things were normal again...

Warm and comfortable, Jek plopped himself down in one of the few whole, sound chairs that was left to him. With a crisp snap, he opened the newspaper, eyes flitting straight to the top headline. "World Saved from Doom Fleet." He nodded with a knowing grin, not much surprised by the news...

Hardly had he sat, and the blast of the horn began to die away. He listened for a few seconds to be sure, understandably loath to do anything about it. Of course, it continued to grow weaker. Jek just shook his head, folding the paper up. "Oh, well," he said to himself. None of the other stories had looked that interesting anyway.

Taking up an overcoat and his musket – the one special-forged by his fellow Knights – Jek opened the front door, nearly jumping back with sudden surprise. Just outside, a man darkened his doorway, his hand extended up and out in a fist – caught the very moment before he would have knocked. The two stood for a spell, looking at each other in an awkward silence. It was the lighthouse inspector.

"Well, I'll be," Jek said. "Today's inspection day, isn't it?"

"That's right," inspector Howitzerov replied, expressionless. They went back to their standing. The rain gushed ever on.

"Why don't you come in?" Jek finally said. "Let me take your coat."

"Thank you," the inspector replied, accepting Jek's help.

Jek took the heavy soaked thing across the room and splayed it in front of the fireplace, then picked up a poker to prod the embers. "We have a fire going," he called back. "You can certainly take a while to warm yourself, if you want. Dinner, dessert and breakfast will be done soon, if you're hungry."

"No, but thank you anyway," the inspector answered, taking out his clipboard and starting to etch on it straight away. "If it's all the same to you, I'd sooner have this done and over with."

"No problem," Jek said. He watched the inspector stoop over the same destroyed dresser with which he had begun the previous examination. He ran his finger over a chunk of the top. Another dust-test...

"This is filthy," he said, rubbing his finger and thumb together. "Surely it hasn't been dusted in weeks."

"We just got in last night," Jek explained. "There wasn't time for it."

The inspector grunted. "Still, it will cost you a significant deduction."

Jek grinned. "I figured." Suddenly, he remembered about the horn. Though by now, he couldn't even hear it anymore. "Sounds like the foghorn needs tending to," he said. "I'll go take care of it..."

"Don't bother. All this blasted rain hasn't allowed for much fog. I'd be surprised if there is even a patch of it left by now. Let us rather continue your inspection on the second floor."

"Alright," Jek shrugged.

* * *

As they reached the upstairs, inspector Howitzerov stopped in his tracks as he looked up from his clipboard, perhaps for the first time since he fetched it. The floor was still littered by fragments of the old reserve lens. But that was not so much what got the inspector's attention. Moreover, he noticed the floating creature who was there, handling three brooms, currently engaged with trying to tidy up the mess…

"Good day to you, Mr. Inspector," Baegulgog said, inclining himself in the air. "I am sorry about the clutter on the floor. It shall be dealt with presently, as you see. But perhaps you will be glad to know I have remedied my blunder!" He pointed with his one free tentacle, indicating a very large parcel in the corner. Jek went over, pulling the protective cover off…

"Behold!" Baegulgog went on. "A new backup lens!"

"Indeed," the inspector said softly, wide-eyed. As if catching himself in his wonder, he quickly returned to his clipboard. "That is a good turn. But redeeming a previous mistake is not going to help the score of the inspection, I'm afraid." He paused for a moment, his face scrunching with some sudden befuddlement. "How did you afford the replacement, Mr. Clerk? Surely not on Dronehood salary… if in fact you are even paid at all…"

"He simply redeemed the requisition order," a voice intruded. The chair behind the desk swiveled, revealing its huge reptilian occupant, as she held out a piece of paper. "Here is the receipt, if you care to peruse it," Parissah said.

"*You*!" the inspector recoiled. "What the devil are you doing back here?"

"Is it not customary for all parties to return to the scene of the crime?" came another voice, while a second huge figure ascended the steps behind them. Jek did experience some of his old fear, hoping the stairs and the upper floor could hold up under the weight of all these large creatures…

"The upstart public defender too?" the inspector marveled, backing away in yet another direction as he identified Horus Templar. "This is a strange gathering! I cannot imagine what would prompt it… unless this is some tasteless joke at my expense…"

"It is nothing of the sort!" bellowed yet *another* voice, fell and terrible, brimming with commanding power. Zedulon alighted in the broken window. "It is an errand beyond the scope of your imagination which unites us. We shall arise to face it soon enough… if there can be any end to these trifling formalities that so hinder!"

"*Proconsul Zedulon*," the inspector gasped, kneeling in the presence of a mighty sovereign. "Pray thou excuseth the arrogance of a lowly peasant. Bewildered am-eth I, who find-est-eth myself in the midst of such company."

"Oh, but don't mind us," a rival voice said – huge like the Proconsul's, but not terrible. The enormous armored head of Enscharaulgk craned down to the windows beside Zedulon, filling them. "As my old pal Zedulon has told you, we're really just passing through."

"*My word*," the inspector gasped again. "The Grand Inquisitor himself!" The man was quite overcome. He rested a shaky palm on his forehead, where it rested some seconds above wide eyes. "I think I need a bit of air," he said at length. "Come, proprietor Jek. Let's have a look at the grounds…" He walked unsteadily for the door to the outside stair.

"But your coat's still downstairs," Jek reminded him.

"And there it may stay!" the inspector replied tersely. "I need to get out of here before any more unexpected guests arrive…"

No sooner had he said this, and there was a knock at the door in front of him. "Now who in all the Undervoid could that be?" the inspector barked. "The way this is going, I shouldn't be surprised if Onyxadon himself was at the door!"

Jek opened the door, and just outside was another titanic dragon head, black and ethereal, grinning horribly. "Well-guessed, little man," Onyxadon said. The inspector stumbled back flat on the floor, spilling the pages of his clipboard, shielding himself against the menace of the ages.

"Hey, now! Get out of here!" Jek waved O'nyxon off, quite annoyed by his exasperating tendencies. "Can't you see the man's having a rough day?"

"Oh, very well," Onyxadon sighed. "But I don't see I did any differently than the rest. Spoil-sports and hypocrites, the lot of you…" His skeletal appearance streaked in a million mirky strands up into the sky, and his darkness passed. The inspector fumbled with his papers on the floor, hastily gathering them up.

"Here, let me help…" Jek offered, starting to stoop…

"No! Thank you," the inspector insisted, shooting prematurely to his feet, reaching back down for more papers. "I will be quite alright. *Eventually*, no doubt." He marched out the doorway with Jek following close. As he crossed the threshold into the storm, one of his papers fell from his folded arms. A wind gust gathered it up at once, setting it flying on a familiar course. But Jek saw it coming, and with one hand up and out he caught it flat… just in time. He smiled to himself, looking back at his companions, and then past them, at the old walls of Brighamok's Lighthouse. *They haven't changed a bit*, he thought. Some things never did…

* * *

"That is a rather gaudy thing," the inspector said, frowning up at the one object on the property that *had* changed. "I dare say it is most out-of-place on such strictly regulated grounds." He scrawled more on his clipboard, as best he could in the torrential downpour.

Jek paid him little mind, looking up at the great memorial they had brought with them. It was a statue, carved in a good likeness of a friend of his, even if the features were (forgivably) a bit more stately than the man himself had been. The sculpture had one hand rolled up, resting against the hip, and the other turned out, with an open mouth full of teeth that weren't nearly crooked enough. It certainly captured his manner – a perfect snapshot of one of his countless crochety anecdotes. Beside him, there was also a beautifully carven steed – the proudest and most heroic image of a racehorse that Jek had ever seen – a late addition to the memorial, which had been included at the insistence of Baegulgog. Jek still had no idea what the story was there… and he couldn't decide whether the statues complimented each other or clashed. But he didn't trouble about it. He just admired the handiwork, basking in memories. Stressful, terrifying, happy memories…

"And how is that for an epitaph!" the inspector demanded suddenly, pointing down at the base of the statue with his pen. "'The Old Man'?" he scoffed. "But what ever was the fellow's *name*?"

Jek looked at the plaque himself. There it was indeed, in big, bold script:

The
Old
Man

…and below it in smaller script, read in parentheses: "*and Charles the Horse*."

But Jek was struck suddenly – and delightfully – seeing the words lined up, one over the other… the three capital letters forming a column. And all at once, he had an answer for the inspector…

"*Tom*," Jek stated. "His name was *Tom*."

"Well, someone should have informed the engraver," inspector Howitzerov quipped…

* * *

A short time later, after they had surveyed the rest of the property, Jek found himself still beside Howitzerov as he worked furiously to finish his report, both of them standing near the crest of the hill overlooking the sea. Finally, his pen came to a screeching rest, and he tore a sheet free of the board, handing it to Jek. "Here is your copy of the report," he said. "I'm afraid you did not pass inspection. The accumulation of dust alone was enough to put you over. Please report with this to town, and submit yourself for execution."

Jek shook his head somberly. "Sorry, but I can't. Diplomatic immunity, and all. My wife and I are emmisaries of the Inquisition now… and auxiliary Knights, too. We're going to be going on another Quest, in a little while."

The inspector fumed, finally having endured all he could take. "But you *must* be executed! That is the penalty! It is my job to conduct these inspections, and to dole out the consequences of failure! If I can't be allowed to do my job properly, then what am I even doing here?!"

Jek set his jaw, and grinned at the poor, frustrated inspector. "*What are you even doing here*?" he repeated back to him, shaking his head. He turned, and reaching one arm around the inspector's back, slapping him reassuringly on the shoulder blade, he looked to the coast. His eyes settled on his wife – on Aaliyah – who stood atop the hill ahead of him, already gazing out intently over the ocean. He suppressed another moment of amusement. It was the wrong ocean. Their ultimate object may well have been in the exact opposite direction she was looking! But he didn't let it ruin the solemnity of the moment. He studied her with eyes full of pride, and of love. From this vantage, he could see only the right side of her face, outlined starkly against the stormy horizon. It was as beautiful to him as the left side. Perhaps more so.

"Cheer up, pal," he assuaged the inspector. "If I can figure out what I'm doing here... what I'm *really* doing here... I'd say anybody can."

Acknowledgements

Foremost thanks, appreciation, and recognition go to Rachael V, who has done more for the betterment of this book than can be recalled. She made the wonderful first edition cover image! She convinced me of much-needed chapter breaks. She volunteered many terrific ideas, from simple chapter titles and quotations... to entire features of the world and the story which I can hardly wait to explore (hint-hint: sequel)! And, perhaps most crucially of all, she had the good sense and the stubbornness necessary to see that my ending was missing something, and to keep after me about it until I finally went back in and made it right. Second only to Rachael, I must thank John V, another indispensable beta reader, advocate, creative consultant and collaborator. It was listening to him talk about his own fantasy campaign that got me thinking about an adventure in a series of islands in the first place. Between the two of them, I had all the help and encouragement an aspiring author could ever need. Thank you both! Though no thanks are really adequate...

As to the great authors who came before me, I would be most remiss not to here honor J.R.R. Tolkien, Patrick F. McManus, and Michael Crichton. To be sure, I could never have devised this story without standing on the shoulders of giants, and homaging all manner of epics and shorter pieces. Among many other storytellers that have ignited my imagination over the years, I must also give special credit to George Lucas, Gene Roddenberry, Christopher Nolan, and the incomparable Chuck Norris. Also in need of much thanks is Erle Stanley Gardner, whose legal drama stories are quite shamelessly homaged here...

Additional appreciation and honor must go to some of the great film composers: Hans Zimmer, John Williams, and Howard Shore, in particular. Sometimes more than the films themselves, the incredible music these men have written has been some of the best imagination fuel anyone could wish for.

A very special acknowledgement to David J. Williams, Martin Cirulis and Arinn Dembo, as well as Aaron Kambeitz, Rob Cunningham, and Alex Garden (and many others). I don't honestly know if I'm allowed to even mention the masterpieces they've worked on together, but for crying out loud, look it up! It was their work which prompted the Inquisition – a true cornerstone of this whole book, and any books that may follow. Together, they have told one of the very greatest stories I've ever known. I only wish their recognition could be in proportion with the quality of their craftsmanship.

I particularly need to thank my grandma and Dale and Fran C. for listening to me talk about this whole thing way too much. And my folks, who have had much more patience with me over the years than they probably should have. And Gilbert, who was the first to endure this story in its entirety, and many forced hours of me prattling on about it besides.

Finally, I wish to thank anyone else who read any part of this book before it was published, or even had so much as a passing thought to do so. Life is busy and this is a long, long book... and even the slightest interest anyone showed in it meant a lot!

Doodles of Some Things in the Book

(Starts on Next Page)

AVARICAN
INQUISITOR

CHIEF
KATYDID

DIRE HERON
PLAGUE DOCTOR

DRONEHOOD
CLERK v1

ENSCHARAULGK v1
MASK

ETHON
Z

MEDUSEL DAN
FRONT
SIDE

MEDUSELDAN
QUEEN

MEDUSELDAN SWORDSDRONE

ONYXADON

POSTAL
SQUIRE v1

PUBLIC
DEFENDER

The Glowy Lady

THAER

For More from E.L. Ward...

Visit his personal site, at:

https://www.booksofelward.com

His vast arsenal of backlist titles includes the following:

TITLES IN THE ORPHAN UNIVERSE

HERON PROPHECIES SERIES

The Chocolate Prophecy

HORUS TEMPLAR – PUBLIC DEFENDER SERIES

Horus Templar and the Case of the Wimpy War-Criminal
Horus Templar and the Case of the Iniquitous Inquisitor
Horus Templar and the Case of the Draft-Dodging Drone
Horus Templar and the Case of the Dubious Decedent

E.L. Ward is proud to partner with:

MALOB ARTS

Check out his and other creative works at:

www.malobarts.com

Made in the USA
Monee, IL
03 October 2022